'An outstanding debut fantasy . . . this is the type of assured, rich first novel most writers can only dream of producing. The fantasy world has a new star'

Publishers Weekly

'I haven't been so gripped by a new fantasy series in years. It's certain to become a classic'   *The Times*

'Pacy, witty and entertaining, *The Name of the Wind* is a rattling read'   *SFX*

'*The Name of the Wind* has everything . . . it's humorous and terrifying and completely believable'   Tad Williams

'It is a rare and great pleasure to find a fantasist writing not only with the accuracy of language that is essential to fantasy-making, but with true music in the words as well. Wherever Pat Rothfuss goes with the big story that begins with *The Name of the Wind*, he'll carry us with him as a good singer carries us through a song'   Ursula Le Guin

D1321906

The Name of the Wind

THE KINGKILLER CHRONICLE: DAY ONE

PATRICK ROTHFUSS

First published in Great Britain in 2007 by
Gollancz
An imprint of the Orion Publishing Group
Orion House, 5 Upper St Martin's Lane,
London WC2H 9EA
An Hachette UK Company

This edition published in Great Britain in 2011 by Gollancz

A CIP catalogue record for this book
is available from the British Library

Typeset at The Spartan Press Ltd,
Lymington, Hants

Printed and bound in Great Britain at CPI Group (UK) Ltd,
Croydon, CRO 4YY

The Orion Publishing Group's policy is to use papers that
are natural, renewable and recyclable products and made
from wood grown in sustainable forests. The logging and
manufacturing processes are expected to conform to the
environmental regulations of the country of origin.

www.patrickrothfuss.com
www.orionbooks.co.uk

INTRODUCTION

A letter to Patrick Rothfuss from Stephen Deas.

Dear Pat,

A few years ago, my wife Michaela came home with a new book: *The Name of the Wind*. Life was all downhill from there. I guess you just about remember us from your visit to the UK, and if you do, you probably remember us going on, both of us, about how much we liked your tale of Kvothe. But what you don't know is how it went on after that. How much Michaela liked *The Name of the Wind* even more than my own fantasies, rather like wishing you had someone else's kid instead of your own. Days of it. Weeks. Months. Years. The relentless crushing comparison, burning away every vestige of self-respect until all that remains now is a bitter hollow shell, seething with bilious rage. Sort of like Lord Voldemort without the magic although at least I get to keep my nose.

Well hey – what goes around, comes around. Karma and fate and possibly a dark sacrifice to an elder god or two and now here I am. I scratch the emaciated claws that were once hands and I contemplate the delicious taste . . . of *revenge*.

But.

But the trouble is, I've read, and I've read it again. Just to know, y'know. To see for myself, in case I was wrong, in case it was all a myth. And therein lies my problem. I simply can't hold it against you, because really, honestly yes, it *is* that damn good. A novel is as much about the journey as it is about the destination, and this is the most painstakingly perfectly rendered scenery it has been my pleasure to watch slide by. It reminds me of Robert Silverberg at his best. Or maybe it's how Mervyn Peake might have been if he'd been force-fed every episode of *Buffy the Vampire-Slayer* on continuous loop for a few weeks. It simply has the most exquisitely compelling prose of any fantasy novel I've ever read, and the dialogue must make even Joss Whedon turn nervously in his sleep. You could probably rewrite a laundry list into an elegant piece of haunting poetry. So I'd curse you, Mr New York Times number one bestselling author, with your beard that secretly aspires to world domination and your disturbingly comprehensive knowledge of Anglo-Saxon names of a certain nature, your eloquent self-deprecating wit, your jaw-dropping fund-raisers for Heifer International and your spine-tingling soul-stopping 'It was a silence of three parts' that tells us the ride is about to begin once more, but that would be like cursing the sun; and what's the point of that when you can simply lie back and bask in its warmth?

So bask sir, for it's an honour and a privilege to welcome Kvothe the Kingkiller to the stage: Long may he reign; but before I go, I have one last thing to say.

Touched. By. A. Viking.

My work here is done.

Stephen Deas

Stephen Deas (www.stephendeas.com) is the author of The Memory of Flames trilogy (THE ADAMANTINE PALACE, THE KING OF THE CRAGS and THE ORDER OF THE SCALES) and THE THIEF-TAKER'S APPRENTICE.

Stephen has donated his fee for this introduction to the Heifer International charity which is dedicated to helping to end hunger and poverty around the world.

www.heifer.org

Acknowledgments

To . . .

. . . all the readers of my early drafts. You are legion, too many to name, but not too many to love. I kept writing because of your encouragement. I kept improving because of your criticism. If not for you, I would not have won . . .

. . . the Writers of the Future contest. If not for their workshop, I would never have met my wonderful anthology-mates from volume 18 or . . .

. . . Kevin J. Anderson. If not for his advice, I would never have ended up with . . .

. . . Matt Bialer, the best of agents. If not for his guidance, I would never have sold the book to . . .

. . . Betsy Wolheim, beloved editor and president of DAW. If not for her, you would not be holding this book. A similar book, perhaps, but this book would not exist.

And, lastly, to Mr. Bohage, my high school history teacher. In 1989 I told him I'd mention him in my first novel. I keep my promises.

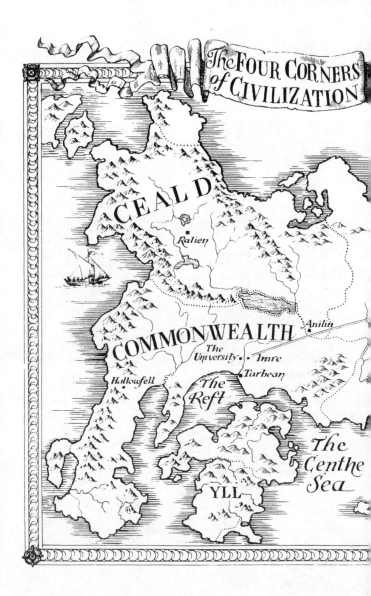

The FOUR CORNERS of CIVILIZATION

CEALD

Ralien

COMMONWEALTH

The University • Imre

Anilin

Tarbean

Hallowfell

The Reft

The Centhe Sea

YLL

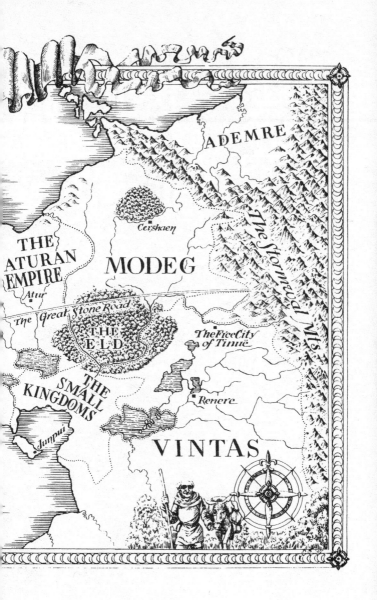

To my mother,
who taught me to love books and opened the
door to Narnia, Pern, and Middle Earth.

And to my father,
who taught me that if I was going to do something,
I should take my time and do it right.

PROLOGUE

A Silence of Three Parts

IT WAS NIGHT AGAIN. The Waystone Inn lay in silence, and it was a silence of three parts.

The most obvious part was a hollow, echoing quiet, made by things that were lacking. If there had been a wind it would have sighed through the trees, set the inn's sign creaking on its hooks, and brushed the silence down the road like trailing autumn leaves. If there had been a crowd, even a handful of men inside the inn, they would have filled the silence with conversation and laughter, the clatter and clamour one expects from a drinking house during the dark hours of night. If there had been music . . . but no, of course there was no music. In fact there were none of these things, and so the silence remained.

Inside the Waystone a pair of men huddled at one corner of the bar. They drank with quiet determination, avoiding serious discussions of troubling news. In doing this they added a small, sullen silence to the larger, hollow one. It made an alloy of sorts, a counterpoint.

The third silence was not an easy thing to notice. If you listened for an hour, you might begin to feel it in the wooden floor underfoot and in the rough, splintering barrels behind the bar. It was in the weight of the black stone hearth that held the heat of a long-dead fire. It was in the slow back and forth of a white linen cloth rubbing along the grain of the bar. And it was in the hands of the man who stood there, polishing a stretch of mahogany that already gleamed in the lamplight.

The man had true-red hair, red as flame. His eyes were dark and distant, and he moved with the subtle certainty that comes from knowing many things.

The Waystone was his, just as the third silence was his. This was appropriate, as it was the greatest silence of the three, wrapping the others inside itself. It was deep and wide as autumn's ending. It was heavy as a great river-smooth stone. It was the patient, cut-flower sound of a man who is waiting to die.

CHAPTER ONE

A Place for Demons

IT WAS FELLING NIGHT, and the usual crowd had gathered at the Waystone Inn. Five wasn't much of a crowd, but five was as many as the Waystone ever saw these days, times being what they were.

Old Cob was filling his role as storyteller and advice dispensary. The men at the bar sipped their drinks and listened. In the back room a young innkeeper stood out of sight behind the door, smiling as he listened to the details of a familiar story.

'When he awoke, Taborlin the Great found himself locked in a high tower. They had taken his sword and stripped him of his tools: key, coin, and candle were all gone. But that weren't even the worst of it, you see . . .' Cob paused for effect, '. . . cause the lamps on the wall were burning blue!'

Graham, Jake, and Shep nodded to themselves. The three friends had grown up together, listening to Cob's stories and ignoring his advice.

Cob peered closely at the newer, more attentive member of his small audience, the smith's prentice. 'Do you know what that meant, boy?' Everyone called the smith's prentice 'boy' despite the fact that he was a hand taller than anyone there. Small towns being what they are, he would most likely remain 'boy' until his beard filled out or he bloodied someone's nose over the matter.

The boy gave a slow nod. 'The Chandrian.'

'That's right,' Cob said approvingly. 'The Chandrian. Everyone knows that blue fire is one of their signs. Now he was—'

'But how'd they find him?' the boy interrupted. 'And why din't they kill him when they had the chance?'

'Hush now, you'll get all the answers before the end,' Jake said. 'Just let him tell it.'

'No need for all that, Jake,' Graham said. 'Boy's just curious. Drink your drink.'

'I drank me drink already,' Jake grumbled. 'I need t'nother but the innkeep's still skinning rats in the back room.' He raised his voice and knocked his empty mug hollowly on the top of the mahogany bar. 'Hoy! We're thirsty men in here!'

The innkeeper appeared with five bowls of stew and two warm, round loaves of bread. He pulled more beer for Jake, Shep, and Old Cob, moving with an air of bustling efficiency.

The story was set aside while the men tended to their dinners. Old Cob tucked away his bowl of stew with the predatory efficiency of a lifetime bachelor. The others were still blowing steam off their bowls when he finished the last of his loaf and returned to his story.

'Now Taborlin needed to escape, but when he looked around, he saw his cell had no door. No windows. All around him was nothing but smooth, hard stone. It was a cell no man had ever escaped.

'But Taborlin knew the names of all things, and so all things were his to command. He said to the stone: *"Break!"* and the stone broke. The wall tore like a piece of paper, and through that hole Taborlin could see the sky and breathe the sweet spring air. He stepped to the edge, looked down, and without a second thought he stepped out into the open air . . .'

The boy's eyes went wide. 'He didn't!'

Cob nodded seriously. 'So Taborlin fell, but he did not despair. For he knew the name of the wind, and so the wind obeyed him. He spoke to the wind and it cradled and caressed him. It bore him to the ground as gently as a puff of thistledown and set him on his feet softly as a mother's kiss.

'And when he got to the ground and felt his side where they'd stabbed him, he saw that it weren't hardly a scratch. Now maybe it was just a piece of luck,' Cob tapped the side of his nose knowingly. 'Or maybe it had something to do with the amulet he was wearing under his shirt.'

'What amulet?' the boy asked eagerly through a mouthful of stew.

Old Cob leaned back on his stool, glad for the chance to elaborate. 'A few days earlier, Taborlin had met a tinker on the road. And even though Taborlin didn't have much to eat, he shared his dinner with the old man.'

'Right sensible thing to do,' Graham said quietly to the boy. 'Everyone knows: "A tinker pays for kindness twice".'

'No no,' Jake grumbled. 'Get it right: "A tinker's advice pays kindness twice".'

The innkeeper spoke up for the first time that night. 'Actually, you're missing more than half,' he said, standing in the doorway behind the bar.

> *'A tinker's debt is always paid:*
> *Once for any simple trade.*
> *Twice for freely-given aid.*
> *Thrice for any insult made.'*

The men at the bar seemed almost surprised to see Kote standing there. They'd been coming to the Waystone every Felling night for months and Kote had never interjected anything of his own before. Not that you could expect anything else, really. He'd only been in town for a year or so. He was still a stranger. The smith's prentice had lived here since he was eleven, and he was still referred to as 'that Rannish boy', as if Rannish were some foreign country and not a town less than thirty miles away.

'Just something I heard once,' Kote said to fill the silence, obviously embarrassed.

Old Cob nodded before he cleared his throat and launched back into the story. 'Now this amulet was worth a whole bucket of gold nobles, but on account of Taborlin's kindness, the tinker sold it to him for nothing but an iron penny, a copper penny, and a silver penny. It was black as a winter night and cold as ice to touch, but so long as it was round his neck, Taborlin would be safe from the harm of evil things. Demons and such.'

'I'd give a good piece for such a thing these days,' Shep said darkly. He had drunk most and talked least over the course of the evening. Everyone knew that something bad had happened out on his farm last Cendling night, but since they were good friends they knew better than to press him for the details. At least not this early in the evening, not as sober as they were.

'Aye, who wouldn't?' Old Cob said judiciously, taking a long drink.

'I din't know the Chandrian were demons,' the boy said. 'I'd heard—'

'They ain't demons,' Jake said firmly. 'They were the first six people to refuse Tehlu's choice of the path, and he cursed them to wander the corners—'

'Are you telling this story, Jacob Walker?' Cob said sharply. 'Cause if you are, I'll just let you get on with it.'

The two men glared at each other for a long moment. Eventually Jake looked away, muttering something that could, conceivably, have been an apology.

Cob turned back to the boy. 'That's the mystery of the Chandrian,' he explained. 'Where do they come from? Where do they go after they've done their bloody deeds? Are they men who sold their souls? Demons? Spirits? No one knows.' Cob shot Jake a profoundly disdainful look. 'Though every half-wit *claims* he knows . . .'

The story fell further into bickering at this point, about the nature of the Chandrian, the signs that showed their presence to the wary, and whether the amulet would protect Taborlin from bandits, or mad dogs, or falling off a horse. Things were getting heated when the front door banged open.

Jake looked over. 'It's about time you got in, Carter. Tell this damn fool the difference between a demon and a dog. Everybody kn—' Jake stopped midsentence and rushed to the door. 'God's body, what happened to you?'

Carter stepped into the light, his face pale and smeared with blood. He clutched an old saddle blanket to his chest. It was an odd, awkward shape, as if it were wrapped around a tangle of kindling sticks.

His friends jumped off their stools and hurried over at the sight of him. 'I'm fine,' he said as he made his slow way into the common room. His eyes were wild around the edges, like a skittish horse. 'I'm fine. I'm fine.'

He dropped the bundled blanket onto the nearest table where it knocked hard against the wood, as if it were full of stones. His clothes were crisscrossed with long, straight cuts. His grey shirt hung in loose tatters except where it was stuck to his body, stained a dark, sullen red.

Graham tried to ease him into a chair. 'Mother of God. Sit down, Carter. What happened to you? Sit down.'

Carter shook his head stubbornly. 'I told you, I'm fine. I'm not hurt that bad.'

'How many were there?' Graham said.

'One,' Carter said. 'But it's not what you think—'

'Goddammit. I told you, Carter,' Old Cob burst out with the sort of frightened anger only relatives and close friends can muster. 'I told you for months now. You can't go out alone. Not even as far as Baedn. It ain't safe.' Jake laid a hand on the old man's arm, quieting him.

'Just take a sit,' Graham said, still trying to steer Carter into a chair. 'Let's get that shirt off you and get you cleaned up.'

Carter shook his head. 'I'm fine. I got cut up a little, but the blood is mostly Nelly's. It jumped on her. Killed her about two miles outside town, past the Oldstone Bridge.'

A moment of serious silence followed the news. The smith's prentice laid a sympathetic hand on Carter's shoulder. 'Damn. That's hard. She was gentle as a lamb, too. Never tried to bite or kick when you brought her in for shoes. Best horse in town. Damn. I'm . . .' He trailed off. 'Damn. I don't know what to say.' He looked around helplessly.

Cob finally managed to free himself from Jake. 'I told you,' he repeated, shaking a finger in Carter's direction. 'There's folks out lately that would kill you for a pair of pennies, let alone a horse and cart. What are you going to do now? Pull it yourself?'

There was a moment of uncomfortable quiet. Jake and Cob glared at each other while the rest seemed at a loss for words, unsure how to comfort their friend.

The innkeeper moved carefully through the silence. Arms full, he stepped nimbly around Shep and began to arrange some items on a nearby table: a bowl of hot water, shears, some clean linen, a few glass bottles, needle and gut.

'This never would have happened if he'd listened to me in the first place,' Old Cob muttered. Jake tried to quiet him, but Cob brushed him aside. 'I'm just tellin' the truth. It's a damn shame about Nelly, but he better listen now or he'll end up dead. You don't get lucky twice with those sort of men.'

Carter's mouth made a thin line. He reached out and pulled the edge of the bloody blanket. Whatever was inside flipped over once and snagged on the cloth. Carter tugged harder and there was a clatter like a bag of flat river stones upended onto the tabletop.

It was a spider as large as a wagon wheel, black as slate.

The smith's prentice jumped backward and hit a table, knocking it over and almost falling to the ground himself. Cob's face went slack. Graham, Shep, and Jake made wordless, startled sounds and moved away, raising their hands to their faces. Carter took a step backward that was almost like a nervous twitch. Silence filled the room like a cold sweat.

The innkeeper frowned. 'They can't have made it this far west yet,' he said softly.

If not for the silence, it is unlikely anyone would have heard him. But they did. Their eyes pulled away from the thing on the table to stare mutely at the red-haired man.

Jake found his voice first. 'You know what this is?'

The innkeeper's eyes were distant. 'Scrael,' he said distractedly. 'I'd thought the mountains—'

'Scrael?' Jake broke in. 'Blackened body of God, Kote. You've seen these things before?'

'What?' The red-haired innkeeper looked up sharply, as if suddenly remembering where he was. 'Oh. No. No, of course not.' Seeing that he was the only one within arm's length of the dark thing, he took a measured step away. 'Just something I heard.' They stared at him. 'Do you remember the trader that came through about two span ago?'

They all nodded. 'Bastard tried to charge me ten pennies for a half-pound of salt,' Cob said reflexively, repeating the complaint for perhaps the hundredth time.

'Wish I'd bought some,' Jake mumbled. Graham nodded a silent agreement.

'He was a filthy shim,' Cob spat, seeming to find comfort in the familiar words. 'I might pay two in a tight time, but ten is robbery.'

'Not if there are more of those on the road,' Shep said darkly.

All eyes went back to the thing on the table.

'He told me he'd heard of them over near Melcombe,' Kote said quickly, watching everyone's faces as they studied the thing on the table. 'I thought he was just trying to drive up his prices.'

'What else did he say?' Carter asked.

The innkeeper looked thoughtful for a moment, then shrugged. 'I didn't get the whole story. He was only in town for a couple hours.'

'I don't like spiders,' the smith's prentice said. He remained on the other side of a table some fifteen feet away. 'Cover it up.'

'It's not a spider,' Jake said. 'It's got no eyes.'

'It's got no mouth either,' Carter pointed out. 'How does it eat?'

'What does it eat?' Shep said darkly.

The innkeeper continued to eye the thing curiously. He leaned closer, stretching out a hand. Everyone edged even farther away from the table.

'Careful,' Carter said. 'Its feet are sharp like knives.'

'More like razors,' Kote said. His long fingers brushed the scrael's black, featureless body. 'It's smooth and hard, like pottery.'

'Don't go messing with it,' the smith's prentice said.

Moving carefully, the innkeeper took one of the long, smooth legs and tried to break it with both hands like a stick. 'Not pottery,' he amended. He set it against the edge of the table and leaned his weight against it. It broke with a sharp *crack*. 'More like stone.' He looked up at Carter. 'How did it get all these cracks?' He pointed at the thin fractures that crazed the smooth black surface of the body.

'Nelly fell on it,' Carter said. 'It jumped out of a tree and started to climb all over her, cutting her up with its feet. It moved so fast. I didn't even know what was going on.' Carter finally sank into the chair at Graham's urging. 'She got tangled in her harness and fell on it, broke some of its legs. Then it came after me, got on me, crawling all over.' He crossed his arms in front of his bloody chest and shuddered. 'I managed to get it off me and stomped it hard as I could. Then it got on me again . . .' He trailed off, his face ashen.

The innkeeper nodded to himself as he continued to prod the thing. 'There's no blood. No organs. It's just grey inside.' He poked it with a finger. 'Like a mushroom.'

'Great Tehlu, just leave it alone,' the smith's prentice begged. 'Sometimes spiders twitch after you kill them.'

'Listen to yourselves,' Cob said scathingly. 'Spiders don't get big as pigs. You know what this is.' He looked around, making eye contact with each of them. 'It's a demon.'

They looked at the broken thing. 'Oh, come on now,' Jake said, disagreeing mostly out of habit. 'It's not like . . .' He made an inarticulate gesture. 'It can't just . . .'

Everyone knew what he was thinking. Certainly there were demons in the world. But they were like Tehlu's angels. They were like heroes and kings. They belonged in stories. They belonged *out there*. Taborlin the Great called up fire and lightning to destroy demons. Tehlu broke them in his hands and sent them howling into the nameless void. Your childhood friend didn't stomp one to death on the road to Baedn-Bryt. It was ridiculous.

Kote ran his hand through his red hair, then broke the silence. 'There's one way to tell for sure,' he said, reaching into his pocket. 'Iron or fire.' He brought out a bulging leather purse.

'And the name of God,' Graham pointed out. 'Demons fear three things: cold iron, clean fire, and the holy name of God.'

The innkeeper's mouth pressed itself into a straight line that was not quite a frown. 'Of course,' he said as he emptied his purse onto the table then fingered through the jumbled coins: heavy silver talents and thin silver bits, copper jots, broken ha'pennies, and iron drabs. 'Does anyone have a shim?'

'Just use a drab,' Jake said. 'That's good iron.'

'I don't want good iron,' the innkeeper said. 'A drab has too much carbon in it. It's almost steel.'

'He's right,' the smith's prentice said. 'Except it's not carbon. You use coke to make steel. Coke and lime.'

The innkeeper nodded deferentially to the boy. 'You'd know best, young master. It's your business after all.' His long fingers finally found a shim in the pile of coins. He held it up. 'Here we are.'

'What will it do?' Jake asked.

'Iron kills demons,' Cob's voice was uncertain, 'but this one's already dead. It might not do anything.'

'One way to find out.' The innkeeper met each of their eyes briefly, as if measuring them. Then he turned purposefully back to the table, and they edged farther away.

Kote pressed the iron shim to the black side of the creature, and there was a short, sharp crackling sound, like a pine log snapping in a hot fire. Everyone startled, then relaxed when the black thing remained motionless. Cob and the others exchanged shaky smiles, like boys spooked by a ghost story. Their smiles went sour as the room filled with the sweet, acrid smell of rotting flowers and burning hair.

The innkeeper pressed the shim onto the table with a sharp *click*. 'Well,' he said, brushing his hands against his apron. 'I guess that settles that. What do we do now?'

————————

Hours later, the innkeeper stood in the doorway of the Waystone and let his eyes relax to the darkness. Footprints of lamplight from the inn's windows fell across the dirt road and the doors of the smithy across the way. It was not a large road, or well travelled. It didn't seem to lead anywhere, as some roads do. The innkeeper drew a deep breath of autumn air and looked around restlessly, as if waiting for something to happen.

He called himself Kote. He had chosen the name carefully when he came to this place. He had taken a new name for most of the usual reasons, and for a few unusual ones as well, not the least of which was the fact that names were important to him.

Looking up, he saw a thousand stars glittering in the deep velvet of a night with no moon. He knew them all, their stories and their names. He knew them in a familiar way, the way he knew his own hands.

Looking down, Kote sighed without knowing it and went back inside. He locked the door and shuttered the wide windows of the inn, as if to distance himself from the stars and all their varied names.

He swept the floor methodically, catching all the corners. He washed the tables and the bar, moving with a patient efficiency. At the end of an hour's work, the water in his bucket was still clean enough for a lady to wash her hands in.

Finally, he pulled a stool behind the bar and began to polish the vast array of bottles nestled between the two huge barrels. He wasn't nearly as crisp and efficient about this chore as he had been with the others, and it soon became obvious the polishing was only an excuse to touch and hold. He even hummed a little, although he did not realise it, and would have stopped himself if he had known.

As he turned the bottles in his long, graceful hands the familiar motion eased a few tired lines from his face, making him seem younger, certainly not yet thirty. Not even near thirty. Young for an innkeeper. Young for a man with so many tired lines remaining on his face.

———

Kote came to the top of the stairs and opened the door. His room was austere, almost monkish. There was a black stone fireplace in the center of the room, a pair of chairs, and a small desk. The only other furniture was a narrow bed with a large, dark chest at its foot. Nothing decorated the walls or covered the wooden floor.

There were footsteps in the hall, and a young man stepped into the room carrying a bowl of stew that steamed and smelled of pepper. He was dark and charming, with a quick smile and cunning eyes. 'You haven't been this late in weeks,' he said as he handed over the bowl. 'There must have been good stories tonight, Reshi.'

Reshi was another of the innkeeper's names, a nickname almost. The sound of it tugged one corner of his mouth into a wry smile as he sank into the deep chair in front of the fire. 'So, what did you learn today, Bast?'

'Today, master, I learned why great lovers have better eyesight than great scholars.'

'And why is that, Bast?' Kote asked, amusement touching the edges of his voice.

Bast closed the door and returned to sit in the second chair, turning it to face his teacher and the fire. He moved with a strange delicacy and grace, as if he were close to dancing. 'Well Reshi, all the rich books are found inside where the light is bad. But lovely girls tend to be out in the sunshine and therefore much easier to study without risk of injuring one's eyes.'

Kote nodded. 'But an exceptionally clever student could take a book outside, thus bettering himself without fear of lessening his much-loved faculty of sight.'

'I thought the same thing, Reshi. Being, of course, an exceptionally clever student.'

'Of course.'

'But when I found a place in the sun where I could read, a beautiful girl came along and kept me from doing anything of the sort,' Bast finished with a flourish.

Kote sighed. 'Am I correct in assuming you didn't manage to read any of *Celum Tinture* today?'

Bast managed to look somewhat ashamed.

Looking into the fire, Kote tried to assume a stern face and failed. 'Ah Bast, I hope she was lovely as a warm wind in the shade. I'm a bad teacher to say it, but I'm glad. I don't feel up to a long bout of lessons right now.' There was a moment of silence. 'Carter was attacked by a scraeling tonight.'

Bast's easy smile fell away like a cracked mask, leaving his face stricken and pale. 'The scrael?' He came halfway to his feet as if he would bolt from the room, then gave an embarrassed frown and forced himself back down into his chair. 'How do you know? Who found his body?'

'He's still alive, Bast. He brought it back. There was only one.'

'There's no such thing as one scraeling,' Bast said flatly. 'You know that.'

'I know,' Kote said. 'The fact remains there was only one.'

'And he *killed* it?' Bast said. 'It couldn't have been a scraeling. Maybe—'

'Bast, it was one of the scrael. I saw it.' Kote gave him a serious look. 'He was lucky, that's all. Even so he was badly hurt. Forty-eight stitches. I used up nearly all my gut.' Kote picked up his bowl of stew. 'If anyone asks, tell them my grandfather was a caravan guard who taught me how to clean and stitch a wound. They were too shocked to ask about it tonight, but tomorrow some of them might get curious. I don't want that.' He blew into his bowl, raising a cloud of steam around his face.

'What did you do with the body?'

'*I* didn't do anything with it,' Kote said pointedly. '*I* am just an innkeeper. This sort of thing is quite beyond me.'

'Reshi, you can't just let them muddle through this on their own.'

Kote sighed. 'They took it to the priest. He did all the right things for all the wrong reasons.'

Bast opened his mouth, but Kote continued before he could say anything. 'Yes, I made sure the pit was deep enough. Yes, I made sure there was rowan wood in the fire. Yes, I made sure it burned long and hot before they buried it. And yes, I made sure that no one kept a piece of it as a souvenir.' He scowled, his eyebrows drawing together. 'I'm not an idiot, you know.'

Bast visibly relaxed, settling back into his chair. 'I know you're not, Reshi. But I wouldn't trust half these people to piss leeward without help.' He looked thoughtful for a moment. 'I can't imagine why there was only one.'

'Maybe they died coming over the mountains,' Kote suggested. 'All but this one.'

'It's possible,' Bast admitted reluctantly.

'Maybe it was that storm from a couple of days back,' Kote pointed out. 'A real wagon-tipper, as we used to say back in the troupe. All the wind and rain might have scattered one loose from the pack.'

'I like your first idea better, Reshi,' Bast said uncomfortably. 'Three or four scrael would go through this town like . . . like . . .'

'Like a hot knife through butter?'

'More like several hot knives through several dozen farmers,' Bast said dryly. 'These people can't defend themselves. I bet there aren't six swords in this whole town. Not that swords would do much good against the scrael.'

There was a long moment of thoughtful silence. After a moment Bast began to fidget. 'Any news?'

Kote shook his head. 'They didn't get to the news tonight. Carter disrupted things while they were still telling stories. That's something, I suppose. They'll be back tomorrow night. It'll give me something to do.'

Kote poked his spoon idly into the stew. 'I should have bought the scrael from Carter,' he mused. 'He could've used the money for a new horse. People would have come from all over to see it. We could have had some business for a change.'

Bast gave him a speechless, horrified look.

Kote made a pacifying gesture with the hand that held the spoon. 'I'm joking, Bast.' He gave a weak smile. 'Still, it would have been nice.'

'No Reshi, it most certainly would *not* have been nice,' Bast said emphatically. ' "People would have come from all over to see it," ' he repeated derisively. 'Indeed.'

'The *business* would have been nice,' Kote clarified. 'Busy-ness would be nice.' He jabbed his spoon into the stew again. 'Anything would be nice.'

They sat for a long moment. Kote scowling down into the bowl of stew in his hands, his eyes far away. 'It must be awful for you here, Bast,' he said at last. 'You must be numb with boredom.'

Bast shrugged. 'There are a few young wives in town. A scattering of daughters.' He grinned like a child. 'I tend to make my own fun.'

'That's good, Bast.' There was another silence. Kote took another spoonful, chewed, swallowed. 'They thought it was a demon, you know.'

Bast shrugged. 'It might as well be, Reshi. It's probably the best thing for them to think.'

'I know. I encouraged them, in fact. But you know what that means.' He met Bast's eyes. 'The blacksmith is going to be doing a brisk business in the next couple of days.'

Bast's expression went carefully blank. 'Oh.'

Kote nodded. 'I won't blame you if you want to leave, Bast. You have better places to be than this.'

Bast's expression was shocked. 'I couldn't leave, Reshi.' He opened and closed his mouth a few times, at a loss for words. 'Who else would teach me?'

Kote grinned, and for a moment his face showed how truly young he was. Behind the weary lines and the placid innkeeper's expression he looked no older than his dark-haired companion. 'Who indeed?' He gestured toward the door with his spoon. 'Go and do your reading then, or bother someone's daughter. I'm sure you have better things to do than watch me eat.'

'Actually . . .'

'Begone demon!' Kote said, switching to a thickly accented Temic through half a mouthful of stew. *'Tehus antausa eha!'*

Bast burst into startled laughter and made an obscene gesture with one hand.

Kote swallowed and changed languages. *'Aroi te denna-leyan!'*

'Oh come now,' Bast reproached, his smile falling away. 'That's just insulting.'

'By earth and stone, I abjure you!' Kote dipped his fingers into the cup by his side and flicked droplets casually in Bast's direction. 'Glamour be banished!'

'With cider?' Bast managed to look amused and annoyed at the same time as he daubed a bead of liquid from the front of his shirt. 'This had better not stain.'

Kote took another bite of his dinner. 'Go soak it. If the situation becomes desperate, I recommend you avail yourself of the numerous solvent formulae extant in *Celum Tinture*. Chapter thirteen, I believe.'

'Fine.' Bast stood and walked to the door, stepping with his strange, casual grace. 'Call if you need anything.' He closed the door behind himself.

Kote ate slowly, mopping up the last of the stew with a piece of bread. He looked out of the window as he ate, or tried to, as the lamplight turned its surface mirrorlike against the dark behind it.

His eyes wandered the room restlessly. The fireplace was made of the same black rock as the one downstairs. It stood in the center of the room, a minor feat of engineering of which Kote was rather proud. The bed was small, little more than a cot, and if you were to touch it you would find the mattress almost nonexistent.

A skilled observer might notice there was something his gaze avoided. The same way you avoid meeting the eye of an old lover at a formal dinner, or that of an old enemy sitting across the room in a crowded alehouse late at night.

Kote tried to relax, failed, fidgeted, sighed, shifted in his seat, and without willing it his eyes fell on the chest at the foot of the bed.

It was made of roah, a rare, heavy wood, dark as coal and smooth as polished glass. Prized by perfumers and alchemists, a piece the size of your thumb was easily worth gold. To have a chest made of it went far beyond extravagance.

The chest was sealed three times. It had a lock of iron, a lock of copper, and a lock that could not be seen. Tonight the wood filled the room with the almost imperceptible aroma of citrus and quenching iron.

When Kote's eyes fell on the chest they did not dart quickly away. They did not slide slyly to the side as if he would pretend it wasn't there at all. But in a moment of looking, his face regained all the lines the simple pleasures of the day had slowly smoothed away. The comfort of his bottles and books was erased in a second, leaving nothing behind his eyes but emptiness and ache. For a moment fierce longing and regret warred across his face.

Then they were gone, replaced by the weary face of an innkeeper, a man who called himself Kote. He sighed again without knowing it and pushed himself to his feet.

It was a long time before he walked past the chest to bed. Once in bed, it was a long time before he slept.

───────

As Kote had guessed, they came back to the Waystone the next night for dinner and drinks. There were a few half-hearted attempts at stories, but they died out quickly. No one was really in the mood.

So it was still early in the evening when the discussion turned to matters of greater import. They chewed over the rumours that had come into town, most of them troubling. The Penitent King was having a difficult time with the rebels in Resavek. This caused some concern, but only in a general way. Resavek was a long way off, and even Cob, the most worldly of them, would be hard pressed to find it on a map.

They discussed the war in their own terms. Cob predicted a third levy tax after the harvests were in. No one argued, though there hadn't been a three-bleeder year in living memory.

Jake guessed the harvest would be good enough so the third levy wouldn't break most families. Except the Bentleys, who were on hard times anyway. And the Orissons, whose sheep kept disappearing. And Crazy Martin, who had planted all barley this year. Every farmer with half a brain had planted beans. That was one good thing about all the fighting – soldiers ate beans, and prices would be high.

After a few more drinks, deeper concerns were voiced. Deserter soldiers and other opportunists were thick on the roads, making even short trips risky. The roads were always bad, of course, in the same way that winter was always cold. You complained, took sensible precautions, and got on with the business of living your life.

But this was different. Over the last two months the roads had become so bad that people had stopped complaining. The last caravan had two wagons and four guards. The merchant had been asking ten pennies for half a pound of salt, fifteen for a loaf of sugar. He didn't have any pepper, or cinnamon, or chocolate. He did have one small sack of coffee, but he wanted two silver talents for that. At first people had laughed at his prices. Then, when he held firm, folk had spat and cursed at him.

That had been two span ago: twenty-two days. There had not been another serious trader since, even though this was the season for it. So despite the third levy tax looming large in everyone's minds, people were looking in their purses and wishing they'd bought a little something, just in case the snow came early.

No one spoke of the previous night, of the thing they had burned and buried. Other folk were talking, of course. The town was alive with gossip. Carter's wounds ensured that the stories were taken half seriously, but not much more than half. The word 'demon' was being spoken, but it was with smiles half-hidden behind raised hands.

Only the six friends had seen the thing before it was burned. One of them had been wounded and the others had been drinking. The priest had seen it too, but it was his job to see demons. Demons were good for his business.

The innkeeper had seen it too, apparently. But he wasn't from around here. He couldn't know the truth that was so apparent to everyone born and raised in this little town: stories were told here, but they happened somewhere else. This was not a place for demons.

Besides, things were bad enough without borrowing trouble. Cob and the rest knew there was no sense talking about it. Trying to convince folk would only make them a laughingstock, like Crazy Martin, who had been trying to dig a well inside his own house for years now.

Still, each of them bought a piece of cold-wrought iron from the smith, heavy as they could swing, and none of them said what they were thinking. Instead they complained that the roads were bad and getting worse. They talked about merchants, and deserters, and levies, and not enough salt to last the winter. They reminisced that three years ago no one would have even thought of locking their doors at night, let alone barring them.

The conversation took a downward turn from there, and even though none of them said what they were thinking, the evening ended on a grim note. Most evenings did these days, times being what they were.

CHAPTER TWO

A Beautiful Day

I T WAS ONE OF those perfect autumn days so common in stories and so rare in the real world. The weather was warm and dry, ideal for ripening a field of wheat or corn. On both sides of the road the trees were changing colour. Tall poplars had gone a buttery yellow while the shrubby sumac encroaching on the road was tinged a violent red. Only the old oaks seemed reluctant to give up the summer, and their leaves remained an even mingling of gold and green.

Everything said, you couldn't hope for a nicer day to have a half dozen ex-soldiers with hunting bows relieve you of everything you owned.

'She's not much of a horse, sir,' Chronicler said. 'One small step above a dray, and when it rains she—'

The man cut him off with a sharp gesture. 'Listen friend, the king's army is paying good money for anything with four legs and at least one eye. If you were stark mad and riding a hobbyhorse down the road, I'd still take it off you.'

Their leader had an air of command about him. Chronicler guessed he had been a low ranking officer not long ago. 'Just hop down,' he said seriously. 'We'll get this done with and you can be on your way.'

Chronicler climbed down from his horse. He had been robbed before and knew when there was nothing to be gained by discussion. These fellows knew their business. No energy was wasted on bravado or idle threats. One of them looked over the horse, checking hooves, teeth, and harness. Two others went through his saddlebags with a military efficiency, laying all his worldly possessions out on the ground. Two blankets, a hooded cloak, the flat leather satchel, and his heavy, well-stocked travelsack.

'That's all of it, Commander,' one of the men said. 'Except for about twenty pounds of oats.'

The commander knelt down and opened the flat leather satchel, peering inside.

'There's nothing but paper and pens in there,' Chronicler said.

The commander turned to look back over his shoulder. 'You a scribe then?'

Chronicler nodded. 'It's my livelihood, sir. And no real use to you.'

The man looked through the satchel, found it to be true, and set it aside. Then he upended the travelsack onto Chronicler's spread cloak and poked idly through the contents.

He took most of Chronicler's salt and a pair of bootlaces. Then, much to the scribe's dismay, he picked up the shirt Chronicler had bought back in Linwood. It was fine linen dyed a deep, royal blue, too nice for travelling. Chronicler hadn't even had the chance to wear it yet. He sighed.

The commander left everything else lying on the cloak and got to his feet. The others took turns going through Chronicler's things.

The commander spoke up, 'You only have one blanket, don't you Janns?' One of the men nodded. 'Take one of his then, you'll need a second before winter's through.'

'His cloak is in better shape than mine, sir.'

'Take it, but leave yours. The same for you, Witkins. Leave your old tinderbox if you're taking his.'

'I lost mine, sir,' Witkins said. 'Else I would.'

The whole process was surprisingly civilised. Chronicler lost all of his needles but one, both extra pairs of socks, a bundle of dried fruit, a loaf of sugar, half a bottle of alcohol, and a pair of ivory dice. They left him the rest of his clothes, his dried meat, and a half-eaten loaf of incredibly stale rye bread. His flat leather satchel remained untouched.

While the men repacked his travelsack, the commander turned to Chronicler. 'Let's have the purse then.'

Chronicler handed it over.

'And the ring.'

'There's hardly any silver in it,' Chronicler mumbled as he unscrewed it from his finger.

'What's that around your neck?'

Chronicler unbuttoned his shirt, revealing a dull ring of metal hanging from a leather cord. 'Just iron, sir.'

The commander came close and rubbed it between his fingers before letting it fall back against Chronicler's chest. 'Keep it then. I'm not one to come between a man and his religion,' he said, then emptied the purse into one hand, making a pleasantly surprised noise as he prodded through the coins with his finger. 'Scribing pays better than I thought,' he said as he began to count out shares to his men.

'I don't suppose you could spare me a penny or two out of that?' Chronicler asked. 'Just enough for a couple of hot meals?'

The six men turned to look at Chronicler, as if they couldn't quite believe what they had heard.

The commander laughed. 'God's body, you certainly have a heavy pair, don't you?' There was a grudging respect in his voice.

'You seem a reasonable fellow,' Chronicler said with a shrug. 'And a man's got to eat.'

Their leader smiled for the first time. 'A sentiment I can agree with.' He took out two pennies and brandished them before putting them back into Chronicler's purse. 'Here's a pair for your pair, then.' He tossed Chronicler the purse and stuffed the beautiful royal-blue shirt into his saddlebag.

'Thank you, sir,' Chronicler said. 'You might want to know that that bottle one of your men took is wood alcohol I use for cleaning my pens. It'll go badly if he drinks it.'

The commander smiled and nodded. 'You see what comes of treating people well?' he said to his men as he pulled himself up onto his horse. 'It's been a pleasure, sir scribe. If you get on your way now, you can still make Abbott's Ford by dark.'

When Chronicler could no longer hear their hoofbeats in the distance, he repacked his travelsack, making sure everything was well stowed. Then he tugged off one of his boots, stripped out the lining, and removed a tightly wrapped bundle of coins stuffed deep into the toe. He moved some of these into his purse, then unfastened his pants, produced another bundle of coins from underneath several layers of clothes, and moved some of that money into his purse as well.

The key was to keep the proper amount in your purse. Too little and they would be disappointed and prone to look for more. Too much and they would be excited and might get greedy.

There was a third bundle of coins baked into the stale loaf of bread that only the most desperate of criminals would be interested in. He left that alone for now, as well as the whole silver talent he had hidden in a jar of ink.

Over the years he had come to think of the last as more of a luck piece. No one had ever found that.

He had to admit, it was probably the most civil robbery he'd ever been through. They had been genteel, efficient, and not terribly savvy. Losing the horse and saddle was hard, but he could buy another in Abbott's Ford and still have enough money to live comfortably until he finished this foolishness and met up with Skarpi in Treya.

Feeling an urgent call of nature, Chronicler pushed his way through the bloodred sumac at the side of the road. As he was rebuttoning his pants, there was sudden motion in the underbrush as a dark shape thrashed its way free of some nearby bushes.

Chronicler staggered back, crying out in alarm before he realised it was nothing more than a crow beating its wings into flight. Chuckling at his own foolishness, he straightened his clothes and made his way back to the road through the sumac, brushing away invisible strands of spiderweb that clung tickling to his face.

As he shouldered his travelsack and satchel, Chronicler found himself feeling remarkably lighthearted. The worst had happened, and it hadn't been that bad. A breeze tussled through the trees, sending poplar leaves spinning like golden coins down onto the rutted dirt road. It was a beautiful day.

CHAPTER THREE

Wood and Word

KOTE WAS LEAFING IDLY through a book, trying to ignore the silence of the empty inn when the door opened and Graham backed into the room.

'Just got done with it.' Graham maneuvered through the maze of tables with exaggerated care. 'I was gonna bring it in last night, but then I thought "one last coat of oil, rub it, and let dry". Can't say I'm sorry I did. Lord and lady, it's beautiful as anything these hands have ever made.'

A small line formed between the innkeeper's eyebrows. Then, seeing the flat bundle in the man's arms, he brightened. 'Ahhh! The mounting board!' Kote smiled tiredly. 'I'm sorry Graham. It's been so long. I'd almost forgotten.'

Graham gave him a bit of a strange look. 'Four month ain't long for wood all the way from Aryen, not with the roads being as bad as they are.'

'Four months,' Kote echoed. He saw Graham watching him and hurried to add, 'That can be a lifetime if you're waiting for something.' He tried to smile reassuringly, but it came out sickly.

In fact, Kote himself seemed rather sickly. Not exactly unhealthy, but hollow. Wan. Like a plant that's been moved into the wrong sort of soil and, lacking something vital, has begun to wilt.

Graham noted the difference. The innkeeper's gestures weren't as extravagant. His voice wasn't as deep. Even his eyes weren't as bright as they had been a month ago. Their colour seemed duller. They were less sea-foam, less green-grass than they had been. Now they were like riverweed, like the bottom of a green glass bottle. And his hair had been bright before, the colour of flame. Now it seemed – red. Just red-hair colour, really.

Kote drew back the cloth and looked underneath. The wood was a dark charcoal colour with a black grain, heavy as a sheet of iron. Three dark pegs were set above a word chiselled into the wood.

'Folly,' Graham read. 'Odd name for a sword.'

Kote nodded, his face carefully blank. 'How much do I owe you?' he asked quietly.

Graham thought for a moment. 'After what ye've given me to cover the cost of the wood . . .' There was a cunning glimmer in the man's eye. 'Around one and three.'

Kote handed over two talents. 'Keep the rest. It's difficult wood to work with.'

'That it is,' Graham said with some satisfaction. 'Like stone under the saw. Try a chisel, like iron. Then, after all the shouting was done, I couldn't char it.'

'I noticed that,' Kote said with a flicker of curiosity, running a finger along the darker groove the letters made in the wood. 'How did you manage it?'

'Well,' Graham said smugly, 'after wasting half a day, I took it over to the smithy. Me and the boy managed to sear it with a hot iron. Took us better than two hours to get it black. Not a wisp of smoke, but it made a stink like old leather and clover. Damnedest thing. What sort of wood don't burn?'

Graham waited a minute, but the innkeeper gave no signs of having heard. 'Where would'e like me to hang it then?'

Kote roused himself enough to look around the room. 'You can leave that to me, I think. I haven't quite decided where to put it.'

Graham left a handful of iron nails and bid the innkeeper good day. Kote remained at the bar, idly running his hands over the wood and the word. Before too long Bast came out of the kitchen and looked over his teacher's shoulder.

There was a long moment of silence like a tribute given to the dead.

Eventually, Bast spoke up. 'May I ask a question, Reshi?'

Kote smiled gently. 'Always, Bast.'

'A troublesome question?'

'Those tend to be the only worthwhile kind.'

They remained staring at the object on the bar for another silent moment, as if trying to commit it to memory. *Folly.*

Bast struggled for a moment, opening his mouth, then closing it with a frustrated look, then repeating the process.

'Out with it,' Kote said finally.

'What were you thinking?' Bast said with an odd mixture of confusion and concern.

Kote was a long while in answering. 'I tend to think too much, Bast. My greatest successes came from decisions I made when I stopped thinking and simply did what felt right. Even if there was no good explanation for what I did.' He smiled wistfully. 'Even if there were very good reasons for me *not* to do what I did.'

Bast ran a hand along the side of his face. 'So you're trying to avoid second-guessing yourself?'

Kote hesitated. 'You could say that,' he admitted.

'*I* could say that, Reshi,' Bast said smugly. 'You, on the other hand, would complicate things needlessly.'

Kote shrugged and turned his eyes back to the mounting board. 'Nothing to do but find a place for it, I suppose.'

'Out here?' Bast's expression was horrified.

Kote grinned wickedly, a measure of vitality coming back into his face. 'Of course,' he said, seeming to savour Bast's reaction. He looked speculatively at the walls and pursed his lips. 'Where did you put it, anyway?'

'In my room,' Bast admitted. 'Under my bed.'

Kote nodded distractedly, still looking at the walls. 'Go get it then.' He made a small shooing gesture with one hand, and Bast hurried off, looking unhappy.

The bar was decorated with glittering bottles, and Kote was standing on the now-vacant counter between the two heavy oak barrels when Bast came back into the room, black scabbard swinging loosely from one hand.

Kote paused in the act of setting the mounting board atop one of the barrels and cried out in dismay, 'Careful, Bast! You're carrying a lady there, not swinging some wench at a barn dance.'

Bast stopped in his tracks and dutifully gathered it up in both hands before walking the rest of the way to the bar.

Kote pounded a pair of nails into the wall, twisted some wire, and hung the mounting board firmly on the wall. 'Hand it up, would you?' he asked with an odd catch in his voice.

Using both hands, Bast held it up to him, looking for a moment like a squire offering up a sword to some bright-armoured knight. But there was no knight there, just an innkeeper, just a man in an apron who called himself Kote. He took the sword from Bast and stood upright on the counter behind the bar.

He drew the sword without a flourish. It shone a dull grey-white in the room's autumn light. It had the appearance of a new sword. It was not notched or rusted. There were no bright scratches skittering along its dull grey side. But though it was unmarred, it was old. And while it was obviously a sword, it was not a familiar shape. At least no one in this town would have found it familiar. It looked as if an alchemist had distilled a dozen swords, and when the crucible had cooled this was lying in the bottom: a sword in its pure form. It was slender and graceful. It was deadly as a sharp stone beneath swift water.

Kote held it a moment. His hand did not shake.

Then he set the sword on the mounting board. Its grey-white metal shone against the dark roah behind it. While the handle could be seen, it was dark enough to be almost indistinguishable from the wood. The word beneath it, black against blackness, seemed to reproach: *Folly*.

Kote climbed down, and for a moment he and Bast stood side by side, silently looking up.

Bast broke the silence. 'It *is* rather striking,' he said, as if he regretted the truth. 'But . . .' He trailed off, trying to find appropriate words. He shuddered.

Kote clapped him on the back, oddly cheerful. 'Don't bother being disturbed on my account.' He seemed more lively now, as if his activity lent him energy. 'I like it,' he said with sudden conviction, and hung the black scabbard from one of the mounting board's pegs.

Then there were things to be done. Bottles to be polished and put back in place. Lunch to be made. Lunch clutter to be cleaned. Things were cheerful for a while in a pleasant, bustling way. The two talked of small matters as they worked. And while they moved around a great deal, it was obvious they were reluctant to finish whatever task they were close to completing, as if they both dreaded the moment when the work would end and the silence would fill the room again.

Then something odd happened. The door opened and noise poured into the Waystone like a gentle wave. People bustled in, talking and dropping bundles of belongings. They chose tables and threw their coats over the backs of chairs. One man, wearing a shirt of heavy metal rings, unbuckled a sword and leaned it against a wall. Two or three wore knives on their belts. Four or five called for drinks.

Kote and Bast watched for a moment, then moved smoothly into action. Kote smiled and began pouring drinks. Bast darted outside to see if there were horses that needed stabling.

In ten minutes the inn was a different place. Coins rang on the bar. Cheese and fruit were set on platters and a large copper pot was hung to simmer in the kitchen. Men moved tables and chairs about to better suit their group of nearly a dozen people.

Kote identified them as they came in. Two men and two women, wagoneers, rough from years of being outside and smiling to be spending a night out of the wind. Three guards with hard eyes, smelling of iron. A tinker with a potbelly and a ready smile showing his few remaining teeth. Two young men, one sandy-haired, one dark, well dressed and well-spoken: travellers sensible enough to hook up with a larger group for protection on the road.

The settling-in period lasted an hour or two. Prices of rooms were dickered over. Friendly arguments started about who slept with whom. Minor necessities were brought in from wagons or saddlebags. Baths were requested and water heated. Hay was taken to the horses, and Kote topped off the oil in all the lamps.

The tinker hurried outside to make use of the remaining daylight. He walked his two-wheel mule cart through the town's streets. Children crowded around, begging for candy and stories and shims.

When it became apparent that nothing was going to be handed out, most of them lost interest. They formed a circle with a boy in the middle and started to clap, keeping the beat with a children's song that had been ages old when their grandparents had chanted it:

> *'When the hearthfire turns to blue,*
> *What to do? What to do?*
> *Run outside. Run and hide.'*

Laughing, the boy in the middle tried to break out of the circle while the other children pushed him back.

'Tinker,' the old man's voice rang out like a bell. 'Pot mender. Knife grinder. Willow-wand water-finder. Cut cork. Motherleaf. Silk scarves off the city streets. Writing paper. Sweetmeats.'

This drew the attention of the children. They flocked back to him, making a small parade as he walked down the street, singing, 'Belt leather. Black pepper. Fine lace and bright feather. Tinker in town tonight, gone tomorrow. Working through the evening light. Come wife. Come daughter, I've small cloth and rose water.' After a couple of minutes he settled outside the Waystone, set up his sharpening wheel and began to grind a knife.

As the adults began to gather around the old man, the children returned to their game. A girl in the centre of the circle put one hand over her eyes and tried to catch the other children as they ran away, clapping and chanting:

> *'When his eyes are black as crow?*
> *Where to go? Where to go?*
> *Near and far. Here they are.'*

The tinker dealt with everyone in turn, sometimes two or three at a time. He traded sharp knives for dull ones and a small coin. He sold shears and needles, copper pots and small bottles that wives hid quickly after buying them. He traded buttons and bags of cinnamon and salt. Limes from Tinuë, chocolate from Tarbean, polished horn from Aerueh . . .

All the while the children continued to sing:

> *'See a man without a face?*
> *Move like ghosts from place to place.*
> *What's their plan? What's their plan?*
> *Chandrian. Chandrian.'*

Kote guessed the travellers had been together a month or so, long enough to become comfortable with each other, but not long enough to be squabbling over small things. They smelled of road dust and horses. He breathed it in like perfume.

Best of all was the noise. Leather creaking. Men laughing. The fire cracked and spat. The women flirted. Someone even knocked over a chair. For the first time in a long while there was no silence in the Waystone Inn. Or if there was, it was too faint to be noticed, or too well hidden.

Kote was in the middle of it all, always moving, like a man tending a large, complex machine. Ready with a drink just as a person called for it, he talked and listened in the right amounts. He laughed at jokes, shook hands, smiled, and whisked coins off the bar as if he truly needed the money.

Then, when the time for songs came and everyone had sung their favourites and still wanted more, Kote led them from behind the bar, clapping to keep a beat. With the fire shining in his hair, he sang 'Tinker Tanner', with more verses than anyone had heard before, and no one minded in the least.

———————

Hours later, the common room had a warm, jovial feel to it. Kote was kneeling on the hearth, building up the fire, when someone spoke behind him.

'Kvothe?'

The innkeeper turned, wearing a slightly confused smile. 'Sir?'

It was one of the well-dressed travellers. He swayed a little. 'You're Kvothe.'

'Kote, sir,' Kote replied in an indulgent tone that mothers use on children and innkeepers use on drunks.

'Kvothe the Bloodless.' The man pressed ahead with the dogged persistence of the inebriated. 'You looked familiar, but I couldn't finger it.' He smiled proudly and tapped a finger to his nose. 'Then I heard you sing, and I knew it was you. I heard you in Imre once. Cried my eyes out afterward. I never heard anything like that before or since. Broke my heart.'

The young man's sentences grew jumbled as he continued, but his face remained earnest. 'I knew it couldn't be you. But I thought it was. Even though. But who else has your hair?' He shook his head, trying unsuccessfully to clear it. 'I saw the place in Imre where you killed him. By the fountain. The cobblestones are all shathered.' He frowned and concentrated on the word. '*Shattered*. They say no one can mend them.'

The sandy-haired man paused again. Squinting for focus, he seemed surprised by the innkeeper's reaction.

The red-haired man was grinning. 'Are you saying I look like Kvothe? *The* Kvothe? I've always thought so myself. I have an engraving of him in back. My assistant teases me for it. Would you tell him what you just told me?'

Kote threw a final log onto the fire and stood. But as he stepped from the hearth, one of his legs twisted underneath him and he fell heavily to the floor, knocking over a chair.

Several of the travellers hurried over, but the innkeeper was already on his feet, waving people back to their seats. 'No, no. I'm fine. Sorry to startle anyone.' In spite of his grin it was obvious he'd hurt himself. His face was tight with pain, and he leaned heavily on a chair for support.

'Took an arrow in the knee on my way through the Eld three summers ago. It gives out every now and then.' He grimaced and said wistfully, 'It's what made me give up the good life on the road.' He reached down to touch his oddly bent leg tenderly.

One of the mercenaries spoke up. 'I'd put a poultice on that, or it'll swell terrible.'

Kote touched it again and nodded. 'I think you are wise, sir.' He turned to the sandy-haired man who stood swaying slightly by the fireplace, 'Could you do me a favour, son?'

The man nodded dumbly.

'Just close the flue.' Kote gestured toward the fireplace. 'Bast, will you help me upstairs?'

Bast hurried over and drew Kote's arm around his shoulders. Kote leaned on him with every other step as they made their way through the doorway and up the stairs.

'Arrow in the leg?' Bast asked under his breath. 'Are you really that embarrassed from taking a little fall?'

'Thank God you're as gullible as they are,' Kote said sharply as soon as they were out of sight. He began to curse under his breath as he climbed a few more steps, his knee obviously uninjured.

Bast's eyes widened, then narrowed.

Kote stopped at the top of the steps and rubbed his eyes. 'One of them knows who I am.' Kote frowned. 'Suspects.'

'Which one?' Bast asked with a mix of apprehension and anger.

'Green shirt, sandy hair. The one nearest to me by the fireplace. Give him something to make him sleep. He's already been drinking. No one will think twice if he happens to pass out.'

Bast thought briefly. 'Nighmane?'

'Mhenka.'

Bast raised an eyebrow, but nodded.

Kote straightened. 'Listen three times, Bast.'

Bast blinked once and nodded.

Kote spoke crisply and cleanly. 'I was a city-licensed escort from Ralien. Wounded while successfully defending a caravan. Arrow in right knee. Three years ago. Summer. A grateful Cealdish merchant gave me money to start an inn. His name is Deolan. We were travelling from Purvis. Mention it casually. Do you have it?'

'I hear you three times, Reshi,' Bast replied formally.

'Go.'

───────────

Half an hour later Bast brought a bowl to his master's room, reassuring him that everything was well downstairs. Kote nodded and gave terse instructions that he not be disturbed for the rest of the night.

Closing the door behind himself, Bast's expression was worried. He stood at the top of the stairs for some time, trying to think of something he could do.

It is hard to say what troubled Bast so much. Kote didn't seem noticeably changed in any way. Except, perhaps, that he moved a little slower, and whatever small spark the night's activity had lit behind his eyes was dimmer now. In fact, it could hardly be seen. In fact, it may not have been there at all.

Kote sat in front of the fire and ate his meal mechanically, as if he were simply finding a place inside himself to keep the food. After the last bite he sat staring into nothing, not remembering what he had eaten or what it tasted like.

The fire snapped, making him blink and look around the room. He looked down at his hands, one curled inside the other, resting in his lap. After a moment, he lifted and spread them, as if warming them by the fire. They were graceful, with long, delicate fingers. He watched them intently, as if expecting them to do something on their own. Then he lowered them to his lap, one hand lightly cupping the other, and returned to watching the fire. Expressionless, motionless, he sat until there was nothing left but grey ash and dully glowing coals.

As he was undressing for bed, the fire flared. The red light traced faint lines across his body, across his back and arms. All the scars were smooth and silver, streaking him like lightning, like lines of gentle remembering. The flare of flame revealed them all briefly, old wounds and new. All the scars were smooth and silver except one.

The fire flickered and died. Sleep met him like a lover in an empty bed.

───────────

The travellers left early the next morning. Bast tended to their needs, explaining his master's knee was swollen quite badly and he didn't feel up to taking the stairs so early in the day. Everyone understood except for the sandy-haired merchant's son, who was too groggy to understand much of anything. The guards exchanged smiles and rolled their eyes while the tinker gave an impromptu sermon on the subject of temperance. Bast recommended several unpleasant hangover cures.

After they left, Bast tended to the inn, which was no great chore, as there were no customers. Most of his time was spent trying to find ways to amuse himself.

Some time after noon, Kote came down the stairs to find him crushing walnuts on the bar with a heavy leather-bound book. 'Good morning, Reshi.'

'Good morning, Bast,' Kote said. 'Any news?'

'The Orrison boy stopped by. Wanted to know if we needed any mutton.'

Kote nodded, almost as if he had been suspecting the news. 'How much did you order?'

Bast made a face. 'I hate mutton, Reshi. It tastes like wet mittens.'

Kote shrugged and made his way to the door. 'I've got some errands to run. Keep an eye on things, will you?'

'I always do.'

Outside the Waystone Inn the air lay still and heavy on the empty dirt road that ran through the centre of town. The sky was a featureless grey sheet of cloud that looked as if it wanted to rain but couldn't quite work up the energy.

Kote walked across the street to the open front of the smithy. The smith wore his hair cropped short and his beard thick and bushy. As Kote watched, he carefully drove a pair of nails through a scythe blade's collar, fixing it firmly onto a curved wooden handle. 'Hello Caleb.'

The smith leaned the scythe up against the wall. 'What can I do for you, Master Kote?'

'Did the Orrison boy stop by your place too?' Caleb nodded. 'They still losing sheep?' Kote asked.

'Actually, some of the lost ones finally turned up. Torn up awful, practically shredded.'

'Wolves?' Kote asked.

The smith shrugged. 'It's the wrong time of year, but what else would it be? A bear? I guess they're just selling off what they can't watch over properly, them being shorthanded and all.'

'Shorthanded?'

'Had to let their hired man go because of taxes, and their oldest son took the king's coin early this summer. He's off fighting the rebels in Menat now.'

'Meneras,' Kote corrected gently. 'If you see their boy again, let him know I'd be willing to buy about three halves.'

'I'll do that.' The smith gave the innkeeper a knowing look. 'Is there anything else?'

'Well,' Kote looked away, suddenly self-conscious. 'I *was* wondering if you have any rod-iron lying around,' he said, not meeting the smith's eye. 'It doesn't have to be anything fancy mind you. Just plain old pig-iron would do nicely.'

Caleb chuckled. 'I didn't know if you were going to stop by at all. Old Cob and the rest came by day before yesterday.' He walked over to a work-bench and lifted up a piece of canvas. 'I made a couple of extras just in case.'

Kote picked up a rod of iron about two feet long and swung it casually with one hand. 'Clever man.'

'I know my business,' the smith said smugly. 'You need anything else?'

'Actually,' Kote said as he settled the bar of iron comfortably against his shoulder, 'there is one other thing. Do you have a spare apron and set of forge gloves?'

'Could have,' Caleb said hesitantly. 'Why?'

'There's an old bramble patch behind the inn.' Kote nodded in the direction of the Waystone. 'I'm thinking of tearing it up so I can put in a garden next year. But I don't fancy losing half my skin doing it.'

The smith nodded and gestured for Kote to follow him into the back of the shop. 'I've got my old set,' he said as he dug out a pair of heavy gloves and a stiff leather apron; both were charred dark in places and stained with grease. 'They're not pretty, but they'll keep the worst of it off you, I suppose.'

'What are they worth to you?' Kote asked, reaching for his purse.

The smith shook his head, 'A jot would be a great plenty. They're no good to me or the boy.'

The innkeeper handed over a coin and the smith stuffed them into an old burlap sack. 'You sure you want to do it now?' The smith asked. 'We haven't had rain in a while. The ground'll be softer after the spring thaw.'

Kote shrugged. 'My granda always told me that fall's the time to root up something don't want coming back to trouble you.' Kote mimicked the quaver of an old man's voice. ' "Things are too full of life in the spring

months. In the summer, they're too strong and won't let go. Autumn . . ." '
He looked around at the changing leaves on the trees.' "Autumn's the time.
In autumn everything is tired and ready to die." '

———————————

Later that afternoon Kote sent Bast to catch up on his sleep. Then he moved
listlessly around the inn, doing small jobs left over from the night before.
There were no customers. When evening finally came he lit the lamps and
began to page disinterestedly through a book.

Fall was supposed to be the year's busiest time, but travellers were scarce
lately. Kote knew with bleak certainty how long winter would be.

He closed the inn early, something he had never done before. He didn't
bother sweeping. The floor didn't need it. He didn't wash the tables or the
bar, none had been used. He polished a bottle or two, locked the door, and
went to bed.

There was no one around to notice the difference. No one except Bast,
who watched his master, and worried, and waited.

CHAPTER FOUR

Halfway to Newarre

CHRONICLER WALKED. Yesterday he had limped, but today there was no part of his feet that didn't hurt, so limping did no good. He had searched for horses in Abbott's Ford and Rannish, offering outrageous prices for even the most broken-down animals. But in small towns like these, people didn't have horses to spare, especially not with harvest fast approaching.

Despite a hard day's walking, he was still on the road when night fell, making the rutted dirt road a stumbling ground of half-seen shapes. After two hours of fumbling through the dark, Chronicler saw light flickering through the trees and abandoned any thought of making it to Newarre that night, deciding a farmstead's hospitality would be welcome enough.

He left the road, blundering through the trees toward the light. But the fire was farther away than he had thought, and larger. It wasn't lamplight from a house, or even sparks from a campfire. It was a bonfire roaring in the ruins of an old house, little more than two crumbling stone walls. Huddled into the corner those two walls made was a man. He wore a heavy hooded cloak, bundled up as if it were full winter and not a mild autumn evening.

Chronicler's hopes rose at the sight of a small cook fire with a pot hanging over it. But as he came close, he caught a foul scent mingling with the woodsmoke. It reeked of burning hair and rotting flowers. Chronicler quickly decided that whatever the man was cooking in the iron pot, he wanted none of it. Still, even a place next to a fire was better than curling up by the side of the road.

Chronicler stepped into the circle of firelight. 'I saw your f—' He stopped as the figure sprang quickly to its feet, a sword held with both hands. No, not a sword, a long, dark cudgel of some sort, too regularly shaped to be a piece of firewood.

Chronicler stopped dead in his tracks. 'I was just looking for a place to sleep,' he said quickly, his hand unconsciously clutching at the circle of iron that hung around his neck. 'I don't want any trouble. I'll leave you to your dinner.' He took a step backward.

The figure relaxed, and the cudgel dropped to grate metallically against a stone. 'Charred body of God, what are you doing out here at this time of night?'

'I was headed to Newarre and saw your fire.'

'You just followed a strange fire into the woods at night?' The hooded figure shook his head. 'You might as well come here.' He motioned Chronicler closer, and the scribe saw he was wearing thick leather gloves. 'Tehlu anyway, have you had bad luck your whole life, or have you been saving it all up for tonight?'

'I don't know who you're waiting for,' Chronicler said, taking a step backwards. 'But I'm sure you'd rather do it alone.'

'Shut up and listen,' the man said sharply. 'I don't know how much time we have.' He looked down and rubbed at his face. 'God, I never know how much to tell you people. If you don't believe me, you'll think I'm crazy. If you *do* believe me, you'll panic and be worse than useless.' Looking back up, he saw Chronicler hadn't moved. 'Get over here, damn you. If you go back out there you're as good as dead.'

Chronicler glanced over his shoulder into the dark of the forest. 'Why? What's out there?'

The man gave a short, bitter laugh and shook his head in exasperation. 'Honestly?' He ran his hand absentmindedly though his hair, brushing his hood back in the process. In the firelight his hair was impossibly red, his eyes a shocking, vibrant green. He looked at Chronicler, sizing him up. 'Demons,' he said. 'Demons in the shape of big, black spiders.'

Chronicler relaxed. 'There's no such thing as demons.' From his tone it was obvious he'd said the same thing many, many times before.

The red-haired man gave an incredulous laugh. 'Well, I guess we can all go home then!' He flashed a manic grin at Chronicler. 'Listen, I'm guessing you're an educated man. I respect that, and for the most part, you're right.' His expression went serious. 'But here and now, tonight, you're wrong. Wrong as wrong can be. You don't want to be on that side of the fire when you figure that out.'

The flat certainty in the man's voice sent a chill down Chronicler's back. Feeling more than slightly foolish, he stepped delicately around to the other side of the bonfire.

The man sized him up quickly. 'I don't suppose you have any weapons?' Chronicler shook his head. 'It doesn't really matter. A sword wouldn't do you much good.' He handed Chronicler a heavy piece of firewood. 'You probably won't be able to hit one, but it's worth a try. They're fast. If one of them gets on you, just fall down. Try to land on it, crush it with your body. Roll on it. If you get hold of one, throw it into the fire.'

He drew the hood back over his head, speaking quickly. 'If you have any extra clothes, put them on. If you have a blanket you could wrap—'

He stopped suddenly and looked out across the circle of firelight. 'Get your back against the wall,' he said abruptly, bringing his iron cudgel up with both hands.

Chronicler looked past the bonfire. Something dark was moving in the trees.

They came into the light, moving low across the ground: black shapes, many-legged and large as cart wheels. One, quicker than the rest, rushed into the firelight without hesitating, moving with the disturbing, sinuous speed of a scuttling insect.

Before Chronicler could raise his piece of firewood, the thing skirted sideways around the bonfire and sprang at him, quick as a cricket. Chronicler threw up his hands just as the black thing struck his face and chest. Its cold, hard legs scrabbled for a hold and he felt bright stripes of pain across the backs of his arm. Staggering away, the scribe felt his heel snag on the rough ground, and he began to topple over backward, arms flailing wildly.

As he fell, Chronicler caught one last glimpse of the circle of firelight. More of the black things were scuttling out of the dark, their feet beating a quick staccato rhythm against roots and rocks and leaves. On the other side of the fire the man in the heavy cloak held his iron cudgel ready with both hands. He stood perfectly still, perfectly silent, waiting.

Still falling backwards with the dark thing on top of him, Chronicler felt a dull, dark explosion as the back of his head struck the stone wall behind him. The world slowed, turned blurry, then black.

———

Chronicler opened his eyes to a confusing mass of dark shapes and firelight. His skull throbbed. There were several lines of bright, clear pain crossing the backs of his arms and a dull ache that pulled at his left side every time he drew in a breath.

After a long moment of concentration the world came into a blurry focus. The bundled man sat nearby. He was no longer wearing his gloves, and his heavy cloak hung off his body in loose tatters, but other than that he seemed unscathed. His hood was up, hiding his face.

'You're awake?' the man asked curiously. 'That's good. You can never be sure with a head wound.' The hood tilted a bit. 'Can you talk? Do you know where you are?'

'Yes,' Chronicler said thickly. It seemed to take far too much effort to make a single word.

'Even better. Now, third time pays for all. Do you think you can stand up and lend me a hand? We need to burn and bury the bodies.'

Chronicler moved his head a bit and felt suddenly dizzy and nauseous. 'What happened?'

'I might have broken a couple of your ribs,' the man said. 'One of them was all over you. I didn't have a lot of options.' He shrugged. 'I'm sorry, for whatever that's worth. I've already stitched up the cuts on your arms. They should heal up nicely.'

'They're gone?'

The hood nodded once. 'The scrael don't retreat. They're like wasps from a hive. They keep attacking until they die.'

A horrified look spread over Chronicler's face. 'There's a hive of these things?'

'Dear God, no. There were just these five. Still, we have to burn and bury them, just to be sure. I already cut the wood we'll need: ash and rowan.'

Chronicler gave a laugh that sounded slightly hysterical. 'Just like the children's song:

> *"Let me tell you what to do.*
> *Dig a pit that's ten by two.*
> *Ash and elm and rowan too—" '*

'Yes indeed,' the bundled man said dryly. 'You'd be surprised at the sorts of things hidden away in children's songs. But while I don't think we need to dig the entire ten feet down, I wouldn't refuse a little help . . .' He trailed off meaningfully.

Chronicler moved one hand to feel the back of his head gingerly, then

looked at his fingers, surprised that they weren't covered in blood. 'I think
I'm fine,' he said as he cautiously levered himself up onto one elbow and
from there into a sitting position. 'Is there any—' His eyes flickered and he
went limp, falling bonelessly backwards. His head struck the ground,
bounced once, and came to rest tilted slightly to one side.

————————

Kote sat patiently for a few long moments, watching the unconscious man.
When there was no movement other than the chest slowly rising and falling,
he came stiffly to his feet and knelt at Chronicler's side. Kote lifted one eyelid, then the other and grunted at what he saw, not seeming particularly
surprised.

'I don't suppose there's any chance of you waking up again?' he asked
without much hope in his voice. He tapped Chronicler's pale cheek lightly.
'No chance at—' A drop of blood spotted Chronicler's forehead, followed
quickly by another.

Kote straightened up so that he was no longer leaning over the unconscious man and wiped the blood away as best he could, which wasn't very
well, as his hands were covered in blood themselves. 'Sorry,' he said absently.

He gave a deep sigh and pushed back his hood. His red hair was matted
down against his head, and half his face was smeared with drying blood.
Slowly he began to peel away the tattered remains of his cloak. Underneath
was a leather blacksmith's apron, wildly scored with cuts. He removed that as
well, revealing a plain grey shirt of homespun. Both his shoulders and his left
arm were dark and wet with blood.

Kote fingered the buttons of his shirt for a moment, then decided against
removing it. Climbing gingerly to his feet, he picked up the spade and
slowly, painfully, began to dig.

CHAPTER FIVE

Notes

IT WAS WELL PAST midnight by the time Kote made it back to Newarre with Chronicler's limp body slung across his lacerated shoulders. The town's houses and shops were dark and silent, but the Waystone Inn was full of light.

Bast stood in the doorway, practically dancing with irritation. When he spotted the approaching figure he rushed down the street, waving a piece of paper angrily. 'A note? You sneak out and leave me a *note?*' He hissed angrily. 'What am I, some dockside whore?'

Kote turned around and shrugged Chronicler's limp body into Bast's arms. 'I knew you would just argue with me, Bast.'

Bast held Chronicler easily in front of him. 'It wasn't even a *good* note. "If you are reading this I am probably dead." What sort of a note is that?'

'You weren't supposed to find it till morning,' Kote said tiredly as they began to walk down the street to the inn.

Bast looked down at the man he was carrying, as if noticing him for the first time. 'Who is this?' He shook him a little, eyeing him curiously before slinging him easily over one shoulder like a burlap sack.

'Some unlucky sod who happened to be on the road at the wrong time,' Kote said dismissively. 'Don't shake him too much. His head might be on a little loose.'

'What the hell did you sneak off for, anyway?' Bast demanded as they entered the inn. 'If you're going to leave a note it should at least tell me what—' Bast's eyes widened as he saw Kote in the light of the inn, pale and streaked with blood and dirt.

'You can go ahead and worry if you want,' Kote said dryly. 'It's every bit as bad as it looks.'

'You went out hunting for them, didn't you?' Bast hissed, then his eyes widened. 'No. You kept a piece of the one Carter killed. I can't believe you. You lied to me. To *me!*'

Kote sighed as he trudged up the stairs. 'Are you upset by the lie, or the fact that you didn't catch me at it?' he asked as he began to climb.

Bast spluttered. 'I'm upset that you thought you couldn't trust me.'

They let their conversation lapse as they opened one of the many empty rooms on the second floor, undressed Chronicler, and tucked him snugly into bed. Kote left the man's satchel and travelsack on the floor nearby.

Closing the door to the room behind him, Kote said, 'I trust you Bast, but I wanted you safe. I knew I could handle it.'

'I could have helped, Reshi.' Bast's tone was injured. 'You know I would have.'

'You can still help, Bast,' Kote said as he made his way to his room and sat heavily on the edge of his narrow bed. 'I need some stitching done.' He began to unbutton his shirt. 'I could do it myself. But the tops of my shoulders and my back are hard to reach.'

'Nonsense, Reshi. I'll do it.'

Kote made a gesture to the door. 'My supplies are down in the basement.'

Bast sniffed disdainfully. 'I will use my own needles, thank you very much. Good honest bone. None of your nasty jagged iron things, stabbing you like little slivers of hate.' He shivered. 'Stream and stone, it's frightening how primitive you people are.' Bast bustled out of the room, leaving the door open behind him.

Kote slowly removed his shirt, grimacing and sucking his breath through his teeth as the dried blood stuck and tugged against the wounds. His face went stoic again when Bast came back into the room with a basin of water and began to clean him off.

As the dried blood was washed away a wild scoring of long, straight cuts became clear. They gaped redly against the innkeeper's fair skin, as if he had been slashed with a barber's razor or a piece of broken glass. There were perhaps a dozen cuts in all, most of them on the tops of his shoulders, a few across his back and along his arms. One started on the top of his head and ran down his scalp to behind his ear.

'I thought you weren't supposed to bleed, Reshi,' Bast said. 'Bloodless and all that.'

'Don't believe everything you hear in stories, Bast. They lie to you.'

'Well you aren't nearly as bad off as I thought,' Bast said, wiping his hands clean. 'Though by all rights you should have lost a piece of your ear. Were they wounded like the one that attacked Carter?'

'Not that I could see,' Kote said.

'How many were there?'

'Five.'

'Five?' Bast said, aghast. 'How many did the other fellow kill?'

'He distracted one of them for a while,' Kote said generously.

'*Anpauen,* Reshi,' Bast said, shaking his head as he threaded a bone needle with something thinner and finer than gut. 'You should be dead. You should be dead *twice.*'

Kote shrugged. 'It's not the first time I should be dead, Bast. I'm a fair hand at avoiding it.'

Bast bent to his work. 'This will sting a bit,' he said, his hands strangely gentle. 'Honestly Reshi, I can't see how you've managed to stay alive this long.'

Kote shrugged again and closed his eyes. 'Neither do I, Bast,' he said. His voice was tired and grey.

———

Hours later, the door to Kote's room cracked open and Bast peered inside. Hearing nothing but slow, measured breathing, the young man walked softly to stand beside the bed and bent over the sleeping man. Bast eyed the colour of his cheeks, smelled his breath, and lightly touched his forehead, his wrist, and the hollow of his throat above his heart.

Then Bast drew a chair alongside the bed and sat, watching his master, listening to him breathe. After a moment he reached out and brushed the unruly red hair back from his face, like a mother would with a sleeping child. Then he began to sing softly, the tune lilting and strange, almost a lullaby:

> '*How odd to watch a mortal kindle*
> *Then to dwindle day by day.*
> *Knowing their bright souls are tinder*
> *And the wind will have its way.*
> *Would I could my own fire lend.*
> *What does your flickering portend?*'

Bast's voice faded until at last he sat motionless, watching the rise and fall of his master's silent breathing through the long hours of morning's early dark.

CHAPTER SIX

The Price of Remembering

IT WAS EARLY EVENING of the next day before Chronicler came down the stairs to the common room of the Waystone Inn. Pale and unsteady, he carried his flat leather satchel under one arm.

Kote sat behind the bar, paging through a book. 'Ah, our unintentional guest. How's the head?'

Chronicler raised a hand to touch the back of his head. 'Throbs a bit when I move around too quickly. But it's still working.'

'Glad to hear it,' Kote said.

'Is this . . .' Chronicler hesitated, looking around. 'Are we in Newarre?'

Kote nodded. 'You are, in fact, in the middle of Newarre.' He made a dramatic sweeping gesture with one hand. 'Thriving metropolis. Home to dozens.'

Chronicler stared at the red-haired man behind the bar. He leaned against one of the tables for support. 'God's charred body,' he said breathlessly. 'It really is you, isn't it?'

The innkeeper looked puzzled. 'I beg your pardon?'

'I know you're going to deny it,' Chronicler said. 'But what I saw last night . . .'

The innkeeper held up a hand, quieting him. 'Before we discuss the possibility that you've addled your wits with that crack to the head, tell me, how is the road to Tinuë?'

'What?' Chronicler asked, irritated. 'I wasn't heading to Tinuë. I was . . . oh. Well even aside from last night, the road's been pretty rough. I was robbed off by Abbot's Ford, and I've been on foot ever since. But it was all worth it since you're actually here.' The scribe glanced at the sword hanging over the bar and drew a deep breath, his expression becoming vaguely anxious. 'I'm not here to cause trouble, mind you. I'm not here because of the price on your head.' He gave a weak smile. 'Not that I could hope to trouble you—'

'Fine,' the innkeeper interrupted as he pulled out a white linen cloth and began to polish the bar. 'Who are you then?'

'You can call me Chronicler.'

'I didn't ask what I could call you,' Kote said. 'What is your name?'

'Devan. Devan Lochees.'

Kote stopped polishing the bar and looked up. 'Lochees? Are you related to Duke . . .' Kote trailed off, nodding to himself. 'Yes, of course you are. Not *a* chronicler, *the* Chronicler.' He stared hard at the balding man, looking him up and down. 'How about that? The great debunker himself.'

Chronicler relaxed slightly, obviously pleased to have his reputation precede him. 'I wasn't trying to be difficult before. I haven't thought of myself as Devan in years. I left that name behind me long ago.' He gave the innkeeper a significant look. 'I expect you know something of that yourself . . .'

Kote ignored the unspoken question. 'I read your book years ago. *The Mating Habits of the Common Draccus*. Quite the eye-opener for a young man with his head full of stories.' Looking down he began moving the white cloth along the grain of the bar again. 'I'll admit, I was disappointed to learn that dragons didn't exist. That's a hard lesson for a boy to learn.'

Chronicler smiled. 'Honestly, I was a little disappointed myself. I went looking for a legend and found a lizard. A fascinating lizard, but a lizard just the same.'

'And now you're here,' Kote said. 'Have you come to prove that I don't exist?'

Chronicler laughed nervously. 'No. You see, we heard a rumour—'

' "*We?*" ' Kote interrupted.

'I've been travelling with an old friend of yours. Skarpi.'

'Taken you under his wing, has he?' Kote said to himself. 'How about that? Skarpi's apprentice.'

'More of a colleague, really.'

Kote nodded, still expressionless. 'I might have guessed he would be the first to find me. Rumourmongers, both of you.'

Chronicler's smile grew sour, and he swallowed the first words that came to his lips. He struggled for a moment to recapture his calm demeanour.

'So what can I do for you?' Kote set aside the clean linen cloth and gave his best innkeeper's smile. 'Something to eat or drink? A room for the night?'

Chronicler hesitated.

'I have it all right here.' Kote gestured expansively behind the bar. 'Old wine, smooth and pale? Honey mead? Dark ale? Sweet fruit liquor! Plum? Cherry? Green apple? Blackberry?' Kote pointed out the bottles in turn. 'Come now, surely you must want something?' As he spoke, his smile widened, showing too many teeth for a friendly innkeeper's grin. At the same time his eyes grew cold, and hard, and angry.

Chronicler dropped his gaze. 'I'd thought that—'

'You *thought*,' Kote said derisively, dropping all pretense of a smile. 'I very much doubt it. Otherwise, you might have *thought*,' he bit off the word, 'of how much danger you were putting me in by coming here.'

Chronicler's face grew red. 'I'd heard that Kvothe was fearless,' he said hotly.

The innkeeper shrugged. 'Only priests and fools are fearless, and I've never been on the best of terms with God.'

Chronicler frowned, aware that he was being baited. 'Listen,' he continued calmly, 'I was extraordinarily careful. No one except Skarpi knew I was coming. I didn't mention you to anyone. I didn't expect to actually find you.'

'Imagine my relief,' Kote said sarcastically.

Obviously disheartened, Chronicler spoke, 'I'll be the first to admit that my coming here may have been a mistake.' He paused, giving Kote the opportunity to contradict him. Kote didn't. Chronicler gave a small, tight sigh and continued, 'But what's done is done. Won't you even consider . . .'

Kote shook his head. 'It was a long time ago—'

'Not even two years,' Chronicler protested.

'—and I am not what I was,' Kote continued without pausing.

'And what was that, exactly?'

'Kvothe,' he said simply, refusing to be drawn any further into an explanation. 'Now I am Kote. I tend to my inn. That means beer is three shims and a private room costs copper.' He began polishing the bar again with a fierce intensity. 'As you said, "done is done". The stories will take care of themselves.'

'But—'

Kote looked up, and for a second Chronicler saw past the anger that lay glittering on the surface of his eyes. For a moment he saw the pain underneath, raw and bloody, like a wound too deep for healing. Then Kote looked away and only the anger remained. 'What could you possibly offer me that is worth the price of remembering?'

'Everyone thinks you're dead.'

'You don't get it, do you?' Kote shook his head, stuck between amusement and exasperation. 'That's the whole point. People don't look for you when you're dead. Old enemies don't try to settle scores. People don't come asking you for stories,' he said acidly.

Chronicler refused to back down. 'Other people say you're a myth.'

'I am a myth,' Kote said easily, making an extravagant gesture. 'A very special kind of myth that creates itself. The best lies about me are the ones *I* told.'

'They say you never existed,' Chronicler corrected gently.

Kote shrugged nonchalantly, his smile fading an imperceptible amount.

Sensing weakness, Chronicler continued. 'Some stories paint you as little more than a red-handed killer.'

'I'm that too.' Kote turned to polish the counter behind the bar. He shrugged again, not as easily as before. 'I've killed men and things that were more than men. Every one of them deserved it.'

Chronicler shook his head slowly. 'The stories are saying "assassin" not "hero". Kvothe the Arcane and Kvothe Kingkiller are two very different men.'

Kote stopped polishing the bar and turned his back to the room. He nodded once without looking up.

'Some are even saying that there is a new Chandrian. A fresh terror in the night. His hair as red as the blood he spills.'

'The important people know the difference,' Kote said as if he were trying to convince himself, but his voice was weary and despairing, without conviction.

Chronicler gave a small laugh. 'Certainly. For now. But you of all people should realise how thin the line is between the truth and a compelling lie. Between history and an entertaining story.' Chronicler gave his words a minute to sink in. 'You know which will win, given time.'

Kote remained facing the back wall, hands flat on the counter. His head was bowed slightly, as if a great weight had settled onto him. He did not speak.

Chronicler took an eager step forward, sensing victory. 'Some people say there was a woman—'

'What do they know?' Kote's voice cut like a saw through bone. 'What do they know about what happened?' He spoke so softly that Chronicler had to hold his breath to hear.

'They say she—' Chronicler's words stuck in his suddenly dry throat as the room grew unnaturally quiet. Kote stood with his back to the room, a stillness in his body and a terrible silence clenched between his teeth. His right hand, tangled in a clean white cloth, made a slow fist.

Eight inches away a bottle shattered. The smell of strawberries filled the air alongside the sound of splintering glass. A small noise inside so great a stillness, but it was enough. Enough to break the silence into small, sharp slivers. Chronicler felt himself go cold as he suddenly realised what a dangerous game he was playing. *So this is the difference between telling a story and being in one,* he thought numbly, *the fear.*

Kote turned. 'What can any of them know about her?' he asked softly. Chronicler's breath stopped when he saw Kote's face. The placid innkeeper's expression was like a shattered mask. Underneath, Kote's expression was haunted, eyes half in this world, half elsewhere, remembering.

Chronicler found himself thinking of a story he had heard. One of the many. The story told of how Kvothe had gone looking for his heart's desire. He had to trick a demon to get it. But once it rested in his hand, he was forced to fight an angel to keep it. *I believe it,* Chronicler found himself thinking. *Before it was just a story, but now I can believe it. This is the face of a man who has killed an angel.*

'What can any of them know about me?' Kote demanded, a numb anger in his voice. 'What can they know about any of this?' He made a short, fierce gesture that seemed to take in everything, the broken bottle, the bar, the world.

Chronicler swallowed against the dryness in his throat. 'Only what they're told.'

Tat tat, tat-tat. Liquor from the broken bottle began to patter an irregular rhythm onto the floor. 'Ahhhh,' Kote sighed out a long breath. *Tat-tat, tat-tat, tat.* 'Clever. You'd use my own best trick against me. You'd hold my story a hostage.'

'I would tell the truth.'

'Nothing but the truth could break me. What is harder than the truth?' A sickly, mocking smile flickered across his face. For a long moment, only the gentle tapping of drops against the floor kept the silence at bay.

Finally Kote walked through the doorway behind the bar. Chronicler stood awkwardly in the empty room, unsure whether or not he had been dismissed.

A few minutes later Kote returned with a bucket of soapy water. Without looking in the storyteller's direction, he began to gently, methodically, wash his bottles. One at a time, Kote wiped their bottoms clean of the strawberry wine and set them on the bar between himself and Chronicler, as if they might defend him.

'So you went looking for a myth and found a man,' he said without inflection, without looking up. 'You've heard the stories and now you want the truth of things.'

Radiating relief, Chronicler set his satchel down on one of the tables, surprised at the slight tremor in his hands. 'We got wind of you a while back. Just a whisper of a rumour. I didn't really expect . . .' Chronicler paused, suddenly awkward. 'I thought you would be older.'

'I am,' Kote said. Chronicler looked puzzled, but before he could say anything the innkeeper continued. 'What brings you into this worthless little corner of the world?'

'An appointment with the Earl of Baedn-Bryt,' Chronicler said, puffing himself up slightly. 'Three days from now, in Treya.'

The innkeeper paused mid-polish. 'You expect to make it to the earl's manor in four days?' he asked quietly.

'I am behind schedule,' Chronicler admitted. 'My horse was stolen near Abbott's Ford.' He glanced out the window at the darkening sky. 'But I'm willing to lose some sleep. I'll be off in the morning and out of your hair.'

'Well I wouldn't want to cost you any sleep,' Kote said sarcastically, his eyes gone hard again. 'I can tell the whole thing in one breath.' He cleared his throat. ' "I trouped, travelled, loved, lost, trusted and was betrayed". Write that down and burn it for all the good it will do you.'

'You needn't take it that way,' Chronicler said quickly. 'We can take the whole night if you like. And a few hours in the morning as well.'

'How gracious,' Kote snapped. 'You'll have me tell my story in an *evening*? With no time to collect myself? No time to prepare?' His mouth made a thin line. 'No. Go dally with your earl. I'll have none of it.'

Chronicler spoke quickly, 'If you're certain you'll need—'

'Yes.' Kote set a bottle down hard on the bar, hard. 'It's safe to say I'll need more time than that. And you'll get none of it tonight. A real story takes time to prepare.'

Chronicler frowned nervously and ran his hands through his hair. 'I could spend tomorrow collecting your story . . .' He trailed off at the sight of Kote shaking his head. After a pause he started again, almost talking to himself. 'If I pick up a horse in Baedn, I can give you all day tomorrow, most of the night, and a piece of the following day.' He rubbed his forehead. 'I hate riding at night, but—'

'I'll need three days,' Kote said. 'I'm quite sure of it.'

Chronicler blanched. 'But . . . the earl.'

Kote waved a hand dismissively.

'No one needs three days,' Chronicler said firmly. 'I interviewed Oren Velciter. *Oren Velciter*, mind you. He's eighty years old, and done two hundred years' worth of living. Five hundred, if you count the lies. He sought *me* out,' Chronicler said with particular emphasis. 'He only took two days.'

'That is my offer,' the innkeeper said simply. 'I'll do this properly or not at all.'

'Wait!' Chronicler brightened suddenly. 'I've been thinking about this all backwards,' he said, shaking his head at his own foolishness. 'I'll just visit the earl, then come back. You can have all the time you like then. I could even bring Skarpi back with me.'

Kote gave Chronicler a look of profound disdain. 'What gives you the slightest impression that I would be here when you came back?' he asked incredulously. 'For that matter, what makes you think you're free to simply walk out of here, knowing what you know?'

Chronicler went very still. 'Are—' He swallowed and started again. 'Are you saying that—'

'The story will take three days,' Kote interrupted. 'Starting tomorrow. *That* is what I am saying.'

Chronicler closed his eyes and ran his hand over his face. The earl would be furious, of course. No telling what it might take to get back in his good graces. Still . . . 'If that's the only way that I can get it, I accept.'

'I'm glad to hear it.' The innkeeper relaxed into a half smile. 'Come now, is three days really so unusual?'

Chronicler's serious expression returned. 'Three days is quite unusual. But then again—' Some of the self-importance seemed to leak out of him. 'Then again,' he made a gesture as if to show how useless words were. 'You are Kvothe.'

The man who called himself Kote looked up from behind his bottles. A full-lipped smile played about his mouth. A spark was kindling behind his eyes. He seemed taller.

'Yes, I suppose I am,' Kvothe said, and his voice had iron in it.

CHAPTER SEVEN

Of Beginnings and the Names of Things

SUNLIGHT POURED INTO THE Waystone. It was a cool, fresh light, fitted for beginnings. It brushed past the miller as he set his water-wheel turning for the day. It lit the forge the smith was rekindling after four days of cold metal work. It touched draft horses hitched to wagons and sickle blades glittering sharp and ready at the beginning of an autumn day.

Inside the Waystone, the light fell across Chronicler's face and touched a beginning there, a blank page waiting the first words of a story. The light flowed across the bar, scattered a thousand tiny rainbow beginnings from the coloured bottles, and climbed the wall towards the sword, as if searching for one final beginning.

But when the light touched the sword there were no beginnings to be seen. In fact, the light the sword reflected was dull, burnished, and ages old. Looking at it, Chronicler remembered that though it was the beginning of a day, it was also late autumn and growing colder. The sword shone with the knowledge that dawn was a small beginning compared to the ending of a season: the ending of a year.

Chronicler pulled his eyes away from the sword, aware that Kvothe had said something, but not knowing what. 'I beg your pardon?'

'How do people normally go about relating their stories?' Kvothe asked.

Chronicler shrugged. 'Most simply tell me what they remember. Later, I record events in the proper order, remove the unnecessary pieces, clarify, simplify, that sort of thing.'

Kvothe frowned. 'I don't think that will do.'

Chronicler gave him a shy smile. 'Storytellers are always different. They prefer their stories be left alone. But they also prefer an attentive audience. I usually listen and record later. I have a nearly perfect memory.'

'*Nearly perfect* doesn't quite suit me.' Kvothe pressed a finger against his lips. 'How fast can you write?'

Chronicler gave a knowing smile. 'Faster than a man can talk.'

Kvothe raised an eyebrow. 'I'd like to see that.'

Chronicler opened his satchel. He brought out a stack of fine, white paper and a bottle of ink. After arranging them carefully, he dipped a pen and looked expectantly at Kvothe.

Kvothe sat forward in his chair and spoke quickly, 'I am. We are. She is. He was. They will be.' Chronicler's pen danced and scratched down the page as Kvothe watched it. 'I, Chronicler do hereby avow that I can neither read nor write. Supine. Irreverent. Jackdaw. Quartz. Lacquer. Eggoliant. *Lhin ta Lu soren hea*. "There was a young widow from Faeton, whose morals were hard as a rock. She went to confession, for her true obsession—"' Kvothe leaned farther forward to watch as Chronicler wrote. 'Interesting – oh, you may stop.'

Chronicler smiled again and wiped his pen on a piece of cloth. The page in front of him held a single line of incomprehensible symbols. 'Some sort of cipher?' Kvothe wondered aloud. 'Very neatly done, too. I'll bet you don't spoil many pages.' He turned the sheet to look at the writing more carefully.

'I never spoil pages,' Chronicler said haughtily.

Kvothe nodded without looking up.

'What does "eggoliant" mean?' Chronicler asked.

'Hmmm? Oh, nothing. I made it up. I wanted to see if an unfamiliar word would slow you down.' He stretched, and pulled his chair closer to Chronicler's. 'As soon as you show me how to read this, we can begin.'

Chronicler looked doubtful. 'It's a very complex—' Seeing Kvothe frown, he sighed. 'I'll try.'

Chronicler drew a deep breath and began to write a line of symbols as he spoke. 'There are around fifty different sounds we use to speak. I've given each of them a symbol consisting of one or two pen strokes. It's all sound. I could conceivably transcribe a language I don't even understand.' He pointed. 'These are different vowel sounds.'

'All vertical lines,' Kvothe said, looking intently at the page.

Chronicler paused, thrown off his stride. 'Well . . . yes.'

'The consonants would be horizontal then? And they would combine like this?' Taking the pen, Kvothe made a few marks of his own on the page. 'Clever. You'd never need more than two or three for a word.'

Chronicler watched Kvothe quietly.

Kvothe didn't notice, his attention on the paper. 'If this is "am" then these must be the *ah* sounds,' he motioned to a group of characters Chronicler had penned. '*Ah, ay, aeh, auh*. That would make these the *oh*s.' Kvothe nodded to himself and pressed the pen back into Chronicler's hand. 'Show me the consonants.'

Chronicler penned them down numbly, reciting the sounds as he wrote. After a moment, Kvothe took the pen and completed the list himself, asking the dumbfounded Chronicler to correct him if he made a mistake.

Chronicler watched and listened as Kvothe completed the list. From beginning to end the whole process took about fifteen minutes. He made no mistakes.

'Wonderfully efficient system,' Kvothe said appreciatively. 'Very logical. Did you design it yourself?'

Chronicler took a long moment before he spoke, staring at the rows of characters on the page in front of Kvothe. Finally, disregarding Kvothe's question, Chronicler asked, 'Did you really learn Tema in a day?'

Kvothe gave a faint smile and looked down at the table. 'That's an old story. I'd almost forgotten. It took a day and a half, actually. A day and a half with no sleep. Why do you ask?'

'I heard about it at the University. I never really believed it.' He looked down at the page of his cipher in Kvothe's neat handwriting. 'All of it?'

Kvothe looked puzzled. 'What?'

'Did you learn the whole language?'

'No. Of course not,' Kvothe said rather testily. 'Only a portion of it. A large portion to be sure, but I don't believe you can ever learn all of anything, let alone a language.'

Kvothe rubbed his hands together. 'Now, are you ready?'

Chronicler shook his head as if to clear it, set out a new sheet of paper, and nodded.

Kvothe held up a hand to keep Chronicler from writing, and spoke, 'I've never told this story before, and I doubt I'll ever tell it again.' Kvothe leaned forward in his chair. 'Before we begin, you must remember that I am of the Edema Ruh. We were telling stories before Caluptena burned. Before there were books to write in. Before there was music to play. When the first fire kindled, we Ruh were there spinning stories in the circle of its flickering light.'

Kvothe nodded to the scribe. 'I know your reputation as a great collector of stories and recorder of events.' Kvothe's eyes became hard as flint, sharp as broken glass. 'That said, do not presume to change a word of what I say. If I seem to wander, if I seem to stray, remember that true stories seldom take the straightest way.'

Chronicler nodded solemnly, trying to imagine the mind that could break apart his cipher in a piece of an hour. A mind that could learn a language in a day.

Kvothe gave a gentle smile and looked around the room as if fixing it in his memory. Chronicler dipped his pen and Kvothe looked down at his folded hands for as long as it takes to draw three deep breaths.

Then he began to speak.

'In some ways, it began when I heard her singing. Her voice twinning, mixing with my own. Her voice was like a portrait of her soul: wild as a fire, sharp as shattered glass, sweet and clean as clover.'

Kvothe shook his head. 'No. It began at the University. I went to learn magic of the sort they talk about in stories. Magic like Taborlin the Great. I wanted to learn the name of the wind. I wanted fire and lightning. I wanted answers to ten thousand questions and access to their archives. But what I found at the University was much different than a story, and I was much dismayed.

'But I expect the true beginning lies in what led me to the University. Unexpected fires at twilight. A man with eyes like ice at the bottom of a well. The smell of blood and burning hair. The Chandrian.' He nodded to himself. 'Yes. I suppose that is where it all begins. This is, in many ways, a story about the Chandrian.'

Kvothe shook his head, as if to free himself from some dark thought. 'But I suppose I must go even further back than that. If this is to be something resembling my book of deeds, I can spare the time. It will be worth it if I am remembered, if not flatteringly, then at least with some small amount of accuracy.

'But what would my father say if he heard me telling a story this way? "Begin at the beginning." Very well, if we are to have a telling, let's make it a proper one.'

Kvothe sat forward in his chair.

'In the beginning, as far as I know, the world was spun out of the nameless void by Aleph, who gave everything a name. Or, depending on the version of the tale, found the names all things already possessed.'

Chronicler let slip a small laugh, though he did not look up from his page or pause in his writing.

Kvothe continued, smiling himself. 'I see you laugh. Very well, for simplicity's sake, let us assume I am the centre of creation. In doing this, let us pass over innumerable boring stories: the rise and fall of empires, sagas of heroism, ballads of tragic love. Let us hurry forward to the only tale of any real importance.' His smile broadened. 'Mine.'

My name is Kvothe, pronounced nearly the same as 'Quothe'. Names are important as they tell you a great deal about a person. I've had more names than anyone has a right to.

The Adem call me Maedre. Which, depending on how it's spoken, can mean 'The Flame', 'The Thunder', or 'The Broken Tree'.

'The Flame' is obvious if you've ever seen me. I have red hair, bright. If I had been born a couple of hundred years ago I would probably have been burned as a demon. I keep it short but it's unruly. When left to its own devices, it sticks up and makes me look as if I have been set afire.

'The Thunder' I attribute to a strong baritone and a great deal of stage training at an early age.

I've never thought of 'The Broken Tree' as very significant. Although in retrospect I suppose it could be considered at least partially prophetic.

My first mentor called me E'lir because I was clever and I knew it. My first real lover called me Dulator because she liked the sound of it. I have been called Shadicar, Lightfinger, and Six-String. I have been called Kvothe the Bloodless, Kvothe the Arcane, and Kvothe Kingkiller. I have earned those names. Bought and paid for them.

But I was brought up as Kvothe. My father once told me it meant 'to know'.

I have, of course, been called many other things. Most of them uncouth, although very few were unearned.

I have stolen princesses back from sleeping barrow kings. I burned down the town of Trebon. I have spent the night with Felurian and left with both my sanity and my life. I was expelled from the University at a younger age than most people are allowed in. I tread paths by moonlight that others fear to speak of during day. I have talked to Gods, loved women, and written songs that make the minstrels weep.

You may have heard of me.

CHAPTER EIGHT

Thieves, Heretics, and Whores

IF THIS STORY IS to be something resembling my book of deeds, we must begin at the beginning. At the heart of who I truly am. To do this, you must remember that before I was anything else, I was one of the Edema Ruh.

Contrary to popular belief, not all travelling performers are of the Ruh. My troupe was not some poor batch of mummers, japing at crossroads for pennies, singing for our suppers. We were court performers, Lord Greyfallow's Men. Our arrival in most towns was more of an event than the Midwinter Pageantry and Solinade Games rolled together. There were usually at least eight wagons in our troupe and well over two dozen performers: actors and acrobats, musicians and hand magicians, jugglers and jesters: my family.

My father was a better actor and musician than any you have ever seen. My mother had a natural gift for words. They were both beautiful, with dark hair and easy laughter. They were Ruh down to their bones, and that, really, is all that needs to be said.

Save perhaps that my mother was a noble before she was a trouper. She told me my father had lured her away from 'a miserable dreary hell' with sweet music and sweeter words. I could only assume she meant Three Crossings, where we went to visit relatives when I was very young. Once.

My parents were never really married, by which I mean they never bothered making their relationship official with any church. I'm not embarrassed by the fact. They considered themselves married and didn't see much point in announcing it to any government or God. I respect that. In truth, they seemed more content and faithful than many officially married couples I have seen since.

Our patron was Baron Greyfallow, and his name opened many doors that would ordinarily be closed to the Edema Ruh. In return we wore his colors, green and grey, and added to his reputation wherever we went. Once a year we spent two span at his manor, entertaining him and his household.

It was a happy childhood, growing up in the center of an endless fair. My father would read to me from the great monologues during the long wagon rides between towns. Reciting mostly from memory, his voice would roll down the road for a quarter mile. I remember reading along, coming in on the secondary parts. My father would encourage me to try particularly good sections myself, and I learned to love the feel of good words.

My mother and I would make up songs together. Other times my parents would act out romantic dialogues while I followed along in the books. They seemed like games at the time. Little did I know how cunningly I was being taught.

I was a curious child: quick with questions and eager to learn. With acrobats and actors as my teachers, it is little wonder that I never grew to dread lessons as most children do.

The roads were safer in those days, but cautious folk would still travel with our troupe for safety's sake. They supplemented my education. I learned an eclectic smattering of Commonwealth law from a travelling barrister too drunk or too pompous to realise he was lecturing an eight-year-old. I learned woodcraft from a huntsman named Laclith who travelled with us for nearly a whole season.

I learned the sordid inner workings of the royal court in Modeg from a . . . courtesan. As my father used to say: 'Call a jack a jack. Call a spade a spade. But always call a whore a lady. Their lives are hard enough, and it never hurts to be polite'.

Hetera smelled vaguely of cinnamon, and at nine years old I found her fascinating without exactly knowing why. She taught me I should never do anything in private that I didn't want talked about in public, and cautioned me to not talk in my sleep.

And then there was Abenthy, my first real teacher. He taught me more than all the others set end to end. If not for him, I would never have become the man I am today.

I ask that you not hold it against him. He meant well.

————————

'You'll have to move along,' the mayor said. 'Camp outside town and no one will bother you so long as you don't start any fights or wander off with anything that isn't yours.' He gave my father a significant look. 'Then be on your merry way tomorrow. No performances. They're more trouble than they're worth.'

'We *are* licensed,' my father said, pulling out a folded piece of parchment from the inner pocket of his jacket. 'Charged to perform, in fact.'

The mayor shook his head and made no motion to look at our writ of patronage. 'It makes folk rowdy,' he said firmly. 'Last time there was an unholy row during the play. Too much drinking, too much excitement. Folks tore the doors off the public house and smashed up the tables. The hall belongs to the town, you see. The town bears the expense of the repairs.'

By this time our wagons were drawing attention. Trip was doing some juggling. Marion and his wife were putting on an impromptu string-puppet show. I was watching my father from the back of our wagon.

'We certainly would not want to offend you *or* your patron,' the mayor said. 'However the town can ill afford another evening such as that. As a gesture of goodwill I'm willing to offer you a copper each, say twenty pennies, simply to be on your way and not make any trouble for us here.'

Now you have to understand that twenty pennies might be a good bit of money for some little ragamuffin troupe living hand-to-mouth. But for us it was simply insulting. He should have offered us forty to play for the evening, free use of the public hall, a good meal, and beds at the inn. The last we would graciously decline, as their beds were no doubt lousy and those in our wagons were not.

If my father was surprised or insulted, he did not show it. 'Pack up!' He shouted over one shoulder.

Trip tucked his juggling stones into various pockets without so much as a flourish. There was a disappointed chorus from several dozen townsfolk as the puppets stopped midjape and were packed away. The mayor looked relieved, brought out his purse, and pulled out two silver pennies.

'I'll be sure to tell the baron of your generosity,' my father said carefully as the mayor lay the pennies into his hand.

The mayor froze midmotion. 'Baron?'

'Baron Greyfallow.' My father paused, looking for some spark of recognition on the mayor's face. 'Lord of the eastern marshes, Hudumbran-by-Thiren, and the Wydeconte Hills.' My father looked around at the horizon. 'We *are* still in the Wydeconte Hills, aren't we?'

'Well yes,' the mayor said. 'But Squire Semelan . . .'

'Oh, we're in *Semelan's* fief!' my father exclaimed, looking around as if just now getting his bearings. 'Thin gentleman, tidy little beard?' He brushed his chin with his fingers. The mayor nodded numbly. 'Charming fellow, lovely singing voice. Met him when we were entertaining the baron last Midwinter.'

'Of course,' the mayor paused significantly. 'Might I see your writ?'

I watched as the mayor read it. It took him a little while, as my father had not bothered to mention the majority of the baron's titles such as the Viscount of Montrone and Lord of Trelliston. The upshot was this: it was true that the Squire Semelan controlled this little town and all the land around it, but Semelan owed fealty directly to Greyfallow. In more concrete terms, Greyfallow was captain of the ship; Semelan scrubbed the planking and saluted him.

The mayor refolded the parchment and handed it back to my father. 'I see.'

That was all. I remember being stunned when the mayor didn't apologise or offer my father more money.

My father paused as well, then continued, 'The city is your jurisdiction, sir. But we'll perform either way. It will either be here or just outside the city limits.'

'Ye can't use the public house,' the mayor said firmly. 'I won't have it wrecked again.'

'We can play right here,' my father pointed to the market square. 'It will be enough space, and it keeps everyone right here in town.'

The mayor hesitated, though I could hardly believe it. We sometimes chose to play on the green because the local buildings weren't big enough. Two of our wagons were built to become stages for just that eventuality. But in my whole eleven years of memory I could barely count on both hands the times we'd been *forced* to play the green. We had never played outside the city limits.

But we were spared that. The mayor nodded at last and gestured my father closer. I slipped out the back of the wagon and moved close enough to catch the end of what he said, '—God-fearing folk around here. Nothing vulgar or heretical. We had a double handful of trouble with the last troupe that came through here, two fights, folks missing their laundry, and one of Branston's daughters got herself in a family way.'

I was outraged. I waited for my father to show the mayor the sharp side of his tongue, to explain the difference between mere travelling performers and Edema Ruh. We didn't steal. We would never let things get so out of control that a bunch of drunks ruined the hall where we were playing.

But my father did nothing of the sort, he just nodded and walked back toward our wagon. He gestured and Trip started juggling again. The puppets reemerged from their cases.

As he came around the wagon he saw me standing, half-hidden beside the horses. 'I'm guessing you heard the whole thing from the look on your face,' he said with a wry grin. 'Let it go, my boy. He gets full marks for honesty if not for grace. He just says out loud what other folk keep in the quiet of their hearts. Why do you think I have everyone stay in pairs when we go about our business in bigger towns?'

I knew it for the truth. Still, it was a hard pill for a young boy to swallow. 'Twenty pennies,' I said scathingly. 'As if he were offering us charity.'

That was the hardest part of growing up Edema Ruh. We are strangers everywhere. Many folk view us as vagabonds and beggars, while others deem us little more than thieves, heretics, and whores. It's hard to be wrongfully accused, but it's worse when the people looking down on you are clods who have never read a book or travelled more than twenty miles from the place they were born.

My father laughed and roughed my hair. 'Just pity him, my boy. Tomorrow we'll be on our way, but he'll have to keep his own disagreeable company until the day he dies.'

'He's an ignorant blatherskate,' I said bitterly.

He lay a firm hand on my shoulder, letting me know I'd said enough. 'This is what comes of getting too close to Atur, I suppose. Tomorrow we'll head south: greener pastures, kinder folk, prettier women.' He cupped an ear toward the wagon and nudged me with his elbow.

'I can hear everything you say,' my mother called sweetly from inside. My father grinned and winked at me.

'So what play are we going to do?' I asked my father. 'Nothing vulgar, mind you. They're God-fearing folk in these parts.'

He looked at me. 'What would you pick?'

I gave it a long moment's thought. 'I'd play something from the Brightfield Cycle. *The Forging of the Path* or somesuch.'

My father made a face. 'Not a very good play.'

I shrugged. 'They won't know the difference. Besides, it's chock full of Tehlu, so no one will complain about it being vulgar.' I looked up at the sky. 'I just hope it doesn't rain on us halfway through.'

My father looked up at the clouds. 'It will. Still, there are worse things than playing in the rain.'

'Like playing in the rain and getting shimmed on the deal?' I asked.

The mayor hurried up to us, moving at a fast walk. There was a thin sheen of sweat on his forehead and he was puffing a little bit, as if he'd been running. 'I talked it over with a few members of the council and we decided that it would be quite all right for you to use the public house if you would care to.'

My father's body language was perfect. It was perfectly clear he was offended but far too polite to say anything. 'I certainly wouldn't want to put you out . . .'

'No, no. No bother at all. I insist, in fact.'

'Very well, if you insist.'

The mayor smiled and hurried away.

'Well that's a little better,' my father sighed. 'No need to tighten our belts yet.'

'Halfpenny a head. That's right. Anyone without a head gets in free. Thank you, sir.'

Trip was working the door, making sure everyone paid to see the play. 'Halfpenny a head. Though by the rosy glow in your lady's cheeks I should be charging you for a head and a half. Not that it's any of my business, mind you.'

Trip had the quickest tongue of anyone in the troupe, which made him the best man for the job of making sure no one tried to fast-talk or bully their way inside. Wearing his green and grey jester's motley, Trip could say just about anything and get away with it.

'Hello, mum, no charge for the little one, but if he starts to squawk you'd best give him the tit quick or take him outside.' Trip carried on his unending patter. 'That's right, halfpenny. Yes, sir, empty head still pays full price.'

Though it was always fun to watch Trip work, most of my attention was on a wagon that had rolled into the other end of town about a quarter hour ago. The mayor had argued with the old man driving it, then stormed off. Now I saw the mayor heading back to the wagon accompanied by a tall fellow carrying a long cudgel, the constable unless I missed my guess.

My curiosity got the best of me and I made my way towards the wagon, doing my best to stay out of sight. The mayor and the old man were arguing again by the time I got close enough to hear. The constable stood nearby, looking irritated and anxious.

'. . . told you. I don't have a license. I don't *need* a license. Does a peddler need a license? Does a tinker need a license?'

'You're not a tinker,' the mayor said. 'Don't try to pass yourself off as one.'

'I'm not trying to pass myself off as anything,' the old man snapped. 'I'm a tinker and a peddler, and I'm more than both. I'm an *arcanist,* you great dithering heap of idiot.'

'My point exactly,' the mayor said doggedly. 'We're God-fearing people in these parts. We don't want any meddling with dark things better left alone. We don't want the trouble your kind can bring.'

'My kind?' the old man said. 'What do you know about my kind? There probably hasn't been an arcanist through these parts in fifty years.'

'We like it that way. Just turn around and go back the way you came.'

'Like hell if I'm spending a night in the rain because of your thick head,' the old man said hotly. 'I don't need your permission to rent a room or do business in the street. Now get away from me or I'll show you firsthand what sort of trouble *my kind* can be.'

Fear flashed across the mayor's face before it was overwhelmed by outrage. He gestured over one shoulder at the constable. 'Then you'll spend the night in jail for vagrancy and threatening behavior. We'll let you on your way in the morning if you've learned to keep a civil tongue in your head.' The constable advanced on the wagon, his cudgel held cautiously at his side.

The old man stood his ground and raised one hand. A deep, red light welled up from the front corners of his wagon. 'That's far enough,' he said ominously. 'Things could get ugly otherwise.'

After a moment's surprise, I realised the strange light came from a pair of sympathy lamps the old man had mounted on his wagon. I had seen one before, in Lord Greyfallow's library. They were brighter than gaslight, steadier than candles or lamps, and lasted nearly forever. They were also terribly expensive. I was willing to bet that no one in this little town had ever heard of them, let alone seen one.

The constable stopped in his tracks when the light began to swell. But when nothing else seemed to happen, he set his jaw and kept walking toward the wagon.

The old man's expression grew anxious. 'Now hold on a moment,' he said as the red light from the wagon started to fade. 'We don't want . . .'

'Shut your clepper, you old shit-fire,' the constable said. He snatched at the arcanist's arm as if he were sticking his hand into an oven. Then, when nothing happened, he smiled and grew more confident. 'Don't think I won't knock you a good one to keep you from working any more of your devilry.'

'Well done, Tom,' the mayor said, radiating relief. 'Bring him along and we'll send someone back for the wagon.'

The constable grinned and twisted the old man's arm. The arcanist bent at the waist and gasped a short, painful breath.

From where I hid, I saw the arcanist's face change from anxious, to pained, to angry all in a second. I saw his mouth move.

A furious gust of wind came out of nowhere, as if a storm had suddenly burst with no warning. The wind struck the old man's wagon and it tipped onto two wheels before slamming back down onto four. The constable staggered and fell as if he had been struck by the hand of God. Even where I hid nearly thirty feet away the wind was so strong that I was forced to take a step forward, as if I'd been pushed roughly from behind.

'Begone!' the old man shouted angrily. 'Trouble me no longer! I will set fire to your blood and fill you with a fear like ice and iron!' There was something familiar about his words, but I couldn't put my finger on it.

Both the mayor and the constable turned tail and ran, their eyes white and wild as startled horses'.

The wind faded as quickly as it had come. The whole sudden burst couldn't have lasted more than five seconds. As most of the townsfolk were gathered around the public house, I doubted anyone had seen it except for me, the mayor, the constable, and the old man's donkeys who stood placidly in their harness, utterly unperturbed.

'Leave this place clean of your foul presence,' the arcanist muttered to himself as he watched them go. 'By the power of my name I command it to be so.'

I finally realised why his words seemed so familiar. He was quoting lines from the exorcism scene in *Daeonica*. Not many folk knew that play.

The old man turned back to his wagon and began to extemporise. 'I'll turn you into butter on a summer day. I'll turn you into a poet with the soul of a priest. I'll fill you with lemon custard and push you out a window.' He spat. 'Bastards.'

His irritation seemed to leave him and he heaved a great, weary sigh. 'Well that couldn't have gone much worse,' the old man muttered as he rubbed at the shoulder of the arm the constable had twisted. 'Do you think they'll come back with a mob behind them?'

For a second I thought the old man was talking to me. Then I realised the truth. He was talking to his donkeys.

'I don't think so either,' he said to them. 'But I've been wrong before. Let's stay near the edge of town and have a look at the last of the oats, shall we?'

He clambered up into the back of the wagon and came down with a wide bucket and a nearly empty burlap sack. He upended the sack into the bucket and seemed disheartened by the results. He took out a handful for himself before nudging the bucket toward the donkeys with his foot. 'Don't give me that look,' he said to them. 'It's short rations all around. Besides, you can graze.' He petted one donkey while he ate his handful of rough oats, stopping occasionally to spit out a husk.

It struck me as very sad, this old man all alone on the road with no one to talk to but his donkeys. It's hard for us Edema Ruh, but at least we had each other. This man had no one.

'We've wandered too far from civilisation, boys. The folk that need me don't trust me, and the ones that trust me can't afford me.' The old man peered into his purse. 'We've got a penny and a half, so our options are limited. Do we want to be wet tonight or hungry tomorrow? We're not going to do any business, so it will probably be one or the other.'

I slunk around the edge of the building until I could see what was written on the side of the old man's wagon. It read:

ABENTHY: ARCANIST EXTRAORDINARY.
Scribe. Dowser. Chemist. Dentist.
Rare Goods. All Alements Tended.
Lost Items Found. Anything Mended.
No Horoscopes. No Love Potions. No Malefaction.

Abenthy noticed me as soon as I stepped out from behind the building where I'd been hiding. 'Hello there. Can I help you?'

'You've misspelled "ailments",' I pointed out.

He looked surprised. 'It's a joke, actually,' he explained. 'I brew a bit.'

'Oh. Ale,' I said, nodding. 'I get it.' I brought my hand out of my pocket. 'Can you sell me anything for a penny?'

He seemed stuck between amusement and curiosity. 'What are you looking for?'

'I'd like some lacillium.' We had performed *Farien the Fair* a dozen times in the last month, and it had filled my young mind with intrigue and assassination.

'Are you expecting someone to poison you?' he said, somewhat taken aback.

'Not really. But it seems to me that if you wait around until you know you need an antidote, it's probably too late to pick one up.'

'I suppose I could sell you a penny's worth,' he said. 'That would be about a dose for a person your size. But it's dangerous stuff in its own right. It only cures certain poisons. You can hurt yourself if you take it at the wrong time.'

'Oh,' I said. 'I didn't know that.' In the play it was touted as an infallible cure-all.

Abenthy tapped his lips thoughtfully. 'Can you answer me a question in the meantime?' I nodded. 'Whose troupe is that?'

'In a way it's mine,' I said. 'But in another way, it's my father's because he runs the show and points which way the wagons go. But it's Baron Greyfallow's too, because he's our patron. We're Lord Greyfallow's Men.'

The old man gave me an amused look. 'I've heard of you. Good troupe. Good reputation.'

I nodded, not seeing any point in false modesty.

'Do you think your father might be interested in taking on any help?' he asked. 'I don't claim to be much of an actor, but I'm handy to have around. I could make you face paint and rouge that aren't all full of lead and mercury and arsenic. I can do lights, too, quick, clean, and bright. Different colours if you want them.'

I didn't have to think too hard about it; candles were expensive and vulnerable to drafts, torches were dirty and dangerous. And everyone in the troupe learned the dangers of cosmetics at an early age. It was hard to become an old, seasoned trouper when you painted poison on yourself every third day and ended up raving mad by the time you were twenty-five.

'I may be overstepping myself a little,' I said as I held out my hand for him to shake. 'But let me be the first to welcome you to the troupe.'

If this is to be a full and honest account of my life and deeds, I feel I should mention that my reasons for inviting Ben into our troupe were not entirely altruistic. It's true that quality cosmetics and clean lights were a welcome addition to our troupe. It's also true that I'd felt sorry for the old man alone on the road.

But underneath it all I was moved by my curiosity. I had seen Abenthy do something I could not explain, something strange and wonderful. Not his trick with the sympathy lamps – I recognised that for what it was: show-manship, a bluff to impress ignorant townsfolk.

What he had done afterwards was different. He called the wind and the wind came. It was magic. Real magic. The sort of magic I'd heard about in stories of Taborlin the Great. The sort of magic I hadn't believed in since I was six. Now I didn't know what to believe.

So I invited him into our troupe, hoping to find answers to my questions. Though I didn't know it at the time, I was looking for the name of the wind.

CHAPTER NINE

Riding in the Wagon with Ben

ABENTHY WAS THE FIRST arcanist I ever met, a strange, exciting figure to a young boy. He was knowledgeable in all the sciences: botany, astronomy, psychology, anatomy, alchemy, geology, chemistry . . .

He was portly, with twinkling eyes that moved quickly from one thing to another. He had a strip of dark grey hair running around the back of his head, but (and this is what I remember most about him) no eyebrows. Rather, he had them, but they were in a perpetual state of regrowing from being burned off in the course of his alchemical pursuits. It made him look surprised and quizzical all at once.

He spoke gently, laughed often, and never exercised his wit at the expense of others. He cursed like a drunken sailor with a broken leg, but only at his donkeys. They were called Alpha and Beta, and Abenthy fed them carrots and lumps of sugar when he thought no one was looking. Chemistry was his particular love, and my father said he'd never known a man to run a better still.

By his second day in our troupe I was making a habit of riding in his wagon. I would ask him questions and he would answer. Then he would ask for songs and I would pluck them out for him on a lute I borrowed from my father's wagon.

He would even sing from time to time. He had a bright, reckless tenor that was always wandering off, looking for notes in the wrong places. More often than not he stopped and laughed at himself when it happened. He was a good man, and there was no conceit in him.

Not long after he joined our troupe, I asked Abenthy what it was like being an arcanist.

He gave me a thoughtful look. 'Have you ever known an arcanist?'

'We paid one to mend a cracked axle on the road once.' I paused to think. 'He was heading inland with a caravan of fish.'

Abenthy made a dismissive gesture. 'No, no, boy. I'm talking about *arcanists*. Not some poor chill-charmer who works his way back and forth across caravan routes, trying to keep fresh meat from rotting.'

'What's the difference?' I asked, sensing it was expected of me.

'Well,' he said. 'That might take a bit of explaining . . .'

'I've got nothing but time.'

Abenthy gave me an appraising look. I'd been waiting for it. It was the look that said, 'You don't sound as young as you look.' I hoped he'd come to grips with it fairly soon. It gets tiresome being spoken to as if you are a child, even if you happen to be one.

He took a deep breath. 'Just because someone knows a trick or two doesn't mean they're an arcanist. They might know how to set a bone or read Eld Vintic. Maybe they even know a little sympathy. But—'

'Sympathy?' I interrupted as politely as possible.

'You'd probably call it magic,' Abenthy said reluctantly. 'It's not, really.' He shrugged. 'But even knowing sympathy doesn't make you an arcanist. A true arcanist has worked his way through the Arcanum at the University.'

At his mention of the Arcanum, I bristled with two dozen new questions. Not so many, you might think, but when you added them to the half-hundred questions I carried with me wherever I went, I was stretched nearly to bursting. Only through a severe effort of will did I remain silent, waiting for Abenthy to continue on his own.

Abenthy, however, noticed my reaction. 'So, you've heard about the Arcanum, have you?' He seemed amused. 'Tell me what you've heard, then.'

This small prompt was all the excuse I needed. 'I heard from a boy in Temper Glen that if your arm's cut off they can sew it back on at the University. Can they really? Some stories say Taborlin the Great went there to learn the names of all things. There's a library with a thousand books. Are there really that many?'

He answered the last question, the others having rushed by too quickly for him to respond. 'More than a thousand, actually. Ten times ten thousand books. More than that. More books than you could ever read.' Abenthy's voice grew vaguely wistful.

More books than I could read? Somehow I doubted that.

Ben continued. 'The people you see riding with caravans – charmers who keep food from spoiling, dowsers, fortune-tellers, toad eaters – aren't real arcanists any more than all travelling performers are Edema Ruh. They might know a little alchemy, a little sympathy, a little medicine.' He shook his head. 'But they're *not* arcanists.

'A lot of people pretend to be. They wear robes and put on airs to take advantage of the ignorant and gullible. But here's how you tell a true arcanist.'

Abenthy pulled a fine chain over his head and handed it to me. It was the first time I had ever seen an Arcanum guilder. It looked rather unimpressive, just a flat piece of lead with some unfamiliar writing stamped onto it.

'That is a true *gilthe*. Or guilder if you prefer,' Abenthy explained with some satisfaction. 'It's the only sure way to be certain of who is and who isn't an arcanist. Your father asked to see mine before he let me ride with your troupe. It shows he's a man of the world.' He watched me with a sly disinterest. 'Uncomfortable, isn't it?'

I gritted my teeth and nodded. My hand had gone numb as soon as I'd touched it. I was curious to study the markings on its front and back, but after the space of two breaths, my arm was numb to the shoulder, as if I had slept on it all night. I wondered if my whole body would go numb if I held it long enough.

I was prevented from finding out, as the wagon hit a bump and my numbed hand almost let Abenthy's guilder fall to the footboard of the wagon. He snatched it up and slipped it back over his head, chuckling.

'How can you stand it?' I asked, trying to rub a little feeling back into my hand.

'It only feels that way to other people,' he explained. 'To its owner, it's just warm. That's how you can tell the difference between an arcanist and someone who has a knack for finding water or guessing at the weather.'

'Trip has something like that,' I said. 'He rolls sevens.'

'That's a little different,' Abenthy laughed. 'Not anything so unexplainable as a knack.' He slouched a little farther down into his seat. 'Probably for the best. A couple of hundred years ago, a person was as good as dead if folk saw he had a knack. The Tehlins called them demon signs, and burned folk if they had them.' Abenthy's mood seemed to have taken a downward turn.

'We had to break Trip out of jail once or twice,' I said, trying to lighten the tone of the conversation. 'But no one actually tried to burn him.'

Abenthy gave a tired smile. 'I suspect Trip has a pair of clever dice or an equally clever skill which probably extends to cards as well. I thank you for your timely warning, but a knack is something else entirely.'

I can't abide being patronised. 'Trip can't cheat to save his life,' I said a little more sharply than I had intended. 'And anyone in the troupe can tell good dice from bad. Trip throws sevens. It doesn't matter whose dice he uses, he rolls sevens. If he bets on someone, they roll sevens. If he so much as bumps a table with loose dice on it, seven.'

'Hmmm.' Abenthy nodded to himself. 'My apologies. That does sound like a knack. I'd be curious to see it.'

I nodded. 'Take your own dice. We haven't let him play for years.' A thought occurred to me. 'It might not still work.'

He shrugged. 'Knacks don't go away so easily as that. When I was growing up in Staup, I knew a young man with a knack. Uncommonly good with plants.' Abenthy's grin was gone as he looked off at something I couldn't see. 'His tomatoes would be red while everyone else's vines were still climbing. His squash were bigger and sweeter, his grapes didn't hardly have to be bottled before they started being wine.' He trailed off, his eyes far away.

'Did they burn him?' I asked with the morbid curiosity of the young.

'What? No, of course not. I'm not that old.' He scowled at me in mock severity. 'There was a drought and he got run out of town. His poor mother was heartbroken.'

There was a moment of silence. Two wagons ahead of us, I heard Teren and Shandi rehearsing lines from *The Swineherd and the Nightingale*.

Abenthy seemed to be listening as well, in an offhand way. After Teren got himself lost halfway through Fain's garden monologue, I turned back to face him. 'Do they teach acting at the University?' I asked.

Abenthy shook his head, slightly amused by the question. 'Many things, but not that.'

I looked over at Abenthy and saw him watching me, his eyes danced.

'Could you teach me some of those other things?' I asked.

He smiled, and it was as easy as that.

———

Abenthy proceeded to give me a brief overview of each of the sciences. While his main love was for chemistry, he believed in a rounded education. I learned how to work the sextant, the compass, the slipstick, the abacus. More important, I learned to do without.

Within a span I could identify any chemical in his cart. In two months I could distill liquor until it was too strong to drink, bandage a wound, set a bone, and diagnose hundreds of sicknesses from symptoms. I knew the process for making four different aphrodisiacs, three concoctions for contraception, nine for impotence, and two philtres referred to simply as 'maiden's helper'. Abenthy was rather vague about the purpose of the last of these, but I had some strong suspicions.

I learned the formulae for a dozen poisons and acids and a hundred medicines and cure-alls, some of which even worked. I doubled my herb lore in theory if not in practice. Abenthy started to call me Red and I called him Ben, first in retaliation, then in friendship.

Only now, far after the fact, do I recognise how carefully Ben prepared me for what was to come at the University. He did it subtly. Once or twice a day, mixed in with my normal lectures, Ben would present me with a little mental exercise I would have to master before we went on to anything else. He made me play Tirani without a board, keeping track of the stones in my head. Other times he would stop in the middle of a conversation and make me repeat everything said in the last few minutes, word for word.

This was levels beyond the simple memorisation I had practiced for the stage. My mind was learning to work in different ways, becoming stronger. It felt the same way your body feels after a day of splitting wood, or swimming, or sex. You feel exhausted, languorous, and almost Godlike. This feeling was similar, except it was my intellect that was weary and expanded, languid and latently powerful. I could feel my mind starting to awaken.

I seemed to gain momentum as I progressed, like when water starts to wash away a dam made of sand. I don't know if you understand what a geometric progression is, but that is the best way to describe it. Through it all Ben continued to teach me mental exercises that I was half convinced he constructed out of sheer meanness.

CHAPTER TEN

Alar and Several Stones

BEN HELD UP A chunk of dirty fieldstone slightly bigger than his fist. 'What will happen if I let go of this rock?'

I thought for a bit. Simple questions during lesson time were very seldom simple. Finally I gave the obvious answer. 'It will probably fall.'

He raised an eyebrow. I had kept him busy over the last several months, and he hadn't had the leisure to accidentally burn them off. 'Probably? You sound like a sophist, boy. Hasn't it always fallen before?'

I stuck my tongue out at him. 'Don't try to boldface your way through this one. That's a fallacy. You taught me that yourself.'

He grinned. 'Fine. Would it be fair to say you believe it will fall?'

'Fair enough.'

'I want you to believe it will fall up when I let go of it.' His grin widened. I tried. It was like doing mental gymnastics. After a while I nodded. 'Okay.'

'How well do you believe it?'

'Not very well,' I admitted.

'I want you to believe this rock will float away. Believe it with a faith that will move mountains and shake trees.' He paused and seemed to take a different tack. 'Do you believe in God?'

'Tehlu? After a fashion.'

'Not good enough. Do you believe in your parents?'

I gave a little smile. 'Sometimes. I can't see them right now.'

He snorted and unhooked the slapstick he used to goad Alpha and Beta when they were being lazy. 'Do you believe in this, E'lir?' He only called me E'lir when he thought I was being especially willfully obstinate. He held out the stick for my inspection.

There was a malicious glitter in his eye. I decided not to tempt fate. 'Yes.'

'Good.' He slapped the side of the wagon with it, producing a sharp *crack*. One of Alpha's ears pivoted around at the noise, uncertain as to whether or not it was directed at her. 'That's the sort of belief I want. It's called *Alar: riding-crop belief*. When I drop this stone it will float away, free as a bird.'

He brandished the slapstick a bit. 'And none of your petty philosophy or I'll make you sorry you ever took a shining to that little game.'

I nodded. I cleared my mind with one of the tricks I'd already learned, and bore down on believing. I started to sweat.

After what may have been ten minutes I nodded again.

He let go of the rock. It fell.

I began to get a headache.

He picked the rock back up. 'Do you believe that it floated?'

'No!' I sulked, rubbing my temples.

'Good. It didn't. Never fool yourself into perceiving things that don't exist. It's a fine line to walk, but sympathy is not an art for the weak willed.'

He held out the rock again. 'Do you believe it will float?'

'It didn't!'

'It doesn't matter. Try again.' He shook the stone. 'Alar is the cornerstone of sympathy. If you are going to impose your will on the world, you must have control over what you believe.'

I tried and I tried. It was the most difficult thing I had ever done. It took me almost all afternoon.

Finally Ben was able to drop the rock and I retained my firm belief that it wouldn't fall despite evidence to the contrary.

I heard the thump of the rock and I looked at Ben. 'I've got it,' I said calmly, feeling more than a little smug.

He looked at me out of the corner of his eye, as if he didn't quite believe me but didn't want to admit it. He picked at the rock absently with one fingernail, then shrugged and held it up again. 'I want you to believe the rock will fall and that the rock will not fall when I let go of it.' He grinned.

I went to bed late that night. I had a nosebleed and a smile of satisfaction. I held the two separate beliefs loosely in my mind and let their singing discord lull me into senselessness.

Being able to think about two disparate things at once, aside from being wonderfully efficient, was roughly akin to being able to sing harmony with yourself. It turned into a favorite game of mine. After two days of practicing I was able to sing a trio. Soon I was doing the mental equivalent of palming cards and juggling knives.

There were many other lessons, though none were quite so pivotal as the Alar. Ben taught me Heart of Stone, a mental exercise that let you set aside your emotions and prejudices and let you think clearly about whatever you wished. Ben said a man who truly mastered Heart of Stone could go to his sister's funeral without ever shedding a tear.

He also taught me a game called Seek the Stone. The point of the game was to have one part of your mind hide an imaginary stone in an imaginary room. Then you had another, separate part of your mind try to find it.

Practically, it teaches valuable mental control. If you can really play Seek the Stone, then you are developing an iron-hard Alar of the sort you need for sympathy.

However, while being able to think about two things at the same time is terribly convenient, the training it takes to get there is frustrating at best, and at other times rather disturbing.

I remember one time I looked for the stone for almost an hour before I consented to ask the other half of me where I'd hidden it, only to find I hadn't hidden the stone at all. I had merely been waiting to see how long I would look before giving up. Have you ever been annoyed and amused with yourself at the same time? It's an interesting feeling, to say the very least.

Another time I asked for hints and ended up jeering at myself. It's no wonder that many arcanists you meet are a little eccentric, if not downright cracked. As Ben had said, sympathy is not for the weak of mind.

CHAPTER ELEVEN

The Binding of Iron

I SAT IN THE back of Abenthy's wagon. It was a wonderful place for me, home to a hundred bottles and bundles, saturated with a thousand smells. To my young mind it was usually more fun than a tinker's cart, but not today.

It had rained heavily the night before, and the road was a thick morass of mud. Since the troupe was not on any particular schedule, we had decided to wait for a day or two to give the roads time to dry. It was a fairly common occurrence, and it happened to fall at the perfect time for Ben to further my education. So I sat at the wooden worktable in the back of Ben's wagon and chafed at wasting the day listening to him lecture me about things I already understood.

My thoughts must have been apparent, because Abenthy sighed and sat down beside me. 'Not quite what you expected, eh?'

I relaxed a bit, knowing his tone meant a temporary reprieve from the lecture. He gathered up a handful of the iron drabs that were sitting on the table and clinked them together thoughtfully in his hand.

He looked at me. 'Did you learn to juggle all at once? Five balls at a time? Knives too?'

I flushed a bit at the memory. Trip hadn't even let me try three balls at first. He'd made me juggle two. I'd even dropped them a couple of times. I told Ben so.

'Right,' Ben said. 'Master this trick and you get to learn another.' I expected him to stand up and start back into the lesson, but he didn't.

Instead he held out the handful of iron drabs. 'What do you know about these?' He clattered them together in his hand.

'In what respect?' I asked. 'Physically, chemically, historically—'

'Historically,' he grinned, 'Astound me with your grasp of historical minutiae, E'lir.' I had asked him what E'lir meant once. He claimed it meant 'wise one', but I had my doubts from the way his mouth had quirked when he said it.

'A long time ago, the people who—'

'How long ago?'

I frowned at him in mock severity. 'Roughly two thousand years ago. The nomadic folk who roamed the foothills around the Shalda Mountains were brought together under one chieftain.'

'What was his name?'

'Heldred. His sons were Heldim and Heldar. Would you like his entire lineage, or should I get to the point?' I glowered at him.

'Sorry, sir.' Ben sat up straight in his seat and assumed such an aspect of rapt attention that we both broke into grins.

I started again. 'Heldred eventually controlled the foothills around the Shalda. This meant that he controlled the mountains themselves. They started to plant crops, their nomadic lifestyle was abandoned, and they slowly began to—'

'Get to the point?' Abenthy asked. He tossed the drabs onto the table in front of me.

I ignored him as best I could. 'They controlled the only plentiful and easily accessible source of metal for a great distance and soon they were the most skilled workers of those metals as well. They exploited this advantage and gained a great deal of wealth and power.

'Until this point barter was the most common method of trade. Some larger cities coined their own currency, but outside those cities the money was only worth the weight of the metal. Bars of metal were better for bartering, but full bars of metal were inconvenient to carry.'

Ben gave me his best bored-student face. The effect was only slightly inhibited by the fact that he had burned his eyebrows off again about two days ago. 'You're not going to go into the merits of representational currency, are you?'

I took a deep breath and resolved not to pester Ben so much when he was lecturing me. 'The no-longer-nomads, called the Cealdim by now, were the first to establish a standardised currency. By cutting one of these smaller bars into five pieces you get five drabs.' I began to piece two rows of five drabs each together to illustrate my point. They resembled little ingots of metal. 'Ten drabs are the same as a copper jot; ten jots—'

'Good enough,' Ben broke in, startling me. 'So these two drabs,' he held a pair out for my inspection, 'Could have come from the same bar, right?'

'Actually, they probably cast them individually . . .' I trailed off under a glare. 'Sure.'

'So there's something still connecting them, right?' He gave me the look again.

I didn't really agree, but knew better than to interrupt. 'Right.'

He set them both on the table. 'So when you move one, the other should move, right?'

I agreed for the sake of argument, then reached out to move one. But Ben stopped my hand, shaking his head. 'You've got to remind them first. You've got to convince them, in fact.'

He brought out a bowl and decanted a slow blob of pine pitch into it. He dipped one of the drabs into the pitch and stuck the other one to it, spoke several words I didn't recognise, and slowly pulled the bits apart, strands of pitch stretching between them.

He set one on the table, keeping the other in his hand. Then he muttered something else and relaxed.

He raised his hand, and the drab on the table mimicked the motion. He danced his hand around and the brown piece of iron bobbed in the air.

He looked from me to the coin. 'The law of sympathy is one of the most basic parts of magic. It states that the more similar two objects are, the greater the sympathetic link. The greater the link, the more easily they influence each other.'

'Your definition is circular.'

He set down the coin. His lecturer's facade gave way to a grin as he tried with marginal success to wipe the pitch off of his hands with a rag. He thought for a while. 'Seems pretty useless doesn't it?'

I gave a hesitant nod, trick questions were fairly common around lesson time.

'Would you rather learn how to call the wind?' His eyes danced at me. He murmured a word and the canvas ceiling of the wagon rustled around us.

I felt a grin capture my face, wolfish.

'Too bad, E'lir.' His grin was wolfish too, and savage. 'You need to learn your letters before you can write. You need to learn the fingerings on the strings before you play and sing.'

He pulled out a piece of paper and jotted a couple of words on it. 'The trick is in holding the Alar firm in your mind. You need to believe they are connected. You need to *know* they are.' He handed me the paper. 'Here is the phonetic pronunciation. It's called the Sympathetic Binding of Parallel Motion. Practice.' He looked even more lupine than before, old and grizzled with no eyebrows.

He left to wash his hands. I cleared my mind using Heart of Stone. Soon I was floating on a sea of dispassionate calm. I stuck the two bits of metal together with pine pitch. I fixed in my mind the Alar, the riding-crop belief, that the two drabs were connected. I said the words, pulled the coins apart, spoke the last word, and waited.

No rush of power. No flash of hot or cold. No radiant beam of light struck me.

I was rather disappointed. At least as disappointed as I could be in the Heart of Stone. I lifted the coin in my hand, and the coin on the table lifted itself in a similar fashion. It was magic, there was no doubt about that. But I felt rather underwhelmed. I had been expecting . . . I don't know what I'd been expecting. It wasn't this.

The rest of that day was spent experimenting with the simple sympathetic binding Abenthy had taught me. I learned that almost anything could be bound together. An iron drab and a silver talent, a stone and a piece of fruit, two bricks, a clod of earth and one of the donkeys. It took me about two hours to figure out that the pine pitch wasn't necessary. When I asked him, Ben admitted that it was merely an aid for concentration. I think he was surprised that I figured it out without being told.

Let me sum up sympathy very quickly since you will probably never need to have anything other than a rough comprehension of how these things work.

First, energy cannot be created or destroyed. When you are lifting one drab and the other rises off the table, the one in your hand feels as heavy as if you're lifting both, because, in fact, you are.

That's in theory. In practice, it feels like you're lifting three drabs. No sympathetic link is perfect. The more dissimilar the items, the more energy is lost. Think of it as a leaky aqueduct leading to a water wheel. A good sympathetic link has very few leaks, and most of the energy is used. A bad link is full of holes; very little of the effort you put into it goes towards what you want it to do.

For instance I tried linking a piece of chalk to a glass bottle of water. There was very little similarity between the two, so even though the bottle of water might have weighed two pounds, when I tried to lift the chalk it felt like sixty pounds. The best link I found was a tree branch I had broken in half.

After I understood this little piece of sympathy, Ben taught me others. A dozen dozen sympathetic bindings. A hundred little tricks for channelling power. Each of them was a different word in a vast vocabulary I was just beginning to speak. Quite often it was tedious, and I'm not telling you the half of it.

Ben continued giving me a smattering of lessons in other areas: history, arithmetic, and chemistry. But I grabbed at whatever he could teach me about sympathy. He doled out his secrets sparingly, making me prove I'd mastered one before giving me another. But I seemed to have a knack for it above and beyond my natural penchant for absorbing knowledge, so there was never too long a wait.

I don't mean to imply that the road was always smooth. The same curiosity that made me such an eager student also led me into trouble with fair regularity.

One evening as I was building up my parents' cookfire, my mother caught me chanting a rhyme I had heard the day before. Not knowing that she was behind me, she overheard as I knocked one stick of firewood against another and absentmindedly recited:

> 'Seven things has Lady Lackless
> Keeps them underneath her black dress
> One a ring that's not for wearing
> One a sharp word, not for swearing
> Right beside her husband's candle
> There's a door without a handle
> In a box, no lid or locks
> Lackless keeps her husband's rocks
> There's a secret she's been keeping
> She's been dreaming and not sleeping
> On a road, that's not for travelling
> Lackless likes her riddle ravelling.'

I had heard a little girl chant it as she played hop-skip. I'd only heard it twice, but it had stuck in my head. It was memorable, as most child rhymes are.

But my mother heard me and came over to stand by the fire. 'What were you just saying, sweet?' Her tone wasn't angry, but I could tell she wasn't pleased either.

'Something I heard back in Fallows,' I said evasively. Running off with town children was a largely forbidden activity. *Distrust turns quickly to dislike*, my father told new members of our troupe, *so stay together when you're in town, and be polite.* I laid some heavier sticks on the fire and let the flames lick them.

My mother was silent for a while, and I was beginning to hope she would leave it alone, when she said, 'It's not a nice thing to be singing. Have you stopped to think what it's about?'

I hadn't, actually. It seemed mostly nonsense rhyme. But when I ran it back through my head, I saw the rather obvious sexual innuendo. 'I do. I didn't think about it before.'

Her expression grew a little gentler, and she reached down to smooth my hair, 'Always think about what you're singing, honey.'

I seemed to be out of trouble, but I couldn't keep from asking, 'How is it any different than parts of *For All His Waiting*? Like when Fain asks Lady Perial about her hat? "I heard about it from so many men I wished to see it for myself and try the fit." It's pretty obvious what he's really talking about.'

I watched her mouth grow firm, not angry, but not pleased. Then something in her face changed. 'You tell me what the difference is,' she said.

I hated bait questions. The difference was obvious: one would get me in trouble, the other wouldn't. I waited a while to make it clear I had given the matter proper consideration before I shook my head.

My mother knelt lightly in front of the fire, warming her hands. 'The difference is . . . go fetch me the tripod, would you?' She gave me a gentle push, and I scampered off to get it from the back of our wagon as she continued, 'The difference is between saying something *to* a person, and saying something *about* a person. The first might be rude, but the second is always gossip.'

I brought the tripod back and helped her set it over the fire. 'Also, Lady Perial is just a character. Lady Lackless is a real person, with feelings that can be hurt.' She looked up at me.

'I didn't know,' I protested guiltily.

I must have struck a sufficiently piteous figure because she gathered me in for a hug and a kiss. 'It's nothing to cry over, sweet one. Just remember to always think about what you're doing.' She ran her hand over my head and smiled like the sun. 'I imagine you could make it up to both Lady Lackless and myself if you found some sweet nettle for the pot tonight.'

Any excuse to escape judgment and play for a while in the tangle of trees by the roadside was good enough for me. I was gone almost before the words left her mouth.

———————

I should also make it clear that much of the time I spent with Ben was my free time. I was still responsible for my normal duties in the troupe. I acted the part of the young page when needed. I helped paint scenery and sew costumes. I rubbed down the horses at night and rattled the sheet of tin backstage when we needed thunder onstage.

But I didn't bemoan the loss of my free time. A child's endless energy and my own insatiable lust for knowledge made the following year one of the happiest times I can remember.

CHAPTER TWELVE

Puzzle Pieces Fitting

T OWARDS THE END OF the summer I accidentally overheard a conversation that shook me out of my state of blissful ignorance. When we are
children we seldom think of the future. This innocence leaves us free to
enjoy ourselves as few adults can. The day we fret about the future is the day
we leave our childhood behind.

It was evening, and the troupe was camped by the side of the road. Abenthy
had given me a new piece of sympathy to practice: The Maxim of Variable
Heat Transferred to Constant Motion, or something pretentious like that.

It was tricky, but it had fallen into place like a puzzle piece fitting. It had
taken about fifteen minutes, and from Abenthy's tone I guessed he had
expected it to take three or four hours at least.

So I went looking for him. Partly to get my next lesson, and partly so that
I could be just a little bit smug.

I tracked him down to my parents' wagon. I heard the three of them long
before I saw them. Their voices were just murmurs, the distant music that a
conversation makes when it's too dim for words. But as I was coming close
I heard one word clearly: *Chandrian.*

I pulled up short when I heard that. Everyone in the troupe knew my
father was working on a song. He'd been teasing old stories and rhymes from
townsfolk for over a year wherever we stopped to play.

For months it was stories about Lanre. Then he started gathering old
faerie stories too, legends about bogies and shamble-men. Then he began to
ask questions about the Chandrian . . .

That was months ago. Over the last half year he had asked more about the
Chandrian and less about Lanre, Lyra, and the rest. Most songs my father set

to writing were finished in a single season, while this one was stretching toward its second year.

You should know this as well, my father never let word or whisper of a song be heard before it was ready to play. Only my mother was allowed into his confidence, as her hand was always in any song he made. The cleverness in the music was his. The best words were hers.

When you wait a few span or month to hear a finished song, the anticipation adds savour. But after a year excitement begins to sour. By now, a year and a half had passed and folk were almost mad with curiosity. This occasionally led to hard words when someone was caught wandering a little too close to our wagon while my father and mother were working.

So I moved closer to my parents' fire, stepping softly. Eavesdropping is a deplorable habit, but I have developed worse ones since.

'. . . much about them,' I heard Ben say. 'But I'm willing.'

'I'm glad to talk with an educated man on the subject.' My father's strong baritone was a contrast to Ben's tenor. 'I'm weary of these superstitious country folk, and the . . .'

Someone added wood to the fire and I lost my father's words in the crackling that followed. Stepping as quickly as I dared, I moved into the long shadow of my parents' wagon.

'. . . like I'm chasing ghosts with this song. Trying to piece together this story is a fool's game. I wish I'd never started it.'

'Nonsense,' my mother said. 'This will be your best work, and you know it.'

'So you think there is an original story all the others stem from?' Ben asked. 'A historical basis for Lanre?'

'All the signs point to it,' my father said. 'It's like looking at a dozen grandchildren and seeing ten of them have blue eyes. You know the grandmother had blue eyes, too. I've done this before, I'm good at it. I wrote "Below the Walls" the same way. But . . .' I heard him sigh.

'What's the problem then?'

'The story's older,' my mother explained. 'It's more like he's looking at great-great-grandchildren.'

'And they're scattered to the four corners,' my father groused. '*And* when I finally do find one, it's got five eyes: two greens, a blue, a brown, and a chartreuse. Then the next one has only one eye, and it changes colour. How am I supposed to draw conclusions from that?'

Ben cleared his throat. 'A disturbing analogy,' he said. 'But you're welcome to pick my brain about the Chandrian. I've heard a lot of stories over the years.'

'The first thing I need to know is how many there actually are,' my father said. 'Most stories say seven, but even that's conflicted. Some say three, others five, and in *Felior's Fall* there are a full thirteen of them: one for each pontifet in Atur, and an extra for the capitol.'

'That I can answer,' Ben said. 'Seven. You can hold to that with some certainty. It's part of their name, actually. *Chaen* means seven. *Chaen-dian* means "seven of them". Chandrian.'

'I didn't know that,' my father said. '*Chaen*. What language is that? Yllish?'

'Sounds like Tema,' my mother said.

'You've got a good ear,' Ben said to her. 'It's Temic, actually. Predates Tema by about a thousand years.'

'Well that simplifies things,' I heard my father say. 'I wish I'd asked you a month ago. I don't suppose you know why they do what they do?' I could tell by my father's tone that he didn't really expect an answer.

'That's the real mystery, isn't it?' Ben chuckled. 'I think that's what makes them more frightening than the rest of the bogey-men you hear about in stories. A ghost wants revenge, a demon wants your soul, a shamble-man is hungry and cold. It makes them less terrible. Things we understand we can try to control. But Chandrian come like lightning from a clear blue sky. Just destruction. No rhyme or reason to it.'

'My song will have both,' my father said with grim determination. 'I think I've dug up their reason, after all this while. I've teased it together from bits and pieces of story. That's what's so galling about this, to have the harder part of this done and have all these small specifics giving me such trouble.'

'You think you know?' Ben said curiously. 'What's your theory?'

My father gave a low chuckle. 'Oh no Ben, you'll have to wait with the others. I've sweated too long over this song to give away the heart of it before it's finished.'

I could hear the disappointment in Ben's voice. 'I'm sure this is all just an elaborate ruse to keep me travelling with you,' he groused. 'I won't be able to leave until I've heard the blackened thing.'

'Then help us finish it,' my mother said. 'The Chandrian's signs are another key piece of information we can't nail down. Everyone agrees there are signs that warn of their presence, but nobody agrees on what they are.'

'Let me think . . .' Ben said. 'Blue flame is obvious, of course. But I'd hesitate to attribute that to the Chandrian in particular. In some stories it's a sign of demons. In others it's fae creatures, or magic of any sort.'

'It shows bad air in mines, too,' my mother pointed out.

'Does it?' my father asked.

She nodded. 'When a lamp burns with a blue haze you know there's firedamp in the air.'

'Good lord, firedamp in a coal mine,' my father said. 'Blow out your light and get lost in the black, or leave it burn and blow the whole place to flinders. That's more frightening than any demon.'

'I'll also admit to the fact that certain arcanists occasionally use prepared candles or torches to impress gullible townsfolk,' Ben said, clearing his throat self-consciously.

My mother laughed. 'Remember who you're talking to, Ben. We'd never hold a little showmanship against a man. In fact, blue candles would be just the thing the next time we play *Daeonica*. If you happened to find a couple tucked away somewhere, that is.'

'I'll see what I can do,' Ben said, his voice amused. 'Other signs . . . one of them is supposed to have eyes like a goat, or no eyes, or black eyes. I've heard that one quite a bit. I've heard that plants die when the Chandrian are around. Wood rots, metal rusts, brick crumbles . . .' He paused. 'Though I don't know if that's several signs, or all one sign.'

'You begin to see the trouble I'm having,' my father said morosely. 'And there's still the question as to if they all share the same signs, or have a couple each.'

'I've told you,' my mother said, exasperated. 'One sign for each of them. It makes the most sense.'

'My lady wife's favorite theory,' my father said. 'But it doesn't fit. In some stories the only sign is blue flame. In others you have animals going crazy and no blue flame. In others you have a man with black eyes *and* animals going mad *and* blue flame.'

'I've told you how to make sense of that,' she said, her irritated tone indicating they'd had this particular discussion before. 'They don't always have to be together. They could go out in threes or fours. If one of them makes fires dim, then it'll look the same as if they *all* made the fires dim. That would account for the differences in the stories. Different numbers and different signs depending on how they're grouped together.'

My father grumbled something.

'That's a clever wife you've got there, Arl.' Ben spoke up, breaking the tension. 'How much will you sell her for?'

'I need her for my work, unfortunately. But if you're interested in a short-term rental, I'm sure we could arrange a reas—' There was a fleshy thump followed by a slightly pained chortle in my father's baritone. 'Any other signs that spring to mind?'

'They're supposed to be cold to the touch. Though how anyone could know that is beyond me. I've heard that fires don't burn around them. Though that directly contradicts the blue flame. It could—'

The wind picked up, stirring the trees. The rustling leaves drowned out what Ben said. I took advantage of the noise to creep a few steps closer.

'. . . being "yoked to shadow", whatever that means,' I heard my father say as the wind died down.

Ben grunted. 'I couldn't say either. I heard a story where they were given away because their shadows pointed the wrong way, towards the light. And there was another where one of them was referred to as "shadow-hamed". It was "*something* the shadow-hamed". Damned if I can remember the name though . . .'

'Speaking of names, that's another point I'm having trouble with,' my father said. 'There are a couple of dozen I've collected that I'd appreciate your opinion on. The most—'

'Actually, Arl,' Ben interrupted, 'I'd appreciate it if you didn't say them out loud. Names of people, that is. You can scratch them in the dirt if you'd like, or I could go fetch a slate, but I'd be more comfortable if you didn't actually *say* any of them. Better safe than sore, as they say.'

There was a deep piece of silence. I stopped midsneak with one foot off the ground, afraid they'd heard me.

'Now don't go looking at me like that, either of you,' Ben said testily.

'We're just surprised, Ben,' came my mother's gentle voice. 'You don't seem the superstitious type.'

'I'm not,' Ben said. 'I'm careful. There's a difference.'

'Of course,' my father said. 'I'd never—'

'Save it for the paying customers, Arl,' Ben cut him off, irritation plain in his voice. 'You're too good an actor to show it, but I know perfectly well when someone thinks I'm daft.'

'I just didn't expect it, Ben,' my father said apologetically. 'You're educated, and I'm so tired of people touching iron and tipping their beer as soon as I mention the Chandrian. I'm just reconstructing a story, not meddling with dark arts.'

'Well, hear me out. I like both of you too well to let you think of me as an old fool,' Ben said. 'Besides, I have something to talk with you about later, and I'll need you to take me seriously for that.'

The wind continued to pick up, and I used the noise to cover my last few steps. I edged around the corner of my parents' wagon and peered through a veil of leaves. The three of them were sitting around the campfire. Ben was sitting on a stump, huddled in his frayed brown cloak. My parents were opposite him, my mother leaning against my father, a blanket draped loosely around them.

Ben poured from a clay jug into a leather mug and handed it to my mother. His breath fogged as he spoke. 'How do they feel about demons off in Atur?' he asked.

'Scared.' My father tapped his temple. 'All that religion makes their brains soft.'

'How about off in Vintas?' Ben asked. 'Fair number of them are Tehlins. Do they feel the same way?'

My mother shook her head. 'They think it's a little silly. They like their demons metaphorical.'

'What are they afraid of at night in Vintas then?'

'The Fae,' my mother said.

My father spoke at the same time. 'Draugar.'

'You're both right, depending on which part of the country you're in,' Ben said. 'And here in the Commonwealth people laugh up their sleeves at both ideas.' He gestured at the surrounding trees. 'But here they're careful come autumn-time for fear of drawing the attention of shamble-men.'

'That's the way of things,' my father said. 'Half of being a good trouper is knowing which way your audience leans.'

'You still think I've gone cracked in the head,' Ben said, amused. 'Listen, if tomorrow we pulled into Biren and someone told you there were shamble-men in the woods, would you believe them?' My father shook his head. 'What if two people told you?' Another shake.

Ben leaned forward on his stump. 'What if a dozen people told you, with perfect earnestness, that shamble-men were out in the fields, eating—'

'Of course I wouldn't believe them,' my father said, irritated. 'It's ridiculous.'

'Of course it is,' Ben agreed, raising a finger. 'But the real question is this: Would you go into the woods?'

My father sat very still and thoughtful for a moment.

Ben nodded. 'You'd be a fool to ignore half the town's warning, even though you don't believe the same thing they do. If not shamble-men, what are you afraid of?'

'Bears.'

'Bandits.'

'Good sensible fears for a trouper to have,' Ben said. 'Fears that towns-folk don't appreciate. Every place has its little superstitions, and everyone laughs at what the folk across the river think.' He gave them a serious look. 'But have either of you ever heard a humorous song or story about the Chandrian? I'll bet a penny you haven't.'

My mother shook her head after a moment's thought. My father took a long drink before joining her.

'Now I'm not saying that the Chandrian are out there, striking like light-ning from the clear blue sky. But folk everywhere are afraid of them. There's usually a reason for that.'

Ben grinned and tipped his clay cup, pouring the last drizzle of beer out onto the earth. 'And names are strange things. Dangerous things.' He gave them a pointed look. 'That I know for true *because* I am an educated man. If I'm a mite superstitious too . . .' He shrugged. 'Well, that's my choice. I'm old. You have to humour me.'

My father nodded thoughtfully. 'It's odd I never noticed that everyone treats the Chandrian the same. It's something I should've seen.' He shook his head as if to clear it. 'We can come back to names later, I suppose. What was it you wanted to talk about?'

I prepared to sneak off before I was caught, but what Ben said next froze me in place before I took a single step.

'It's probably hard to see, being his parents and all. But your young Kvothe is rather bright.' Ben refilled his cup, and held out the jug to my father, who declined it. 'As a matter of fact, "bright" doesn't begin to cover it, not by half.'

My mother watched Ben over the top of her mug. 'Anyone who spends a little time with the boy can see that, Ben. I don't see why anyone would make a point of it. Least of all, you.'

'I don't think you really grasp the situation,' Ben said, stretching his feet almost into the fire. 'How easily did he pick up the lute?'

My father seemed a little surprised by the sudden change of topic. 'Fairly easily, why?'

'How old was he?'

My father tugged thoughtfully at his beard for a moment. In the silence my mother's voice was like a flute. 'Eight.'

'Think back to when you learned to play. Can you remember how old you were? Can you remember the sort of difficulties you had?' My father continued to tug on his beard, but his face was more reflective now, his eyes far away.

Abenthy continued. 'I'll bet he learned each chord, each fingering after being shown just once, no stumbling, no complaining. And when he did make a mistake it was never more than once, right?'

My father seemed a little perturbed. 'Mostly, but he did have trouble, just the same as anyone else. E chord. He had a lot of trouble with greater and diminished E.'

My mother broke in softly. 'I remember too, dear, but I think it was just his small hands. He was awfully young . . .'

'I bet it didn't stall him for long,' Ben said quietly. 'He does have marvellous hands; my mother would have called them magician's fingers.'

My father smiled. 'He gets them from his mother, delicate, but strong. Perfect for scrubbing pots, eh woman?'

My mother swatted him, then caught one of his hands in her own and unfolded it for Ben to see. 'He gets them from his father, graceful and gentle. Perfect for seducing young nobles' daughters.' My father started to protest, but she ignored him. 'With his eyes and those hands there won't be a woman safe in all the world when he starts hunting after the ladies.'

'Courting, dear,' my father corrected gently.

'Semantics,' she shrugged. 'It's all a chase, and when the race is done, I think I pity women chaste who run.' She leaned back against my father, keeping his hand in her lap. She tilted her head slightly and he took his cue, leaning in to kiss the corner of her mouth.

'Amen,' Ben said, raising his mug in salute.

My father put his other arm around her and gave her a squeeze. 'I still don't see what you're getting at, Ben.'

'He does everything that way, quick as a whip, hardly ever makes mistakes. I'll bet he knows every song you've ever sung to him. He knows more about what's in my wagon than I do.'

He picked up the jug and uncorked it. 'It's not just memorisation though. He understands. Half the things I've been meaning to show him he's already figured out for himself.'

Ben refilled my mother's cup. 'He's eleven. Have you ever known a boy his age who talks the way he does? A great deal of it comes from living in such an enlightened atmosphere.' Ben gestured to the wagons. 'But most eleven-year-olds' deepest thoughts have to do with skipping stones, and how to swing a cat by the tail.'

My mother laughed like bells, but Abenthy's face was serious. 'It's true, lady. I've had older students that would have loved to do half as well.' He grinned. 'If I had his hands, and one quarter his wit, I'd be eating off silver plates inside a year.'

There was a lull. My mother spoke softly, 'I remember when he was just a little baby, toddling around. Watching, always watching. With clear bright eyes that looked like they wanted to swallow up the world.' Her voice had a little quaver in it. My father put his arm around her and she rested her head on his chest.

The next silence was longer. I was considering sneaking away when my father broke it. 'What is it you suggest we do?' His voice was a mix of mild concern and fatherly pride.

Ben smiled gently. 'Nothing except to think about what options you might give him when the time comes. He will leave his mark on the world as one of the best.'

'The best what?' my father rumbled.

'Whatever he chooses. If he stays here I don't doubt he will become the next Illien.'

My father smiled. Illien is the troupers' hero. The only truly famous Edema Ruh in all of history. All our oldest, best songs are his songs.

What's more, if you believed the stories, Illien reinvented the lute in his lifetime. A master luthier, Illien transformed the archaic, fragile, unwieldy court lute into the marvellous, versatile, seven-string trouper's lute we use today. The same stories claim Illien's own lute had eight strings in all.

'Illien. I like that thought,' my mother said. 'Kings coming from miles away to hear my little Kvothe play.'

'His music stopping barroom brawls and border wars.' Ben smiled.

'The wild women in his lap,' my father enthused, 'laying their breasts on his head.'

There was a moment of stunned silence. Then my mother spoke slowly, with an edge to her voice. 'I think you mean "wild beasts laying their heads in his lap"'.'

'Do I?'

Ben coughed and continued. 'If he decides to become an arcanist, I bet he'll have a royal appointment by the time he's twenty-four. If he gets it into his head to be a merchant I don't doubt he'll own half the world by the time he dies.'

My father's brows knitted together. Ben smiled and said, 'Don't worry about the last one. He's too curious for a merchant.'

Ben paused as if considering his next words very carefully. 'He'd be accepted into the University, you know. Not for years, of course. Seventeen is about as young as they go, but I have no doubts about . . .'

I missed the rest of what Ben said. The University! I had come to think of it in the same way most children think of the Fae court, a mythical place reserved for dreaming about. A school the size of a small town. Ten times ten thousand books. People who would know the answers to any question I could ever ask . . .

It was quiet when I turned my attention back to them.

My father was looking down at my mother, nestled under his arm. 'How about it, woman? Did you happen to bed down with some wandering God a dozen years ago? That might solve our little mystery.'

She swatted at him playfully, and a thoughtful look crossed her face. 'Come to think of it, there was a night, about a dozen years ago, a man came to me. He bound me with kisses and cords of chorded song. He robbed me of my virtue and stole me away.' She paused, 'But he didn't have red hair. Couldn't be him.'

She smiled wickedly at my father, who appeared a little embarrassed. Then she kissed him. He kissed her back.

That's how I like to remember them today. I snuck away with thoughts of the University dancing in my head.

CHAPTER THIRTEEN

Interlude — Flesh with Blood Beneath

IN THE WAYSTONE INN there was a silence. It surrounded the two men sitting at a table in an otherwise empty room. Kvothe had stopped speaking, and while he seemed to be staring down at his folded hands, in reality his eyes were far away. When he finally pulled his gaze upwards, he seemed almost surprised to find Chronicler sitting across the table, pen poised above his inkwell.

Kvothe let out his breath self-consciously and motioned Chronicler to set down his pen. After a moment Chronicler complied, wiping the nib of the pen on a clean cloth before setting it down.

'I could use a drink,' Kvothe announced suddenly, as if he were surprised. 'I haven't told many stories lately, and I find myself unreasonably dry.' He rose smoothly from the table and began to make his way through the maze of empty tables toward the empty bar. 'I can offer you almost anything, dark ale, pale wine, spiced cider, chocolate, coffee . . .'

Chronicler raised an eyebrow. 'Chocolate would be wonderful, if you have it. I wouldn't expect to find that sort of thing this far from . . .' He cleared his throat politely. 'Well, anywhere.'

'We have everything here at the Waystone,' Kvothe said, making an offhand gesture to the empty room. 'Excepting any customers, of course.' He brought an earthenware jug up from underneath the bar, then set it on the bar with a hollow sound. He sighed before calling out, 'Bast! Bring up some cider, would you?'

An indistinct reply echoed from a doorway at the back of the room.

'Bast,' Kvothe chided, seemingly too quiet to be heard.

'Shag down here and get it yourself, you hack!' the voice shouted up from the basement. 'I'm in the middle of something.'

'Hired help?' Chronicler asked.

Kvothe leaned his elbows on the bar and smiled indulgently.

After a moment, the sound of someone climbing a set of wooden stairs in hard-soled boots echoed from the doorway. Bast stepped into the room, muttering under his breath.

He was dressed simply: black long-sleeved shirt tucked into black pants; black pants tucked into soft black boots. His face was sharp and delicate, almost beautiful, with striking blue eyes.

He carried a jug to the bar, walking with a strange and not unpleasant grace. 'One customer?' he said reproachfully. 'You couldn't get it yourself? You pulled me away from *Celum Tinture*. You've been harping on me to read it for nearly a month now.'

'Bast, do you know what they do to students at the University who eavesdrop on their teachers?' Kvothe asked archly.

Bast put a hand on his chest and began to protest his innocence.

'Bast . . .' Kvothe gave him a stern look.

Bast closed his mouth and for a moment looked as if he was about to try and offer some explanation, then his shoulders slumped. 'How did you know?'

Kvothe chuckled. 'You've been avoiding that book for a mortal age. Either you had suddenly become an exceptionally dedicated student, or you were doing something incriminating.'

'What *do* they do to students at the University who eavesdrop?' Bast asked curiously.

'I haven't the slightest idea. *I* was never caught. I think making you sit and listen to the rest of my story should be punishment enough. But I forget myself,' Kvothe said, gesturing to the common room. 'We are neglecting our guest.'

Chronicler seemed anything but bored. As soon as Bast entered the room, Chronicler began to watch him curiously. As the conversation continued, Chronicler's expression had grown by degrees more puzzled and more intent.

In fairness, something ought to be said about Bast. At first glance, he looked to be an average, if attractive, young man. But there was something different about him. For instance, he wore soft black leather boots. At least, if you looked at him that's what you saw. But if you happened to catch a glimpse of him from the corner of your eye, and if he were standing in the right type of shadow, you might see something else entirely.

And if you had the right sort of mind, the sort of mind that actually *sees* what it looks at, you might notice that his eyes were odd. If your mind had the rare talent of not being fooled by its own expectations, you might notice something else about them, something strange and wonderful.

Because of this, Chronicler had been staring at Kvothe's young student, trying to decide what was different about him. By the time their conversation was through, Chronicler's gaze would be considered intense at the very least, and rude by most. When Bast finally turned from the bar, Chronicler's eyes widened perceptibly, and the colour drained from his already pale face.

Chronicler reached inside his shirt and tugged something from around his neck. He set it on the table at arm's length, between himself and Bast. All this was done in half a second, and his eyes never left the dark-haired young man at the bar. Chronicler's face was calm as he pressed the metal disk firmly onto the table with two fingers.

'Iron,' he said. His voice sounding with strange resonance, as if it were an order to be obeyed.

Bast doubled over as if punched in the stomach, baring his teeth and making a noise halfway between a growl and a scream. Moving with an unnatural, sinuous speed, he drew one hand back to the side of his head and tensed himself to spring.

It all happened in the time it takes to draw a sharp breath. Still, somehow, Kvothe's long-fingered hand caught Bast's wrist. Unaware or uncaring, Bast leaped toward Chronicler only to be brought up short, as if Kvothe's hand were a shackle. Bast struggled furiously to free himself, but Kvothe stood behind the bar, arm outstretched, motionless as steel or stone.

'Stop!' Kvothe's voice struck the air like a commandment, and in the stillness that followed, his words were sharp and angry. 'I will have no fighting among my friends. I have lost enough without that.' His eyes caught Chronicler. 'Undo that, or I will break it.'

Chronicler paused, shaken. Then his mouth moved silently, and with a slight tremor he drew his hand away from the circle of dull metal that lay upon the table.

Tension poured out of Bast, and for a moment he hung limply as a rag doll from the wrist Kvothe still held, standing behind the bar. Shakily, Bast managed to find his feet and lean against the bar. Kvothe gave him a long, searching look, then released his wrist.

Bast slumped onto the stool without taking his eyes from Chronicler. He moved gingerly, like a man with a tender wound.

And he had changed. The eyes that watched Chronicler were still a striking ocean blue, but now they showed themselves to be all one colour, like gems or deep forest pools, and his soft leather boots had been replaced with graceful cloven hooves.

Kvothe motioned Chronicler forward imperiously, then turned to grab two thick glasses and a bottle seemingly at random. He set the glasses down as Bast and Chronicler eyed each other uneasily.

'Now,' Kvothe said angrily, 'you've both acted understandably, but that does not by any means mean that either of you has behaved well. So, we might as well start over altogether.'

He drew a deep breath. 'Bast, let me introduce you to Devan Lochees, also known as Chronicler. By all accounts a great teller, rememberer, and recorder of stories. In addition, unless I have suddenly lost all my wit, an accomplished member of the Arcanum, at least Re'lar, and one of perhaps two score people in the world who knows the name of iron.

'However,' Kvothe continued, 'in spite of these accolades he seems to be a bit innocent of the ways of the world. As demonstrated by his plentiful lack of wit in making a near-suicidal attack on what I guess is the first of the folk he has ever had the luck to see.'

Chronicler stood impassively throughout the introduction, watching Bast as if he were a snake.

'Chronicler, I would like you to meet Bastas, son of Remmen, Prince of Twilight and the Telwyth Mael. The brightest, which is to say the *only* student I've had the misfortune to teach. Glamourer, bartender, and, not last, my friend.

'Who, over the course of a hundred and fifty years of life, not to mention nearly two years of my personal tutelage, has managed to avoid learning a few important facts. The first being this: attacking a member of the Arcanum skilled enough to make a binding of iron is foolish.'

'He attacked me!' said Bast hotly.

Kvothe looked at him coolly. 'I didn't say it was unjustified. I said it was foolish.'

'I would have won.'

'Very likely. But you would have been hurt, and he would be hurt or dead. Do you remember that I had introduced him as my guest?'

Bast was silent. His expression remained belligerent.

'Now,' said Kvothe with a brittle cheerfulness. 'You've been introduced.'

'Pleased,' Bast said icily.

'Likewise,' Chronicler returned.

'There is no reason for you two to be anything other than friends,' Kvothe continued, an edge creeping into his voice. 'And that is not how friends greet each other.'

Bast and Chronicler stared at each other, neither moved.

Kvothe's voice grew quiet. 'If you do not stop this foolishness, you may both leave now. One of you will be left with a slim sliver of story, and the other can search out a new teacher. If there is one thing I will not abide, it is the folly of a willful pride.'

Something about the low intensity of Kvothe's voice broke the stare between them. And when they turned to look at him it seemed that some-one very different was standing behind the bar. The jovial innkeeper was gone, and in his place stood someone dark and fierce.

He's so young, Chronicler marvelled. *He can't be more than twenty-five. Why didn't I see it before? He could break me in his hands like a kindling stick. How did I ever mistake him for an innkeeper, even for a moment?*

Then he saw Kvothe's eyes. They had deepened to a green so dark they were nearly black. *This is who I came to see,* Chronicler thought to himself, *this is the man who counselled kings and walked old roads with nothing but his wit to guide him. This is the man whose name has become both praise and curse at the University.*

Kvothe stared at Chronicler and Bast in turn; neither could meet his eye for very long. After an awkward pause, Bast extended his hand. Chronicler hesitated for a bare moment before reaching out quickly, as if he were sticking his hand into a fire.

Nothing happened, both of them seemed moderately surprised.

'Amazing, isn't it?' Kvothe addressed them bitingly. 'Five fingers and flesh with blood beneath. One could almost believe that on the other end of that hand lay a person of some sort.'

Guilt crept into the expressions of the two men. They let go of each other's hands.

Kvothe poured something from the green bottle into the glasses. This simple gesture changed him. He seemed to fade back into himself, until there was little left of the dark-eyed man who'd stood behind the bar a moment ago. Chronicler felt a pang of loss as he stared at the innkeeper with one hand hidden in a linen rag.

'Now.' Kvothe pushed the glasses toward them. 'Take these drinks, sit at that table, and talk. When I come back, I don't want to find either one of you dead or the building on fire. Fair?'

Bast gave an embarrassed smile as Chronicler picked up the glasses and moved back to the table. Bast followed him and almost sat down before returning to grab the bottle too.

'Not too much of that,' Kvothe cautioned as he stepped into the back room. 'I don't want you giggling through my story.'

The two at the table began a tense, halting conversation as Kvothe moved into the kitchen. Several minutes later he emerged, bringing out cheese and a loaf of dark bread, cold chicken and sausage, butter and honey.

They moved to a larger table as Kvothe brought the platters out, bustling about and looking every bit the innkeeper. Chronicler watched him covertly, finding it hard to believe that this man humming to himself and cutting sausage could be the same person who had stood behind the bar just minutes ago, dark-eyed and terrible.

As Chronicler gathered his paper and quills, Kvothe studied the angle of the sun through the window, a pensive look on his face. Eventually he turned to Bast. 'How much did you manage to overhear?'

'Most of it, Reshi,' Bast smiled. 'I have good ears.'

'That's good. We don't have time to backtrack.' He drew a deep breath. 'Let's get back to it then. Brace yourselves, the story takes a turn now. Downward. Darker. Clouds on the horizon.'

CHAPTER FOURTEEN

The Name of the Wind

WINTER IS A SLOW time of year for a travelling troupe, but Abenthy put it to good use and finally got around to teaching me sympathy in earnest. However, as is often the case, especially for children, the anticipation proved much more exciting than the reality.

It would be wrong to say that I was disappointed with sympathy. But honestly, I *was* disappointed. It was not what I expected magic to be.

It was useful. There was no denying that. Ben used sympathy to make light for our shows. Sympathy could start a fire without flint or lift a heavy weight without cumbersome ropes and pulleys.

But the first time I'd seen him, Ben had somehow called the wind. That was no mere sympathy. That was storybook magic. That was the secret I wanted more than anything.

Spring thaw was well behind us and the troupe was riding through the forests and fields of the western Commonwealth. I was riding along, as normal, in the front of Ben's wagon. Summer was just deciding to make itself known again and everything was green and growing.

Things had been quiet for about an hour. Ben was drowsing with the reins held loosely in one hand when the wagon hit a stone and jarred us both out of our respective reveries.

Ben pulled himself more upright in his seat, and addressed me in a tone I had grown to think of as Have-I-Got-a-Puzzle-for-You. 'How would you bring a kettle of water to a boil?'

Looking around I saw a large boulder by the side of the road. I pointed.

'That stone should be warm from sitting in the sun. I'd bind it to the water in the kettle, and use the heat in the stone to bring the water to boil.'

'Stone to water isn't very efficient,' Ben chided me. 'Only about one part in fifteen would end up warming the water.'

'It would work.'

'I'll grant you that. But it's sloppy. You can do better, E'lir.'

He then proceeded to shout at Alpha and Beta, a sign that he was in a genuine good mood. They took it as calmly as ever, in spite of the fact that he accused them of things I'm sure no donkey has ever willingly done, especially not Beta, who possessed impeccable moral character.

Stopping midtirade, he asked, 'How would you bring down that bird?' He gestured to a hawk riding the air above a wheat field to the side of the road.

'I probably wouldn't. It's done nothing to me.'

'Hypothetically.'

'I'm saying that, hypothetically, I wouldn't do it.'

Ben chuckled. 'Point made, E'lir. Precisely *how* wouldn't you do it? Details please.'

'I'd get Teren to shoot it down.'

He nodded thoughtfully. 'Good, good. However, it is a matter between you and the bird. That hawk,' he gestured indignantly, 'has said something uncouth about your mother.'

'Ah. Then my honour demands I defend her good name myself.'

'Indeed it does.'

'Do I have a feather?'

'No.'

'Tehlu hold and—' I bit off the rest of what I was going to say at his disapproving look. 'You never make it easy, do you?'

'It's an annoying habit I picked up from a student who was too clever for his own good.' He smiled. 'What could you do even if you had a feather?'

'I'd bind it to the bird and lather it with lye soap.'

Ben furrowed his brow, such as it was. 'What kind of binding?'

'Chemical. Probably second catalytic.'

A thoughtful pause. 'Second catalytic . . .' He scratched at his chin. 'To dissolve the oil that makes the feather smooth?'

I nodded.

He looked up at the bird. 'I've never thought of that,' he said with a kind of quiet admiration. I took it as a compliment.

'Nevertheless,' he looked back to me, 'you have no feather. How do you bring it down?'

I thought for several minutes, but couldn't think of anything. I decided to try and turn this into a different sort of lesson.

'I would,' I said casually, 'simply call the wind, and make it strike the bird from the sky.'

Ben gave me a calculating look that told me he knew exactly what I was up to. 'And how would you do that, E'lir?'

I sensed he might be ready to finally tell me the secret he had been keeping all through the winter months. At the same time I was struck with an idea.

I drew in a deep breath and spoke the words to bind the air in my lungs to the air outside. I fixed the Alar firmly in my mind, put my thumb and forefinger in front of my pursed lips, and blew between them.

There was a light puff of wind at my back that tousled my hair and caused the tarpaulin covering the wagon to pull taut for a moment. It might have been nothing more than a coincidence, but nevertheless, I felt an exultant smile overflow my face. For a second I did nothing but grin like a maniac at Ben, his face dull with disbelief.

Then I felt something squeeze my chest, as if I was deep underwater.

I tried to draw a breath but couldn't. Mildly confused, I kept trying. It felt as if I'd just fallen flat on my back and had the air driven from me.

All in a rush I realised what I had done. My body exploded into a cold sweat and I grabbed frantically at Ben's shirt, pointing at my chest, my neck, my open mouth.

Ben's face turned from shocked to ashen as he looked at me.

I realised how still everything was. Not a blade of grass was stirring. Even the sound of the wagon seemed muted, as if far off in the distance.

Terror screamed through my mind, drowning out any thought. I began to claw at my throat, ripping my shirt open. My heart thundered through the ringing in my ears. Pain stabbed through my straining chest as I gasped for air.

Moving more quickly than I had ever seen before, Ben grabbed me by the tatters of my shirt and sprang from the seat of the wagon. Landing in the grass by the side of the road, he dashed me to the ground with such a force that, if I'd had any air in my lungs, it would have been driven out of me.

Tears streaked my face as I thrashed blindly. I knew that I was going to die. My eyes felt hot and red. I raked madly at the earth with hands that were numb and cold as ice.

I was aware of someone shouting, but it seemed very far away. Ben kneeled above me, but the sky was getting dim behind him. He seemed almost distracted, as if he were listening to something I couldn't hear.

Then he looked at me, all I remember were his eyes, they seemed far away and filled with a terrible power, dispassionate and cold.

He looked at me. His mouth moved. He called the wind.

A leaf in lightning, I shook. And the thunderclap was black.

———————

The next thing I remember was Ben helping me to my feet. I was dimly aware of the other wagons stopping and curious faces peering at us. My mother came away from our wagon and Ben met her halfway, chuckling and saying something reassuring. I couldn't make out the words as I was focused on breathing deep, in and out.

The other wagons trundled on, and I followed Ben mutely back to his wagon. He made a show of puttering around, checking the cords that held the tarpaulin tight. I collected my wits and was helping as best I could when the final wagon in the troupe passed us.

When I looked up, Ben's eyes were furious. 'What were you thinking?' he hissed. 'Well? What? What were you thinking?' I'd never seen him like this before, his whole body drawn up into a tight knot of anger. He was shaking with it. He drew back his arm to strike me . . . then stopped. After a moment his hand fell to his side.

Moving methodically he checked the last couple of ropes and climbed back onto the wagon. Not knowing what else to do, I followed him.

Ben twitched the reins and Alpha and Beta tugged the wagon into motion. We were last in line now. Ben stared straight ahead. I fingered the torn front of my shirt. It was tensely silent.

In hindsight, what I had done was glaringly stupid. When I bound my breath to the air outside, it made it impossible for me to breathe. My lungs weren't strong enough to move that much air. I would have needed a chest like an iron bellows. I would have had as much luck trying to drink a river or lift a mountain.

We rode for about two hours in an uncomfortable silence. The sun was brushing the tops of the trees when Ben finally drew in a deep breath and let it out in an explosive sigh. He handed me the reins.

When I looked back at him I realised for the first time how old he was. I had always known he was nearing his third score of years, but I'd never seen him look it before.

'I lied to your mother back there, Kvothe. She saw the end of what happened and was worried about you.' His eyes didn't move from the wagon ahead of ours as he spoke. 'I told her we were working on something for a performance. She's a good woman. She deserves better than lies.'

We rode on in an endless agony of silence, but it was still a few hours before sunset when I heard voices calling 'Greystone!' down the line. The bump of our wagon turning onto the grass jostled Ben from his brooding.

He looked around and saw the sun was still in the sky. 'Why are we stopping so early? Tree across the road?'

'Greystone.' I gestured up ahead to the slab of stone that loomed over the tops of the wagons ahead of us.

'What?'

'Every once in a while we run across one by the road.' I gestured again to the greystone peering over the tops of smaller trees by the roadside. Like most greystones it was a crudely hewn rectangle about a dozen feet tall. The wagons gathering around it seemed rather insubstantial compared to the stone's solid presence. 'I've heard them called standing stones, but I've seen a lot of them that weren't standing, just lying on their sides. We always stop for the day when we find one, unless we're in a terrible hurry.' I stopped, realising I was babbling.

'I've known them by a different name. Waystones,' Ben said quietly. He looked old and tired. After a moment he asked, 'Why do you stop when you find one?'

'We just always do. It's a break from the road.' I thought for a moment. 'I think they're supposed to be good luck.' I wished I had more to say to keep the conversation going, his interest piqued, but I couldn't think of anything else.

'I suppose they could be at that.' Ben guided Alpha and Beta into a spot on the far side of the stone, away from most of the other wagons. 'Come back for dinner or soon afterwards. We need to talk.' He turned without looking at me and began to unhitch Alpha from the wagon.

I'd never seen Ben in a mood like this before. Worried that I'd ruined things between us, I turned and ran to my parents' wagon.

I found my mother sitting in front of a fresh fire, slowly adding twigs to build it up. My father sat behind her, rubbing her neck and shoulders. They both looked up at the sound of my feet running towards them.

'Can I eat with Ben tonight?'

My mother looked up at my father, then back to me. 'You shouldn't make yourself a nuisance, dear.'

'He invited. If I go now, I can help him set up for the night.'

She wiggled her shoulders, and my father started rubbing them again. She smiled at me. 'Fair enough, but don't keep him up until the wee hours.' She smiled at me. 'Give me a kiss.' She held out her arms and I gave her a hug and a kiss.

My father gave me a kiss too. 'Let me have your shirt. It'll give me something to do while your mother fixes dinner.' He skinned me out of it and fingered the torn edges. 'This shirt is wholly holey, more than it has any right to be.'

I started to stammer out an explanation but he waved it aside. 'I know, I know, it was all for the greater good. Try to be more careful, or I'll make you sew it yourself. There's a fresh one in your trunk. Bring me needle and thread while you're in there, if you'd be so kind.'

I made a dash into the back of the wagon and drew on a fresh shirt. While I rummaged around for needle and thread I heard my mother singing:

> *'In evening when the sun is setting fast,*
> *I'll watch for you from high above*
> *The time for your return is long since past*
> *But mine is ever-faithful love.'*

My father answered:

> *'In evening when the light is dying*
> *My feet at last are homeward turning*
> *The wind is through the willows sighing*
> *Please keep the hearthfire burning.'*

When I came out of the wagon, he had her in a dramatic dip and was giving her a kiss. I set the needle and thread next to my shirt and waited. It seemed like a good kiss. I watched with a calculating eye, dimly aware that at some point in the future I might want to kiss a lady. If I did, I wanted to do a decent job of it.

After a moment my father noticed me and stood my mother back on her feet. 'That will be ha'penny for the show, Master Voyeur,' he laughed. 'What are you still here for, boy? I'll bet you the same ha'penny that a question slowed you down.'

'Why do we stop for the greystones?'

'Tradition, my boy,' he said grandly, throwing his arms wide. 'And superstition. They are one and the same, anyway. We stop for good luck and because everyone enjoys an unexpected holiday.' He paused. 'I used to know a bit of poem about them. How did it go . . . ?

> *'Like a drawstone even in our sleep*
> *Standing stone by old road is the way*
> *To lead you ever deeper into Fae.*
> *Laystone as you lay in hill or dell*
> *Greystone leads to* something something "ell".'

My father stood for a second or two looking off into space and tugging at his lower lip. Finally he shook his head. 'Can't remember the end of that last line. Lord but I dislike poetry. How can anyone remember words that aren't put to music?' His forehead creased with concentration as he mouthed the words silently to himself.

'What's a drawstone?' I asked.

'It's an old name for loden-stones,' my mother explained. 'They're pieces of star-iron that draw all other iron toward themselves. I saw one years ago in a curiosity cabinet.' She looked up at my father who was still muttering to himself. 'We saw the loden-stone in Peleresin, didn't we?'

'Hmmm? What?' The question jogged him out of his reverie. 'Yes. Peleresin.' He tugged at his lip again and frowned. 'Remember this, son, if you forget everything else. A poet is a musician who can't sing. Words have to find a man's mind before they can touch his heart, and some men's minds are woeful small targets. Music touches their hearts directly no matter how small or stubborn the mind of the man who listens.'

My mother made a slightly unladylike snort. 'Elitist. You're just getting old.' She gave a dramatic sigh. 'Truly, all the more's the tragedy; the second thing to go is a man's memory.'

My father puffed up into an indignant pose but my mother ignored him and said to me, 'Besides, the only tradition that keeps troupes by the greystone is laziness. The poem should run like this:

> *'Whatever the season*
> *That I'm on the road*
> *I look for a reason*
> *Loden or laystone*
> *To lay down my load.'*

My father had a dark glimmer in his eye as he moved behind her. 'Old?' He spoke in a low voice as he began to rub her shoulders again. 'Woman, I have a mind to prove you wrong.'

She smiled a wry smile. 'Sir, I have a mind to let you.'

I decided to leave them to their discussion and started to scamper back to Ben's wagon when I heard my father call out behind me, 'Scales after lunch tomorrow? And the second act of *Tinbertin?*'

'Okay.' I burst into a jog.

When I got back to Ben's wagon he had already unhitched Alpha and Beta and was rubbing them down. I started to set up the fire, surrounding dry leaves with a pyramid of progressively larger twigs and branches. When I was finished I turned to where Ben sat.

More silence. I could almost see him picking out his words as he spoke. 'How much do you know about your father's new song?'

'The one about Lanre?' I asked. 'Not much. You know what he's like. No one hears it until it's finished. Not even me.'

'I'm not talking about the song itself,' Ben said. 'The story behind it. Lanre's story.'

I thought about the dozens of stories I'd heard my father collect over the last year, trying to pick out the common threads. 'Lanre was a prince,' I said. 'Or a king. Someone important. He wanted to be more powerful than anyone else in the world. He sold his soul for power but then something went wrong and afterwards I think he went crazy, or he couldn't ever sleep again, or . . .' I stopped when I saw Ben shaking his head.

'He didn't sell his soul,' Ben said. 'That's just nonsense.' He gave a great sigh that seemed to leave him deflated. 'I'm doing this all wrong. Never mind your father's song. We'll talk about it after he finishes it. Knowing Lanre's story might give you some perspective.'

Ben took a deep breath and tried again. 'Suppose you have a thoughtless six-year-old. What harm can he do?'

I paused, unsure what sort of answer he wanted. Straightforward would probably be best. 'Not much.'

'Suppose he's twenty, and still thoughtless, how dangerous is he?'

I decided to stick with the obvious answers. 'Still not much, but more than before.'

'What if you give him a sword?'

Realisation started to dawn on me, and I closed my eyes. 'More, much more. I understand, Ben. Really I do. Power is okay, and stupidity is usually harmless. Power and stupidity together are dangerous.'

'I never said *stupid*,' Ben corrected me. 'You're clever. We both know that. But you can be thoughtless. A clever, thoughtless person is one of the most terrifying things there is. Worse, I've been teaching you some dangerous things.'

Ben looked at the fire I'd laid out, then picked up a leaf, mumbled a few words, and watched a small flame flicker into life in the center of the twigs and tinder. He turned to look at me. 'You could kill yourself doing something as simple as that.' He gave a sickly grin. 'Or looking for the name of the wind.'

He started to say something else, then stopped and rubbed his face with his hands. He gave a great sigh that seemed to deflate him. When he took his hands away, his face was tired. 'How old are you again?'

'Twelve next month.'

He shook his head. 'It's so easy to forget that. You don't act your age.' He poked at the fire with a stick, 'I was eighteen when I began at the University,' he said. 'I was twenty before I knew as much as you do now.' He stared into the fire. 'I'm sorry Kvothe. I need to be alone tonight. I need to do some thinking.'

I nodded silently. I went to his wagon, gathered tripod and kettle, water and tea. I brought them back and quietly laid them beside Ben. He was still staring into the fire when I turned away.

Knowing my parents wouldn't expect me back for a while, I headed into the forest. I had some thinking of my own to do. I owed Ben that much. I wished I could do more.

It took a full span of days before Ben was his normal, jovial self again. But even then things weren't the same between us. We were still fast friends, but there was something between us, and I could tell he was consciously holding himself apart.

Lessons ground to a near standstill. He halted my fledgling study of alchemy, limiting me to chemistry instead. He refused to teach me any sygaldry at all, and on top of everything else, he began to ration what little sympathy he thought safe for me.

I chafed at the delays, but held my peace, trusting that if I showed myself to be responsible and meticulously careful, he would eventually relax and things would return to normal. We were family, and I knew that any trouble between us would eventually be smoothed over. All I needed was time.

Little did I know our time was quickly drawing to an end.

CHAPTER FIFTEEN

Distractions and Farewells

THE TOWN WAS CALLED Hallowfell. We stopped for a handful of days because there was a good wainwright there, and nearly all our wagons needed tending or mending of some sort. While we were waiting, Ben got the offer he couldn't refuse.

She was a widow, fairly wealthy, fairly young, and to my inexperienced eyes, fairly attractive. The official story was that she needed someone to tutor her young son. However, anyone who saw the two of them walking together knew the truth behind that story.

She had been the brewer's wife, but he had drowned two years ago. She was trying to run the brewery as best she could, but she didn't really have the know-how to do a good job of it . . .

As you can see, I don't think anyone could have built a better snare for Ben if they had tried.

———

Plans were changed and the troupe stayed on at Hallowfell for a few extra days. My twelfth birthday was moved up and combined with Ben's going away party.

To truly understand what it was like, you must realise that nothing is so grand as a troupe showing off for one another. Good entertainers try to make each performance seem special, but you need to remember that the show they're putting on for you is the same one they've put on for hundreds of other audiences. Even the most dedicated troupes have an occasional lacklustre performance, especially when they know they can get away with it.

Small towns, rural inns, those places didn't know good entertainment from bad. Your fellow performers did.

Think then, how do you entertain the people who have seen your act a thousand times? You dust off the old tricks. You try out some new ones. You hope for the best. And, of course, the grand failures are as entertaining as the great successes.

I remember the evening as a wonderful blur of warm emotion, tinged in bitter. Fiddles, lutes, and drums, everyone played and danced and sang as they wished. I dare say we rivalled any faerie revel you can bring to mind.

I got presents. Trip gave me a belt knife with a leather grip, claiming that all boys should have something they can hurt themselves with. Shandi gave me a lovely cloak she had made, scattered with little pockets for a boy's treasures. My parents gave me a lute, a beautiful thing of smooth dark wood. I had to play a song of course, and Ben sang with me. I slipped a little on the strings of the unfamiliar instrument, and Ben wandered off looking for notes once or twice, but it was nice.

Ben opened up a small keg of mead he had been saving for 'just such an occasion'. I remember it tasting the way I felt, sweet and bitter and sullen.

Several people had collaborated to write 'The Ballad of Ben, Brewer Supreme'. My father recited it as gravely as if it were the Modegan royal lineage while accompanying himself on a half harp. Everyone laughed until they hurt, and Ben twice as much as everyone else.

At some point in the night, my mother swept me up and danced around in a great spinning circle. Her laughter sang out like music trailing in the wind. Her hair and skirt spun around me as she twirled. She smelled comforting, the way only mothers do. That smell, and the quick laughing kiss she gave me did more to ease the dull ache of Ben's leaving than all the entertainments combined.

Shandi offered to do a special dance for Ben, but only if he came into her tent to see it. I'd never seen Ben blush before, but he did it well. He hesitated, and when he refused it was obviously about as easy for him as tearing out his own soul. Shandi protested and pouted prettily, saying she'd been practicing it for a long time. Finally she dragged him into the tent, their disappearance encouraged by a cheer from the entire troupe.

Trip and Teren staged a mock sword fight that was one part breathtaking swordplay, one part dramatic soliloquy (provided by Teren), and one part buffoonery that I'm sure Trip must have invented on the spot. It ranged all over the camp. In the course of the fight Trip managed to break his sword, hide under a lady's dress, fence with a sausage, and perform such fantastical acrobatics that it's a miracle he didn't seriously injure himself. Although he did split his trousers up the back.

Dax set himself alight while attempting a spectacular bit of fire breathing and had to be doused. All he suffered was a bit of singed beard and a slightly bruised pride. He recovered quickly under Ben's tender ministrations, a mug of mead, and a reminder that not everyone was cut out to have eyebrows.

My parents sang 'The Lay of Sir Savien Traliard'. Like most of the great songs, Sir Savien was written by Illien, and generally considered to be his crowning work.

It's a beautiful song, made more so by the fact that I'd only heard my father perform the whole thing a handful of times before. It's hellishly complex, and my father was probably the only one in the troupe who could do it justice. Though he didn't particularly show it, I knew it was taxing even for him. My mother sang the counter-harmony, her voice soft and lilting. Even the fire seemed subdued when they took a breath. I felt my heart lift and dive. I wept as much for the glory of two voices so perfectly enmeshed as for the tragedy of the song.

Yes, I cried at the end of it. I did then, and I have every time since. Even a reading of the story aloud will bring tears to my eyes. In my opinion, anyone who isn't moved by it is less than human inside.

There was a momentary quiet after they finished, wherein everyone wiped their eyes and blew their noses. Then, after a suitable period of recovery had elapsed, someone called out, 'Lanre! Lanre!'

The shout was taken up by several other people. 'Yes, Lanre!'

My father gave a wry smile and shook his head. He never performed any part of a song until it was finished.

'C'mon, Arl!' Shandi called out. 'You've been stewing it long enough. Let some out of the pot.'

He shook his head again, still smiling. 'It's not ready yet.' He bent down and carefully set his lute into its case.

'Let's have a taste, Arliden.' It was Teren this time.

'Yeah, for Ben's sake. It's not fair that he should have to hear you mumble over it for all this while and not get . . .'

'. . . are wondering what you're doing in that wagon with your wife if it's not . . .'

'Sing it!'

'Lanre!'

Trip quickly organised the whole troupe into a great chanting, howling mass that my father managed to withstand for almost a minute before he stooped and lifted his lute back out of the case. Everyone cheered.

The crowd hushed as soon as he sat back down. He tuned a string or two, even though he'd only just set it down. He flexed his fingers and struck a few soft, experimental notes, then swept into the song so gently that I caught myself listening to it before I knew it had begun. Then my father's voice spoke over the rise and fall of the music.

> '*Sit and listen all, for I will sing*
> *A story, wrought and forgotten in a time*
> *Old and gone. A story of a man.*
> *Proud Lanre, strong as the spring*
> *Steel of the sword he had at ready hand.*
> *Hear how he fought, fell, and rose again,*
> *To fall again. Under shadow falling then.*
> *Love felled him, love for native land,*
> *And love of his wife Lyra, at whose calling*
> *Some say he rose, through doors of death*
> *To speak her name as his first reborn breath.*'

My father drew a breath and paused, his mouth open as if he would continue. Then a wide, wicked grin spread across his face and he bent to tuck his lute safely away. There was an outcry and a great deal of complaining, but everyone knew they had been lucky to hear as much as they had. Someone else struck up a song for dancing, and the protests faded away.

My parents danced together, her head on his chest. Both had their eyes closed. They seemed so perfectly content. If you can find someone like that, someone who you can hold and close your eyes to the world with, then you're lucky. Even if it only lasts for a minute or a day. The image of them gently swaying to the music is how I picture love in my mind even after all these years.

Afterwards, Ben danced with my mother, his steps sure and stately. I was struck by how beautiful they looked together. Ben, old, grey, and portly, with his lined face and half-burned eyebrows. My mother, slender, fresh, and bright, pale and smooth-skinned in the firelight. They complemented each other by contrast. I ached knowing I might never see them together again.

By this time the sky was beginning to brighten in the east. Everyone gathered to say their final good-byes.

I can't remember what I said to him before we left. I know it felt woefully inadequate, but I knew he understood. He made me promise not to get myself into any trouble, tinkering with the things he had taught me.

He stooped a bit and gave me a hug, then tousled my hair. I didn't even mind. In semiretaliation I tried to smooth out his eyebrows, something I'd always wanted to try.

His expression was marvellous in its surprise. He gathered me into another hug. Then he stepped away.

My parents promised to steer the troupe back towards the town when we were in the area. All the troupers said they wouldn't need much steering. But, even as young as I was, I knew the truth. It would be a great long time before I saw him again. Years.

I don't remember starting out that morning, but I do remember trying to sleep and feeling quite alone except for a dull, bittersweet ache.

───────

When I awoke later in the afternoon I found a package resting next to me. Wrapped in sackcloth and tied with twine, there was a bright piece of paper with my name fixed to the top, waving in the wind like a little flag.

Unwrapping it, I recognised the book's binding. It was *Rhetoric and Logic*, the book Ben had used to teach me argument. Out of his small library of a dozen books it was the only one I hadn't read from cover to cover. I hated it.

I cracked it open and saw writing on the inside cover. It said:

> **Kvothe,**
> **Defend yourself well at the University. Make me proud.**
> **Remember your father's song. Be wary of folly.**
> **Your friend,**
> **Abenthy**

Ben and I had never discussed my attending the University. Of course I had dreams of going there, someday. But they were dreams I hesitated to share with my parents. Attending the University would mean leaving my parents, my troupe, everyone and everything I had ever known.

Quite frankly, the thought was terrifying. What would it be like to settle in one place, not just for an evening or a span of days, but for months? Years? No more performing? No tumbling with Trip, or playing the bratty young noble's son in *Three Pennies for Wishing?* No more wagons? No one to sing with?

I'd never said anything aloud, but Ben would have guessed. I read his inscription again, cried a bit, and promised him that I would do my best.

CHAPTER SIXTEEN

Hope

OVER THE NEXT MONTHS my parents did their best to patch the hole left by Ben's absence, bringing in the other troupers to fill my time productively and keep me from moping.

You see, in the troupe age had little to do with anything. If you were strong enough to saddle the horses, you saddled the horses. If your hands were quick enough, you juggled. If you were clean shaven and fit the dress, you played Lady Reythiel in *The Swineherd and the Nightingale*. Things were generally as simple as that.

So Trip taught me how to jape and tumble. Shandi walked me though the courtly dances of a half dozen countries. Teren measured me against the hilt of his sword and judged that I had grown tall enough to begin the basics of swordplay. Not enough to actually fight, he stressed. But enough so I could make a good show of it on stage.

The roads were good this time of year, so we made excellent time travelling north through the Commonwealth: fifteen, twenty miles a day as we searched out new towns to play. With Ben gone, I rode with my father more often, and he began my formal training for the stage.

I already knew a great deal, of course. But what I had picked up was an undisciplined hodgepodge. My father systematically went about showing me the true mechanics of the actor's trade. How slight changes in accent or posture make a man seem oafish, or sly, or silly.

Lastly, my mother began teaching me how to comport myself in polite society. I knew a little from our infrequent stays with Baron Greyfallow, and thought I was quite genteel enough without having to memorise forms of address, table manners, and the elaborate snarled rankings of the peerage. Eventually, I told my mother exactly that.

'Who cares if a Modegan viscount outranks a Vintish spara-thain?' I protested. 'And who cares if one is "your grace" and the other is "my lord"?'

'They care,' my mother said firmly. 'If you perform for them, you need to conduct yourself with dignity and learn to keep your elbow out of the soup.'

'Father doesn't worry about which fork to use and who outranks who,' I groused.

My mother frowned, her eyes narrowing.

'Who outranks *whom*,' I said grudgingly.

'Your father knows more than he lets on,' my mother said. 'And what he doesn't know he breezes past due to his considerable charm. That's how he gets by.' She took my chin and turned my face toward her. Her eyes were green with a ring of gold around the pupil. 'Do you just want to get by? Or do you want to make me proud?'

There was only one answer to that. Once I knuckled down to learn it, it was just another type of acting. Another script. My mother made rhymes to help me remember the more nonsensical elements of etiquette. And together we wrote a dirty little song called 'The Pontifex Always Ranks Under a Queen'. We laughed over it for a solid month, and she strictly forbade me to sing it to my father, lest he play it in front of the wrong people someday and get us all into serious trouble.

———————

'Tree!' The shout came faintly down the line. 'Threeweight oak!'

My father stopped in the middle of the monologue he had been reciting for me and gave an irritated sigh. 'That'll be as far as we get today then,' he grumbled, looking up at the sky.

'Are we stopping?' my mother called from inside the wagon.

'Another tree across the road,' I explained.

'I swear,' my father said, steering the wagon to a clear space at the side of the road. 'Is this the king's road or isn't it? You'd think we were the only people on it. How long ago was that storm? Two span?'

'Not quite,' I said. 'Sixteen days.'

'And trees still blocking the road! I've a mind to send the consulate a bill for every tree we've had to cut and drag out of the way. This will put us another three hours behind schedule.' He hopped from the wagon as it rolled to a halt.

'I think it's nice,' my mother said, walking around from the back of the wagon. 'Gives us the chance for something hot,' she gave my father a significant look, 'to eat. It gets frustrating making do with whatever you can grab at the end of the day. A body wants more.'

My father's mood seemed to temper considerably. 'There is that,' he said.

'Sweet?' my mother called to me. 'Do you think you could find me some wild sage?'

'I don't know if it grows around here,' I said with the proper amount of uncertainty in my voice.

'No harm in looking,' she said sensibly. She looked at my father from the corner of her eye. 'If you can find enough, bring back an armload. We'll dry it for later.'

Typically, whether or not I found what I was looking for didn't matter very much.

It was my habit to wander away from the troupe in the evenings. I usually had some sort of errand to run while my parents set up for dinner. But it was just an excuse for us to get away from each other. Privacy is hard to come by on the road, and they needed it as much as I did. So if it took me an hour to gather an armload of firewood they didn't mind. And if they hadn't started dinner by the time I came back, well, that was only fair, wasn't it?

I hope they spent those last few hours well. I hope they didn't waste them on mindless tasks: kindling the evening fire and cutting vegetables for dinner. I hope they sang together, as they so often did. I hope they retired to our wagon and spent time in each other's arms. I hope they lay near each other afterward and spoke softly of small things. I hope they were together, busy with loving each other, until the end came.

It is a small hope, and pointless really. They are just as dead either way.

Still, I hope.

———————

Let us pass over the time I spent alone in the woods that evening, playing games that children invent to amuse themselves. The last carefree hours of my life. The last moments of my childhood.

Let us pass over my return to the camp just as the sun was beginning to set. The sight of bodies strewn about like broken dolls. The smell of blood and burning hair. How I wandered aimlessly about, too disoriented for proper panic, numb with shock and dread.

I would pass over the whole of that evening, in fact. I would spare you the burden of any of it if one piece were not necessary to the story. It is vital. It is the hinge upon which the story pivots like an opening door. In some ways, this is where the story begins.

So let's have done with it.

———————

Scattered patches of smoke hung in the still evening air. It was quiet, as if everyone in the troupe was listening for something. As if they were all holding their breath. An idle wind tussled the leaves in the trees and wafted a patch of smoke like a low cloud towards me. I stepped out of the forest and through the smoke, heading into the camp.

I left the cloud of smoke and rubbed some of the sting from my eyes. As I looked around I saw Trip's tent lying half collapsed and smoldering in his fire. The treated canvas burned fitfully, and the acrid grey smoke hung close to the ground in the quiet evening air.

I saw Teren's body lying by his wagon, his sword broken in his hand. The green and grey he normally wore was wet and red with blood. One of his legs was twisted unnaturally and the splintered bone showing through the skin was very, very white.

I stood, unable to look away from Teren, the grey shirt, the red blood, the white bone. I stared as if it were a diagram in a book I was trying to understand. My body grew numb. I felt as if I was trying to think through syrup.

Some small rational part of me realised I was in deep shock. It repeated the fact to me again and again. I used all Ben's training to ignore it. I did not want to think about what I saw. I did not want to know what had happened here. I did not want to know what any of this meant.

After I don't know how long, a wisp of smoke broke my line of vision. I sat down next to the nearest fire in a daze. It was Shandi's fire, and a small pot hung simmering, boiling potatoes, strangely familiar among the chaos.

I focused on the kettle. Something normal. I used a stick to poke at the contents and saw that they were finished cooking. Normal. I lifted the kettle from the fire and set it on the ground next to Shandi's body. Her clothes hung in tatters about her. I tried to brush her hair away from her face and my hand came back sticky with blood. The firelight reflected in her flat, empty eyes.

I stood and looked about aimlessly. Trip's tent was entirely aflame by now, and Shandi's wagon was standing with one wheel in Marion's campfire. All the flames were tinged with blue, making the scene dreamlike and surreal.

I heard voices. Peering around the corner of Shandi's wagon I saw several unfamiliar men and women sitting around a fire. My parents' fire. A dizziness swept over me and I reached out a hand to steady myself against the wagon's wheel. When I gripped it, the iron bands that reinforced the wheel crumbled in my hand, flaking away in gritty sheets of brown rust. When I pulled my hand away the wheel creaked and began to crack. I stepped back as it gave way, the wagon splintering as if its wood were rotten as an old stump.

I now stood in full view of the fire. One of the men tumbled backward and came to his feet with his sword out. His motion reminded me of quick-silver rolling from a jar onto a tabletop: effortless and supple. His expression was intent, but his body was relaxed, as if he had just stood and stretched.

His sword was pale and elegant. When it moved, it cut the air with a brittle sound. It reminded me of the quiet that settles on the coldest days in winter when it hurts to breathe and everything is still.

He was two dozen feet from me, but I could see him perfectly in the fading light of sunset. I remember him as clearly as I remember my own mother, sometimes better. His face was narrow and sharp, with the perfect beauty of porcelain. His hair was shoulder length, framing his face in loose curls the colour of frost. He was a creature of winter's pale. Everything about him was cold and sharp and white.

Except his eyes. They were black like a goat's but with no iris. His eyes were like his sword, and neither one reflected the light of the fire or the setting sun.

He relaxed when he saw me. He dropped the tip of his sword and smiled with perfect ivory teeth. It was the expression a nightmare wore. I felt a stab of feeling penetrate the confusion I clutched around me like a thick protective blanket. Something put both its hands deep into my chest and clutched. It may have been the first time in my life I was ever truly afraid.

Back by the fire, a bald man with a grey beard chuckled. 'Looks like we missed a little rabbit. Careful Cinder, his teeth may be sharp.'

The one called Cinder sheathed his sword with the sound of a tree crack-ing under the weight of winter ice. Keeping his distance, he knelt. Again I was reminded of the way mercury moved. Now on eye level with me, his expres-sion grew concerned behind his matte-black eyes. 'What's your name, boy?'

I stood there, mute. Frozen as a startled fawn.

Cinder sighed and dropped his gaze to the ground for a moment. When he looked back up at me I saw pity staring at me with hollow eyes.

'Young man,' he said, 'wherever are your parents?' He held my gaze for a moment and then looked over his shoulder back towards the fire where the others sat.

'Does anyone know where his parents are?'

Some of them smiled, hard and brittle, as if enjoying a particularly good joke. One or two of them laughed aloud. Cinder turned back to me and the pity fell away like a cracked mask, leaving only the nightmare smile upon his face.

'Is this your parents' fire?' he asked with a terrible delight in his voice.

I nodded numbly.

His smile slowly faded. Expressionless, he looked deep into me. His voice was quiet, cold, and sharp. 'Someone's parents,' he said, 'have been singing entirely the wrong sort of songs.'

'Cinder.' A cool voice came from the direction of the fire.

His black eyes narrowed in irritation. 'What?' he hissed.

'You are approaching my displeasure. This one has done nothing. Send him to the soft and painless blanket of his sleep.' The cool voice caught slightly on the last word, as if it were difficult to say.

The voice came from a man who sat apart from the rest, wrapped in shadow at the edge of the fire. Though the sky was still bright with sunset and nothing stood between the fire and where he sat, shadow pooled around him like thick oil. The fire snapped and danced, lively and warm, tinged with blue, but no flicker of its light came close to him. The shadow gathered thicker around his head. I could catch a glimpse of a deep cowl like some priests wear, but underneath the shadows were so deep it was like looking down a well at midnight.

Cinder glanced briefly at the shadowed man, then turned away. 'You are as good as a watcher, Haliax,' he snapped.

'And you seem to forget our purpose,' the dark man said, his cool voice sharpening. *'Or does your purpose simply differ from my own?'* The last words were spoken carefully, as if they held special significance.

Cinder's arrogance left him in a second, like water poured from a bucket. 'No,' he said, turning back toward the fire. 'No, certainly not.'

'That is good. I hate to think of our long acquaintance coming to an end.'

'As do I.'

'Refresh me again as to our relationship, Cinder,' the shadowed man said, a deep sliver of anger running through his patient tone.

'I . . . I am in your service—' Cinder made a placating gesture.

'You are a tool in my hand,' the shadowed man interrupted gently. *'Nothing more.'*

A hint of defiance touched Cinder's expression. He paused. 'I wo—'

The soft voice went as hard as a rod of Ramston steel. *'Ferula.'*

Cinder's quicksilver grace disappeared. He staggered, his body suddenly rigid with pain.

'You are a tool in my hand,' the cool voice repeated. *'Say it.'*

Cinder's jaw clenched angrily for a moment, then he convulsed and cried out, sounding more like a wounded animal than a man. 'I am a tool in your hand,' he gasped.

'Lord Haliax.'

'I am a tool in your hand, Lord Haliax,' Cinder amended as he crumpled, trembling, to his knees.

'Who knows the inner turnings of your name, Cinder?' The words were spoken with a slow patience, like a schoolmaster reciting a forgotten lesson.

Cinder wrapped shaking arms around his midsection and hunched over, closing his eyes. 'You, Lord Haliax.'

'Who keeps you safe from the Amyr? The singers? The Sithe? From all that would harm you in the world?' Haliax asked with calm politeness, as if genuinely curious as to what the answer might be.

'You, Lord Haliax.' Cinder's voice was a quiet shred of pain.

'And whose purpose do you serve?'

'Your purpose, Lord Haliax.' The words were choked out. 'Yours. None other.' The tension left the air and Cinder's body suddenly went slack. He fell forwards onto his hands and beads of sweat fell from his face to patter on the ground like rain. His white hair hung limp around his face. 'Thank you, lord,' he gasped out earnestly. 'I will not forget again.'

'You will. You are too fond of your little cruelties. All of you.' Haliax's hooded face swept back and forth to look at each of the figures sitting around the fire. They stirred uncomfortably. *'I am glad I decided to accompany you today. You are straying, indulging in whimsy. Some of you seem to have forgotten what it is we seek, what we wish to achieve.'* The others sitting around the fire stirred uneasily.

The hood turned back to Cinder. *'But you have my forgiveness. Perhaps if not for these reminders, it would be I who would forget.'* There was an edge to the last of his words. *'Now, finish what—'* His cool voice trailed away as his shadowed hood slowly tilted to look toward the sky. There was an expectant silence.

Those sitting around the fire grew perfectly still, their expressions intent. In unison they tilted their heads as if looking at the same point in the twilit sky. As if trying to catch the scent of something on the wind.

A feeling of being watched pulled at my attention. I felt a tenseness, a subtle change in the texture of the air. I focused on it, glad for the distraction, glad for anything that might keep me from thinking clearly for just a few more seconds.

'They come,' Haliax said quietly. He stood, and shadow seemed to boil outward from him like a dark fog. 'Quickly. To me.'

The others rose from their seats around the fire. Cinder scrambled to his feet and staggered a half dozen steps toward the fire.

Haliax spread his arms and the shadow surrounding him bloomed like a flower unfolding. Then, each of the others turned with a studied ease and took a step toward Haliax, into the shadow surrounding him. But as their feet came down they slowed, and gently, as if they were made of sand with wind blowing across them, they faded away. Only Cinder looked back, a hint of anger in his nightmare eyes.

Then they were gone.

I will not burden you with what followed. How I ran from body to body, frantically feeling for the signs of life as Ben had taught me. My futile attempt at digging a grave. How I scrabbled in the dirt until my fingers were bloody and raw. How I found my parents . . .

It was in the darkest hours of the night when I found our wagon. Our horse had dragged it nearly a hundred yards down the road before he died. It seemed so normal inside, so tidy and calm. I was struck by how much the back of the wagon smelled like the two of them.

I lit every lamp and candle in the wagon. The light was no comfort, but it was the honest gold of real fire, untinged with blue. I took down my father's lute case. I lay in my parent's bed with the lute beside me. My mother's pillow smelled of her hair, of an embrace. I did not mean to sleep, but sleep took me.

I woke coughing with everything in flames around me. It had been the candles, of course. Still numb with shock, I gathered a few things into a bag. I was slow and aimless, unafraid as I pulled Ben's book from under my burning mattress. What horror could a simple fire hold for me now?

I put my father's lute into its case. It felt like I was stealing, but I couldn't think of anything else that would remind me of them. Both their hands had brushed its wood a thousand thousand times.

Then I left. I walked into the forest and kept going until dawn began to brighten the eastern edges of the sky. As the birds began to sing I stopped and set down my bag. I brought out my father's lute and clutched it to my body. Then I began to play.

My fingers hurt, but I played anyway. I played until my fingers bled on the strings. I played until the sun shone through the trees. I played until my arms ached. I played, trying not to remember, until I fell asleep.

CHAPTER SEVENTEEN

Interlude – Autumn

KVOTHE HELD OUT A hand to Chronicler, then turned to his student, frowning. 'Stop looking at me like that, Bast.'

Bast looked close to tears. 'Oh, Reshi,' he choked out. 'I had no idea.'

Kvothe gestured as if cutting the air with the side of his hand. 'There's no reason you should Bast, and no reason to make an issue out of it.'

'But Reshi . . .'

Kvothe gave his student a severe look. 'What, Bast? Should I weep and tear my hair? Curse Tehlu and his angels? Beat my chest? No. That is low drama.' His expression softened somewhat. 'I appreciate your concern, but this is just a piece of the story, not even the worst piece, and I am *not* telling it to garner sympathy.'

Kvothe pushed his chair back from the table and came to his feet. 'Besides, all of this happened long ago.' He made a dismissive gesture. 'Time is the great healer, and so on.'

He rubbed his hands together. 'Now, I'm going to bring in enough wood to get us though the night. There'll be a chill if I'm any judge of weather. You can get a couple of loaves ready to bake while I'm out, and try to collect yourself. I refuse to tell the rest of this story with you making blubbery cow eyes at me.'

With that, Kvothe walked behind the bar and out through the kitchen towards the back door of the inn.

Bast scrubbed roughly at his eyes, then watched his master go. 'He's fine so long as he's busy,' Bast said softly.

'I beg your pardon?' Chronicler said reflexively. He shifted awkwardly in his seat, as if he wanted to get to his feet, but couldn't think of a polite way to excuse himself.

Bast gave a warm smile, his eyes a human blue again. 'I was so excited when I heard who you were, that he was going to tell his story. His mood's been so dark lately, and there's nothing to shake him out of it, nothing to do but sit and brood. I'm sure that remembering the good times will . . .' Bast grimaced. 'I'm not saying this very well. I'm sorry for earlier. I wasn't thinking straight.'

'N—no,' Chronicler stammered hastily. 'I'm the one – it was my fault, I'm sorry.'

Bast shook his head. 'You were just surprised, but you only tried to bind me.' His expression grew a little pained. 'Not that it was pleasant, mind. It feels like being kicked between your legs, but all over your body. It makes you feel sick, and weak, but it's just pain. It wasn't like you'd actually wounded me.' Bast looked embarrassed. 'I was going to do more than hurt you. I might have killed you before I even stopped to think.'

Before an uncomfortable silence developed, Chronicler said, 'Why don't we take his word that we were both suffering from blinding idiocy, and leave it at that?' Chronicler managed a sickly smile that was heartfelt in spite of the circumstances. 'Peace?' he extended his hand.

'Peace.' They shook hands with much more genuine warmth than they had earlier. As Bast reached across the table his sleeve pulled back to reveal a bruise blossoming around his wrist.

Bast self-consciously pulled his cuff back into place. 'From when he grabbed me,' he said quickly. 'He's stronger than he looks. Don't mention it to him. He'll only feel bad.'

———

Kvothe emerged from the kitchen and shut the door behind himself. Looking around, he seemed surprised that it was a mild autumn afternoon rather than the springtime forest of his story. He lifted the handles of a flat-bottomed barrow and trundled it out into the woods behind the inn, his feet crunching in the fallen leaves.

Not too far into the trees was the winter's wood supply. Cord on cord of oak and ash were stacked to make tall, crooked walls between the trunks of trees. Kvothe tossed two pieces of firewood into the wheelbarrow where they struck the bottom like a muted drum. Another two followed them. His motions were precise, his face blank, his eyes far away.

As he continued to load the barrow, he moved slower and slower, like a machine winding down. Eventually he stopped completely and stood for a long minute, still as stone. Only then did his composure break. And even with no one there to see, he hid his face in his hands and wept quietly, his body wracked with wave on wave of heavy, silent sobs.

CHAPTER EIGHTEEN

Roads to Safe Places

PERHAPS THE GREATEST FACULTY our minds possess is the ability to cope with pain. Classic thinking teaches us of the four doors of the mind, which everyone moves through according to their need.

First is the door of sleep. Sleep offers us a retreat from the world and all its pain. Sleep marks passing time, giving us distance from the things that have hurt us. When a person is wounded they will often fall unconscious. Similarly, someone who hears traumatic news will often swoon or faint. This is the mind's way of protecting itself from pain by stepping through the first door.

Second is the door of forgetting. Some wounds are too deep to heal, or too deep to heal quickly. In addition, many memories are simply painful, and there is no healing to be done. The saying 'time heals all wounds' is false. Time heals most wounds. The rest are hidden behind this door.

Third is the door of madness. There are times when the mind is dealt such a blow it hides itself in insanity. While this may not seem beneficial, it is. There are times when reality is nothing but pain, and to escape that pain the mind must leave reality behind.

Last is the door of death. The final resort. Nothing can hurt us after we are dead, or so we have been told.

———

After my family was killed, I wandered deep into the forest and slept. My body demanded it, and my mind used the first door to dull the pain. The wound was covered until the proper time for healing could come. In self-defense, a good portion of my mind simply stopped working – went to sleep, if you will.

While my mind slept, many of the painful parts of the previous day were ushered through the second door. Not completely. I did not forget what had happened, but the memory was dulled, as if seen through thick gauze. If I wanted to, I could have brought to memory the faces of the dead, the memories of the man with black eyes. But I did not want to remember. I pushed those thoughts away and let them gather dust in a seldom-used corner of my mind.

I dreamed, not of blood, glassy eyes, and the smell of burning hair, but of gentler things. And slowly the wound began to grow numb . . .

I dreamed I was walking through the forest with plain-faced Laclith, the woodsman who had travelled with our troupe when I was younger. He walked silently through the underbrush while I kicked up more noise than a wounded ox dragging an overturned cart.

After a long period of comfortable silence I stopped to look at a plant. He came quietly up behind me. 'Sagebeard,' he said. 'You can tell by the edge.' He reached past me and gently stroked the appropriate part of the leaf. It did look like a beard. I nodded.

'This is willow. You can chew the bark to lessen pains.' It was bitter and slightly gritty. 'This is itchroot, don't touch the leaves.' I didn't. 'This is baneberry, the small fruits are safe to eat when red but never when shading from green to yellow to orange.

'This is how you set your feet when you want to walk silently.' It made my calves ache. 'This is how you part the brush quietly, leaving no sign of your passing. This is where you find the dry wood. This is how you keep the rain off when you don't have canvas. This is paterroot. You can eat it but it tastes bad. These,' he gestured, 'straightrod, orangestripe, never eat them. The one with little knobs on it is burrum. You should only eat it if you have just eaten something like straightrod. It will make you keck up whatever's in your stomach.

'This is how you set a snare that won't kill a rabbit. This snare will.' He looped the string first one way, then another.

As I watched his hands manipulate the string I realised it was no longer Laclith, but Abenthy. We were riding in the wagon and he was teaching me how to tie sailors' knots.

'Knots are interesting things,' Ben said as he worked. 'The knot will either be the strongest or the weakest part of the rope. It depends entirely on how well one makes the binding.' He held up his hands, showing me an impossibly complex pattern spread between his fingers.

His eyes glittered. 'Any questions?'

'Any questions?' my father said. We had stopped early for the day because of a greystone. He sat tuning his lute and was finally going to play his song for my mother and me. We had been waiting so long. 'Are there any questions?' he repeated, as he sat with his back against the great grey stone.

'Why do we stop at the waystones?'

'Tradition mostly. But some people say they marked old roads—' My father's voice changed and became Ben's voice, '—safe roads. Sometimes roads to safe places, sometimes safe roads leading into danger.' Ben held one hand out to it, as if feeling the warmth of a fire. 'But there is a power in them. Only a fool would deny that.'

Then Ben was no longer there, and there was not one standing stone, but many. More than I had ever seen in one place before. They formed a double circle around me. One stone was set across the top of two others, forming a huge arch with thick shadow underneath. I reached out to touch it . . .

And awoke. My mind had covered a fresh pain with the names of a hundred roots and berries, four ways to light a fire, nine snares made from nothing but a sapling and string, and where to find fresh water.

I thought very little on the other matter of the dream. Ben had never taught me sailors' knots. My father had never finished his song.

I took inventory of what I had with me: a canvas sack, a small knife, a ball of string, some wax, a copper penny, two iron shims, and *Rhetoric and Logic,* the book Ben had given me. Aside from my clothes and my father's lute, I had nothing else.

I set out looking for drinking water. 'Water comes first,' Laclith had told me. 'Anything else you can do without for days.' I considered the lay of the land and followed some animal trails. By the time I found a small spring-fed pool nestled among some birch trees, I could see the sky purpling into dusk behind the trees. I was terribly thirsty, but caution won out and I took only a small drink.

Next I collected dry wood from the hollows of trees and under canopies. I set a simple snare. I hunted for and found several stalks of motherleaf and spread the sap onto my fingers where they were bloody and torn. The stinging helped distract me from remembering how I had hurt them.

Waiting for the sap to dry, I took my first casual look around. Oaks and birches crowded each other for space. Their trunks made patterns of alternating light and dark beneath the canopy of branches. A small rivulet ran from the pool across some rocks and away to the east. It may have been beautiful, but I didn't notice. I couldn't notice. To me the trees were shelter, the undergrowth a source of nourishment, and the pool reflecting moonlight only reminded me of my thirst.

There was also a great rectangular stone lying on its side near the pool. A few days earlier I would have recognised it as a greystone. Now I saw it as an efficient windbreak, something to put my back against as I slept.

Through the canopy I saw the stars were out. That meant it had been several hours since I had tried the water. Since it hadn't made me sick, I decided it must be safe and took a long drink.

Rather than refreshing me, all my drink did was make me aware of how hungry I was. I sat on the stone by the edge of the pool. I stripped the leaves from the stalks of motherleaf and ate one. It was rough, papery, and bitter. I ate the rest, but it didn't help. I took another drink of water, then lay down to sleep, not caring that the stone was cold and hard, or at least pretending not to care.

———

I awoke, took a drink, and went to check the snare I had set. I was surprised to find a rabbit already struggling against the cord. I took out my small knife and remembered how Laclith had shown me to dress a rabbit. Then I thought of the blood and how it would feel on my hands. I felt sick and vomited. I cut loose the rabbit and walked back to the pool.

I took another drink of water and sat on the stone. I felt a little light-headed and wondered if it was from hunger.

After a moment my head cleared and I chided myself for my foolishness. I found some shelf fungus growing on a dead tree and ate it after washing it in the pool. It was gritty and tasted like dirt. I ate all I could find.

I set a new snare, one that would kill. Then, smelling rain in the air, I returned to the greystone to make a shelter for my lute.

CHAPTER NINETEEN

Fingers and Strings

IN THE BEGINNING I was almost like an automaton, thoughtlessly performing the actions that would keep me alive.

I ate the second rabbit I caught, and the third. I found a patch of wild strawberries. I dug for roots. By the end of the fourth day, I had everything I needed to survive: a stone-lined fire pit, a shelter for my lute. I had even assembled a small stockpile of foodstuffs that I could fall back on in case of emergency.

I also had one thing I did not need: time. After I had taken care of immediate needs, I found I had nothing to do. I think this is when a small part of my mind started to slowly reawaken itself.

Make no mistake, I was not myself. At least I was not the same person I had been a span of days before. Everything I did I attended to with my whole mind, leaving no part of me free for remembering.

I grew thinner and more ragged. I slept in rain or sun, on soft grass, moist earth, or sharp stones with an intensity of indifference that only grief can promote. The only notice I took of my surroundings was when it rained, because then I could not bring out my lute to play, and that pained me.

Of course I played. It was my only solace.

By the end of the first month, my fingers had calluses hard as stones and I could play for hours upon hours. I played and played again all of the songs I knew from memory. Then I played the half-remembered songs as well, filling in the forgotten parts as best I could.

Eventually I could play from when I woke until the time I slept. I stopped playing the songs I knew and started inventing new ones. I had made up songs before; I had even helped my father compose a verse or two. But now I gave it my whole attention. Some of those songs have stayed with me to this day.

Soon after that I began playing . . . how can I describe it?

I began to play something other than songs. When the sun warms the grass and the breeze cools you, it feels a certain way. I would play until I got the feeling right. I would play until it sounded like Warm Grass and Cool Breeze.

I was only playing for myself, but I was a harsh audience. I remember spending nearly three whole days trying to capture Wind Turning a Leaf.

By the end of the second month, I could play things nearly as easily as I saw and felt them: Sun Setting Behind the Clouds, Bird Taking a Drink, Dew in the Bracken.

Somewhere in the third month I stopped looking outside and started looking inside for things to play. I learned to play Riding in the Wagon with Ben, Singing with Father by the Fire, Watching Shandi Dance, Grinding Leaves When It Is Nice Outside, Mother Smiling . . .

Needless to say, playing these things hurt, but it was a hurt like tender fingers on lute strings. I bled a bit and hoped that I would callous soon.

Towards the end of summer, one of the strings broke, broke beyond repair. I spent the better part of the day in a mute stupor, unsure of what to do. My mind was still numb and mostly asleep. I focused with a dim shadow of my usual cleverness on my problem. After realising that I could neither make a string nor acquire a new one, I sat back down and began to learn to play with only six strings.

In a span I was nearly as good with six strings as I had been with seven. Three span later I was trying to play Waiting While it Rains when a second string broke.

This time I didn't hesitate, I stripped off the useless string and started to learn again.

It was midway through Reaping when the third string broke. After trying for nearly half a day, I realised that three broken strings were too many. So I packed a small dull knife, half a ball of string, and Ben's book into a tattered canvas sack. Then I shouldered my father's lute and began to walk.

I tried humming Snow Falling with the Late Autumn Leaves; Calloused Fingers and a Lute With Four Strings, but it wasn't the same as playing it.

My plan was to find a road and follow it to a town. I had no idea how far I was from either, in which direction they might lie, or what their names might be. I knew I was somewhere in the southern Commonwealth, but the precise location was buried, tangled up with other memories that I was not eager to unearth.

The weather helped me make up my mind. Cool autumn was turning to winter's chill. I knew the weather was warmer to the south. So, lacking any better plan, I set the sun on my left shoulder and tried to cover as much distance as I could.

The next span was an ordeal. The little food I'd brought with me was soon gone, and I had to stop and forage when I was hungry. Some days I couldn't find water, and when I did I had nothing I could use to carry it. The small wagon track joined a bigger road, which joined a larger road yet. My feet chafed and blistered against the insides of my shoes. Some nights were bitter cold.

There were inns, but aside from the occasional drink I stole from horse troughs, I gave them a wide berth. There were a few small towns as well, but I needed someplace larger. Farmers have no need for lute strings.

At first, whenever I heard a wagon or a horse approaching I found myself limping off to hide by the side of the road. I had not spoken with another human since the night my family was killed. I was more akin to a wild animal than a boy of twelve. But eventually the road became too large and well travelled, and I found myself spending more time hiding than walking. I finally braved the traffic and was relieved when I was largely ignored.

———————

I had been walking for less than an hour one morning when I heard a wagon coming up behind me. The road was wide enough for two wagons to run abreast, but I moved to the grass at the edge of the road anyway.

'Hey, boy!' a rough male voice behind me yelled. I didn't turn around. 'Hullo, boy!'

I moved farther off the road into the grass without looking behind me. I kept my eyes on the ground beneath my feet.

The wagon pulled slowly alongside me. The voice bellowed twice as loud as before, 'Boy. Boy!'

I looked up and saw a weathered old man squinting against the sun. He could have been anywhere from forty to seventy years old. There was a thick-shouldered, plain-faced young man sitting next to him on the wagon. I guessed they were father and son.

'Are ye deaf, boy?' The old man pronounced it *deef.*

I shook my head.

'Ye dumb then?'

I shook my head again. 'No.' It felt strange talking to someone. My voice sounded odd, rough and rusty from disuse.

He squinted at me. 'You goin' into the city?'

I nodded, not wanting to talk again.

'Get in then.' He nodded toward the back of the wagon. 'Sam won't mind pulling a little whippet like yuself.' He patted the rump of his mule.

It was easier to agree than run away. And the blisters on my feet were stinging from the sweat in my shoes. I moved to the back of the open cart and climbed on, pulling my lute after me. The back of the open wagon was about three-quarters full of large burlap bags. A few round, knobby squash had spilled from an open sack and were rolling aimlessly around on the floor.

The old man shook the reins. 'Hup!' and the mule grudgingly picked up its pace. I picked up the few loose squash and tucked them into the bag that had fallen open. The old farmer gave me a smile over his shoulder. 'Thanks, boy. I'm Seth, and this here is Jake. You might want to be sittin' down, a bad bump could tip ye over the side.' I sat on one of the bags, tense for no good reason, not knowing what to expect.

The old farmer handed the reins to his son and brought a large brown loaf of bread out of a sack that sat between the two of them. He casually tore off a large chunk, spread a thick dab of butter onto it, and handed it back to me.

This casual kindness made my chest ache. It had been half a year since I had eaten bread. It was soft and warm and the butter was sweet. I saved a piece for later, tucking it into my canvas sack.

After a quiet quarter of an hour, the old man turned halfway around. 'Do you play that thing, boy?' He gestured to the lute case.

I clutched it closer to my body. 'It's broken.'

'Ah,' he said, disappointed. I thought he was going to ask me to get off, but instead he smiled and nodded to the man beside him. 'We'll just have to be entertainin' you instead.'

He started to sing 'Tinker Tanner', a drinking song that is older than God. After a second his son joined in, and their rough voices made a simple harmony that set something inside me aching as I remembered other wagons, different songs, a half-forgotten home.

CHAPTER TWENTY

Bloody Hands Into Stinging Fists

I T WAS AROUND NOON when the wagon turned onto a new road, this one wide as a river and paved with cobbles. At first there were only a handful of travellers and a wagon or two, but to me it seemed like a great crowd after such a long time alone.

We went deeper into the city, and low buildings gave way to taller shops and inns. Trees and gardens were replaced by alleys and cart vendors. The great river of a road grew clogged and choked with the flotsam of a hundred carts and pedestrians, dozens of wains and wagons and the occasional mounted man.

There was the sound of horses' hooves and people shouting, the smell of beer and sweat and garbage and tar. I wondered which city this was, and if I'd been here before, before—

I gritted my teeth and forced myself to think of other things.

'Almost there,' Seth raised his voice above the din. Eventually the road opened out into a market. Wagons rolled on the cobbles with a sound like distant thunder. Voices bargained and fought. Somewhere in the distance a child was crying shrill and high. We rode aimlessly for a while until he found an empty corner in front of a bookshop.

Seth stopped the wagon and I hopped out as they were stretching away the kinks from the road. Then, with a sort of silent agreement, I helped them unload the lumpy sacks from the back of the wagon and pile them to one side.

A half an hour later we were resting among the piled sacks. Seth looked at me, shading his eyes with a hand. 'What are ye doin' in town today, boy?'

'I need lute strings,' I said. Only then did I realise I didn't know where my father's lute was. I looked around wildly. It wasn't in the wagon where

I'd left it, or leaning against the wall, or on the piles of squash. My stomach clenched until I spotted it underneath some loose burlap sacking. I walked over to it and picked it up with shaking hands.

The older farmer grinned at me and held out a pair of the knobby squash we'd been unloading. 'How would your mother like it if you brought home a couple of the finest orange butter squash this side of the Eld?'

'No, I can't,' I stammered, pushing away a memory of raw fingers digging in the mud and the smell of burning hair. 'I m—mean, you've already . . .' I trailed off, clutching my lute closer to my chest and moving a couple of steps away.

He looked at me more closely, as if seeing me for the first time. Suddenly self-conscious, I imagined how I must look: ragged and half-starved. I hugged the lute and backed farther away. The farmer's hands fell to his side and his smile faded. 'Ah, lad,' he said softly.

He set the squash down, then turned back to me and spoke with a gentle seriousness. 'Me and Jake will be here selling until round about sundown. If you find what you're looking for by then, you'd be welcome back on the farm with us. The missus and me could sure use an extra hand some days. You'd be more than welcome. Wouldn't he Jake?'

Jake was looking at me too, pity written across his honest face. 'Sure enough, Pa. She said so right afore we left.'

The old farmer continued to look at me with serious eyes. 'This is Seaward Square.' He said, pointing at his feet. 'We'll be here till dark, maybe a little after. You come back if'n you want a ride.' His eyes turned worried. 'You hear me? You can come back with us.'

I continued to back away, step by step, not sure why I was doing it. Only knowing that if I went with him I would have to explain, would have to remember. Anything was better than opening that door . . .

'No. No, thank you,' I stammered. 'You've helped so much. I'll be fine.' I was jostled from behind by a man in a leather apron. Startled, I turned and ran.

I heard one of them call out behind me, but the crowd drowned them out. I ran, my heart heavy in my chest.

———————

Tarbean is big enough that you cannot walk from one end to the other in a single day. Not even if you avoid getting lost or accosted in the tangled web of twisting streets and dead end alleys.

It was too big, actually. It was vast, immense. Seas of people, forests of buildings, roads wide as rivers. It smelled like urine and sweat and coal smoke and tar. If I had been in my right mind, I never would have gone there.

In the fullness of time, I became lost. I took a turn too early or too late, then tried to compensate by cutting through an alley like a narrow chasm between two tall buildings. It wound like a gully carved by a river that had left to find a cleaner bed. Garbage drifted up the walls and filled the cracks between buildings and the alcove doorways. After I had taken several turns I caught the rancid smell of something dead.

I turned a corner and staggered against a wall as pain stars blinded me. I felt rough hands grab hold of my arms.

I opened my eyes to see an older boy. He was twice my size with dark hair and savage eyes. The dirt that smudged his face gave him the appearance of having a beard, making his young face strangely cruel.

Two other boys jerked me away from the wall. I yelped as one of them twisted my arm. The older boy smiled at the sound and ran a hand through his hair. 'What are you doin' here, Nalt? You lost?' His grin broadened.

I tried to pull away but one of the boys twisted my wrist and I gasped, 'No.'

'I think he's lost, Pike,' the boy on my right said. The one on my left elbowed me sharply in the side of the head and the alley tilted crazily around me.

Pike laughed.

'I'm looking for the Woodworks,' I muttered, slightly stunned.

Pike's expression turned murderous. His hands grabbed my shoulders. 'Did I ask you a question?' he shouted. 'Did I say you could talk?' He slammed his forehead into my face and I felt a sharp *crack* followed by an explosion of pain.

'Hey, Pike.' The voice seemed to come from an impossible direction. A foot nudged my lute case, tipping it over. 'Hey Pike, look at this.'

Pike looked down at the hollow *thump* as the lute case fell flat against the ground. 'What did you steal, Nalt?'

'I didn't steal it.'

One of the boys holding my arms laughed. 'Yeah, your uncle gave it to you so you could sell it to buy medicine for your sick grandma.' He laughed again while I tried to blink the tears out of my eyes.

I heard three clicks as the latches were undone. Then came the distinctive harmonic thrum as the lute was taken out of its case.

'Your grandma is gonna be mighty sorry you lost this, Nalt,' Pike's voice was quiet.

'Tehlu crush us!' the boy on my right exploded. 'Pike, ya know how much one of them's worth? Gold, Pike!'

'Don't say Tehlu's name like that,' said the boy on my left.

'What?'

' "Do not call on Tehlu save in the greatest need, for Tehlu judges every thought and deed," ' he recited.

'Tehlu and his great glowing penis can piss all over me if that thing isn't worth twenty talents. That means we can get at least six from Diken. Do you know what you can do with that much money?'

'You won't get the chance to do anything with it if you don't quit saying things like that. Tehlu watches over us, but he is vengeful.' The second boy's voice was reverent and afraid.

'You've been sleeping in the church again haven't you? You get religion like I get fleas.'

'I'll tie your arms in a knot.'

'Your ma's a penny whore.'

'Don't talk about my mom, Lin.'

'*Iron* pennies.'

By this time I had managed to blink my eyes free from the tears and I could see Pike squatting in the alley. He seemed fascinated by my lute. My beautiful lute. He had a dreamy look in his eyes as he held it, turning it over and over in his dirty hands. A slow horror was dawning on me through the haze of fear and pain.

As the two voices grew louder behind me, I began to feel a hot anger inside. I tensed. I couldn't fight them, but I knew if I got hold of my lute and made it into a crowd I could lose them and be safe again.

'. . . but she kept humping away anyway. But now she only got a halfpenny a throw. That's why your head is so soft. You're lucky you don't have a dent. So don't feel bad, that's why you get religious so easy.' The first boy finished triumphantly.

I felt only a tenseness on my right side. I tensed too, ready to spring.

'But thanks for the warning. I hear Tehlu likes to hide behind big clumps of horseshit and th—'

Suddenly both of my arms were free as one boy tackled the other into the wall. I sprinted the three steps to Pike, grabbed the lute by the neck, and pulled.

But Pike was quicker than I'd expected, or stronger. The lute didn't come away in my hand. I was jerked to a halt and Pike was pulled to his feet.

My frustration and anger boiled over. I let go of the lute and threw myself at Pike. I clawed madly at his face and neck, but he was a veteran of too many street fights to let me get close to anything vital. One of my fingernails tore a line of blood across his face from ear to chin. Then he was against me, pressing me back until I hit the alley wall.

My head struck brick, and I would have fallen if Pike hadn't been grinding me into the crumbling wall. I gasped for breath and only then realised I'd been screaming all the while.

He smelled like old sweat and rancid oil. His hands pinned my arms to my sides as he pressed me harder into the wall. I was dimly aware that he must have dropped my lute.

I gasped for breath again and flailed blindly, knocking my head against the wall again. I found my face pressed into his shoulder and bit down hard. I felt his skin break under my teeth and tasted blood.

Pike screamed and jerked away from me. I drew a breath and winced at a tearing pain in my chest.

Before I could move or think, Pike grabbed me again. He bludgeoned me up against the wall once, twice. My head whipsawed back and forth, caroming off the wall. Then he grabbed me by the throat, spun me around, and threw me to the ground.

That's when I heard the noise, and everything seemed to stop.

After my troupe was murdered, there were times when I would dream of my parents, alive and singing. In my dream their deaths had been a mistake, a misunderstanding, a new play they had been rehearsing. And for a few moments I had relief from the great blanketing grief that was constantly crushing me. I hugged them and we laughed at my foolish worry. I sang with them, and for a moment everything was wonderful. Wonderful.

But I always woke up, alone in the dark by the forest pool. What was I doing out here? Where were my parents?

Then I would remember everything, like a wound ripping open. They were dead and I was terribly alone. And that great weight that had been lifted for just a moment would come crushing down again, worse than before because I wasn't ready for it. Then I would lay on my back, staring into the dark with my chest aching and my breath coming hard, knowing deep inside that nothing would ever be right, ever again.

When Pike threw me to the ground, my body was almost too numb to feel my father's lute being crushed underneath me. The sound it made was like a dying dream, and it brought that same sick, breathless ache back to my chest.

I looked around and saw Pike breathing heavily and clutching his shoulder. One of the boys was kneeling on the chest of the other. They weren't wrestling anymore, both were looking in my direction, stunned.

I stared numbly at my hands, bloody where slivers of wood had pierced the skin.

'Little bastard bit me,' Pike said quietly, as if he couldn't quite believe what had happened.

'Get off me,' said the boy lying on his back.

'I said you shouldn't say those things. Look what happened.'

Pike's expression twisted and his face went a livid red. 'Bit me!' he shouted and swung a vicious kick at my head.

I tried to get out of the way without doing any more damage to the lute. His kick caught me in the kidney and sent me sprawling into the wreckage again, splintering it even further.

'See what happens when you mock Tehlu's name?'

'Shut up about Tehlu. Get off me and grab that thing. It might still be worth something to Diken.'

'Look what you did!' Pike continued to howl above me. A kick caught me in the side and rolled me halfway over. The edges of my vision started to darken. I almost welcomed it as a distraction. But the deeper pain was still there, untouched. I balled my bloody hands into stinging fists.

'These knob things still seem okay. They're silvery, I'll bet we can get something for them.'

Pike pulled back his foot again. I tried to put up my hands to keep it away, but my arms just twitched and Pike kicked me in the stomach.

'Grab that bit over there . . .'

'Pike. Pike!'

Pike kicked me in the stomach again and I vomited weakly onto the cobblestones.

'You there, stop! City Watch!' A new voice shouted. A heartbeat of stillness was followed by a scuffle and a flurry of pattering feet. A second later, heavy boots pounded past and faded in the distance.

I remember the ache in my chest. I blacked out.

———

I was shaken out of darkness by someone turning my pockets inside out. I tried unsuccessfully to open my eyes.

I heard a voice muttering to itself, 'Is this all I get for saving your life? Copper and a couple of shims? Drinks for an evening? Worthless little sod.' He coughed deep in his chest and the smell of stale liquor washed over me. 'Screaming like that. If you hadn't sounded like a girl I wouldn't have run all this way.'

I tried to say something, but it dribbled out as a groan.

'Well, you're alive. That's something, I suppose.' I heard a grunt as he stood up, then the heavy thumping of his boots faded away into silence.

After a while I found I could open my eyes. My vision was blurry and my nose felt larger than the rest of my head. I prodded it delicately. Broken. Remembering what Ben had taught me, I put one hand on each side of it and twisted it sharply back into place. I clenched my teeth against a cry of pain, and my eyes filled with tears.

I blinked them away and was relieved when I saw the street without the painful blurriness of a moment ago. The contents of my small sack lay next to me on the ground: a half ball of string, a small dull knife, *Rhetoric and Logic,* and the remainder of a piece of bread the farmer had given me for lunch. It seemed like forever ago.

The farmer. I thought of Seth and Jake. Soft bread and butter. Songs while riding in a wagon. Their offer of a safe place, a new home . . .

A sudden memory was followed by a sudden sickening panic. I looked around the alley, my head aching from the sudden movement. Sifting the garbage with my hands I found some terribly familiar shards of wood. I stared at them mutely as the world darkened imperceptibly around me. I darted a look at the thin strip of sky visible overhead and saw it was purpling into twilight.

How late was it? I hurried to gather my possessions, treating Ben's book more gently than the rest, and limped off in what I hoped was the direction of Seaward Square.

The last of twilight had faded from the sky by the time I found the square. A few wagons rolled sluggishly among the few straggling customers. I limped wildly from corner to corner of the square, searching madly for the old farmer who had given me a ride. Searching for the sight of one of those ugly, knobby squash.

When I finally found the bookstore Seth had parked beside, I was panting and staggering. Seth and his wagon were nowhere to be seen. I sank down into the empty space their wagon had left and felt the aches and pains of a dozen injuries that I had forced myself to ignore.

I felt them out, one by one. I had several painful ribs, although I couldn't tell if they were broken or if the cartilage was torn. I was dizzy and nauseous when I moved my head too quickly, probably a concussion. My nose was broken, and I had more bruises and scrapes than I could conveniently count. I was also hungry.

The last being the only thing I could do anything about, I took what was left of my piece of bread from earlier in the day and ate it. It wasn't enough, but it was better than nothing. I took a drink from a horse trough and was thirsty enough not to care that the water was brackish and sour.

I thought of leaving, but it would take me hours of walking in my current condition. Besides, there was nothing waiting for me on the outskirts of the city except miles upon miles of harvested farmland. No trees to keep the wind away. No wood to make a fire. No rabbits to set traps for. No roots to dig. No heather for a bed.

I was so hungry my stomach was a hard knot. Here at least I could smell chicken cooking somewhere. I would have gone looking for the smell, but I was dizzy, and my ribs hurt. Maybe tomorrow someone would give me something to eat. Right now I was too tired. I wanted nothing more than to sleep.

The cobblestones were losing the last of the sun's heat and the wind was picking up. I moved back into the doorway of the bookshop to get out of the wind. I was almost asleep when the owner of the shop opened the door and kicked at me, telling me to shove off or he'd call the guard. I limped away as quickly as I could.

After that I found some empty crates in an alley. I curled up behind them, bruised and weary. I closed my eyes and tried not to remember what it was like to go to sleep warm and full, surrounded by people who loved you.

That was the first night of nearly three years I spent in Tarbean.

CHAPTER TWENTY-ONE

Basement, Bread and Bucket

I T WAS JUST AFTER lunchtime. Rather, it would have been after lunchtime if I'd had anything to eat. I was begging in Merchant's Circle and so far the day had profited me two kicks (one guard, one mercenary), three shoves (two wagoneers, one sailor), one new curse concerning an un-likely anatomical configuration (also from the sailor), and a spray of spittle from a rather unendearing elderly man of indeterminate occupation.

And one iron shim. Though I attributed it more to the laws of probability than from any human kindness. Even a blind pig finds an acorn once in a while.

I had been living in Tarbean for nearly a month, and the day before I had tried my hand at stealing for the first time. It was an inauspicious beginning. I'd been caught with my hand in a butcher's pocket. This had earned me such a tremendous blow to the side of the head that today I was dizzy when I tried to stand or move about quickly. Hardly encouraged by my first foray into thievery, I had decided that today was a begging day. As such, it was about average.

Hunger knotted my stomach, and a single shim's worth of stale bread wasn't going to help much. I was considering moving to a different street when I saw a boy run up to a younger beggar across the way. They talked excitedly for a moment then hurried off.

I followed of course, showing a pale shadow of my former burning curiosity. Besides, anything that moved the two of them away from a busy street corner in the middle of the day was bound to be worth my while. Maybe the Tehlins were giving out bread again. Or a fruit cart had tipped over. Or the guard was hanging someone. That would be worth half an hour of my time.

I followed the boys through the twisting streets until I saw them turn a corner and scurry down a flight of stairs into the basement of a burned-out building. I stopped, my dim spark of curiosity smothered by my common sense.

A moment later they reappeared, each carrying a chunk of flat brown bread. I watched as they wandered past, laughing and shoving at each other. The youngest, no more than six, saw me looking and waved.

'Still some left,' he called through a mouthful of bread. 'Better hurrup though.'

My common sense did a rapid turnaround, and I headed cautiously downward. At the bottom of the steps were a few rotting planks, all that remained of a broken door. Inside I could see a short hallway opening out into a dimly lit room. A young girl with hard eyes pushed past me without looking up. She clutched another piece of bread.

I stepped over the broken pieces of door into the chill, damp dark. After a dozen steps I heard a low moan that froze me where I stood. It was almost an animal sound, but my ear told me it came from a human throat.

I don't know what I expected, but it was nothing like what I found. Two ancient lamps burned fish oil, throwing dim shadows against the dark stone walls. There were six cots in the room, all occupied. Two children that were hardly more than babies shared a blanket on the stone floor, and another was curled up in a pile of rags. A boy my age sat in a dark corner, his head pressed against the wall.

One of the boys moved slightly on his cot, as if stirring in his sleep. But something was wrong with the movement. It was too strained, too tense. I looked closer and saw the truth. He was tied to the cot. All of them were.

He strained against the ropes and made the noise I had heard in the hall. It was clearer now, a long moaning cry. 'Aaaaaaabaaaaaaah.'

For a moment all I could do was think about every story I had ever heard about the Duke of Gibea. About how he and his men had abducted and tortured people for twenty years before the church had gone in and put an end to it.

'What what,' came a voice from the other room. The voice had an odd inflection to it, as if it wasn't really asking a question.

The boy on the cot jerked against his ropes. 'Aaaahbeeeeh.'

A man came through the doorway brushing his hands on the front of his tattered robe. 'What what,' he repeated in the same not-questioning tone. His voice was old and tired around the edges, but at its centre it was patient.

Patient as a heavy stone or a mother cat with kittens. Not the sort of voice I expected a Duke-of-Gibea type to have.

'What what. Hush hush, Tanee. I wan't gone, just stepped away. Now I'm here.' His feet made slapping sounds against the bare stone floor. He was barefoot. I felt the tension slowly spill out of me. Whatever was going on here, it didn't seem nearly as sinister as I had originally thought.

The boy stopped straining against the ropes when he saw the man approaching. 'Eeeeeeaah.' He said, and tugged against the ropes restraining him.

'What?' It was a question this time.

'Eeeeeeaah.'

'Hmmm?' The old man looked around and saw me for the first time. 'Oh. Hello.' He looked back to the boy on the bed. 'Well aren't you the clever one today? Tanee called me in to see we have a visitor!' Tanee's face broke into a terrific grin and he gave a harsh, honking gasp of breath. In spite of the painful sound, it was clear he was laughing.

Turning to look at me, the barefoot man said, 'I don't recognise you. Have you been here before?'

I shook my head.

'Well, I've got some bread, only two days old. If you carry some water for me, you can have as much as you can eat.' He looked at me. 'Does that sound all right?'

I nodded. A chair, table, and an open barrel standing near one of the doors were the only furnishings in the room aside from the cots. Four large, round loaves were stacked on the table.

He nodded too, then began to move carefully towards the chair. He walked gingerly, as if it pained him to set his feet down.

After he reached the chair and sank into it, he pointed to the barrel by the doorway. 'Through the door there's a pump and bucket. Don't bother to hurry, it's na a race.' As he spoke he absentmindedly crossed his legs and began to rub one of his bare feet.

Inefficient circulation, a long-unused part of me thought. *Increased risk of infection and considerable discomfort. Feet and legs should be raised, massaged, and swabbed in a warm infusion of willow bark, camphor, and arrowroot.*

'Don't fill the bucket too full. I don't want you to hurt yourself or spill all over. It's wet enough down here.' He eased his foot back to the floor and bent to gather up one of the tiny children who was beginning to stir restlessly on the blanket.

As I filled the barrel I snuck glances at the man. His hair was grey, but despite that and the slow, tender manner in which he walked, he wasn't very old. Perhaps forty, probably a little less. He wore a long robe, patched and mended to such a degree that I couldn't really guess at its original colour or shape. Though nearly as ragged as I was, he was cleaner. Which isn't to say that he was clean exactly, just cleaner than me. It wasn't hard to be.

His name was Trapis. The patched robe was the only piece of clothing he owned. He spent nearly every moment of his waking life in that damp basement caring for the hopeless people no one else would bother with. Most of them were young boys. Some, like Tanee, had to be restrained so they wouldn't hurt themselves or roll out of their beds. Others, like Jaspin who had gone fever-mad two years ago, had to be restrained so they wouldn't hurt others.

Palsied, crippled, catatonic, spastic, Trapis tended them all with equal and unending patience. I never once heard him complain of anything, not even his bare feet, which were always swollen and must have pained him constantly.

He gave us children what help he could, a bit of food when he had some to spare. To earn a little something to eat we carried water, scrubbed his floor, ran errands, and held the babies so they wouldn't cry. We did whatever he asked, and when there wasn't any food we could always have a drink of water, a tired smile, and someone who looked at us as if we were human, not animals in rags.

Sometimes it seemed that Trapis alone was trying to care for all the hopeless creatures in our corner of Tarbean. In return we loved him with a silent ferocity that only animals can match. If anyone had ever raised a hand to Trapis, a hundred howling children would have torn them to bloody scraps in the middle of the street.

I stopped by his basement often in those first few months, then less and less as time went by. Trapis and Tanee were fine companions. None of us felt the need to talk much, and that suited me fine. But the other street children made me unspeakably nervous, so I visited infrequently, only when I was in desperate need of help, or when I had something to share.

Despite the fact that I was seldom there, it was good to know there was one place in the city where I wouldn't be kicked at, chased, or spit on. It helped when I was out on the rooftops alone, knowing that Trapis and the basement were there. It was almost like a home you could come back to. Almost.

CHAPTER TWENTY-TWO

A Time for Demons

I LEARNED MANY THINGS those first months in Tarbean.

I learned which inns and restaurants threw away the best food, and how rotten food needed to be before it made you sick to eat it.

I learned that the walled complex of buildings near the docks was the Temple of Tehlu. The Tehlins sometimes gave out bread, making us say prayers before we could take our loaf. I didn't mind. It was easier than begging. Sometimes the grey-robed priests tried to get me to come into the church to say the prayers, but I'd heard rumours and ran away whenever I was asked, whether I had my loaf or no.

I learned how to hide. I had a secret place atop an old tannery where three roofs met, making a shelter from the wind and rain. Ben's book I secreted away under the rafters, wrapped in canvas. I handled it only rarely, like a holy relic. It was the last solid piece of my past, and I took every precaution to keep it safe.

I learned that Tarbean is vast. You cannot understand if you have not seen it yourself. It is like the ocean. I can tell you of the waves and water, but you don't begin to get an inkling of its size until you stand on the shore. You don't really understand the ocean until you are in the midst of it, nothing but ocean on all sides, stretching away endlessly. Only then do you realise how small you are, how powerless.

Part of Tarbean's vastness is the fact that it is divided into a thousand small pieces, each with its own personality. There was Downings, Drover Court, the Wash, Middletown, Tallows, Tunning, Dockside, the Tarway, Seamling Lane . . . You could live your whole life in Tarbean and never know all its parts.

But for most practical purposes Tarbean had two pieces: Waterside and Hillside. Waterside is where people are poor. That makes them beggars, thieves, and whores. Hillside is where people are rich. That makes them solicitors, politicians, and courtesans.

I had been in Tarbean for two months when I first thought to try my hand at begging Hillside. Winter gripped the city firmly and the Midwinter Pageantry was making the streets more dangerous than usual.

This was shocking to me. Every winter for the entirety of my young life our troupe had organised the Midwinter Pageantry for some town. Dressed in demon masks, we would terrorise them for the seven days of High Mourning, much to everyone's delight. My father played an Encanis so convincing you'd think we'd conjured him. Most importantly, he could be frightening and careful at the same time. No one was ever hurt when our troupe was in charge.

But in Tarbean it was different. Oh, the *pieces* of the pageantry were all the same. There were still men in garishly painted demon masks skulking about the city, making mischief. Encanis was out there too, in the traditional black mask, making more serious trouble. And though I hadn't seen him, I didn't doubt that silver-masked Tehlu was striding around the better neighborhoods, playing his part. As I said, the *pieces* of the pageantry were the same.

But they played out differently. For one thing, Tarbean was too big for one troupe to provide enough demons. A hundred troupes wouldn't be enough. So, rather than pay for professionals, as would be sensible and safe, the churches in Tarbean took the more profitable path of selling demon masks.

Because of this, on the first day of High Mourning ten thousand demons were set loose on the city. Ten thousand *amateur* demons, with license to make whatever mischief they had minds to.

This might seem like an ideal situation for a young thief to take advantage of, but really the opposite was true. The demons were always thickest Waterside. And while the great majority behaved properly, fleeing at the sound of Tehlu's name and keeping their devilry within reasonable bounds, many did not. Things were dangerous the first few days of High Mourning, and I spent most of my time simply staying out of harm's way.

But as Midwinter approached, things settled down. The number of demons steadily decreased as people lost their masks or tired of the game. Tehlu no doubt eliminated his share as well, but silver mask or no, he was only one man. He could hardly cover the whole of Tarbean in just seven days' time.

I chose the last day of Mourning for my trip Hillside. Spirits are always high on Midwinter's Day, and high spirits mean good begging. Best of all, the ranks of the demons were noticeably thinned, which meant it was reasonably safe to be walking the streets again.

I set out in the early afternoon, hungry because I couldn't find any bread to steal. I remember feeling vaguely excited as I headed towards Hillside. Maybe some part of me remembered what Midwinter had been like with my family: warm meals and warm beds afterward. Maybe I had been infected by the smell of evergreen boughs being gathered into piles and set ablaze in celebration of Tehlu's triumph.

That day I learned two things. I learned why beggars stay Waterside, and I learned that no matter what the church might tell you, Midwinter is a time for demons.

I emerged from an alley and was instantly struck by the difference in atmosphere between this part of the city and where I had come from.

Waterside, merchants wheedled and cajoled customers, hoping to lure them into their shops. Should that fail, they were not shy about bursting into fits of bellicosity: cursing or even openly bullying customers.

Here the shop owners wrung their hands nervously. They bowed and scraped and were unfailingly polite. Voices were never raised. After the brutal reality of things Waterside, it seemed to me as if I had stumbled into a formal ball. Everyone was dressed in new clothes. Everyone was clean, and they all seemed to be participating in some sort of intricate social dance.

But there were shadows here, too. As I surveyed the street I spotted a pair of men lurking in the alleyway across from me. Their masks were quite good, bloodred and fierce. One had a gaping mouth and the other a grimace of pointed white teeth. They were both wearing the traditional black hooded robes, which I approved of. So many of the demons Waterside didn't bother with the proper costume.

The pair of demons slipped out to follow a well-dressed young couple who were strolling idly down the street, arm in arm. The demons stalked them carefully for nearly a hundred feet, then one of them snatched the gentleman's hat and thrust it into a nearby snowdrift. The other grabbed the woman in a rough embrace and lifted her from the ground. She shrieked while the man struggled with the demon for possession of his walking stick, obviously flummoxed by the situation.

Luckily his lady maintained her composure. *'Tehus! Tehus!'* she shouted. *'Tehus antausa eha!'*

At the sound of Tehlu's name the two red-masked figures cowered, then turned and ran off down the street.

Everyone cheered. One of the shopkeepers helped the gentleman retrieve his hat. I was rather surprised by the civility of it all. Apparently even the demons were polite on the good side of town.

Emboldened by what I had seen, I eyed the crowd, looking for my best prospects. I stepped up to a young woman. She wore a powder blue dress and had a wrap of white fur. Her hair was long and golden, curled artfully around her face.

As I stepped forward she looked down at me and stopped. I heard a startled intake of breath as one hand went to her mouth. 'Pennies, ma'am?' I held out my hand and made it tremble just a little. My voice trembled too. 'Please?' I tried to look every bit as small and hopeless as I felt. I shuffled from foot to foot in the thin grey snow.

'You poor dear,' she sighed almost too quietly for me to hear. She fumbled with the purse at her side, either unable or unwilling to take her eyes from me. After a moment she looked inside her purse and brought something out. As she curled my fingers around it I felt the cold, reassuring weight of a coin.

'Thank you, ma'am,' I said automatically. I looked down for a moment and saw silver glinting through my fingers. I opened my hand and saw a silver penny. A whole silver penny.

I gaped. A silver penny was worth ten copper pennies, or fifty iron ones. More than that, it was worth a full belly every night for half a month. For an iron penny I could sleep on the floor at the Red Eye for the night, for two I could sleep on the hearth by the embers of the evening fire. I could buy a rag blanket that I would hide on the rooftops, keeping me warm all winter.

I looked up at the woman, who was still looking down at me with pitying eyes. She couldn't know what this meant. 'Lady, thank you,' my voice cracked. I remembered one of the things that we said back when I lived in the troupe. 'May all your stories be glad ones, and your roads be smooth and short.'

She smiled at me and might have said something, but I got a strange feeling near the base of my neck. Someone was watching me. On the street you either develop a sensitivity to certain things, or your life is miserable and short.

I looked around and saw a shopkeeper talking with a guard and gesturing in my direction. This wasn't some Waterside guard. He was clean-shaven and upright. He wore a black leather jerkin with metal studs and carried a brass-bound club as long as his arm. I caught scraps of what the shopkeeper was saying.

'. . . customers. Who's going to buy chocolate with . . .' He gestured my way again and said something I couldn't catch. '. . . pays you? That's right. Maybe I should mention . . .'

The guard turned his head to look in my direction. I caught his eyes. I turned and ran.

I headed for the first alley I saw, my thin shoes slipping on the light layer of snow that covered the ground. I heard his heavy boots pounding behind me as I turned into a second alley branching off from the first.

My breath was burning in my chest as I looked for somewhere to go, somewhere to hide. But I didn't know this part of the city. There were no piles of trash to worm into, no burned-out buildings to climb through. I felt sharp frozen gravel slice through the thin sole of one of my shoes. Pain tore through my foot as I forced myself to keep running.

I ran into a dead end after my third turning. I was halfway up one of the walls when I felt a hand close around my ankle and pull me to the ground.

My head hit the cobblestones and the world spun dizzily as the guard lifted me off the ground, holding me by one wrist and my hair. 'Clever boy, aren't you?' he panted, his breath hot on my face. He smelled like leather and sweat. 'You're old enough, you should know not to run by now.' He shook me angrily and twisted my hair. I cried out as the alley tilted around me.

He pressed me roughly against a wall. 'You should know enough not to be coming Hillside either.' He shook me. 'You dumb, boy?'

'No,' I said muzzily as I felt for the cool wall with my free hand. 'No.'

My answer seemed to infuriate him. '*No?*' he bit off the word. 'You got me in trouble, boy. I might get written up. If you aren't dumb, then you must need a lesson.' He spun me around and threw me down. I slid in the greasy alley snow. My elbow struck the ground and my arm went numb. The hand clutching a month of food, warm blankets, and dry shoes came open. Something precious flew away and landed without even a clink as it hit the ground.

I hardly noticed. The air hummed before his club cracked against my leg. He snarled at me, 'Don't come Hillside, understand?' The club caught me again, this time across the shoulder blades. 'Everything past Fallow Street is off limits to you little whore's sons. Understand?' he backhanded me across the face and I tasted blood as my head careened off the snow-covered cobbles.

I curled into a ball as he hissed down at me. 'And Mill Street and Mill Market is where I work, so you never. Come. Back. Here. Again.' He punctuated each word with a blow from his stick. 'Understand?'

I lay there shaking in the churned-up snow, hoping it was over. Hoping he would just go away. 'Understand?' He kicked me in the stomach and I felt something tear inside of me.

I cried out and must have babbled something. He kicked me again when I didn't get up, then went away.

I think I passed out or lay in a daze. When I finally came to my senses again, it was dusk. I was cold to the very center of my bones. I crawled around in the muddy snow and wet garbage, searching for the silver penny with fingers so numb with cold they would barely work.

One of my eyes was swelled shut and I could taste blood, but I searched until the last scrap of evening's light was gone. Even after the alley had gone black as tar I kept sifting the snow with my hands, though I knew in my heart of hearts that my fingers were too numb to feel the coin even if I chanced across it.

I used the wall to get to my feet and started to walk. My wounded foot made progress slow. Pain stabbed up my leg with each step, and I tried to use the wall as a crutch to keep some weight off it.

I moved into Waterside, the part of the city that was more a home to me than anywhere else. My foot grew numb and wooden from the cold, and while that worried some rational piece of me, my practical side was just glad there was one less part of me that hurt.

It was miles back to my secret place, and my limping progress was slow. At some point I must have fallen. I don't remember it, but I do remember lying in the snow and realising how delightfully comfortable it was. I felt sleep drawing itself over me like a thick blanket, like death.

I closed my eyes. I remember the deep silence of the deserted street around me. I was too numb and tired to be properly afraid. In my delirium, I imagined death in the form of a great bird with wings of fire and shadow. It hovered above, watching patiently, waiting for me . . .

I slept, and the great bird settled its burning wings around me. I imagined a delicious warmth. Then its claws were in me, tearing me open—

No, it was just the pain of my torn ribs as someone rolled me onto my back.

Blearily, I opened an eye and saw a demon standing over me. In my confused and credulous state, the sight of the man in the demon mask startled me into wakefulness, the seductive warmth I had felt a moment ago vanished, leaving my body limp and leaden.

'It *is*. I told you. There's a kid lying in the snow here!' The demon lifted me to my feet.

Now awake, I noticed his mask was sheer black. This was Encanis, Lord of Demons. He set me unsteadily onto my feet and began to brush away the snow that covered me.

Through my good eye I saw a figure in a livid green mask standing nearby. 'Come on . . .' the other demon said urgently, her voice sounding hollowly from behind the rows of pointed teeth.

Encanis ignored her. 'Are you okay?'

I couldn't think of a response, so I concentrated on keeping my balance as the man continued to brush the snow away with the sleeve of his dark robe. I heard the sound of distant horns.

The other demon looked nervously down the road. 'If we don't keep ahead of them we'll be up to our shins in it,' she hissed nervously.

Encanis brushed the snow out of my hair with his dark gloved fingers, then paused and leaned in closer to look at my face. His dark mask loomed oddly in my blurry vision.

'God's body, Holly, someone's beaten hell out of this kid. On Midwinter's Day, too.'

'Guard,' I managed to croak. I tasted blood when I said the word.

'You're freezing,' Encanis said and began to chafe my arms and legs with his hands, trying to get my blood flowing again. 'You'll have to come with us.'

The horns sounded again, closer. They were mixed with the dim sounds of a crowd.

'Don't be stupid,' the other demon said. 'He's in no shape to go running through the city.'

'He's in no shape to stay here,' Encanis snapped. He continued to massage my arms and legs roughly. Some feeling was slowly returning to them, mostly a stinging, prickly heat that was like a painful mockery of the soothing warmth I had felt a minute ago when I was drifting off to sleep. Pain jabbed at me each time he went over a bruise, but my body was too tired to flinch away.

The green-masked demon came close and laid a hand on her friend's shoulder. 'We have to go now, Gerrek! Someone else will take care of him.' She tried to pull her friend away and met with no success. 'If they find us here with him they'll assume we did it.'

The man behind the black mask swore, then nodded and began to rummage around underneath his robe. 'Don't lie down again,' he said to me in urgent tones. 'And get inside. Somewhere you can warm up.' The crowd sounds were close enough for me to hear individual voices mixed with the noise of horses' hooves and creaking wooden wheels. The man in the black mask held out his hand.

It took me a moment to focus on what he held. A silver talent, thicker and heavier than the penny I had lost. So much money I could hardly think of it. 'Go on, take it.'

He was a form of darkness, black hooded cloak, black mask, black gloves. Encanis stood in front of me holding out a bright bit of silver that caught the moonlight. I was reminded of the scene from *Daeonica* where Tarsus sells his soul.

I took the talent, but my hand was so numb I couldn't feel it. I had to look down to make sure my fingers were gripping it. I imagined I could feel warmth radiating up my arm, I felt stronger. I grinned at the man in the black mask.

'Take my gloves too.' He pulled them off and pushed them against my chest. Then the woman in the green demon mask pulled my benefactor away before I could give him any word of thanks. I watched the two of them go. Their dark robes made them look like pieces of retreating shadow against the charcoal colors of Tarbean's moonlit streets.

Not even a minute passed before I saw the pageantry's torchlight come around the corner towards me. The voices of a hundred men and women singing and shouting crashed over me like waves. I moved away until I felt my back press up against a wall, then I slid weakly sideways until I found a recessed doorway.

I watched the pageantry from my vantage there. People poured by, shouting and laughing. Tehlu stood tall and proud in the back of a wagon drawn by four white horses. His silver mask gleamed in the torchlight. His white robes were immaculate and lined with fur at the cuff and collar. Grey-robed priests followed along beside the wagon, ringing bells and chanting. Many of them wore the heavy iron chains of penitent priests. The sound of the voices and the bells, the chanting and the chains mingled to make a sort of music. All eyes were for Tehlu. No one saw me standing in the shadows of the doorway.

It took nearly ten minutes for all of them to pass, only then did I emerge and begin to make my careful way home. It was slow going, but I felt fortified by the coin I held. I checked the talent every dozen steps or so to reassure myself that my numb hand was still gripping it tightly. I wanted to put on the gloves I had been given, but I feared to drop the coin and lose it in the snow.

I don't know how long it took for me to get back. The walking warmed me slightly, though my feet still felt wooden and numb. When I looked back over my shoulder, my trail was marked by a smear of blood in every other footprint. It reassured me in an odd way. A foot that bleeds is better than one that is frozen solid.

I stopped at the first inn I recognised, the Laughing Man. It was full of music, singing, and celebration. I avoided the front door and went around to the back alley. There were a pair of young girls chatting in the kitchen doorway, avoiding their work.

I limped up to them, using the wall as a crutch. They didn't notice me until I was nearly on top of them. The younger one looked up at me and gasped.

I took a step closer. 'Could one of you bring me food and a blanket? I can pay.' I held out my hand and was frightened by how much it shook. It was smeared with blood from when I had touched the side of my face. The inside of my mouth felt raw. It hurt to talk. 'Please?'

They looked at me for a moment in stunned silence. Then they looked at each other and the older of the two motioned the other inside. The young girl disappeared through the door without a word. The older girl, who might have been sixteen, came closer to me and held out her hand.

I gave her the coin and let my arm fall heavily to my side. She looked at it and disappeared inside after a second long glance at me.

Through the open doorway I heard the warm, bustling sounds of a busy inn: the low murmur of conversation, punctuated with laughter, the bright clink of bottle glass, and the dull thump of wooden tankards on tabletops.

And, threading gently through it all, a lute played in the background. It was faint, almost drowned by the other noise, but I heard it the same way a mother can mark her child crying from a dozen rooms away. The music was like a memory of family, of friendship and warm belonging. It made my gut twist and my teeth ache. For a moment my hands stopped aching from the cold, and instead longed for the familiar feel of music running through them.

I took a slow, shuffling step. Slowly, sliding along the wall, I moved back away from the doorway until I couldn't hear the music anymore. Then I took another step, until my hands hurt with the cold again and the ache in my chest came from nothing more than broken ribs. They were simpler pains, easier to endure.

I don't know how long it was before the two girls came back. The younger one held out a blanket wrapped around something. I hugged it to my aching chest. It seemed disproportionately heavy for its size, but my arms were trembling slightly under their own weight, so it was hard to tell. The older girl held out a small, solid purse. I took it as well, clutching it so tightly my frostburned fingers ached.

She looked at me. 'You can have a corner by the fire in here if you want it.'

The younger girl nodded quickly. 'Nattie won't mind.' She took a step and reached out to take my arm.

I jerked away from her, almost falling. 'No!' I meant to shout but it came out as a weak croak, 'Don't touch me.' My voice was shaking, though I couldn't tell if I was angry or afraid. I staggered away against the wall. My voice was blurry in my ears. 'I'll be fine.'

The younger girl started to cry, her hands hanging useless at her sides.

'I've got somewhere to go.' My voice cracked and I turned away. I hurried off as fast as I could. I wasn't sure what I was running from, unless it was people. That was another lesson I had learned perhaps too well: people meant pain. I heard a few muffled sobs behind me. It seemed a long while before I made it to the corner.

I made it to my hidden place, where the roofs of two buildings met underneath the overhang of a third. I don't know how I managed to climb up there.

Inside the blanket was a whole flask of spiced wine and a loaf of fresh bread nestled next to a turkey breast bigger than both my balled fists. I wrapped myself in the blanket and moved out of the wind as the snow turned to sleet. The brick of the chimney behind me was warm and wonderful.

The first swallow of wine burned my mouth like fire where it was cut. But the second didn't sting nearly so much. The bread was soft and the turkey was still warm.

I woke at midnight when all the bells in the city started ringing. People ran and shouted in the streets. The seven days of High Mourning were behind us. Midwinter was past. A new year had begun.

CHAPTER TWENTY-THREE

The Burning Wheel

I STAYED TUCKED INTO my secret place all that night and woke late the next day to find my body had stiffened into a tight knot of pain. Since I still had food and a little wine I stayed where I was rather than risk falling when I tried to climb down to the street.

It was a sunless day with a damp wind that never seemed to stop. Sleet gusted under the protection of the overhanging roof. The chimney was warm behind me, but it wasn't enough to actually dry out my blanket or drive away the chilly damp that soaked my clothes.

I finished the wine and the bread early on, and after that I spent most of my time gnawing at the turkey bones and trying to warm up snow in the empty wine flask so I could drink it. Neither proved very productive, and I ended up eating mouthfuls of slushy snow that left me shivering with the taste of tar in my mouth.

Despite my injuries I dropped off to sleep in the afternoon and woke late at night filled with the most wonderful warmth. I pushed away my blanket and rolled away from the now too-hot chimney only to wake near dawn, shivering and soaked through to the skin. I felt strange, dizzy and fuddled. I huddled back against the chimney and spent the rest of the day drifting in and out of a restless, fevered sleep.

I have no memory of how I made it off the rooftop, delirious with fever and nearly crippled. I don't remember making my way the three-quarters of a mile through Tallows and the Crates. I only remember falling down the stairs that led to Trapis' basement, my purse of money clutched tight in my hand. As I lay there shivering and sweating I heard the faint slapping of his bare feet on the stone.

'What what,' he said gently as he picked me up. 'Hush hush.'

Trapis nursed me through the long days of my fever. He wrapped me in blankets, fed me, and when my fever showed no signs of breaking on its own, he used the money I'd brought to buy a bittersweet medicine. He kept my face and hands wet and cool while murmuring his patient, gentle, 'What what. Hush hush,' while I cried out from endless fever dreams of my dead parents, the Chandrian, and a man with empty eyes.

I woke clear-headed and cool.

'Oooohreeee,' Tanee said loudly from where he was tied to his cot.

'What what. Hush hush, Tanee.' Trapis said as he put down one of the babies and picked up the other. It looked around owlishly with wide, dark eyes, but seemed unable to support its own head. It was quiet in the room.

'Ooooooohreeee,' Tanee said again.

I coughed, trying to clear my throat.

'There's a cup on the floor next to you,' Trapis said, brushing a hand along the head of the baby he held.

'OOOOOH OOHRRRREE EEEEEEHHAA!' Tanee bellowed, strange half-gasps punctuating his cry. The noise agitated several of the others who moved restlessly in their cots. The older boy sitting in the corner raised his hands to the sides of his head and began to moan. He started rocking back and forth, gently at first, but then more and more violently so that when he came forward his head knocked against the bare stone of the wall.

Trapis was at his side before the boy could do himself any real harm. He put his arms around the rocking boy. 'Hush hush, Loni. Hush hush.' The boy's rocking slowed but did not entirely subside. 'Tanee, you know better than to make all that noise.' His voice was serious, but not stern. 'Why are you making trouble? Loni could hurt himself.'

'Oorrahee,' Tanee said softly. I thought I could detect a note of remorse in his voice.

'I think he wants a story,' I said, surprising myself by speaking.

'Aaaa,' Tanee said.

'Is that what you want, Tanee?'

'Aaaa.'

There was a quiet moment. 'I don't know any stories,' he said.

Tanee remained stubbornly silent.

Everyone knows one story, I thought. *Everyone knows at least one.*

'Ooooooree!'

Trapis looked around at the quiet room, as if looking for an excuse. 'Well,' he said reluctantly. 'It has been a while since we had a story, hasn't it?' He looked down at the boy in his arms. 'Would you like a story, Loni?'

Loni nodded a violent affirmation, nearly battering Trapis' cheek with the back of his head.

'Will you be good and sit by yourself, so I can tell a story?'

Loni stopped rocking almost immediately. Trapis slowly unwrapped his arms and stepped away. After a long look to make sure the boy wouldn't hurt himself, he stepped carefully back to his chair.

'Well,' he muttered softly to himself as he stooped to pick up the baby he had set aside. 'Do I have a story?' He spoke very quietly to the child's wide eyes. 'No. No, I don't. Can I remember one? I suppose I had better.'

He sat for a long moment, humming to the child in his arms, a thoughtful expression on his face. 'Yes, of course.' He sat up taller in his chair. 'Are you ready?'

———

This is a story from long ago. Back before any of us were born. Before our fathers were born, too. It was a long time ago. Maybe – maybe four hundred years. No, more than that. Probably a thousand years. But maybe not quite as much as that.

It was a bad time in the world. People were hungry and sick. There were famines and great plagues. There were many wars and other bad things in this time, because there was no one to stop them.

But the worst thing in this time was that there were demons walking the land. Some of them were small and troublesome, creatures who lamed horses and spoiled milk. But there were many worse than those.

There were demons who hid in men's bodies and made them sick or mad, but those were not the worst. There were demons like great beasts that would catch and eat men while they were still alive and screaming, but they were not the worst. Some demons stole the skins of men and wore them like clothes, but even they were not the worst.

There was one demon that stood above the others. Encanis, the swallowing darkness. No matter where he walked, shadows hid his face, and scorpions that stung him died of the corruption they had touched.

Now Tehlu, who made the world and who is lord over all, watched the world of men. He saw that demons made sport of us and killed us and ate our bodies. Some men he saved, but only a few. For Tehlu is just and saves only the worthy, and in these times few men acted even for their own good, let alone the good of others.

Because of this, Tehlu was unhappy. For he had made the world to be a good place for men to live. But his church was corrupt. They stole from the poor and did not live by the laws he had given . . .

No, wait. There was no church yet, and no priests either. Just men and women, and some of them knew who Tehlu was. But even those were wicked, so when they called on Lord Tehlu for help he felt no desire to aid them.

But after years of watching and waiting, Tehlu saw a woman pure of heart and spirit. Her name was Perial. Her mother had raised her to know Tehlu, and she worshiped him as well as her poor circumstances allowed. Although her own life was hard, Perial prayed only for others, and never for herself.

Tehlu watched her for long years. He saw her life was hard, full of misfortune and torment at the hands of demons and bad men. But she never cursed his name or ceased her praying, and she never treated any person other than with kindness and respect.

So late one night, Tehlu went to her in a dream. He stood before her, and seemed to be made entirely of fire or sunlight. He came to her in splendour and asked her if she knew who he was.

'Sure enough,' she said. You see, she was very calm about it because she thought she was just having an odd dream. 'You're Lord Tehlu.'

He nodded and asked her if she knew why he had come to her.

'Are you going to do something for my neighbor Deborah?' she asked. Because that's who she had prayed for before she went to sleep. 'Are you going to lay your hand on her husband Losel and make him a better man? The way he treats her isn't right. Man should never lay a hand on woman, save in love.'

Tehlu knew her neighbours. He knew they were wicked people who had done wicked things. Everyone in the village was wicked but her. Everyone in the world was. He told her so.

'Deborah has been very kind and good to me,' Perial said. 'And even Losel, who I don't care for, is one of my neighbours all the same.'

Tehlu told her that Deborah spent time in many different men's beds, and Losel drank every day of the week, even on Mourning. No, wait – there wasn't any Mourning yet. But he drank a lot at any rate. Sometimes he grew so angry that he beat his wife until she could not stand or even cry aloud.

Perial was quiet for a long moment in her dream. She knew Tehlu spoke the truth, but while Perial was pure of heart, she was not a fool. She had suspected her neighbours of doing the things Tehlu said. Even now that she knew for certain, she cared for her neighbours all the same. 'You won't help her?'

Tehlu said that the man and wife were each other's fitting punishment. They were wicked and the wicked should be punished.

Perial spoke out honestly, perhaps because she thought she was dreaming, but perhaps she would have said the same thing had she been awake, for Perial said what was in her heart. 'It's not their fault that the world is full of hard choices and hunger and loneliness,' she said. 'What can you expect of people when demons are their neighbours?'

But though Tehlu listened to her wise words with his ears, he told her that mankind was wicked, and the wicked should be punished.

'I think you know very little about what it is to be a man,' she said. 'And I would still help them if I could,' she told him resolutely.

SO YOU SHALL, Tehlu told her, and reached out to lay his hand on her heart. When he touched her she felt like she were a great golden bell that had just rung out its first note. She opened her eyes and knew then that it had been no normal dream.

Thus it was that she was not surprised to discover she was pregnant. In three months she gave birth to a perfect dark-eyed baby boy. She named him Menda. The day after he was born, Menda could crawl. In two days he could walk. Perial was surprised, but not worried, for she knew the child was a gift from God.

Nevertheless, Perial was wise. She knew that people might not understand. So she kept Menda close by her, and when her friends and neighbours came to visit, she sent them away.

But this could only last a little while, for in a small town there are no secrets. Folk knew that Perial was not married. And while children born out of wedlock were common during this time, children who grew to manhood in less than two months were not. They were afraid that she might have lain down with a demon, and that her child was a demon's child. Such things were not unheard of in those dark times, and the people were afraid.

So everyone gathered together on the first day of the seventh span, and made their way to the tiny house where Perial lived by herself with her son. The town smith, whose name was Rengen, led them. 'Show us the boy,' he yelled. But there was no response from the house. 'Bring out the boy, and show us he is nothing but a human child.'

The house remained quiet, and though there were many men among them, no one wanted to enter a house that might have a demon's child inside. So the smith cried out again, 'Perial, bring out young Menda, or we will burn your house around you.'

The door opened, and a man stepped out. None of them recognised who it was, because even though he was only seven span from the womb, Menda looked to be a young man of seventeen. He stood proud and tall, with coal-black hair and eyes. 'I am the one you think is Menda,' he said in a voice both powerful and deep. 'What do you want of me?'

The sound of his voice made Perial gasp inside the cottage. Not only was this the first time Menda had ever spoken, but she recognised his voice as the same one that had spoken to her in a dream, months ago.

'What do you mean, we think you are Menda?' asked the smith, gripping his hammer tightly. He knew that there were demons that looked like men, or wore their skins like costumes, the way a man might hide beneath a sheepskin.

The child who was not a child spoke again. 'I am Perial's son, but I am not Menda. And I am not a demon.'

'Touch the iron of my hammer then,' said Rengen, for he knew all demons feared two things, cold iron and clean fire. He held out his heavy forge hammer. It shook in his hands, but no one thought the less of him for it.

He who was not Menda stepped forward and lay both hands on the iron head of the hammer. Nothing happened. From the doorway of her house where she watched, Perial burst into tears, for though she trusted Tehlu, some part of her had held a mother's worry for her son.

'I am not Menda, though that is what my mother called me. I am Tehlu, lord above all. I have come to free you from demons and the wickedness of your own hearts. I am Tehlu, son of myself. Let the wicked hear my voice and tremble.'

And they did tremble. But some of them refused to believe. They called him a demon and threatened him. They spoke hard, frightened words. Some threw stones and cursed him, and spat toward him and his mother.

Then Tehlu grew angry, and he might have slain them all, but Perial leaped forward and laid a restraining hand on his shoulder. 'What more can you expect?' she asked him quietly. 'From men who live with demons for their neighbours? Even the best dog will bite that has been kicked enough.'

Tehlu considered her words and saw that she was wise. So he looked over his hands at Rengen, looked deep into his heart and said, 'Rengen, son of Engen, you have a mistress who you pay to lie with you. Some men come to you for work and you cheat or steal from them. And though you pray loudly, you do not believe I, Tehlu, made the world and watch over all who live here.'

When Rengen heard this, he grew pale and dropped his hammer to the ground. For what Tehlu said to him was true. Tehlu looked at all the men and women there. He looked into their hearts and spoke of what he saw. All of them were wicked, so much that Rengen was among the best of them.

Then Tehlu drew a line in the dirt of the road so that it lay between himself and all those who had come. 'This road is like the meandering course of a life. There are two paths to take, side by side. Each of you are already travelling that side. You must choose. Stay on your own path, or cross to mine.'

'But the road is the same, isn't it? It still goes to the same place,' someone asked.

'Yes.'

'Where does the road lead?'

'Death. All lives end in death, excepting one. Such is the way of things.'

'Then what does it matter which side a man is on?' It was Rengen asking these questions. He was a large man, one of the few that was taller than dark-eyed Tehlu. But he was shaken by all that he had seen and heard in the past few hours. 'What is on our side of the road?'

'Pain,' Tehlu said in a voice as hard and cold as stone. 'Punishment.'

'And your side?'

'Pain now,' Tehlu said in the same voice. 'Punishment now, for all that you have done. It cannot be avoided. But I am here too, this is my path.'

'How do I cross?'

'Regret, repent, and cross to me.'

Rengen stepped over the line to stand beside his God. Then Tehlu bent to pick up the hammer that the smith had dropped. But instead of giving it back, he struck Rengen with it as if it were a lash. Once. Twice. Thrice. And the third blow sent Rengen to his knees sobbing and crying out in pain. But after the third blow, Tehlu laid the hammer aside and knelt to look Rengen in the face. 'You were the first to cross,' he said softly so only the smith could hear. 'It was a brave thing, a hard thing to do. I am proud of you. You are no longer Rengen, now you are Wereth, the forger of the path.' Then

Tehlu embraced him with both arms, and his touch took much of the pain
from Rengen who was now Wereth. But not all, for Tehlu spoke truly when
he said that punishment cannot be avoided.

One by one they crossed, and one by one Tehlu struck them down with
the hammer. But after each man or woman fell, Tehlu knelt and spoke to
them, giving them new names and healing some of their hurt.

Many of the men and women had demons hiding inside them that fled
screaming when the hammer touched them. These people Tehlu spoke with
a while longer, but he always embraced them in the end, and they were all
grateful. Some of them danced for the joy of being free of such terrible
things living inside them.

In the end, seven stayed on the other side of the line. Tehlu asked them
three times if they would cross, and three times they refused. After the third
asking Tehlu sprang across the line and he struck each of them a great blow,
driving them to the ground.

But not all were men. When Tehlu struck the fourth, there was the sound
of quenching iron and the smell of burning leather. For the fourth man had
not been a man at all, but a demon wearing a man's skin. When it was
revealed, Tehlu grabbed the demon and broke it in his hands, cursing its
name and sending it back to the outer darkness that is the home of its kind.

The remaining three let themselves be struck down. None of them were
demons, though demons fled the bodies of some who fell. After he was done,
Tehlu did not speak to the six who did not cross, nor did he kneel to
embrace them and ease their wounds.

The next day, Tehlu set off to finish what he had begun. He walked from
town to town, offering each village he met the same choice he had given
before. Always the results were the same, some crossed, some stayed, some
were not men at all but demons, and those he destroyed.

But there was one demon who eluded Tehlu. Encanis, whose face was all
in shadow. Encanis, whose voice was like a knife in the minds of men.
Wherever Tehlu stopped to offer men the choice of path, Encanis had
been there just before, killing crops and poisoning wells. Encanis, setting men
to murder one another and stealing children from their beds at night.

At the end of seven years, Tehlu's feet had carried him all through the
world. He had driven out the demons that plagued us. All but one. Encanis
ran free and did the work of a thousand demons, destroying and despoiling
wherever he went.

So Tehlu chased and Encanis fled. Soon Tehlu was a span of days behind the demon, then two days, then half a day. Finally he was so close he felt the chill of Encanis' passing and could spy places where he had set his hands and feet, for they were marked with a cold, black frost.

Knowing he was pursued, Encanis came to a great city. The Lord of Demons called forth his power and the city was brought to ruin. He did this hoping Tehlu would delay so he could make his escape, but the Walking God paused only to appoint priests who cared for the people of the ruined town.

For six days Encanis fled, and six great cities he destroyed. But on the seventh day, Tehlu drew near before Encanis could bring his power to bear and the seventh city was saved. That is why seven is a lucky number, and why we celebrate on Caenin.

Encanis was now hard pressed and bent his whole thought upon escape. But on the eighth day Tehlu did not pause to sleep or eat. And thus it was that at the end of Felling Tehlu caught Encanis. He leaped on the demon and struck him with his forge hammer. Encanis fell like a stone, but Tehlu's hammer shattered and lay in the dust of the road.

Tehlu carried the demon's limp body all through the long night, and on the morning of the ninth day he came to the city of Atur. When men saw Tehlu carrying the demon's senseless form, they thought Encanis dead. But Tehlu knew that such a thing was not easily done. No simple blade or blow could kill him. No cell of bars could keep him safe within.

So Tehlu carried Encanis to the smithy. He called for iron, and people brought all they owned. Though he had taken no rest nor a morsel of food, all through the ninth day Tehlu laboured. While ten men worked the bellows, Tehlu forged the great iron wheel.

All night he worked, and when the first light of the tenth morning touched him, Tehlu struck the wheel one final time and it was finished. Wrought all of black iron, the wheel stood taller than a man. It had six spokes, each thicker than a hammer's haft, and its rim was a handspan across. It weighed as much as forty men, and was cold to the touch. The sound of its name was terrible, and none could speak it.

Tehlu gathered the people who were watching and chose a priest among them. Then he set them to dig a great pit in the center of the town, fifteen feet wide and twenty feet deep.

With the sun rising Tehlu laid the body of the demon on the wheel. At the first touch of iron, Encanis began to stir in his sleep. But Tehlu chained him tightly to the wheel, hammering the links together, sealing them tighter than any lock.

Then Tehlu stepped back, and all saw Encanis shift again, as if disturbed by an unpleasant dream. Then he shook and came awake entirely. Encanis strained against the chains, his body arching upward as he pulled against them. Where the iron touched his skin it felt like knives and needles and nails, like the searing pain of frost, like the sting of a hundred biting flies. Encanis thrashed on the wheel and began to howl as the iron burned and bit and froze him.

To Tehlu the sound was like a sweet music. He lay down on the ground beside the wheel and slept a deep sleep, for he was very tired.

When he awoke, it was evening of the tenth day. Encanis was still bound to the wheel, but he no longer howled and fought like a trapped animal. Tehlu bent and with great effort lifted one edge of the wheel and set it leaning against a tree that grew nearby. As soon as he came close, Encanis cursed him in languages no one knew, scratching and biting.

'You brought this on yourself,' Tehlu said.

That night there was a celebration. Tehlu sent men to cut a dozen evergreens and use them to kindle a bonfire in the bottom of the deep pit they had dug.

All night the townsfolk danced and sang around the burning fire. They knew the last and most dangerous of the world's demons was finally caught.

And all night Encanis hung from his wheel and watched them, motionless as a snake.

When the morning of the eleventh day came, Tehlu went to Encanis a third and final time. The demon looked worn and feral. His skin was sallow and his bones pressed tight against his skin. But his power still lay around him like a dark mantle, hiding his face in shadow.

'Encanis,' Tehlu said. 'This is your last chance to speak. Do it, for I know it is within your power.'

'Lord Tehlu, I am not Encanis.' For that brief moment the demon's voice was pitiful, and all who heard it were moved to sorrow. But then there was a sound like quenching iron, and the wheel rung like an iron bell. Encanis' body arched painfully at the sound then hung limply from his wrists as the ringing of the wheel faded.

'Try no tricks, dark one. Speak no lies,' Tehlu said sternly, his eyes as dark and hard as the iron of the wheel.

'What then?' Encanis hissed, his voice like the rasp of stone on stone. 'What? Rack and shatter you, what do you want of me?'

'Your road is very short, Encanis. But you may still choose a side on which to travel.'

Encanis laughed. 'You will give me the same choice you give the cattle? Yes then, I will cross to your side of the path, I regret and rep—'

The wheel rung again, like a great bell tolling long and deep. Encanis threw his body tight against the chains again and the sound of his scream shook the earth and shattered stones for half a mile in each direction.

When the sounds of wheel and scream had faded, Encanis hung panting and shaking from his chains. 'I told you to speak no lie, Encanis,' Tehlu said, pitiless.

'My path then!' Encanis shrieked. 'I do not regret! If I had my choice again, I would only change how fast I ran. Your people are like cattle my kind feed on! Bite and break you, if you gave me half an hour I would do such things that these wretched gawping peasants would go mad with fear. I would drink their children's blood and bathe in women's tears.' He might have said more, but his breath was short as he strained against the chains that held him.

'So,' Tehlu said, and stepped close to the wheel. For a moment it seemed like he would embrace Encanis, but he was merely reaching for the iron spokes of the wheel. Then, straining, Tehlu lifted the wheel above his head. He carried it, arms upstretched, towards the pit, and threw Encanis in.

Through the long hours of night, a dozen evergreens had fed the fire. The flames had died in the early morning, leaving a deep bed of sullen coals that glimmered when the wind brushed them.

The wheel struck flat, with Encanis on top. There was an explosion of spark and ash as it landed and sank inches deep into the hot coals. Encanis was held over the coals by the iron that bound and burned and bit at him.

Though he was held away from the fire itself, the heat was so intense that Encanis' clothes charred black and began to crumble without bursting into flame. The demon thrashed against his bonds, settling the wheel more firmly into the coals. Encanis screamed, because he knew that even demons can die from fire or iron. And though he was powerful, he was bound and burning. He felt the metal of the wheel grow hot beneath him, blackening the flesh of his arms and legs. Encanis screamed, and even as his skin began to smoke and char, his face was still hidden in a shadow that rose from him like a tongue of darkening flame.

Then Encanis grew silent, and the only sound was the hiss of sweat and blood as they fell from the demon's straining limbs. For a long moment everything was still. Encanis strained against the chains that held him to the wheel, and it seemed that he would strain until his muscles tore themselves from bone and sinew both.

Then there was a sharp sound like a bell breaking and the demon's arm jerked free of the wheel. Links of chain, now glowing red from the heat of the fire, flew upward to land smoking at the feet of those who stood above. The only sound was the sudden, wild laughter of Encanis, like breaking glass.

In a moment the demon's second hand was free, but before he could do more, Tehlu flung himself into the pit and landed with such force that the iron rang with it. Tehlu grabbed the hands of the demon and pressed them back against the wheel.

Encanis screamed in fury and in disbelief, for though he was forced back onto the burning wheel, and though he felt the strength of Tehlu was greater than chains he had broken, he saw Tehlu was burning in the flames.

'Fool!' he wailed. 'You will die here with me. Let me go and live. Let me go and I will trouble you no further.' And the wheel did not ring out, for Encanis was truly frightened.

'No,' said Tehlu. 'Your punishment is death. You will serve it.'

'Fool! Madling!' Encanis thrashed to no avail. 'You are burning in the flames with me, you will die as I do!'

'To ash all things return, so too this flesh will burn. But I am Tehlu. Son of myself. Father of myself. I was before, and I will be after. If I am a sacrifice then it is to myself alone. And if I am needed and called in the proper ways then I will come again to judge and punish.'

So Tehlu held him to the burning wheel, and none of the demon's threats or screaming moved him the least part of an inch. So it was that Encanis passed from the world, and with him went Tehlu who was Menda. Both of them burned to ash in the pit in Atur. That is why the Tehlin priests wear robes of ashen grey. And that is how we know Tehlu cares for us, and watches us, and keeps us safe from—

Trapis broke off his story as Jaspin began to howl and thrash against his restraints. I slid softly back into unconsciousness as soon as I no longer had the story to hold my attention.

After that, I began to harbour a suspicion that never entirely left me. Was Trapis a Tehlin priest? His robe was tattered and dirty, but it might have been the proper grey long ago. Parts of his story had been awkward and stumbling, but some were stately and grand, as if he had been reciting them from some half-forgotten memory. Of sermons? Of his readings from the *Book of the Path?*

I never asked. And though I stopped by his basement frequently in the months that followed, I never heard Trapis tell another story again.

CHAPTER TWENTY-FOUR

Shadows Themselves

THROUGH ALL MY TIME in Tarbean, I continued to learn, though most of the lessons were painful and unpleasant.

I learned how to beg. It was a very practical application of acting with a very difficult audience. I did it well, but Waterside money was tight and an empty begging bowl meant a cold, hungry night.

Through dangerous trial and error I discovered the proper way to slit a purse and pick a pocket. I was especially good at the latter. Locks and latches of all kinds soon gave up their secrets to me. My nimble fingers were put to a use my parents or Abenthy never would have guessed.

I learned to run from anyone with an unnaturally white smile. Denner resin slowly bleaches your teeth, so if a sweet-eater lives long enough for their teeth to grow fully white, chances are they have already sold everything they have worth selling. Tarbean is full of dangerous people, but none as dangerous as a sweet-eater filled with the desperate craving for more resin. They will kill you for a pair of pennies.

I learned how to lash together makeshift shoes out of rags. Real shoes became a thing of dreams for me. The first two years it seemed like my feet were always cold, or cut, or both. But by the third year my feet were like old leather and I could run barefoot for hours over the rough stones of the city and not feel it at all.

I learned not to expect help from anyone. In the bad parts of Tarbean a call for help attracts predators like the smell of blood on the wind.

I was sleeping on the rooftops, snugged tightly into my secret place where three roofs met. I awoke from a deep sleep to the sound of harsh laughter and pounding feet in the alley below me.

The slapping footsteps stopped and more laughter followed the sound of ripping cloth. Slipping to the edge of the roof, I looked down to the alley below. I saw several large boys, almost men. They were dressed as I was, rags and dirt. There may have been five, maybe six of them. They moved in and out of the shadows like shadows themselves. Their chests heaved from their run and I could hear their breath from the roof above.

The object of the chase was in the middle of the alley: a young boy, eight years old at the most. One of the older boys was holding him down. The young boy's bare skin shone pale in the moonlight. There was another sound of ripping cloth, and the boy gave a soft cry that ended in a choked sob.

The others watched and talked in low urgent tones with each other, wearing hard, hungry smiles.

I'd been chased before at night, several times. I'd been caught too, months ago. Looking down, I was surprised to find a heavy red roof tile in my hand, ready to throw.

Then I paused, looking back to my secret place. I had a rag blanket and a half a loaf of bread there. My rainy-day money was hidden here, eight iron pennies I had hoarded for when my luck turned bad. And most valuable of all, Ben's book. I was safe here. Even if I hit one of them, the rest would be on the roof in two minutes. Then, even if I got away, I wouldn't have anywhere to go.

I set down the tile. I went back to what had become my home, and curled myself into the shelter of the niche underneath the overhanging roof. I twisted my blanket in my hands and clenched my teeth, trying to shut out the low rumble of conversation punctuated by coarse laughter and quiet, hopeless sobbing from below.

CHAPTER TWENTY-FIVE

Interlude — Eager for Reasons

KVOTHE GESTURED FOR CHRONICLER to set down his pen and stretched, lacing his fingers together above his head. 'It's been a long time since I remembered that,' he said. 'If you are eager to find the reason I became the Kvothe they tell stories about, you could look there, I suppose.'

Chronicler's forehead wrinkled. 'What do you mean, exactly?'

Kvothe paused for a long moment, looking down at his hands. 'Do you know how many times I've been beaten over the course of my life?'

Chronicler shook his head.

Looking up, Kvothe grinned and tossed his shoulders in a nonchalant shrug. 'Neither do I. You'd think that sort of thing would stick in a person's mind. You'd think I would remember how many bones I've had broken. You'd think I'd remember the stitches and bandages.' He shook his head. 'I don't. I remember that young boy sobbing in the dark. Clear as a bell after all these years.'

Chronicler frowned. 'You said yourself that there was nothing you could have done.'

'I could have,' Kvothe said seriously, 'and I didn't. I made my choice and I regret it to this day. Bones mend. Regret stays with you forever.'

Kvothe pushed himself away from the table. 'That's enough of Tarbean's darker side, I imagine.' He came to his feet and gave a great stretch, arms over his head.

'Why, Reshi?' The words poured out of Bast in a sudden gush. 'Why did you stay there when it was so awful?'

Kvothe nodded to himself, as if he had been expecting the question. 'Where else was there for me to go, Bast? Everyone I knew was dead.'

'Not everyone,' Bast insisted. 'There was Abenthy. You could have gone to him.'

'Hallowfell was hundreds of miles away, Bast,' Kvothe said wearily as he wandered to the other side of the room and moved behind the bar. 'Hundreds of miles without my father's maps to guide me. Hundreds of miles without wagons to ride or sleep in. Without help of any sort, or money, or shoes. Not an impossible journey, I suppose. But for a young child, still numb with the shock of losing his parents . . .'

Kvothe shook his head. 'No. In Tarbean at least I could beg or steal. I'd managed to survive in the forest for a summer, barely. But over the winter?' He shook his head. 'I would have starved or frozen to death.'

Standing at the bar, Kvothe filled his mug and began to add pinches of spice from several small containers, then walked toward the great stone fireplace, a thoughtful expression on his face. 'You're right, of course. Anywhere would have been better than Tarbean.'

He shrugged, facing the fire. 'But we are all creatures of habit. It is far too easy to stay in the familiar ruts we dig for ourselves. Perhaps I even viewed it as fair. My punishment for not being there to help when the Chandrian came. My punishment for not dying when I should have, with the rest of my family.'

Bast opened his mouth, then closed it and looked down at the tabletop, frowning.

Kvothe looked over his shoulder and gave a gentle smile. 'I'm not saying it's rational, Bast. Emotions by their very nature are not reasonable things. I don't feel that way now, but back then I did. I remember.' He turned back to the fire. 'Ben's training has given me a memory so clean and sharp I have to be careful not to cut myself sometimes.'

Kvothe took a mulling stone from the fire and dropped it into his wooden mug. It sank with a sharp hiss. The smell of searing clove and nutmeg filled the room.

Kvothe stirred his cider with a long-handled spoon as he made his way back to the table. 'You must also remember that I was not in my right mind. Much of me was still in shock, sleeping if you will. I needed something, or someone, to wake me up.'

He nodded to Chronicler, who casually shook his writing hand to loosen it, then unstoppered his inkwell.

Kvothe leaned back in his seat. 'I needed to be reminded of things I had forgotten. I needed a reason to leave. It was years before I met someone who could do those things.' He smiled at Chronicler. 'Before I met Skarpi.'

CHAPTER TWENTY-SIX

Lanre Turned

I HAD BEEN IN Tarbean for years at this point. Three birthdays had slipped by unnoticed and I was just past fifteen. I knew how to survive Waterside. I had become an accomplished beggar and thief. Locks and pockets opened to my touch. I knew which pawnshops bought goods 'from uncle' with no questions asked.

I was still ragged and frequently hungry, but I was in no real danger of starving. I had been slowly building my rainy-day money. Even after a hard winter that had frequently forced me to pay for a warm spot to sleep, my hoard was over twenty iron pennies. It was like a dragon's treasure to me.

I had grown comfortable there. But aside from the desire to add to my rainy-day money I had nothing to live for. Nothing driving me. Nothing to look forward to. My days were spent looking for things to steal and ways to entertain myself.

But that had changed a few days earlier in Trapis' basement. I had heard a young girl speaking in an awed voice about a storyteller who spent all his time in a Dockside bar called the Half-Mast. Apparently, every sixth bell he told a story. Any story you asked for, he knew. What's more, she said that he had a bet going. If he didn't know your story, he would give you a whole talent.

I thought about what the girl had said for the rest of the day. I doubted it was true, but I couldn't help thinking about what I could do with a whole silver talent. I could buy shoes, and maybe a knife, give money to Trapis, and still double my rainy-day fund.

Even if the girl was lying about the bet, I was still interested. Entertainment was hard to come by on the streets. Occasionally some ragamuffin troupe would mum a play on a street corner or I'd hear a fiddler in a pub. But most real entertainment cost money, and my hard-won pennies were too precious to squander.

But there was a problem. Dockside wasn't safe for me.

I should explain. More than a year before, I had seen Pike walking down the street. It had been the first time I'd seen him since my first day in Tarbean when he and his friends had jumped me in that alley and destroyed my father's lute.

I followed him carefully for the better part of a day, keeping my distance and staying in the shadows. Eventually he went home to a little box alley Dockside where he had his own version of my secret place. His was a nest of broken crates he had cobbled together to keep the weather off.

I perched on the roof all night, waiting until he left the next morning. Then I made my way down to his nest of crates and looked around. It was cozy, filled with the accumulated small possessions of several years. He had a bottle of beer, which I drank. There was also half a cheese that I ate, and a shirt that I stole, as it was slightly less raggedy than my own.

Further searching revealed various odds and ends, a candle, a ball of string, some marbles. Most surprising were several pieces of sailcloth with charcoal drawings of a woman's face. I had to search for nearly ten minutes until I found what I was really looking for. Hidden away behind everything else was a small wooden box that showed signs of much handling. It held a bundle of dried violets tied with a white ribbon, a toy horse that had lost most of its string mane, and a lock of curling blond hair.

It took me several minutes with flint and steel to get the fire going. The violets were good tinder and soon greasy clouds of smoke were billowing high into the air. I stood by and watched as everything Pike loved went up in flames.

But I stayed too long, savouring the moment. Pike and a friend came running down the box alley, drawn by the smoke, and I was trapped. Furious, Pike jumped me. He was taller by six inches and outweighed me by fifty pounds. Worse, he had a piece of broken glass wrapped with twine at one end, making a crude knife.

He stabbed me once in the thigh right above my knee before I smashed his hand into the cobblestones, shattering the knife. After that he still gave me a black eye and several broken ribs before I managed to kick him squarely between the legs and get free. As I pelted away he limped after me, shouting that he would kill me for what I'd done.

I believed him. After patching up my leg, I took every bit of rainy-day money I had saved and bought five pints of dreg, a cheap, foul liquor strong enough to blister the inside of your mouth. Then I limped into Dockside and waited for Pike and his friends to spot me.

It didn't take long, I let him and two of his friends follow me for half a mile, past Seamling Lane and into Tallows. I kept to the main roads, knowing they wouldn't dare attack me in broad daylight when people were around.

But when I darted into a side alley, they hurried to catch up, suspecting I was trying to make a run for it. However, when they turned the corner no one was there.

Pike thought to look up just as I was pouring the bucket of dreg onto him from the edge of the low roof above. It doused him, splashing across his face and chest. He screamed and clutched at his eyes as he went to his knees. Then I struck the phosphorus match I'd stolen, and dropped it onto him, watching it sputter and flare as it fell.

Full of the pure, hard hatred of a child, I hoped he would burst into a pillar of flame. He didn't, but did catch fire. He screamed again and staggered around while his friends swatted at him, trying to put him out. I left while they were busy.

It had been over a year ago and I hadn't seen Pike since. He hadn't tried to find me, and I had stayed well clear of Dockside, sometimes going miles out of my way rather than pass near it. It was a kind of truce. However, I didn't doubt that Pike and his friends remembered what I looked like, and were willing to settle the score if they spotted me.

After thinking it over, I decided it was too dangerous. Even the promise of free stories and a chance at a silver talent wasn't worth stirring things up with Pike again. Besides, what story would I ask for?

The question rolled around in my head for the next few days. What story would I ask for? I jostled up against a dockworker and was cuffed away before I could get my hand all the way into his pocket. What story? I begged on the street corner opposite the Tehlin church. What story? I stole three loaves of bread and took two of them down to Trapis as a gift. What story?

Then, as I lay on the rooftops in my secret place where three roofs met, it came to me just as I was about to drift off to sleep. Lanre. Of course. I could ask him for the real story of Lanre. The story my father had been . . .

My heart stuttered in my chest as I suddenly remembered things I had avoided for years: my father idly strumming at his lute, my mother beside him in the wagon, singing. Reflexively, I began to draw away from the memories, the way you might pull your hand back from a fire.

But I was surprised to find these memories held only a gentle ache, not the deep pain I expected. Instead I found a small, budding excitement at the thought of hearing a story my father would have sought out. A story he himself might have told.

Still, I knew it to be sheer folly to go running Dockside for the sake of a story. All the hard practicality Tarbean had taught me over the years urged me to stay in my familiar corner of the world, where I was safe . . .

———

The first thing I saw on entering the Half-Mast was Skarpi. He was sitting on a tall stool at the bar, an old man with eyes like diamonds and the body of a driftwood scarecrow. He was thin and weathered with thick white hair on his arms and face and head. The whiteness of it stood out from his deep brown tan, making him seem splashed with wave foam.

At his feet were a group of twenty children, some few my age, most younger. They were a strange mix to see, ranging from grubby, shoeless urchins like myself, to reasonably well-dressed, well-scrubbed children who probably had parents and homes.

None of them looked familiar to me, but I never knew who might be a friend of Pike's. I found a place near the door with my back to the wall and sank down onto my haunches.

Skarpi cleared his throat once or twice in a way that made me thirsty. Then, with ritual significance, he looked mournfully into the clay mug that sat in front of him and carefully turned it upside down on the bar.

The children surged forward, pressing coins onto the bar. I did a quick count: two iron halfpennies, nine shims, and a drab. Altogether, just a little over three iron pennies in Commonwealth coin. Maybe he was no longer offering the silver talent bet. More likely the rumour I'd heard was wrong.

The old man nodded almost imperceptibility to the bartender. 'Fallows Red.' His voice was deep and rough, almost hypnotic. The bald man behind the bar gathered up the coins and deftly poured wine into Skarpi's wide clay cup.

'So, what would everyone like to hear about today?' Skarpi rumbled. His deep voice rolling out like distant thunder.

There was a moment of silence that again struck me as ritualistic, almost reverent. Then a babble burst forth from all the children at once.

'I want a faerie story!'

'. . . Oren and the fight at Mnat's . . .'

'Yes, Oren Velciter! The one with Baron . . .'

'Lartam . . .'

'Myr Tariniel!'

'Illien and the Bear!'

'Lanre,' I said, almost without meaning to.

The room went still again as Skarpi took a drink. The children watched him with a familiar intensity I couldn't quite identify.

Skarpi sat calmly in the middle of the quiet. 'Did I,' his voice rolled out slowly, like dark honey, 'hear someone say Lanre?' He looked directly at me, his blue eyes clear and sharp.

I nodded, not knowing what to expect.

'I want to hear about the dry lands over the Stormwal,' one of the younger girls complained. 'About the sand snakes that come out of the ground like sharks. And the dry men who hide under the dunes and drink your blood instead of water. And—' She was cuffed quickly into silence from a dozen different directions by the children surrounding her.

Silence fell sharply as Skarpi took another drink. Watching the children as they watched Skarpi, I realised what they reminded me of: a person anxiously watching a clock. I guessed that when the old man's drink was gone, the story he told would be over as well.

Skarpi took another drink, no more than a sip this time, then set his cup down and pivoted on his stool to face us. 'Who would like to hear the story of a man who lost his eye and gained a better sight?'

Something about the tone of his voice or the reaction of the other children told me this was a purely rhetorical question. 'So, Lanre and the Creation War. An old, old story.' His eyes swept over the children. 'Sit and listen for I will speak of the shining city as it once was, years and miles away . . .'

Once, years and miles away, there was Myr Tariniel. The shining city. It sat among the tall mountains of the world like a gem on the crown of a king.

Imagine a city as large as Tarbean, but on every corner of every street there was a bright fountain, or a green tree growing, or a statue so beautiful it would make a proud man cry to look at it. The buildings were tall and graceful, carved from the mountain itself, carved of a bright white stone that held the sun's light long after evening fell.

Selitos was lord over Myr Tariniel. Just by looking at a thing Selitos could see its hidden name and understand it. In those days there were many who could do such things, but Selitos was the most powerful namer of anyone alive in that age.

Selitos was well loved by the people he protected. His judgments were strict and fair, and none could sway him through falsehood or dissembling. Such was the power of his sight that he could read the hearts of men like heavy-lettered books.

Now in those days there was a terrible war being fought across a vast empire. The war was called the Creation War, and the empire was called Ergen. And despite the fact that the world has never seen an empire as grand or a war so terrible, both of them only live in stories now. Even history books that mentioned them as doubtful rumour have long since crumbled into dust.

The war had lasted so long that folk could hardly remember a time when the sky wasn't dark with the smoke of burning towns. Once there had been hundreds of proud cities scattered through the empire. Now there were merely ruins littered with the bodies of the dead. Famine and plague were everywhere, and in some places there was such despair that mothers could no longer muster enough hope to give their children names. But eight cities remained. They were Belen, Antus, Vaeret, Tinusa, Emlen, and the twin cities of Murilla and Murella. Last was Myr Tariniel, greatest of them all and the only one unscarred by the long centuries of war. It was protected by the mountains and brave soldiers. But the true cause of Myr Tariniel's peace was Selitos. Using the power of his sight he kept watch over the mountain passes leading to his beloved city. His rooms were in the city's highest towers so he could see any attack long before it came to be a threat.

The other seven cities, lacking Selitos' power, found their safety elsewhere. They put their trust in thick walls, in stone and steel. They put their trust in strength of arm, in valour and bravery and blood. And so they put their trust in Lanre.

Lanre had fought since he could lift a sword, and by the time his voice began to crack he was the equal of a dozen older men. He married a woman named Lyra, and his love for her was a passion fiercer than fury.

Lyra was terrible and wise, and held a power just as great as his. For while Lanre had the strength of his arm and the command of loyal men, Lyra knew the names of things, and the power of her voice could kill a man or still a thunderstorm.

As the years passed, Lanre and Lyra fought side by side. They defended Belen from a surprise attack, saving the city from a foe that should have overwhelmed them. They gathered armies and made the cities recognise the need for allegiance. Over the long years they pressed the empire's enemies back. People who had grown numb with despair began to feel warm hope kindling inside. They hoped for peace, and they hung those flickering hopes on Lanre.

Then came the Blac of Drossen Tor. *Blac* meant 'battle' in the language of the time, and at Drossen Tor there was the largest and most terrible battle of this large and terrible war. They fought unceasing for three days in the light of the sun, and for three nights unceasing by the light of the moon. Neither side could defeat the other, and both were unwilling to retreat.

Of the battle itself I have only one thing to say. More people died at Drossen Tor than there are living in the world today.

Lanre was always where the fight was thickest, where he was needed most. His sword never left his hand or rested in its sheath. At the very end of things, covered in blood amid a field of corpses, Lanre stood alone against a terrible foe. It was a great beast with scales of black iron, whose breath was a darkness that smothered men. Lanre fought the beast and killed it. Lanre brought victory to his side, but he bought it with his life.

After the battle was finished and the enemy was set beyond the doors of stone, survivors found Lanre's body, cold and lifeless near the beast he had slain. Word of Lanre's death spread quickly, covering the field like a blanket of despair. They had won the battle and turned the tide of the war, but each of them felt cold inside. The small flame of hope that each of them cherished began to flicker and fade. Their hopes had hung on Lanre, and Lanre was dead.

In the midst of silence Lyra stood by Lanre's body and spoke his name. Her voice was a commandment. Her voice was steel and stone. Her voice told him to live again. But Lanre lay motionless and dead.

In the midst of fear Lyra knelt by Lanre's body and breathed his name. Her voice was a beckoning. Her voice was love and longing. Her voice called him to live again. But Lanre lay cold and dead.

In the midst of despair Lyra fell across Lanre's body and wept his name. Her voice was a whisper. Her voice was echo and emptiness. Her voice begged him to live again. But Lanre lay breathless and dead.

Lanre was dead. Lyra wept brokenly and touched his face with trembling hands. All around men turned their heads, because the bloody field was less horrible to look upon than Lyra's grief.

But Lanre heard her calling. Lanre turned at the sound of her voice and came to her. From beyond the doors of death Lanre returned. He spoke her name and took Lyra in his arms to comfort her. He opened his eyes and did his best to wipe away her tears with shaking hands. And then he drew a deep and living breath.

The survivors of the battle saw Lanre move and they marvelled. The flickering hope for peace each of them had nurtured for so long flared like hot fire inside them.

'Lanre and Lyra!' they shouted, their voices like thunder. 'Our lord's love is stronger than death! Our lady's voice has called him back! Together they have beaten death! Together, how can we help but be victorious?'

So the war continued, but with Lanre and Lyra fighting side by side the future seemed less grim. Soon everyone knew the story of how Lanre had died, and how his love and Lyra's power had drawn him back. For the first time in living memory people could speak openly of peace without being seen as fools or madmen.

Years passed. The empire's enemies grew thin and desperate and even the most cynical of men could see the end of the war was drawing swiftly near.

Then rumours began to spread: Lyra was ill. Lyra had been kidnapped. Lyra had died. Lanre had fled the empire. Lanre had gone mad. Some even said Lanre had killed himself and gone searching for his wife in the land of the dead. There were stories aplenty, but no one knew the truth of things.

In the midst of these rumours, Lanre arrived in Myr Tariniel. He came alone, wearing his silver sword and haubergeon of black iron scales. His armour fit him closely as a second skin of shadow. He had wrought it from the carcass of the beast he had killed at Drossen Tor.

Lanre asked Selitos to walk with him outside the city. Selitos agreed, hoping to learn the truth of Lanre's trouble and offer him what comfort a friend can give. They often kept each other's counsel, for they were both lords among their people.

Selitos had heard the rumours, and he was worried. He feared for Lyra's health, but more he feared for Lanre. Selitos was wise. He understood how grief can twist a heart, how passions drive good men to folly.

Together they walked the mountain paths. Lanre leading the way, they came to a high place in the mountains where they could look out over the land. The proud towers of Myr Tariniel shone brightly in the last light of the setting sun.

After a long time Selitos said, 'I have heard terrible rumours concerning your wife.'

Lanre said nothing, and from his silence Selitos knew that Lyra was dead.

After another long pause Selitos tried again. 'Though I do not know the whole of the matter, Myr Tariniel is here for you, and I will lend whatever aid a friend can give.'

'You have given me enough, old friend.' Lanre turned and placed his hand on Selitos' shoulder. '*Silanxi,* I bind you. By the name of stone, be still as stone. *Aeruh,* I command the air. Lay leaden on your tongue. *Selitos,* I name you. May all your powers fail you but your sight.'

Selitos knew that in all the world there were only three people who could match his skill in names: Aleph, Iax, and Lyra. Lanre had no gift for names – his power lay in the strength of his arm. For him to attempt to bind Selitos by his name would be as fruitless as a boy attacking a soldier with a willow stick.

Nevertheless, Lanre's power lay on him like a great weight, like a vise of iron, and Selitos found himself unable to move or speak. He stood, still as stone and could do nothing but marvel: how had Lanre come by such power?

In confusion and despair, Selitos watched night settle in the mountains. With horror he saw that some of the encroaching blackness was, in fact, a great army moving upon Myr Tariniel. Worse still, no warning bells were ringing. Selitos could only stand and watch as the army crept closer in secret.

Myr Tariniel was burned and butchered, the less that is said of it the better. The white walls were charred black and the fountains ran with blood. For a night and a day Selitos stood helpless beside Lanre and could do nothing more than watch and listen to the screams of the dying, the ring of iron, the crack of breaking stone.

When the next day dawned on the blackened towers of the city, Selitos found he could move. He turned to Lanre and this time his sight did not fail him. He saw in Lanre a great darkness and a troubled spirit. But Selitos still felt the fetters of enchantment binding him. Fury and puzzlement warred within him, and he spoke. 'Lanre, what have you done?'

Lanre continued to look out over the ruins of Myr Tariniel. His shoulders stooped as though he bore a great weight. There was a weariness in his voice when he spoke. 'Was I accounted a good man, Selitos?'

'You were counted among the best of us. We considered you beyond reproach.'

'Yet I did this.'

Selitos could not bring himself to look upon his ruined city. 'Yet you did this,' he agreed. 'Why?'

Lanre paused. 'My wife is dead. Deceit and treachery brought me to it, but her death is on my hands.' He swallowed and turned to look out over the land.

Selitos followed his eyes. From the vantage high in the mountains he saw plumes of dark smoke rising from the land below. Selitos knew with certainty and horror that Myr Tariniel was not the only city that had been destroyed. Lanre's allies had brought about the ruin of the last bastions of the empire.

Lanre turned. 'And I *counted among the best*.' Lanre's face was terrible to look upon. Grief and despair had ravaged it. 'I, considered wise and good, did all this!' He gestured wildly. 'Imagine what unholy things a lesser man must hold within his secret heart.' Lanre faced Myr Tariniel and a sort of peace came over him. 'For them, at least, it is over. They are safe. Safe from the thousand evils of the everyday. Safe from the pains of an unjust fate.'

Selitos spoke softly, 'Safe from the joy and wonder . . .'

'There is no joy!' Lanre shouted in an awful voice. Stones shattered at the sound and the sharp edges of echo came back to cut at them. 'Any joy that grows here is quickly choked by weeds. I am not some monster who destroys out of a twisted pleasure. I sow salt because the choice is between weeds and nothing.' Selitos saw nothing but emptiness behind his eyes.

Selitos stooped to pick up a jagged shard of mountain glass, pointed at one end.

'Will you kill me with a stone?' Lanre gave a hollow laugh. 'I wanted you to understand, to know it was not madness that made me do these things.'

'You are not mad,' Selitos admitted. 'I see no madness in you.'

'I hoped, perhaps, that you would join me in what I aim to do.' Lanre spoke with a desperate longing in his voice. 'This world is like a friend with a mortal wound. A bitter draught given quickly only eases pain.'

'Destroy the world?' Selitos said softly to himself. 'You are not mad, Lanre.

What grips you is something worse than madness. I cannot cure you.' He fingered the needle-sharp point of the stone he held.

'Will you kill me to cure me, old friend?' Lanre laughed again, terrible and wild. Then he looked at Selitos with sudden, desperate hope in his hollow eyes. 'Can you?' he asked. 'Can you kill me, old friend?'

Selitos, his eyes unveiled, looked at his friend. He saw how Lanre, nearly mad with grief, had sought the power to bring Lyra back to life again. Out of love for Lyra, Lanre had sought knowledge where knowledge is better left alone, and gained it at a terrible price.

But even in the fullness of his hard-won power, he could not call Lyra back. Without her, Lanre's life was nothing but a burden, and the power he had taken up lay like a hot knife in his mind. To escape despair and agony, Lanre had killed himself. Taking the final refuge of all men, attempting to escape beyond the doors of death.

But just as Lyra's love had drawn him back from past the final door before, so this time Lanre's power forced him to return from sweet oblivion. His new-won power burned him back into his body, forcing him to live.

Selitos looked at Lanre and understood all. Before the power of his sight, these things hung like dark tapestries in the air about Lanre's shaking form.

'I can kill you,' Selitos said, then looked away from Lanre's expression suddenly hopeful. 'For an hour, or a day. But you would return, pulled like iron to a loden-stone. Your name burns with the power in you. I can no more extinguish it than I could throw a stone and strike down the moon.'

Lanre's shoulders bowed. 'I had hoped,' he said simply. 'But I knew the truth. I am no longer the Lanre you knew. Mine is a new and terrible name. I am Haliax and no door can bar my passing. All is lost to me, no Lyra, no sweet escape of sleep, no blissful forgetfulness, even madness is beyond me. Death itself is an open doorway to my power. There is no escape. I have only the hope of oblivion after everything is gone and the Aleu fall nameless from the sky.' And as he said this Lanre hid his face in his hands, and his body shook with silent, racking sobs.

Selitos looked out on the land below and felt a small spark of hope. Six plumes of smoke rose from the land below. Myr Tariniel was gone, and six cities destroyed. But that meant all was not lost. One city still remained . . .

In spite of all that had happened, Selitos looked at Lanre with pity, and when he spoke it was with sadness in his voice. 'Is there nothing, then? No hope?' He lay one hand on Lanre's arm. 'There is sweetness in life. Even after all of this, I will help you look for it. If you will try.'

'No,' said Lanre. He stood to his full height, his face regal behind the lines of grief. 'There is nothing sweet. I will sow salt, lest the bitter weeds grow.'

'I am sorry,' Selitos said, and stood upright as well.

Then Selitos spoke in a great voice, 'Never before has my sight been clouded. I failed to see the truth inside your heart.'

Selitos drew a deep breath. 'By my eye I was deceived, never again . . .' He raised the stone and drove its needle point into his own eye. His scream echoed among the rocks as he fell to his knees gasping. 'May I never again be so blind.'

A great silence descended, and the fetters of enchantment fell away from Selitos. He cast the stone at Lanre's feet and said, 'By the power of my own blood I bind you. By your own name let you be accursed.'

Selitos spoke the long name that lay in Lanre's heart, and at the sound of it the sun grew dark and wind tore stones from the mountainside.

Then Selitos spoke. 'This is my doom upon you. May your face be always held in shadow, black as the toppled towers of my beloved Myr Tariniel.

'This is my doom upon you. Your own name will be turned against you, that you shall have no peace.

'This is my doom upon you and all who follow you. May it last until the world ends and the Aleu fall nameless from the sky.'

Selitos watched as a darkness gathered about Lanre. Soon nothing could be seen of his handsome features, only a vague impression of nose and mouth and eyes. All the rest was shadow, black and seamless.

Then Selitos stood and said, 'You have beaten me once through guile, but never again. Now I see truer than before and my power is upon me. I cannot kill you, but I can send you from this place. Begone! The sight of you is all the fouler, knowing that you once were fair.'

But even as he spoke them, the words were bitter in his mouth. Lanre, his face in shadow darker than a starless night, was blown away like smoke upon the wind.

Then Selitos bowed his head and wept hot tears of blood upon the earth.

———

It wasn't until Skarpi stopped speaking that I noticed how lost in the story I had become. He tilted his head back and drained the last of the wine from his wide clay cup. He turned it upside-down and set it on the bar with a dull thump of finality.

There was a small clamour of questions, comments, pleas, and thanks from children who had remained still as stones throughout the story. Skarpi made a small gesture to the barkeep who set out a mug of beer as the children began to trickle out onto the street.

I waited until the last of them had left before I approached him. He turned those diamond-blue eyes on me and I stammered.

'Thank you. I wanted to thank you. My father would have loved that story. It's the . . .' I broke off. 'I wanted to give you this.' I brought out an iron halfpenny. 'I didn't know what was going on, so I didn't pay.' My voice seemed rusty. This was probably more than I had spoken in a month.

He looked closely at me. 'Here are the rules,' he said, ticking them off on his gnarled fingers. 'One: don't talk while I'm talking. Two: give a small coin, *if* you have it to spare.'

He looked at the ha'penny on the bar.

Not wanting to admit how much I needed it, I sought for something else to say. 'Do you know many stories?'

He smiled, and the network of lines that crossed his face turned to make themselves part of that smile. 'I only know one story. But oftentimes small pieces seem to be stories themselves.' He took a drink. 'It's growing all around us. In the manor houses of the Cealdim and in the workshops of the Cealdar, over the Stormwal in the great sand sea. In the low stone houses of the Adem, full of silent conversation. And sometimes.' He smiled. 'Sometimes the story is growing in squalid backstreet bars, Dockside in Tarbean.' His bright eyes looked deep into me, as if I were a book that he could read.

'There's no good story that doesn't touch the truth,' I said, repeating something my father used to say, mostly to fill the silence. It felt strange talking to someone again, strange but good. 'There's as much truth here as anywhere, I suppose. It's too bad, the world could do with a little less truth and a little more . . .' I trailed off, not knowing what I wanted more of. I looked down at my hands and found myself wishing they were cleaner.

He slid the halfpenny towards me. I picked it up and he smiled. His rough hand lit lightly as a bird on my shoulder. 'Every day except Mourning. Sixth bell, more or less.'

I started to leave, then stopped. 'Is it true? The story.' I made an inarticulate gesture. 'The part you told today?'

'All stories are true,' Skarpi said. 'But this one really happened, if that's what you mean.' He took another slow drink, then smiled again, his bright eyes dancing. 'More or less. You have to be a bit of a liar to tell a story the right way. Too much truth confuses the facts. Too much honesty makes you sound insincere.'

'My father used to say the same thing.' As soon as I mentioned him a confusing welter of emotions rose up in me. Only when I saw Skarpi's eyes following me did I realise I was backing nervously toward the exit. I stopped and forced myself to turn and walk out the door. 'I'll be here, if I can.'

I heard the smile in his voice behind me. 'I know.'

CHAPTER TWENTY-SEVEN

His Eyes Unveiled

I LEFT THE BAR smiling, unmindful of the fact that I was still Dockside and in danger. I felt buoyant knowing I would have the chance to hear another story soon. It had been a long time since I had looked forward to anything. I went back to my street corner and proceeded to waste three hours begging, not gaining so much as a thin shim for my efforts. Even this failed to dampen my spirits. Tomorrow was Mourning, but the day after there would be stories!

But as I sat there, I felt a vague unease creep over me. A feeling that I was forgetting something impinged on my too-rare happiness. I tried to ignore it, but it stayed with me all day and into the next, like a mosquito I couldn't see, let alone swat. By the end of the day, I was certain I had forgotten something. Something about the story Skarpi had told.

It is easy for you to see, no doubt, hearing the story like this, conveniently arranged and narrated. Keep in mind that I had been living like an animal in Tarbean for nearly three years. Pieces of my mind were still asleep, and my painful memories had been gathering dust behind the door of forgetfulness. I had grown used to avoiding them, the same way a cripple keeps weight off an injured leg.

Luck smiled on me the next day, and I managed to steal a bundle of rags off the back of a wagon and sell them to a ragman for four iron pennies. Too hungry to worry about tomorrow, I bought a thick slice of cheese and a warm sausage, then a whole loaf of fresh bread and a warm apple tart. Finally, on a whim, I went to the back door of the nearby inn and spent my final penny on a mug of strong beer.

I sat on the steps of a bakery across the street from the inn and watched people coming and going as I enjoyed my best meal in months. Soon twilight faded into darkness and my head began to spin pleasantly from the beer. But as the food settled in my belly, the nagging sensation returned, stronger than before. I frowned, irritated that something would spoil an otherwise perfect day.

Night deepened until the inn across the street stood in a pool of light. A few women hovered near the doorway to the inn. They murmured in low voices and gave knowing looks to the men who walked past.

I drank off the last of the beer and was about to cross the street and return the mug when I saw a flicker of torchlight approaching. Looking down the street, I saw the distinctive grey of a Tehlin priest and decided to wait until he had passed. Drunk on Mourning and just recently a thief, I guessed the less contact I had with the clergy the better off I'd be.

He was hooded, and the torch he carried was between us, so I couldn't see his face. He approached the group of nearby women and there was a low murmur of discussion. I heard the distinctive chink of coins and sunk further into the shadow of the doorway.

The Tehlin turned and headed back the way he had come. I remained still, not wanting to draw his attention, not wanting to have to run for safety while my head was spinning. This time, however, the torch was not between us. When he turned to look in my direction, I could see nothing of his face, only darkness under the cowl of his hood, only shadow.

He continued on his way, unaware of my presence, or uncaring. But I stayed where I was, unable to move. The image of the hooded man, his face hidden in shadow, had thrown open a door in my mind and memories were spilling out. I was remembering a man with empty eyes and a smile from a nightmare, remembering the blood on his sword. Cinder, his voice like a chill wind: 'Is this your parents' fire?'

Not him, the man behind him. The quiet one who had sat beside the fire. The man whose face was hidden in shadow. Haliax. This had been the half-remembered thing hovering on the edge of my awareness since I had heard Skarpi's story.

I ran to the rooftops and wrapped myself in my rag blanket. Pieces of story and memory slowly fit together. I began to admit impossible truths to myself. The Chandrian were real. Haliax was real. If the story Skarpi had told was true, then Lanre and Haliax were the same person. The Chandrian had killed my parents, my whole troupe. Why?

Other memories bubbled to the surface of my mind. I saw the man with black eyes, Cinder, kneeling in front of me. His face expressionless, his voice sharp and cold. 'Someone's parents,' he had said, 'have been singing entirely the wrong sort of songs.'

They had killed my parents for gathering stories about them. They had killed my whole troupe over a song. I sat awake all night with little more than these thoughts running through my head. Slowly I came to realise them as the truth.

What did I do then? Did I swear I would find them, kill them all for what they had done? Perhaps. But even if I did, I knew in my heart it was impossible. Tarbean had taught me hard practicality. Kill the Chandrian? Kill Lanre? How could I even begin? I would have more luck trying to steal the moon. At least I knew where to look for the moon at night.

But there was one thing I could do. Tomorrow I would ask Skarpi for the real truth behind his stories. It wasn't much, but it was all I had. Revenge might be beyond me, at least for now. But I still had a hope of knowing the truth.

I held tight to that hope through the dark hours of night, until the sun rose and I fell asleep.

CHAPTER TWENTY-EIGHT

Tehlu's Watchful Eye

THE NEXT DAY I came blearily awake to the sound of the hour being struck. I counted four bells, but didn't know how many I might have slept through. I blinked the sleep from my eyes and tried to gauge the time from the position of the sun. About sixth bell. Skarpi would be starting his story now.

I ran through the streets. My bare feet slapped on rough cobbles, splashing through puddles and taking shortcuts through alleyways. Everything became a blur around me as I pulled in great lungfuls of the damp, stagnant, city air.

I almost burst into the Half-Mast at a dead run and settled in against the back wall by the door. I dimly realised there were more people in the inn than usual this early in the evening. Then Skarpi's story pulled me in and I could do nothing but listen to his deep rolling voice and watch his sparkling eyes.

———

. . . Selitos One-Eye stood forward and said, 'Lord, if I do this thing will I be given the power to avenge the loss of the shining city? Can I confound the plots of Lanre and his Chandrian who killed the innocent and burned my beloved Myr Tariniel?'

Aleph said, 'No. All personal things must be set aside, and you must punish or reward only what you yourself witness from this day forth.'

Selitos bowed his head. 'I am sorry, but my heart says to me I must try to stop these things before they are done, not wait and punish later.'

Some of the Ruach murmured agreement with Selitos and went to stand with him, for they remembered Myr Tariniel and were filled with rage and hurt at Lanre's betrayal.

Selitos went to Aleph and knelt before him. 'I must refuse, for I cannot forget. But I will oppose him with these faithful Ruach beside me. I see their hearts are pure. We will be called the Amyr in memory of the ruined city. We will confound Lanre and any who follow him. Nothing will prevent us from attaining the greater good.'

Most of the Ruach hung back from Selitos, too. They were afraid, and they did not wish to become involved in great matters.

But Tehlu stood forward saying, 'I hold justice foremost in my heart. I will leave this world behind that I might better serve it, serving you.' He knelt before Aleph, his head bowed, his hands open at his sides.

Others came forward. Tall Kirel, who had been burned but left living in the ash of Myr Tariniel. Deah, who had lost two husbands to the fighting, and whose face and mouth and heart were hard and cold as stone. Enlas, who would not carry a sword or eat the flesh of animals, and who no man had ever known to speak hard words. Fair Geisa, who had a hundred suitors in Belen before the walls fell. The first woman to know the unasked-for touch of man.

Lecelte, who laughed easily and often, even when there was woe thick about him. Imet, hardly more than a boy, who never sang and killed swiftly without tears. Ordal, the youngest of them all, who had never seen a thing die, stood bravely before Aleph, her golden hair bright with ribbon. And beside her came Andan, whose face was a mask with burning eyes, whose name meant anger.

They came to Aleph, and he touched them. He touched their hands and eyes and hearts. The last time he touched them there was pain, and wings tore from their backs that they might go where they wished. Wings of fire and shadow. Wings of iron and glass. Wings of stone and blood.

Then Aleph spoke their long names and they were wreathed in a white fire. The fire danced along their wings and they became swift. The fire flickered in their eyes and they saw into the deepest hearts of men. The fire filled their mouths and they sang songs of power. Then the fire settled on their foreheads like silver stars and they became at once righteous and wise and terrible to behold. Then the fire consumed them and they were gone forever from mortal sight.

None but the most powerful can see them, and only then with great difficulty and at great peril. They mete out justice to the world, and Tehlu is the greatest of them all—

————————

'I have heard enough.' The speaker wasn't loud, but he may as well have shouted. When Skarpi told a story, any interruption was like chewing a grain of sand in a mouthful of bread.

From the back of the room, two men in dark cloaks came towards the bar: one tall and proud, one short and hooded. As they walked I saw a flash of grey robe beneath their cloaks: Tehlin priests. Worse, I saw two other men with armour under their cloaks. I hadn't seen it while they were sitting, but now that they were moving it was painfully obvious they were church strongmen. Their faces were grim, and the lines of their cloaks spoke of swords to me.

I wasn't the only one who saw. The children were trickling out the door. The smarter ones tried to appear casual, but some broke into a run before they got outside. Against common sense three children stayed. There was a Cealdish boy with lace on his shirt, a little girl with bare feet, and myself.

'I believe we have all heard enough,' the taller of the two priests said with quiet severity. He was lean, with sunken eyes that smoldered like half hidden coals. A carefully trimmed beard the colour of soot sharpened the edges of his knife blade face.

He handed his cloak to the shorter, hooded priest. Underneath he wore the pale grey robe of the Tehlins. Around his neck was a set of silver scales. My heart sunk deep into the pit of my stomach. Not just a priest, but a Justice. I saw the other two children slip out the door.

The Justice spoke, 'Under Tehlu's watchful eye, I charge you with heresy.'

'Witnessed,' said the second priest from within his hood.

The Justice motioned to the mercenaries. 'Bind him.'

This the mercenaries did with rough efficiency. Skarpi endured the whole thing placidly, without saying a word.

The Justice watched his bodyguard begin to tie Skarpi's wrists, then turned his body slightly away, as if dismissing the storyteller from his mind. He took a long look around the room, his inspection finally ending with the bald, aproned man behind the bar.

'T–Tehlu's blessing be upon you!' the owner of the Half-Mast stammered explosively.

'It is,' the Justice said simply. He took another long look around the room. Finally he turned his head to the second priest who stood back from the bar. 'Anthony, would a fine place such as this be harbouring heretics?'

'Anything is possible, Justice.'

'Ahhh,' the Justice said softly and looked slowly around the room, once again ending with an inspection of the man behind the bar.

'Can I offer your honours a drink? If'n it please you?' the owner offered quickly.

There was only silence.

'I mean . . . a drink for you and your brothers. A fine barrel of fallow white? To show my thanks. I let him stay because his stories were interesting, at first.' He swallowed hard and hurried on, 'But then he started to say wicked things. I was afraid to throw him out, because he is obviously mad, and everyone knows God's displeasure falls heavy on those who raise their hands to madmen . . .' His voice broke, leaving the room suddenly quiet. He swallowed, and I could hear the dry click his throat made from where I stood by the door.

'A generous offer,' the Justice said finally.

'Very generous,' echoed the shorter priest.

'However, strong drink sometimes tempts men to wicked actions.'

'Wicked,' whispered the priest.

'And some of our brothers have taken vows against the temptations of the flesh. I must refuse.' The Justice's voice dripped pious regret.

I managed to catch Skarpi's eye, he gave me a little half-smile. My stomach churned. The old storyteller didn't seem to have any idea what sort of trouble he was in. But at the same time, deep inside me, something selfish was saying, *if you'd come earlier and found out what you needed to know, it wouldn't be so bad now, would it?*

The barman broke the silence. 'Could you take the price of the barrel then, sirs? If not the barrel itself.'

The Justice paused, as if thinking.

'For the sake of the children,' the bald man pleaded. 'I know you will use the money for them.'

The Justice pursed his lips. 'Very well,' he said after a moment, 'for the sake of the children.'

The shorter priest's voice had an unpleasant edge. 'The children.'

The owner managed a weak smile.

Skarpi rolled his eyes at me and winked.

'You would think,' Skarpi's voice rolled out like thick honey, 'fine churchmen such as yourselves could find better things to do than arresting storytellers and extorting money from honest men.'

The clinking of the barman's coins trailed off and the room seemed to hold its breath. With a studied casualness, the Justice turned his back toward Skarpi and spoke over one shoulder toward the shorter priest. 'Anthony, we seem to have found a courteous heretic, how strange and wonderful! We should sell him to a Ruh troupe; in a way he resembles a talking dog.'

Skarpi spoke to the man's back. 'It's not as if I expect you to bound off looking for Haliax and the Seven yourself. "Small deeds for small men," I always say. I imagine the trouble is in finding the job small enough for men such as yourselves. But you are resourceful. You could pick trash, or check brothel beds for lice when you are visiting.'

Turning, the Justice snatched the clay cup off the bar and dashed it against Skarpi's head, shattering it. 'Do not speak in my presence!' he crackled. 'You know nothing!'

Skarpi shook his head a little, as if to clear it. A trickle of red lined its way down his driftwood face, down into one of his sea-foam eyebrows. 'I suppose that could be true. Tehlu always said—'

'Do not speak his name!' the Justice screamed, his face a livid red. 'Your mouth dirties it. It is a blasphemy upon your tongue.'

'Oh come now, Erlus.' Skarpi chided as though talking to a small child. 'Tehlu hates you even more than the rest of the world does, which is quite a bit.'

The room became unnaturally still. The Justice's face grew pale. 'God have mercy on you,' he said in a cold, trembling voice.

Skarpi looked at the Justice mutely for a moment. Then he started to laugh. Great, booming, helpless laughter from the bottom of his soul.

The eyes of the Justice flicked to one of the men who had tied the storyteller. With no preamble the grim-faced man struck Skarpi with a tight fist. Once in the kidney, once in the back of the neck.

Skarpi crumpled to the ground. The room was silent. The sound of his body hitting the wood planking of the floor seemed to fade before the echoes of his laughter did. At a gesture from the Justice, one of the guards picked the old man up by the scruff of his neck. He dangled like a rag doll, his feet trailing on the ground.

But Skarpi was not unconscious, merely stunned. The storyteller's eyes rolled around to focus on the Justice. 'Mercy on *my* soul.' He gave a weak croak that might have been a chuckle on a better day. 'You don't know how funny that sounds coming from you.'

Skarpi seemed to address the air in front of him. 'You should run, Kvothe. There's nothing to be gained by meddling with these sort of men. Head to the rooftops. Stay where they won't see you for a while. I have friends in the church who can help me, but there's nothing you can do here. Go.'

Since he wasn't looking at me when he spoke, there was a moment of confusion. The Justice gestured again and one of the guards struck Skarpi a blow to the back of the head. His eyes rolled back, and his head lolled forwards. I slipped out the door, onto the street.

I took Skarpi's advice and was on a rooftop running before they left the bar.

CHAPTER TWENTY-NINE

The Doors of My Mind

UP ONTO THE ROOFTOPS and back to my secret place, I wrapped myself in my blanket and cried. I cried as if something inside me had broken and everything was rushing out.

When I had worn myself out with sobbing it was deep into the night. I lay there looking at the sky, weary but unable to sleep. I thought of my parents and of the troupe, and was surprised to find the memories less bitter than before.

For the first time in years, I used one of the tricks Ben had taught me for calming and sharpening the mind. It was harder than I remembered, but I did it.

If you have ever slept the whole night without moving, then awoke in the morning, your body stiff with inaction. If you can remember how that first terrific stretch feels, pleasant and painful, then you may understand how my mind felt after all these years, stretching awake on the rooftops of Tarbean.

I spent the rest of that night opening the doors of my mind. Inside I found things long forgotten: my mother fitting words together for a song, diction for the stage, three recipes for tea to calm nerves and promote sleep, finger scales for the lute.

My music. Had it really been years since I held a lute?

I spent a long time thinking about the Chandrian, about what they had done to my troupe, what they had taken from me. I remembered blood and the smell of burning hair and felt a deep, sullen anger burning in my chest. I will admit I thought dark, vengeful thoughts that night.

But my years in Tarbean had instilled an iron-hard practicality. I knew revenge was nothing more than a childish fantasy. I was fifteen. What could I possibly do?

I did know one thing. It had come to me as I lay remembering. It was something Haliax had said to Cinder. *Who keeps you safe from the Amyr? The singers? The Sithe? From all that would harm you in the world?*

The Chandrian had enemies. If I could find them, they would help me. I had no idea who the singers or the Sithe were, but everyone knew that the Amyr were church knights, the strong right hand of the Aturan Empire. Unfortunately, everyone also knew that there had been no Amyr in three hundred years. They had been disbanded when the Aturan Empire collapsed.

But Haliax had spoken of them as if they still existed. And Skarpi's story implied that the Amyr had begun with Selitos, not with the Aturan Empire as I had always been taught. There was obviously more to the story, more that I needed to know.

The more I thought on it, the more questions arose. The Chandrian obviously didn't kill everyone who gathered stories or sang songs about them. Everyone knew a story or two about them, and every child at one point has sung the silly rhyme about their signs. What made my parent's song so different?

I had questions. There was only one place for me to go, of course.

I looked over my meagre possessions. I had a rag blanket and a burlap sack with some straw that I used for a pillow. I had a pint bottle with a cork in it, half full of clean water. A piece of canvas sailcloth that I weighted down with bricks and used as a windbreak on cold nights. A crude pair of salt-dice and a single, tatty shoe that was too small for me, but that I hoped to trade for something else.

And twenty-seven iron pennies in common coin. My rainy-day money. A few days ago it had seemed like a vast treasure trove, but now I knew it would never be enough.

As the sun was rising, I removed *Rhetoric and Logic* from its hiding place underneath a rafter. I unwrapped the scrap of treated canvas I used to protect it and was relieved to find it dry and well. I felt the smooth leather in my hands. I held it to my face and smelled the back of Ben's wagon, spice and yeast with the bitter tang of acids and chemical salts mingled in. It was the last tangible piece of my past.

I opened it to the first page and read the inscription Ben had made more than three years ago.

Kvothe,
Defend yourself well at the University. Make me proud.
Remember your father's song. Be wary of folly.
Abenthy.

I nodded to myself and turned the page.

CHAPTER THIRTY

The Broken Binding

THE SIGN OVER THE doorpost read: THE BROKEN BINDING. I took it to be an auspicious sign and walked in.

A man sat behind a desk. I assumed he was the owner. He was tall and reedy with thinning hair. He looked up from a ledger, his expression vaguely irritated.

Deciding to keep niceties to a minimum, I walked to his desk and handed him the book. 'How much would you give me for this?'

He leafed through it professionally, feeling the paper between his fingers, checking the binding. He shrugged. 'A couple of jots.'

'It's worth more than that!' I said indignantly.

'It's worth what you can get for it,' he said matter-of-factly. 'I'll give you one and a half.'

'Two talents and I have the option to buy it back for a month.'

He gave a short, barking laugh. 'This is not a pawnshop.' He slid the book across the desk towards me with one hand as he picked up his pen with the other.

'Twenty days?'

He hesitated, then gave the book another cursory once-over and brought out his purse. He pulled out two heavy silver talents. It was more money than I'd seen in one place for a long, long time.

He slid them across the desk. I restrained the desire to snatch them up immediately and said, 'I'll need a receipt.'

This time he gave me such a long hard look that I began to get a little nervous. It was only then I realised how I must look, covered in a year's worth of alley dirt, trying to get a receipt for a book I'd obviously stolen.

Eventually he gave another bland shrug and scratched out a note on a slip of paper. At the bottom of it he drew a line and made a motion with his pen. 'Sign here.'

I looked at the paper. It read:

I, by signing below, hereby attest to the fact that I can neither read nor write.

I looked up at the owner. He held a straight face. I dipped the pen and carefully wrote the letters 'D D' as if they were initials.

He fanned the ink dry and slid my 'receipt' across the desk toward me. 'What does D stand for?' he asked with the barest hint of a smile.

'Defeasance,' I said. 'It means to render something null and void, usually a contract. The second D is for Decrepitate. Which is the act of throwing someone into a fire.' He gave me a blank look. 'Decrepication is the punishment for forgery in Junpui. I think false receipts fall in that category.'

I made no move to touch the money or the receipt. There was a tense silence.

'This isn't Junpui,' he said, his face carefully composed.

'True enough,' I admitted. 'You have a keen sense of defalcation. Perhaps I should add a third D.'

He gave another sharp, barking laugh and smiled. 'You've convinced me, young master.' He pulled out a fresh slip of paper and set it in front of me. 'You write me a receipt, and I will sign it.'

I took up the pen and wrote. 'I the undersigned, do agree to return the copy of the book *Rhetoric and Logic* with the inscription "to Kvothe" to the bearer of this note in exchange for two silver pennies, provided he present this receipt before the date—'

I looked up. 'What day is it?'

'Shuden. The thirty-fifth.'

I had fallen out of the habit of keeping track of the date. On the streets, one day is largely the same as the next, save that people are a little more drunk on Hepten, a little more generous on Mourning.

But if it was the thirty-fifth then I only had five days to get to the University. I knew from Ben that admissions only lasted until Cendling. If I missed them, I would have to wait two months for the next term to start.

I filled in the date on the receipt and drew a line for the bookseller to sign. He looked a little bemused as I slid the paper toward him. What's more, he didn't notice that the receipt read pennies instead of talents. Talents were worth significantly more. This meant he had just agreed to give me back the book for less money than he had bought it for.

My satisfaction damped itself when it occurred to me how foolish all of this was. Pennies or talents, I wouldn't have enough money to buy the book back in two span. If everything went well I wouldn't even be in Tarbean tomorrow.

Despite its uselessness, the receipt helped ease the sting of parting with the last thing I owned from my childhood. I blew on the paper, folded it carefully into a pocket, and collected my two silver talents. I was surprised when the man held out his hand to me.

He smiled in an apologetic way. 'Sorry about the note. But you didn't look like you'd be coming back.' He gave a little shrug. 'Here.' He pressed a copper jot into my hand.

I decided that he was not an altogether bad fellow. I smiled back at him and for a second I almost felt guilty about how I'd written the receipt.

I also felt guilty about the three pens I'd stolen, but only for a second. And since there was no convenient way to give them back, I stole a bottle of ink before I left.

CHAPTER THIRTY-ONE

The Nature of Nobility

THE TWO TALENTS HAD a reassuring weight to them that had nothing to do with how heavy they were. Anyone who has been without money for a long time will know what I'm talking about. My first investment was a good leather purse. I wore it underneath my clothes, tight against my skin.

Next was a real breakfast. A plateful of hot eggs and a slice of ham. Bread that was fresh and soft, plenty of honey and butter on the side, and a glass of milk not two days from the cow. It cost me five iron pennies. It may be the best meal I ever ate.

It felt strange sitting at a table, eating with a knife and fork. It felt strange being around people. It felt strange having a person bring me food.

As I mopped up the remnants of my breakfast with an end of bread, I realised that I had a problem.

Even in this slightly grubby inn Waterside, I was attracting attention. My shirt was nothing more than an old burlap sack with holes for my arms and head. My trousers were made out of canvas and too big by several degrees. They reeked of smoke, grease, and stagnant alley water. I'd been holding them up with a length of rope I had dug out of some trash. I was filthy, barefoot, and I stank.

Should I buy clothes or try to find a bath? If I bathed first, I would have to wear my old clothes afterward. However, if I tried to buy clothes looking the way I did now, I might not even be let into the store. And I doubted that anyone would want to measure me for a fit.

The innkeep came to take my plate, and I decided on a bath first, mainly because I was sick to death of smelling like a week-dead rat. I smiled up at him. 'Where can I find a bath near here?'

'Here, if you have a couple of pennies.' He looked me over. 'Or I'll work you an hour instead, a good hard hour. The hearth could use scrubbing.'

'I'll need a lot of water, and soap.'

'Two hours then, I've got dishes too. Hearth first, then bath, then dishes. Fair?'

An hour or so later my shoulders ached and the hearth was clean. He showed me to a back room with a large wooden tub and a grate on the floor. There were pegs along the walls for clothes, and a sheet of tin nailed to the wall served as a crude mirror.

He brought me a brush, a bucket of steaming water, and a cake of lye soap. I scrubbed until I was sore and pink. The innkeeper brought a second bucket of hot water, then a third. I gave a silent prayer of thanks that I didn't seem to be lousy. I had probably been too filthy for any self-respecting louse to take up residence.

As I rinsed myself for the last time, I looked at my discarded clothes. Cleaner than I'd been in years, I didn't want to touch them, let alone wear them. If I tried to wash them they'd simply fall apart.

I dried myself off and I used the rough brush to pull through the snarls in my hair. It was longer than it had seemed when it was dirty. I wiped the fog from the makeshift mirror and was surprised. I looked old, older at any rate. Not only that, I looked like some young noble's son. My face was lean and fair. My hair needed a bit of a trim, but was shoulder-length and straight, as was the current fashion. The only thing missing was a noble's clothes.

And that gave me an idea.

Still naked, I wrapped myself in a towel and left by the back door. I took my purse but kept it out of sight. It was a little before noon and people were everywhere. Needless to say, quite a few eyes were turned in my direction. I ignored them and set a brisk pace, not trying to hide. I composed my features into an impassive, angry mask without a trace of embarrassment.

I stopped by a father and son loading burlap sacks into a cart. The son was about four years older than me and head and shoulders taller. 'Boy,' I snapped. 'Where can I buy some clothes around here?' I looked pointedly at his shirt. 'Decent clothes,' I amended.

He looked at me, his expression somewhere between confusion and anger. His father hurriedly took off his hat and stepped in front of his son. 'Your lordship might try Bentley's. It's plain stuff, but it's only a street or two away.'

I darkened my expression. 'Is it the only place about?'

He gaped. 'Well . . . it could . . . there's one . . .'

I waved him impatiently into silence. 'Where is it? Simply point, since your wits have left you.'

He pointed and I strode off. As I walked I remembered one of the young page parts I used to play in the troupe. The page's name was Dunstey, an insufferably petulant little boy with an important father. He was perfect. I gave my head an imperious tilt, set my shoulders a little differently and made a couple of mental adjustments.

I threw open the door and stormed in. There was a man in a leather apron who I can only assume was Bentley. He was fortyish, thin, and balding. He jumped at the sound of his door banging against the wall. He turned to look at me, his expression incredulous.

'Fetch me a robe, lack-wit. I'm sick of being gawked at by you and every other mewler that decided to go marketing today.' I slouched into a chair and sulked. When he didn't move I glared at him. 'Did I stutter? Are my needs perhaps inobvious?' I tugged at the edge of my towel to demonstrate.

He stood there, gaping.

I lowered my voice menacingly, 'If you don't bring me something to wear—' I stood up and shouted, '—I'll tear this place apart! I'll ask my father for your stones as a Midwinter gift. I'll have his dogs mount your dead corpse. DO YOU HAVE ANY IDEA WHO I AM?'

Bently scurried away, and I threw myself back into the chair. A customer I hadn't noticed until now made a hurried exit, stopping briefly to curtsy to me before she left.

I fought back the urge to laugh.

After that it was surprisingly easy. I kept him running about for half an hour, bringing me one piece of clothing or another. I mocked the material, the cut, and workmanship of everything he brought out. In short, I was the perfect little brat.

In truth I couldn't have been more pleased. The clothing was plain but well made. Indeed, compared to what I had been wearing an hour before, a clean burlap sack would have been a great step up.

If you haven't spent much time in court or in large cities, you won't understand why this was so easy for me to accomplish. Let me explain.

Nobles' sons are one of nature's great destructive forces, like floods or tornadoes. When you're struck with one of these catastrophes, the only thing an average man can do is grit his teeth and try to minimise the damage.

Bentley knew this. He marked the shirt and trousers and helped me out of them. I got back into the robe he had given me, and he began sewing like the devil was breathing down his neck.

I flounced back into the chair. 'You might as well ask. I can tell you're dying of curiosity.'

He looked up briefly from his stitching. 'Sir?'

'The circumstances surrounding my current state of undress.'

'Ah, yes.' He tied off the thread and began on the trousers. 'I will admit to a slight curiosity. No more than proper. I'm not one to pry into anyone's business.'

'Ah,' I nodded, pretending disappointment. 'A laudable attitude.'

There followed a long moment, the only sound was that of the thread being drawn through cloth. I fidgeted. Finally, I continued as if he had asked me, 'A whore stole my clothes.'

'Really, sir?'

'Yes, she tried to get me to trade them for my purse, the bitch.'

Bentley looked up briefly, genuine curiosity on his face. 'Wasn't your purse with your clothes, sir?'

I looked shocked. 'Certainly not! "A gentleman's hand is never far away from his purse". So my father says.' I waved my purse at him to make my point.

I noticed him trying to suppress a laugh and it made me feel a little better. I'd made the man miserable for almost an hour, the least I could give him was a story to tell his friends.

'She told me if I wanted to keep my dignity, then I'd give her my purse and walk home wearing my clothes.' I shook my head scornfully. ' "Wanton," I said to her, "A gentleman's dignity isn't in his clothes. If I handed over my purse simply to save myself an embarrassment then I would be handing over my dignity".'

I looked thoughtful for a second, then spoke softly as if thinking aloud. 'It only follows that a gentleman's dignity is in his purse then.' I looked at the purse in my hands, and gave a long pause. 'I think I heard my father say something of the sort the other day.'

Bentley gave a laugh that he turned into a cough, then stood up and shook out the shirt and trousers. 'There you go, sir, fit you like a glove now.' A hint of a smile played around his lips as he handed them to me.

I slid out of the robe and pulled on the trousers. 'They'll get me home, I suppose. How much for your trouble, Bentley?' I asked.

He thought for a second. 'One and two.'

I began to lace up my shirt and said nothing.

'Sorry, sir,' he said quickly. 'Forgot who I was dealing with.' He swallowed. 'One even would do nicely.'

Taking out my purse, I put one silver talent into his hand and looked him in the eye. 'I will be needing some change.'

His mouth made a thin line, but he nodded and handed me back two jots.

I tucked the coins away and tied my purse firmly underneath my shirt, then gave him a meaningful look and patted it.

I saw the smile tug at his lips again. 'Good-bye, sir.'

I picked up my towel, left the store, and started my altogether less conspicuous walk back to the inn where I had found breakfast and a bath.

'What can I get for you, young sir?' the innkeeper asked as I approached the bar. He smiled and wiped his hands on his apron.

'A stack of dirty dishes and a rag.'

He squinted at me, then smiled and laughed. 'I'd thought you'd run off naked through the streets.'

'Not quite naked.' I laid his towel on the bar.

'There was more dirt than boy before. And I would have bet a solid mark your hair was black. You really don't look the same.' He marvelled mutely for a second. 'Would you like your old clothes?'

I shook my head. 'Throw them away – actually, burn them, and make sure no one accidentally breathes the smoke.' He laughed again. 'I did have some other items though.' I reminded him.

He nodded and tapped the side of his nose. 'Right enough. Just a second.' He turned and disappeared though a doorway behind the bar.

I let my attention wander around the room. It seemed different now that I wasn't attracting hostile stares. The fieldstone fireplace with the black kettle simmering. The slightly sour smells of varnished wood and spilled beer. The low rumble of conversation . . .

I've always had a fondness for taverns. It comes from growing up on the road, I think. A tavern is a safe place, a refuge of sorts. I felt very comfortable just then, and it occurred to me that it wouldn't be a bad life, owning a place like this.

'Here you go then.' The innkeeper laid down three pens, a jar of ink, and my receipt from the bookstore. 'These gave me almost as much of a puzzle as why you had run off without your clothes.'

'I'm going to the University.' I explained.

He raised an eyebrow. 'A little young, aren't you?'

I felt a nervous chill at his words, but shrugged it off. 'They take all kinds.'

He nodded politely as if that explained why I had shown up barefoot and reeking of back alleys. After waiting for a while to see if I'd elaborate, the barman poured himself a drink. 'No offense, but you don't exactly look to be the sort who would want to be washin' dishes anymore.'

I opened my mouth to protest; an iron penny for an hour's work was a bargain I was hesitant to pass up. Two pennies was the same as a loaf of bread, and I couldn't count all the times that I had been hungry in the last year.

Then I saw my hands resting on the bar. They were pink and clean, I almost didn't recognise them for my own.

I realised then I didn't want to do the dishes. I had more important things to do. I stood back from the bar and got a penny from my purse. 'Where's the best place to find a caravan leaving for the north?' I asked.

'Drover's Lot, up Hillside. Quarter mile past the mill on Green Street.'

I felt a nervous chill when Hillside was mentioned. I ignored it as best I could and nodded. 'You have a lovely inn here. I'd count myself lucky to have one as nice when I've grown up.' I handed him the penny.

He broke into a huge smile and handed back the penny. 'With such nice compliments, you come back any time.'

CHAPTER THIRTY-TWO

Coppers, Cobblers and Crowds

IT WAS ABOUT AN hour before noon when I stepped out onto the street. The sun was out and the cobblestones were warm beneath my feet. As the noise of the market rose to an irregular hum around me, I tried to enjoy the pleasant sensation of having a full belly and a clean body.

But there was a vague unease in the pit of my stomach, like the feeling you get when someone's staring at the back of your head. It followed me until my instincts got the better of me and I slipped into a side alley quick as a fish.

As I stood pressed against a wall, waiting, the feeling faded. After a few minutes, I began to feel foolish. I trusted my instincts, but they gave false alarms every now and again. I waited a few more minutes just to be sure, then moved back into the street.

The feeling of vague unease returned almost immediately. I ignored it while trying to find out where it was coming from. But after five minutes I lost my nerve and turned onto a side street, watching the crowd to see who was following me.

No one. It took a nerve-wracking half hour and two more alleys before I finally figured out what it was.

It felt strange to be walking with the crowd.

Over the last couple of years crowds had become a part of the scenery of the city to me. I might use a crowd to hide from a guard or a storekeeper. I might move *through* a crowd to get where I was going. I might even be going in the same direction as the crowd, but I was never a part of it.

I was so used to being ignored, I almost ran from the first merchant who tried to sell me something.

Once I knew what was bothering me, the greater part of my uneasiness left. Fear tends to come from ignorance. Once I knew what the problem was, it was just a problem, nothing to fear.

———————

As I've mentioned, Tarbean has two main sections: Hillside and Waterside. Waterside was poor. Hillside was rich. Waterside stank. Hillside was clean. Waterside had thieves. Hillside had bankers— I'm sorry, burglars.

I have already told the story of my one ill-auspiced venture Hillside. So perhaps you will understand why, when the crowd in front of me happened to part for a moment, I saw what I was looking for. A member of the guard. I ducked through the nearest door, my heart pounding.

I spent a moment reminding myself that I wasn't the same filthy little urchin who'd been beaten years ago. I was well-dressed and clean. I looked like I belonged here. But old habits die slow deaths. I fought to control a deep red anger, but couldn't tell if I was angry at myself, the guard, or the world in general. Probably a little of each.

'Be right with you,' came a cheerful voice from a curtained doorway.

I looked around the shop. Light from the front window fell across a crowded workbench and dozens of shelved pairs of shoes. I decided I could have picked a worse store to wander into.

'Let me guess—' came the voice again from the back. A grandfather-grey man emerged from behind the curtain carrying a long piece of leather. He was short and stooped, but his face smiled at me through his wrinkles. '—you need shoes.' He smiled timidly, as if the joke was a pair of old boots that had worn out long ago, but were too comfortable to give up. He looked down at my feet. I looked too, in spite of myself.

I was barefoot of course. I hadn't had shoes for so long that I never even thought about them anymore. At least not during the summer. In the winter, I dreamed of shoes.

I looked up. The old man's eyes were dancing, as if he couldn't decide whether laughing would cost him his customer or not. 'I guess I need shoes,' I admitted.

He laughed and guided me into a seat, measuring my bare feet with his hands. Thankfully the streets were dry, so my feet were merely dusty from the cobblestones. If there had been rain they would have been embarrassingly filthy.

'Let's see what you like, and if I have anything of a size for you. If not, I can make or change a pair to fit you in an hour or two. So, what would you be wanting shoes for? Walking? Dancing? Riding?' He leaned back on his stool and grabbed a pair off a shelf behind him.

'Walking.'

'Thought so.' He deftly rolled a pair of stockings onto my feet, as if all his customers came in barefoot. He tucked my feet into a pair of something black with buckles. 'How's those feel? Put a little weight on to make sure.'

'I—'

'They're tight. I thought so. Nothing more annoying that a shoe that pinches.' He stripped me out of them, and into another pair, quick as a whip. 'How about these?' They were a deep purple and made of velvet or felt.

'They—'

'Not quite what you're looking for? Don't blame you really, wear out terrible fast. Nice color though, good for chasing the ladies.' He patted a new pair onto my feet. 'How about these?'

They were a simple brown leather, and fit like he'd measured my feet before he'd made them. I pressed my foot to the ground, and it hugged me. I had forgotten how wonderful a good shoe can feel. 'How much?' I asked apprehensively.

Instead of answering he stood, and started searching the shelves with his eyes. 'You can tell a lot about a person by their feet,' he mused. 'Some men come in here, smiling and laughing, shoes all clean and brushed, socks all powdered up. But when the shoes are off, their feet smell just fearsome. Those are the people that hide things. They've got bad smelling secrets and they try to hide 'em, just like they try to hide their feet.'

He turned to look at me. 'It never works though. Only way to stop your feet from smelling is to let them air out a bit. Could be the same thing with secrets. I don't know about that, though. I just know about shoes.'

He began to look through the clutter of his workbench. 'Some of these young men from the court come in, fanning their faces and moaning about the latest tragedy. But their feet are so pink and soft. You know they've never walked anywhere on their own. You know they've never really been hurt.'

He finally found what he was looking for, holding up a pair of shoes similar to the pair I wore. 'Here we go. These were my Jacob's when he was your age.' He sat on his stool and unlaced the pair of shoes I was wearing.

'Now you,' he continued, 'have old soles for a boy so young: scars, calluses. Feet like these could run barefoot all day on stone and not need shoes. A boy your age only gets these feet one way.'

He looked up at me, making it a question. I nodded.

He smiled and lay a hand on my shoulder. 'How do they feel?'

I stood up to test them. If anything, they were more comfortable than the newer pair for being a little broken in.

'Now, this pair,' he waved the shoes he held, 'are new. They haven't been walked a mile, and for new shoes like these I charge a talent, maybe a talent and two.' He pointed at my feet. 'Those shoes, on the other hand, are used, and I don't sell used shoes.'

He turned his back on me and started to tidy his workbench rather aimlessly, humming to himself. It took me a second to recognise the tune: 'Leave the Town, Tinker.'

I knew that he was trying to do me a favour, and a week ago I would have jumped at the opportunity for free shoes. But for some reason I didn't feel right about it. I quietly gathered up my things and left a pair of copper jots on his stool before I left.

Why? Because pride is a strange thing, and because generosity deserves generosity in return. But mostly because it felt like the right thing to do, and that is reason enough.

———

'Four days. Six days if raining.'

Roent was the third wagoneer I'd asked about going north to Imre, the town nearest the University. He was a thick-bodied Cealdish man with a fierce black beard that hid most of his face. He turned away and barked curses in Siaru at a man loading a wagon with bolts of cloth. When he spoke his native language, he sounded like an angry rockslide.

His rough voice lowered to a rumble as he turned back to me. 'Two coppers. Jots. Not pennies. You can ride in a wagon if there is space. You can sleep underneath at night if you want. You eat in the evening with us. Lunch is just bread. If a wagon gets stuck, you help push.'

There was another pause while he shouted at the men. There were three wagons being packed with trade goods while the fourth was achingly familiar, one of the wheeled houses I had spent most of my early life riding. Roent's wife, Reta, sat in the front of that wagon. Her mien wavered from severe, when she watched the men loading the wagons, to smiling when she spoke with a girl standing nearby.

I assumed the girl was a passenger like myself. She was my age, perhaps a year older, but a year makes a great deal of difference at that time of life. The Tahl have a saying about children of our age. *The boy grows upward, but the girl grows up.*

She was dressed practically for travelling, pants and shirt, and was just young enough for it not to seem improper. Her bearing was such that if she had been a year older, I would have been forced to see her as a lady. As it was, when she spoke with Reta she moved back and forth between a genteel grace and a childlike exuberance. She had long, dark hair, and . . .

Simply said, she was beautiful. It had been a long time since I had seen anything beautiful.

Roent followed my gaze and continued. 'Everyone helps set camp at night. Everyone takes a turn watching. You fall asleep during your watch, you get left behind. You eat with us, whatever my wife cooks. You complain, you get left behind. You walk too slow, you get left behind. You bother the girl . . .' He ran a hand through his thick dark beard. 'Bad things happen.'

Hoping to turn his thoughts in a different direction, I spoke up, 'When will the wagons be done loading?'

'Two hours,' he said with a grim certainty, as if defying the workers to contradict him.

One of the men stood upright atop a wagon, shading his eyes with a hand. He called out, raising his voice over the sound of horses, wagons, and men that filled the square. 'Don't let him scare you off, kid. He's decent enough after all the growling.' Roent pointed a stern finger, and the man turned back to his work.

I hardly needed to be convinced. A man who travels with his wife is usually to be trusted. Besides, the price was fair, and he was leaving today. I took this opportunity to pull a pair of jots from my purse and hold them out to Roent.

He turned to me. 'Two hours.' He held up thick fingers to make his point. 'You are late, you get left behind.'

I nodded solemnly. *'Rieusa, tu kialus A'isha tua.'* Thank you for bringing me close to your family.

Roent's great shaggy eyebrows went up. He recovered quickly and gave a quick nod that was almost a small bow. I looked around the square, trying to get my bearings.

'Someone's full of surprises.' I turned around to see the worker who had shouted to me from the wagon. He held out his hand. 'Derrik.'

I shook his hand, feeling awkward. It had been so long since I'd made simple conversation with someone that I felt strange and hesitant. 'Kvothe.'

Derrik put his hands behind him and stretched his back with a grimace.
He stood head and shoulders taller than me, twenty or so, tall and blond. 'You
gave Roent a bit of a turn there. Where'd you learn to speak Siaru?'

'An arcanist taught me a little,' I explained. I watched as Roent went to
speak to his wife. The dark-haired girl looked in my direction and smiled. I
looked away, not knowing what to make of it.

He shrugged. 'I'll leave you to fetch your things, then. Roent's all growl
and not much gruff, but he won't wait once the wagons are packed.'

I nodded, even though my 'things' were nonexistent. I did have a little
shopping to do. They say you can find anything in Tarbean if you have
enough money. For the most part, they are right.

———————

I made my way down the stairs to Trapis' basement. It felt strange to make
the trip wearing shoes. I was used to the cool damp of stone underfoot when
I came to pay a visit.

As I made my way down the short hallway, a boy in rags emerged from
the inner rooms holding a small winter apple. He pulled up short when he
saw me, then scowled, his eyes narrow and suspicious. Looking down, he
brushed roughly past me.

Without even thinking about it, I slapped his hand away from my
purse and turned to look at him, too stunned for words. He bolted outside,
leaving me confused and disturbed. We never stole from each other here. Out
on the streets it was everyone for themselves, but Trapis' basement was the
closest thing to a sanctuary we had, like a church. None of us would risk
spoiling that.

I took the last few steps into the main room and was relieved to see that
everything else seemed normal. Trapis wasn't there, probably off collecting
charity to help him care for his children. There were six cots, all full, and
more children lying on the floor. Several grubby urchins stood around a
bushel basket on the table, clutching winter apples. They turned to stare at
me, their expressions flinty and spiteful.

It dawned on me then. None of them recognised me. Clean and well-
dressed, I looked like some regular boy come wandering in. I didn't belong.

Just then Trapis came back, carrying several flat loaves of bread under one
arm and a squalling child in the other. 'Ari,' he called to one of the boys

standing near the bushel basket. 'Come help. We've got a new visitor and she needs changing.'

The boy hurried over and took the child out of Trapis' arms. He lay the bread on the table next to the bushel basket and all the children's eyes fixed on him attentively. My stomach went sour. Trapis hadn't even looked at me. What if he didn't recognise me? What if he told me to leave? I didn't know if I could cope with that, I began to edge toward the door.

Trapis pointed to the children one at a time. 'Let me see. David, you empty and scrub the drinking barrel. It's getting brackish. When he's done Nathan can fill it from the pump.'

'Can I take twice?' Nathan asked. 'I need some for my brother.'

'Your brother can come for his own bread,' Trapis said gently, then looked more closely at the boy, sensing something. 'Is he hurt?'

Nathan nodded, looking at the floor.

Trapis laid a hand on the boy's shoulder. 'Bring him down. We'll see to him.'

'It's his leg.' Nathan blurted, seeming close to tears. 'It's all hot, and he can't walk!'

Trapis nodded and gestured to the next child. 'Jen, you help Nathan bring his brother back.' They hurried out. 'Tam, since Nathan's gone, you carry the water instead.'

'Kvothe, you run for soap.' He held out a halfpenny. 'Go to Marna's in the Wash. You'll get better from her if you tell her who it's for.'

I felt a sudden lump form in my throat. He knew me. I can't hope to explain to you how much of a relief it was. Trapis was the closest thing I had to a family. The thought of him not knowing me had been horrifying.

'I don't have time to run an errand, Trapis.' I said hesitantly. 'I'm leaving. I'm heading inland, to Imre.'

'Are you then?' he asked, then paused and gave me a second, closer look. 'Well then, I guess you are.'

Of course. Trapis never saw the clothes, only the child inside them. 'I stopped by to let you know where my things are. On the roof of the candle works there's a place where three roofs meet. There are some things there, a blanket, a bottle. I don't need any of it anymore. It's a good place to sleep if anyone needs one, dry. No one goes there . . .' I trailed off.

'That's kind of you. I'll send one of the boys round,' Trapis said. 'Come here.' He came forward and gathered me into a clumsy hug, his beard tickling the side of my face. 'I'm always glad to see one of you get away,' he said softly to me. 'I know you'll do just fine for yourself, but you can always come back if you need to.'

One of the girls on a nearby cot began to thrash and moan. Trapis pulled away from me and turned to look. 'What what,' he said as he hurried over to tend to her, his bare feet slapping on the floor. 'What what. Hush hush.'

CHAPTER THIRTY-THREE

A Sea of Stars

I RETURNED TO DROVER'S Lot with a travelsack swinging by one shoulder. It held a change of clothes, a loaf of trail bread, some jerked meat, a skin of water, needle and thread, flint and steel, pens and ink. In short, everything an intelligent person takes on a trip in the event they might need it.

However, my proudest acquisition was a dark blue cloak that I had bought off a fripperer's cart for only three jots. It was warm, clean, and, unless I missed my guess, only one owner from new.

Now let me say this: when you're travelling a good cloak is worth more than all your other possessions put together. If you've nowhere to sleep, it can be your bed and blanket. It will keep the rain off your back and the sun from your eyes. You can conceal all manner of interesting weaponry beneath it if you are clever, and a smaller assortment if you are not.

But beyond all that, two facts remain to recommend a cloak. First, very little is as striking as a well-worn cloak, billowing lightly about you in the breeze. And second, the best cloaks have innumerable little pockets that I have an irrational and overpowering attraction towards.

As I have said, this was a good cloak, and it had a number of such pockets. Squirreled away in them I had string and wax, some dried apple, a tinderbox, a marble in a small leather sack, a pouch of salt, hook-needle and gut.

I'd made a point of spending all my carefully hoarded Commonwealth coin, keeping my hard Cealdish currency for my trip. Pennies spent well enough here in Tarbean, but Cealdish money was solid no matter where in the four corners you found yourself.

A final flurry of preparation was being made as I arrived. Roent paced around the wagons like a restless animal, checking everything again and

again. Reta watched the workers with a stern eye and a quick word for anything that wasn't being done to her satisfaction. I was comfortably ignored
until we headed out of the city, towards the University.

――――――

As the miles rolled away, it was as if a great weight slowly fell away from me.
I revelled in the feel of the ground through my shoes, the taste of the air, the
quiet hush of wind brushing through the spring wheat in the fields. I found
myself grinning for no good reason, save that I was happy. We Ruh are not
meant to stay in one place for so long. I took a deep breath and nearly
laughed out loud.

I kept to myself as we travelled, not being used to the company of others.
Roent and the mercenaries were willing to leave me alone. Derrik joked
with me off and on, but generally found me too reserved for his tastes.

That left the other passenger, Denna. We didn't speak until the first day's
ride was nearly done. I was riding with one of the mercenaries, absently
peeling the bark from a willow switch. While my fingers worked, I studied
the side of her face, admiring the line of her jaw, the curve of her neck into
her shoulder. I wondered why she was travelling alone, and where she was
going. In the middle of my musing she turned to look in my direction and
caught me staring at her.

'Penny for your thought?' she asked, brushing at an errant strand of hair.

'I was wondering what you're doing here,' I said half-honestly.

Smiling, she held my eyes. 'Liar.'

I used an old stage trick to keep myself from blushing, gave my best
unconcerned shrug, and looked down at the willow wand I was peeling.
After a few minutes, I heard her return to her conversation with Reta. I
found myself strangely disappointed.

After camp was set and dinner was cooking, I idled around the wagons,
examining the knots Roent used to lash his cargo into place. I heard a
footfall behind me and turned to see Denna approaching. My stomach
rolled over and I took a short breath to compose myself.

She stopped about a dozen feet from me. 'Have you figured it out yet?'
she asked.

'Excuse me?'

'Why I'm here.' She smiled gently. 'I've been wondering the same thing
for most my life, you see. I thought if you had any ideas . . .' she gave me a
wry, hopeful look.

I shook my head, too uncertain of the situation to find the humour in it. 'All I've been able to guess is that you're going somewhere.'

She nodded seriously. 'That's as much as I've guessed too.' She paused to look at the circle the horizon made around us. The wind caught her hair and she brushed it back again. 'Do you happen to know where I'm going?'

I felt a smile begin a slow creep onto my face. It felt odd. I was out of practice smiling. 'Don't *you* know?'

'I have suspicions. Right now I'm thinking Anilin.' She rocked onto the edges of her feet, then back to the flats. 'But I've been wrong before.'

A silence settled over our conversation. Denna looked down at her hands, fidgeting with a ring on her finger, twisting it. I caught a glimpse of silver and a pale blue stone. Suddenly she dropped her hands to her sides and looked up at me. 'Where are you going?'

'The University.'

She arched an eyebrow, looking ten years older. 'So certain.' She smiled and was suddenly young again. 'How does it feel to know where you are going?'

I couldn't think of a reply, but was saved from the need for one by Reta calling us for supper. Denna and I walked toward the campfire, together.

———

The beginning of the next day was spent in a brief, awkward courtship. Eager, but not wanting to *seem* eager, I made a slow dance around Denna before finally finding some excuse to spend time with her.

Denna, on the other hand, seemed perfectly at ease. We spent the rest of the day as if we were old friends. We joked and told stories. I pointed out the different types of clouds and what they told of the weather to come. She showed me the shapes they held: a rose, a harp, a waterfall.

So passed the day. Later, when lots were being drawn to see who had which turn at watch, Denna and I drew the first two shifts. Without discussing it, we shared the four hours of watch together. Talking softly so as to not wake the others, we sat close by the fire and spent the time watching very little but each other.

The third day was much the same. We passed the time pleasantly, not in long conversation, but more often watching the scenery, saying whatever happened to come to our minds. That night we stopped at a wayside inn where Reta bought fodder for the horses and a few other supplies.

Reta retired early with her husband, telling each of us that she'd arranged for our dinners and beds with the innkeeper. The former was quite good, bacon and potato soup with fresh bread and butter. The latter was in the stables, but it was still a long sight better than what I was used to in Tarbean.

The common room smelled of smoke and sweat and spilled beer. I was glad when Denna asked if I wanted to take a walk. Outside was the warm quiet of a windless spring night. We talked as we wended our slow way through the wild bit of forest behind the inn. After a while we came to a wide clearing circling a pond.

On the edge of the water were a pair of waystones, their surfaces silver against the black of the sky, the black of the water. One stood upright, a finger pointing to the sky. The other lay flat, extending into the water like a short stone pier.

No breath of wind disturbed the surface of the water. So as we climbed out onto the fallen stone the stars reflected themselves in double fashion; as above, so below. It was as if we were sitting amid a sea of stars.

We spoke for hours, late into the night. Neither of us mentioned our pasts. I sensed that there were things she would rather not talk about, and by the way she avoided questioning me, I think she guessed the same. We spoke of ourselves instead, of fond imaginings and impossible things. I pointed to the skies and told her the names of stars and constellations. She told me stories about them I had never heard before.

My eyes were always returning to Denna. She sat beside me, arms hugging her knees. Her skin was more luminous than the moon, her eyes wider than the sky, deeper than the water, darker than the night.

It slowly began to dawn on me that I had been staring at her wordlessly for an impossible amount of time. Lost in my thoughts, lost in the sight of her. But her face didn't look offended or amused. It almost looked as if she were studying the lines of my face, almost as if she were waiting.

I wanted to take her hand. I wanted to brush her cheek with my fingertips. I wanted to tell her that she was the first beautiful thing I had seen in three years. That the sight of her yawning to the back of her hand was enough to drive the breath from me. How I sometimes lost the sense of her words in the sweet fluting of her voice. I wanted to say that if she were with me then somehow nothing could ever be wrong for me again.

In that breathless second I almost asked her. I felt the question boiling up from my chest. I remember drawing a breath then hesitating – what could I say? Come away with me? Stay with me? Come to the University? No. Sudden certainty tightened in my chest like a cold fist. What could I ask her? What could I offer? Nothing. Anything I said would sound foolish, a child's fantasy.

I closed my mouth and looked across the water. Inches away, Denna did the same. I could feel the heat of her. She smelled like road dust, and honey, and the smell the air holds seconds before a heavy summer rain.

Neither of us spoke. I closed my eyes. The closeness of her was the sweetest, sharpest thing my life had ever known.

CHAPTER THIRTY-FOUR

Yet to Learn

THE NEXT MORNING I blearily awoke after two hours of sleep, bundled myself onto one of the wagons and proceeded to drowse away the morning. It was nearly noon before I realised that we had taken on another passenger at the inn last night.

His name was Josn, and he had paid Roent for passage to Anilin. He had an easy manner and an honest smile. He seemed an earnest man. I did not like him.

My reason was simple. He spent the entire day riding next to Denna. He flattered her outrageously and joked with her about becoming one of his wives. She seemed unaffected by the late hours we had kept the night before, looking as bright and fresh as ever.

The result was that I spent the day being irritated and jealous while acting unconcerned. Since I was too proud to join their conversation, I was left to myself. I spent the day thinking sullen thoughts, trying to ignore the sound of his voice and occasionally remembering the way Denna had looked last night with the moon reflecting off the water behind her.

That night I was planning to ask Denna to go for a walk after everyone turned in for the night. But before I could approach her, Josn went to one of the wagons and brought back a large black case with brass buckles along the side. The sight of it made my heart turn sideways in my chest.

Sensing the group's anticipation, though not mine in particular, Josn slowly undid the brass clasps and drew out his lute with an air of studied nonchalance. It was a trouper's lute, its long, graceful neck and round bowl were painfully familiar. Sure of everyone's attention, he cocked his head and strummed, pausing to listen to the sound. Then, nodding to himself, he started to play.

He had a fair tenor and reasonably clever fingers. He played a ballad, then a light, quick drinking song, then a slow, sad melody in a language that I didn't recognise but suspected might be Yllish. Lastly he played 'Tinker Tanner', and everyone came in on the chorus. Everyone but me.

I sat still as stone with my fingers aching. I wanted to play, not listen. *Want* isn't strong enough a word. I was hungry for it, starved. I'm not proud of the fact that I thought about stealing his lute and leaving in the dark of the night.

He finished the song with a flourish, and Roent clapped his hands a couple of times to get everyone's attention. 'Time for sleep. You sleep too late—'

Derrik broke in, gently teasing. '. . . *we get left behind*. We know, Master Roent. We'll be ready to roll with the light.'

Josn laughed and flipped open his lute case with his foot. But before he could put it away I called over to him. 'Could I see that for a second?' I tried to keep the desperation out of my voice, tried to make it sound like idle curiosity.

I hated myself for the question. Asking to hold a musician's instrument is roughly similar to asking to kiss a man's wife. Nonmusicians don't understand. An instrument is like a companion and a lover. Strangers ask to touch and hold with annoying regularity. I knew better, but I couldn't help myself. 'Just for a second?'

I saw him stiffen slightly, reluctant. But keeping friendly appearances is a minstrel's business just as much as music. 'Certainly,' he said with a jocularity that I saw as false but was probably convincing for the others. He strode over to me and held it out. 'Be careful . . .'

Josn took a couple of steps back and gave a very good appearance of being at ease. But I saw how he stood with his arms slightly bent, ready to rush forward and whisk the lute away from me if the need arose.

I turned it over in my hands. Objectively, it was nothing special. My father would have rated it as one short step above firewood. I touched the wood. I cradled it against my chest.

I spoke without looking up. 'It's beautiful,' I said softly, my voice rough with emotion.

It was beautiful. It was the most beautiful thing I had seen in three years. More beautiful than the sight of a spring field after three years of living in that pestilent cesspit of a city. More beautiful than Denna. Almost.

I can honestly say that I was still not really myself. I was only four days away from living on the streets. I was not the same person I had been back in the days of the troupe, but neither was I yet the person you hear about in stories. I had changed because of Tarbean. I had learned many things it would have been easier to live without.

But sitting beside the fire, bending over the lute, I felt the hard, unpleasant parts of myself that I had gained in Tarbean crack. Like a clay mould around a now-cool piece of iron they fell away, leaving something clean and hard behind.

I sounded the strings, one at a time. When I hit the third it was ever so slightly off and I gave one of the tuning pegs a minute adjustment without thinking.

'Here now, don't go touching those,' Josn tried to sound casual, 'you'll turn it from true.' But I didn't really hear him. The singer and all the rest couldn't have been farther away from me if they'd been at the bottom of the Centhe Sea.

I touched the last string and tuned it too, ever so slightly. I made a simple chord and strummed it. It rang soft and true. I moved a finger and the chord went minor in a way that always sounded to me as if the lute were saying *sad*. I moved my hands again and the lute made two chords whispering against each other. Then, without realising what I was doing, I began to play.

The strings felt strange against my fingers, like reunited friends who have forgotten what they have in common. I played soft and slow, sending notes no farther than the circle of our firelight. Fingers and strings made a careful conversation, as if their dance described the lines of an infatuation.

Then I felt something inside me break and music began to pour out into the quiet. My fingers danced; intricate and quick they spun something gossamer and tremulous into the circle of light our fire had made. The music moved like a spiderweb stirred by a gentle breath, it changed like a leaf twisting as it falls to the ground, and it felt like three years Waterside in Tarbean, with a hollowness inside you and hands that ached from the bitter cold.

I don't know how long I played. It could have been ten minutes or an hour. But my hands weren't used to the strain. They slipped and the music fell to pieces like a dream on waking.

I looked up to see everyone perfectly motionless, their faces ranging from shock to amazement. Then, as if my gaze had broken some spell, everyone stirred. Roent shifted in his seat. The two mercenaries turned and raised eyebrows at each other. Derrik looked at me as if he had never seen me before.

Reta remained frozen, her hand held in front of her mouth. Denna lowered her face into her hands and began to cry in quiet, hopeless sobs.

Josn simply stood. His face was stricken and bloodless as if he had been stabbed.

I held out the lute, not knowing whether to thank him or apologise. He took it numbly. After a moment, unable to think of anything to say, I left them sitting by the fire and walked toward the wagons.

And that is how Kvothe spent his last night before he came to the University, with his cloak as both his blanket and his bed. As he lay down, behind him was a circle of fire, and before him lay shadow like a mantle, gathered. His eyes were open, that much is certain, but who among us can say they know what he was seeing?

Look behind him instead, to the circle of light that the fire has made, and leave Kvothe to himself for now. Everyone deserves a moment or two alone when they desire it. And if by chance there were tears, let us forgive him. He was just a child, after all, and had yet to learn what sorrow really was.

CHAPTER THIRTY-FIVE

A Parting of Ways

THE WEATHER HELD FAIR, which meant that the wagons rolled into Imre just as the sun was setting. My mood was sullen and hurt. Denna had shared a wagon with Josn the whole of the day, and I, being foolish and proud, had kept my distance.

A whirl of activity sprang up as soon as the wagons rolled to a stop. Roent began to argue with a clean-shaven man in a velvet hat before he had brought his wagon to a full stop. After the initial bout of bargaining, a dozen men began unloading bolts of cloth, barrels of molasses, and burlap sacks of coffee. Reta cast a stern eye over the lot of them. Josn scuttled around, trying to keep his luggage from being damaged or stolen.

My own luggage was easier to manage, as I only had my travelsack. I retrieved it from between some bolts of cloth and moved away from the wagons. I slung it over one shoulder and looked around for Denna.

I found Reta instead. 'You were a great help on the road,' she said clearly. Her Aturan was much better than Roent's, with hardly any trace of a Siaru accent at all. 'It is nice to have someone along who can unhitch a horse without being led by the hand.' She held out a coin to me.

I took it without thinking. It was a reflex action from my years as a beggar. Like the reverse of jerking your hand back from a fire. Only after the coin was in my hand did I take a closer look at it. It was a whole copper jot, fully half of what I had paid to travel with them to Imre. When I looked back up, Reta was heading back towards the wagons.

Not sure what to think, I wandered over to where Derrick sat on the edge of a horse trough. He shaded his eyes against the evening sun with one hand as he looked up at me. 'On your way then? I almost thought you might stick with us for a while.'

I shook my head. 'Reta just gave me a jot.'

He nodded. 'I'm not terribly surprised. Most folks are nothing but dead weight.' He shrugged. 'And she appreciated your playing. Have you ever thought of trying out as a minstrel? They say Imre's a good place for it.'

I steered the conversation back to Reta. 'I don't want Roent to be angry with her. He seems to take his money pretty seriously.'

Derrick laughed. 'And she doesn't?'

'I gave my money to Roent,' I clarified. 'If he'd wanted to give some of it back, I think he'd do it himself.'

Derrick nodded. 'It's not their way. A man doesn't give money away.'

'That's my point,' I said. 'I don't want her to get in trouble.'

Derrick waved his hands back and forth, cutting me off. 'I'm not doing a good job explaining myself,' he said. 'Roent knows. He might have even sent her over to do it. But grown Cealdish men don't give away money. It's seen as womanish behaviour. They don't even buy things if they can help it. Didn't you notice that Reta was the one who bargained for our rooms and food at the inn a few nights ago?'

I did remember, now that he mentioned it. 'But why?' I asked.

Derrick shrugged. 'There isn't any why. It's just the way they do things. That's why so many Cealdish caravans are husband-wife teams.'

'Derrick!' Roent's voice came from behind the wagons.

He sighed as he stood up. 'Duty calls,' he said. 'See you around.'

I tucked the jot into my pocket and thought about what Derrick had said. The truth was, my troupe had never gone so far north as to make it into the Shald. It was unnerving to think I wasn't as world-wise as I'd thought.

I slung my travelsack over my shoulder and looked around one last time, thinking that perhaps it would be best if I left without any troublesome good-byes. Denna was nowhere to be seen. That settled it then. I turned to leave . . .

. . . and found her standing behind me. She smiled a little awkwardly with her hands clasped behind her back. She was lovely as a flower, and totally unconscious of it. I was suddenly short of breath, and I forgot myself, my irritation, my hurt.

'You're still going?' She asked.

I nodded.

'You could come to Anilin with us,' she suggested. 'They say the streets are paved with gold there. You could teach Josn to play that lute he carries around.' She smiled. 'I've asked him, and he's said he wouldn't mind.'

I considered it. For half a heartbeat I almost threw my whole plan aside just to stay with her a little longer. But the moment passed and I shook my head.

'Don't look like that,' she chided me with a smile. 'I'll be there for a while, if things don't work out for you here.' She trailed off hopefully.

I didn't know what I *could* do if things didn't work out for me here. I was hanging all my hopes on the University. Besides, Anilin was hundreds of miles away. I barely owned the clothes on my back. How would I find her?

Denna must have seen my thoughts reflected on my face. She smiled playfully. 'I guess I'll just have to come looking for you, then.'

We Ruh are travellers. Our lives are composed of meetings and partings, with brief, bright acquaintances in-between. Because of this I knew the truth. I felt it, heavy and certain in the pit of my stomach: I would never see her again.

Before I could say anything she looked nervously behind her. 'I had better go. Watch for me.' She flashed her impish smile again before turning to walk away.

'I will,' I called after her. 'I'll see you where the roads meet.'

She glanced back and hesitated for a moment, then waved and ran off into the early evening twilight.

CHAPTER THIRTY-SIX

Less Talents

I SPENT THE NIGHT sleeping outside the city limits of Imre in a soft bed of heather. The next day I woke late, washed in a nearby stream, and made my way west to the University.

As I walked, I watched the horizon for the largest building in the University. From Ben's descriptions I knew what it would look like: featureless, grey, and square as a block. Larger than four granaries stacked together. No windows, no decorations, and only one set of great stone doors. Ten times ten thousand books. The Archives.

I had come to the University for many reasons, but that was at the heart of it. The Archives held answers, and I had many, many questions. First and foremost, I wanted to know the truth about the Chandrian and the Amyr. I needed to know how much of Skarpi's story was the truth.

When the road crossed the Omethi River, there was an old stone bridge. I don't doubt that you know the type. It was one of those ancient, mammoth pieces of architecture scattered throughout the world, so old and solidly built that they have become part of the landscape, not a soul wondering who built them, or why. This one was particularly impressive, over two hundred feet long and wide enough for two wagons to pass each other, it stretched over the canyon the Omethi had carved into the rock. When I reached the crest of the bridge I saw the Archives for the first time in my life, rising like some great greystone over the trees to the west.

The University lay at the heart of a small city. Though truthfully, I hesitate to call it a city at all. It was nothing like Tarbean with its twisting alleys and garbage smell. It was more of a town, with wide roads and clean air. Lawns and gardens were spaced between small houses and shops.

But since this town had grown up to serve the peculiar needs of the University, a careful observer could note small differences in the services the town provided. For instance, there were two glassblowers, three fully stocked apothecaries, two binderies, four booksellers, two brothels, and a truly disproportionate number of taverns. One of them had a large wooden sign nailed to its door proclaiming, NO SYMPATHY! I wondered what non-arcane visitors might think of the warning.

The University itself consisted of about fifteen buildings that bore little resemblance to each other. Mews had a circular central hub with eight wings radiating in each direction so it looked like a compass rose. Hollows was simple and square, with stained glass windows showing Teccam in a classic pose: standing barefoot in the mouth of his cave, speaking to a group of students. Mains was the most distinctive building of the lot: it covered nearly an acre and a half and looked like it had been cobbled together from a number of smaller, mismatched buildings.

As I approached the Archives, its grey, windowless surface reminded me of an immense greystone. It was hard to believe after all the years of waiting that I was finally there. I circled around it until I found the entrance, a massive pair of stone doors standing wide open. Over them, chiselled deep into the stone, were the words *Vorfelan Rhinata Morie*. I didn't recognise the language. It wasn't Siaru . . . maybe Yllish, or Temic. Yet another question I needed answers for.

Through the stone doors was a small antechamber with a more ordinary set of wooden doors inside. I tugged them open and felt cool, dry air brush past me. The walls were bare grey stone, lit with the distinctive unwavering reddish light of sympathy lamps. There was a large wooden desk with several large, ledger-type books lying open atop it.

At the desk sat a young man who looked to be a full-blooded Ceald, with the characteristic ruddy complexion and dark hair and eyes.

'Can I help you?' he asked, his voice thick with the harsh burr a Siaru accent makes.

'I'm here for the Archives,' I said stupidly. My stomach was dancing with butterflies. My palms were sweaty.

He looked me over, obviously wondering at my age. 'Are you a student?'

'Soon,' I said. 'I haven't been through admissions yet.'

'You'll need to do that first,' he said seriously. 'I can't let anyone in unless they're in the book.' He gestured at the ledgers on the desk in front of him.

The butterflies died. I didn't bother to hide my disappointment. 'Are you sure I can't look around just for a couple of minutes? I've come an awfully long way . . .' I looked at the two sets of double doors leading out of the room, one labelled TOMES the other STACKS. Behind the desk a smaller door was labeled SCRIVS ONLY.

His expression softened somewhat. 'I cannot. There would be trouble.' He looked me over again. 'Are you really going through admissions?' his skepticism was obvious even through his thick accent.

I nodded. 'I just came here first.' I said looking around the empty room, eyeing the closed doors, trying to think of some way to persuade him to let me in.

He spoke before I could think of anything. 'If you're really going, you should hurry. Today is the last day. Sometimes they don't go much longer than noon.'

My heart beat hard and quick in my chest. I'd assumed they would run all day. 'Where are they?'

'Hollows.' He gestured toward the outer door. 'Down, then left. Short building with . . . colour-windows. Two big . . . trees out front.' He paused. 'Maple? Is that the word for a tree?'

I nodded and hurried outside, soon I was pelting down the road.

———

Two hours later I was in Hollows, fighting down a sour stomach and climbing up onto the stage of an empty theatre. The room was dark except for the wide circle of light that held the masters' table. I walked to stand at the edge of the light and waited. Slowly the nine masters stopped talking among themselves and turned to look at me.

They sat at a huge, crescent-shaped table. It was raised, so even seated they were looking down on me. They were serious-looking men, ranging in age from mature to ancient.

There was a long moment of silence before the man sitting at the centre of the crescent motioned me forward. I guessed he was the Chancellor. 'Come up where we can see you. That's right. Hello. Now, what's your name, boy?'

'Kvothe, sir.'

'And why are you here?'

I looked him in the eye. 'I want to attend the University. I want to be an arcanist.' I looked around at each of them. Some seemed amused. None looked particularly surprised.

'You are aware,' the Chancellor said. 'That the University is for continuing one's education. Not beginning it?'

'Yes, Chancellor. I know.'

'Very well,' he said. 'May I have your letter of introduction?'

I didn't hesitate. 'I'm afraid I don't have one, sir. Is it absolutely necessary?'

'It is customary to have a sponsor,' he explained. 'Preferably an arcanist. Their letter tells us what you know. Your areas of excellence and weakness.'

'The arcanist I learned from was named Abenthy, sir. But he never gave me a letter of introduction. Might I tell you myself?'

The Chancellor nodded gravely, 'Unfortunately, we have no way of knowing that you actually have studied with an arcanist without proof of some kind. Do you have anything that can corroborate your story? Any other correspondence?'

'He gave me a book before we parted ways, sir. He inscribed it to me and signed his name.'

The Chancellor smiled. 'That should do nicely. Do you have it with you?'

'No.' I let some honest bitterness creep into my voice. 'I had to pawn it in Tarbean.'

Sitting to the left of the Chancellor, Master Rhetorician Hemme made a disgusted noise at my comment, earning him an irritated look from the Chancellor. 'Come, Herma,' Hemme said, slapping his hand on the table. 'The boy is obviously lying. I have important matters to attend to this afternoon.'

The Chancellor gave him a vastly irritated look. 'I have not given you leave to speak, Master Hemme.' The two of them stared at each other for a long moment before Hemme looked away, scowling.

The Chancellor turned back to me, then his eye caught some movement from one of the other masters. 'Yes, Master Lorren?'

The tall, thin master looked at me passively. 'What was the book called?'

'*Rhetoric and Logic,* sir.'

'And where did you pawn it?'

'The Broken Binding, on Seaward Square.'

Lorren turned to look at the Chancellor. 'I will be leaving for Tarbean tomorrow to fetch necessary materials for the upcoming term. If it is there I will bring it back. The matter of the boy's claim can be settled then.'

The Chancellor gave a small nod. 'Thank you, Master Lorren.' He settled himself back into his chair and folded his hands in front of himself. 'Very well, then. What would Abenthy's letter tell us, if he had written it?'

I took a good breath. 'He would say that I knew by heart the first ninety sympathetic bindings. That I could double-distill, perform titration, calcify, sublimate, and precipitate solution. That I am well versed in history, argument, grammars, medicine, and geometry.'

The Chancellor did his best to not look amused. 'That's quite a list. Are you sure you didn't leave anything out?'

I paused. 'He probably would have also mentioned my age, sir.'

'How old are you, boy?'

'Kvothe, sir.'

A smile tugged at the Chancellor's face. 'Kvothe.'

'Fifteen, sir.' There was a rustle as the masters each took some small action, exchanged glances, raised eyebrows, shook their heads. Hemme rolled his eyes skyward.

Only the Chancellor did nothing. 'How exactly would he have mentioned your age?'

I gave a thin sliver of a smile. 'He would have urged you to ignore it.'

There was a breath of silence. The Chancellor drew a deep breath and leaned back in his seat. 'Very well. We have a few questions for you. Would you like to begin, Master Brandeur?' He made a gesture toward one end of the crescent table.

I turned to face Brandeur. Portly and balding, he was the University's Master Arithmetician. 'How many grains are in thirteen ounces?'

'Six thousand two hundred and forty,' I said immediately.

He raised his eyebrows a little. 'If I had fifty silver talents and converted them to Vintish coin and back, how much would I have if the Cealdim took four percent each time?'

I started the ponderous conversion between currencies, then smiled as I realised it was unnecessary. 'Forty-six talents and eight drabs, if he's honest. Forty-six even if he's not.'

He nodded again, looking at me more closely. 'You have a triangle,' he said slowly. 'One side is seven feet. Another side, three feet. One angle is sixty degrees. How long is the other side?'

'Is the angle between the two sides?' He nodded. I closed my eyes for the space of half a breath, then opened them again. 'Six feet six inches. Dead even.'

He made a *hmmmpfh* noise and looked surprised. 'Good enough. Master Arwyl?'

Arwyl asked his question before I had time to turn and to face him. 'What are the medicinal properties of hellebore?'

'Anti-inflammatory, antiseptic, mild sedative, mild analgesic. Blood purifier.' I said, looking up at the grandfatherly, spectacled old man. 'Toxic if used excessively. Dangerous for women who are with child.'

'Name the component structures that comprise the hand.'

I named all twenty-seven bones, alphabetically. Then the muscles from largest to smallest. I listed them quickly, matter-of-factly, pointing out their locations on my own upraised hand.

The speed and accuracy of my answers impressed them. Some of them hid it, others wore it openly on their faces. The truth was, I needed to impress them. I knew from my previous discussions with Ben that you needed money or brains to get into the University. The more of one you had, the less of the other you needed.

So I was cheating. I had snuck into Hollows through a back entrance, acting the part of an errand boy. Then I'd picked two locks and spent more than an hour watching other students' interviews. I heard hundreds of questions and thousands of answers.

I also heard how high the other students' tuitions were set. The lowest had been four talents and six jots, but most were double that. One student had been charged over thirty talents for his tuition. It would be easier for me to get a piece of the moon than that much money.

I had two copper jots in my pocket and no way to get a bent penny more. So I needed to impress them. More than that. I needed to confound them with my intelligence. To dazzle them.

I finished listing the muscles of the hand and started in on the ligatures when Arwyl waved me into silence and asked his next question. 'When do you bleed a patient?'

The question brought me up short. 'When I want him to die?' I asked dubiously.

He nodded, mostly to himself. 'Master Lorren?'

Master Lorren was pale and seemed unnaturally tall even while sitting. 'Who was the first declared king of Tarvintas?'

'Posthumously? Feyda Calanthis. Otherwise it would be his brother, Jarvis.'

'Why did the Aturan Empire collapse?'

I paused, taken aback by the scope of the question. None of the other students had been asked anything so broad as this. 'Well sir,' I said slowly to give myself a moment or two to organise my thoughts. 'Partly because Lord Nalto was an inept egomaniac. Partly because the church went into upheaval and denounced the Order Amyr who were a large part of the strength of Atur. Partly because the military was fighting three different wars of conquest at the same time, and high taxes fomented rebellion in lands already inside the empire.'

I watched the master's expression, hoping he would give some sign when he had heard enough. 'They also debased their currency, undercut the universality of the iron law, and antagonised the Adem.' I shrugged. 'But of course it's more complicated than that.'

Master Lorren's expression remained unchanged, but he nodded. 'Who was the greatest man who ever lived?'

Another unfamiliar question. I thought for a minute. 'Illien.'

Master Lorren blinked once, expressionless. 'Master Mandrag?'

Mandrag was clean-shaven and smooth-faced, with hands stained a half hundred different colours and seemed to be made all of knuckle and bone. 'If you needed phosphorus where would you get it?'

His tone sounded for a moment so much like Abenthy's that I forgot myself and spoke without thinking. 'An apothecary?' One of the masters on the other side of the table chuckled and I bit my too-quick tongue.

He gave me a faint smile, and I drew a faint breath. 'Barring access to an apothecary.'

'I could render it from urine,' I said quickly. 'Given a kiln and enough time.'

'How much would you need to gain two ounces pure?' He cracked his knuckles absentmindedly.

I paused to consider, as this was a new question too. 'At least forty gallons, Master Mandrag, depending on the quality of the material.'

There was a long pause as he cracked his knuckles one at a time. 'What are the three most important rules of the chemist?'

This I knew from Ben. 'Label clearly. Measure twice. Eat elsewhere.'

He nodded, still wearing the faint smile. 'Master Kilvin?'

Kilvin was Cealdish, his thick shoulders and bristling black beard reminded me of a bear. 'Right,' he grumbled, folding his thick hands in front of him. 'How would you make an ever-burning lamp?'

Each of the other eight masters made some sort of exasperated noise or gesture.

'What?' Kilvin demanded, looking around at them, irritated. 'It is my question. The asking is mine.' He turned his attention back to me. 'So. How would you make it?'

'Well,' I said slowly. 'I would probably start with a pendulum of some sort. Then I would bind it to—'

'*Kraem*. No. Not like this.' Kilvin growled out a couple words and pounded his fist on the table, each thump as his hand came down was accompanied by a staccato burst of reddish light that welled up from his hand. 'No sympathy. I do not want an ever-*glowing* lamp. I want an ever-*burning* one.' He looked at me again showing his teeth, as if he were going to eat me.

'Lithium salt?' I asked without thinking, then backpedaled. 'No, a sodium oil that burned in an enclosed . . . no, damn.' I mumbled my way to a stop. The other applicants hadn't had to deal with questions like these.

He cut me off with a short sideways gesture of his hand. 'Enough. We will talk later. Elxa Dal.'

It took me a moment to remember that Elxa Dal was the next master. I turned to him. He looked like the archetypal sinister magician that seems to be a requirement in so many bad Aturan plays. Severe dark eyes, lean face, short black beard. For all that, his expression was friendly enough. 'What are the words for the first parallel kinetic binding?'

I rattled them off glibly.

He didn't seem surprised. 'What was the binding that Master Kilvin used just a moment ago?'

'Capacatorial Kinetic Luminosity.'

'What is the synodic period?'

I looked at him oddly. 'Of the moon?' The question seemed a little out of sync with the other two.

He nodded.

'Seventy-two and a third days, sir. Give or take a bit.'

He shrugged and gave a wry smile, as if he'd expected to catch me with the last question. 'Master Hemme?'

Hemme looked at me over steepled fingers. 'How much mercury would it take to reduce two gills of white sulfur?' he asked pompously, as if I'd already given the wrong answer.

One of the things I'd learned during my hour of quiet observation was this: Master Hemme was the king-high bastard of the lot. He took delight in students' discomfort and did everything he could to badger and unsettle them. He had a fondness for trick questions.

Luckily, this was one I had watched him use on other students. You see, you *can't* reduce white sulfur with mercury. 'Well,' I drew the word out, pretending to think it through. Hemme's smug smile grew wider by the second. 'Assuming you mean *red* sulfur, it would be about forty-one ounces. Sir.' I smiled a sharp smile at him. All teeth.

'Name the nine prime fallacies,' he snapped.

'Simplification. Generalisation. Circularity. Reduction. Analogy. False causality. Semantism. Irrelevancy. . . .' I paused, not being able to remember the formal name of the last one. Ben and I had called it Nalt, after Emperor Nalto. It galled me, not being able to recall its real name, as I had read it in *Rhetoric and Logic* just a few days ago.

My irritation must have shown on my face. Hemme glowered at me as I paused, saying. 'So you don't know everything after all?' He leaned back into his seat with a satisfied expression.

'I wouldn't be here if I didn't think I had anything to learn,' I said bitingly before I managed to get my tongue under control again. From the other side of the table, Kilvin gave a deep chuckle.

Hemme opened his mouth, but the Chancellor silenced him with a look before he could say anything else. 'Now then,' the Chancellor began, 'I think—'

'I too would ask some questions,' the man to the Chancellor's right said. He had an accent that I couldn't quite place. Or perhaps it was that his voice held a certain resonance. When he spoke, everyone at the desk stirred slightly, then grew still, like leaves touched by the wind.

'Master Namer,' the Chancellor said with equal parts deference and trepidation.

Elodin was younger than the others by at least a dozen years. Cleanshaven with deep eyes. Medium height, medium build, there was nothing particularly striking about him, except for the way he sat at the table, one moment watching something intently, the next minute bored and letting his attention wander among the high beams of the ceiling above. He was almost like a child who had been forced to sit down with adults.

I felt Master Elodin look at me. Actually felt it. I suppressed a shiver. *'Soheketh ka Siaru krema'teth tu?'* he asked. *How well do you speak Siaru?*

'Rieusa, ta krelar deala tu.' Not very well, thank you.

He lifted a hand, his index finger pointing upwards. 'How many fingers am I holding up?'

I paused for a moment, which was more consideration than the question seemed to warrant. 'At least one,' I said. 'Probably no more than six.'

He broke into a broad smile and brought his other hand up from underneath the table, it had two fingers upright. He waved them back and forth for the other masters to see, nodding his head from side to side in an absent, childish way. Then he lowered his hands to the table in front of him, and grew suddenly serious. 'Do you know the seven words that will make a woman love you?'

I looked at him, trying to decide if there was more to the question. When nothing more was forthcoming, I answered simply, 'No.'

'They exist.' He reassured me, and sat back with a look of contentment. 'Master Linguist?' He nodded to the Chancellor.

'That seems to cover most of academia,' the Chancellor said almost to himself. I had the impression that something had unsettled him, but he was too composed for me to tell exactly what. 'You will forgive me if I ask a few things of a less scholarly nature?'

Having no real choice, I nodded.

He gave me a long look that seemed to stretch several minutes. 'Why didn't Abenthy send a letter of recommendation with you?'

I hesitated. Not all travelling entertainers are as respectable as our troupe, so, understandably, not everyone respected them. But I doubted that lying was the best course of action. 'He left my troupe three years ago. I haven't seen him since.'

I saw each of the masters look at me. I could almost hear them doing the mental arithmetic, calculating my age backwards.

'Oh come now,' Hemme said disgustedly and moved as if he would stand.

The Chancellor gave him a dark look, silencing him. 'Why do you wish to attend the University?'

I stood dumbfounded. It was the one question I was completely unprepared for. What could I say? *Ten thousand books. Your Archives. I used to have dreams of reading there when I was young.* True, but too childish. *I want revenge against the Chandrian.* Too dramatic. *To become so powerful that no one will ever be able to hurt me again.* Too frightening.

I looked up to the Chancellor and realised I'd been quiet for a long while. Unable to think of anything else, I shrugged and said, 'I don't know, sir. I guess I'll have to learn that too.'

The Chancellor's eyes had taken on a curious look by this point but he pushed it aside as he said, 'Is there anything else you would like to say?' He had asked the question of the other applicants, but none of them had taken advantage of it. It seemed almost rhetorical, a ritual before the masters discussed the applicant's tuition.

'Yes, please,' I said, surprising him. 'I have a favour to ask beyond mere admission.' I took a deep breath, letting their attention settle on me. 'It has taken me nearly three years to get here. I may seem young, but I belong here as much, if not more, than some rich lordling who can't tell salt from cyanide by tasting it.'

I paused. 'However, at this moment I have two jots in my purse and nowhere in the world to get more than that. I have nothing worth selling that I haven't already sold.

'Admit me for more than two jots and I will not be able to attend. Admit me for less and I will be here every day, while every night I will do what it takes to stay alive while I study here. I will sleep in alleys and stables, wash dishes for kitchen scraps, beg pennies to buy pens. I will do whatever it takes.' I said the last words fiercely, almost snarling them.

'But admit me free, and give me three talents so I can live and buy what I need to learn properly, and I will be a student the likes of which you have never seen before.'

There was a half-breath of silence, followed by a thunderclap of a laugh from Kilvin. 'HA!' he roared. 'If one student in ten had half his fire I'd teach with a whip and chair instead of chalk and slate.' He brought his hand down hard on the table in front of him.

This sparked everyone to begin talking at the same time in their own varied tones. The Chancellor made a little wave in my direction and I took the chance to seat myself in the chair that stood at the edge of the circle of light.

The discussion seemed to go on for quite a long while. But even two or three minutes would have seemed like an eternity, sitting there while a group of old men debated my future. There was no actual shouting, but a fair amount of hand waving, most of it by Master Hemme, who seemed to have taken the same dislike of me that I had for him.

It wouldn't have been so bad if I could have understood what they were saying, but even my finely tuned eavesdropper's ears couldn't quite make out what was being said.

Their talking died down suddenly, and then the Chancellor looked in my direction, motioning me forward.

'Let it be recorded,' he said formally, 'that Kvothe, son of—' He paused and then looked at me inquiringly.

'Arliden,' I supplied. The name sounded strange to me after all these years. Master Lorren turned to look in my direction, blinking once.

'. . . son of Arliden, is admitted into the University for the continuance of his education on the forty-third of Caitelyn. His admission into the Arcanum contingent upon proof that he has mastered the basic principles of sympathy. Official sponsor being one Kilvin, Master Artificer. His tuition shall be set at the rate of less three talents.'

I felt a great dark weight settle inside me. Three talents might as well be all the money in the world for any hope I had in earning it before the term began. Working in kitchens, running errands for pennies, I might be able to save that much in a year, if I was lucky.

I held a desperate hope that I could cutpurse that much in time. But I knew the thought to be just that, desperate. People with that sort of money generally knew better than to leave it hanging in a purse.

I didn't realise that the masters had left the table until one of them approached me. I looked up to see the Master Archivist approaching me.

Lorren was taller than I would have guessed, over six and a half feet. His long face and hands made him look almost stretched. When he saw he had my attention, he asked, 'Did you say your father's name was Arliden?'

He asked it very calmly, with no hint of regret or apology in his voice. It suddenly made me very angry, that he should stifle my ambitions of getting into the University then come over and ask about my dead father as easy as saying good morning.

'Yes.' I said tightly.

'Arliden the bard?'

My father always thought of himself as a trouper. He never called himself bard or minstrel. Hearing him referred to in that way irritated me even more, if that were possible. I didn't deign to reply, merely nodded once, sharply.

If he thought my response terse he didn't show it. 'I was wondering which troupe he performed in.'

My thin restraint burst. 'Oh, you were *wondering*,' I said with every bit of venom my troupe-sharpened tongue could muster. 'Well maybe you can wonder a while longer. I'm stuck in ignorance now. I think you can abide a while with a little piece of it yourself. When I come back after earning my three talents, maybe then you can ask me again.' I gave him a fierce look, as if hoping to burn him with my eyes.

His reaction was minimal, it wasn't until later that I found getting any re-action from Master Lorren was about as likely as seeing a stone pillar wink.

He looked vaguely puzzled at first, then slightly taken aback, then, as I glared up at him, he gave a faint, thin smile and mutely handed me a piece of paper.

I unfolded and read it. It read: 'Kvothe. Spring term. Tuition: -3. Tln.' *Less* three talents. Of course.

Relief flooded me. As if it were a great wave that swept my legs from beneath me, I sat suddenly on the floor and wept.

CHAPTER THIRTY-SEVEN

Bright-Eyed

LORREN LED THE WAY across a courtyard. 'That is what most of the dis-cussion was about,' Master Lorren explained, his voice as passionless as stone. 'You had to have a tuition. Everyone does.'

I had recovered my composure and apologised for my terrible manners. He nodded calmly and offered to escort me to the office of the bursar to ensure that there was no confusion regarding my admission 'fee'.

'After it was decided to admit you in the manner you had suggested—' Lorren gave a brief but significant pause, leading me to believe that it had not been quite as simple as that '—there was the problem that there was no precedent set for giving out funds to enrolling students.' He paused again. 'A rather unusual thing.'

Lorren led me into another stone building, through a hallway, and down a flight of stairs. 'Hello, Riem.'

The bursar was an elderly, irritable man who became more irritable when he discovered he had to give money to me rather than the other way around. After I got my three talents, Master Lorren led me out of the building.

I remembered something and dug into my pocket, glad for an excuse to divert the conversation. 'I have a receipt from the Broken Binding.' I handed him the piece of paper, wondering what the owner would think when the University's Master Archivist showed up to redeem the book a filthy street urchin had sold him. 'Master Lorren, I appreciate your agreeing to do this, and I hope you won't think me ungrateful if I ask another favour . . .'

Lorren glanced at the receipt before tucking it into a pocket, and looked at me intently. No, not intently. Not quizzically. There was no expression on his face at all. No curiosity. No irritation. Nothing. If not for the fact that his eyes were focused on me, I would have thought he'd forgotten I was there. 'Feel free to ask,' he said.

'That book. It's all I have left from . . . that time in my life. I would very much like to buy it back from you someday, when I have the money.'

He nodded, still expressionless. 'That can be arranged. Do not waste your worry on its safety. It will be kept as carefully as any book in the Archives.'

Lorren raised a hand, gesturing to a passing student.

A sandy-haired boy pulled up short and approached nervously. Radiating deference, he made a nod that was almost like a bow to the Master Archivist. 'Yes, Master Lorren?'

Lorren gestured to me with one of his long hands. 'Simmon, this is Kvothe. He needs to be shown about, signed to classes and the like. Kilvin wants him in Artificing. Trust to your judgment otherwise. Will you tend to it?'

Simmon nodded again and brushed his hair out of his eyes. 'Yes, sir.'

Without another word, Lorren turned and walked away, his long strides making his black masters' robes billow out behind him.

Simmon was young for a student, though still a couple of years my senior. He stood taller than me, but his face was still boyish, his manner boyishly shy.

'Do you have somewhere to stay yet?' he asked as we started to walk. 'Room at an inn or anything?'

I shook my head. 'I just got in today. I haven't thought much further than getting though admissions.'

Simmon chuckled. 'I know what that's like. I still get sweaty at the beginning of each term.' He pointed to the left, down a wide lane lined with trees. 'Let's head to Mews first then.'

I stopped walking. 'I don't have a lot of money,' I admitted. I hadn't planned on getting a room. I was used to sleeping outside, and I knew I would need to save my three talents for clothes, food, paper, and next term's tuition. I couldn't count on the masters' generosity two terms in a row.

'Admissions didn't go that well, huh?' Simmon said sympathetically as he took my elbow and steered me towards another one of the grey University buildings. This one was three stories tall, many-windowed, and had several wings radiating out from a central hub. 'Don't feel bad about it. I got nervous and pissed myself the first time through. Figuratively.'

'I didn't do that badly,' I said, suddenly very conscious of the three talents in my purse. 'But I think I offended Master Lorren. He seemed a little . . .'

'Chilly?' Simmon asked. 'Distant? Like an unblinking pillar of stone?' He laughed. 'Lorren is always like that. Rumour has it that Elxa Dal has a standing offer of ten gold marks to anyone who can make him laugh.'

'Oh,' I relaxed a little. 'That's good. He's the last person I'd want to get on the wrong side of. I'm looking forward to spending a lot of time in the Archives.'

'Just handle the books gently and you'll get along fine. He's pretty detached for the most part, but be careful around his books.' He raised his eyebrows and shook his head. 'He's fiercer than a mother bear protecting her cubs. In fact, I'd rather get caught by a mother bear than have Lorren see me folding back a page.'

Simmon kicked at a rock, sending it skipping down the cobblestones. 'Okay. You've got options in the Mews. A talent will get you a bunk and a meal chit for the term.' He shrugged. 'Nothing fancy, but it keeps the rain off. You can share a room for two talents or get one all to yourself for three.'

'What's a meal chit?'

'Meals are three a day over in the Mess.' He pointed to a long, low-roofed building across the lawn. 'The food isn't bad so long as you don't think too hard about where it might have come from.'

I did some quick arithmetic. A talent for two month's worth of meals and a dry place to sleep was as good a deal as I could hope for. I smiled at Simmon. 'Sounds like just the thing.'

Simmon nodded as he opened the door into the Mews. 'Bunks it is, then. Come on, let's find a steward and get you signed up.'

The bunks for non-Arcanum students were on the fourth floor of the east wing of Mews, farthest from the bathing facilities on the ground floor. The accommodations were as Sim had described, nothing fancy. But the narrow bed had clean sheets, and there was a trunk with a lock where I could keep my meagre possessions.

All the lower bunks had already been claimed, so I took an upper one in the far corner of the room. As I looked out of one of the narrow windows from on top of my bunk, I was reminded of my secret place high on Tarbean's rooftops. The similarity was oddly comforting.

Lunch was a bowl of steaming-hot potato soup, beans, narrow rashers of fatty bacon, and fresh brown bread. The room's large plank tables were nearly half full, seating about two hundred students. The room was full of the low murmur of conversation, punctuated by laughter and the metallic sound of spoons and forks scraping against the tin trays.

Simmon steered me to the back corner of the long room. Two other students looked up as we approached.

Simmon made a one-handed gesture to me as he set down his tray. 'Everyone, meet Kvothe. Our newest dewy-eyed first-termer.' He gestured from one person to the next. 'Kvothe, these are the worst students the Arcanum has to offer: Manet and Wilem.'

'Already met him,' Wilem said. He was the dark-haired Cealdim from the Archives. 'You really were headed to admissions,' he said, mildly surprised. 'I thought you were dealing me false iron.' He reached out his hand for me to shake. 'Welcome.'

'Tehlu anyway,' Manet muttered, looking me over. He was at least fifty years old with wild hair and a grizzled beard. He wore a slightly dishevelled look, as if he'd only woken up a few minutes ago. 'Am I as old as I feel? Or is he as young as he looks?'

'Both,' Simmon said cheerfully as he sat down. 'Kvothe, Manet here has been in the Arcanum for longer than all of us put together.'

Manet snorted. 'Give me some credit. I've been in the Arcanum longer than any of you have been alive.'

'And still a lowly E'lir,' Wilem said, his thick Siaru accent made it hard to tell if he was being sarcastic or not.

'Huzzah to being an E'lir,' Manet said earnestly. 'You boys will regret it if you move any farther up the ranks. Trust me. It's just more hassle and higher tuitions.'

'We want our guilders, Manet,' Simmon said. 'Preferably sometime before we're dead.'

'The guilder is overrated too,' Manet said, tearing off a piece of bread and dunking it in his soup. The exchange had an easy feel, and I guessed this was a familiar conversation.

'How'd you do?' Simmon asked Wilem eagerly.

'Seven and eight,' Wilem grumbled.

Simmon looked surprised. 'What in God's name happened? Did you punch one of them?'

'Fumbled my cipher,' Wilem said sullenly. 'And Lorren asked about the influence of subinfudation on Modegan currency. Kilvin had to translate. Even then I could not answer.'

'My soul weeps for you,' Sim said lightly. 'You trounced me these last two terms, I was bound to catch a break sooner or later. I got five talents even this term.' He held out his hand. 'Pay up.'

Wilem dug into his pocket and handed Sim a copper jot.

I looked at Manet. 'Aren't you in on it?'

The wild-haired man huffed a laugh and shook his head. 'There'd be some long odds against me,' he said, his mouth half full.

'Let's hear it,' Simon said with a sigh. 'How much this term?'

'One and six,' Manet said, grinning like a wolf.

Before anyone could think to ask me what my tuition was, I spoke up. 'I heard about someone getting a thirty-talent tuition. Do they usually get that high?'

'Not if you have the good sense to stay low in the rankings,' Manet grumbled.

'Only nobility,' Wilem said. '*Kraemlish* bastards with no business having their study here. I think they stoke up high tuitions just so they can complain.'

'I don't mind,' Manet said. 'Take their money. Keep my tuition low.'

I jumped as a tray clattered down onto the other side of the table. 'I assume you're talking about me.' The owner of the tray was blue-eyed and handsome with a carefully trimmed beard and high Modegan cheekbones. He was dressed in rich, muted colours. On his hip was a knife with a worked-wire hilt. The first weapon I'd seen anyone wearing at the University.

'Sovoy?' Simmon looked stunned. 'What are you doing here?'

'I ask myself the same thing.' Sovoy looked down at the bench. 'Are there no proper chairs in this place?' He took his seat, moving with an odd combination of graceful courtliness and stiff, affronted dignity. 'Excellent. Next, I'll be eating with a trencher and throwing bones to the dogs over my shoulder.'

'Etiquette dictates it be the left shoulder, your highness,' Manet said around a mouthful of bread, grinning.

Sovoy's eyes flashed angry, but before he could say anything Simmon spoke up, 'What happened?'

'My tuition was sixty-eight strehlaum,' he said indignantly.

Simmon looked nonplussed. 'Is that a lot?'

'It is. A lot,' Sovoy said sarcastically. 'And for no good reason. I answered their questions. This is a grudge, plain and simple. Mandrag does not like me.

Neither does Hemme. Besides, everyone knows they squeeze the nobility twice as hard as you lot, bleeding us dry as stones.'

'Simmon's nobility,' Manet pointed a spoon. 'He seems to do fine for himself.'

Sovoy exhaled sharply through his nose. 'Simmon's father is a paper duke bowing to a tin king in Atur. My father's stables have longer bloodlines than half you Aturan nobles.'

Simmon stiffened slightly in his seat, though he didn't look up from his meal.

Wilem turned to face Sovoy, his dark eyes going hard. But before he could say anything Sovoy slumped, rubbing his face in one hand. 'I'm sorry, Sim, my house and name to you. It's just . . . things were going to be better this term, but now they're worse instead. My allowance wouldn't even cover my tuition, and no one will extend me more credit. Do you know how humiliating that is? I've had to give up my rooms at the Golden Pony. I'm on the third floor of Mews. I almost had to share a room. What would my father say if he knew?'

Simmon, his mouth full, shrugged and made a gesture with his spoon that seemed to indicate that there was no offence taken.

'Maybe things would go better for you if you didn't go in there looking like a peacock.' Manet said. 'Leave off the silk when you go through admissions.'

'Is that how it is?' Sovoy said, his temper flaring again. 'Should I abase myself? Rub ashes in my hair? Tear my clothes?' As he grew angrier, his lilting accent became more pronounced. 'No. They are none of them better men than me. I need not bow to them.'

There was a moment of uncomfortable silence at the table. I noticed more than a few of the surrounding students were watching the show from the nearby tables.

'*Hylta tiam,*' Sovoy continued. 'There is nothing in this place I do not hate. Your weather is wild and uncivilised. Your religion barbaric and prudish. Your whores are intolerably ignorant and unmannerly. Your language barely has the subtlety to express how wretched this place is . . .'

Sovoy's voice grew softer the longer he spoke, until he almost seemed to be speaking to himself. 'My blood goes back fifty generations, older than tree or stone. And I am come to this,' he put his head against the palms of his hands and looked down at his tin tray. 'Barley bread. Gods all around us, a man is meant to eat wheat.'

I watched him while chewing a mouthful of the fresh brown bread. It tasted wonderful.

'I don't know what I was thinking,' Sovoy said suddenly, getting to his feet. 'I can't deal with this.' He stormed off, leaving his tray on the table.

'That's Sovoy,' Manet said to me in an offhand manner. 'Not a bad sort, though he's usually not nearly as drunk as that.'

'He's Modegan?'

Simmon laughed. 'You don't get more Modegan than Sovoy.'

'You should not prod at him,' Wilem said to Manet. His rough accent made it hard for me to tell if he was rebuking the older student, but his dark Cealdish face showed definite reproach. As a foreigner, I guessed he sympathised with Sovoy's difficulty adjusting to the language and culture of the Commonwealth.

'He *is* having a rough time of it,' Simmon admitted. 'Remember when he had to let his manservant go?'

Mouth full, Manet made a gesture with both hands as if playing an imaginary violin. He rolled his eyes, his expression vastly unsympathetic.

'He had to sell his rings this time around,' I added. Wilem, Simmon, and Manet turned to look at me curiously. 'There were pale lines on his fingers.' I explained, holding up my hand to demonstrate.

Manet gave me a close looking over. 'Well now! Our new student seems to be all manner of clever.' He turned to Wilem and Simmon. 'Lads, I'm in a betting mood. I'll wager two jots that our young Kvothe makes it into the Arcanum before the end of his third term.'

'Three terms?' I said, surprised. 'They told me all I had to do was prove I mastered the basic principles of sympathy.'

Manet gave me a gentle smile. 'They tell everyone that. Principles of Sympathy is one of the classes you'll have to slog through before they elevate you to E'lir.' He turned back to Wil and Sim expectantly. 'How about it? Two jots?'

'I'll bet.' Wilem gave me a small, apologetic shrug. 'No offense. I play the odds.'

'What'll you be studying then?' Manet asked as they shook on it.

The question caught me off guard. 'Everything, I guess.'

'You sound like me thirty years ago,' Manet chuckled. 'Where are you going to start?'

'The Chandrian,' I said. 'I'd like to know as much about them as possible.'

Manet frowned, then burst out laughing. 'Well that's fine and good, I suppose. Sim here studies faeries and piksies. Wil there believes in all manner of silly damn Cealdish sky spirits and such.' He puffed himself up absurdly. 'I'm big on imps and shamble-men myself.'

I felt my face get hot with embarrassment.

'God's body, Manet,' Sim cut him off. 'What has got into you?'

'I just bet two jots on a boy who wants to study bedtime stories,' Manet groused, gesturing to me with his fork.

'He meant folklore. That sort of thing.' Wilem turned to look at me. 'You looking to work in the Archives?'

'Folklore's a piece of it,' I hedged quickly, eager to save face. 'I want to see if different cultures' folktales conform to Teccam's theory of narrative septagy.'

Sim turned back to Manet. 'See? Why are you so twitchy today? When's the last time you slept?'

'Don't take that tone with me,' Manet grumbled. 'I caught a few hours last night.'

'And which night was that?' Sim pressed.

Manet paused, looking down at his tray. 'Felling night?'

Wilem shook his head, muttering something in Siaru.

Simmon looked horrified. 'Manet, yesterday was Cendling. Has it been two days since you've slept?'

'Probably not,' Manet said uncertainly. 'I always lose track of things during admissions. There aren't any classes. It throws off my schedule. Besides, I've been caught up in a project in the Fishery.' He trailed off, scrubbing at his face with his hands, then looked up at me. 'They're right. I'm a little off my head right now. Teccam's septagy, folklore and all that. It's a bit bookish for me, but a fine thing to study. I didn't mean any offence.'

'None taken.' I said easily and nodded at Sovoy's tray. 'Slide that over here, would you? If our young noble's not coming back, I'll have his bread.'

After Simmon took me to sign up for classes, I made my way to the Archives, eager to have a look around after all these years of dreaming.

This time when I entered the Archives, there was a young gentleman sitting behind the desk, tapping a pen on a piece of paper that bore the marks of much rewriting and crossing out. As I approached, he scowled and scratched out another line. His face was built to scowl. His hands were soft and pale. His blinding white linen shirt and richly-dyed blue vest reeked of money. The part of me that was not long removed from Tarbean wanted to pick his pocket.

He tapped his pen for another few moments before laying it down with a vastly irritated sigh. 'Name,' he said without looking up.

'Kvothe.'

He flipped through the ledger, found a particular page and frowned. 'You're not in the book.' He glanced up briefly and scowled again before turning back to whatever verse he was laboring over. When I made no signs of leaving he flicked his fingers as if shooing away a bug. 'Feel free to piss off.'

'I've just—'

Ambrose put down his pen again. 'Listen,' he said slowly, as if explaining to a simpleton. 'You're not in the book,' he made an exaggerated gesture toward the ledger with both hands. 'You don't get inside.' He made another gesture to the inner doors. 'The end.'

'I've just gone through admissions—'

He tossed up his hands, exasperated. 'Then of course you're not in the book.'

I dug into a pocket for my admission slip. 'Master Lorren gave me this himself.'

'I don't care if he carried you here pig-a-back,' Ambrose said, pointedly redipping his pen. 'Now quit wasting my time. I have things to do.'

'Wasting *your* time?' I demanded, my temper finally wearing thin. 'Do you have any idea what I've gone through to get here?'

Ambrose looked up at me, his expression growing suddenly amused. 'Wait, let me guess,' he said, laying his hands flat on the table and pushing himself to his feet. 'You were always smarter than the other children back in Clodhump, or whatever little one-whore town you're from. Your ability to read and count left the local villagers awestruck.'

I heard the outer door open and shut behind me, but Ambrose didn't pay it any attention as he walked around to lean against the front of the desk. 'Your parents knew you were special so they saved up for a couple years, bought you a pair of shoes, and sewed the pig blanket into a shirt.' He reached out to rub the fabric of my new clothes between his fingers.

'It took months of walking, hundreds of miles bumping along in the backs of mule carts. But in the end . . .' He made an expansive gesture with both hands. 'Praise Tehlu and all his angels! Here you are! All bright-eyed and full of dreams!'

I heard laughter and turned to see that two men and a young woman had come in during his tirade. 'God's body, Ambrose. What's got you started?'

'Goddamn first-termers,' Ambrose groused as he headed back around to sit behind the desk. 'Come in here dressed like rag piles and act like they own the place.'

The three newcomers walked toward the doors marked STACKS. I fought down a hot flush of embarrassment as they looked me up and down. 'Are we still heading to the Eolian tonight?'

Ambrose nodded. 'Of course. Sixth bell.'

'Aren't you going to check to see if they're in the book?' I asked as the door closed behind them.

Ambrose turned back to me, his smile bright, brittle, and by no means friendly. 'Listen, I'm going to give you a little advice for free. Back home you were something special. Here you're just another kid with a big mouth. So address me as Re'lar, go back to your bunk, and thank whatever pagan God you pray to that we're not in Vintas. My father and I would chain you to a post like a rabid dog.'

He shrugged. 'Or don't. Stay here. Make a scene. Start to cry. Better yet, take a swing at me.' He smiled. 'I'll give you a thrashing and get you thrown out on your ear.' He picked up his pen and turned back to whatever he was writing.

I left.

You might think that this encounter left me disheartened. You might think I felt betrayed, my childhood dreams of the University cruelly shattered.

Quite the contrary. It reassured me. I had been feeling rather out of my element until Ambrose let me know, in his own special way, that there wasn't much difference between the University and the streets of Tarbean. No matter where you are, people are basically the same.

Besides, anger can keep you warm at night, and wounded pride can spur a man to wondrous things.

CHAPTER THIRTY-EIGHT

Sympathy in the Mains

MAINS WAS THE OLDEST building at the University. Over the centuries it had grown slowly in all directions, engulfing smaller buildings and courtyards as it spread. It had the look of an ambitious architectural breed of lichen that was trying to cover as many acres as it could.

It was a hard place to find your way around. Hallways took odd turns, dead-ended unexpectedly, or took long, rambling, roundabout paths. It could easily take twenty minutes to walk from one room to another, despite the fact that they were only fifty feet apart. More experienced students knew shortcuts, of course: which workrooms and lecture halls to cut through to reach your destination.

At least one of the courtyards had been completely isolated and could only be accessed by climbing though a window. Rumour had it that there were some rooms bricked off entirely, some with students still inside. Their ghosts were rumoured to walk the halls at night, bewailing their fate and complaining about the food in the Mess.

My first class was held in Mains. Luckily, I had been warned by my bunkmates that Mains was difficult to navigate, so despite getting lost, I still arrived with time to spare.

When I finally found the room for my first class, I was surprised to find it resembled a small theatre. Seats rose in tiered semicircles around a small raised stage. In larger cities my troupe had performed in places not unlike this one. The thought relaxed me as I found a seat in the back.

I was a jangling mass of excitement as I watched other students slowly trickle into the room. Everyone was older than me by at least a few years. I reviewed the first thirty sympathetic bindings in my head as the theatre filled with anxious students. There were perhaps fifty of us in all, making the room about three-quarters full. Some had pen and paper with hardbacks to write on. Some had wax tablets. I hadn't brought anything, but that didn't worry me overmuch. I've always had an excellent memory.

Master Hemme entered the room and made his way onto the stage to stand behind a large stone worktable. He looked impressive in his dark masters' robes, and it was bare seconds before the whispering, shuffling theatre of students hushed to silence.

'So you want to be arcanists?' he said. 'You want magic like you've heard about in bedtime stories. You've listened to songs about Taborlin the Great. Roaring sheets of fire, magic rings, invisible cloaks, swords that never go dull, potions to make you fly.' He shook his head, disgusted. 'Well if that's what you're looking for, you can leave now, because you won't find it here. It doesn't exist.'

At this point a student came in, realised he was late, and moved quickly into a vacant seat. Hemme spotted him though. 'Hello, glad you chose to attend. What is your name?'

'Gel,' the boy said nervously. 'I'm sorry. I had a bit of a hard time . . .'

'Gel,' Hemme interrupted. 'Why are you here?'

Gel gaped for a moment before managing to say, 'For Principles of Sympathy?'

'I do not appreciate tardiness in my class. For tomorrow, you may prepare a report on the development of the sympathy clock, its differences from the previous, more arbitrary clocks that used harmonic motion, and its effect on the accurate treatment of time.'

The boy twisted in his seat. 'Yes, sir.'

Hemme seemed satisfied with the reaction. 'Very well. What is sympathy, then?'

Another boy hurried in clutching a hardback. He was young, by which I mean he looked to be no more than two years older than me. Hemme stopped him before he could make it into a seat. 'Hello there,' he said in an over-courteous tone. 'And you are?'

'Basil, sir,' the boy stood awkwardly in the aisle. I recognised him. I had spied on his admissions interview.

'Basil, you wouldn't happen to be from Yll, would you?' Hemme asked, smiling sharply.

'No, sir.'

'Ahhh,' Hemme said, feigning disappointment. 'I had heard that Yllish

tribes use the sun to tell time, and as such, have no true concept of punctu-
ality. However, as you are not Yllish, I can see no excuse for being late. Can
you?'

Basil's mouth worked silently for a moment, as if to make some excuse,
then apparently decided better of it. 'No sir.'

'Good. For tomorrow, you can prepare a report on Yll's lunar calendar
compared to the more accurate, civilised Aturan calendar that you should be
familiar with by now. Be seated.'

Basil slunk wordlessly into a nearby seat like a whipped dog.

Hemme gave up all pretext of lecture and lay in wait for the next tardy
student. Thus it was that the hall was tensely silent when she stepped hesitantly into the room.

It was a young woman of about eighteen. A rarity of sorts. The ratio of
men to women in the University is about ten to one.

Hemme's manner softened when she entered the room. He moved
quickly up the steps to greet her. 'Ah, my dear. I am suddenly pleased that
we have not yet begun today's discussion.' He took her by the elbow and led
her down a few of the steps to the first available seat.

She was obviously embarrassed by the attention. 'I'm sorry, Master
Hemme. Mains is bigger than I'd guessed.'

'No worry,' Hemme said in a kindly fashion. 'You're here and that's what
matters.' He solicitously helped her arrange her paper and ink before
returning to the stage.

Once there, it seemed as if he might actually lecture. But before he began
he looked back to the girl. 'I'm sorry miss.' She was the only woman in the
room. 'Poor manners on my part. What is your name?'

'Ria.'

'Ria, is that short for Rian?'

'Yes, it is,' she smiled.

'Rian, would you please cross your legs?'

The request was made with such an earnest tone that not even a titter
escaped the class. Looking puzzled, Rian crossed her legs.

'Now that the gates of hell are closed,' Hemme said in his normal, rougher
tones. 'We can begin.'

And so he did, ignoring her for the rest of the lecture. Which, as I see it,
was an inadvertent kindness.

It was a long two and a half hours. I listened attentively, always hoping that
he would come to something I hadn't learned from Abenthy. But there was

nothing. I quickly realised that while Hemme *was* discussing the principles of sympathy, he was doing it at a very, very basic level. This class was a colossal waste of my time.

After Hemme dismissed the class I ran down the stairs and caught him just as he was leaving through a lower door. 'Master Hemme?'

He turned to face me. 'Oh yes, our boy prodigy. I wasn't aware you were in my class. I didn't go too fast for you, did I?'

I knew better than to answer that honestly. 'You covered the basics very clearly, sir. The principles you mentioned today will lay a good foundation for the other students in the class.' Diplomacy is a large part of being a trouper.

He puffed up a bit at my perceived compliment, then looked more closely at me. '*Other* students?' He asked.

'I'm afraid I'm already familiar with the basics, sir. I know the three laws and the fourteen corollaries. As well as the first ninety—'

'Yes, yes. I see,' he cut me off. 'I'm rather busy right at the moment. We can speak of this tomorrow, before class.' He turned and walked briskly away.

Half a loaf being better than none, I shrugged and headed for the Archives. If I wasn't going to learn anything from Hemme's lectures, I might as well start educating myself.

This time when I entered the Archives there was a young woman sitting behind the desk. She was strikingly beautiful with long, dark hair and clear, bright eyes. A notable improvement over Ambrose to be sure.

She smiled as I approached the desk. 'What's your name?'

'Kvothe,' I said. 'Son of Arliden.'

She nodded and began to page through the ledger.

'What's yours?' I asked to fill the silence.

'Fela,' she said without looking up. Then nodded to herself and tapped the ledger. 'There you are, go on in.'

There were two sets of double doors leading out of the antechamber, one marked STACKS and the other TOMES. Not knowing the difference between the two, I headed to the ones labeled STACKS. That was what I wanted. Stacks of books. Great heaps of books. Shelf after endless shelf of books.

I had my hands on the handles of the doors before Fela's voice stopped me. 'I'm sorry. It's your first time in here, isn't it?'

I nodded, not letting go of the door's handles. I was so close. What was going to happen now?

'The stacks are Arcanum only.' She said apologetically. She stood up and walked around the desk to the other set of doors. 'Here, let me show you.'

I reluctantly let go of the door's handles and followed her.

Using both hands, she tugged one of the heavy wooden doors open, revealing a large, high-ceilinged room filled with long tables. A dozen students were scattered throughout the room, reading. The room was well-lit with the unwavering light of dozens of sympathy lamps.

Fela leaned close to me and spoke in a soft voice. 'This is the main reading area. You'll find all the necessary tomes used for most of the basic classes.' She blocked the door open with her foot and pointed along one wall to a long section of shelving with three or four hundred books. More books than I had ever seen in one place before.

Fela continued to speak softly. 'It's a quiet place. No talking above a whisper.' I'd noticed that the room was almost unnaturally quiet. 'If you want a book that isn't there, you can submit a request at the desk,' she pointed. 'They'll find the book and bring it out to you.'

I turned to ask her a question, and only then realised how close she was standing. It says a great deal about how enamored I was with the Archives that I failed to notice one of the most attractive women in the University standing less than six inches away. 'How long does it usually take them to find a book?' I asked quietly, trying not to stare at her.

'It varies,' she brushed her long black hair back over her shoulder. 'Sometimes we're busier than others. Some people are better at finding the appropriate books.' She shrugged and some of her hair swung back down to brush against my arm. 'Usually no more than an hour.'

I nodded, disappointed by not being able to browse the whole of the Archives, but still excited to be inside. Once again, half a loaf was better than none. 'Thanks, Fela.' I went inside, and she let the door swing shut behind me.

But she came after me just a moment later. 'One last thing,' she said quietly. 'I mean, it goes without saying, but this is your first time here . . .' Her expression was serious. 'The books don't leave this room. Nothing leaves the Archives.'

'Of course,' I said. 'Naturally.' I hadn't known.

Fela smiled and nodded. 'I just wanted to make sure. A couple of years ago we had a young gent who was used to carrying off books from his father's library. I'd never even seen Lorren frown before that, or talk much above a whisper. But when he caught that boy in the street with one of his books . . .' She shook her head as if she couldn't hope to explain what she had seen.

I tried to picture the tall, somber master angry and failed. 'Thanks for the warning.'

'Don't mention it.' Fela headed back out into the entrance hall.

I approached the desk she had pointed out to me. 'How do I request a book?' I asked the scriv quietly.

He showed me a large log book half filled with student's names and their requests. Some were requests for books with specific titles or authors, but others were more general requests for information. One of the entries caught my eye: 'Basil – Yllish lunar calendar. History of Aturan calendar.' I looked around the room and saw the boy from Hemme's class hunched over a book, taking notes.

I wrote: 'Kvothe – The history of the Chandrian. Reports of the Chandrian and their signs: black eyes, blue flame, etc.'

I went to the shelves next and started looking over the books. I recognised one or two from my studies with Ben. The only sound in the room was the occasional scratch of a pen on paper, or the faint, bird-wing sound of a page turning. Rather than being unsettling, I found the quiet strangely comforting. Later I was to find out that the place was nicknamed 'Tombs' because of its cryptlike quiet.

Eventually a book called *The Mating Habits of the Common Draccus* caught my eye and I took it over to one of the reading tables. I picked it because it had a rather stylish embossed dragon on the cover, but when I started reading I discovered it was an educated investigation into several common myths.

I was halfway through the title piece explaining how the myth of the dragon in all likelihood evolved from the much more mundane draccus when a scriv appeared at my elbow. 'Kvothe?' I nodded and he handed me a small book with a blue cloth cover.

Opening it, I was instantly disappointed. It was a collection of faerie stories. I flipped through it, hoping to find something useful, but it was filled with sticky-sweet adventure stories meant to amuse children. You know the sort: brave orphans trick the Chandrian, win riches, marry princesses, and live happily ever after.

I sighed and closed the book. I had half expected this. Until the Chandrian killed my family, I thought they were nothing more than children's stories too. This sort of search wasn't going to get me anywhere.

After walking to the desk I thought for a long moment before writing a new line in the request-ledger: 'Kvothe – The history of the Order Amyr. The origins of the Amyr. The practices of the Amyr.' I reached the end of the line and rather than start another one I stopped and looked up at the scriv behind the desk. 'I'll take anything on the Amyr, really,' I said.

'We're a little busy right now,' he said, gesturing to the room. Another dozen or so students had filtered in since I had arrived. 'But we'll bring something out to you as soon as we can.'

I returned to the table and flipped through the children's book again before abandoning it for the bestiary. The wait was much longer this time, and I was learning about the strange summer hibernation of Susquinian when I felt a light touch on my shoulder. I turned, expecting to see a scriv with an armload of books, or maybe Basil come to say hello. I was startled by the sight of Master Lorren looming over me in his dark masters' robes.

'Come,' he said softly, and gestured for me to follow.

Not knowing what might be the matter, I followed him out of the reading room. We walked behind the scriv's desk and down a flight of stairs to a small featureless room with a table and two chairs. The Archives was filled with little rooms like this, reading holes, designed to give members of the Arcanum a place to sit privately and study.

Lorren lay the request-ledger from Tomes on the table. 'I noticed your request while assisting one of the newer scrivs in his duties,' he said. 'You have an interest in the Chandrian and the Amyr?' he asked.

I nodded.

'Is this in regard to an assignment from one of your instructors?'

For a moment I thought about telling him the truth. About what had happened to my parents. About the story I had heard in Tarbean.

But Manet's reaction to my mention of the Chandrian had shown me how foolish that would be. Until I'd seen the Chandrian myself, I didn't believe in them. If anyone would have claimed to have seen them, I would have thought they were crazy.

At best Lorren would think I was delusional, at worst, a foolish child. I was suddenly pointedly aware of the fact that I was standing in one of the cornerstones of civilisation, talking to the Master Archivist of the University.

It put things in a new perspective for me. The stories of an old man in some Dockside tavern suddenly seemed very far away and insignificant.

I shook my head. 'No sir. It's merely to satisfy my curiosity.'

'I have a great respect for curiosity,' Lorren said with no particular inflection. 'Perhaps I can satisfy yours a bit. The Amyr were a part of the church back when the Aturan Empire was still strong. Their credo was *Ivare Enim Euge* which roughly translates as "for the greater good". They were equal part knight-errant and vigilante. They had judiciary powers, and could act as judges in both the religious and secular courts. All of them, to varying degrees, were exempt from the law.'

I knew most of this already. 'But where did they come from?' I asked. It was as close as I dared come to mentioning Skarpi's story.

'They evolved from travelling judges,' Lorren said. 'Men who went from town to town, bringing the rule of law to small Aturan towns.'

'They originated in Atur then?'

He looked at me. 'Where else would they have originated?'

I couldn't bring myself to tell him the truth: that because of an old man's story I suspected the Amyr might have roots much older than the Aturan Empire. That I hoped they might still exist somewhere in the world today.

Lorren took my silence as a response. 'A piece of advice,' he said gently. 'The Amyr are dramatic figures. When we are young we all pretend to be Amyr and fight battles with willow-switch swords. It is natural for boys to be attracted to those stories.' He met my eyes. 'However, a man, an *arcanist*, must focus himself on the present day. He must attend to practical things.'

He held my eyes as he continued to speak. 'You are young. Many will judge you by that fact alone.' I drew a breath, but he held up a hand. 'I am not accusing you of engaging in boyish fancy. I am advising you to avoid the *appearance* of boyish fancy.' He gave me a level look, his face as calm as always.

I thought of the way Ambrose had treated me and nodded, feeling colour rise to my cheeks.

Lorren brought out a pen and drew a series of hashes through my single line of writing in the ledger book. 'I have a great respect for curiosity,' he said. 'But others do not think as I do. I would not see your first term unnecessarily complicated by such things. I expect things will be difficult enough for you without that additional worry.'

I bowed my head, feeling as if I'd somehow disappointed him. 'I understand. Thank you, sir.'

CHAPTER THIRTY-NINE

Enough Rope

THE NEXT DAY I was ten minutes early to Hemme's class, sitting in the front row. I hoped to catch Hemme before the class started, thereby saving myself from having to sit through another one of his lectures.

Unfortunately, he did not appear early. The lecture hall was full when he entered by the hall's lower door and climbed the three steps onto the raised wooden stage. He looked around the hall, eyes searching me out. 'Ah yes, our young prodigy. Stand up, would you?'

Uncertain as to what was going on, I stood.

'I have pleasant news for everyone,' he said. 'Mr. Kvothe here has assured me as to his complete grasp of the principles of sympathy. In doing so, he has offered to give today's lecture.' He made an expansive gesture for me to join him on the stage. He smiled at me with hard eyes. 'Mr. Kvothe?'

He was mocking me, of course, expecting me to slink down into my seat, cowed and ashamed.

But I had had enough of bullies in my life. So I climbed onto the stage and shook his hand. Using a good stage voice I spoke to the students, 'I thank Master Hemme for this opportunity. I only hope that I can help him shed some light on this most important subject.'

Having started this little game, Hemme was unable to stop it without looking foolish. As he shook my hand he gave me the look a wolf gives a treed cat. Smiling to himself, he left the stage to assume my recently vacated seat in the front row. Confident of my ignorance, he was willing to let the charade continue.

I would never have got away with it if not for two of Hemme's numerous flaws. First, his general stupidity in not believing what I had told him the day before. Second, his desire to see me embarrassed as thoroughly as possible.

Plainly said, he was giving me enough rope to hang myself with. Apparently he didn't realise that once a noose is tied, it will fit one neck as easily as another.

I faced the class. 'Today I will be presenting an example of the laws of sympathy. However, as time is limited I will need help with the preparations.' I pointed to a student at random. 'Would you be so good as to bring me one of Master Hemme's hairs, please?'

Hemme offered one up with an exaggerated graciousness. As the student brought it up to me, Hemme smiled in genuine amusement, certain that the more grandiose my preparations were, the greater my embarrassment would be in the end.

I took advantage of this slight delay to look over what equipment I had to work with. A brazier sat off to one side of the stage, and a quick rifling of the drawers in the worktable revealed chalk, a prism, sulfur matches, an enlarging glass, some candles, and a few oddly-shaped blocks of metal. I took three of the candles and left the rest.

I took Master Hemme's hair from the student and recognised him as Basil, the boy Hemme had browbeat yesterday. 'Thank you, Basil. Would you bring that brazier over here and get it burning as quickly as you can?' As he brought it closer I was delighted to see that it was equipped with a small bellows. While he poured alcohol onto the coal and struck a spark to it, I addressed the class.

'The concepts of sympathy are not entirely easy to grasp. But underneath everything there remain three simple laws.'

'First is the Doctrine of Correspondence which says, "similarity enhances sympathy". Second is the Principle of Consanguinity, which says, "a piece of a thing can represent the whole of a thing". Third is the Law of Conservation, which says "energy cannot be destroyed nor created". Correspondence, Consanguinity, and Conservation. The three C's.'

I paused and listened to the sound of a half hundred pens scratching down my words. Beside me, Basil pumped industriously at the bellows. I realised I could grow to enjoy this.

'Don't worry if it doesn't make sense yet. The demonstration should make everything abundantly clear.' Looking down, I saw the brazier was warming nicely. I thanked Basil and hung a shallow metal pan above the coals and dropped two of the candles in to melt.

I set a third candle in a holder on the table and used one of the sulfur matches in the drawer to set it alight. Next, I moved the pan off the heat and poured its now-melted contents carefully onto the table, forming a fist-sized blob of soft wax. I looked back up at the students.

'In sympathy, most of what you are doing is redirecting energy. Sympathetic links are how the energy travels.' I pulled out the wicking and began kneading the wax into a roughly human-shaped doll. 'The first law I mentioned, "Similarity enhances sympathy", simply means that the more things resemble each other, the stronger the sympathetic link between them will be.'

I held the crude doll up for the class to inspect. 'This,' I said, 'is Master Hemme.' Laughter muttered back and forth across the hall. 'Actually, this is my sympathetic representation of Master Hemme. Would anyone like to take a guess as to why it is not a very good one?'

There was a moment of silence. I let it stretch out for a while, a cold audience. Hemme had traumatised them yesterday and they were slow in responding. Finally, from the back of the room, a student said, 'It's the wrong size?'

I nodded and continued to look around the room.

'He isn't made of wax either.'

I nodded. 'It does bear some small resemblance to him, in general shape and proportion. Nevertheless, it is a very poor sympathetic representation. Because of that, any sympathetic link based off it would be rather weak. Perhaps two per cent efficiency. How could we improve it?'

There was another silence, shorter than the first. 'You could make it bigger,' someone suggested. I nodded and waited. Other voices called out, 'You could carve Master Hemme's face on it.' 'Paint it.' 'Give it a little robe.' Everyone laughed.

I held up my hand for quiet and was surprised by how quickly it fell. 'Practicality aside, assume you did all these things. A six-foot, fully-clothed, masterfully carved Master Hemme stands beside me.' I gestured. 'Even with all that effort the best you might hope for is ten or fifteen per cent sympathetic link. Not very good, not very good at all.

'This brings me to the second law, Consanguinity. An easy way of thinking of it is, "once together, always together". Due to Master Hemme's generosity I have one of his hairs.' I held it up, and ceremoniously stuck it to the head of the doll. 'And as easy as this, we have a sympathetic link that will work at thirty to thirty-five per cent.'

I had been watching Hemme. While at first he had seemed a little wary, he had lapsed back into a self-satisfied smirk. He knew that without the appropriate binding and properly focused Alar, all the wax and hair in the world wouldn't do one whit of good.

Sure that he had taken me for a fool, I gestured to the candle and asked him, 'With your permission, Master?' He made a magnanimous wave of compliance and settled back into his chair, folding his arms in front of him, confident in his safety.

Of course I did know the binding. I'd told him so. And Ben had taught me about the Alar, the riding-crop belief, back when I was twelve.

But I didn't bother with either. I put the doll's foot into the candle flame, which guttered and smoked.

There was a tense, held-breath quiet as everyone stretched in their seats to get a look at Master Hemme.

Hemme shrugged, feigning astonishment. But his eyes had the look of a jaw trap about to close. A smirk tugged at one corner of his mouth, and he began to rise from his seat. 'I feel nothing. Wh—'

'Exactly.' I said, cracking my voice like a whip, startling the students' attentions back to me. 'And why is that?' I looked expectantly at the lecture hall.

'Because of the third law that I had mentioned, Conservation. "Energy cannot be destroyed or created, merely lost or found". If I were to hold a candle underneath our esteemed teacher's foot, very little would occur. And since only about thirty per cent of the heat is getting through, we do not even get that small result.'

I paused to let them think for a moment. 'This is the prime problem in sympathy. Where do we get the energy? Here, however, the answer is simple.'

I blew out the candle and relit it from the brazier. Muttering the few necessary words underneath my breath. 'By adding a second sympathetic link between the candle and a more substantial fire . . .' I broke my mind into two pieces, one binding Hemme and the doll together, the other connecting the candle and the brazier. 'We get the desired effect.'

I casually moved the foot of the wax doll into the space about an inch above the candle's wick, which is actually the hottest part of the flame.

There was a startled exclamation from where Hemme was sitting.

Without looking in his direction I continued speaking to the class in the driest of tones. 'And it appears that this time we are successful.' The class laughed.

I blew out the candle. 'This is also a good example of the power that a clever sympathist commands. Imagine what would happen if I were to throw this doll into the fire itself?' I held it over the brazier.

As if on cue, Hemme stormed onto the stage. It may have been my imagination, but it seemed to me that he was favouring his left leg slightly.

'It appears that Master Hemme wishes to resume your instruction at this point.' Laughter rippled through the room, louder this time. 'I thank you all: students and friends. And thus my humble lecture ends.'

At this point I used one of the tricks of the stage. There is a certain inflection of voice and body language that signals a crowd to applaud. I cannot explain how exactly it is done, but it had its intended effect. I nodded my head to them and turned to face Hemme amidst applause which, though far from deafening, was probably more than any he had ever received.

As he took the last few steps towards me I almost backed away. His face was a fearsome red and a vein pulsed at his temple as if it were about to explode.

For my own part, my stage training helped me maintain my composure, I returned his gaze levelly and held out my hand for him to shake. It was with no small amount of satisfaction that I watched him give a quick glance to the still applauding class, swallow, and shake my hand.

His handshake was painfully tight. It might have become worse if I hadn't made a slight gesture over the brazier with the wax doll. His face went from its livid red to an ashen white more quickly than I would have believed possible. His grip underwent a similar transformation and I regained my hand.

With another nod toward the seated students, I left the lecture hall without a backward glance.

CHAPTER FORTY

On the Horns

A FTER HEMME DISMISSED HIS class, news of what I had done spread through the University like wildfire. I guessed from the student's reactions that Master Hemme was not particularly well loved. As I sat on a stone bench outside the Mews, passing students smiled in my direction. Others waved or gave laughing thumbs-up.

While I enjoyed the notoriety, a cold anxiety was slowly growing in my gut. I'd made an enemy of one of the nine masters. I needed to know how much trouble I was in.

———

Dinner in the Mess was brown bread with butter, stew, and beans. Manet was there, his wild hair making him look like a great white wolf. Simmon and Sovoy groused idly about the food, making grim speculations as to what manner of meat was in the stew. To me, less than a span away from the streets of Tarbean, it was a marvellous meal indeed.

Nevertheless, I was rapidly losing my appetite in the face of what I was hearing from my friends.

'Don't get me wrong,' Sovoy said. 'You've got a great weighty pair on you. I'll never call *that* into question. But still . . .' he gestured with his spoon. 'They're going to string you up for this.'

'If he's lucky,' Simmon said. 'I mean, we are talking about malfeasance here, aren't we?'

'It's not a big deal,' I said with more assurance than I felt. 'I gave him a little bit of a hotfoot, that's all.'

'Any harmful sympathy falls under malfeasance.' Manet pointed at me with his piece of bread, his wild, grizzled eyebrows arching seriously over his nose. 'You've got to pick your battles, boy. Keep your head down around the masters. They can make your life a real hell once you get into their bad books.'

'He started it,' I said sullenly though a mouthful of beans.

A young boy jogged up to the table, breathless. 'You're Kvothe?' He asked, looking me over.

I nodded, my stomach suddenly turning over.

'They want you in the Masters' Hall.'

'Where is it?' I asked. 'I've only been here a couple of days.'

'Can one of you show him?' the boy asked, looking around at the table. 'I've got to go and tell Jamison I found him.'

'I'll do it,' Simmon said pushing away his bowl. 'I'm not hungry anyway.'

Jamison's runner boy took off, and Simmon started to get to his feet.

'Hold on,' I said, pointing to my tray with my spoon. 'I'm not finished here.'

Simmon's expression was anxious. 'I can't believe you're eating,' he said. '*I* can't eat. How can you eat?'

'I'm hungry,' I said. 'I don't know what's waiting in the Masters' Hall, but I'm guessing I'd rather have a full stomach for it.'

'You're going on the horns,' Manet said. 'It's the only reason they'd call you there at this time of night.'

I didn't know what he meant by that, but I didn't want to advertise my ignorance to everyone in the room. 'They can wait until I'm done.' I took another bite of stew.

Simmon returned to his seat and poked idly at his food. Truth be told, I wasn't really hungry any more, but it galled me to be pulled away from a meal after all the times I'd been hungry in Tarbean.

When Simmon and I finally got to our feet, the normal clamour in the Mess quieted as folk watched us leave. They knew where I was headed.

Outside, Simmon put his hands in his pockets and headed roughly in the direction of Hollows. 'All kidding aside, you're in a good bit of trouble, you know.'

'I was hoping Hemme would be embarrassed and keep quiet about it,' I admitted. 'Do they expel many students?' I tried to make it sound like a joke.

'There hasn't been anyone this term,' Sim said with his shy, blue-eyed smile. 'But it's only the second day of classes. You might set some sort of record.'

'This isn't funny,' I said, but found myself wearing a grin regardless. Simmon could always make me smile, no matter what was going on.

Sim led the way, and we reached Hollows far too soon for my liking. Simmon raised a hand in a hesitant farewell as I opened the door and made my way inside.

I was met by Jamison. He oversaw everything that wasn't under direct control of the masters: the kitchens, the laundry, the stables, the stockrooms. He was nervous and birdlike. A man with the body of a sparrow and the eyes of a hawk.

Jamison escorted me into a large windowless room with a familiar crescent-shaped table. The Chancellor sat at the center, as he had during admissions. The only real difference was that this table was not elevated, and the seated masters were close to eye level with me.

The eyes I met were not friendly. Jamison escorted me to the front of the crescent table. Seeing it from this angle made me understand the references to being 'on the horns'. Jamison retreated to a smaller table of his own, dipping a pen.

The Chancellor steepled his fingers and spoke without preamble. 'On the fourth of Caitelyn, Hemme called the masters together.' Jamison's pen scratched across a piece of paper, occasionally dipping back into the inkwell at the top of the desk. The Chancellor continued formally, 'Are all the masters present?'

'Master Physicker,' said Arwyl.

'Master Archivist,' said Lorren, his face impassive as ever.

'Master Arithmetician,' Brandeur said, cracking his knuckles absently.

'Master Artificer,' grumbled Kilvin without looking up from the tabletop.

'Master Alchemist,' said Mandrag.

'Master Rhetorician,' Hemme's face was fierce and red.

'Master Sympathist,' said Elxa Dal.

'Master Namer.' Elodin actually smiled at me. Not just a perfunctory curling of the lips, but a warm, toothy grin. I drew a bit of a shaky breath, relieved that at least one person present didn't seem eager to hang me up by my thumbs.

'And Master Linguist,' said the Chancellor. 'All eight . . .' He frowned. 'Sorry. Strike that. All *nine* masters are present. Present your grievance, Master Hemme.'

Hemme did not hesitate. 'Today, first-term student Kvothe, not of the Arcanum, did perform sympathetic bindings on me with malicious intent.'

'Two grievances are recorded against Kvothe by Master Hemme,' the Chancellor said sternly, not taking his eyes away from me. 'First grievance, unauthorised use of sympathy. What is the proper discipline for this, Master Archivist?'

'For unauthorised use of sympathy leading to injury, the offending student will be bound and whipped a number of times, not less than two nor more than ten, singly, across the back.' Lorren said it as if reading off directions for a recipe.

'Number of lashes sought?' The Chancellor looked at Hemme.

Hemme paused to consider. 'Five.'

I felt the blood drain from my face and I forced myself to take a slow, deep breath through my nose to calm myself.

'Does any master object to this?' The Chancellor looked around the table, but all mouths were silent, all eyes were stern. 'The second grievance: malfeasance. Master Archivist?'

'Four to fifteen single lashes and expulsion from the University.' Lorren said in a level voice.

'Lashes sought?'

Hemme stared directly at me. 'Eight.'

Thirteen lashes and expulsion. A cold sweat swept over me and I felt nausea in the pit of my stomach. I had known fear before. In Tarbean it was never far away. Fear kept you alive. But I had never before felt such a desperate helplessness. A fear not just for my body being hurt, but for my entire life being ruined. I began to get light-headed.

'Do you understand these grievances set against you?' The Chancellor asked sternly.

I took a deep breath. 'Not exactly, sir.' I hated the way my voiced sounded, tremulous and weak.

The Chancellor held up a hand and Jamison lifted his pen from the paper. 'It is against the laws of the University for a student who is not a member of the Arcanum to use sympathy without permission from a master.'

His expression darkened. 'And it is always, *always,* expressly forbidden to cause harm with sympathy, especially to a master. A few hundred years ago arcanists were hunted down and burned for things of that sort. We do not tolerate that sort of behaviour here.'

I heard a hard edge creep into the Chancellor's voice, only then did I sense how truly angry he was. He took a deep breath. 'Now, do you understand?'

I nodded shakily.

He made another motion to Jamison, who set his pen back to the paper. 'Do you, Kvothe, understand these grievances set against you?'

'Yes, sir.' I said, as steadily as I could. Everything seemed too bright, and my legs were trembling slightly. I tried to force them to be still, but it only seemed to make them shake all the more.

'Do you have anything to say in your defense?' the Chancellor asked curtly.

I just wanted to leave. I felt the stares of the masters bearing down on me. My hands were wet and cold. I probably would have shaken my head and slunk from the room had the Chancellor not spoken again.

'Well?' The Chancellor repeated testily. 'No defense?'

The words struck a chord in me. They were the same words that Ben had used a hundred times as he drilled me endlessly in argument. His words came back, admonishing me: *What? No defense? Any student of mine must be able to defend his ideas against an attack. No matter how you spend your life, your wit will defend you more often than a sword. Keep it sharp!*

I took another deep breath, closed my eyes and concentrated. After a long moment, I felt the cool impassivity of the Heart of Stone surround me. My trembling stopped.

I opened my eyes and heard my own voice say, 'I had permission for my use of sympathy, sir.'

The Chancellor gave me a long, hard look before saying, 'What?'

I held the Heart of Stone around me like a calming mantle. 'I had permission from Master Hemme, both express and implied.'

The masters stirred in their seats, puzzled.

The Chancellor looked far from pleased. 'Explain yourself.'

'I approached Master Hemme after his first lecture and told him I was already familiar with the concepts he had discussed. He told me we would discuss it the next day.

'When he arrived for class the next day, he announced that I would be giving the lecture in order to demonstrate the principles of sympathy. After observing what materials were available, I gave the class the first demonstration my master gave me.' Not true, of course. As I've already mentioned, my first lesson involved a handful of iron drabs. It was a lie, but a plausible lie.

Judging by the masters' expressions, this was news to them. Somewhere deep in the Heart of Stone, I relaxed, glad that the master's irritation was based on Hemme's angrily abridged version of the truth.

'You gave a demonstration before the class?' the Chancellor asked before I could continue. He glanced at Hemme, then back to me.

I played innocent. 'Just a simple one. Is that unusual?'

'It is a little odd,' he said, looking at Hemme. I could sense his anger again, but this time it didn't seem to be directed at me.

'I thought it might be the way you proved your knowledge of the material and moved to a more advanced class,' I said innocently. Another lie, but again, plausible.

Elxa Dal spoke up, 'What did the demonstration involve?'

'A wax doll, a hair from Hemme's head, and a candle. I would have picked a different example, but my materials were limited. I thought that might be another part of the test, making do with what you were given.' I shrugged again. 'I couldn't think of any other way to demonstrate all three laws with the materials on hand.'

The Chancellor looked at Hemme. 'Is what the boy says true?'

Hemme opened his mouth as if he would deny it, then apparently remembered that an entire classroom full of students had witnessed the exchange. He said nothing.

'Damn it, Hemme,' Elxa Dal burst out. 'You let the boy make a simulacra of you, then bring him here on malfeasance?' He spluttered. 'You deserve worse than you got.'

'E'lir Kvothe could not have hurt him with just a candle,' Kilvin muttered. He gave his fingers a puzzled look, as if he were working something out in his head. 'Not with hair and wax. Maybe blood and clay . . .'

'Order.' The Chancellor's voice was too quiet to be called a shout, but it carried the same authority. He shot looks at Elxa Dal and Kilvin. 'Kvothe, answer Master Kilvin's question.'

'I made a second binding between the candle and a brazier to illustrate the Law of Conservation.'

Kilvin didn't look up from his hands. 'Wax and hair?' He grumbled as if not entirely satisfied with my explanation.

I gave a half-puzzled, half-embarrassed look and said, 'I don't understand it myself, sir. I should have got a ten per cent transference at best. It shouldn't have been enough to blister Master Hemme, let alone burn him.'

I turned to Hemme. 'I really didn't mean any harm, sir,' I said in my best distraught voice. 'It was just supposed to be a bit of a hotfoot to make you jump. The fire hadn't been going more than five minutes, and I didn't imagine that a fresh fire at ten per cent could hurt you.' I even wrung my hands a little, every bit the distraught student. It was a good performance. My father would have been proud.

'Well it did,' Hemme said bitterly. 'And where is the damn mommet anyway? I demand you return it at once!'

'I'm afraid I can't, sir. I destroyed it. It was too dangerous to leave lying around.'

Hemme gave me a shrewd look. 'It's of no real concern,' he muttered.

The Chancellor took up the reins again. 'This changes things considerably. Hemme, do you still set grievance against Kvothe?'

Hemme glared and said nothing.

'I move to strike both grievances,' Arwyl said. The physicker's old voice coming as a bit of a surprise. 'If Hemme set him in front of the class, he gave permission. And it isn't malfeasance if you give him your hair and watch him stick it on the mommet's head.'

'I expected him to have more control over what he was doing,' Hemme said, shooting a venomous look at me.

'It's not malfeasance,' Arwyl said doggedly, glaring at Hemme from behind his spectacles, the grandfatherly lines on his face forming a fierce scowl.

'It would fall under reckless use of sympathy,' Lorren interjected coolly.

'Is that a motion to strike the previous two grievances and replace them with reckless use of sympathy?' asked the Chancellor, trying to regain a semblance of formality.

'Aye,' said Arwyl, still glaring fearsomely at Hemme through his spectacles.

'All for the motion?' The Chancellor said,

There was a chorus of ayes from everyone but Hemme.

'Against?'

Hemme remained silent.

'Master Archivist, what is the discipline for reckless use of sympathy?'

'If one is injured by reckless use of sympathy, the offending student will be whipped, singly, no more than seven times across the back.' I wondered what book Master Lorren was reciting from.

'Number of lashes sought?'

Hemme looked at the other masters' faces, realising the tide had turned against him. 'My foot is blistered halfway to my knee,' he gritted. 'Three lashes.'

The Chancellor cleared his throat. 'Does any master oppose this action?'

'Aye,' Elxa Dal and Kilvin said together.

'Who wishes to suspend the discipline? Vote by show of hands.'

Elxa Dal, Kilvin, and Arwyl raised their hands at once, followed by the Chancellor. Mandrag kept his hand down, as did Lorren, Brandeur, and Hemme. Elodin grinned at me cheerily, but did not raise his hand. I kicked myself for my recent trip to the Archives and the bad impression it made on Lorren. If not for that he might have tipped things in my favour.

'Four and a half in favour of suspending punishment,' the Chancellor said after a pause. 'The discipline stands: three lashes to be served tomorrow, the fifth of Caitelyn, at noon.'

As I was deep into the Heart of Stone, all I felt was a slight analytical curiosity about what it would be like to be publicly whipped. All the masters showed signs of preparing to stand and leave, but before things could be called to a close I spoke up, 'Chancellor?'

He took a deep breath and let it out in a gush. 'Yes?'

'During my admission, you said that my admittance to the Arcanum was granted, contingent upon proof that I had mastered the basic principles of sympathy.' I quoted him nearly word for word. 'Does this constitute proof?'

Both Hemme and the Chancellor opened their mouths to say something. Hemme was louder. 'Look here, you little cocker!'

'Hemme!' the Chancellor snapped. Then he turned to me, 'I'm afraid proof of mastery requires more than a simple sympathetic binding.'

'A double binding,' Kilvin corrected gruffly.

Elodin spoke, seeming to startle everyone at the table. 'I can think of students currently enrolled in the Arcanum who would be hard pressed to complete a double binding, let alone draw enough heat to "blister a man's foot to the knee".' I had forgotten how Elodin's light voice moved through the deep places in your chest when he spoke. He smiled happily at me again.

There was a moment of quiet reflection.

'True enough,' admitted Elxa Dal, giving me a close look.

The Chancellor looked down at the empty table for a minute. Then he shrugged, looked up, and gave a surprisingly jaunty smile. 'All in favour of admitting first-term student Kvothe's reckless use of sympathy as proof of mastery of the basic principles of sympathy vote by show of hands.'

Kilvin and Elxa Dal raised their hands together. Arwyl added his a moment later. Elodin waved. After a pause, the Chancellor raised his hand as well, saying, 'Five and a half in favour of Kvothe's admission to the Arcanum.

Motion passed. Meeting dismissed. Tehlu shelter us, fools and children all.' He said the last very softly as he rested his forehead against the heel of his hand.

Hemme stormed out of the room with Brandeur in tow. Once they were through the door I heard Brandeur ask, 'Weren't you wearing a gram?'

'No, I wasn't.' Hemme snapped. 'And don't take that tone with me, as if this were my fault. You might as well blame someone stabbed in an alley for not wearing armour.'

'We should all take precautions.' Brandeur said, placatingly. 'You know as well as—' Their voices were cut off with the sound of a door closing.

Kilvin stood and shrugged his shoulders, stretching. Looking over to where I stood, he scratched his bushy beard with both hands, a thoughtful look on his face, then strode over to where I stood. 'Do you have your sygaldry yet, E'lir Kvothe?'

I looked at him blankly. 'Do you mean runes, sir? I'm afraid not.'

Kilvin ran his hands through his beard, thoughtfully. 'Do not bother with the Basic Artificing class you have signed for. Instead you will come to my workroom tomorrow. Noon.'

'I'm afraid I have another appointment at noon, Master Kilvin.'

'Hmmm. Yes.' He frowned. 'First bell, then.'

'I'm afraid the boy will be having an appointment with my folk shortly after the whipping, Kilvin,' Arwyl said with a glimmer of amusement in his eyes. 'Have someone bring you to the Medica afterwards, son. We'll stitch you back together.'

'Thank you, sir.'

Arwyl nodded and made his way out of the room.

Kilvin watched him go, then turned to look at me. 'My workshop. Day after tomorrow. Noon.' The tone of his voice implied that it wasn't really a question.

'I would be honoured, Master Kilvin.'

He grunted in response and left with Elxa Dal.

That left me alone with the still-seated Chancellor. We stared at each other while the sound of footsteps faded in the hallway. I brought myself back up out of the Heart of Stone and felt a tangle of anticipation and fear at everything that had just happened.

'I'm sorry to be so much trouble so soon, sir.' I offered hesitantly.

'Oh?' he said. His expression considerably less stern now that we were alone. 'How long had you intended to wait?'

'At least a span, sir.' My brush with disaster had left me feeling giddy with relief. I felt an irrepressible grin bubble onto my face.

'At least a span,' he muttered. The Chancellor put his face into his hands and rubbed, then looked up and surprised me with a wry smile. I realised he wasn't particularly old when his face wasn't locked in a stern expression. Probably only on the far side of forty. 'You don't look like someone who knows he's going to be whipped tomorrow,' he observed.

I pushed the thought aside. 'I imagine I'll heal, sir.' He gave me an odd look, it took me a while to recognise it as the one I'd grown accustomed to in the troupe. He opened his mouth to speak, but I jumped on the words before he could say them. 'I'm not as young as I look, sir. I know it. I just wish other people knew it, too.'

'I imagine they will before too long.' He gave me a long look before pushing himself up from the table. He held out a hand. 'Welcome to the Arcanum.'

I shook his hand solemnly and we parted ways. I worked my way outside and was surprised to see that it was full night. I breathed in a lungful of sweet spring air and felt my grin resurface.

Then someone touched me on the shoulder. I jumped fully two feet into the air and narrowly avoided falling on Simmon in the howling, scratching, biting blur that had been my only method of defense in Tarbean.

He took a step back, startled by the expression on my face.

I tried to slow my pounding heart. 'Simmon. I'm sorry. I'm just . . . try to make a little noise around me. I startle easily.'

'Me too,' he murmured shakily, wiping a hand across his forehead. 'I can't really blame you, though. Riding the horns will do that to the best of us. How did things go?'

'I'm to be whipped and admitted to the Arcanum.'

He looked at me curiously, trying to see if I was making a joke. 'I'm sorry? Congratulations?' He made a shy smile at me. 'Do I buy you a bandage or a beer?'

I smiled back. 'Both.'

———

By the time I got back to the fourth floor of the Mews, rumour of my non-expulsion and admission into the Arcanum had spread ahead of me. I was greeted by a smattering of applause from my bunkmates. Hemme was not well loved. Some of my bunkmates offered awed congratulations while Basil made a special point of coming forward to shake my hand.

I had just climbed up to a sitting position on my bunk and was explaining to Basil the difference between a single whip and a six-tail when the third-floor steward came looking for me. He instructed me to pack up my things, explaining that Arcanum students were located in the west wing.

Everything I owned still fit neatly into my travelsack, so it was no great chore. As the steward led me away there was a chorus of good-byes from my fellow first-term students.

The west wing bunks were similar to those I had left behind. It was still rows of narrow beds, but here they weren't stacked two high. Each bed had a small wardrobe and desk in addition to a trunk. Nothing fancy, but definitely a step up.

The biggest difference was in the attitudes of my bunkmates. There were scowls and glares, though for the most part I was pointedly ignored. It was a chilly reception, especially in light of the welcome I had just received from my non-Arcanum bunkmates.

It was easy to understand why. Most students attend the University for several terms before being admitted into the Arcanum. Everyone here had worked their way up through the ranks the hard way. I hadn't.

Only about three quarters of the bunks were full. I picked one in the back corner, away from the others. I hung my one extra shirt and my cloak in the wardrobe and put my travelsack in the trunk at the foot of my bed.

I lay down and stared at the ceiling. My bunk lay outside the light of the other student's candles and sympathy lamps. I was finally a member of the Arcanum, in some ways exactly where I had always wanted to be.

CHAPTER FORTY-ONE

Friend's Blood

THE NEXT MORNING I woke early, washed up, and grabbed a bite to eat at the Mess. Then, because I had nothing to do before my whipping at noon, I strolled the University aimlessly. I wandered through a few apothecaries and bottle shops, admired the well-kept lawns and gardens.

Eventually I came to rest on a stone bench in a wide courtyard. Too anxious to think of doing anything productive, I simply sat and enjoyed the weather, watching the wind tumble a few scraps of wastepaper along the cobblestones.

It wasn't too long before Wilem strolled over and sat himself next to me without an invitation. His characteristic Cealdish dark hair and eyes made him seem older than Simmon and me, but he still had the slightly awkward look of a boy who wasn't quite used to being man-sized yet.

'Nervous?' he asked with the harsh burr a Siaru accent makes.

'Trying not to think about it, actually,' I said.

Wilem grunted. We were both quiet for a minute while we watched the students walk past. A few of them paused in their conversations to point at me.

I quickly grew tired of their attention. 'Are you doing anything right now?'

'Sitting,' he said simply. 'Breathing.'

'Clever. I can see why you're in the Arcanum. Are you busy for the next hour or so?'

He shrugged and looked at me expectantly.

'Would you show me where Master Arwyl is? He told me to stop by . . . after.'

'Certainly,' he said, pointing to one of the courtyard's outlets. 'Medica is on the other side of Archives.'

We made our way around the massive windowless block that was the Archives. Wilem pointed. 'That is Medica.' It was a large, oddly-shaped building. It looked like a taller, less rambling version of Mains.

'Bigger than I'd thought it would be,' I mused. 'All for teaching medicine?'

He shook his head. 'They do much business in tending the sick. They never turn anyone away because they can't pay.'

'Really?' I looked at Medica again, thinking of Master Arwyl. 'That's surprising.'

'You need not pay in *advance,*' he clarified. 'After you recover,' he paused and I heard the clear implication, *if you recover,* 'you settle accounts. If you have no hard coin, you work until your debt is . . .' He paused. 'What is the word for *sheyem*?' he asked, holding out his hands with the palms up and moving them up and down as if they were the pans of a scale.

'Weighed?' I suggested.

He shook his head. 'No. *Sheyem.*' He stressed the word, and brought his hands even with each other.

'Oh,' I mimicked the gesture. 'Balanced.'

He nodded. 'You work until your debt is *balanced* with the Medica. Few leave without settling their debts.'

I gave a grim chuckle. 'Not that surprising. What's the point of running away from an arcanist who has a couple drops of your blood?'

We eventually came to another courtyard. In the center of it was a pennant pole with a stone bench underneath it. I didn't need to guess who was going to be tied to it in an hour or so. There were about a hundred students milling around, giving things an oddly festive air.

'It's not usually this big,' Wilem said apologetically. 'But a few masters cancelled classes.'

'Hemme, I'm guessing, and Brandeur.'

Wilem nodded. 'Hemme hauls grudges.' He paused to give emphasis to his understatement. 'He'll be there with his whole coterie.' He pronounced the last word slowly. 'Is that the right word? *Coterie*?'

I nodded, and Wilem looked vaguely self-satisfied. Then he frowned. 'That makes me remember something strange in your language. People are always asking me about the road to Tinuë. Endlessly they say, "how is the road to Tinuë?" What does it mean?'

I smiled. 'It's an idiomatic piece of the language. That means—'

'I know what an idiom is,' Wilem interrupted. 'What does this one mean?'

'Oh,' I said, slightly embarrassed. 'It's just a greeting. It's kind of like asking "how is your day?" or "how is everything going?" '

'That is also an idiom.' Wilem grumbled. 'Your language is thick with nonsense. I wonder how any of you understand each other. *How is everything going?* Going where?' He shook his head.

'Tinuë, apparently.' I grinned at him. '*Tuan volgen oketh ama.*' I said, using one of my favorite Siaru idioms. It meant 'don't let it make you crazy' but it translated literally as: 'don't put a spoon in your eye over it'.

We turned away from the courtyard and walked around the University aimlessly for a while. Wilem pointed out a few more notable buildings, including several good taverns, the alchemy complex, the Cealdish laundry, and both the sanctioned and unsanctioned brothels. We strolled past the featureless stone walls of the Archives, past a cooper, a bookbinder, an apothecary . . .

A thought occurred to me. 'Do you know much herb lore?'

He shook his head. 'Chemistry mostly, and I dapple in the Archives with Puppet sometimes.'

'Dabble,' I said, emphasising the *buh* sound for him. 'Dapple is something else. Who's Puppet?'

Wil paused. 'Hard to describe.' He waved a hand to dismiss the question. 'I'll introduce you later. What do you need to know about herbs?'

'Nothing really. Could you do me a favour?' He nodded and I pointed to the nearby apothecary. 'Go buy me two scruples of nahlrout.' I held up two iron drabs. 'This should cover it.'

'Why me?' he asked warily.

'Because I don't want the fellow in there giving me the "you're awfully young" look.' I frowned. 'I don't want to have to deal with that today.'

I was nearly dancing with anxiety by the time Wilem got back. 'He was busy,' he explained, seeing the impatient expression on my face. He handed me a small paper packet and a loose jingle of change. 'What is it?'

'It's to settle my stomach,' I said. 'Breakfast isn't sitting too well, and I don't fancy throwing up halfway through being whipped.'

I bought us cider at a nearby pub, using mine to wash down the nahlrout, trying not to grimace at the bitter, chalky taste. Before too long we heard the belling tower striking noon.

'I think I must go to class,' Wil tried to mention it nonchalantly, but it came out almost strangled. He looked up at me, embarrassed and a little pale under his dark complexion. 'I am not fond of blood.' He gave a shaky smile. 'My blood . . . friend's blood . . .'

'I don't plan on doing much bleeding,' I said. 'But don't worry. You got me through the hard part, the waiting. Thank you.'

We parted ways, and I fought down a wave of guilt. After knowing me less than three days Wil had gone out of his way to help me. He could have taken the easy route and resented my quick admittance into the Arcanum as many others did. Instead he had done a friend's duty, helping me pass a difficult time, and I had repaid him with lies.

———

As I walked toward the pennant pole, I felt the weight of the crowd's eyes on me. How many were there? Two hundred? Three? After a certain point is reached the numbers cease to matter, and all that remains is the faceless mass of a crowd.

My stage training held me firm under their stares. I walked steadily towards the pennant pole amid a sea of susurrus murmurings. I didn't carry myself proudly, as I knew that might turn them against me. I was not repentant, either. I carried myself well, as my father had taught me, with neither fear nor regret on my face.

As I walked, I felt the nahlrout begin to take firm hold of me. I felt perfectly awake while everything around me grew almost painfully bright. Time seemed to slow as I approached the center of the courtyard. As my feet came down on the cobblestones I watched the small puffs of dust they raised. I felt a breath of wind catch the hem of my cloak and curl underneath to cool the sweat between my shoulder blades. It seemed for a second that, should I wish to, I could count the faces in the crowd around me, like flowers in a field.

I spotted none of the masters in the crowd except for Hemme. He stood near the pennant pole, looking piglike in his smugness. He folded his arms in front of himself, letting the sleeves of his black master's robe hang loosely at his sides. He caught my eye and his mouth quirked up into a soft smirk that I knew was meant for me.

I resolved that I would bite out my own tongue before I gave him the satisfaction of appearing frightened, or even concerned. Instead I gave him a wide, confident smile then looked away, as if he didn't concern me in the least.

Then I was at the pennant pole. I heard someone reading something, but the words were just a vague buzzing to me as I removed my cloak and lay it across the back of a stone bench that sat at the base of the pole. Then I began to unbutton my shirt, as casually as if I were preparing to take a bath.

A hand on my wrist stopped me. The man that had read the announcement gave me a smile that tried to be comforting. 'You don't need to go shirtless,' he said. 'It'll save you from a bit of the sting.'

'I'm not going to ruin a perfectly good shirt,' I said.

He gave me an odd look, then shrugged and ran a length of rope through an iron ring above our heads. 'I'll need your hands.'

I gave him a flat look. 'You don't need to worry about my running off.'

'It's to keep you from falling over if you pass out.'

I gave him a hard look. 'If I pass out you may do whatever you wish,' I said firmly. 'Until then, I will not be tied.'

Something in my voice gave him pause. He didn't offer me any argument as I climbed onto the stone bench beneath the pole and stretched to reach the iron ring. I gripped it firmly with both hands. Smooth and cool, I found it oddly comforting. I focused on it as I lowered myself into the Heart of Stone.

I heard people moving away from the base of the pole. Then the crowd quieted and there was no sound but the soft hiss and crack of the whip being loosened behind me. I was relieved I was to be whipped with a single headed whip. In Tarbean I had seen the terrible bloody hash a six-tail can make of a man's back.

There was a sudden hush. Then, before I could brace myself, there came a sharper crack than the ones before. I felt a line of dim red fire trace down my back.

I gritted my teeth. But it wasn't as bad as I'd thought it would be. Even with the precautions I had taken, I expected a sharper, fiercer pain.

Then the second lash came. Its crack was louder, and I heard it through my body rather than with my ears. I felt an odd looseness across my back. I held my breath, knowing I was torn and bleeding. Everything went red for a moment and I leaned against the rough, tarred wood of the pennant pole.

The third lash came before I was ready for it. It licked up to my left shoulder, then tore nearly all the way down to my left hip. I grit my teeth, refusing to make a sound. I kept my eyes open and watched the world grow black around the edges for a moment before snapping back into sharp, bright focus.

Then, ignoring the burning across my back, I set my feet on the bench and loosened my clenched fingers from the iron ring. A young man jumped forward as if he expected to have to catch me. I gave him a scathing look and he backed away. I gathered my shirt and cloak, laid them carefully over one arm, and left the courtyard, ignoring the silent crowd around me.

CHAPTER FORTY-TWO

Bloodless

'IT COULD BE WORSE, that much is certain.' Master Arwyl's round face was serious as he circled me. 'I was hoping you would simply welt. But I should have known better with your skin.'

I sat on the edge of a long table deep inside the Medica. Arwyl prodded my back gently as he chattered on, 'But, as I say, it could be worse. Two cuts, and as cuts go, you couldn't have done better. Clean, shallow, and straight. If you do as I tell you, you'll have nothing but smooth silver scars to show the ladies how brave you are.' He stopped in front of me and raised his white eyebrows enthusiastically behind the round rings of his spectacles, 'Eh?'

His expression wrung a smile from me.

He turned to the young man that stood by the door, 'Go and fetch the next Re'lar on the list. Tell them only that they are to bring what is needful to repair a straight, shallow laceration.' The boy turned and left, his feet pattering away in the distance.

'You will provide excellent practice for one of my Re'lar,' Arwyl said cheerfully. 'Your cut is a good straight one, with little chance of complication, but there is not much to you.' He prodded my chest with a wrinkled finger, and made a *tsk* noise with his tongue against his teeth. 'Just bones and a little wrapping. It is easier for us if we have more meat to work with.

'But,' he shrugged, bringing his shoulders almost to his ears, and back down, 'things are not always ideal. That is what a young physicker must learn more than anything.'

He looked up at me as if expecting a response. I nodded seriously.

It seemed to satisfy him, and his squinting smile returned. He turned and opened a cabinet that stood against one of the walls, 'Give me just a moment and I will numb the burning that must be all across your back.' He clinked a few bottles together as he rummaged around on its shelves.

'It's all right, Master Arwyl,' I said stoically. 'You can stitch me closed the way I am.' I had two scruples of nahlrout numbing me, and I knew better than to mix anesthetics if I could avoid it.

He paused with one arm deep into the cabinet, and had to withdraw it to turn and look at me. 'Have you ever had stitches before, my boy?'

'Yes,' I said honestly.

'Without anything to soften the pain?'

I nodded again.

As I sat on the table, my eyes were slightly higher than his. He looked up at me skeptically. 'Let me see then,' he said, as if he didn't quite believe me.

I pulled my pantleg up over my knee, gritting my teeth as the motion tugged on my back. Eventually I revealed a handspan worth of scar on my outer thigh above my knee from when Pike had stabbed me with his bottleglass knife back in Tarbean.

Arwyl looked at it closely, holding his glasses with one hand. He gave it one gentle prod with his index finger before straightening. 'Sloppy,' he pronounced with a mild distaste.

I had thought it was a rather good job. 'My cord broke halfway through,' I said stiffly. 'I wasn't working under ideal circumstances.'

Arwyl was silent for a while, stroking his upper lip with a finger as he watched me through half-lidded eyes. 'And do you enjoy this sort of thing?' he asked dubiously.

I laughed at his expression, but it was cut short when dull pain blossomed across my back. 'No, Master. I was just taking care of myself as best I could.'

He continued looking at me, still stroking his lower lip. 'Show me where the gut broke.'

I pointed. It isn't the sort of thing that you forget.

He gave the old scar a closer examination, and prodded it again before looking up. 'You may be telling me the truth.' He shrugged. 'I do not know. But I would think that if—' he trailed off and peered speculatively into my eyes. Reaching up he pulled one of the lids back. 'Look up,' he said perfunctorily.

Frowning at whatever he saw, Arwyl picked up one of my hands, pressed the tip of my fingernail firmly, and watched intently for a second or two. His frown deepened as he moved closer to me, took hold of my chin with one hand, opened my mouth, and smelled it.

'Tennasin?' He asked, then answered his own question. 'No. Nahlrout, of course. I must be getting old to not notice it sooner. It also explains why you're not bleeding all over my nice clean table.' He gave me a serious look. 'How much?'

I didn't see any way of denying it. 'Two scruples.'

Arwyl was silent for a while as he looked at me. After a moment he removed his spectacles and rubbed them fiercely against his cuff. Replacing them, he looked straight at me, 'It is no surprise that a boy might fear a whipping enough to drug himself for it.' He looked sharply at me. 'But why, if he was so afraid, would he remove his shirt beforehand?' He frowned again. 'You will explain all of this to me. If you've lied to me before, admit it and all will be well. I know boys tell foolish stories sometimes.'

His eyes glittered behind the glass of his spectacles. 'But if you lie to me now, neither I nor any of mine will stitch you. I will not be lied to.' He crossed his arms in front of himself. 'So. Explain. I do not understand what is going on here. That, more than anything else, I do not like.'

My last resort then, the truth. 'My teacher, Abenthy, taught me as much as he could about the physicker's arts,' I explained. 'When I ended up living on the streets of Tarbean I took care of myself.' I gestured to my knee. 'I didn't wear my shirt today because I only have two shirts, and it has been a long time since I have had as many as that.'

'And the nahlrout?' he asked.

I sighed, 'I don't fit in here, sir. I'm younger than everyone, and a lot of people think I don't belong. I upset a lot of students by getting into the Arcanum so quickly. And I've managed to get on the wrong side of Master Hemme. All those students, and Hemme, and his friends, they're all watching me, waiting for some sign of weakness.'

I took a deep breath. 'I took the nahlrout because I didn't want to faint. I needed to let them know they couldn't hurt me. I've learned that the best way to stay safe is to make your enemies think you can't be hurt.' It sounded ugly to say it so starkly, but it was the truth. I looked at him defiantly.

There was a long silence as Arwyl looked at me, his eyes narrowing slightly behind his spectacles, as if he were trying to see something inside me. He brushed his upper lip with his finger again before he began, slowly, to speak.

'I suppose if I were older,' he said, quietly enough to be speaking to himself, 'I would say that you were being ridiculous. That our students are adults, not squabbling, bickersome boys.'

He paused again, still stroking his lip absentmindedly. Then his eyes crinkled upward around the edges as he smiled at me. 'But I am not so old as that. *Hmmm.* Not yet. Not by half. Anyone who thinks boys are innocent and sweet has never been a boy himself, or has forgotten it. And anyone who thinks men aren't hurtful and cruel at times must not leave his house often. And he has certainly never been a physicker. We see the effects of cruelty more than any other.'

Before I could respond he said, 'Close your mouth, E'lir Kvothe, or I will feel obliged to put some vile tonic in it. Ahhh, here they come.' The last was said to two students entering the room, one was the same assistant who had shown me here, the other was, surprisingly, a young woman.

'Ah, Re'lar Mola,' Arwyl enthused, all signs of our serious discussion passing lightly from his face. 'You have heard that your patient has two straight, clean lacerations. What have you brought to remedy the situation?'

'Boiled linen, hook needle, gut, alcohol, and iodine,' she said, crisply. She had green eyes that stood out in her pale face.

'What?' Arwyl demanded. 'No sympathy wax?'

'No, Master Arwyl,' she responded, paling a little at his tone.

'And why not?'

She hesitated. 'Because I don't need it.'

Arwyl seemed mollified. 'Yes. Of course you don't. Very good. Did you wash before you came here?'

Mola nodded, her short blonde hair bobbing with the motion of her head.

'Then you have wasted your time and effort,' he said sternly. 'Think of all the germs of disease that you might have gathered in the long walk through the passageway. Wash again and we will begin.'

She washed with a thorough briskness at a nearby basin. Arwyl helped me lay facedown on the table.

'Has the patient been numbed?' she asked. Though I couldn't see her face, I heard a shadow of doubt in her voice.

'Anesthetised,' Arwyl corrected. 'You have a good eye for detail, Mola. No, he has not. Now, what would you do if E'lir Kvothe reassured you that that he has no need for such things? He claims to have self-control like a bar of Ramston steel and will not flinch when you stitch him.' Arwyl's tone was serious, but I could detect a hint of amusement hiding underneath.

Mola looked at me, then back to Arwyl. 'I would tell him that he was being foolish,' she said after a brief pause.

'And if he persisted in his claims that he needed no numbing agent?'

There was a longer pause from Mola. 'He doesn't seem to be bleeding much at all, so I would proceed. I would also make it clear to him that if he moved overmuch, I would tie him to the table and treat him as I saw fit for his well-being.'

'Hmmm,' Arwyl seemed a little surprised at her response. 'Yes. Very good. So, Kvothe, do you still wish to forgo an anesthetic?'

'Thank you,' I said politely. 'I do not need one.'

'Very well,' Mola said, as if resigning herself. 'First we will clean and sterilise the wound.' The alcohol stung, but that was the worst of it. I tried my best to relax as Mola talked her way through the procedure. Arwyl kept up a steady stream of comments and advice. I occupied my mind with other things and tried not to twitch at the nahlrout-dulled jabs of the needle.

She finished quickly and proceeded to bandage me with a quick efficiency I admired. As she helped me to a sitting position and wound linen around me, I wondered if all Arwyl's students were as well-trained as this one.

She was making her final knots behind me when I felt a vague, feather-like touch on my shoulder, almost insensible through the nahlrout that numbed me. 'He has lovely skin.' I heard her muse, presumably to Arwyl.

'Re'lar!' Arwyl said severely. 'Such comments are not professional. I am disappointed by your lack of sense.'

'I was referring to the nature of the scar he can expect to have,' she responded scathingly. 'I imagine it will be little more than a pale line, provided he can avoid tearing open his wound.'

'Hmmm,' Arwyl said. 'Yes, of course. And how should he avoid that?'

Mola walked around to stand in front of me. 'Avoid motions like this,' she extended her hands in front of her, 'or this,' she held them high over her head. 'Avoid over-quick motions of any kind – running, jumping, climbing. The bandage may come off in two days. Do not get it wet.' She looked away from me, to Arwyl.

He nodded. 'Very good, Re'lar. You are dismissed.' He looked at the younger boy who had watched mutely throughout the procedure, 'You may go as well, Geri. If anyone asks, I will be in my study. Thank you.'

In a moment Arwyl and I were alone again. He stood motionless, one hand covering his mouth as I eased my way carefully into my shirt. Finally, he seemed to reach a decision, 'E'lir Kvothe, would you like to study here at the Medica?'

'Very much so, Master Arwyl,' I said honestly.

He nodded to himself, hand still held against his lips, 'Come back in four days. If you are clever enough to keep from tearing out your stitches, I will have you here.' His eyes twinkled.

CHAPTER FORTY-THREE

The Flickering Way

B UOYED BY THE STIMULANT effects of the nahlrout and feeling very little pain, I made my way to the Archives. Since I was now a member of the Arcanum, I was free to explore the stacks, something I'd been waiting my whole life to do.

Better still, so long as I didn't ask for any help from the scrivs, nothing would be recorded in the Archive's ledger books. That meant I could research the Chandrian and the Amyr to my heart's content, and no one, not even Lorren, need ever know about my 'childish' pursuits.

Entering the reddish light of the Archives I found both Ambrose and Fela sitting behind the entry desk. A mixed blessing if ever there was one.

Ambrose was leaning towards her, speaking in a low voice. She had the distinctly uncomfortable look of a woman who knows the futility of a polite refusal. One of his hands rested on her knee, while the other arm was draped across the back of her chair, his hand resting on her neck. He meant for it to look tender and affectionate, but there was a tension in her body like that of a startled deer. The truth was he was holding her there, the same way you hold a dog by the scruff of its neck to keep it from running off.

As the door thumped closed behind me Fela looked up, met my eyes, then looked down and away, ashamed by her predicament. As if she'd done anything. I had seen that look too many times on the streets of Tarbean. It sparked an old anger in me.

I approached the desk, making more noise than necessary. Pen and ink lay on the other end of the desk, and a piece of paper three-quarters full of rewriting and crossing out. From the looks of things, Ambrose had been trying to compose a poem.

I reached the edge of the desk and stood for a moment. Fela looked everywhere except at me or Ambrose. She shifted in her seat, uncomfortable, but obviously not wanting to make a scene. I cleared my throat pointedly.

Ambrose looked over his shoulder, scowling. 'You have damnable timing, E'lir. Come back later.' He turned away again, dismissing me.

I snorted and leaned over the desk, craning my neck to look at the sheet of paper he'd left lying there. '*I* have damnable timing? Please, you have thirteen syllables in a line here.' I tapped a finger onto the page. 'It's not iambic either. I don't know if it's anything metrical at all.'

He turned to look at me again, his expression irritated. 'Mind your tongue, E'lir. The day I come to you for help with poetry is the day—'

'. . . is the day you have two hours to spare,' I said. 'Two long hours, and that's just for getting started. "So same can the humble thrush well know its north?" I mean, I don't even know how to begin to criticise that. It practically mocks itself.'

'What do you know of poetry?' Ambrose said without bothering to turn around.

'I know a limping verse when I hear it,' I said. 'But this isn't even limping. A limp has rhythm. This is more like someone falling down a set of stairs. Uneven stairs. With a midden at the bottom.'

'It is a sprung rhythm,' he said, his voice stiff and offended. 'I wouldn't expect you to understand.'

'Sprung?' I burst out with an incredulous laugh. 'I understand that if I saw a horse with a leg this badly "sprung", I'd kill it out of mercy, then burn its poor corpse for fear the local dogs might gnaw on it and die.'

Ambrose finally turned around to face me, and in so doing he had to take his right hand off Fela's knee. A half-victory, but his other hand remained on her neck, holding her in her chair with the appearance of a casual caress.

'I thought you might stop by today,' he said with a brittle cheerfulness. 'So I already checked the ledger. You're not in the lists yet. You'll have to stick with Tomes or come back later, after they've updated the books.'

'No offense, but would you mind checking again? I'm not sure I can trust the literacy of someone who tries to rhyme "north" with "worth". No wonder you have to hold women down to get them to listen to it.'

Ambrose stiffened and his arm slid off the back of the chair to fall at his side. His expression was pure venom. 'When you're older, E'lir, you'll understand that what a man and a woman do together—'

'What? In the privacy of the entrance hall of the Archives?' I gestured around us. 'God's body, this isn't some brothel. And, in case you hadn't noticed, she's a student, not some brass nail you've paid to bang away at. If you're going to force yourself on a woman, have the decency to do it in an alleyway. At least that way she'll feel justified screaming about it.'

Ambrose's face flushed furiously and it took him a long moment to find his voice. 'You don't know the first thing about women.'

'There, at least, we can agree,' I said easily. 'In fact, that's the reason I came here today. I wanted to do some research. Find a book or two on the subject.' I struck the ledger with two fingers, hard. 'So look up my name and let me in.'

Ambrose flipped the book open, found the proper page, and turned the book around to face me. 'There. If you can find your name on that list, you are welcome to peruse the stacks at your leisure.' He gave a tight smile. 'Otherwise feel free to come back in a span or so. We should have things updated by then.'

'I had the masters send along a note just in case there was any confusion about my admission to the Arcanum.' I said, and drew my shirt up over my head, turning so he could see the broad expanse of bandages covering my back. 'Can you read it from there, or do I need to come closer?'

There was a pointed silence from Ambrose, so I lowered my shirt and turned to face Fela, ignoring him entirely. 'My lady scriv,' I said to her with a bow. A very slight bow, as my back wouldn't permit a deep one. 'Would you be so good as to help me locate a book concerning women? I have been instructed by my betters to inform myself on this most subtle subject.'

Fela gave a faint smile and relaxed a bit. She had continued sitting stiff and uncomfortable after Ambrose had taken his hand away. I guessed that she knew Ambrose's temperament well enough to know that if she bolted away and embarrassed him, he would make her pay for it later. 'I don't know if we have anything like that.'

'I would settle for a primer,' I said with a smile. 'I have it on good report that I don't know the first thing about them, so anything would further my knowledge.'

'Something with pictures?' Ambrose spat.

'If our search degenerates to that level I'll be sure to call on you,' I said without looking in his direction. I smiled at Fela. 'Perhaps a bestiary,' I said gently. 'I hear they are singular creatures, much different than men.'

Fela's smile blossomed and she gave a small laugh. 'We could have a look around, I suppose.'

Ambrose scowled in her direction.

She made a placating gesture towards him. 'Everyone knows he's in the Arcanum, Ambrose,' she said. 'What's the harm of just letting him in?'

Ambrose glared at her. 'Why don't you run along to Tomes and play the good little fetch-and-carry girl?' he said coldly. 'I can handle things out here by myself.'

Moving stiffly, Fela got up from the desk, gathered up the book she'd been trying to read, and headed into Tomes. As she pulled the door open, I like to think she gave me a brief look of gratitude and relief. But perhaps it was only my imagination.

As the door swung shut behind her, the room seemed to grow a little dimmer. I am not speaking poetically. The light truly seemed to dim. I looked at the sympathy lamps hanging around the room, wondering what was wrong.

But a moment later I felt a slow, burning sensation begin to creep across my back and realised the truth. The nahlrout was wearing off.

Most powerful painkillers have serious side effects. Tennasin occasionally produces delirium or fainting. Lacillium is poisonous. Ophalum is highly addictive. Mhenka is perhaps the most powerful of all, but there are reasons they call it 'devil root'.

Nahlrout was less powerful than these, but much safer. It was a mild anesthetic, a stimulant, and a vascular constrictor, which is why I hadn't bled like a stuck pig when they'd whipped me. Best of all, it had no major side effects. Still, there is always a price to be paid. Once nahlrout wears off, it leaves you physically and mentally exhausted.

Regardless, I had come here to see the stacks. I was now a member of the Arcanum and I didn't intend to leave until I'd been inside the Archives. I turned back to the desk, my expression resolute.

Ambrose gave me a long, calculating look before heaving a sigh. 'Fine,' he said. 'How about a deal? You keep quiet about what you saw here today, and I'll bend the rules and let you in even though you aren't officially in the book.' He looked a little nervous. 'How does that sound?'

Even as he spoke I could feel the stimulant effect from the nahlrout fading. My body felt heavy and tired, my thoughts grew sluggish and syrupy. I reached up to rub at my face with my hands, and winced as the motion tugged sharply at the stitches all across my back. 'That'll be fine,' I said thickly.

Ambrose opened up one of the ledger books and sighed as he turned the pages. 'Since this is your first time in the Archives proper, you'll have to pay the stack fee.'

My mouth tasted strangely of lemons. That was a side effect Ben had never mentioned. It was distracting, and after a moment I saw that Ambrose was looking up at me expectantly. 'What?'

He gave me a strange look. 'The stack fee.'

'There wasn't any fee before,' I said. 'When I was in the Tomes.'

Ambrose looked up at me as if I were an idiot. 'That's because it's the *stack* fee.' He looked back down at the ledger. 'Normally you pay it in addition to your first term's Arcanum tuition. But since you've jumped rank on us, you'll need to tend to it now.'

'How much is it?' I asked, feeling for my purse.

'One talent,' he said. 'And you *do* have to pay before you can go in. Rules are Rules.'

After paying for my bunk in Mews, a talent was nearly all my remaining money. I was keenly aware of the fact that I needed to hoard my resources to save for next term's tuition. As soon as I couldn't pay, I would have to leave the University.

Still, it was a small price to pay for something I'd dreamed about for most of my life. I pulled a talent out of my purse and handed it over. 'Do I need to sign in?'

'Nothing so formal as that,' Ambrose said as he opened a drawer and pulled out a small metal disk. Stupefied from the side effects of the nahlrout, it took me a moment to recognise it for what it was: a handheld sympathy lamp.

'The Stacks aren't lit,' Ambrose said matter-of-factly. 'There's too much space in there, and it would be bad for the books in the long term. Hand lamps cost a talent and a half.'

I hesitated.

Ambrose nodded to himself and looked thoughtful. 'A lot of folk end up strapped during first term.' He reached down into a lower drawer and rooted around for a long moment. 'Hand lamps are a talent and half, and there's nothing I can do about that.' He brought out a four-inch taper. 'But candles are just a ha'penny.'

Ha'penny for a candle was a remarkably good deal. I brought out a penny. 'I'll take two.'

'This is our last one,' Ambrose said quickly. He looked around nervously before pushing it into my hand. 'Tell you what. You can have it for free.' He smiled. 'Just don't tell anyone. It'll be our little secret.'

I took the candle, more than a little surprised. Apparently I'd frightened him with my idle threat earlier. Either that or this rude, pompous noble's son wasn't half the bastard I'd taken him for.

Ambrose hurried me into the stacks as quickly as possible, leaving me no time to light my candle. When the doors swung shut behind me it was as black as the inside of a sack, with only a faint hint of reddish sympathy light coming around the edges of the door behind me.

As I didn't have any matches with me, I had to resort to sympathy. Ordinarily I could have done it quick as blinking, but my nahlrout-weary mind could barely muster the necessary concentration. I gritted my teeth, fixed the Alar in my mind, and after a few seconds I felt the cold leech into my muscles as I drew enough heat from my own body to bring the wick of the candle sputtering to life.

Books.

With no windows to let in the sunlight, the stacks were utterly dark except for the gentle light of my candle. Stretching away into the darkness were shelf on shelf of books. More books than I could look at if I took a whole day. More books than I could read in a lifetime.

The air was cool and dry. It smelled of old leather, parchment, and for-gotten secrets. I wondered idly how they kept the air so fresh in a building with no windows.

Cupping a hand in front of my candle, I made my flickering way through the shelves, savoring the moment, soaking everything in. Shadows danced wildly back and forth across the ceiling as my candle's flame moved from side to side.

The nahlrout had worn off completely by this point. My back was throb-bing and my thoughts were leaden, as if I had a high fever or had taken a hard blow to the back of the head. I knew I wasn't going to be up for a long bout of reading, but I still couldn't bring myself to leave so soon. Not after everything I'd gone through to get here.

I wandered aimlessly for perhaps a quarter of an hour, exploring. I discovered several small stone rooms with heavy wooden doors and tables inside. They were obviously meant as a place where small groups could meet and talk without disturbing the perfect quiet of the Archives.

I found stairwells leading down as well as up. The Archives was six stories tall, but I hadn't known it extended underground as well. How deep did it go? How many tens of thousands of books were waiting under my feet?

I can hardly describe how comforting it was in the cool, quiet dark. I was perfectly content, lost among the endless books. It made me feel safe, knowing that the answers to all my questions were here, somewhere waiting.

It was quite by accident that I found the four-plate door.

It was made of a solid piece of grey stone the same color as the surrounding walls. Its frame was eight inches wide, also grey, and also one single seamless piece of stone. The door and frame fit together so tightly that a pin couldn't slide into the crack.

It had no hinges. No handle. No window or sliding panel. Its only features were four hard copper plates. They were set flush with the face of the door, which was flush with the front of the frame, which was flush with the wall surrounding it. You could run your hand from one side of the door to the next and hardly feel the lines of it at all.

In spite of these notable lacks, the expanse of grey stone was undoubtedly a door. It simply was. Each copper plate had a hole in its center, and though they were not shaped in the conventional way, they were undoubtedly keyholes. The door sat still as a mountain, quiet and indifferent as the sea on a windless day. This was not a door for opening. It was a door for staying closed.

In its center, between the untarnished copper plates, a word was chiseled deep into the stone: VALARITAS.

There were other locked doors in the University, places where dangerous things were kept, where old and forgotten secrets slept: silent and hidden. Doors whose opening was forbidden. Doors whose thresholds no one crossed, whose keys had been destroyed or lost, or locked away themselves for safety's sake.

But they all paled in comparison to the four-plate door. I lay my palm on the cool, smooth face of the door and pushed, hoping against hope that it might swing open to my touch. But it was solid and unmoving as a greystone. I tried to peer through the holes in the copper plates but couldn't see anything by the light of my single candle.

I wanted to get inside so badly I could taste it. It probably shows a perverse element of my personality that even though I was finally inside the Archives, surrounded by endless secrets, that I was drawn to the one locked door I had found. Perhaps it is human nature to seek out hidden things. Perhaps it is simply my nature.

Just then I saw the red, unwavering light of a sympathy lamp approaching through the shelves. It was the first sign I'd seen of any other students in the archives. I took a step back and waited, thinking to ask whoever was coming what was behind the door. What *Valaritas* meant.

The red light swelled and I saw two scrivs turn a corner. They paused, then one of them bolted to where I stood and snatched my candle away, spilling hot wax on my hand in the process of extinguishing it. His expression couldn't have been more horrified if he had found me carrying a freshly severed head.

'What are you doing with an open flame in here?' he demanded in the loudest whisper I had ever heard. He lowered his voice and waved the now extinguished candle at me. 'Charred body of God, what's the matter with you?'

I rubbed at the hot wax on the back of my hand. Trying to think clearly through the fog of pain and exhaustion. *Of course,* I thought, remembering Ambrose's smile as he pressed the candle into my hands and hurried me though the door. *'Our little secret.' Of course. I should have known.*

One of the scrivs led me out of the Stacks while the other ran to fetch Master Lorren. When we emerged into the entryway, Ambrose managed to look confused and shocked. He overacted the part, but it was convincing enough for the scriv accompanying me. 'What's he doing in here?'

'We found him wandering around,' the scriv explained. *'With a candle.'*

'What?' Ambrose's expression was perfectly aghast. 'Well *I* didn't sign him in,' Ambrose said. He flipped open one of the ledger books. 'Look. See for yourself.'

Before anything else could be said, Lorren stormed into the room. His normally placid expression was fierce and hard. I felt myself sweat cold and I thought of what Teccam wrote in his Theophany: *There are three things all wise men fear: the sea in storm, a night with no moon, and the anger of a gentle man.*

Lorren towered over the entry desk. 'Explain,' he demanded of the nearby scriv. His voice was a tight coil of fury.

'Micah and I saw a flickering light in the stacks and we went to see if someone was having trouble with their lamp. We found him near the southeast stairwell with this.' The scriv held up the candle. His hand shook slightly under Lorren's glare.

Lorren turned to the desk where Ambrose sat. 'How did this happen, Re'lar?'

Ambrose raised his hands helplessly. 'He came in earlier and I wouldn't admit him because he wasn't in the book. We bickered for a while, Fela was here for most of it.' He looked at me. 'Eventually I told him he'd have to leave. He must have snuck in when I went into the back room for more ink.' Ambrose shrugged. 'Or maybe he slipped in past the desk in Tomes.'

I stood there, stupefied. What little part of my mind wasn't leaden with fatigue was preoccupied with the screaming pain across my back. 'That . . . that's not true.' I looked up at Lorren. 'He let me in. He sent Fela away, then let me in.'

'What?' Ambrose gaped at me, momentarily speechless. For all that I didn't like him, I must give him credit for a masterful performance. 'Why in God's name would I do that?'

'Because I embarrassed you in front of Fela,' I said. 'He sold me the candle, too.' I shook my head trying to clear my head. 'No, he gave it to me.'

Ambrose's expression was amazed. 'Look at him.' He laughed. 'The little cocker is drunk or something.'

'I was just whipped!' I protested. My voice sounded shrill in my own ears.

'Enough!' Lorren shouted, looming over us like a pillar of anger. The scrivs went pale at the sound of him.

Lorren turned away from me, and made a brief, contemptuous gesture towards the desk. 'Re'lar Ambrose is officially remanded for laxity in his duty.'

'What?' Ambrose's indignant tone wasn't feigned this time.

Lorren frowned at him, and Ambrose closed his mouth. Turning to me, he said, 'E'lir Kvothe is banned from the Archives.' He made a sweeping gesture with the flat of his hand.

I tried to think of something I could say in my defense. 'Master, I didn't mean—'

Lorren rounded on me. His expression, always so calm before, was filled with such a cold, terrible anger that I took a step away from him without meaning to. 'You *mean*?' he said. 'I care nothing for your *intentions*, E'lir Kvothe, deceived or otherwise. All that matters is the reality of your actions. Your hand held the fire. Yours is the blame. That is the lesson all adults must learn.'

I looked down at my feet, tried desperately to think of something I could say. Some proof I could offer. My leaden thoughts were still plodding along when Lorren strode out of the room.

'I don't see why I should be punished for his stupidity,' Ambrose groused to the other scrivs as I made my way numbly to the door. I made the mistake of turning around and looking at him. His expression was serious, carefully controlled.

But his eyes were vastly amused, full of laughter. 'Honestly boy,' he said to me. 'I don't know what you were thinking. You'd think a member of the Arcanum would have more sense.'

I made my way to the Mess, the wheels of my thoughts turning slowly as I plodded along. I fumbled my meal chit into one of the dull tin trays and collected a portion of steamed pudding, a sausage, and some of the ever-present beans. I looked dully around the room until I spotted Simmon and Manet sitting in their usual place at the northeast corner of the hall.

I drew a fair amount of attention as I walked to the table. Understandable, as it was scarcely two hours since I'd been tied to the pennant pole and publicly lashed. I heard someone whisper, '. . . didn't bleed when they whipped him. I was there. Not one drop.'

It was the nahlrout, of course. It had kept me from bleeding. It had seemed like such a good idea at the time. Now it seemed petty and foolish. Ambrose would never have managed to gull me so easily if my naturally suspicious nature hadn't been fuddled. I'm sure I could have found some way to explain things to Lorren if I'd had my wits about me.

As I made my way to the far corner of the room, I realised the truth. I had traded away my access to the Archives in exchange for a little notoriety.

Still, there was nothing to do but make the best of it. If a bit of reputation was all I had to show for this debacle, I'd have to do my best to build on it. I kept my shoulders straight as I made my way across the room to Simmon and Manet and set down my food.

'There's no such thing as a stack fee, is there?' I asked quietly as I slid into my seat, trying not to grimace at the pain across my back.

Sim looked at me blankly. 'Stack fee?'

Manet chortled into his bowl of beans. 'It's been a few years since I heard that. Back when I worked as a scriv we'd trick the first-termers into giving us a penny to use the Archives. Called it a stack fee.'

Sim gave him a disapproving look. 'That's horrible.'

Manet held up his hands defensively in front of his face. 'Just a little harmless fun.' Manet looked me over. 'Is that what your long face is for? Somebody cull you for a copper?'

I shook my head. I wasn't going to announce that Ambrose had tricked me out of a whole talent. 'Guess who just got banned from the Archives?' I said gravely as I tore the crust off my bread and dropped it into my beans.

They looked at me blankly. After a moment Simmon took the obvious guess. 'Ummm . . . you?'

I nodded and began to spoon up my beans. I wasn't really hungry, but I hoped a little food in my stomach might help shake off the sluggishness of the nahlrout. Besides, it went against my nature to pass up an opportunity for a meal.

'You got suspended on your first day?' Simmon said. 'That's going to make studying your Chandrian folklore a whole lot harder.'

I sighed. 'You could say that.'

'How long did he suspend you for?'

'He said *banned*,' I answered. 'He didn't mention a time limit.'

'Banned?' Manet looked up at me. 'He hasn't banned anyone in a dozen years. What'd you do? Piss on a book?'

'Some of the scrivs found me inside with a candle.'

'Merciful Tehlu.' Manet lay down his fork, his expression serious for the first time. 'Old Lore must have been furious.'

'Furious is exactly the right word,' I said.

'What possessed you to go in there with an open flame?' Simmon asked.

'I couldn't afford a hand lamp,' I said. 'So the scriv at the desk gave me a candle instead.'

'He didn't,' Sim said. 'No scriv would . . .'

'Hold on,' Manet said. 'Was this a dark-haired fellow? Well-dressed? Severe eyebrows?' He made an exaggerated scowl.

I nodded tiredly. 'Ambrose. We met yesterday. Got off on the wrong foot.'

'He's hard to avoid,' Manet said carefully, with a significant look to the people sitting around us. I noticed that more than a few were casually listening to our conversation. 'Someone should have warned you to keep clear of him,' he added in a softer tone.

'God's mother,' Simmon said. 'Of all the people you don't want to start a pissing contest with . . .'

'Well, it's been started,' I said. I was starting to feel a little more like myself again, less cotton-headed and weary. Either the side effects of the nahlrout were fading, or my anger was slowly burning away the haze of exhaustion. 'He'll find out I can piss along with the best of them. He'll wish he'd never met me, let alone meddled with my affairs.'

Simmon looked a little nervous. 'You really shouldn't threaten other students,' he said with a little laugh, as if trying to pass my comment off as a joke. More softly, he said. 'You don't understand. Ambrose is heir to a barony off in Vintas.' He hesitated, looking to Manet. 'Lord, how do I even start?'

Manet leaned forward and spoke in more confidential tones as well. 'He's not one of those nobility who dabble here for a term or two then leave. He's been for years, climbed his way up to Re'lar. He's not some seventh son either. He's the firstborn heir. And his father is one of the twelve most powerful men in all of Vintas.'

'Actually he's sixteenth in the peerage,' Sim said matter-of-factly. 'You've got the royal family, the prince regents, Maer Alveron, Duchess Samista, Aculeus and Meluan Lackless . . .' He trailed off under Manet's glare.

'He has money,' Manet said simply. 'And the friends that money buys.'

'And people who want to curry favour with his father,' Simmon added.

'The point is,' Manet said seriously, 'you don't want to cross him. Back in his first year here, one of the alchemists got on Ambrose's bad side. Ambrose bought his debt from the moneylender in Imre. When the fellow couldn't pay, they clapped him into debtor's prison.' Manet tore a piece of bread in half and daubed butter onto it. 'By the time his family got him out he had lung consumption. Fellow was a wreck. Never came back to his studies.'

'And the masters just let this happen?' I demanded.

'All perfectly legal,' Manet said, still keeping his voice low. 'Even so, Ambrose wasn't so silly that he bought the fellow's debt *himself*.' Manet made a dismissive gesture. 'He had someone else do that, but he made sure everyone knew he was responsible.'

'And there was Tabetha,' Sim said darkly. 'She made all that noise about how Ambrose had promised to marry her. She just disappeared.'

This certainly explained why Fela had been so hesitant to offend him. I made a placating gesture to Sim. 'I'm not threatening anyone,' I said innocently, pitching my voice so anyone who was listening could easily hear. 'I'm just quoting one of my favorite pieces of literature. It's from the fourth act of *Daeonica* where Tarsus says:

> *'Upon him I will visit famine and a fire.*
> *Till all around him desolation rings*
> *And all the demons in the outer dark*
> *Look on amazed and recognise*
> *That vengeance is the business of a man.'*

There was a moment of stunned silence nearby. It spread a bit farther through the Mess than I'd expected. Apparently I'd underestimated the number of people who were listening. I turned my attention back to my meal and decided to let it go for now. I was tired, and I hurt, and I didn't particularly want any more trouble today.

'You won't need this piece of information for a while,' Manet said quietly after a long period of silence. 'What with being banned from the Archives and all. Still, I'm supposing you'd rather know . . .' He cleared his throat uncomfortably. 'You don't have to buy a hand lamp. You just sign them out at the desk and return them when you're done.' He looked at me as if anxious about what sort of reaction the information might provoke.

I nodded wearily. I'd been right before. Ambrose wasn't half the bastard I thought he was. He was ten times the bastard.

CHAPTER FORTY-FOUR

The Burning Glass

THE FISHERY WAS WHERE most of the University's works of hands were made. The building held shops for glassblowers, joiners, potters, and glaziers. There was also a full forge and smelt-works that would figure prominently in any metallurgist's daydreams.

Kilvin's workshop was located in the Artificery or, as it was more commonly called, the Fishery. It was big as the inside of a granary, holding at least two dozen thick-timbered worktables strewn with countless, nameless tools and projects in progress. The workshop was the heart of the Fishery, and Kilvin was the heart of the workshop.

When I arrived, Kilvin was in the process of bending a twisted length of iron rod into what I could only assume was a more desirable shape. Seeing me peering in, he left it firmly clamped to the table and walked to meet me, wiping his hands on his shirt.

He looked me over critically. 'Are you well, E'lir Kvothe?'

I'd gone wandering earlier and found some willow bark to chew. My back still burned and itched, but it was bearable. 'Well enough, Master Kilvin.'

He nodded. 'Good. Boys your age shouldn't worry over such small things. Soon again you will be as sound as stone.'

I was trying to think up a polite response when my eye was drawn to something over our heads.

Kilvin followed my gaze up over his shoulder. When he saw what I was looking at, a grin split his great bearded face. 'Ahhh,' he said with fatherly pride. 'My lovelies.'

High among the high rafters of the workshop a half hundred glass spheres hung from chains. They were of varying sizes, though none were much larger than a man's head.

And they were burning.

Seeing my expression, Kilvin made a gesture. 'Come,' he said, and led me to a narrow stairway made of wrought iron. Reaching the top, we stepped out onto a series of slim iron walkways twenty-five feet above the ground, weaving their way among the thick timbers that supported the roof. After a moment of maneuvering through the maze of timber and iron, we came to the hanging row of glass spheres with fires burning inside them.

'These,' Kilvin gestured, 'are my lamps.'

It was only then that I realised what they were. Some were filled with liquid and wicking, much like ordinary lamps, but most of them were utterly unfamiliar. One contained nothing but a boiling grey smoke that flickered sporadically. Another sphere contained a wick hanging in empty air from a silver wire, burning with a motionless white flame despite its apparent lack of fuel.

Two hanging side by side were twins save that one had a blue flame and the other was a hot-forge-orange. Some were small as plums, others large as melons. One held what looked like a piece of black coal and a piece of white chalk, and where the two pieces were pressed together, an angry red flame burned outward in all directions.

Kilvin let me look for a long while before he moved closer. 'Among the Cealdar there are legends of ever-burning lamps. I believe that such a thing was once within the scope of our craft. Ten years I have been looking. I have made many lamps, some of them very good, very long burning.' He looked at me. 'But none of them ever-burning.'

He walked down the line to point at one of the hanging spheres. 'Do you know this one, E'lir Kvothe?' It held nothing but a knob of greenish-greyish wax that was burning with a greenish-greyish tongue of flame. I shook my head.

'Hmmm. You should. White lithium salt. I thought of it three span before you came to us. It is good so far, twenty-four days and I expect many more.' He looked at me. 'Your guessing this thing surprised me, as it took me ten years to think of it. Your second guess, sodium oil, was not as good. I tried it years ago. Eleven days.'

He moved all the way to the end of the row, pointing at the empty sphere with the motionless white flame. 'Seventy days,' he said proudly. 'I do not hope that this will be the one, for hoping is a foolish game. But if it burns six more days it will be my best lamp in these ten years.'

He watched it for a while, his expression oddly soft. 'But I do not hope,' he said resolutely. 'I make new lamps and take my measurements. That is the only way to make progress.'

Wordlessly he led me back down to the floor of the workshop. Once there, he turned to me. 'Hands,' he said in a peremptory way. He held out his own huge hands expectantly.

Not knowing what he wanted, I raised my hands in front of me. He took them in his own, his touch surprisingly gentle. He turned them over, looking at them carefully. 'You have Cealdar hands,' he said in a grudging compliment. He held his own up for me to see. They were thick-fingered, with wide palms. He made two fists that looked more like mauls than balled hands. 'I had many years before these hands could learn to be Cealdar hands. You are lucky. You will work here.' Only by the quizzical tilting of his head did he make the gruff grumble of a statement into an invitation.

'Oh, yes. I mean, thank you, sir. I'm honoured that you wo—'

He cut me off with an impatient gesture. 'Come to me if you have any thoughts on the ever-burning lamp. If your head is as clever as your hands look . . .' What might have been a smile was hidden by his thick beard, but a grin shone in his dark eyes as he hesitated teasingly, almost playfully. 'If,' he repeated, holding up a finger, its tip as large as the ball of a hammer's head. 'Then me and mine will show you things.'

———

'You need to figure out who you're going to suck up to,' Simmon said. 'A master has to sponsor you to Re'lar. So you should pick one and stick to him like shit on his shoe.'

'Lovely,' Sovoy said dryly.

Sovoy, Wilem, Simmon and I were sitting at an out of the way table in the back of Anker's, isolated from the Felling-night crowd that filled the room with a low roar of conversation. My stitches had come out two days earlier and we were celebrating my first full span in the Arcanum.

We were none of us particularly drunk. But then again, none of us were particularly sober, either. Our exact positioning between those two points is a matter of pointless conjecture, and I will waste no time on it.

'I simply concentrate on being brilliant,' Sovoy said. 'Then wait for the masters to realise it.'

'How did that work out with Mandrag?' Wilem said with a rare smile.

Sovoy gave Wilem a dark look. 'Mandrag is a horse's ass.'

'That explains why you threatened him with your riding crop,' Wilem said.

I covered my mouth to stifle a laugh. 'Did you really?'

'They're not telling the whole story,' Sovoy said, affronted. 'He passed me over for promotion in favour of another student. He was keeping me back so he could use me as indentured labour, rather than raise me to Re'lar.'

'And you threatened him with your crop.'

'We had an argument,' Sovoy said calmly. 'And I happened to have my crop in my hand.'

'You waved it at him,' Wilem said.

'I'd been riding!' Sovoy said hotly. 'If I'd been whoring before class and waved a corset at him, no one would have thought twice about it!'

There was a moment of silence at our table.

'I'm thinking twice about it right now,' Simmon said before bursting into laughter with Wilem.

Sovoy fought down a smile as he turned to face me. 'Sim is right about one thing. You should concentrate your efforts on one subject. Otherwise you'll end up like Manet, the eternal E'lir.' He stood and straightened his clothes. 'Now, how do I look?'

Sovoy wasn't fashionably dressed in the strictest sense, as he clung to the Modegan styles rather than the local ones. But there was no denying that he cut quite a figure in the muted colours of his fine silks and suedes.

'What does it matter?' Wilem asked. 'Are you trying to set up a tryst with Sim?'

Sovoy smiled. 'Unfortunately, I must leave you. I have an engagement with a lady, and I doubt our rounds will bring us to this side of town tonight.'

'You didn't tell us you had a date,' Sim protested. 'We can't play corners with just three.'

It was something of a concession that Sovoy was here with us at all. He'd sniffed a bit at Wil and Sim's choice of taverns. Anker's was low-class enough so that the drinks were cheap, but high-class enough so that you didn't have to worry about someone picking a fight or throwing up on you. I liked it.

'You are good friends and good company,' Sovoy said. 'But none of you are female, nor, with the possible exception of Simmon, are you lovely.' Sovoy winked at him. 'Honestly, who among you wouldn't throw the others over if there was a lady waiting?'

We murmured a grudging agreement. Sovoy smiled; his teeth were very white and straight. 'I'll send the girl over with more drinks,' he said as he turned to go. 'To ease the bitter sting of my departure.'

'He's not a bad sort,' I mused after he left. 'For nobility.'

Wilem nodded. 'It's like he knows he's better than you, but doesn't look down on you for it because he knows it's not your fault.'

'So who are you going to cozy up to?' Sim asked, resting his elbows on the table. 'I'm guessing not Hemme.'

'Or Lorren,' I said bitterly. 'Damn Ambrose twelve ways. I would have loved to work in the Archives.'

'Brandeur's out too,' Sim said. 'If Hemme has a grudge, Brandeur helps him carry it.'

'How about the Chancellor?' Wilem asked. 'Linguistics? You already speak Siaru, even if your accent is barbaric.'

I shook my head. 'What about Mandrag? I've got a lot of experience with chemistry. It'd be a small step into alchemy.'

Simmon laughed. 'Everyone thinks chemistry and alchemy are so similar, but they're really not. They're not even related. They just happen to live in the same house.'

Wilem gave a slow nod. 'That's a nice way of putting it.'

'Besides,' Simmon said. 'Mandrag brought in about twenty new E'lir last term. I heard him complaining about how crowded things were.'

'You've got a long haul if you go through Medica,' Wilem said. 'Arwyl is stubborn as pig iron. There is no bending him.' He made a gesture with his hand as if chopping something into sections while he spoke. 'Six terms E'lir. Eight terms Re'lar. Ten terms El'the.'

'At least,' Simmon added. 'Mola's been a Re'lar with him for almost three years now.'

I tried to think of how I could come up with six years' worth of tuition. 'I might not have the patience for that,' I said.

The serving girl appeared with a tray of drinks. Anker's was only half full, so she'd been running just enough to bring roses to her cheeks. 'Your gentleman friend paid for this round and the next,' she said.

'I like Sovoy more and more,' Wilem said.

'However,' she held Wil's drink out of his reach. 'He *didn't* pay for putting his hand on my ass,' she looked each of us in the eye. 'I'll trust the three of you to settle that debt before you leave.'

Sim stammered an apology. 'He . . . he doesn't mean . . . In his culture that sort of thing is more common.'

She rolled her eyes, her expression softening. 'Well in this culture a healthy tip makes a fine apology.' She handed Wil his drink and turned to leave, resting her empty tray on one hip.

We watched her go, each of us thinking our own private thoughts.

'I noticed he had his rings back,' I mentioned eventually.

'He played a brilliant round of bassat last night,' Simmon said. 'Made six doublings in a row and cracked the bank.'

'To Sovoy,' Wilem held up his tin mug. 'May his luck keep him in classes and us in drinks.' We toasted and drank, then Wilem brought us back to the matter at hand. 'That leaves you with Kilvin and Elxa Dal.' He held up two fingers.

'What about Elodin?' I interrupted.

They both gave me blank looks. 'What about him?' Simmon asked.

'He seems nice enough,' I said. 'Couldn't I study under him?'

Simmon burst out laughing. Wilem gave a rare grin. 'What?' I demanded.

'Elodin doesn't teach anything,' Sim explained. 'Except maybe advanced oddness.'

'He has to teach something,' I protested. 'He's a master, isn't he?'

'Sim is right. Elodin is cramped.' Wil tapped the side of his head.

'Cracked,' Simmon corrected.

'Cracked,' Wil repeated.

'He does seem a little . . . strange,' I said.

'You *do* pick things up quick,' Wilem said dryly. 'No wonder you made it into the Arcanum at such a tender age.'

'Ease off, Wil, he's hardly been here a span.' Simmon turned to me. 'Elodin used to be Chancellor about five years ago.'

'Elodin?' I couldn't hide my incredulity. 'But he's so young and . . .' I trailed off, not wanting to say the first word that came to my mind: *crazy*.

Simmon finished my sentence. '. . . brilliant. And not that young if you consider that he was admitted to the University when he was barely fourteen.' Simmon looked at me. 'He was a full arcanist by eighteen. Then he stayed around as a giller for a few years.'

'Giller?' I interrupted.

'Gillers are arcanists who stay at the University,' Wil said. 'They do a lot of the teaching. You know Cammar in the Fishery?'

I shook my head.

'Tall, scarred.' Wil gestured to one side of his face. 'Only one eye?'

I nodded somberly. Cammar was hard to miss. The left side of his face was a web of scars that radiated out, leaving bald strips running through his black hair and beard. He wore a patch over the hollow of his left eye. He was a walking object lesson about how dangerous work in the Fishery could be. 'I've seen him around. He's a full arcanist?'

Wil nodded. 'He's Kilvin's second in command. He teaches sygaldry to the newer students.'

Sim cleared his throat. 'As I was saying, Elodin was the youngest ever admitted, youngest to make arcanist, and youngest to be Chancellor.'

'Even so,' I said. 'You have to admit he's a little odd to be Chancellor.'

'Not back then,' Simmon said soberly. 'That was before it happened.'

When nothing more was forthcoming I prompted, 'It?'

Wil shrugged. 'Something. They do not speak on it. They locked him in the Crockery until he got most of his marbles back.'

'I don't like thinking about it,' Simmon said, shifting uncomfortably in his chair. 'I mean, a couple of students go crazy every term, right?' He looked at Wilem. 'Remember Slyhth?' Wil nodded somberly. 'It might happen to any of us.'

There was a moment of silence as the two of them sipped their drinks, not looking at anything in particular. I wanted to ask for specifics, but I could tell that it was a touchy subject.

'Anyway,' Sim said in a low voice. 'I heard they didn't let him out of the Crockery. I heard he escaped.'

'No arcanist worth his salt can be kept in a cell,' I said. 'That's not surprising.'

'Have you ever been there?' Simmon asked. 'It's built to keep arcanists locked up. All meshed stone. Wards on the doors and windows.' He shook his head. 'I can't imagine how someone could get out, even one of the masters.'

'All this is beside the path,' Wilem said firmly, bringing us back to task. 'Kilvin has welcomed you to the Fishery. Impressing him will be your best chance at making Re'lar.' He looked back and forth between us. 'Agreed?'

'Agreed,' Simmon said.

I nodded, but the wheels in my head were spinning. I was thinking about Taborlin the Great, who knew the names of all things. I thought about the stories Skarpi had told back in Tarbean. He hadn't mentioned arcanists, only namers.

And I thought of Elodin, Master Namer, and how I might approach him.

CHAPTER FORTY-FIVE

Interlude – Some Tavern Tale

AT A GESTURE FROM Kvothe, Chronicler wiped off the nib of his pen and shook out his hand. Bast gave a great, seated stretch, his arms arching over the back of the chair.

'I'd almost forgotten how quickly it all happened,' Kvothe mused. 'Those were probably the first stories anyone ever told about me.'

'They're still telling them at the University,' Chronicler said. 'I've heard three different versions of the class you taught. Your whipping, too. Is that when they started calling you Kvothe the Bloodless?'

Kvothe nodded. 'Possibly.'

'If we're asking questions, Reshi,' Bast said sheepishly, 'I was wondering why you didn't go looking for Skarpi?'

'What could I have done, Bast? Smeared my face with lampblack and staged a daring midnight rescue?' Kvothe gave a brief humorless laugh. 'They'd taken him in on *heresy*. All I could do was hope he truly had friends in the church.'

Kvothe drew a deep breath and sighed. 'But the simplest reason is the least satisfying one, I suppose. The truth is this: I wasn't living in a story.'

'I don't think I'm understanding you, Reshi,' Bast said, puzzled.

'Think of all the stories you've heard, Bast. You have a young boy, the hero. His parents are killed. He sets out for vengeance. What happens next?'

Bast hesitated, his expression puzzled. Chronicler answered the question instead. 'He finds help. A clever talking squirrel. An old drunken swordsman. A mad hermit in the woods. That sort of thing.'

Kvothe nodded. 'Exactly! He finds the mad hermit in the woods, proves himself worthy, and learns the names of all things, just like Taborlin the

Great. Then with these powerful magics at his beck and call, what does he do?'

Chronicler shrugged. 'He finds the villains and kills them.'

'Of course,' Kvothe said grandly. 'Clean, quick, and easy as lying. We know how it ends practically before it starts. That's why stories appeal to us. They give us the clarity and simplicity our real lives lack.'

Kvothe leaned forward. 'If this were some tavern tale, all half-truth and senseless adventure, I would tell you how my time at the University was spent with a purity of dedication. I would learn the ever-changing name of the wind, ride out, and gain my revenge against the Chandrian.' Kvothe snapped his fingers sharply. 'Simple as that.

'But while that might make for an entertaining story, it would not be the truth. The truth is this. I had mourned my parent's death for three years, and the pain of it had faded to a dull ache.'

Kvothe made a conciliatory gesture with one hand, and smiled a tight smile. 'I won't lie to you. There were times late at night when I lay sleepless and desperately alone in my narrow bunk in the Mews, times when I was choked with a sorrow so endless and empty that I thought it would smother me.

'There were times when I would see a mother holding her child, or a father laughing with his son, and anger would flare up in me, hot and furious with the memory of blood and the smell of burning hair.'

Kvothe shrugged. 'But there was more to my life than revenge. I had very real obstacles to overcome close at hand. My poverty. My low birth. The enemies I made at the University were more dangerous to me than any of the Chandrian.'

He gestured for Chronicler to pick up his pen. 'But for all that, we still see that even the most fanciful of stories hold a shred of truth, because I did find something very near to the mad hermit in the woods.' Kvothe smiled. 'And I *was* determined to learn the name of the wind.'

CHAPTER FORTY-SIX

The Ever-Changing Wind

ELODIN PROVED A DIFFICULT man to find. He had an office in Hollows, but never seemed to use it. When I visited Ledgers and Lists, I discovered he only taught one class: Unlikely Maths. However, this was less than helpful in tracking him down, as according to the ledger, the time of the class was 'now' and the location was 'everywhere'.

In the end, I spotted him through sheer luck across a crowded courtyard. He was wearing his black masters' robes, which was something of a rarity. I was on my way to the Medica for observation but decided I'd rather be late for my class than miss the opportunity to speak with him.

By the time I struggled through the midday crowd and caught up with him, we were on the northern edge of the University, following a wide dirt road that led into the forest. 'Master Elodin,' I said, pelting up to him. 'I was hoping I could talk with you.'

'A sad little hope,' he said without breaking stride or looking in my direction. 'You should aim higher. A young man ought to be afire with high ambitions.'

'I hope to study naming then,' I said, falling into step beside him.

'Too high,' he said matter-of-factly. 'Try again. Somewhere in-between.' The dirt road curved, and trees blocked the sight of the University's buildings behind us.

'I hope you'll accept me as a student?' I tried again. 'And teach me whatever you think best?'

Elodin stopped walking abruptly and turned to face me. 'Fine,' he said. 'Go find me three pinecones.' He made a circle with his thumb and finger. 'This big, without any of the little bits broken off.' He sat down right in the middle of the road and made a shooing motion with his hand. 'Go on. Hurry.'

I darted off into the surrounding trees. It took me about five minutes to find three pinecones of the appropriate type. By the time I got back to the road I was dishevelled and bramble-scratched. Elodin was nowhere to be seen.

I looked around stupidly, then cursed, dropped the pinecones, and took off running, following the road north. I caught up with him fairly quickly, as he was just idling along, looking at the trees.

'So what did you learn?' Elodin asked.

'That you want to be left alone?'

'You *are* quick.' He spread his arms dramatically and intoned. 'Here endeth the lesson! Here endeth my profound tutelage of E'lir Kvothe!'

I sighed. If I left now, I could still catch my class in the Medica, but part of me suspected that this might be a test of some sort. Perhaps Elodin was simply making sure that I was genuinely interested before he accepted me as a student. That is the way it usually goes in stories: the young man has to prove his dedication to the old hermit in the woods before he's taken under his wing.

'Will you answer a few questions?' I asked.

'Fine,' he said, holding up his hand with his thumb and forefinger curled in. 'Three questions. If you agree to leave me be afterwards.'

I thought for a moment. 'Why don't you want to teach me?'

'Because the Edema Ruh make exceptionally poor students,' he said brusquely. 'They are fine for rote learning, but the study of naming requires a level of dedication that ravel such as yourself rarely possess.'

My temper flared so hot and quick that I actually felt my skin flush. It started at my face and burned down my chest and arms. It made the hair on my arms prickle.

I took a deep breath. 'I'm sorry that your experience with the Ruh has left something to be desired,' I said carefully. 'Let me assure you that—'

'Ye Gods,' Elodin sighed, disgusted. 'A bootlicker too. You lack the requisite spine and testicular fortitude to study under me.'

Hot words boiled up inside me. I fought them down. He was trying to bait me.

'You aren't telling me the truth,' I said. 'Why don't you want to teach me?'

'For the same reason I don't want a puppy!' Elodin shouted, waving his arms in the air like a farmer trying to startle crows out of a field. 'Because you're too short to be a namer. Your eyes are too green. You have the wrong number of fingers. Come back when you're taller and you've found a decent pair of eyes.'

We stared at each other for a long while. Finally he shrugged and started walking again. 'Fine. I'll show you why.'

We followed the road north. Elodin strolled along, picking up stones and tossing them into the trees. He jumped to snatch leaves from low-hanging branches, his masters' robes billowing ridiculously. At one point he stopped and stood motionless and intent for nearly half an hour, staring at a fern swaying slowly in the wind.

But I kept the tip of my tongue firmly between my teeth. I didn't ask, 'Where are we going?' or 'What are you looking at?' I knew a hundred stories about young boys who squandered questions or wishes by chatting them away. I had two questions left, and I was going to make them count.

Eventually we emerged from the forest, and the road became a path leading up a vast lawn to a huge manor house. Bigger than the Artificery, it had elegant lines, a red tile roof, high windows, arched doorways and pillars. There were fountains, flowers, hedges . . .

But something wasn't quite right. The closer we got to the gates, the more I doubted this was some nobleman's estate. Maybe it was something about the design of the gardens, or the fact that the wrought-iron fence surrounding the lawns was nearly ten feet tall and unclimbable to my well-trained thief's eye.

Two serious-eyed men opened the gate, and we continued up the path toward the front doors. Elodin looked at me. 'Have you heard of Haven yet?'

I shook my head.

'It has other names: the Rookery, the Crockery . . .'

The University asylum. 'It's huge. How . . .' I stopped before asking the question.

Elodin grinned, knowing he'd almost caught me. 'Jeremy,' he called out to the large man who stood at the front door. 'How many guests do we have today?'

'The desk could give you a count, sir,' he said uncomfortably.

'Take a wild guess,' Elodin said. 'We're all friends here.'

'Three-twenty?' the man said with a shrug. 'Three-fifty?'

Elodin rapped on the thick timber door with a knuckle, and the man scrambled to unlock it. 'How many more could we fit if we needed?' Elodin asked him.

'Another hundred-fifty easy.' Jeremy said, tugging the huge door open. 'More in a pinch, I suppose.'

'See, Kvothe?' Elodin winked at me. 'We're ready.'

The entryway was huge, with stained glass windows and vaulted ceilings. The floor was marble polished to a mirror sheen.

The place was eerily silent. I couldn't understand it. The Reftview Asylum in Tarbean was only a fraction the size of this place, and it sounded like a brothel full of angry cats. You could hear it from a mile away over the din of the city.

Elodin strolled up to a large desk where a young woman stood. 'Why isn't anyone outside, Emmie?'

She gave him an uneasy smile. 'They're too wild today, sir. We think there's a storm coming in.' She pulled a ledger book off the shelf. 'The moon's getting full, too. You know how it gets.'

'Sure do.' Elodin crouched down and began to unlace his shoes. 'Where did they stash Whin this time?'

She flipped a few pages in the ledger. 'Second floor east. 247.'

Elodin stood back up and set his shoes on the desk. 'Keep an eye on these, would you?' She gave him an uncertain smile and nodded.

I choked down another mouthful of questions. 'It seems like the University goes to an awful lot of expense here,' I commented.

Elodin ignored me and turned to climb a wide marble staircase in his stocking feet. Then we entered a long, white hallway lined with wooden doors. For the first time I could hear the sounds I had expected in a place like this. Moans, weeping, incessant chattering, screaming, all very faint.

Elodin ran for a few steps, then stopped, his stocking feet gliding across the smooth marble floor, his masters' robes streaming out behind him. He repeated this: a few quick steps, then a long slide with his arms held out to the sides for balance.

I continued to pace along beside him. 'I'd think the masters would find other, more academic uses for the University's funds.'

Elodin didn't look at me. *Step. Step step step.* 'You're trying to get me to answer questions you're not asking.' *Slide.* 'It's not going to work.'

'You're trying to trick me into asking questions,' I pointed out. 'It seems only fair.'

Step step step. Slide. 'So why the hell are you bothering with me, anyway?'

Elodin asked. 'Kilvin likes you well enough. Why not hitch your star to his wagon?'

'I think you know things I can't learn anywhere else.'

'Things like what?'

'Things I've wanted to know since I first saw someone call the wind.'

'Name of the wind, was it?' Elodin raised his eyebrows. *Step. Step. Step-step-step.* 'That's tricky.' *Sliiiiiide.* 'What makes you think I know anything about calling the wind?'

'Process of elimination,' I said. 'None of the other masters do that sort of thing, so it must be your bailiwick.'

'By your logic I should also be in charge of Solinade dances, needlework, and horse thieving.'

We came to the end of the hall. Midslide, Elodin nearly bowled over a huge, broad-shouldered man carrying a hardback. 'Beg your pardon, sir,' he said, though it obviously wasn't his fault.

'Timothy,' Elodin pointed a long finger at him. 'Come with us.'

Elodin led the way through several shorter hallways, eventually coming to a heavy wooden door with a sliding panel at eye level. Elodin opened it and peered through. 'How's he been?'

'Quiet,' the hulking man said. 'I don't think he's slept much.'

Elodin tried the latch, then turned to the broad-shouldered man, his face going grim. 'You locked him in?'

The man stood a full head taller than Elodin and probably weighed twice as much, but the blood drained from his face as the shoeless master glared at him. 'Not me, Master Elodin. It's . . .'

Elodin cut him off with a sharp gesture. 'Unlock it.'

Timothy fumbled with a ring of keys.

Elodin continued to stare him down. 'Alder Whin is not to be confined. He may come and go as he pleases. Nothing is to be put in his food unless he specifically asks for it. I am holding you responsible for this, Timothy Generoy.' Elodin poked him in the chest with a long finger. 'If I find out that Whin has been sedated or restrained I'll ride you naked through the streets of Imre like a little pink pony.' He glared. 'Go.'

The fellow left as quickly as he could manage without actually breaking into a run.

Elodin turned to me. 'You can come in, but don't make any noises or sudden movements. Don't talk unless he talks to you. If you do talk, keep your voice low. Understand?'

I nodded and he opened the door.

The room wasn't what I'd expected. Tall windows let the daylight in, revealing a sizable bed and a table with chairs. The walls, ceiling, and floor were all padded with thick white cloth, muffling even the faint noises from the hallway. The blankets had been pulled off the bed and a thin man of about thirty was bundled up in them, huddled against the wall.

Elodin closed the door and the mousy man flinched a little. 'Whin?' he said softly, moving closer. 'What happened?'

Alder Whin looked up owlishly. A thin stick of a man, he was bare-chested under the blanket, his hair in wild disarray, his eyes round and wide. He spoke softly, his voice cracking a little. 'I was fine. I was doing fine. But all the people talking, dogs, cobblestones . . . I just can't be around that right now.'

Whin pressed himself against the wall and the blanket fell off his bony shoulder. I was startled to see a lead guilder around his neck. This man was a full-fledged arcanist.

Elodin nodded. 'Why are you on the floor?'

Whin looked over at the bed, panic in his eyes. 'I'll fall,' he said softly, his voice somewhere between horror and embarrassment. 'And there are springs and slats. Nails.'

'How are you now?' Elodin asked gently. 'Would you like to come back with me?'

'*Nooooo.*' Whin gave a hopeless, despairing cry, screwing his eyes closed and pulling the blanket closer around himself. His thin, reedy voice made his plea more heart-wrenching than if he'd howled it.

'It's fine. You can stay,' Elodin said softly. 'I'll be back to visit.'

Whin opened his eyes at this, looking agitated. 'Don't bring thunder,' he said urgently. He reached one thin hand out of his blanket and clutched at Elodin's shirt. 'But I do need a catwhistle and bluedown, and bones too.' His tone was urgent. 'Tentbones.'

'I'll bring them,' Elodin reassured him, gesturing for me to back out of the room. I did.

Elodin closed the door behind us, his expression grim. 'Whin knew what he was getting into when he became my giller.' He turned and began to walk down the hall. 'You don't. You don't know anything about the University. About the risks involved. You think this place is a faerie land, a playground. It's not.'

'That's right,' I snapped. 'It's a playground and all the other children are jealous because I got to play "get whipped bloody and banned from the Archives" and they didn't.'

Elodin stopped walking and turned to look at me. 'Fine. Prove me wrong. Prove that you've thought this through. Why does a University with under fifteen hundred students need an asylum the size of the royal palace?'

My mind raced. 'Most students are from well-to-do families,' I said. 'They've led easy lives. When forced to . . .'

'Wrong,' Elodin said dismissively, turning to walk down the hall. 'It is because of what we study. Because of the way we train our minds to move.'

'So ciphering and grammar make people crazy,' I said, taking care to phrase it as a statement.

Elodin stopped walking and wrenched open the nearest door. Panicked screaming burst out into the hallway. '. . . IN ME! THEY'RE IN ME! THEY'RE IN ME! THEY'RE IN ME!' Through the open door I could see a young man thrashing against the leather restraints that bound him to the bed at wrist, waist, neck, and ankle.

'Trigonometry and diagrammed logic don't do this,' Elodin said, looking me in the eye.

'THEY'RE IN ME! THEY'RE IN ME! THEY'RE IN—' The screaming continued in an unbroken chant, like the endless, mindless barking of a dog at night. '—ME! THEY'RE IN ME! THEY'RE IN ME! THEY'RE—'

Elodin closed the door. Though I could still hear the screaming faintly through the thick door, the near-silence was stunning. 'Do you know why they call this place the Rookery?' Elodin asked.

I shook my head.

'Because it's where you go if you're a-ravin'.' He smiled a wild smile. He laughed a terrible laugh.

———

Elodin led me through a long series of hallways to a different wing of the Crockery. Finally we turned a corner and I saw something new: a door made entirely of copper.

Elodin took a key from his pocket and unlocked it. 'I like to stop in when I'm back in the neighborhood,' he said casually as he opened the door. 'Check my mail. Water the plants and such.'

He pulled off one of his socks, tied a knot in it, and used it to wedge the door open. 'It's a nice place to visit, but, you know . . .' He tugged on the door, making sure it wouldn't swing closed. 'Not again.'

The first thing I noticed about the room was something strange about the air. At first I thought it might be soundproofed like Alder Whin's, but looking around I saw the walls and ceilings were bare grey stone. Next I thought the air might be stale, except when I drew a breath I smelled lavender and fresh linen. It was almost like there was a pressure on my ears, as if I were deep underwater, except of course that I wasn't. I waved a hand in front of me, almost expecting the air to feel different, thicker. It didn't.

'Pretty irritating, huh?' I turned around to see Elodin watching me. 'I'm surprised you noticed, actually. Not many do.'

The room was a definite step above Alder Whin's. It had a four-post bed with curtains, an overstuffed couch, an empty bookcase, and a large table with several chairs. Most notable were the huge windows looking out over the lawns and gardens. I could see a balcony outside, but there didn't seem to be any way to get to it.

'Watch this,' Elodin said. He picked up one of the high-backed wooden chairs, lifted it with both hands, spun in a circle, and flung it hard at the window. I cringed, but instead of a terrible crash, there was just a dull splintering of wood. The chair fell to the floor in a ruined tangle of timber and upholstery.

'I used to do that for hours,' Elodin said, drawing a deep breath and looking around the room fondly. 'Good times.'

I went to look at the windows. They were thicker than usual, but not *that* thick. They seemed normal except for faint reddish streaks running through them. I glanced at the window frame. It was copper too. I looked slowly around at the room, eyeing its bare stone walls, feeling its strangely heavy air. I noticed the door didn't even have a handle on the inside, let alone a lock. *Why would anyone go through all the trouble of making a solid copper door?*

I decided on my second question. 'How did you get out?'

'Finally,' Elodin said with a tinge of exasperation.

He slouched onto the couch. 'You see, once upon a time Elodin the Great found himself locked in a high tower.' He gestured to the room around us. 'He had been stripped of his tools: his coin, key, and candle. Furthermore, his cell had no door worth mentioning. No window that could be breached.' He made dismissive gestures at each of these. 'Even the name of the wind was hidden from him by the clever machinations of his captors.'

Elodin got up from the couch and began to pace the room. 'All around him was nothing but smooth hard stone. It was a cell no man had ever escaped.'

He stopped pacing and held up a finger dramatically. 'But Elodin the Great knew the names of all things, and so all things were his to command.' He faced the grey wall beside the windows. 'He said to the stone: "BREAK" and the . . .'

Elodin trailed off, his head tilting to one side curiously. His eyes narrowed. 'Sod me, they changed it,' he said quietly to himself. 'Huh.' He stepped closer to the wall and lay a hand on it.

I let my attention wander. Wil and Sim had been right, the man was cracked in the head. What would happen if I ran out of the room, unstuck the door, and slammed it? Would the other masters thank me?

'Oh,' Elodin said suddenly, laughing. 'That was half-clever of them.' He took two steps back from the wall. '*CYAERBASALIEN.*'

I saw the wall move. It rippled like a hanging rug thumped with a stick. Then it simply . . . fell. Like dark water poured from a bucket, tons of fine grey sand spilled across the floor in a sudden rush, burying Elodin's feet up to his shins.

Sunlight and birdsong poured into the room. Where there had been a foot of solid grey stone before, there was now a gaping hole big enough to drive a cart through.

But the hole wasn't completely clear, some green material was spread across the opening. It almost looked like a dirty, tangled net, but it was too irregular for netting. It was more like a thick, tattered cobweb.

'That wasn't there before,' Elodin said apologetically as he pulled his feet free of the grey sand. 'It was much more dramatic the first time, let me assure you.'

I simply stood, stunned by what I'd just seen. This wasn't sympathy. This wasn't anything I'd ever seen before. All I could think of was the old line from a hundred half-remembered stories: *And Taborlin the Great said to the stone: 'BREAK!' and the stone broke . . .*

Elodin wrenched off one of the chair's legs and used it to batter at the tangled green web that stretched across the opening. Parts of it broke easily or flaked away. Where it was thicker he used the leg as a lever to bend pieces aside. Where it bent or broke it glimmered bright in the sunlight. *More copper,* I thought. *Veins of copper running through the blocks of stone that made the wall.*

Elodin dropped the chair leg and ducked through the gap. Through the window I saw him lean against the white stone railing on the balcony.

I followed him outside. As soon as I stepped onto the balcony, the air no longer felt strangely heavy and still.

'Two years,' he said, looking out over the gardens. 'Able to see this balcony but not stand on it. Able to see the wind, but not hear it, not feel it on my face.' He swung one leg up over the stone railing so he was sitting on it, then dropped a few feet to land on the flat piece of roof just underneath. He wandered out across the roof, away from the building.

I hopped the rail myself and followed him to the edge of the roof. We were only about twenty feet up, but the gardens and fountains spreading out on all sides made for a spectacular view. Elodin stood perilously near the edge, his masters' robe flapping around him like a dark flag. He looked rather impressive, actually, if you were willing to ignore the fact that he was still only wearing one sock.

I went to stand beside him on the edge of the roof. I knew what my third question had to be. 'What do I have to do,' I asked, 'to study naming under you?'

He met my eye calmly, appraising me. 'Jump,' he said. 'Jump off this roof.'

That's when I realised that all of this had been a test. Elodin had been taking my measure ever since we met. He had a grudging respect for my tenacity, and he had been surprised that I noticed something odd about the air in his room. He was on the verge of accepting me as a student.

But he needed more, proof of my dedication. A demonstration. A leap of faith.

And as I stood there, a piece of story came to mind. *So Taborlin fell, but he did not despair. For he knew the name of the wind, and so the wind obeyed him. It cradled and caressed him. It bore him to the ground as gently as a puff of thistledown. It set him on his feet softly as a mother's kiss.*

Elodin knew the name of the wind.

Still looking him in the eye, I stepped off the edge of the roof.

Elodin's expression was marvellous. I have never seen a man so astonished. I spun slightly as I fell, so he stayed in my line of vision. I saw him raise one hand slightly, as if making a belated attempt to grab hold of me.

I felt weightless, like I was floating.

Then I struck the ground. Not gently, like a feather settling down. Hard. Like a brick hitting a cobblestone street. I landed on my back with my left arm beneath me. My vision went dark as the back of my head struck the ground and all the air was driven from my body.

I didn't lose consciousness. I just lay there, breathless and unable to move. I remember thinking, quite earnestly, that I was dead. That I was blind.

Eventually my sight returned, leaving me blinking against the sudden brightness of the blue sky. Pain tore through my shoulder and I tasted blood. I couldn't breathe. I tried to roll off my arm, but my body wouldn't listen to me. I had broken my neck . . . my back . . .

After a long, terrifying moment, I managed to gasp a shallow breath, then another. I gave a sigh of relief and realised that I had at least one broken rib in addition to everything else, but I moved my fingers slightly, then my toes. They worked. I hadn't broken my spine.

As I lay there, counting my blessings and broken ribs, Elodin stepped into my field of vision.

He looked down at me. 'Congratulations,' he said. 'That was the stupidest thing I've ever seen.' His expression was a mix of awe and disbelief. 'Ever.'

———

And that is when I decided to pursue the noble art of artificing. Not that I had a lot of other options. Before helping me limp to the Medica, Elodin made it clear that anyone stupid enough to jump off a roof was too reckless to be allowed to hold a spoon in his presence, let alone study something as 'profound and volatile' as naming.

Nevertheless, I wasn't terribly put out by Elodin's refusal. Storybook magic or no, I was not eager to study under a man whose first set of lessons had left me with three broken ribs, a mild concussion, and a dislocated shoulder.

CHAPTER FORTY-SEVEN

Barbs

ASIDE FROM ITS ROCKY start, my first term went fairly smoothly. I studied in the Medica, learning more about the body and how to heal it. I practiced my Siaru with Wilem and helped him with his Aturan in exchange.

I joined the ranks of the Artificery, studying how to blow glass, mix alloys, draw wire, inscribe metal, and sculpt stone.

Most evenings I came back to Kilvin's workshop to work. I chipped casings off bronze castings, washed glassware, and ground ore for alloys. It was not demanding work, but every span Kilvin gave me a copper jot, sometimes two. I suspected there was a great tally board in that methodical mind of his, carefully marking down the hours each person worked.

I learned things of a less academic nature as well. Some of my Arcanum bunkmates taught me a card game called dogsbreath. I returned the favour by giving an impromptu lesson in psychology, probability, and manual dexterity. I won almost two whole talents before they stopped inviting me back to their games.

I became tight friends with Wilem and Simmon. I had some few others, but not many, and none so close as Wil and Sim. My swift rise to E'lir alienated me from most of the other students. Whether they resented or admired me, most students held themselves apart.

And there was Ambrose. To deem us simply enemies is to lose the true flavour of our relationship. It was more like the two of us entered into a business partnership in order to more efficiently pursue our mutual interest of hating each other.

However, even with my vendetta against Ambrose, I still had a great deal of time on my hands. Since I wasn't able to spend it in the Archives, I spent some time nurturing my budding reputation.

You see, my dramatic entrance to the University had made quite a stir. I'd made my way into the Arcanum in three days instead of the usual three terms. I was the youngest member by almost two years. I had openly defied one of the masters in front of his own class and avoided expulsion. When whipped, I hadn't cried out or bled.

On top of everything else, I had apparently managed to infuriate Master Elodin to such an extent that he had thrown me off the roof of the Crockery. I let that story circulate uncorrected, as it was preferable to the embarrassing truth.

All together, it was enough to start a steady stream of rumour around me, and I decided to take advantage of it. Reputation is like a sort of armour, or a weapon you can brandish if need be. I decided that if I was going to be an arcanist, I might as well be a well-known arcanist.

So I let slip a few pieces of information: I had been admitted without a letter of recommendation. The masters had given me three talents to attend, rather than make me pay a tuition. I had survived for years on the streets of Tarbean, living off my wits.

I even started a few rumours that were pure nonsense, lies so outrageous that people would repeat them despite the fact that they were obviously untrue. I had demon blood in me. I could see in the dark. I only slept an hour each night. When the moon was full I would talk in my sleep, speaking a strange language no one could understand.

Basil, my former bunkmate from Mews, helped me start these rumours. I would make up the stories, he would tell a few people, then together we would watch them spread like a fire in a field. It was an amusing hobby.

But my ongoing feud with Ambrose added to my reputation more than anything else. Everyone was stunned that I dared openly defy a powerful noble's firstborn son.

We had several dramatic encounters that first term. I won't bore you with the details. We'd cross paths and he would make some offhand comment loud enough for everyone in the room to hear. Or he would sneer at me under the guise of a compliment. 'You *must* tell me who cuts your hair . . .'

Anyone with a lick of common sense knew how to deal with arrogant nobility. The tailor I had terrorised back in Tarbean knew what to do. You take your lumps, duck your head, and get the whole thing over as quickly as possible.

But I *always* fought back, and while Ambrose was intelligent and reasonably well-spoken, he was no match for my trouper's tongue. I had been raised on the stage, and my sharp Ruh wits ensured that I got the better of our exchanges.

Still Ambrose continued to seek me out, like a dog too stupid to avoid a porcupine. He would snap at me and leave with a face full of barbs. And each time we parted ways we hated each other just a little more.

People noticed, and by the end of the term I had a reputation for reckless bravery. But the truth is, I was merely fearless.

There's a difference, you see. In Tarbean I'd learned real fear. I feared hunger, pneumonia, guards with hobnail boots, older boys with bottleglass knives. Confronting Ambrose required no real bravery on my part. I simply couldn't muster any fear of him. I saw him as a puffed-up clown. I thought he was harmless.

I was a fool.

CHAPTER FORTY-EIGHT

Interlude – A Silence of a Different Kind

Bast sat in the Waystone Inn and tried to keep his hands motionless in his lap. He had counted fifteen breaths since Kvothe had spoken last, and the innocent silence that had gathered like a clear pool around the three men was beginning to darken into a silence of a different kind. Bast took another breath – sixteen – and braced himself against the moment he feared would come.

It would not be to Bast's credit to say that he was afraid of nothing, as only fools and priests are never afraid. But it is true that very few things unnerved him. Heights, for instance, he didn't care for very much. And the great summer storms that came through these parts that blackened the sky and tore up deep-rooted oaks made him feel uncomfortably small and helpless.

But when you came down to it, nothing really frightened him, not storms, not tall ladders, not even the scrael. Bast was brave by being largely fearless. Nothing would turn him pale, or if it did, he didn't stay pale for very long.

Oh, certainly he didn't relish the thought of someone hurting him. Stabbing him with bitter iron, searing him with hot coals, that sort of thing. But just because he didn't like the thought of his blood on the outside didn't mean he was really afraid of those things. He just didn't want them to happen. To really fear something you have to dwell on it. And since there was nothing that preyed on Bast's waking mind in this fashion, there was nothing his heart truly feared.

But hearts can change. Ten years ago he had lost his grip climbing a tall rennel tree to pick fruit for a girl he fancied. After he slipped, he had hung for a long minute, head down, before falling. In that long minute, a small fear rooted inside him, and had stayed with him ever since.

In the same way, Bast had learned a new fear of late. A year ago he had been fearless as any sane man can hope to be, but now Bast feared silence. Not the ordinary silence that came from a simple absence of things moving about and making noise. Bast feared the deep, weary silence that gathered around his master at times, like an invisible shroud.

Bast breathed in again – seventeen. He fought not to wring his hands as he waited for the deep silence to invade the room. He waited for it to crys-tallise and show its teeth on the edges of the cool quiet that had pooled in the Waystone. He knew how it came, like the frost that bleeds out of the winter ground, hardening the clear water that an early thaw leaves in wagon ruts.

But before Bast could draw another breath, Kvothe straightened in his chair and made a motion for Chronicler to lay down his pen. Bast nearly wept as he sensed the silence scatter like a dark bird startled into flight.

Kvothe gave a sigh that hovered between annoyance and resignation. 'I will admit,' he said. 'That I am not sure how to approach the next part of the story.'

Afraid to let the silence stretch for too long, Bast chirruped, 'Why don't you simply talk about what is most important first? Then you can go back and touch on other things, if you need to.'

'As if it were as simple as that,' Kvothe said sharply. 'What is most important? My magic or my music? My triumphs or my follies?'

Bast flushed a deep crimson and bit his lips.

Kvothe let out his breath in a sudden rush. 'I'm sorry, Bast. It's good advice, as all of your seemingly inane advice turns out to be.' He pushed his chair back from the table. 'But before we continue, the real world has certain calls on me that I can no longer ignore. If you will please excuse me for a moment?'

Chronicler and Bast stood as well, stretching their legs and attending to calls of their own. Bast lit the lamps. Kvothe produced more cheese and bread and hard spiced sausage. They ate, and some small effort was made at polite conversation, but their minds were elsewhere, dwelling on the story.

Bast ate half of everything. Chronicler accounted for a sizable, though more modest amount. Kvothe had a bite or two before he spoke. 'Onward then. Music and magic. Triumph and folly. Think now. What does our story need? What vital element is it lacking?'

'Women, Reshi,' Bast said immediately. 'There's a real paucity of women.'

Kvothe smiled. 'Not *women*, Bast. A woman. *The* woman.' Kvothe looked at Chronicler. 'You have heard bits and pieces, I don't doubt. I will tell you the truth of her. Though I fear I may not be equal to the challenge.'

Chronicler picked up his pen, but before he could dip it, Kvothe held up a hand. 'Let me say one thing before I start. I've told stories in the past, painted pictures with words, told hard lies and harder truths. Once, I sang colours to a blind man. Seven hours I played, but at the end he said he saw them, green and red and gold. That, I think, was easier than this. Trying to make you understand her with nothing more than words. You have never seen her, never heard her voice. You cannot know.'

Kvothe motioned for Chronicler to pick up his pen. 'But still, I will try. She is in the wings now, waiting for her cue. Let us set the stage for her arrival . . .'

CHAPTER FORTY-NINE

The Nature of Wild Things

A S WITH ALL TRULY wild things, care is necessary in approaching them. Stealth is useless. Wild things recognise stealth for what it is, a lie and a trap. While wild things might play games of stealth, and in doing so may even occasionally fall prey to stealth, they are never truly caught by it.

So. With slow care rather than stealth we must approach the subject of a certain woman. Her wildness is of such degree, I fear approaching her too quickly even in a story. Should I move recklessly, I might startle even the idea of her into sudden flight.

So in the name of slow care, I will speak of how I met her. And to do that, I must speak of the events that brought me, quite unwillingly, across the river and into Imre.

———————

I finished my first term with three silver talents and a single jot. Not long ago, it would have seemed like all the money in the world to me. Now I simply hoped it would be enough for one more term's tuition and a bunk in the Mews.

The last span of every term at the University was reserved for admissions exams. Classes were cancelled and the masters spent several hours of each day conducting examinations. Your next term's tuition was based on your performance. A lottery determined what day and hour you would go through admissions.

A great deal hung on the brief interview. Missing a few questions could easily double your tuition. Because of this, slots later in the span were highly prized, as they gave students more time to study and prepare. There was a vigourous trade in appointment times after the lottery was held. Money and favours were bartered as everyone vied for a time that suited them.

I was lucky enough to draw a midmorning hour on Cendling, the last day of admissions. If I'd wanted to, I could have sold my slot, but I preferred to take the extra time to study. I knew my performance would have to be brilliant, as several of the masters were now less than impressed by me. My previous trick of spying was out of the question. I now knew it was grounds for expulsion, and I couldn't risk that.

Despite the long days I spent studying with Wil and Sim, admissions were difficult. I breezed through many of the questions, but Hemme was openly hostile, asking questions with more than one answer so that nothing I said could be correct. Brandeur was difficult as well, clearly helping Hemme carry his grudge. Lorren was unreadable, but I sensed his disapproval rather than seeing it on his face.

Afterwards, I fidgeted while the masters discussed my tuition. Voices were calm and muted at first, then became somewhat louder. Eventually, Kilvin stood and shook a finger at Hemme while shouting and pounding the table with his other hand. Hemme maintained more composure than I would have if I had been faced with twenty stone of furious, bellowing artificer.

After the Chancellor managed to regain control of things, I was called forward and given my receipt. 'E'lir Kvothe. Fall term. Tuition: 3 Tln. 9 Jt. 7 Fe.'

Eight jots more than I had. As I walked out of the Masters' Hall, I ignored the sinking feeling in my gut and tried to think of a way I could lay hands on more money by tomorrow noon.

I made a brief stop at the two Cealdish moneychangers on this side of the river. As I suspected, they wouldn't lend me a thin shim. While I wasn't surprised, the experience was sobering, reminding me again of how different I was from the other students. They had families paying their tuition, granting them allowances to cover their living expenses. They had reputable names they could borrow against in a pinch. They had possessions they could pawn or sell. If worse came to worst, they had homes to return to.

I had none of these things. If I couldn't come up with eight more jots for tuition, I had nowhere in the world I could go.

Borrowing from a friend seemed like the simplest option, but I valued my handful of friends too much to risk losing them over money. As my father used to say: 'There are two sure ways to lose a friend, one is to borrow, the other to lend'.

Besides, I did my best to keep my desperate poverty to myself. Pride is a foolish thing, but it is a powerful force. I wouldn't ask them for money except as my very last resort.

I briefly considered trying to cutpurse the money, but I knew it was a bad idea. If I were caught with my hand in someone's pocket, I would get more than a cuff round the head. At best I'd be jailed and forced to stand against the iron law. At worst, I'd end up on the horns and expelled for Conduct Unbecoming a Member of the Arcanum. I couldn't risk it.

I needed a gaelet, one of the dangerous men who lend money to desperate people. You might have heard them referred to romantically as copper hawks, but more often they're referred to as shim-galls, or lets. Regardless of the name, they exist everywhere. The hard part is finding them. They tend to be rather secretive as their business is semi-legal at best.

But living in Tarbean had taught me a thing or two. I spent a couple of hours visiting the seedier taverns around the University, making casual conversations, asking casual questions. Then I visited a pawnshop called the Bent Penny, and asked a few more pointed questions. Finally I learned where I needed to go. Over the river, to Imre.

CHAPTER FIFTY

Negotiations

IMRE LAY A LITTLE over two miles from the University, on the eastern side of the Omethi River. Since it was a mere two days in a fast coach from Tarbean, a great many wealthy nobles, politicians, and courtiers made their homes there. It was conveniently close to the governing hub of the Commonwealth, while being a comfortable distance from the smell of rotten fish, hot tar, and the vomit of drunken sailors.

Imre was a haven for the arts. There were musicians, dramatists, sculptors, dancers, and the practitioners of a hundred other smaller arts, even the lowest art of all: poetry. Performers came because Imre offered what every artist needs most – an appreciative, affluent audience.

Imre also benefited by its proximity to the University. Access to plumbing and sympathy lamps improved the quality of the town's air. Quality glass was easy to come by, so windows and mirrors were commonplace. Eyeglasses and other ground lenses, while expensive, were readily available.

Despite this, there was little love lost between the two towns. Most of Imre's citizens did not like the thought of a thousand minds tinkering with dark forces better left alone. Listening to the average citizen speak, it was easy to forget that this part of the world had not seen an arcanist burned for nearly three hundred years.

To be fair, it should be mentioned that the University had a vague contempt for Imre's populace, too, viewing them as self-indulgent and decadent. The arts that were viewed so highly in Imre were seen as frivolous by those at the University. Often, students who quit the University were said to have 'gone over the river', the implication being that minds that were too weak for academia had to settle for tinkering with the arts.

And both sides of the river were, ultimately, hypocrites. University students complained about frivolous musicians and fluffhead actors, then lined up to pay for performances. Imre's population griped about unnatural arts being practiced two miles away, but when an aqueduct collapsed or someone fell suddenly sick, they were quick to call on engineers and doctors trained at the University.

All in all, it was a long-standing and uneasy truce where both sides complained while maintaining a grudging tolerance. Those people did have their uses after all, you just wouldn't want your daughter marrying one . . .

Since Imre was such a haven for music and drama, you might think I spent a great deal of time there, but nothing could be further from the truth. I had been there only once. Wilem and Simmon had taken me to an inn where a trio of skilled musicians played: lute, flute, and drum. I bought a short beer for ha'penny and relaxed, fully intending to enjoy an evening with my friends . . .

But I couldn't. Bare minutes after the music started I practically fled the room. I doubt very much you'll be able to understand why, but I suppose I have to explain if things are to make any sense at all.

I couldn't stand being near music and not be a part of it. It was like watching the woman you love bedding down with another man. No. Not really. It was like . . .

It was like the sweet-eaters I'd seen in Tarbean. Denner resin was highly illegal, of course, but that didn't matter in most parts of the city. The resin was sold wrapped in waxy paper, like a sucking candy or a toffee. Chewing it filled you with euphoria. Bliss. Contentment.

But after a few hours you were shaking, filled with a desperate hunger for more, and that hunger grew worse the longer you used it. Once in Tarbean I saw a young girl of no more than sixteen with the telltale hollow eyes and unnaturally white teeth of the hopelessly addicted. She was begging a sailor for a sweet, which he held tauntingly out of reach. He told her it was hers if she stripped naked and danced for him, right there in the street.

She did, not caring who might be watching, not caring that it was nearly Midwinter and she stood in four inches of snow. She pulled off her clothes and danced desperately, her thin limbs pale and shaking, her movements pathetic and jerky. Then, when the sailor laughed and shook his head, she fell to her knees in the snow, begging and weeping, clutching frantically at his legs, promising him anything, anything . . .

That is how I felt, watching the musicians play. I couldn't stand it. The

everyday lack of my music was like a toothache I had grown used to. I could live with it. But having what I wanted dangled in front of me was more than I could bear.

So I avoided Imre until the problem of my second term's tuition forced me back across the river. I had learned that Devi was the person anyone could ask for a loan, no matter how desperate the circumstances.

———

So I crossed the Omethi by Stonebridge and made my way to Imre. Devi's place of business was through an alley and up a narrow balcony staircase behind a butcher's shop. This part of Imre reminded me of Waterside in Tarbean. The cloying smell of rancid fat from the butcher shop below made me thankful for the cool autumn breeze.

I hesitated in front of the heavy door, looking down into the alley. I was about to become involved in dangerous business. A Cealdish moneylender could take you to court if you didn't repay your loan. A gaelet would simply have you beaten, or robbed, or both. This was not smart. I was playing with fire.

But I didn't have any better options. I took a deep breath, squared my shoulders, and knocked on the door.

I wiped my sweaty palms against my cloak, hoping to keep them reasonably dry for when I shook Devi's hand. I had learned in Tarbean that the best way to deal with this type of man was to act with confidence and self-assurance. They were in the business of taking advantage of other people's weakness.

I heard the sound of a heavy bolt being drawn back, then the door opened, revealing a young girl with straight, strawberry-blonde hair framing a pixielike face. She smiled at me, cute as a new button. 'Yes?'

'I'm looking for Devi,' I said.

'You've found her,' she said easily. 'Come on in.'

I stepped inside and she closed the door behind her, sliding the iron bolt home. The room was windowless, but well-lit and filled with the scent of lavender, a welcome change from the smell of the alley. There were hangings on the walls, but the only real furniture was a small desk, a bookshelf, and a large canopy bed with the curtains drawn around it.

'Please,' she said, gesturing to the desk. 'Have a seat.'

She settled herself behind the desk, folding her hands across the top. The way she carried herself made me rethink her age. I'd misjudged her because of her small size, but even so, she couldn't be much older than her early twenties, hardly what I had expected to find.

Devi blinked prettily at me.

'I need a loan,' I said.

'How about your name, first?' She smiled. 'You already know mine.'

'Kvothe.'

'Really?' She arched an eyebrow. 'I've heard a thing or two about you.' She looked me up and down. 'I thought you'd be taller.'

I could say the same. I was caught off balance by the situation. I'd been ready for a muscular thug and negotiations filled with thinly veiled threats and bravado. I didn't know what to make of this smiling waif. 'What have you heard?' I asked to fill the silence. 'Nothing bad, I hope.'

'Good and bad.' She grinned. 'But nothing boring.'

I folded my hands to keep from fidgeting. 'So how exactly do we do this?'

'Not much for banter, are you?' she said, giving a brief, disappointed sigh. 'Fair enough, straight to business. How much do you need?'

'Only about a talent,' I said. 'Eight jots, actually.'

She shook her head seriously, her strawberry-blonde hair swinging back and forth. 'I can't do that, I'm afraid. It's not worth my while to make ha'penny loans.'

I frowned. 'How much is worth your while?'

'Four talents,' she said. 'That's the minimum.'

'And the interest?'

'Fifty percent every two months. So if you're looking to borrow as little as possible, it'll be two talents at the end of the term. You can pay off the whole debt for six if you like. But until I get all the principle back, it's two talents every term.'

I nodded, not terribly surprised. It was roughly four times what even the most avaricious moneylender would charge. 'But I'm paying interest on money I don't really need.'

'No,' she said, meeting my eyes seriously. 'You're paying interest on money you borrowed. That's the deal.'

'How about two talents?' I said. 'Then at the end—'

Devi waved her hands, cutting me off. 'We aren't bargaining here. I'm just informing you as to the conditions of the loan.' She smiled apologetically. 'I'm sorry I didn't make that clear from the beginning.'

I looked at her, the set of her shoulders, the way she met my eyes. 'Okay,' I said, resigned. 'Where do I sign?'

She gave me a slightly puzzled look, her forehead furrowing slightly. 'No need to sign anything.' She opened a drawer and pulled out a small brown bottle with a glass stopper. She laid a long pin next to it on the desk. 'Just a little blood.'

I sat frozen in my chair, my arms at my sides. 'Don't worry,' she reassured me. 'The pin's clean. I only need about three good drops.'

I finally found my voice. 'You've got to be kidding.'

Devi cocked her head to one side, a tiny smile curling one edge of her mouth. 'You didn't know?' she said, surprised. 'It's rare that anyone comes here without knowing the whole story.'

'I can't believe anyone actually . . .' I stalled, at a loss for words.

'Not everyone does,' she said. 'I usually do business with students and ex-students. Folk on this side of the river would think I was some sort of witch or a demon or some nonsense like that. Members of the Arcanum know exactly why I want blood, and what I can do with it.'

'You're a member of the Arcanum too?'

'Former,' she said, her smile fading a little. 'I made Re'lar before I left. I know enough so that with a little blood, you can never hide from me. I can dowse you out anywhere.'

'Among other things,' I said, incredulously, thinking of the wax mommet I'd made of Hemme at the beginning of the term. That was just hair. Blood was much more effective at creating a link. 'You could kill me.'

She gave me a frank look. 'You're awfully thick to be the Arcanum's bright new star. Think it through. Would I stay in business if I made a habit of malfeasance?'

'The masters know about this?'

She laughed. 'God's body, of course not. Neither does the constable, the bishop, or my mother.' She pointed to her chest, then to me. 'I know and you know. That's usually enough to ensure a good working relationship between the two of us.'

'What about *unusually*?' I asked. 'What if I don't have your money at the end of the term? What then?'

She spread her hands and shrugged carelessly. 'Then we work something out between the two of us. Like rational people. Maybe you work for me. Tell me secrets. Do me favours.' She smiled and gave me a slow, lecherous looking over, laughing at my discomfiture. 'If worse comes to worst, and you end up being extraordinarily uncooperative, I could probably sell your blood to someone to recover my loss. Everyone has enemies.' She shrugged easily.

'But I've never had things descend to that level. The threat is usually enough to keep people in line.'

She looked at the expression on my face and her shoulders slumped a little. 'Come on now,' she said gently. 'You came here expecting some thick-necked gaelet with scarred knuckles. You were ready to make a deal with someone ready to beat twelve distinct colours of hell out of you if you were a day late. My way is better. Simpler.'

'This is insane,' I said, getting to my feet. 'Absolutely not.'

Devi's cheerful expression faded. 'Get ahold of yourself,' she said, plainly growing exasperated. 'You're acting like some farmer who thinks I'm trying to buy his soul. It's just a little blood so I can keep tabs on you. It's like collateral.' She made a calming gesture with both hands, as if smoothing the air. 'Fine, I'll tell you what. I'll let you borrow half the minimum.' She looked at me expectantly. 'Two talents. Does that make it easier?'

'No,' I said. 'I'm sorry to have wasted your time, but I can't do it. Are there any other gaelets around?'

'Of course,' she said coolly. 'But I don't feel particularly inclined to give out that sort of information.' She tilted her head quizzically. 'By the way, today's Cendling, isn't it? Don't you need your tuition by noon tomorrow?'

'I'll find them on my own then,' I snapped.

'I'm sure you will, clever boy like you.' Devi waved me away with the back of her hand. 'Feel free to let yourself out. Think fond thoughts of Devi in two months' time, when some thug is kicking the teeth out of your pretty little head.'

After leaving Devi's I paced the streets of Imre, restless and irritated, trying to get my thoughts in order. Trying to think of a way around my problem.

I had a decent chance of paying off the two-talent loan. I hoped to move up the ranks in the Fishery soon. Once I was allowed to pursue my own projects, I could start earning real money. All I needed was to stay in classes long enough. It was just a matter of time.

That's really what I was borrowing: time. One more term. Who knew what opportunities might present themselves in the next two months?

But even as I tried to talk myself into it, I knew the truth. It was a bad idea. It was begging for trouble. I would swallow my pride and see if Wil or Sim or Sovoy could lend me the eight jots I needed. I sighed, resigning myself to a term of sleeping outside and scavenging meals where I could find them. At least it couldn't be worse than my time in Tarbean.

I was just about to head back to the University when my restless pacing took me by a pawnshop's window. I felt the old ache in my fingers . . .

'How much for the seven-string lute?' I asked. To this day I do not remember actually entering the store.

'Four talents even,' the owner said brightly. I guessed he was new to the job, or drunk. Pawnbrokers are never cheerful, not even in rich cities like Imre.

'Ah,' I said, not bothering to hide my disappointment. 'Could I take a look at it?'

He handed it over. It wasn't much to look at. The grain of the wood was uneven, the varnish rough and scratched. Its frets were made of gut and badly in need of replacing, but that was of little concern to me, as I typically played fretless anyway. The bowl was rosewood, so the sound of it wouldn't be terribly subtle. But on the other hand, rosewood would carry better in a crowded taproom, cutting through the murmur of idle conversation. I tapped the bowl with a finger and it gave off a resonant hum. Solid, but not pretty. I began to tune it so I would have an excuse to hold it a while longer.

'I might be able to go as low as three and five,' the man behind the counter said.

My ears pricked up as I heard something in his tone: desperation. It occurred to me that an ugly, used lute might not sell very well in a city full of nobility and prosperous musicians. I shook my head. 'The strings are old.' Actually they were fine, but I hoped he didn't know that.

'True,' he said, reassuring me of his ignorance, 'but strings are cheap.'

'I suppose,' I said doubtfully. With a deliberate plan, I set each of the strings just a hair out of tune with the others. I struck a chord and listened to the grating sound. I gave the lute's neck a sour, speculative look. 'I think the neck might be cracked.' I strummed a minor chord that sounded even less appealing. 'Does that sound cracked to you?' I strummed it again, harder.

'Three and two?' He asked hopefully.

'It's not for me,' I said, as if correcting him. 'It's for my little brother. The little bastard won't leave mine alone.'

I strummed again and grimaced. 'I may not like the little sprit very much, but I'm not cruel enough to buy him a lute with a sour neck.' I paused significantly. When nothing was forthcoming, I prompted him. 'Not for three and two.'

'Three even?' he said hopefully.

To all appearances I held the lute casually, carelessly. But in my heart I was clutching it with a white-knuckled fierceness. I cannot hope for you to understand this. When the Chandrian killed my troupe, they destroyed every piece of family and home I had ever known. But in some ways it had been worse when my father's lute was broken in Tarbean. It had been like losing a limb, an eye, a vital organ. Without my music, I had wandered Tarbean for years, half-alive, like a crippled veteran or one of the walking dead.

'Listen,' I said to him frankly. 'I've got two and two for you.' I pulled out my purse. 'You can take it, or this ugly thing can gather dust on a high shelf for the next ten years.'

I met his eye, careful to keep my face from showing how badly I needed it. I would do anything to keep this lute. I would dance naked in the snow. I would clutch at his legs, shaking and frantic, promising him anything, anything . . .

I counted out two talents and two jots onto the counter between us, nearly all of the money I had saved for this term's tuition. Each coin made a hard click as I pressed it to the table.

He gave me a long look, measuring me. I clicked down one more jot and waited. And waited. When he finally reached out his hand for the money, his haggard expression was the same one I was used to seeing on pawnbroker's faces.

Devi opened the door and smiled. 'Well now, I honestly didn't think I'd see you again. Come in.' She bolted the door behind me and walked over to her desk. 'I can't say I'm disappointed, though.' She looked over her shoulder and flashed her impish smile. 'I was looking forward to doing a little business with you.' She sat down. 'So, two talents then?'

'Four would be better, actually,' I said. Just enough for me to afford tuition and a bunk in the Mews. I could sleep outside in the wind and rain. My lute deserved better.

'Wonderful,' she said as she pulled out the bottle and pin.

I needed the tips of my fingers intact, so I pricked the back of my hand and let three drops of blood slowly gather and fall into the small brown bottle. I held it out to Devi.

'Go ahead and drop the pin in there too.'

I did.

Devi swabbed the bottle's stopper with a clear substance and slid it into the mouth of the bottle. 'A clever little adhesive from your friends over the river,' she explained. 'This way, I can't open the bottle without breaking it. When you pay off your debt, you get it back intact and can sleep safe knowing I haven't kept any for myself.'

'Unless you have the solvent,' I pointed out.

Devi gave me a pointed look. 'You're not big on trust, are you?' She rummaged around in a drawer, brought out some sealing wax, and began to warm it over the lamp on her desk. 'I don't suppose you have a seal, or ring or anything like that?' she asked as she smeared the wax across the top of the bottle's stopper.

'If I had jewelry to sell, I wouldn't be here,' I said frankly and pressed my thumb into the wax. It left a recognisable print. 'But that should do.'

Devi etched a number on the side of the bottle with a diamond stylus, then brought out a slip of paper. She wrote for a moment then fanned it with a hand, waiting for it to dry. 'You can take this to any moneylender on either side of the river,' she said cheerfully as she handed it to me. 'Pleasure doing business with you. Don't be a stranger.'

———

I headed back to the University with money in my purse and the comforting weight of the lute strap hanging from my shoulder. It was secondhand, ugly, and had cost me dearly in money, blood, and peace of mind.

I loved it like a child, like breathing, like my own right hand.

CHAPTER FIFTY-ONE

Tar and Tin

AT THE BEGINNING OF my second term, Kilvin gave me permission to study sygaldry. This raised a few eyebrows, but none in the Fishery where I'd proven myself to be a hard worker and a dedicated student.

Sygaldry, simply put, is a set of tools for channelling forces. Like sympathy made solid.

For example, if you engraved one brick with the rune *ule* and another with the rune *doch,* the two runes would cause the bricks to cling to each other, as if mortared in place.

But it's not as simple as that. What really happens is the two runes tear the bricks apart with the strength of their attraction. To prevent this you have to add the rune *aru* to each of the bricks. *Aru* is the rune for clay, and it makes the two pieces of clay cling to each other, solving your problem.

Except that *aru* and *doch* don't fit together. They're the wrong shape. To get them to fit you have to add a few linking runes, *gea* and *teh*. Then, for balance, you have to add *gea* and *teh* to the other brick, too. Then the bricks cling to each other without breaking.

But only if the bricks are made out of clay. Most bricks aren't. So, generally, it is a better idea to mix iron into the ceramic of the brick before it is fired. Of course, that means you have to use *fehr* instead of *aru*. Then you have to switch *teh* and *gea* so the ends come together properly . . .

As you can see, mortar is a simpler and more reliable route for holding bricks together.

I studied my sygaldry under Cammar. The scarred, one-eyed man was Kilvin's gatekeeper. Only after you were able to prove your firm grasp of sygaldry to him could you move on to a loose apprenticeship with one of the more experienced artificers. You assisted them with their projects, and in return they showed you the finer points of the craft.

There were one hundred ninety-seven runes. It was like learning a new language, except there were nearly two hundred unfamiliar letters, and you had to invent your own words a lot of the time. Most students took at least a month of study before Cammar judged them ready to move on. Some students took an entire term.

Start to finish, it took me seven days.

How?

First, I was driven. Other students could afford to stroll through their studies. Their parents or patrons would cover the expense. I, on the other hand, needed to climb the ranks in the Fishery quickly so I could earn money working on my own projects. Tuition wasn't even my first priority anymore, Devi was.

Second, I was brilliant. Not just your run-of-the-mill brilliance either. I was extraordinarily brilliant.

Lastly, I was lucky. Plain and simple.

———

I stepped across the patchwork rooftops of Mains with my lute slung across my back. It was a dim, cloudy twilight, but I knew my way around by now. I kept to the tar and tin, knowing that red tiles or grey slate made for treacherous footing.

At some point in the remodelling of Mains, one of the courtyards had become completely isolated. It could only be accessed by clambering through a high window in one of the lecture halls or by climbing down a gnarled apple tree, if you happened to be on the roof.

I came here to practice my lute. My bunk in Mews was not convenient. Not only was music viewed as frivolous on this side of the river, but I would only make more enemies by playing while my bunkmates tried to sleep or study. So I came here. It was perfect, secluded, and practically on my doorstep.

The hedges had gone wild and the lawn was a riot of weeds and flowering plants. But there was a bench under the apple tree that was perfectly suited to my needs. Usually I came late at night, when Mains was locked and abandoned. But today was Theden, that meant that if I ate dinner quickly, I had nearly an hour between Elxa Dal's class and my work in the Fishery. Plenty of time for some practice.

However, when I reached the courtyard tonight, I saw lights through the windows. Brandeur's lecture was running late today.

So I stayed on the rooftop. The windows to the lecture hall were shut, so there wasn't much chance of my being overheard.

I put my back to a nearby chimney and began to play. After about ten minutes the lights went out, but I decided to stay where I was rather than waste time climbing down.

I was halfway through 'Ten Tap Tim' when the sun slipped out from behind the clouds. Golden light covered the rooftop, spilling over the edge of the roof into a thin slice of the courtyard below.

That's when I heard the noise. A sudden rustling, like a startled animal down in the courtyard. But then there was something else, a noise unlike anything a squirrel or rabbit would make in the hedge. It was a hard noise, a vaguely metallic thud, as if someone had dropped a heavy bar of iron.

I stopped playing, the half-finished melody still running through my head. Was another student down there, listening? I put my lute back in its case before I made my way over to the lip of the roof and looked down.

I couldn't see through the thick hedge that covered most of the eastern edge of the courtyard. Had a student climbed through the window?

The sunset was fading quickly, and by the time I made it down the apple tree most of the courtyard lay in shadow. I could see from here that the high window was closed; no one had come in that way. Even though it was quickly growing dark, curiosity won over caution and I made my way into the hedge.

There was quite a lot of space there. Portions of the hedge were nearly hollow, a green shell of living branches, leaving enough room to crouch comfortably. I made note of the place as a good space for sleeping if I didn't have enough money for a bunk in the Mews next term.

Even in the fading light I could see I was the only one there. There wasn't room for anything bigger than a rabbit to hide. In the dim light I couldn't spot anything that could have made the metallic noise, either.

Humming the catchy chorus of 'Ten Tap Tim', I crawled through to the other end of the hedge. Only when I came through the other side did I notice the drainage grate. I'd seen similar ones scattered throughout the University, but this one was older and larger. In fact, the opening might be large enough for a person to fit through, if the grate were removed.

Hesitantly, I curled a hand around one of the cool metal bars and pulled. The heavy grate pivoted on a hinge and came up about three inches before stopping. In the dim light I couldn't tell why it wouldn't go any farther. I pulled harder, but couldn't budge it. Finally I gave up and dropped it back into place. It made a hard noise, vaguely metallic. Like someone had dropped a heavy bar of iron.

Then my fingers felt something that my eyes missed: a maze of grooves etching the surface of the bars. I looked closer and recognised some of the runes I was learning under Cammar: *ule* and *doch*.

Then something clicked in my head. The chorus of 'Ten Tap Tim' suddenly fit together with the runes I'd been studying under Cammar for the last handful of days.

> Ule and *doch* are
> Both for binding
> *Reh* for seeking
> *Kel* for finding
> *Gea* key
> *Teh* lock
> *Pesin* water
> *Resin* rock

Before I could go any further, sixth bell struck. The sound startled me from my reverie. But when I reached out to steady myself, my hand didn't come to rest on leaves and dirt. It touched something round and hard and smooth: a green apple.

I emerged from the hedge and made my way to the northwest corner where the apple tree stood. No apples were on the ground. It was too early in the year for that. What's more, the iron grate was on the opposite side of the small courtyard. It couldn't have rolled that far. It must have been carried.

Unsure of what to think, but knowing I was late for my evening shift in the Fishery, I climbed the apple tree, gathered up my lute, and hurried to Kilvin's shop.

Later that night I fit the rest of the runes to music. It took a few hours, but when I was done it was like having a reference sheet in my head. The next day Cammar put me through an extensive two-hour examination, which I passed.

For the next stage of my education in the Fishery, I was apprenticed to Manet, the old, wild-haired student I'd met during my first days at the University. Manet had been attending the University for nearly thirty years, and everyone knew him as the eternal E'lir. But despite the fact that we held the same rank, Manet had more hands-on experience in the Fishery than any dozen higher-ranking students combined.

Manet was patient and considerate. In fact, he reminded me of my old teacher, Abenthy. Except Abenthy had wandered the world like a restless tinker, and it was common knowledge that Manet desired nothing more than to stay at the University for the rest of his life if he could manage it.

Manet started small, teaching me simple formulae of the sort required for twice-tough glass and heat funnels. Under his tutelage, I learned artificing as quickly as I learned everything, and it wasn't long before we worked our way up to more complex projects like heat-eaters and sympathy lamps.

Truly high-level artificing such as sympathy clocks or gearwins were still beyond my reach, but I knew that it was just a matter of time. Unfortunately, time was proving to be in short supply.

CHAPTER FIFTY-TWO

Burning

OWNING A LUTE AGAIN meant I had my music back, but I quickly realised I was three years out of practice. My work in the Artificery over the last couple of months had toughened and strengthened my hands, but not in entirely the right ways. It took several frustrating days before I could play comfortably for even an hour at a time.

I might have progressed more quickly had I not been so busy with my other studies. I had two hours of each day in the Medica, running or standing, an average of two hours of lecture and ciphering each day in Mathematics, and three hours of studying under Manet in the Fishery, learning the tricks of the trade.

And then there was advanced sympathy with Elxa Dal. Out of class, Elxa Dal was charming, soft-spoken, and even a little ridiculous when the mood was on him. But when he taught, his personality strode back and forth between mad prophet and galley-slave drummer. Every day in his class I burned another three hours of time and five hours worth of energy.

Combined with my paid work in Kilvin's shop, this left me with barely enough time to eat, sleep, and study, let alone give my lute the time it deserved.

Music is a proud, temperamental mistress. Give her the time and attention she deserves, and she is yours. Slight her and there will come a day when you call and she will not answer. So I began sleeping less to give her the time she needed.

After a span of this schedule, I was tired. After three span I was still fine, but only through a grim, set-jaw type of determination. Somewhere around the fifth span I began to show definite signs of wear.

———

It was during that fifth span that I was enjoying a rare, shared lunch with Wilem and Simmon. They had their lunches from a nearby tavern. I couldn't afford a drab for an apple and meat pie, so I had snuck some barley bread and a gristly sausage out of the Mess.

We sat on the stone bench beneath the pennant pole where I'd been whipped. The place had filled me with dread after my whipping, but I forced myself to spend time there to prove to myself that I could. After it no longer unnerved me, I sat there because the stares of the students amused me. Now I sat there because I was comfortable. It was my place.

And, because we spent a fair amount of time together, it had become Wilem and Simmon's place too. If they thought my choice an odd one, they didn't speak of it.

'You haven't been around very much,' Wilem said around a mouthful of meat pie. 'Been sick?'

'Right,' Simmon said sarcastically. 'He's been sick a whole month.'

Wilem glared at him and grumbled, reminding me of Kilvin for a moment.

His expression made Simmon laugh. 'Wil's more polite than I am. I'm betting you've been spending all your free hours walking to Imre and back. Courting some fabulously attractive young bard.' He gestured at the lute case that lay at my side.

'He looks like he's been sick.' Wilem looked at me with a critical eye. 'Your woman hasn't been taking care of you.'

'He's lovesick,' Simmon said knowingly. 'Can't eat. Can't sleep. You think of her when you should be trying to memorise your cipher.'

I couldn't think of anything to say.

'See?' Simmon said to Wil. 'She's stolen his tongue as well as his heart. All his words are for her. He can spare none for us.'

'Can't spare any time, either,' Wilem said into his rapidly dwindling meat pie.

It was true of course – I had been neglecting my friends even more than I had been neglecting myself. I felt a flush of guilt wash over me. I couldn't tell them the full truth, that I needed to make the most of this term because it would very likely be my last. I was flat broke.

If you cannot understand why I couldn't bring myself to tell them this, then I doubt you have ever been truly poor. I doubt you can really understand how embarrassing it is to only own two shirts, to cut your own hair as best you can because you can't afford a barber. I lost a button and couldn't spare a shim to buy a matching one. I tore out the knee of my pants and had to make do with the wrong colour thread for mending. I couldn't afford salt for my meals, or drinks on my rare evenings out with friends.

The money I earned in Kilvin's shop was spent on essentials: ink, soap, lute strings . . . the only other thing I could afford was pride. I couldn't bear the thought of my two best friends knowing how desperate my situation was.

If I suffered a piece of extraordinary good luck I might be able to muster two talents to pay the interest on my debt to Devi. But it would require a direct act of God for me to somehow gather enough money to pay that *and* next term's tuition as well. After I was forced out of the University and squared my debt with Devi, I didn't know what I'd do. Pull up stakes and head for Anilin to look for Denna, perhaps.

I looked at them, not knowing what to say. 'Wil, Simmon, I'm sorry. It's just that I've been so busy lately.'

Simmon grew a little more serious, and I saw that he was earnestly hurt at my unexplained absence. 'We're busy too, you know. I've got rhetoric and chemistry *and* I'm learning Siaru.' He turned to Wil and scowled. 'You should know I'm beginning to hate your language, you shim bastard.'

'*Tu kralim,*' the young Ceald replied amiably.

Simmon turned back to me, and spoke with remarkable candour. 'It's just that we'd like to see you more often than once every handful of days as you run from Mains to the Fishery. Girls are wonderful, I'll admit, but when one takes one of my friends away, I get a little jealous.' He gave a sudden, sunny smile. 'Not that I think of you in that way, of course.'

I found it hard to swallow past the sudden lump in my throat. I couldn't remember the last time I'd been missed. For a long time, I hadn't had anyone to miss me. I felt the beginning of hot tears in the back of my throat. 'Really, there isn't a girl. I mean it.' I swallowed hard trying to regain my composure.

'Sim, I think we've been missing something here.' Wilem was looking at me oddly. 'Take a good look at him.'

Simmon gave me a similar, analytical stare. That look from the two of them was enough to unnerve me, pushing me back from the edge of tears.

'Now,' Wilem said as if lecturing. 'How many terms has our young E'lir been attending the University?'

Realisation poured into Sim's honest face. 'Oh.'

'Anyone care to tell me?' I said petulantly.

Wilem ignored my question. 'What classes are you taking?'

'Everything,' I said, glad to have an excuse to complain. 'Geometry, Observation in the Medica, Advanced Sympathy with Elxa Dal, and I've got my apprenticeship under Manet in the Fishery.'

Simmon looked a little shocked. 'No wonder you look like you haven't slept in a span of days,' he said.

Wilem nodded to himself. 'And you're still working in Kilvin's shop, aren't you?'

'A couple hours every night.'

Simmon was aghast. 'And you're learning an instrument at the same time? Are you insane?'

'The music is the only thing that keeps me grounded,' I said, reaching down to touch my lute. 'And I'm not learning to play. I just need practice.'

Wilem and Simmon exchanged looks. 'How long do you think he has?'

Simmon looked me over. 'Span and a half, tops.'

'What do you mean?'

Wilem leaned forward. 'We all bite off too much sooner or later. But some students don't know when to spit their mouthful. They burn out. They quit, or botch their exams. Some crack.' He tapped his head. 'It usually happens to students in their first year.' He gave me a significant look.

'I haven't bitten off too much,' I said.

'Look in a mirror,' Wilem suggested frankly.

I opened my mouth to reassure Wil and Sim that I was fine, but just then I heard the hour being struck, and I only had time for a hurried good-bye. Even so, I had to run to make it to Advanced Sympathy on time.

Elxa Dal stood between two medium sized braziers. In his well-trimmed beard and dark master's robe, he still reminded me of the stereotypical evil magician that appears in so many bad Aturan plays. 'What each of you must remember is that the sympathist is tied to flame,' he said. 'We are its master and its servant.'

He tucked his hands into his long sleeves and began to pace again. 'We are the masters of fire, for we have dominion over it.' Elxa Dal struck a nearby brazier with the flat of his hand, making it ring softly. Flames kindled in the coal and began to lick hungrily upward. 'The energy in all things belongs to the arcanist. We command fire and fire obeys.' Dal walked slowly to the other corner of the room. The brazier at his back dimmed while the one he walked towards sparked to life and began to burn. I appreciated his showmanship.

Dal stopped and faced the class again. 'But we are also servants of fire. Because fire is the most common form of energy, and without energy, our prowess as sympathists is of little use.' He turned his back to the class and began erasing formulae from the slate board. 'Gather your materials, and we'll see who has to knock heads with E'lir Kvothe today.' He began to chalk up a list of all the students' names. Mine was at the top.

Three span ago, Dal had started making us compete against each other. He called it duelling. And though it was a welcome break from the monotony of lecture, this most recent activity had a sinister element too.

A hundred students left the Arcanum every year, perhaps a quarter of them with their guilders. That meant that every year there were a hundred more people in the world that had been trained in the use of sympathy. People who, for one reason or another, you might have to pit your will against later in life. Though Dal never said as much, we knew we were being taught something beyond mere concentration and ingenuity. We were being taught how to fight.

Elxa Dal kept careful track of the results. In the class of thirty-eight, I was the only one to remain undefeated. By this point, even the most thickheaded and grudging students were being forced to admit that my quick admittance to the Arcanum was something other than a fluke.

Duelling could also be profitable in a small way, as there was a bit of clandestine betting. When we wanted to bet on our own duels, Sovoy and I placed bets for each other. Though as a rule I usually didn't have much money to spare.

Thus it was no coincidence that Sovoy and I bumped into each other while we were gathering our materials. I handed him two jots underneath the table.

He slid them into his pocket without looking at me. 'Goodness,' he said quietly. 'Someone's pretty confident today.'

I shrugged nonchalantly, though in truth I was a little nervous. I had started the term penniless, and been scraping by ever since. But yesterday Kilvin had paid me for a span's work in the Fishery: two jots. All the money I had in the world.

Sovoy began to rummage around in a drawer, bringing out sympathy wax, twine, and a few pieces of metal. 'I don't know how well I'll be able to do for you. The odds are getting bad. I'm guessing three to one is the best you'll get today. You still interested if it gets that low?'

I sighed. The odds *were* the down side to my undefeated rank. Yesterday they had been two to one, meaning I would have had to risk two pennies for the chance to win one. 'I've got a little something planned,' I said. 'Don't bet until we've set terms. You should get at least three to one against me.'

'*Against* you?' he muttered as he gathered up an armful of paraphernalia. 'Not unless you're going up against Dal.' I turned my face to conceal a slightly embarrassed blush at the compliment.

Dal clapped his hands and everyone rushed to take their proper place. I was paired with a Vintish boy, Fenton. He was one step below me in the class ranking. I respected him as one of the few in the class that could pose a real challenge to me in the right situation.

'Right then,' Elxa Dal said, rubbing his hands together eagerly. 'Fenton, you're lower on the ranks, pick your poison.'

'Candles.'

'And your link?' Dal asked ritualistically. With candles it was always either wicking or wax.

'Wick.' He held up a piece for everyone to see.

Dal turned to me. 'Link?'

I dug into a pocket, and held up my link with a flourish. 'Straw.' There was a murmur from the class at this. It was a ridiculous link. The best I could hope for is a three percent transfer, maybe five. Fenton's wicking would be ten times better.

'Straw?'

'Straw,' I said with slightly more confidence than I felt. If this didn't tip the odds against me I didn't know what would.

'Straw it is then,' Dal said easily. 'E'lir Fenton, since Kvothe is undefeated you will have the choice of source.' A quiet laugh spread through the class.

My stomach dropped. I hadn't expected that. Normally, whoever doesn't pick the game gets to choose the source. I had been planning on choosing brazier, knowing that the quantity of heat would help offset my self-imposed handicap.

Fenton grinned, knowing his advantage. 'No source.'

I grimaced. All we would have to draw from was our own body heat. Difficult in the best of circumstances, not to mention a little dangerous.

I couldn't win. Not only was I going to lose my perfect rank, I had no way to signal Sovoy not to bet my last two jots. I tried to meet his eyes, but he was already caught up in quiet, intense negotiations with a handful of other students.

Fenton and I moved wordlessly to sit on opposite sides of a large work-table. Elxa Dal set two thick stumps of candle down, one in front of each of us. The object was to light your opponent's candle without letting him do the same to yours. This involved splitting your mind into two different pieces, one piece tried to hold the Alar that your piece of wicking (or straw, if you were stupid) was the same as the wick of the candle you were trying to light. Then you drew energy from your source to make it happen.

Meanwhile the second piece of your mind was kept busy trying to maintain the belief that your opponent's piece of wicking was *not* the same as the wick of your candle.

If all of this sounds difficult, believe me, you don't know the half of it.

Making it worse was the fact that neither of us had an easy source to draw from. You had to be careful using yourself as source. Your body is warm for a reason. It responds badly when its heat is pulled away.

At a gesture from Elxa Dal, we began. I immediately devoted my whole mind to the defense of my own candle and began to think furiously. There was no way I could win. It doesn't matter how skilled a fencer you are, you can't help but lose when your opponent has a blade of Ramston steel and you've chosen to fight with a willow switch.

I lowered myself into the Heart of Stone. Then, still devoting most of my mind to the protection of my candle, I muttered a binding between my candle and his. I reached out and tipped my candle on its side, forcing him to make a grab for his before it did the same and rolled away.

I tried to take quick advantage of his distraction and set his candle aflame. I threw myself into it and felt a chill bleed up my arm from my right hand that held the piece of straw. Nothing happened. His candle remained cold and dark.

I cupped my hand around the wick of my candle, blocking his line of sight. It was a petty trick, and largely useless against a skilled sympathist, but my only hope was to rattle him in some way.

'Hey, Fen,' I said. 'Have you heard the one about the tinker, the Tehlin, the farmer's daughter, and the butter churn yet?'

Fen gave no response. His pale face was locked in fierce concentration.

I gave up distraction as a lost cause. Fenton was too smart to be thrown off that way. Besides, I was finding it difficult to maintain the necessary concentration to keep my candle safe. I lowered myself more deeply into the Heart of Stone and forgot the world apart from the two candles and a piece of wick and straw.

After a minute I was covered in a clammy chill sweat. I shivered. Fenton saw this and gave me a smile with bloodless lips. I redoubled my efforts, but his candle ignored my best attempts to force it into flame.

Five minutes passed with the whole class quiet as stones. Most duels lasted no longer than a minute or two, one person quickly proving himself more clever or possessed of a stronger will. Both my arms were cold now. I saw a muscle in Fenton's neck twitch spastically, like a horse's flank trying to shake loose a biting fly. His posture went rigid as he suppressed the urge to shiver. A wisp of smoke began to curl from the wick of my candle.

I bore down. I realised that my breath was hissing through my clenched teeth, my lips pulled back in a feral grin. Fenton didn't seem to notice, his eyes growing glassy and unfocused. I shivered again, so violently that I almost missed seeing the tremour in his hand. Then, slowly, Fenton's head began to nod toward the tabletop. His eyelids drooped. I set my teeth and was rewarded to see a thin curl of smoke rise from the wick of his candle.

Woodenly, Fenton turned to look, but instead of rallying to his own defense he made a slow, leaden gesture of dismissal and lay his head in the crook of his arm.

He didn't look up as the candle near his elbow spat fitfully to life. There was a brief scattering of applause mixed in with exclamations of disbelief.

Someone pounded me on the back. 'How 'bout that? Wore himself out.'

'No,' I said thickly and reached across the table. With clumsy fingers I prized open the hand that held the wicking and saw it had blood on it. 'Master Dal,' I said as quickly as I could manage. 'He's got the chills.' Speaking made me realise how cold my lips felt.

But Dal was already there, bringing a blanket to wrap around the boy. 'You.' He pointed at one of the students at random. 'Bring someone from the Medica. Go!' The student left at a run. 'Foolish,' Master Dal murmured a binding for heat. He looked over at me. 'You should probably walk around a bit. You don't look much better than he does.'

There was no more duelling that day. The rest of the class watched as Fenton revived slowly under Elxa Dal's care. By the time an older El'the from the Medica arrived, Fenton had warmed enough to begin shivering violently. After a quarter hour of warm blankets and careful sympathy, Fenton was able to drink something hot, though his hands still shook.

Once all the hubbub was finished, it was nearly third bell. Master Dal managed to get all the students seated and quiet long enough to say a few words.

'What we saw today was a prime example of binder's chills. The body is a delicate thing and a few degrees of heat lost rapidly can upset the entire system. A mild case of chills is just that, chilling. But more extreme cases can lead to shock and hypothermia.' Dal looked around. 'Can anyone tell me what Fenton's mistake was?' There was a moment of silence, then a hand raised. 'Yes Brae?'

'He used blood. When heat is lost from the blood, the body cools as a whole unit. This is not always advantageous, as the extremities can stand a more drastic temperature loss than the viscera can.'

'Why would anyone consider using blood then?'

'It offers up more heat more rapidly than the flesh.'

'How much would have been safe for him to draw?' Dal looked around the room.

'Two degrees?' someone volunteered.

'One and a half,' Dal corrected, and wrote a few equations on the board to demonstrate how much heat this would provide. 'Given his symptoms, how much do you suppose he actually drew?'

There was a pause. Finally Sovoy spoke up, 'Eight or nine.'

'Very good,' Dal said grudgingly. 'It's nice that at least one of you has been doing the reading.' His expression grew grave. 'Sympathy is not for the weak of mind, but neither is it for the overconfident. If we had not been here to give Fenton the care he needed, he would have slipped quietly asleep and died.' He paused to let the words sink in. 'Better you should know your honest limit than overguess your abilities and lose control.'

Third bell struck, and the room was filled with sudden noise as students stood to leave. Master Dal raised his voice to be heard. 'E'lir Kvothe, would you mind staying behind for a moment?'

I grimaced. Sovoy walked behind me, clapped me on the shoulder, and muttered, 'Luck.' I couldn't tell if he was referring to my victory or wishing me well.

After everyone was gone, Dal turned and set down the rag he had been using to wipe the slate clean. 'So,' he said conversationally. 'How did the numbers work out?'

I wasn't surprised he knew about the betting. 'Eleven to one,' I admitted. I'd made twenty-two jots. A little over two talents. The presence of that money in my pocket warmed me.

He gave me a speculative look. 'How're you feeling? You were a little pale at the end yourself.'

'I had a little shiver,' I lied.

Actually, in the commotion that followed Fenton's collapse I had slipped out and had a frightening few minutes in a back hallway. Shivers that were close to seizures had made it almost impossible to stay on my feet. Luckily, no one had found me shaking in the hallway, my jaw clenched so tight that I feared my teeth might break.

But no one had seen me. My reputation was intact.

Dal gave me a look that told me he might suspect the truth. 'Come over,' he made a motion to one of the still-burning braziers. 'A little warm won't hurt you.'

I didn't argue. As I held my hands to the fire, I felt myself relax a bit. Suddenly I realised how weary I was. My eyes were itchy from too little sleep. My body felt heavy, as if my bones were made of lead.

With a reluctant sigh I pulled my hands back and opened my eyes. Dal was looking closely at my face. 'I've got to go.' I said with a little regret in my voice. 'Thanks for the use of your fire.'

'We're both sympathists,' Dal said, giving me a friendly wave as I gathered my things and headed for the door. 'You're welcome to it any time.'

Later that night in the Mews, Wilem opened his door to my knocking. 'I'll be dammed,' he said. 'Two times in one day. To what do I owe the honour?'

'I think you know,' I grumbled and pushed my way inside the cell-like little room. I leaned my lute case against a wall and fell into a chair. 'Kilvin has banned me from my work in the shop.'

Wilem sat forward on his bed. 'Why's that?'

I gave him a knowing look. 'I expect it's because you and Simmon stopped by and suggested it to him.'

He watched me for a moment, then shrugged. 'You figured it out quicker than I thought you would.' He rubbed the side of his face. 'You don't seem terribly upset.'

I had been furious. Just as my fortune seemed to be turning, I was forced to leave my only paying job because of well-intentioned meddling by my friends. But rather than storm over and rage at them, I'd gone away to the roof of Mains and played for a while to cool my head.

My music calmed me, as it always did. And while I played, I thought things through. My apprenticeship with Manet was going well, but there was simply too much to learn: how to fire the kilns, how to draw wire to the proper consistency, which alloys to choose for the proper effects. I couldn't hope to bull through it the way I had learning my runes. I couldn't earn enough working in Kilvin's shop to pay back Devi at the end of the month, let alone make enough for tuition too.

'I probably would be,' I admitted. 'But Kilvin made me look in a mirror.' I gave him a tired smile. 'I look like hell.'

'You look like beat-up hell,' he corrected me matter-of-factly, then paused awkwardly. 'I'm glad you're not upset.'

Simmon knocked as he pushed the door open. Guilt chased surprise off his face when he saw me sitting there. 'Aren't you supposed to be, um, in the Fishery?' he asked lamely.

I laughed and Simmon's relief was almost tangible. Wilem moved a stack of paper off another chair and Simmon slouched into it.

'All is forgiven,' I said magnanimously. 'All I ask is this: tell me everything you know about the Eolian.'

CHAPTER FIFTY-THREE

Slow Circles

THE EOLIAN IS WHERE our long-sought player is waiting in the wings. I have not forgotten that she is what I am moving towards. If I seem to be caught in a slow circling of the subject, it is only appropriate, as she and I have always moved towards each other in slow circles.

Luckily, Wilem and Simmon had both been to the Eolian. Together they told me what little I didn't already know.

There were a lot of places you could go in Imre to listen to music. In fact, nearly every inn, tavern, and boarding house had some manner of musician strumming, singing, or piping in the background. But the Eolian was different. It hosted the best musicians in the city. If you knew good music from bad, you knew the Eolian had the best.

To get in the front door of the Eolian cost you a whole copper jot. Once you were inside you could stay as long as you wished, and listen to as much music as you liked.

But paying at the door did not give a musician the right to play at the Eolian. A musician who wished to set foot upon the Eolian's stage had to pay for the privilege: one silver talent. That's right, folk paid to play at the Eolian, not the other way around.

Why would anyone pay such an outrageous amount of money simply to play music? Well, some of those who gave their silver were simply the self-indulgent rich. To them, a talent was not a great price to set themselves on such proud display.

But serious musicians paid too. If your performance impressed the audience and the owners enough, you were given a token: a tiny set of silver pipes that could be mounted on a pin or necklace. Talent pipes were recognised as clear marks of distinction at most sizable inns within two hundred miles of Imre.

If you had your set of talent pipes, you were admitted to the Eolian for free and could play whenever the fancy took you.

The only responsibility the talent pipes carried was that of performance. If you had earned your pipes, you could be called upon to play. This was usually not a heavy burden, as the nobility who frequented the Eolian usually gave money or gifts to performers who pleased them. It was the upper class version of buying drinks for the fiddler.

Some musicians played with little hope of actually gaining their pipes. They paid to play because you never knew who might be in the Eolian that night, listening. A good performance of a single song might not get you your pipes, but it might earn you a wealthy patron instead.

A patron.

———

'You'll never guess what I heard,' Simmon said one evening as we sat on our usual bench in the pennant square. We were alone, as Wilem was off making eyes at a serving girl at Anker's. 'Students have been hearing all manner of odd things from Mains at night.'

'Really,' I feigned disinterest.

Simmon pressed on. 'Yes. Some say that it's the ghost of a student who got lost in the building and starved to death.' He tapped the side of his nose with a finger like an old gaffer telling a story. 'They say he wanders the halls even to this day, never able to find his way outside.'

'Ah.'

'Other opinions suggest it's an angry spirit. They say it tortures animals, especially cats. That's the sound the students hear, late at night: tortured cat's guts. Quite a terrifying sound, I understand.'

I looked at him. He seemed almost ready to burst with laughing. 'Oh let it out,' I told him with mock severity. 'Go on. You deserve it for being so terribly clever. Despite the fact that no one uses gut strings in this day and age.'

He chortled delightedly to himself. I picked up one of his sweetcakes and began to eat it, hoping to teach him a valuable lesson in humility.

'So you're still going at it?'

I nodded.

Simmon looked relieved. 'I thought you might have changed your plans. I hadn't seen you carrying your lute around lately.'

'Not necessary,' I explained. 'Now that I have time to practice I don't have to worry about sneaking in a few minutes whenever I can grab them.'

A group of students passed by, one of them waved to Simmon. 'When are you going to do it?'

'This Mourning,' I said.

'So soon?' Sim asked. 'It was only two span ago that you were worried about being rusty. Has it all come back so quickly?'

'Not all of it,' I admitted. 'It'll take years for it to all come back.' I shrugged and popped the last of the sweetcake into my mouth. 'But it's easy again. The music doesn't stop in my hands any more, it just—' I struggled to explain, then shrugged. 'I'm ready.'

Honestly, I would have liked another month's practice, another year's practice before gambling away an entire talent. But there was no time. The term was nearly over. I needed money to stave off my debt to Devi and pay my upcoming tuition. I couldn't wait any longer.

'You sure?' Sim asked. 'I've heard people try for their talent that were really good. Early this term an old man sang a song about . . . about this woman whose husband had gone off to war.'

' "In the Village Smithy", ' I said.

'Whatever,' Simmon said dismissively. 'What I'm saying is that he was really good. I laughed and cried and just hurt all over.' He gave me an anxious look. 'But he didn't get his pipes.'

I covered my own anxiety with a smile. 'You still haven't heard me play, have you?'

'You know damn well I haven't,' he said crossly.

I smiled. I had refused to play for Wilem and Simmon while I was out of practice. Their opinions were nearly as important as those at the Eolian.

'Well, you'll get your chance this Mourning,' I teased. 'Will you come?'

Simmon nodded. 'Wilem too. Barring earthquakes or a rain of blood.'

I looked up at the sunset. 'I should go,' I said, getting to my feet. 'Practice makes the master.'

Sim waved and I headed to the Mess, where I sat down long enough to spoon up my beans and chew through a flat piece of tough grey meat. I took my small loaf of bread with me, drawing a few odd looks from the nearby students.

I headed to my bunk and retrieved my lute from the trunk at the foot of the bed. Then, given the rumours Sim had mentioned, I took one of the trickier ways onto the roof of Mains, shimmying up a series of drainpipes in a sheltered box alley. I didn't want to draw any extra attention to my night-time activities there.

It was fully dark by the time I made it to the isolated courtyard with the apple tree. All the windows were dark. I looked down from the edge of the roof, seeing nothing but shadows.

'Auri,' I called. 'Are you there?'

'You're late,' came the vaguely petulant reply.

'I'm sorry,' I said. 'Do you want to come up tonight?'

A slight pause. 'No. Come down.'

'There's not much moon tonight,' I said in my best encouraging tones. 'Are you sure you don't want to come up?'

I heard a rustle from the hedges below and then saw Auri scamper up the tree like a squirrel. She ran around the edge of the roof, then pulled up short a few dozen feet away.

At my best guess, Auri was only a few years older than me, certainly no more than twenty. She dressed in tattered clothes that left her arms and legs bare, was shorter than me by almost a foot. She was thin. Part of this was simply her tiny frame, but there was more to it than that. Her cheeks were hollow and her bare arms waifishly narrow. Her long hair was so fine that it trailed her, floating in the air like a cloud.

It had taken me a long while to draw her out of hiding. I'd suspected someone was listening to me practice from the courtyard, but it had been nearly two span before I caught a glimpse of her. Seeing that she was half-starved, I began bringing whatever food I could carry away from the Mess and leaving it for her. Even so, it was another span before she had joined me on the roof as I practiced my lute.

The last few days, she'd even started talking. I'd expected her to be sullen and suspicious, but nothing could be further from the truth. She was bright-eyed and enthusiastic. Though I couldn't help but be reminded of myself in Tarbean when I saw her, there was little real resemblance. Auri was scrupu-lously clean and full of joy.

She didn't like the open sky, or bright lights, or people. I guessed she was some student who had gone cracked and run underground before she could be confined to Haven. I hadn't learned much about her, as she was still shy and skittish. When I'd asked her name, she bolted back underground and didn't return for days.

So I picked a name for her, Auri. Though in my heart I thought of her as my little moon-fey.

Auri came a few steps closer, stopped, waited, then darted forward again. She did this several times until she stood in front of me. Standing still, her hair spread in the air around her like a halo. She held both her hands in front of her, just under her chin. She reached out and tugged my sleeve, then pulled her hand back. 'What did you bring me?' She asked excitedly.

I smiled. 'What did you bring *me*?' I teased gently.

She smiled and thrust her hand forward. Something gleamed in the moonlight. 'A key,' she said proudly, pressing it on me.

I took it. It had a pleasing weight in my hand. 'It's very nice,' I said. 'What does it unlock?'

'The moon,' she said, her expression grave.

'That should be useful,' I said, looking it over.

'That's what I thought,' she said. 'That way, if there's a door in the moon you can open it.' She sat cross-legged on the roof and grinned up at me. 'Not that I would encourage that sort of reckless behaviour.'

I squatted down and opened my lute case. 'I brought you some bread.' I handed her the loaf of brown barley bread wrapped in a piece of cloth. 'And a bottle of water.'

'This is very nice as well,' she said graciously. The bottle seemed very large in her hands. 'What's in the water?' she asked as she pulled out the cork and peered down into it.

'Flowers,' I said. 'And the part of the moon that isn't in the sky tonight. I put that in there too.'

She looked back up. 'I already said the moon,' she said with a hint of reproach.

'Just flowers then. And the shine off the back of a dragonfly. I wanted a piece of the moon, but blue-dragonfly-shine was as close as I could get.'

She tipped the bottle up and took a sip. 'It's lovely,' she said, brushing back several strands of hair that were drifting in front of her face.

Auri spread out the cloth and began to eat. She tore small pieces from the loaf and chewed them delicately, somehow making the whole process look genteel.

'I like white bread,' she said conversationally between mouthfuls.

'Me too,' I said as I lowered myself into a sitting position. 'When I can get it.'

She nodded and looked around at the starry night sky and the crescent moon. 'I like it when it's cloudy, too. But this is okay. It's cozy. Like the Underthing.'

'Underthing?' I asked. She was rarely this talkative.

'I live in the Underthing,' Auri said easily. 'It goes all over.'

'Do you like it down there?'

Auri's eyes lit up. 'Holy God yes, it's marvellous. You can just look forever.' She turned to look at me. 'I have news,' she said teasingly.

'What's that?' I asked.

She took another bite and finished chewing before she spoke. 'I went out last night.' A sly smile. 'On top of things.'

'Really?' I said, not bothering to hide my surprise. 'How did you like it?'

'It was lovely. I went looking around,' she said, obviously pleased with herself. 'I saw Elodin.'

'Master Elodin?' I asked. She nodded. 'Was he on top of things, too?'

She nodded again, chewing.

'Did he see you?'

Her smile burst out again making her look closer to eight than eighteen. 'Nobody sees me. Besides, he was busy listening to the wind.' She cupped her hands around her mouth and made a hooting noise. 'There was good wind for listening last night,' she added confidentially.

While I was trying to make sense of what she'd said, Auri finished the last of her bread and clapped her hands excitedly. 'Now play!' she said breathlessly. 'Play! Play!'

Grinning, I pulled my lute out of its case. I couldn't hope for a more enthusiastic audience than Auri.

CHAPTER FIFTY-FOUR

A Place to Burn

'YOU LOOK DIFFERENT TODAY,' Simmon observed. Wilem grunted in agreement.

'I feel different,' I admitted. 'Good, but different.'

The three of us were kicking up dust on the road to Imre. The day was warm and sunny, and we were in no particular hurry.

'You look . . . calm,' Simmon continued, brushing his hand through his hair. 'I wish I felt as calm as you look.'

'I wish *I* felt as calm as I looked,' I mumbled.

Simmon refused to give up. 'You look more solid.' He grimaced. 'No. You look . . . tight.'

'Tight?' Tension forced laughter out of me, leaving me more relaxed. 'How can someone look tight?'

'Just tight.' He shrugged. 'Like a coiled spring.'

'It's the way he's holding himself,' Wilem said, breaking his usual thoughtful silence. 'Standing straight, neck unbent, shoulders back.' He gestured vaguely to illustrate his points. 'When he steps, his whole foot treads the ground. Not just the ball, as if he would run, or the heel, as if he would hesitate. He steps solidly down, claiming the piece of ground for his own.'

I felt a momentary awkwardness as I tried to watch myself, always a futile thing to attempt.

Simmon gave him a sideways look. 'Someone's been spending time with Puppet, haven't they?'

Wilem shrugged a vague agreement and threw a stone into the trees by the side of the road.

'Who is this Puppet you two keep mentioning?' I asked, partly to draw the attention away from myself. 'I'm about to die of terminal curiosity, you know.'

'If anyone could, it would be you,' Wilem said.

'He spends most of his time in the Archives,' Sim said hesitantly, knowing that he was touching on a sore subject. 'It would be hard to introduce you since . . . you know . . .'

We came to Stonebridge, the ancient arch of grey stone that spanned the Omethi River between the University and Imre. Over two hundred feet from one bank to another, and arching more than sixty feet at its peak, Stonebridge had more stories and legends surrounding it than any other University landmark.

'Spit for luck,' Wilem urged, as we began to climb one side, and followed his own advice. Simmon followed suit, spitting over the side with a childlike exuberance.

I almost said, 'Luck has nothing to do with it.' Master Arwyl's words, repeated sternly a thousand times in the Medica. I tasted them on the tip of my tongue for a minute, hesitated, then spat instead.

The Eolian lay at the heart of Imre, its front doors facing out onto the city's central cobblestone courtyard. There were benches, a few flowering trees, and a marble fountain misting water over a statue of a satyr chasing a group of half-clothed nymphs whose attempt at flight seemed token at best. Well-dressed people milled around, nearly a third carrying some sort of musical instrument or another. I counted at least seven lutes.

As we approached the Eolian the doorman tugged at the front of a wide-brimmed hat and made a nodding bow. He was at least six and a half feet tall, deeply tanned and muscular. 'That will be one jot, young master,' he smiled as Wilem handed over a coin.

He turned to me next with the same sunny smile. Looking at the lute case I carried he cocked an eyebrow at me. 'Good to see a new face. You know the rules?'

I nodded and handed him a jot.

He turned to point inside. 'You see the bar?' It was hard to miss fifty feet of winding mahogany that curved through the far end of the room. 'See where the far end turns toward the stage?' I nodded. 'See him on the stool? If you decide to try for your pipes, he's the one you want to talk to. Name's Stanchion.'

We both turned away from the room at the same time. I shrugged my lute higher onto my shoulder. 'Thank you—' I paused, not knowing his name.

'Deoch.' He smiled again in his relaxed way.

A sudden impulse seized me, and I held out my hand. 'Deoch means "to drink". Will you let me buy you one later?'

He looked at me for a long second before he laughed. It was an unrestrained, happy sound that came leaping straight from his chest. He shook my hand warmly. 'I just might at that.'

Deoch released my hand, looking behind me. 'Simmon, did you bring us this one?'

'He brought me, actually.' Simmon seemed put out by my brief exchange with the doorman, but I couldn't guess why. 'I don't think anyone can really take him anywhere.' He handed a jot to Deoch.

'I'll believe that,' Deoch said. 'There's something about him I like. He's a little fae around the edges. I hope he plays for us tonight.'

'I hope so too,' I said, and we moved inside.

I looked around the Eolian as casually as I could manage. A raised circular stage thrust out from the wall opposite the curving mahogany bar. Several spiralling stairways lead to a second level that was much like a balcony. A smaller, third level was visible above that, more like a high mezzanine circling the room.

Stools and chairs ringed tables throughout around the room. Benches were recessed into niches in the walls. Sympathy lamps were mixed with candles, giving the room a natural light without fouling the air with smoke.

'Well that was cleverly done,' Simmon's voice was brittle. 'Merciful Tehlu, warn me before you try any more stunts, will you?'

'What?' I asked. 'The thing with the doorman? Simmon, you are jittery as a teenage whore. He was friendly. I liked him. What's the harm in offering him a drink?'

'Deoch owns this place,' Simmon said sharply. 'And he absolutely hates it when musicians suck up to him. Two span ago he threw someone out of here for trying to tip him.' He gave me a long look. 'Actually threw him. Almost far enough to make it into the fountain.'

'Oh,' I said, properly taken aback. I snuck a look at Deoch as he bantered with someone at the door. I saw the thick muscles in his arm tense and relax as he made a gesture outside. 'Did he seem upset to you?' I asked.

'No, he didn't. That's the damnedest thing.'

Wilem approached us. 'If the two of you will stop fishwiving and come to table, I will buy the first drinks, *lhin?*' We made our way to the table Wilem had picked out, not too far from where Stanchion sat at the bar. 'What do you want to drink?' Wilem asked as Simmon and I sat down and I settled my lutecase into the fourth chair.

'Cinnamon mead,' Simmon said without stopping to think.

'Girl,' Wilem said in a vaguely accusatory way and turned to me.

'Cider,' I said. 'Soft cider.'

'Two girls,' he said, and walked off to the bar.

I nodded toward Stanchion. 'What about him?' I asked Simmon. 'I thought he owned the place?'

'They both do. Stanchion handles the music end of it.'

'Is there anything I should know about him?' I asked, my near catastrophe with Deoch having sharpened my anxiety.

Simmon shook his head. 'I hear he's cheerful enough in his own right, but I've never talked with him. Don't do anything stupid and everything should be fine.'

'Thanks,' I said sarcastically as I pushed my chair back from the table and stood.

Stanchion had a medium build and was handsomely dressed in deep green and black. He had a round, bearded face and a slight paunch that was probably only noticeable because he was sitting. He smiled and motioned me forward with the hand that wasn't holding an impressively tall tankard.

'Ho there,' he said cheerily. 'You have the hopeful look about you. Are you here to play for us tonight?' He raised a speculative eyebrow. Now that I was closer, I noticed that Stanchion's hair was a deep, bashful red that hid if the light struck him the wrong way.

'I hope to, sir,' I said. 'Though I was planning to wait for a while.'

'Oh, certainly. We never let anyone try their talent until the sun is down.' He paused to take a drink, and as he turned his head I saw a golden set of pipes hanging from his ear.

Sighing, he wiped his mouth happily across the back of his sleeve. 'What do you play then, lute?' I nodded. 'Have any idea what you'll use to woo us?'

'That depends sir. Has anyone played "The Lay of Sir Savien Traliard" lately?'

Stanchion raised an eyebrow and cleared his throat. Smoothing his beard with his free hand, he said, 'Well, no. Someone gave it a whirl a few months ago, but he bit off more than he could swallow whole. Missed a couple fingerings then fell apart.' He shook his head. 'Simply said, no. Not lately.'

He took another drink from his tankard, and swallowed thoughtfully before he spoke again. 'Most people find that a song of more moderate difficulty allows them to showcase their talent,' he said carefully.

I sensed his unspoken advice and was not offended. 'Sir Savien' is the most difficult song I had ever heard. My father had been the only one in the troupe with the skill to perform it, and I had only heard him do it perhaps four or five times in front of an audience. It was only about fifteen minutes long, but those fifteen minutes required quick, precise fingering that, if done properly, would set two voices singing out of the lute at once, both a melody and a harmony.

That was tricky, but nothing any skilled lutist couldn't accomplish. However, 'Sir Savien' was a ballad, and the vocal part was a counter melody that ran against the timing of the lute. Difficult. If the song was being done properly, with both a man and a woman alternating the verses, the song was further complicated by the female's counter harmony in the refrains. If it is done well, it is enough to cut a heart. Unfortunately, few musicians could perform calmly in the center of such a storm of song.

Stanchion drank off another solid swallow from his tankard and wiped his beard on his sleeve. 'You singing alone?' he asked, seeming a bit excited in spite of his half-spoken warning. 'Or have you brought someone to sing opposite you? Is one of the boys you came in with a castrati?'

I fought down laughter at the thought of Wilem as a soprano and shook my head. 'I don't have any friends that can sing it. I was going to double the third refrain to give someone the chance to come in as Aloine.'

'Trouper style, eh?' He gave me a serious look. 'Son, it's really not my place to say this, but do you really want to try for your pipes with someone you've never even practiced with?'

It reassured me that he realised how hard it was going to be. 'How many pipes will be here tonight, roughly?'

He thought briefly. 'Roughly? Eight. Maybe a dozen.'

'So in all likelihood there will be at least three women who have earned their talents?'

Stanchion nodded, watching me curiously.

'Well,' I said slowly. 'If what everyone has told me is true, if only real excellence can win the pipes, then one of those women will know Aloine's part.'

Stanchion took another long, slow drink, watching me over the top of his tankard. When he finally set it down he forgot to wipe his beard. 'You're a proud one, aren't you?' he said frankly.

I looked around the room. 'Isn't this the Eolian? I had heard that this is where pride pays silver and plays golden.'

'I like that,' Stanchion said, almost to himself. 'Plays golden.' He slammed his tankard down onto the bar, causing a small geyser of something frothy to erupt from the top. 'Dammit boy, I hope you're as good as you seem to think you are. I could use someone else around here with Illien's fire.' He ran a hand through his own red hair to clarify his double meaning.

'I hope this place is as good as everyone seems to think it is,' I said earnestly. 'I need a place to burn.'

'He didn't throw you out,' Simmon quipped as I returned to the table. 'So I'm guessing it didn't go as badly as it could have.'

'I think it went well,' I said distractedly. 'But I'm not sure.'

'How can you not know?' Simmon objected. 'I saw him laugh. That must mean something good.'

'Not necessarily,' Wilem said.

'I'm trying to remember everything I said to him,' I admitted. 'Sometimes my mouth just starts talking and it takes my mind a little bit to catch up.'

'This happens often, does it?' asked Wilem with one of his rare, quiet smiles.

Their banter began to relax me. 'More and more often,' I confessed, grinning.

We drank and joked about small things, rumours of the masters and the rare female students who caught our attention. We talked about who we liked in the University, but more time was spent mulling over who we didn't like, and why, and what we would do about it given the chance. Such is human nature.

So time passed and the Eolian slowly filled. Simmon gave in to Wilem's taunting and began to drink scutten, a powerful black wine from the foothills of the Shalda mountains, more commonly called cut-tail.

Simmon showed the effects almost immediately, laughing louder, grinning wider, and fidgeting in his seat. Wilem remained his same taciturn self. I bought the next round of drinks, making it large mugs of straight cider for each of us. I responded to Wilem's scowl by telling him that if I made my talent tonight, I would float him home in cut-tail, but if either of them got drunk on me before then, I would personally thrash them and drop them in the river. They settled down an appreciable amount, and began inventing obscene verses to 'Tinker Tanner'.

I left them to it, retreating into my own thoughts. At the forefront of my mind was the fact that Stanchion's unspoken advice might be worth listening to. I tried to think of other songs I could perform that were difficult enough to show my skill, but easy enough to allow me room for artistry.

Simmon's voice drew me back to the here and now. 'C'mon, you're good at rhymes . . .' he urged me.

I replayed the last bit of their conversation that I'd been half listening to. 'Try "in the Tehlin's cassock",' I suggested disinterestedly. I was too nervous to bother explaining that one of my father's vices had been his propensity for dirty limericks.

They chortled delightedly to themselves while I tried to come up with a different song to sing. I hadn't had much luck when Wilem distracted me again.

'What!' I demanded angrily. Then I saw the flat look in Wilem's eyes that he only gets when he sees something he really doesn't like. 'What?' I repeated, more reasonably this time.

'Someone we all know and love,' he said darkly, nodding in the direction of the door.

I couldn't see anyone I recognised. The Eolian was nearly full, and over a hundred people milled about on the ground floor alone. I saw through the open door that night had settled outside.

'His back is to us. He's working his oily charm on a lovely young lady who must not know him . . . to the right of the round gentleman in red.' Wilem directed my attention.

'Son of a bitch,' I said, too stunned for proper profanity.

'I've always figured him for porcine parentage myself,' Wilem said dryly.

Simmon looked around, blinking owlishly. 'What? Who's here?'

'Ambrose.'

'God's balls,' Simmon said and hunched over the tabletop. 'That's all I need. Haven't you two made nice yet?'

'I'm willing to leave him be,' I protested. 'But every time he sees me he can't help but make another jab in my direction.'

'It takes two to argue,' Simmon said.

'Like hell,' I retorted. 'I don't care whose son he is. I won't go belly-up like some timid pup. If he's fool enough to take a poke at me, I'll snap the finger clean off that does the poking.' I took a breath to calm myself, and tried to sound rational. 'Eventually, he'll learn to leave me well enough alone.'

'You could just ignore him,' Simmon said, sounding surprisingly sober. 'Just don't rise to his baiting and he'll tire of it soon enough.'

'No,' I said seriously, looking Simmon in the eye. 'No, he won't.' I liked Simmon, but he was terribly innocent at times. 'Once he thinks I'm weak he'll be on me twice as thick as the day before. I know his type.'

'Here he comes,' Wilem observed, looking casually away.

Ambrose saw me before he made it to our side of the room. Our eyes met, and it was obvious that he hadn't expected to see me there. He said something to one of his ever-present group of bootlickers and they moved off through the crowd in a different direction to claim a table. His eyes moved from me, to Wilem, to Simmon, to my lute, and back to me. Then he turned and walked to the table his friends had claimed. He looked in my direction before he took his seat.

I found it unnerving that he didn't smile. He had always smiled at me before, an over-sad pantomime smile, with mockery in his eyes.

Then I saw something that unnerved me even more. He was carrying a sturdy squared case. 'Ambrose plays lyre?' I demanded of the world in general.

Wilem shrugged. Simmon looked uncomfortable. 'I thought you knew', he said weakly.

'You've seen him here before?' I asked. Sim nodded. 'Did he play?'

'Recited, actually. Poetry. He recited and kind of plucked at the lyre.' Simmon looked like a rabbit about to run.

'Does he have his talent?' I said darkly. I decided then that if Ambrose was a member of this group, I didn't want anything to do with it.

'No,' Simmon squeaked. 'He tried for it, but . . .' He trailed off, looking a little wild around the eyes.

Wilem lay a hand on my arm and made a calming gesture. I took a deep breath, closed my eyes, and tried to relax.

Slowly, I realised that none of this mattered. At most, it simply raised the stakes for tonight. Ambrose wouldn't be able to do anything to disrupt my playing. He would be forced to watch and listen. Listen to me playing 'The

Lay of Sir Savien Traliard', because now there was no question as to what I would be performing tonight.

———————

The evening's entertainment was led by one of the talented musicians from the crowd. He had a lute and showed that he could play it as well as any Edema Ruh. His second song was even better, one that I'd never heard before.

There was a gap of about ten minutes before another talented musician was called onto the stage to sing. This man had a set of reed pipes and played them better than anyone I had ever heard. He followed by singing a haunting eulogy in a minor key. No instrument, just his high clear voice that rose and flowed like the pipes he had played before.

I was pleased to find the skill of the talented musicians to be everything it was rumored to be. But my anxiety increased a proportionate amount. Excellence is excellence's only companion. Had I not already decided to play 'The Lay of Sir Savien Traliard' for purely spiteful reasons, these performances would have convinced me.

There followed another period of five or ten minutes. I realised that Stanchion was deliberately spacing things out to give the audience a chance to move about and make noise between the songs. The man knew his business. I wondered if he had ever been a trouper.

Then we had our first trial of the night. A bearded man of thirty years or so was brought onto the stage by Stanchion and introduced to the audience. He played flute. Played it well. He played two shorter songs that I knew and a third I didn't. He played for perhaps twenty minutes in all, only making one small mistake that I could hear.

After the applause, the flutist remained on stage while Stanchion circulated in the crowd, gathering opinions. A serving boy brought the flutist a glass of water.

Eventually Stanchion came back onto the stage. The room was quiet as the owner drew close and solemnly shook the man's hand. The musician's expression fell, but he managed a sickly smile and a nod to the audience. Stanchion escorted him off the stage and bought something that came in a tall tankard.

The next to try her talent was a young woman, richly dressed with golden hair. After Stanchion introduced her, she sang an aria in a voice so clear and pure that I forgot my anxiety for a while and was ensnared by her song. For a few blessed moments I forgot myself and could do nothing but listen.

Too soon it was over, leaving me with a tender feeling in my chest and a vague prickling in my eyes. Simmon sniffled a little and rubbed self-consciously at his face.

Then she sang a second song while accompanying herself on a half-harp. I watched her intently, and I will admit that it was not entirely for her musical ability. She had hair like ripe wheat. I could see the clear blue of her eyes from where I sat some thirty feet away. She had smooth arms and small delicate hands that were quick against the strings. And the way she held the harp between her legs made me think of . . . well, the things that every boy of fifteen thinks about incessantly.

Her voice was as lovely as before, enough to set a heart aching. Unfortunately, her playing could not match it. She struck wrong notes halfway through her second song, faltered, then recovered before she made it to the end of her performance.

There was a longer pause as Stanchion circulated this time. He milled through the three levels of the Eolian, talking with everyone, young and old, musician and not.

As I watched, Ambrose caught the eye of the woman on stage and gave her one of his smiles that seem so greasy to me and so charming to women. Then, looking away from her, his gaze wandered to my table and our eyes met. His smile faded, and for a long moment we simply watched each other, expressionless. Neither of us smiled mockingly, or mouthed small insulting nothings to the other. Nevertheless, all our smoldering enmity was renewed in those few minutes. I cannot say with certainty which of us looked away first.

After nearly fifteen minutes of gathering opinions, Stanchion mounted the stage again. He approached the golden-haired woman and took her hand as he had the previous musician's. The woman's face fell in much the same way his had. Stanchion led her from the stage and bought her what I guessed was the consolation tankard.

Closely on the heels of this failure was another talented musician who played fiddle, excellent as the two before him. Then an older man was brought onto stage by Stanchion as if he were trying for his talent. However the applause that greeted him seemed to imply that he was as popular as any of the talented musicians who had played before him.

I nudged Simmon. 'Who's this?' I asked, as the grey-bearded man tuned his lyre.

'Threpe,' Simmon whispered back at me. '*Count* Threpe, actually. He plays here all the time, has for years. Great patron of the arts. He stopped trying for his pipes years ago. Now he just plays. Everyone loves him.'

Threpe began to play and I could see immediately why he had never earned his pipes. His voice cracked and wavered as he plucked his lyre. His rhythm varied erratically and it was hard to tell if he struck a wrong note. The song was obviously of his own devising, a rather candid revelation about the personal habits of a local nobleman. But in spite of its lack of classic artistic merit, I found myself laughing along with the rest of the crowd.

When he was done everyone applauded thunderously, some people pounding on the tables or stamping as well. Stanchion went directly onto the stage and shook the count's hand, but Threpe didn't seem disappointed in the least. Stanchion pounded him enthusiastically on the back as he led him down to the bar.

It was time. I stood and gathered up my lute.

Wilem clapped my arm and Simmon grinned at me, trying not to look almost sick with friendly worry. I nodded silently to each of them as I walked over to Stanchion's vacant seat at the end of the bar where it curved toward the stage.

I fingered the silver talent in my pocket, thick and heavy. Some irrational part of me wanted to clutch it, hoard it for later. But I knew that in a few more days a single talent wouldn't do me a bit of good. With a set of talent pipes I could support myself playing at local inns. If I was lucky enough to attract the attention of a patron, I could earn enough to square my debt to Devi and pay my tuition as well. It was a gamble I had to take.

Stanchion came ambling back to his spot at the bar.

'I'll go next, sir. If it's all right with you.' I hoped I didn't look as nervous as I felt. My grip on the lute case was slippery from my sweating palms.

He smiled at me and nodded. 'You've got a good eye for a crowd, boy. This one's ripe for a sad song. Still planning on doing "Savien"?'

I nodded.

He sat down and took a drink. 'Well then, let's just give them a couple minutes to simmer and get their talking over with.'

I nodded and leaned against the bar. I took the time to fret uselessly about things I had no control over. One of the pegs on my lute was loose and I didn't have the money to fix it. There had not been any talented women on stage yet. I felt a twinge of unease at the thought of this being the odd night where the only talented musicians at the Eolian were men, or women who didn't know Aloine's part.

It seemed only a short time before Stanchion stood and raised a questioning eyebrow at me. I nodded and picked up my lute case. It suddenly looked terribly shabby to me. Together we walked up the stairs.

As soon as my foot touched the stage the room hushed to a murmur. At the same time, my nervousness left me, burned away by the attention of the crowd. It has always been that way with me. Offstage I worry and sweat. Onstage I am calm as a windless winter night.

Stanchion bade everyone consider me as a candidate for my talent. His words had a soothing, ritual feel. When he gestured to me, there was no familiar applause, only an expectant silence. In a flash, I saw myself as the audience must see me. Not finely dressed as the others had been, in fact only one step from being ragged. Young, almost a child. I could feel their curiosity drawing them closer to me.

I let it build, taking my time as I unclasped my battered secondhand lute case and removed my battered secondhand lute. I felt their attention sharpen at the homely sight of it. I struck a few quiet chords, then touched the pegs, tuning it ever so slightly. I fingered a few more light chords, testing, listened, and nodded to myself.

The lights shining onto the stage made the rest of the room dim from where I sat. Looking out I saw what seemed to be a thousand eyes. Simmon and Wilem, Stanchion by the bar. Deoch by the door. I felt a vague flutter in my stomach as I saw Ambrose watching me with all the menace of a smoldering coal.

I looked away from him to see a bearded man in red, Count Threpe, an old couple holding hands, a lovely dark-eyed girl . . .

My audience. I smiled at them. The smile drew them closer still, and I sang.

> 'Still! Sit! For though you listen long
> Long would you wait without the hope of song
> So sweet as this. As Illien himself set down
> An age ago. Master work of a master's life
> Of Savien, and Aloine the woman he would take to wife.'

I let the wave of whisper pass through the crowd. Those who knew the song made soft exclamation to themselves, while those who didn't asked their neighbours what the stir was about.

I raised my hands to the strings and drew their attention back to me. The room stilled, and I began to play.

The music came easily out of me, my lute like a second voice. I flicked my fingers and the lute made a third voice as well. I sang in the proud powerful tones of Savien Traliard, greatest of the Amyr. The audience moved under the music like grass against the wind. I sang as Sir Savien, and I felt the audience begin to love and fear me.

I was so used to practicing the song alone that I almost forgot to double the third refrain. But I remembered at the last moment in a flash of cold sweat. This time as I sang it I looked out into the audience, hoping at the end I would hear a voice answering my own.

I reached the end of the refrain before Aloine's first stanza. I struck the first chord hard and waited as the sound of it began to fade without drawing a voice from the audience. I looked calmly out to them, waiting. Every second a greater relief vied with a greater disappointment inside me.

Then a voice drifted onto stage, gentle as a brushing feather, singing . . .

> 'Savien, how could you know
> It was the time for you to come to me?
> Savien, do you remember
> The days we squandered pleasantly?
> How well then have you carried what
> Have tarried in my heart and memory?'

She sang as Aloine, I as Savien. On the refrains her voice spun, twinning and mixing with my own. Part of me wanted to search the audience for her, to find the face of the woman I was singing with. I tried, once, but my fingers faltered as I searched for the face that could fit with the cool moonlight voice that answered mine. Distracted, I touched a wrong note and there was a burr in the music.

A small mistake. I set my teeth and concentrated on my playing. I pushed my curiosity aside and bowed my head to watch my fingers, careful to keep them from slipping on the strings.

And we sang! Her voice like burning silver, my voice an echoing answer. Savien sang solid, powerful lines, like branches of a rock-old oak, all the while Aloine was like a nightingale, moving in darting circles around the proud limbs of it.

I was only dimly aware of the audience now, dimly aware of the sweat on my body. I was so deeply in the music that I couldn't have told you where it stopped and my blood began.

But it did stop. Two verses from the end of the song, the end came. I struck the beginning chord of Savien's verse and I heard a piercing sound that pulled me out of the music like a fish dragged from deep water.

A string broke. High on the neck of the lute it snapped and the tension lashed it across the back of my hand, drawing a thin, bright line of blood.

I stared at it numbly. It should not have broken. None of my strings were worn badly enough to break. But it had, and as the last notes of the music faded into silence I felt the audience begin to stir. They began to rouse themselves from the waking dream that I had woven for them out of strands of song.

In the silence I felt it all unravelling, the audience waking with the dream unfinished, all my work ruined, wasted. And all the while burning inside me was the song, the song. The song!

Without knowing what I did, I set my fingers back to the strings and fell deep into myself. Into years before, when my hands had calluses like stones and my music had come as easy as breathing. Back to the time I had played to make the sound of Wind Turning a Leaf on a lute with six strings.

And I began to play. Slowly, then with greater speed as my hands remembered. I gathered the fraying strands of song and wove them carefully back to what they had been a moment earlier.

It was not perfect. No song as complex as 'Sir Savien' can be played perfectly on six strings instead of seven. But it was whole, and as I played the audience sighed, stirred, and slowly fell back under the spell that I had made for them.

I hardly knew they were there, and after a minute I forgot them entirely. My hands danced, then ran, then blurred across the strings as I fought to keep the lute's two voices singing with my own. Then, even as I watched them, I forgot them, I forgot everything except finishing the song.

The refrain came, and Aloine sang again. To me she was not a person, or even a voice, she was just a part of the song that was burning out of me.

And then it was done. Raising my head to look at the room was like breaking the surface of the water for air. I came back into myself, found my hand bleeding and my body covered in sweat. Then the ending of the song struck me like a fist in my chest, as it always does, no matter where or when I listen to it.

I buried my face in my hands and wept. Not for a broken lute string and the chance of failure. Not for blood shed and a wounded hand. I did not even cry for the boy who had learned to play a lute with six strings in the forest years ago. I cried for Sir Savien and Aloine, for love lost and found and lost again, at cruel fate and man's folly. And so, for a while, I was lost in grief and knew nothing.

CHAPTER FIFTY-FIVE

Flame and Thunder

I HELD ALL OF my mourning for Savien and Aloine to a few moments. Knowing I was still on display, I gathered myself and straightened in my chair to look out at my audience. My silent audience.

Music sounds different to the one who plays it. It is the musician's curse. Even as I sat, the ending I had improvised was fading from my memory. Then came doubt. What if it hadn't been as whole as it had seemed? What if my ending hadn't carried the terrible tragedy of the song to anyone but myself? What if my tears seemed to be nothing more than a child's embarrassing reaction to his own failure?

Then, waiting, I heard the silence pouring from them. The audience held themselves quiet, tense, and tight, as if the song had burned them worse than flame. Each person held their wounded selves closely, clutching their pain as if it were a precious thing.

Then there was a murmur of sobs released and sobs escaping. A sigh of tears. A whisper of bodies slowly becoming no longer still.

Then the applause. A roar like leaping flame, like thunder after lightning.

CHAPTER FIFTY-SIX

Patrons, Maids and Metheglin

I RESTRUNG MY LUTE. It was a fair distraction while Stanchion gathered opinions from the crowd. My hands went through the routine motions of stripping the broken string away while I fretted to myself. Now that the applause had died, my doubts had come to plague me again. Was one song enough to prove my skill? What if the audience's reaction had been due to the power of the song, rather than my playing of it? What of my improvised ending? Perhaps the song had only seemed whole to me . . .

As I finished removing the broken string I gave it an idle look and all my thoughts fell to a jumble at my feet.

It wasn't worn or flawed as I had thought it would be. The broken end was clean, as if it had been cut with a knife or snipped with a pair of scissors.

For a while I simply stared at it dumbly. My lute had been tampered with? Impossible. It was never out of my sight. Besides, I had checked the strings before I left the University, and again before I had come on stage. Then how?

I was running the thought in circles in my head when I noticed the crowd quieting. I looked up in time to see Stanchion take the last step onto the stage. I hurriedly got to my feet to face him.

His expression was pleasant but otherwise unreadable. My stomach tied a knot as he walked toward me, then it fell as he held out his hand the same way he had held it out for the other two musicians who had been found wanting.

I forced my best smile onto my face and reached to take his hand. I was my father's son and a trouper. I would take my refusal with the high dignity of the Edema Ruh. The earth would crack and swallow this glittering, self-important place before I would show a trace of despair.

And somewhere in the watching audience was Ambrose. The earth would have to swallow the Eolian, Imre, and the whole Centhe Sea before I gave him a grain of satisfaction over this.

So I smiled brightly and took Stanchion's hand in my own. As I shook it, something hard pressed into my palm. Looking down I saw a glimmer of silver. My talent pipes.

My expression must have been a delight to watch. I looked back up at Stanchion. His eyes danced and he winked at me.

I turned and held my pipes aloft for everyone to see. The Eolian roared again. This time it roared a welcome.

'You'll have to promise me,' a red-eyed Simmon said seriously, 'That you will never play that song again without warning me first. Ever.'

'Was it that bad?' I smiled giddily at him.

'No!' Simmon almost cried out. 'It's . . . I've never—' He struggled, wordless for a moment, then bowed his head and began to cry hopelessly into his hands.

Wilem put a protective arm around Simmon, who leaned unashamedly against his shoulder. 'Our Simmon has a tender heart,' he said gently. 'I imagine he meant to say that he liked it very much.'

I noticed that Wilem's eyes were red around the edges too. I lay a hand on Simmon's back. 'It hit me hard the first time I heard it too.' I told him honestly. 'My parents performed it during the Midwinter Pageantry when I was nine, and I was a wreck for two hours afterward. They had to cut my part from *The Swineherd and the Nightingale* because I wasn't in any shape to act.'

Simmon nodded and made a gesture that seemed to imply that he was fine but that he didn't expect to be able to talk any time soon and that I should just carry along with whatever it was I was doing.

I looked back at Wilem. 'I forgot that it hits some people this way,' I said lamely.

'I recommend scutten,' Wilem said bluntly. 'Cut-tail, if you insist on the vulgar. But I seem to remember you saying that you would float us home tonight if you got your pipes. Which may be unfortunate, as I happen to be wearing my lead drinking shoes.'

I heard Stanchion chuckle behind me. 'These must be the two non-castrati friends, eh?' Simmon was surprised enough at being called a non-castrati to collect himself slightly, rubbing his nose on his sleeve.

'Wilem, Simmon, this is Stanchion.' Simmon nodded. Wilem gave a slight, stiff bow. 'Stanchion, could you help us to the bar? I've promised to buy them a drink.'

'S,' Wilem said. 'Drinks.'

'Sorry, drink*s*,' I stressed the plural. 'I wouldn't be here if it wasn't for them.'

'Ah,' Stanchion said with a grin. 'Patrons, I understand completely!'

The victory tankard turned out to be the same as the consolation one. It was ready for me when Stanchion finally managed to get us through the throng of people to our new seats at the bar. He even insisted on buying scutten for Simmon and Wilem, saying that patrons have some claim to the spoils of victory as well. I thanked him earnestly from the bottom of my rapidly thinning purse.

While we were waiting for their drinks to come, I tried to peer curiously into my tankard, and found that doing so while it was sitting on the bar would require me to stand on my stool.

'Metheglin,' Stanchion informed me. 'Try it and you can thank me later. Where I'm from, they say a man will come back from the dead to get a drink of it.'

I tipped an imaginary hat to him. 'At your service.'

'Yours and your family's,' he replied politely.

I took a drink from the tall tankard to give myself a chance to collect my wits, and something wonderful happened in my mouth: cool spring honey, clove, cardamom, cinnamon, pressed grape, burnt apple, sweet pear, and clear well water. That is all I have to say of metheglin. If you haven't tried it, then I am sorry I cannot describe it properly. If you have, you don't need me to remind you what it is like.

I was relieved to see the cut-tail had come in moderately sized glasses, with one for Stanchion too. If my friends had received tankards of the black wine, I would have needed a wheelbarrow to get them back to the other side of the river.

'To Savien!' Wilem toasted.

'Hear hear!' Stanchion said, lifting his own glass.

'Savien . . .' Simmon managed, his voice sounding like a stifled sob.

'. . . and Aloine,' I said, and maneuvered my great tankard to touch glasses with them.

Stanchion drank off his Scutten with a nonchalance that made my eyes water. 'So,' he said, 'Before I leave you to the adulation of your peers, I have to ask. Where did you learn to do that? Play missing a string, I mean.'

I thought for a moment. 'Do you want the short or the long of it?'

'I'll take the short for now.'

I smiled. 'Well in that case, it's just something I picked up.' I made a casual gesture as if tossing something away. 'A remnant of my misspent youth.'

Stanchion gave me a long look, his expression amused. 'I suppose I deserve that. I'll take the long version next time.' He took a deep breath and looked around the room, his golden earring swung and caught the light. 'I'm off to mix the crowd. I'll keep them from coming at you all at once.'

I grinned relief. 'Thank you, sir.'

He shook his head and made a preemptory motion to someone behind the bar who quickly fetched him his tankard. 'Earlier tonight "sir" was proper and good. But now it's Stanchion.' He glanced back in my direction, and I smiled and nodded. 'And I should call you?'

'Kvothe,' I said, 'just Kvothe.'

'Just Kvothe,' Wilem toasted behind me.

'And Aloine,' Simmon added, and began to cry softly into the crook of his arm.

Count Threpe was one of the first to come to me. He looked shorter up close, and older. But he was bright-eyed and laughing as he talked about my song.

'Then it broke!' he said, gesturing wildly. 'And all I could think was, *Not now! Not before the ending!* But I saw the blood on your hand and my stomach knotted up. You looked up at us, then down at the strings, and it got quieter and quieter. Then you put your hands back on the lute and all I could think was, *There's a brave boy. Too brave. He doesn't know he can't save the end of a broken song with a broken lute.* But you did!' He laughed as if I'd played a joke on the world, and danced a quick jig step.

Simmon, who had stopped crying and was on his way to becoming well-buttered, laughed along with the count. Wilem didn't seem to know what to make of the man, and watched him with serious eyes.

'You must play at my house some day,' Threpe said, then quickly held up a hand. 'We won't talk of that now, and I won't take up any more of your evening.' He smiled. 'But before I go, I need to ask you one last question. How many years did Savien spend with the Amyr?'

I didn't have to think about it. 'Six. Three years proving himself, three years training.'

'Does six strike you as a good number?'

I didn't know what he was getting at. 'Six isn't exactly a lucky number,' I hedged. 'If I were looking for a good number I'd have to go up to seven.' I shrugged. 'Or down to three.'

Threpe considered this, tapping his chin. 'You're right. But six years with the Amyr means he came back to Aloine on the seventh year.' He dug into a pocket and brought out a handful of coins of at least three different currencies. He sorted seven talents out of the mess and pushed them into my surprised hand.

'My lord,' I stammered. 'I cannot take your money.' It wasn't the money itself that surprised me, but the amount.

Threpe looked confused. 'Whyever not?'

I gaped a little bit, and for a rare moment I was at a loss for words.

Threpe chuckled and closed my hand around the coins. 'It's not a reward for playing. Well, it *is* that, but it's more an incentive for you to keep practicing, keep getting better. It's for the sake of the music.'

He shrugged. 'You see, a laurel needs rain to grow. I can't do much about that. But I can keep that rain off a few musician's heads, can't I?' A sly smile wound its way onto his face. 'So God will tend the laurels and keep them wet. And I will tend the players and keep them dry. And wiser minds than mine will decide when to bring the two together.'

I was silent for a moment. 'I think you might be wiser than you give yourself credit for.'

'Well,' he said, trying not to look pleased. 'Well don't let it get around or people will start expecting great things from me.' He turned and was quickly swallowed by the crowd.

I slid the seven talents into my pocket and felt a great weight lift from my shoulders. It was like a stay of execution. Perhaps literally, as I had no idea how Devi might have encouraged me to pay my debt. I drew my first carefree breath in two months. It felt good.

After Threpe left, one of the talented musicians came to offer his compliments. After him it was a Cealdish moneylender who shook my hand and offered to buy me a drink.

Then there was a minor nobleman, another musician, and a pretty young lady that I thought might be my Aloine until I heard her voice. She was the daughter of a local moneylender, and we talked of small things, briefly, before she moved on. I remembered my manners almost too late and kissed her hand before she left.

They all blurred together after a while. One by one they came to give me their regards, compliments, handshakes, advice, envy, and admiration. Though Stanchion was true to his word and managed to keep them all from coming at me in a mass, it wasn't long before I began having trouble telling one from another. The metheglin wasn't helping matters either.

I'm not sure how long it was before I thought to look for Ambrose. After scanning the room, I nudged Simmon with an elbow until he looked up from the game he and Wilem were playing with shims. 'Where's our best friend?' I asked.

Simmon gave me a blank look and I realised that he was too far into his cups to catch sarcasm. 'Ambrose,' I clarified. 'Where's Ambrose?'

'Scoffered off,' Wilem announced with an edge of bellicosity. 'As soon as you finished playing. Before you'd even got your pipes.'

'He knew. He knew,' Simmon singsonged delightedly. 'He knew you would get them and couldn't bear to watch.'

'Looked bad when he left,' Wilem said with a quiet malice. 'Pale and shaking. Like he'd found out someone'd been lanting in his drinks all night.'

'Maybe someone was,' Simmon said with uncharacteristic viciousness. '*I* would.'

'Shaking?' I asked.

Wilem nodded. 'Trembling. Like someone'd gut-punched him. Linten was giving him an arm to lean on when he left.'

The symptoms sounded familiar, like binder's chills. A suspicion began to form. I pictured Ambrose, listening to me glide through the most beautiful song he'd ever heard, and realising I'm about to win my pipes.

He wouldn't do anything obvious, but perhaps he could find a loose thread, or a long splinter from the table. Either one would provide only the most tenuous sympathetic link to my lute string: one per cent at best, perhaps only a tenth of that.

I imagined Ambrose drawing on his own body's heat, concentrating as the chill slowly worked into his arms and legs. I pictured him, trembling, his breath growing laboured, until finally the string breaks . . .

. . . And I finish the song in spite of him. I grinned at the thought. Pure speculation of course, but something had certainly broken my lute string, and I didn't doubt for a second that Ambrose would try something of the sort. I focused back in on Simmon.

'. . . it up to him and say, *No hard feelings about that time in the Crucible when you mixed my salts and I was nearly blind for a day. No. No really, drink up!* Ha!' Simmon laughed, lost in his own vengeful fantasy.

The flood of well-wishers slowed somewhat: a fellow lutist, the talented piper I'd seen on stage, a local merchant. A heavily perfumed gentleman with long, oiled hair and a Vintic accent clapped me on the back and gave me a purse of money, 'for new strings.' I didn't like him. I kept the purse.

———

'Why does everyone keep going on about that?' Wilem asked me.

'About what?'

'Half the people that come over to shake your hand bubble over about how beautiful the song was. The other half hardly mention the song at all, and all they talk about is how you played with a broken string. It's like they didn't hardly hear the song at all.'

'The first half don't know anything about music,' Simmon said. 'Only people who take their music seriously can really appreciate what our little E'lir here did tonight.'

Wilem grunted thoughtfully. 'It's hard then, what you did?'

'I've never seen anyone play "Squirrel in the Thatch" without a full set of strings,' Simmon told him.

'Well,' he said. 'You made it look easy. Since you have come to your sense in pushing aside that Yllish fruit drink, will you let me buy you a round of fine dark scutten, drink of the kings of Cealdim?'

I know a compliment when I hear it, but I was reluctant to accept as I was just beginning to feel clear-headed again.

Luckily, I was saved from having to make an excuse by Marea coming to pay her respects. She was the lovely, golden-haired harper who had tried for her talent and failed. I thought for a moment that she might be the voice of my Aloine, but after a moment's listening to her, I realised it couldn't be.

She was pretty though. Even prettier than she had seemed on stage, as is not always the case. Talking, I found she was the daughter of one of Imre's councilmen. Against the tumble of her deep golden hair, the soft blue of her gown was a reflection of the deep blue of her eyes.

Lovely as she was, I couldn't give her the concentration she deserved. I itched to be away from the bar to find the voice that had sung Aloine with me. We talked a while, smiled, and parted with kind words and promises to speak again. She disappeared back into the crowd, a wonderful collection of gently moving curves.

'What was that shameful display?' Wilem demanded after she had gone.

'What?' I asked.

'*What?*' he mocked my tone. 'Can you even pretend to be that thick? If a girl as fair as that looked at me with one eye the way she looked at you with two . . . We'd have a room by now, to say it carefully.'

'She was friendly,' I protested. 'And we were talking. She asked me if I would show her some harp fingerings, but it's been a long time since I played harp.'

'It'll be a lot longer if you keep missing passes like that,' Wilem said frankly. 'She was doing everything but taking down another button for you.'

Sim leaned over and lay his hand on my shoulder, the very picture of the concerned friend. 'Kvothe, I've been meaning to talk to you about this very problem. If you honestly couldn't tell that she was interested in you, you might want to admit the possibility that you are impossibly thick when it comes to women. You may want to consider the priesthood.'

'The both of you are drunk,' I said to cover my flush. 'Did you happen to notice from our conversation that she is a councilman's daughter?'

'Did you notice,' Wil replied in the same tone, 'how she looked at you?'

I knew I was woefully inexperienced with women, but I didn't have to admit to it. So I waved his comment away and got down off my stool. 'Somehow I doubt that a quick romp behind the bar was what she had in mind.' I took a drink of water and straightened my cloak. 'Now, I must go find my Aloine and offer her my earnest thanks. How do I look?'

'What does it matter?' Wilem asked.

Simmon touched Wilem's elbow. 'Don't you see? He's after more dangerous game than some low-bodiced councilman's daughter.'

I turned from them with a disgusted gesture and headed off into the crowded room.

I didn't really have any idea how I would find her. Some foolish, romantic part of me thought I would know her when I saw her. If she were half as radiant as her voice, she would shine like a candle in a dark room.

But as I thought these things, the wiser part of me was whispering in my other ear. *Do not hope,* it said. *Do not dare hold hope that any woman could burn as brightly as the voice that sang the part of Aloine.* And while this voice was not comforting, I knew it to be wise. I had learned to listen to it on the streets of Tarbean, where it had kept me alive.

I wandered through the first level of the Eolian, searching without knowing who I was looking for. Occasionally people would smile or wave. After five minutes I had seen all the faces there were to see and moved to the second level.

This was actually a converted balcony, but instead of tiers of seats, there were rising ranks of tables that looked onto the lower level. As I wended my way through the tables looking for my Aloine, my wiser half kept murmuring in my ear. *Do not hope. All you will earn is disappointment. She will not be as beautiful as you imagine, and then you will despair.*

As I finished searching the second level a new fear began to rise in me. She might have left while I was sitting at the bar, drinking in metheglin and praise. I should have gone to her straightaway, fallen to one knee, and thanked her with my whole heart. What if she was gone? What if no one knew who she was or where she had gone? A nervousness settled into the pit of my stomach as I took the stairs to the highest level of the Eolian.

Now look what your hope has brought you, the voice said. *She is gone and all you have is a bright, foolish imagining to torment yourself with.*

The last level was the smallest of the three, hardly more than a thin crescent that hugged three walls, high above the stage. Here, the tables and benches were more widely spaced and sparsely populated. I noticed that the inhabitants of this level were mostly couples and I felt something of a voyeur as I passed from table to table.

Trying to appear casual, I looked at the faces of those who sat talking and drinking. I grew more nervous the closer I came to the last table. It was impossible for me to do so casually, as it was in a corner. The couple sitting there, one light haired and one dark, had their backs to me.

As I approached, the light-haired one laughed and I caught a glimpse of a proud, fine-featured face. A man. I turned my attention to the woman with the long dark hair. My last hope. I knew she would be my Aloine.

Coming round the corner of the table I saw her face. Or rather, his face. They were both men. My Aloine had left. I had lost her, and with that knowledge I felt as if my heart had been tipped from its resting place in my chest to topple and fall somewhere deep inside me near my feet.

They looked up, and the fair-haired one smiled at me. 'Look Thria, young six-string has come to offer us his respects.' He eyed me up and down. 'You're a fair one. Would you like to join us for a drink?'

'No,' I murmured, embarrassed. 'I was just looking for someone.'

'Well you found someone,' he said easily, touching my arm. 'My name is

Fallon and this is Thria. Come and have a drink. I promise to keep Thria here from trying to take you home. He has a terrible weakness for musicians.' He smiled charmingly at me.

I murmured an excuse and took my leave, too distraught to worry whether or not I had made an ass of myself.

As I made my desolate way back to the stairs, my wise self took the opportunity to berate me. *That is what comes of hope*, it said. *No good. Still, you are better having missed her. She could never have been equal to her voice. That voice, fair and terrible as burning silver, like moonlight on river stones, like a feather against your lips.*

I headed to the stairs, eyes on the floor lest anyone try to catch me in a conversation.

Then I heard a voice, a voice like burning silver, like a kiss against my ears. Looking up, my heart lifted and I knew it was my Aloine. Looking up, I saw her and all I could think was, beautiful.

Beautiful.

CHAPTER FIFTY-SEVEN

Interlude – The Parts that Form Us

MOVING SLOWLY, Bast stretched and looked around the room. Finally the short fuse of his patience burned out. 'Reshi?'

'Hmmm?' Kvothe looked at him.

'And then what, Reshi? Did you talk to her?'

'Of course I talked to her. There would be no story if I hadn't. Telling that part is easy. But first I must describe her. I'm not sure how to do it.'

Bast fidgeted.

Kvothe laughed, a fond expression wiping the irritation from his face. 'So is describing a beautiful woman as easy as looking at one for you?'

Bast looked down and blushed, and Kvothe laid a gentle hand on his arm, smiling. 'My trouble, Bast, is that she is very important. Important to the story. I cannot think of how to describe her without falling short of the mark.'

'I . . . I think I understand, Reshi,' Bast said in conciliatory tones. 'I've seen her too. Once.'

Kvothe sat back in his chair, surprised. 'You have, haven't you? I'd forgotten.' He pressed his hands to his lips. 'How would you describe her then?'

Bast brightened at the opportunity. Straightening up in his chair he looked thoughtful for a moment then said. 'She had perfect ears.' He made a delicate gesture with his hands. 'Perfect little ears, like they were carved out of . . . something.'

Chronicler laughed, then looked slightly taken aback, as if he'd surprised himself. 'Her ears?' he asked as if he couldn't be sure if he had heard correctly.

'You know how hard it is to find a pretty girl with the right sort of ears,' Bast said matter-of-factly.

Chronicler laughed again, seeming to find it easier the second time. 'No,' he said. 'No, I'm sure I don't.'

Bast gave the story collector a deeply pitying look. 'Well then, you'll just have to take my word for it. They were exceptionally fine.'

'I think you've struck that chord well enough, Bast,' Kvothe said, amused. He paused for a moment, and when he spoke again it was slowly, his eyes far away. 'The trouble is, she is unlike anyone I have ever known. There was something intangible about her. Something compelling, like heat from a fire. She had a grace, a spark—'

'She had a crooked nose, Reshi,' Bast said, interrupting his master's reverie.

Kvothe looked at him, a line of irritation creasing his forehead. 'What?'

Bast held his hands up defensively. 'It's just something I noticed, Reshi. All the women in your story are beautiful. I can't gainsay you as a whole, as I've never seen any of them. But this one I did see. Her nose was a little crooked. And if we're being honest here, her face was a little narrow for my taste. She wasn't a perfect beauty by any means, Reshi. I should know. I've made some study of these things.'

Kvothe stared at his student for a long moment, his expression solemn. 'We are more than the parts that form us, Bast,' he said with a hint of reproach.

'I'm not saying she wasn't lovely, Reshi,' Bast said quickly. 'She smiled at me. It was . . . it had a sort of . . . it went right down into you, if you understand me.'

'I understand, Bast. But then again, I've met her.' Kvothe looked at Chronicler. 'The trouble comes from comparison, you see. If I say "she was dark haired", you might think, "I've known dark-haired women, some of them lovely". But you would be far off the mark, because that woman would not really have anything in common with her. That other woman wouldn't have her quick wit, her easy charm. She was unlike anyone I have ever met . . .'

Kvothe trailed off, looking down at folded hands. He was quiet for such a long moment that Bast began to fidget, looking around anxiously.

'There's no sense worrying, I suppose,' Kvothe said at last, looking up and motioning to Chronicler. 'If I ruin this as well, it will be a small thing as far as the world is concerned.'

Chronicler picked up his pen, and Kvothe began to speak before he had the chance to dip it. 'Her eyes were dark. Dark as chocolate, dark as coffee, dark as the polished wood of my father's lute. They were set in a fair face, oval. Like a teardrop.'

Kvothe stopped suddenly, as if he had run himself out of words. The silence was so sudden and deep that Chronicler glanced briefly up from his page, something he had not done before. But even as Chronicler looked up, another flood of words burst out of Kvothe.

'Her easy smile could stop a man's heart. Her lips were red. Not the garish painted red so many women believe makes them desirable. Her lips were always red, morning and night. As if minutes before you saw her, she had been eating sweet berries, or drinking heart's blood.

'No matter where she stood, she was in the center of the room.' Kvothe frowned. 'Do not misunderstand. She was not loud, or vain. We stare at a fire because it flickers, because it glows. The light is what catches our eyes, but what makes a man lean close to a fire has nothing to do with its bright shape. What draws you to a fire is the warmth you feel when you come near. The same was true of Denna.'

As Kvothe spoke, his expression twisted, as if each word he spoke rankled him more and more. And while the words were clear, they matched his expression, as if each one was rasped with a rough file before it left his mouth.

'She . . .' Kvothe's head was bowed so low he seemed to be speaking to his hands laying in his lap. 'What am I doing?' He said faintly, as if his mouth was full of grey ash. 'What good can come of this? How can I make any sense of her for you when I have never understood the least piece of her myself?'

Chronicler had written most of this out before he realised that Kvothe had probably not intended him to. He froze for a bare moment, then finished scratching down the rest of the sentence. Then he waited a long, quiet moment, before he stole a look upward at Kvothe.

Kvothe's eyes caught and held him. They were the same dark eyes that Chronicler had seen before. Eyes like an angry God's. For a moment it was all Chronicler could do to not draw back from the table. There was an icy silence.

Kvothe stood and pointed at the paper that lay in front of Chronicler. 'Cross that out,' he grated.

Chronicler blanched, his expression as stricken as if he'd been stabbed.

When he made no move, Kvothe reached down and calmly slid the half-written sheet from under Chronicler's pen. 'If crossing out is something you feel disinclined towards . . .' Kvothe tore the half-written sheet with slow care, the sound bleeding the colour from Chronicler's face.

With terrible deliberateness Kvothe lifted a blank sheet and lay it carefully in front of the stunned scribe. One long finger stabbed at the torn sheet, smearing the still-wet ink. 'Copy to here,' he said in a voice that was cold and motionless as iron. The iron was in his eyes too, hard and dark.

There was no arguing. Chronicler quietly copied to where Kvothe's finger pinned the paper to the table.

Once Chronicler was finished, Kvothe began to speak crisply and clearly, as if he were biting off pieces of ice. 'In what manner was she beautiful? I realise that I cannot say enough. So. Since I cannot say enough, at least I will avoid saying too much.

'Say this, that she was dark haired. There. It was long and straight. She was dark of eye and fair complected. There. Her face was oval, her jaw strong and delicate. Say that she was poised and graceful. There.'

Kvothe took a breath before continuing. 'Finally, say that she was beautiful. That is all that can be well said. That she was beautiful, through to her bones, despite any flaw or fault. She was beautiful, to Kvothe at least. At least? To Kvothe she was most beautiful.' For a moment Kvothe tensed as if he would leap up and tear this sheet away from Chronicler as well.

Then he relaxed, like a sail when the wind leaves it. 'But to be honest, it must be said that she was beautiful to others as well . . .'

CHAPTER FIFTY-EIGHT

Names for Beginning

IT WOULD BE NICE to say that our eyes met and I moved smoothly to her side. It would be nice to say that I smiled and spoke of pleasant things in carefully metered rhyming couplets, like Prince Gallant from some faerie story.

Unfortunately, life is seldom so carefully scripted. In truth, I simply stood. It was Denna, the young woman I had met in Roent's caravan so long ago.

Come to think of it, it had only been half a year. Not so long when you're listening to a story, but half a year is a great long while to live through, especially if you are young. And we were both of us very young.

I caught sight of Denna as she was climbing the final step onto the third level of the Eolian. Her eyes were downcast, her expression thoughtful, almost sad. She turned and began to walk in my direction without lifting her eyes from the floor, without seeing me.

The months had changed her. Where before she had been pretty, now she was lovely as well. Perhaps that difference was only that she wasn't wearing the road clothes I had met her in, but a long dress instead. But it was Denna without a doubt. I even recognised the ring on her finger, silver set with a pale blue stone.

Since we parted ways, I had kept foolish, fond thoughts of Denna hidden in a secret corner of my heart. I had thought of making the trip to Anilin and tracking her down, of meeting her by chance on the road again, of her coming to find me at the University. But deep down I knew these thoughts for nothing more than childish daydreams. I knew the truth: I would never see her again.

But here she was, and I was entirely unprepared. Would she even remember me, the awkward boy she had known for a few days so long ago?

Denna was barely a dozen feet away when she looked up and saw me. Her expression brightened, as if someone had lit a candle inside her and she was glowing from its light. She rushed towards me, closing the distance between us in three excited, skipping steps.

For a moment, she looked as if she would run straight into my arms, but at the last moment she pulled back, darting a glance at the people sitting around us. In the space of half a step, she transformed her delighted head-long run into a demure greeting at arm's length. It was gracefully done, but even so, she had to reach out a hand and steady herself against my chest, lest she stumble into me due to her sudden stop.

She smiled at me then. It was warm and sweet and shy, like a flower un-furling. It was friendly and honest and slightly embarrassed. When she smiled at me, I felt . . .

I honestly cannot think of how I could describe it. Lying would be easier. I could steal from a hundred stories and tell you a lie so familiar you would swallow it whole. I could say my knees went to rubber. That my breath came hard in my chest. But that would not be the truth. My heart did not pound or stop or stutter. That is the sort of thing they say happens in stories. Foolishness. Hyperbole. Tripe. But still . . .

Go out in the early days of winter, after the first cold snap of the season. Find a pool of water with a sheet of ice across the top, still fresh and new and clear as glass. Near the shore the ice will hold you. Slide out farther. Farther. Eventually you'll find the place where the surface just barely bears your weight. There you will feel what I felt. The ice splinters under your feet. Look down and you can see the white cracks darting through the ice like mad, elaborate spiderwebs. It is perfectly silent, but you can feel the sudden sharp vibrations through the bottoms of your feet.

That is what happened when Denna smiled at me. I don't mean to imply I felt as if I stood on brittle ice about to give way beneath me. No. I felt like the ice itself, suddenly shattered, with cracks spiraling out from where she had touched my chest. The only reason I held together was because my thousand pieces were all leaning together. If I moved, I feared I would fall apart.

Perhaps it is enough to say that I was caught by a smile. And though that sounds as if it came from a storybook, it is very near the truth.

Words have never been difficult for me. Quite the opposite in fact – often I find it all too easy to speak my mind, and things go badly because of it. However, here in front of Denna, I was too stunned to speak. I could not have said a sensible word to save my life.

Without thinking, all the courtly manners my mother had drilled into me came to the fore. I reached out smoothly and clasped Denna's outstretched hand in my own, as if she'd offered it to me. Then I took a half step backward and made a genteel three-quarter bow. At the same time my free hand caught hold of the edge of my cloak and tucked it behind my back. It was a flattering bow, courtly without being ridiculouly formal, and safe for a public setting such as this.

What next? A kiss on the hand was traditional, but what sort of kiss was appropriate? In Atur you merely nod over the hand. Cealdish ladies like the moneylender's daughter I had chatted with earlier expected you to brush the knuckles lightly and make a kissing sound. In Modeg you actually press your lips to the back of your own thumb.

But we were in Commonwealth, and Denna showed no foreign accent. A straightforward kiss then. I pressed my lips gently to the back of her hand for the space of time it takes to draw a quick breath. Her skin was warm and smelled vaguely of heather.

'I am at your service, my lady,' I said, standing and releasing her hand. For the first time in my life I understood the true purpose of this sort of formal greeting. It gives you a script to follow when you have absolutely no idea what to say.

'My lady?' Denna echoed, sounding a little surprised. 'Very well, if you insist.' She took hold of her dress with one hand and bobbed a curtsey, somehow managing to make it look graceful and mocking and playful all at once. 'Your lady.' Hearing her voice, I knew my suspicions were true. She was my Aloine.

'What are you doing up here in the third circle alone?' She glanced around the crescent-shaped balcony. '*Are* you alone?'

'I was alone,' I said. Then when I could think of nothing else to say, I borrowed a line from the song fresh in my memory. ' "Now unexpected Aloine beside me stands".'

She smiled at that, flattered. 'How do you mean, unexpected?' she asked.

'I had more than half convinced myself that you had already left.'

'It was a near thing,' Denna said, archly. 'Two hours I waited for my Savien to come.' She sighed tragically, glancing up and to one side like a statue of a saint. 'Finally, filled with despair, I decided Aloine could do the finding this time, and damn the story.' She smiled a wicked smile.

' "So we were ill-lit ships at night . . ." ' I quoted.

'. . . "passing close but all unknown to one another", ' Denna finished.

'*Felward's Falling,*' I said with something that touched the outward boundary of respect. 'Not many people know that play.'

'I am not many people,' she said.

'I will never forget that again,' I bowed my head with exaggerated deference. She snorted derisively. I ignored it and continued in a more serious tone. 'I can't thank you enough for helping me tonight.'

'You can't?' she said. 'Well that's a shame. How much *can* you thank me?'

Without thinking, I reached up to the collar of my cloak and unpinned my talent pipes. 'Only this much,' I said, holding them out to her.

'I . . .' Denna hesitated, somewhat taken aback. 'You can't be serious.'

'Without you, I wouldn't have won them,' I said. 'And I have nothing else of any value, unless you want my lute.'

Denna's dark eyes studied my face, as if she couldn't decide if I was making fun or not. 'I don't think you can give away your pipes . . .'

'I can, actually,' I said. 'Stanchion mentioned if I lost them or gave them away, I'd have to earn another set.' I took her hand, uncurled her fingers, then laid the silver pipes on her palm. 'That means I can do with them as I please, and it pleases me to give them to you.'

Denna stared at the pipes in her hand, then looked at me with deliberate attention, as if she hadn't entirely noticed me before. For a moment I was painfully aware of my appearance. My cloak was threadbare, and even wearing my best clothes I was a short step from shabby.

She looked down again and slowly closed her hand around the pipes. Then she looked up at me, her expression unreadable. 'I think you might be a wonderful person,' she said.

I drew a breath, but Denna spoke first. 'However,' she said, 'this is too great a thanks. More payment than is appropriate for any help I've given you. I would end up in *your* debt.' She caught hold of my hand and pressed the pipes back into it. 'I would rather have you beholden to me.' She grinned suddenly. 'This way you still owe me a favour.'

The room grew noticeably quieter. I looked around, confused due to the fact that I'd forgotten where I was. Denna lay a finger to her lips and pointed over the railing to the stage below. We stepped closer to the edge and looked down to see an old man with a white beard opening an oddly-shaped instrument case. I sucked in a surprised breath when I saw what he was holding.

'What is that thing?' Denna asked.

'It's an old court lute,' I said, unable to keep the amazement out of my voice. 'I've never actually seen one before.'

'That's a lute?' Denna's lips moved silently. 'I count twenty-four strings. How does that even work? That's more than some harps.'

'That's how they made them years ago, before metal strings, before they knew how to brace a long neck. It's incredible. There's more careful engineering in that swan neck than in any three cathedrals.' I watched as the old man tucked his beard out of the way and adjusted himself in his seat. 'I just hope he tuned it before he went onstage,' I added softly. 'Otherwise we'll be waiting an hour while he fiddles with his pegs. My father used to say the old minstrels used to spend two days stringing and two hours of tuning to get two minutes' music from an old court lute.'

It only took the old man about five minutes to get the strings in agreement. Then he began to play.

I am shamed to admit it, but I remember nothing of the song. Despite the fact that I had never seen a court lute, let alone heard one, my mind was too awhirl with thoughts of Denna to absorb much else. As we leaned on the railing side by side, I snuck glances of her out of the corner of my eye.

She hadn't called me by name, or mentioned our meeting before in Roent's caravan. That meant she didn't remember me. Not too surprising, I suppose, that she would forget a ragged boy she'd only known for a few days on the road. Still, it stung a bit, as I'd had fond thoughts of her for months. Still, there was no way to bring it up now without seeming foolish. Better to make a fresh start and hope I was more memorable the second time around.

The song was over before I realised it, and I clapped enthusiastically to make up for my inattention.

'I thought you'd made a mistake when you doubled your chorus earlier,' Denna said to me as the applause died down. 'I couldn't believe you really wanted a stranger to join in. I haven't seen that done anywhere except around campfires at night.'

I shrugged. 'Everyone kept telling me this is where the best musicians played.' I made a sweeping gesture with one hand toward her. 'I trusted someone would know the part.'

She arched an eyebrow. 'It was a near thing,' she said. 'I waited for someone else to jump in instead. I was a little anxious to step in myself.'

I gave her a puzzled look. 'Why? You have a lovely voice.'

She gave a sheepish grimace. 'I'd only heard the song twice before this. I wasn't sure if I'd remember all of it.'

'Twice?'

Denna nodded. 'And the second time was just a span ago. A couple played it during a formal dinner I attended off in Aetnia.'

'Are you serious?' I said incredulously.

She tilted her head back and forth, as if caught in a white lie. Her dark hair fell across her face and she brushed it away absentmindedly. 'Okay, I suppose I did hear the couple rehearse a little right before the dinner . . .'

I shook my head, hardly believing it. 'That's amazing. It's a terribly diffi- cult harmony. And to remember all the lyrics . . .' I marvelled silently for a moment, shaking my head. 'You have an incredible ear.'

'You're not the first man to say that,' Denna said, wryly. 'But you might be the first to say it while actually looking at my ears,' she glanced down meaningfully.

I felt myself beginning to blush furiously when I heard a familiar voice behind us. 'There you are!' Turning, I saw Sovoy, my tall, handsome friend and coconspirator from Advanced Sympathy.

'Here I am,' I said, surprised that he would seek me out. Doubly surprised that he would have the bad grace to interrupt me when I was in a private conversation with a young woman.

'Here we all are.' Sovoy smiled at me as he walked over and put his arm casually around Denna's waist. He made a mock frown at her. 'I scour the bottom levels trying to help you find your singer, while all the while both of you are up here, thick as thieves.'

'We stumbled into each other,' Denna said, laying her hand over his where it rested on her hip. 'I knew you'd come back for your drink, if nothing else . . .' She nodded to a nearby table, empty except for a pair of wineglasses.

Together, they turned and walked arm in arm back to their table. Denna looked over her shoulder at me and gave a sort of a shrug with her eyebrows. I hadn't the slightest idea what the expression meant.

Sovoy waved me over to join them and pulled over an unoccupied chair so I would have a place to sit. 'I couldn't quite believe it was you down there,' he said to me. 'I thought I recognised your voice, but . . .' He gestured, indicating the highest level of the Eolian. 'While the third circle provides a comfortable privacy for young lovers, its view of the stage leaves a little to be desired. I didn't know you played.' He settled a long arm across Denna's shoulders and smiled his charming blue-eyed smile.

'Off and on,' I said flippantly as I sat down.

'Lucky for you I picked the Eolian for our entertainment tonight,' Sovoy said. 'Otherwise you'd have had nothing but echoes and crickets to accompany you.'

'Then I'm in your debt,' I said to him, with a deferential nod.

'Make it up to me by taking Simmon as a partner next time we play corners,' he said. 'That way you're the one to eat the forfeit when the giddy little bastard calls the tall card with nothing but a pair.'

'Done,' I said. 'Though it pains me.' I turned to Denna. 'What of you? I owe you a great favour – how can I repay it? Ask anything and it is yours, should it be within my skill.'

'Anything within your skill,' she repeated playfully. 'What can you do then, besides play so well that Tehlu and his angels would weep to hear?'

'I imagine I could do anything,' I said easily. 'If you would ask it of me.'

She laughed.

'That's a dangerous thing to say to a woman,' Sovoy said. 'Especially this one. She'll have you off to bring her a leaf of the singing tree from the other side of the world.'

She leaned back in her chair and looked at me with dangerous eyes. 'A leaf of the singing tree,' she mused. 'That might be a nice thing to have. Would you bring me one?'

'I would,' I said, and was surprised to find that it was the truth.

She seemed to consider it, then shook her head playfully. 'I couldn't send you journeying so far away. I'll save my favour for another day.'

I sighed. 'So I am left in your debt.'

'Oh no!' she exclaimed. 'Another weight upon my Savien's heart . . .'

'The reason my heart is so heavy is that I fear I might never know your name. I could keep thinking of you as Felurian,' I said. 'But that could lead to unfortunate confusion.'

She gave me an appraising look. 'Felurian? I might like that if I didn't think you were a liar.'

'A liar?' I said indignantly. 'My first thought in seeing you was "Felurian! What have I done? The adulation of my peers below has been a waste of hours. Could I recall the moments I have careless cast away, I could but hope to spend them in a wiser way, and warm myself in light that rivals light of day".'

She smiled. 'A thief *and* a liar. You stole that from the third act of *Daeonica*.'

She knew *Daeonica* too? 'Guilty,' I admitted freely. 'But that doesn't make it untrue.'

She smiled at Sovoy then turned back to me. 'Flattery is fine and good, but it won't win you my name. Sovoy mentioned you were keeping pace with him in the University. That means you meddle with dark forces better left alone. If I give you my name you would have a terrible power over me.' Her mouth was serious, but her smile showed itself around the corners of her eyes, in the tilt of her head.

'That is very true,' I said with equal seriousness. 'But I will make you a bargain. I'll give you my name in exchange. Then I will be in your power as well.'

'You'd sell me my own shirt,' she said. 'Sovoy knows your name. Assuming he hasn't told me already, I could have it from him as easy as breathing.'

'True enough,' Sovoy said, seeming relieved that we remembered he was there. He took up her hand and kissed the back of it.

'He can *tell* you my name,' I said, dismissively. 'But he cannot *give* it to you – only I can do that.' I lay one hand flat on the table. 'My offer stands, my name for yours. Will you take it? Or will I be forced to think of you always as an Aloine, and never as yourself?'

Her eyes danced. 'Very well,' she said. 'I'll have yours first though.'

I leaned forwards, and motioned for her to do the same. She let go of Sovoy's hand and turned an ear toward me. With due solemnity I whispered my name in her ear. 'Kvothe.' She smelled faintly of flowers, which I guessed was a perfume, but beneath that was her own smell, like green grass, like the open road after a light spring rain.

Then she leaned back into her seat and seemed to think of it for a while. 'Kvothe,' she said eventually. 'It suits you. Kvothe.' Her eyes sparkled as if she held some hidden secret. She said it slowly, as if tasting it, then nodded to herself. 'What does it mean?'

'It means many things,' I said in my best Taborlin the Great voice. 'But you will not distract me so easily. I have paid, and now am in your power. Would you give me your name, that I might call you by it?'

She smiled and leaned forward again, I did likewise. Turning my head to the side, I felt an errant strand of her hair brush against me. 'Dianne,' her warm breath was like a feather against my ear. 'Dianne.'

We both sat back in our seats. When I didn't say anything she prompted me, 'Well?'

'I have it,' I assured her. 'As sure as I know my own.'

'Say it then.'

'I am saving it,' I reassured her, smiling. 'Gifts like these should not be squandered.'

She looked at me.

I relented. 'Dianne,' I said. 'Dianne. It suits you as well.'

We looked at each other for a long moment, then I noticed that Sovoy was giving me a not-quite-subtle stare.

'I should get back downstairs,' I said, rising quickly from my seat. 'I've got important people to meet.' I cringed inwardly at the awkwardness of the words as soon as I'd said them, but couldn't think of a less awkward way to take them back.

Sovoy stood and shook my hand, no doubt eager to be rid of me. 'Well done tonight, Kvothe. I'll be seeing you.'

I turned to see Denna standing too. She met my eyes and smiled. 'I hope to see you too.' She held out her hand.

I gave her my best smile. 'There's always hope.' I meant it to seem witty, but the words seemed to turn boorish as soon as they left my mouth. I had to leave before I made an even greater ass of myself. I shook her hand quickly. It was slightly cool to the touch. Soft, delicate, and strong. I did not kiss it, as Sovoy was my friend, and that is not the sort of thing friends do.

CHAPTER FIFTY-NINE

All This Knowing

IN THE FULLNESS OF TIME, and with considerable help from Deoch and Wilem, I became drunk.

Thus it was that three students made their slightly erratic way back to the University. See them as they go, weaving only slightly. It is quiet, and when the belling tower strikes the late hour, it doesn't break the silence so much as it underpins it. The crickets, too, respect the silence. Their calls are like careful stitches in its fabric, almost too small to be seen.

The night is like warm velvet around them. The stars, burning diamonds in the cloudless sky, turn the road beneath their feet a silver grey. The University and Imre are the hearts of understanding and art, the strongest of the four corners of civilisation. Here on the road between the two there is nothing but old trees and long grass bending to the wind. The night is perfect in a wild way, almost terrifyingly beautiful.

The three boys, one dark, one light, and one – for lack of a better word – fiery, do not notice the night. Perhaps some part of them does, but they are young, and drunk, and busy knowing deep in their hearts that they will never grow old or die. They also know that they are friends, and they share a certain love that will never leave them. The boys know many other things, but none of them seem as important as this. Perhaps they are right.

CHAPTER SIXTY

Fortune

THE NEXT DAY I went to the admissions lottery sporting my very first hangover. Weary and vaguely nauseous, I joined the shortest line and tried to ignore the din of hundreds of students milling about, buying, selling, trading, and generally complaining about the slots they'd drawn for their exams.

'Kvothe, Arliden's son,' I said when I finally arrived at the front of the line. The bored looking woman marked my name and I drew a tile out of the black velvet bag. It read 'Hepten: Noon.' Five days from now, plenty of time to prepare.

But as I turned back to the Mews, a thought occurred to me. How much preparation did I really need? More importantly, how much could I genuinely accomplish without access to the Archives?

Thinking it over, I raised my hand over my head with my middle finger and thumb extended, signaling that I had a slot five days from now that I was willing to sell.

It wasn't long before an unfamiliar student wandered close. 'Fourth day,' she said, holding up her own tile. 'I'll give you a jot to trade.' I shook my head. She shrugged and wandered away.

Galven, a Re'lar from the Medica approached me. He held up his index finger, indicating he had a slot later this afternoon. From the circles under his eyes and his anxious expression, I didn't think he was eager to go through testing that soon. 'Will you take five jots?'

'I'd like to get a whole talent . . .'

He nodded, flipping his own tile over between his fingers. It was a fair price. No one wanted to go through admissions on the first day. 'Maybe later. I'll look around a little first.'

As I watched him leave, I marvelled at the difference a single day could make. Yesterday five jots would have seemed like all the money in the world. But today my purse was heavy . . .

I was lost in vague musings about how much money I had actually earned last night when I saw Wilem and Simmon approaching. Wil looked a little pale under his dark Cealdish complexion. I guessed he was feeling the after-effects of our night's carousing too.

Sim, on the other hand, was bright and sunny as ever. 'Guess who drew slots this afternoon?' He nodded over my shoulder. 'Ambrose and several of his friends. It's enough to make me believe in a just universe.'

Turning to search the crowd, I heard Ambrose's voice before I saw him. '. . . from the same bag, that means they did a piss-poor job mixing. They should restart this whole mismanaged sham and . . .'

Ambrose was walking with several well-dressed friends, their eyes sweeping over the crowd, looking for raised hands. Ambrose was a dozen feet away before he finally looked down and realised the hand he was heading towards was mine.

He stopped short, scowling, then gave a sudden barking laugh. 'You poor boy, all the time in the world and no way to spend it. Hasn't Lorren let you back in yet?'

'Hammer and horn,' Wil said wearily behind me.

Ambrose smiled at me. 'Tell you what. I'll give you ha'penny and one of my old shirts for your slot. That way, you'll have something to wear when you're washing that one in the river.' A few of his friends chuckled behind him, looking me up and down.

I kept my expression nonchalant, not wanting to give him any satisfaction. Truth was, I was all too aware of the fact that I only owned two shirts, and after two terms of constant wear they were getting shabby. Shabbier. What's more, I *did* wash them in the river, as I'd never had money to spare for laundry.

'I'll pass,' I said lightly. 'Your shirttails are a little richly dyed for my taste.' I tugged at the front of my own shirt to make my point clear. A few nearby students laughed.

'I don't get it,' I heard Sim say quietly to Wil.

'He's implying Ambrose has the . . .' Wil paused. 'The *Edamete tass*, a disease you get from whores. There is a discharge—'

'Okay, okay,' Sim said quickly. 'I get it. Ick. Ambrose is wearing green too.'

Meanwhile, Ambrose forced himself to chuckle along with the crowd at my joke. 'I suppose I deserve that,' he said. 'Very well, pennies for the poor.' He brought out his purse and shook it. 'How much do you want?'

'Five talents,' I said.

He stared at me, frozen in the act of opening his purse. It was an outrageous price. A few of the spectators nudged each other with their elbows, obviously hoping I'd somehow swindle Ambrose into paying several times what my slot was actually worth.

'I'm sorry,' I asked. 'Do you need that converted?' It was a well-known fact that Ambrose had botched the arithmetic portion of his admissions last term.

'Five is ridiculous,' he said. 'You'd be lucky to get one this late in the day.'

I forced a careless shrug. 'I'd settle for four.'

'You'll settle for one,' Ambrose insisted. 'I'm not an idiot.'

I took a deep breath, let it out again, resigned. 'I don't suppose I could get you to go as high as . . . one and four?' I asked, disgusted by how plaintive my voice sounded.

Ambrose smiled like a shark. 'I tell you what,' he said magnanimously. 'I'll give you one and three. I'm not above a little charity now and again.'

'Thank you sir,' I said meekly. 'It's much appreciated.' I could sense the crowd's disappointment as I rolled over like a dog for Ambrose's money.

'Don't mention it,' Ambrose said smugly. 'Always a pleasure to help out the needy.'

'In Vintish coin, that'll be two nobles, six bits, two pennies, and four shims.'

'I can do my own conversion,' he snapped. 'I've travelled the world with my father's retinue since I was a boy. I know how money spends.'

'Of course you do.' I ducked my head. 'Silly of me.' I looked up curiously. 'You've been to Modeg then?'

'Of course,' he said absentmindedly as he proceeded to dig through his purse, pulling out an assortment of coins. 'I've actually been to high court in Cershaen. Twice.'

'Is it true that the Modegan nobility regard haggling as a contemptible activity for those of any highborn station?' I asked innocently. 'I heard that they consider it a sure sign that the person is either possessed of low blood or fallen on truly desperate times . . .'

Ambrose looked up at me, frozen halfway through the act of digging coins out of his purse. His eyes narrowed.

'Because if that's true, it's terribly kind of you to come down to my level just for the fun of a little bargain.' I grinned at him. 'We Ruh love to dicker.' There was a murmur of laughter from the crowd around us. It had grown to several dozen people at this point.

'That's not it at all,' Ambrose said.

My face became a mask of concern. 'Oh, I'm sorry, m'lord. I had no idea you'd come on hard times . . .' I took several steps toward him, holding out my admissions tile. 'Here, you can have it for just ha'penny. I'm not above a little charity myself.' I stood directly in front of him, holding out the tile. 'Please, I insist, it's always a pleasure to help the needy.'

Ambrose glared furiously. 'Keep it and choke,' he hissed at me in a low voice. 'And remember this when you're eating beans and washing in the river. I'll still be here the day you leave with nothing but your hands in your pockets.' He turned and left, the very picture of affronted dignity.

There was a smattering of applause from the surrounding crowd. I took flourishing bows in all directions.

'How would you score that one?' Wil asked Sim.

'Two for Ambrose. Three for Kvothe.' Sim looked at me. 'Not your best work, really.'

'I didn't get much sleep last night,' I admitted.

'Every time you do this it makes the eventual payback that much worse,' Wil said.

'We can't do anything but snap at each other,' I said. 'The masters made sure of that. Anything too extreme would get us expelled for Conduct Unbecoming a Member of the Arcanum. Why do you think I haven't made his life a hell?'

'You're lazy?' Wil suggested.

'Laziness is one of my best characteristics,' I said easily. 'If I weren't lazy, I might go through the work of translating *Edamete tass* and grow terribly offended when I discover it means "the Edema Drip".' I raised my hand again, thumb and middle finger extended. 'Instead I'll assume it translates directly into the name of the disease: "nemserria", thus preventing any unnecessary strain on our friendship.'

I eventually sold my slot to a desperate Re'lar from the Fishery named Jaxim. I drove a hard bargain, trading him my slot for six jots and a favour to be named later.

Admissions went about as well as could be expected, considering I couldn't study. Hemme was still carrying his grudge. Lorren was cool. Elodin had his head down on the table and seemed to be asleep. My tuition was a full six talents, which put me in an interesting situation . . .

———

The long road to Imre was mostly deserted. The sun brushed through the trees and the wind carried just a hint of the cool that fall would soon be bringing. I headed to the Eolian first to retrieve my lute. Stanchion had insisted that I leave it there last night, lest I break it on my long, inebriated walk home.

As I approached the Eolian, I saw Deoch lounging against the doorpost, walking a coin across the back knuckles of his hand. He smiled when he saw me. 'Ho there! Thought you and your friends would end up in the river by the way you were weaving when you left last night.'

'We were swaying in different directions,' I explained. 'So it balanced out.'

Deoch laughed. 'We've got your lady inside.'

I fought down a flush and wondered how he had known I was hoping to find Denna here. 'I don't know if I would call her *my* lady exactly.' Sovoy was my friend, after all.

He shrugged. 'Whatever you call her, Stanchion's got her behind the bar. I'd go grab her before he gets overly familiar and starts practicing his fingering.'

I felt a flash of rage and barely managed to swallow a mouthful of hot words. *My lute. He was talking about my lute.* I ducked inside quickly, guessing the less Deoch saw of my expression the better it would be.

I wandered through the three levels of the Eolian, but Denna was nowhere to be found. I did run into Count Threpe though, who enthusiastically invited me to have a seat.

'I don't suppose I might persuade you to pay me a visit at my house sometime?' Threpe asked bashfully. 'I'm thinking of having a little dinner, and I know a few people who would love to meet you.' He winked. 'Word about your performance is already getting around.'

I felt a twinge of anxiety, but I knew rubbing elbows with the nobility was something of a necessary evil. 'I'd be honoured to, my lord.'

Threpe grimaced. 'Does it have to be *my lord*?'

Diplomacy is a large part of being a trouper, and a large portion of diplomacy is adherence to title and rank. 'Etiquette, my lord,' I said regretfully.

'Piss on etiquette,' Threpe said petulantly. 'Etiquette is a set of rules people use so they can be rude to each other in public. I was born Dennais first, Threpe second, and count last of all.' He looked imploringly up at me. 'Denn for short?'

I hesitated.

'Here at least,' he pleaded. 'It makes me feel like a weed in a flowerbed when someone starts "lording" me here.'

I relaxed. 'If it makes you happy, Denn.'

He flushed as if I'd flattered him. 'Tell me a bit about yourself, then. Where are you lodging?'

'On the other side of the river,' I said evasively. The bunks in Mews were not exactly glamorous. When Threpe gave me a puzzled look, I continued. 'I attend the University.'

'The University?' he asked, clearly puzzled. 'Are they teaching music now?'

I almost laughed at the thought. 'No no. I'm in the Arcanum.'

I immediately regretted my words. He leaned back in his seat and gave me an uncomfortable look. 'You're a warlock?'

'Oh no,' I said, dismissively. 'I'm just studying. You know, grammar, mathematics . . .' I picked two of the more innocent fields of study I could think of, and he seemed to relax a bit.

'I guess I'd just thought that you were . . .' he trailed off and shook himself. 'Why are you studying there?'

The question caught me off guard. 'I . . . I've always wanted to. There's so much to learn.'

'But you don't need any of that. I mean—' he groped for words. 'The way you play. Surely your patron is encouraging you to focus on your music . . .'

'I don't have a patron, Denn,' I said with a shy smile. 'Not that I'm opposed to the idea, mind you.'

His reaction was not what I expected. 'Damn my blackened luck.' He slapped his hand on the table, hard. 'I assumed someone was being coy, keeping you a secret.' He thumped the table with his fist. 'Damn. Damn. Damn.'

He recovered his composure a little and looked up at me. 'I'm sorry. It's just that . . .' He made a frustrated gesture and sighed. 'Have you ever heard the saying: "One wife, you're happy, two and you're tired—" '

I nodded. ' "—three and they'll hate each other—" '

' "—four and they'll hate you",' Threpe finished. 'Well the same thing is doubly true for patrons and their musicians. I just picked up my third, a struggling flutist.' He sighed and shook his head. 'They bicker like cats in a bag, worried they're not getting enough attention. If only I'd known you were coming along, I would have waited.'

'You flatter me, Denn.'

'I'm kicking myself is what I'm doing,' he sighed and looked guilty. 'That's not fair. Sephran's good at what he does. They're all good musicians, and overprotective of me, just like real wives.' He gave me an apologetic look. 'If I try to bring you in, there'll be hell to pay. I've already had to lie about that little gift I gave you last night.'

'So I'm your mistress then?' I grinned.

Threpe chuckled. 'Let's not carry the analogy too far. I'll be your match-maker instead. I'll help you toward a proper patron. I know everyone with blood or money for fifty miles, so it shouldn't be that hard.'

'That would be a great help,' I said earnestly. 'The social circles on this side of the river are a mystery to me.' A thought occurred to me. 'Speaking of which, I met a young lady last night, and didn't find out much about her. If you're familiar with the town . . .' I trailed off hopefully.

He gave me a knowing look. 'Ahhh, I see.'

'No, no, no,' I protested. 'She's the girl that sang along with me. My Aloine. I was just hoping to find her to pay my respects.'

Threpe looked as if he didn't believe me, but wasn't going to make an issue of it. 'Fair enough, what's her name?'

'Dianne.' Threpe seemed to be waiting for more. 'That's all I know.'

Threpe snorted. 'What did she look like? Sing it if you have to.'

I felt the beginning of a flush on my cheeks. 'She had dark hair to about here,' I gestured a little lower than my shoulder with one hand. 'Young, fair skin.' Threpe watched me expectantly. 'Pretty.'

'I see,' Threpe mused, rubbing his lips. 'Did she have her talent pipes?'

'I don't know. Maybe.'

'Does she live in the city?'

I shrugged my ignorance again, feeling more and more foolish.

Threpe laughed. 'You're going to have to give me more than that.' He looked over my shoulder. 'Wait, there's Deoch. If anyone could spot a girl for you, it'd be him.' He raised his hand. 'Deoch!'

'It's really not that important,' I said hurriedly. Threpe ignored me and waved the broad-shouldered man over to our table.

Deoch strolled over and leaned against a table. 'What can I do for you?'

'Our young singer needs a little information about a lady that he met last night.'

'Can't say I'm surprised, there were quite a crop of lovelies out. One or two asked about you.' He winked at me. 'Who caught your eye?'

'It's not like that,' I protested. 'She was the one who sang my harmony last night. She had a lovely voice and I was hoping to find her so we could do a little singing.'

'I think I know the tune you're talking about.' He gave me a broad, knowing smile.

I felt myself blushing furiously and began to protest again.

'Oh settle down, I'll keep this one between my tongue and teeth. I'll even keep from telling Stanchion, which is as good as telling the whole town. He gossips like a schoolgirl when he's had a cup.' He looked at me expectantly.

'She was slender with deep, coffee-coloured eyes,' I said before I thought about how it sounded. I hurried on before either Threpe or Deoch could make a joke. 'Her name was Dianne.'

'Ahhh.' Deoch nodded slowly to himself, his smile going a little wry. 'I guess I should have known.'

'Does she live here?' Threpe asked. 'I don't believe I know her.'

'You'd remember,' Deoch said. 'But no, I don't think she lives in town. I see her off and on. She travels, always here and gone again.' He rubbed the back of his head and gave me a worried smile. 'I don't know where you might be able to find her. Careful boy, that one will steal your heart. Men fall for her like wheat before a sickle blade.'

I shrugged as if such things couldn't be further from my mind, and was glad when Threpe turned the topic to a piece of gossip about one of the local councilmen. I chuckled at their bickering until my drink was done, then made my farewells and took my leave of them.

Half an hour later I stood on the stairway outside Devi's door, trying to ignore the rancid smell of the butcher's shop below. I counted my money for the third time and thought about my options. I could pay off my entire debt and still afford my tuition, but it would leave me penniless. I had other debts to settle as well, and as much as I wanted to be out from under Devi's thumb, I didn't relish starting the semester without a bit of coin in my pocket.

The door opened suddenly, startling me. Devi's face peered out suspiciously through a narrow crack, then brightened with a smile when she recognised me. 'What are you lurking for?' she asked. 'Gentlemen knock, as a rule.' She opened the door wide to let me in.

'Just weighing my options,' I said as she bolted the door behind me. Her room was much the same as before save that today it smelled of cinnamon, not lavender. 'I hope I won't be inconveniencing you if I only pay the interest this term?'

'Not at all,' she said graciously. 'I like to think of it as an investment on my part.' She gestured me toward a chair. 'Besides, it means I get to see you again. You'd be surprised how few visitors I get.'

'It's probably your location more than your company,' I said.

She wrinkled her nose. 'I know. I settled here at first because it was cheap. Now I feel obliged to stay because my customers know to find me here.'

I laid two talents on the desk and slid them toward her. 'Do you mind a question?'

She gave me a look of impish excitement. 'Is it inappropriate?'

'A bit,' I admitted. 'Has anyone ever tried to report you?'

'Well now,' she sat forward in her chair. 'That can be taken a number of different ways.' She raised an eyebrow over one icy blue eye. 'Are you being threatening, or curious?'

'Curious,' I said quickly.

'I tell you what.' She nodded at my lute. 'Play me a song and I'll tell you the truth.'

I smiled and unlatched the case, drawing out my lute. 'What would you like to hear?'

She thought for a minute. 'Can you play "Leave the Town, Tinker"?'

I played it, quick and easy. She came in enthusiastically on the chorus, and at the end she smiled and clapped like a young girl.

Which, in hindsight, I guess she was. Back then she was an older woman, experienced and self-sure. I, on the other hand, was not quite sixteen.

'Once,' she answered as I put my lute away. 'Two years ago a young gentleman E'lir decided it would be better to inform the constable than to settle his debt.'

I looked up at her. 'And?'

'And that was it.' She shrugged carelessly. 'They came, asked me questions, searched the place. Didn't find anything incriminating, of course.'

'Of course.'

'The next day the young gentleman admitted the truth to the constable. He had made the whole story up because I had spurned his romantic advances.' She grinned. 'The constable was not amused, and the gentleman was fined for slanderous action against a lady of the town.'

I couldn't help but smile. 'I can't say as I'm terribly ...' I trailed off, noticing something for the first time. I pointed at her bookshelf. 'Is that Malcaf's *The Basis of All Matter?*'

'Oh yes,' she said proudly. 'It's new. A partial repayment.' She gestured towards the shelf. 'Feel free.'

I walked over and pulled it out. 'If I'd had this to study from, I wouldn't have missed one of the questions during admissions today.'

'I'd think you'd have your fill of books at the Archives,' she said, her voice thick with envy.

I shook my head. 'I was banned,' I said. 'I've spent about two hours total in the Archives, and half of that was getting thrown out on my ear.'

Devi nodded slowly. 'I'd heard, but you never know which rumours are true. We're in something of the same boat then.'

'I'd say you're slightly better off,' I said looking over her shelves. 'You've got Teccam here, and the *Heroborica.*' I scanned all the titles, looking for anything that might have information about the Amyr or the Chandrian, but nothing looked especially promising. 'You've got *The Mating Habits of the Common Draccus,* too. I was partway through reading that when I was kicked out.'

'That's the latest edition,' she said proudly. 'There's new engravings and a section on the Faen-Moite.'

I ran my fingers down the book's spine, then stepped back. 'It's a nice collection.'

'Well,' she said teasingly. 'If you promise to keep your hands clean, you could come over and do some reading now and again. If you bring your lute and play for me, I might even let you borrow a book or two, so long as you bring them back in a timely fashion.' She gave me a winsome smile. 'We exiles should stick together.'

I spent the long walk back to the University wondering if Devi was being flirtatious or friendly. At the end of the three miles, I hadn't reached anything resembling a decision. I mention this to make something clear. I was clever, a burgeoning hero with an Alar like a bar of Ramston steel. But, first and foremost, I was a fifteen-year-old boy. When it came to women, I was lost as a lamb in the woods.

I found Kilvin in his office, etching runes into a hemisphere of glass for another hanging lamp. I knocked softly on the open door.

He glanced up at me. 'E'lir Kvothe, you are looking better.'

It took me a moment to remember that he was speaking of three span ago when he banned me from my work at the Fishery due to Wilem's meddling. 'Thank you sir. I feel better.'

He cocked his head minutely.

I lowered one hand to my purse. 'I would like to resolve my debt to you.'

Kilvin grunted. 'You owe me nothing.' He looked back down at the table and the project in his hands.

'My debt to the shop, then,' I pressed. 'I've been taking advantage of your good nature for some time now. How much do I owe for the materials I've used during my studies with Manet?'

Kilvin continued to work. 'One talent, seven jots, and three.'

The exactness of the number startled me, as he hadn't checked the ledger in the storeroom. I boggled to think of everything the bearlike man was carrying around in his head. I took the appropriate amount from my purse and set the coins on a relatively clutter-free corner of the table.

Kilvin looked at them. 'E'lir Kvothe, I trust you came to this money honorably.'

His tone was so serious I had to smile. 'I earned it playing in Imre last night.'

'Music across the river pays this well?'

I held my smile and shrugged nonchalantly. 'I don't know if I'll do this well *every* night. This was only my first time, after all.'

Kilvin made a sound somewhere between a snort and a huff and turned his eyes back to his work. 'Elxa Dal's pridefulness is rubbing off on you.' He drew a careful line on the glass. 'Am I correct in assuming that you will no longer be spending evenings in my employ?'

Shocked, it took me a moment to catch my breath. 'I–I wouldn't—I came here to speak with you about—' *about coming back to work in the shop.* The thought of not working for Kilvin hadn't crossed my mind.

'Apparently your music has more profit than working here.' Kilvin gave the coins on the table a significant look.

'But I *want* to work here!' I said wretchedly.

Kilvin's face broke into a great white smile. 'Good. I would not have wanted to lose you to the other side of the river. Music is a fine thing, but metal lasts.' He struck the table with two huge fingers to emphasise his point. Then he made a shooing motion with the hand that held his unfinished lamp. 'Go. Do not be late for work or I will keep you polishing bottles and grinding ore for another term.'

As I left, I thought about what Kilvin had said. It was the first thing he had said to me that I did not agree with wholeheartedly. *Metal rusts,* I thought, *music lasts forever.*

Time will eventually prove one of us right.

———

After I left the Fishery I headed straight to the Horse and Four, arguably the best inn this side of the river. The innkeeper was a bald, portly fellow named Caverin. I showed him my talent pipes and bargained for a pleasant fifteen minutes.

The end result was that in exchange for playing three evenings a span I received free room and board. The Four's kitchens were remarkable, and my room was actually a small suite: bedroom, dressing room, and sitting room. A huge step up from my narrow bunk in the Mews.

But best of all, I would earn two silver talents every month. An almost ridiculous sum of money to someone who had been poor for as long as I had. And that was in addition to whatever gifts or tips the wealthy customers might give me.

Playing here, working in the Fishery, and with a wealthy patron on the horizon, I'd no longer be forced to live like a pauper. I'd be able to buy things I desperately needed: another suit of clothes, some decent pens and paper, new shoes . . .

If you have never been desperately poor, I doubt you can understand the relief I felt. For months I'd been waiting for the other shoe to drop, knowing that any small catastrophe could ruin me. But now I no longer had to live every day worrying about my next term's tuition or the interest on Devi's loan. I was no longer in danger of being forced out of the University.

I had a lovely dinner of venison steak with a leaf salad and a bowl of delicately spiced tomato soup. There were fresh peaches and plums and white bread with sweet cream butter. Though I didn't even ask for it, I was served several glasses of an excellent dark Vintish wine.

Then I retired to my rooms where I slept like a dead man, lost in the vastness of my new feather bed.

CHAPTER SIXTY-ONE

Jackass, Jackass

WITH ADMISSIONS BEHIND ME I had no responsibilities until fall term began. I spent the intervening days catching up on my sleep, working in Kilvin's shop, and enjoying my new, luxurious accommodations at the Horse and Four.

I also spent a considerable amount of time on the road to Imre, usually under the excuse of visiting Threpe or enjoying the camaraderie of the other musicians at the Eolian. But the truth behind the stories was that I was hoping to find Denna.

But my diligence gained me nothing. She seemed to have vanished from the town completely. I asked a few people who I could trust not to make gossip of it, but none of them knew more than Deoch. I briefly entertained the thought of asking Sovoy about her, but discarded it as a bad idea.

After my sixth fruitless trip to Imre I decided to abandon my search. After my ninth I convinced myself it was a waste of valuable time. After my fourteenth trip, I came to the deep realisation that I wouldn't find her. She was well and truly gone. Again.

It was during one of my Denna-less trips to the Eolian that I received some troubling news from Count Threpe. Apparently, Ambrose, firstborn son of the wealthy and influential Baron Jakis, had been busy as a bee in the social circles of Imre. He had spread rumours, made threats, and generally turned the nobility against me. While he couldn't keep me from gaining the respect of my fellow musicians, apparently he *could* keep me from gaining a wealthy patron. It was my first glimpse of the trouble Ambrose could make for a person like me.

Threpe was apologetic and morose, while I seethed with irritation. Together we proceeded to drink an unwise amount of wine and grouse about Ambrose Jakis. Eventually Threpe was called up onto the stage where he sang a scathing little ditty of his own design, satirising one of Tarbean's councilmen. It was met with great laughter and applause.

From there it was a short step for us to begin composing a song about Ambrose. Threpe was an inveterate gossipmonger with a knack for tasteless innuendo, and I have always had a gift for a catchy tune. It took us under an hour to compose our masterwork, which we lovingly titled 'Jackass, Jackass.'

On the surface, it was a ribald little tune about a donkey who wanted to be an arcanist. Our extraordinarily clever pun on Ambrose's surname was as close as we came to mentioning him. But anyone with half a wit could tell who the shoe was meant to fit.

It was late when Threpe and I took the stage, and we weren't the only ones worse for drink. There was thunderous laughter and applause from the majority of the audience, who called for an encore. We gave it to them again, and everyone came in singing on the chorus.

The key to the song's success was its simplicity. You could whistle or hum it. Anyone with three fingers could play it, and if you had one ear and a bucket you could carry the tune. It was catchy, and vulgar, and mean-spirited. It spread through the University like a fire in a field.

―――――――

I tugged open the outer doors of the Archives and stepped into the entry hall, my eyes adjusting to the red tint of the sympathy lamps. The air was dry and cool, rich with the smell of dust, leather, and old ink. I took a breath the way a starving man might outside a bakery.

Wilem was tending the desk. I knew he'd be working. Ambrose wasn't anywhere in the building. 'I'm just here to talk with Master Lorren,' I said quickly.

Wil relaxed. 'He's with someone right now. It might be a while—'

A tall, lean Cealdish man opened the door behind the entry desk. Unlike most Cealdish men he was clean-shaven and wore his hair long, pulled back into a tail. He wore well-mended hunter's leathers, a faded travelling cloak, and high boots, all dusty from the road. As he shut the door behind him, his hand went unconsciously to the hilt of his sword to keep it from striking the wall or the desk.

'*Tetalia tu Kiaure edan A'siath*,' he said in Siaru, clapping Wilem on the shoulder as he walked out from behind the desk. '*Vorelan tua tetam.*'

Wil gave a rare smile, shrugging. '*Lhinsatva. Tua kverein.*'

The man laughed, and as he stepped around the desk I saw he wore a long knife in addition to his sword. I'd never seen anyone armed at the University. Here in the Archives, he looked as out of place as a sheep in the king's court. But his manner was relaxed, confident, as if he couldn't feel more at home.

He stopped walking when he saw me standing there. He cocked his head to the side a little. '*Cyae tsien?*'

I didn't recognise the language. 'I beg your pardon?'

'Oh, sorry,' he said, speaking perfect Aturan. 'You looked Yllish. The red hair fooled me.' He looked at me closer. 'But you're not, are you? You're one of the Ruh.' He stepped forward and held out his hand to me. 'One family.'

I shook it without thinking. His hand was solid as a rock, and his dark Cealdish complexion was tanned even darker than usual, highlighting a few pale scars that ran over his knuckles and up his arms. 'One family,' I echoed, too surprised to say anything else.

'Folk from the family are a rare thing here,' he said easily, walking past me towards the outer door. 'I'd stop and share news, but I've got to make it to Evesdown before sunset or I'll miss my ship.' He opened the outer door and sunlight flooded the room. 'I'll catch you up when I'm back in these parts,' he said, and with a wave, he was gone.

I turned to Wilem. 'Who was that?'

'One of Lorren's gillers,' Wil said. 'Viari.'

'He's a *scriv*?' I said incredulously, thinking of the pale, quiet students who worked in the Archives, sorting, scribing, and fetching books.

Wil shook his head. 'He works in acquisitions. They bring back books from all over the world. They're a different breed entirely.'

'I gathered that,' I said, glancing at the door.

'He's the one Lorren was talking to, so you can go in now,' Wil said, getting to his feet and opening the door behind the massive wooden desk. 'Down at the end of the hall. There's a brass plate on his door. I'd walk you back, but we're short-staffed. I can't leave the desk.'

I nodded and began to walk down the hallway. I smiled to hear Wil softly humming the melody from 'Jackass, Jackass' under his breath. Then the door gave a muffled thump behind me, and the hall was quiet save for the sound of my own breathing. By the time I reached the appropriate door, my hands were clammy with sweat. I knocked.

'Enter,' Lorren called from inside. His voice was like a sheet of smooth grey slate, without the barest hint of inflection or emotion.

I opened the door. Lorren sat behind a huge semicircular desk. Shelves lined the walls from floor to ceiling. The room was so full of books there wasn't more than a palm's breadth of wall visible in the entire room.

Lorren looked at me coolly. Even sitting down he was still nearly as tall as me. 'Good morning.'

'I know I'm banned from the Archives, Master,' I said quickly. 'I hope that I am not violating that by coming to see you.'

'Not if you are here to good purpose.'

'I've come into some money,' I said pulling out my purse. 'And I was hoping to buy back my copy of *Rhetoric and Logic*.'

Lorren nodded and came to his feet. Tall, clean-shaven, and wearing his dark master's robes, he reminded me of the enigmatic Silent Doctor character present in many Modegan plays. I fought off a shiver, trying not to dwell on the fact that the appearance of the Doctor always signalled catastrophe in the next act.

Lorren went to one of the shelves and pulled out a small book. Even at a glimpse I recognised it as mine. A dark stain patterned the cover from the time it had got wet during a storm in Tarbean.

I fumbled with the strings of my purse, surprised to see my hands trembling slightly. 'It was two silver pennies, I believe.'

Lorren nodded.

'Can I offer you anything in addition to that? If you hadn't bought it for me, I would have lost it forever. Not to mention the fact that your purchase helped me gain admittance in the first place.'

'Two silver pennies will be sufficient.'

I lay the coins on his desk, they clattered slightly as I set them down, testament to my shaking hands. Lorren held out the book and I wiped my sweaty hands on my shirt before taking it. I opened it to Ben's inscription and smiled. 'Thank you for taking care of it, Master Lorren. It is precious to me.'

'The care of one more book is little trouble,' Lorren said as he returned to his seat. I waited to see if he might continue. He didn't.

'I . . .' my voice snagged in my throat. I swallowed to clear it. 'I also wanted to say that I was sorry for . . .' I stalled at the thought of actually mentioning open flame in the Archives. '. . . for what I did before.' I finished lamely.

'I accept your apology, Kvothe.' Lorren looked back down at the book he had been reading when I had come in. 'Good morning.'

I swallowed again against the dryness in my mouth. 'I was also wondering when I might hope to regain admittance to the Archives.'

Lorren looked up at me. 'You were caught with live fire among my books,' he said, emotion touching the edges of his voice like a hint of red sunset against the slate-grey clouds.

All of my carefully planned persuasion flew out of my head. 'Master Lorren,' I pleaded. 'I'd been whipped that day and wasn't at my wit's best. Ambrose—'

Lorren raised his long-fingered hand from the desk, his palm facing out, towards me. The careful gesture cut me off more quickly than a slap across the face. His face was expressionless as a blank page. 'Who am I to believe? A Re'lar of three years, or an E'lir of two months? A scriv in my employ, or an unfamiliar student found guilty of Reckless Use of Sympathy?'

I manage to regain a little of my composure. 'I understand your decision, Master Lorren. But is there anything I might do to earn readmittance?' I asked, unable to keep my voice entirely free of desperation. 'Honestly, I would rather be whipped again than spend another term banned. I would give you all the money in my pocket, though it isn't much. I'd work long hours as a scriv, without pay, for the privilege of proving myself to you. I know you're short-staffed during exams . . .'

Lorren looked at me, his placid eyes almost curious. I couldn't help but feel that my plea had affected him. 'All that?'

'All that,' I said earnestly, hope billowing wildly through my chest. 'All that and any other penance you desire.'

'I require but one thing to rescind my ban,' Lorren said.

I fought to keep a manic grin off my face. 'Anything.'

'Demonstrate the patience and prudence which you have heretofore been lacking,' Lorren said flatly, then looked down at the book that lay open on his desk. 'Good morning.'

The next day one of Jamison's errand boys woke me out of a sound sleep in my vast bed at the Horse and Four. He informed me that I was due on the horns at a quarter hour before noon. I was being charged with Conduct Unbecoming a Member of the Arcanum. Ambrose had finally caught wind of my song.

I spent the next several hours feeling vaguely sick to my stomach. This was exactly what I'd hoped to avoid: an opportunity for both Ambrose and Hemme to settle scores with me. Worse still, this was bound to lower Lorren's opinion of me even further, no matter what the outcome.

I arrived in the Masters' Hall early and was relieved to find the atmosphere much more relaxed than when I'd gone on the horns for malfeasance against Hemme. Arwyl and Elxa Dal smiled at me. Kilvin nodded. I was relieved that I had friends among the masters to balance out the enemies I'd made.

'Alright,' the Chancellor said briskly. 'We've got ten minutes before we start admissions. I don't feel like getting behind schedule, so I'm going to move this right along.' He looked around at the rest of the masters and saw only nods. 'Re'lar Ambrose, make your case. Keep it under a minute.'

'You have a copy of the song right there,' Ambrose said hotly. 'It's slanderous. It defames my good name. It's a shameful way for a member of the Arcanum to behave.' He swallowed, his jaw clenching. 'That's all.'

The Chancellor turned to me. 'Anything to say in your defense?'

'It was in poor taste, Chancellor, but I didn't expect it to get around. I only sang it on one occasion, in fact.'

'Fair enough.' The Chancellor looked down at the paper in front of him. He cleared his throat. 'Re'lar Ambrose, are you a donkey?'

Ambrose went stiff. 'No sir,' he said.

'Are you possessed of,' he cleared his throat and read directly off the page. 'A pizzle bound to fizzle?' A few of the masters struggled to control smiles. Elodin grinned openly.

Ambrose flushed. 'No sir.'

'Then I'm afraid I don't see the problem,' the Chancellor said curtly, letting the paper settle to the table. 'I move the charge of Conduct Unbecoming be replaced with Undignified Mischief.'

'Seconded,' Kilvin said.

'All in favour?' All hands went up except for Hemme's and Brandeur's. 'Motion passed. Discipline will be set at a formal letter of apology tendered to—'

'For God's sake, Arthur,' Hemme broke in. 'At least make it a public letter.'

The Chancellor glared at Hemme, then shrugged. '. . . formal letter of apology posted publicly before the fall term. All in favour?' All hands were raised. 'Motion passed.'

The Chancellor leaned forward onto his elbows and looked down at Ambrose. 'Re'lar Ambrose, in the future you will refrain from wasting our time with spurious charges.'

I could feel the anger radiating off Ambrose. It was like standing near a fire. 'Yes sir.'

Before I could feel smug, the Chancellor turned to me. 'And you, E'lir Kvothe, will comport yourself with more decorum in the future.' His stern words were somewhat spoiled by the fact that Elodin had begun cheerfully humming the melody to 'Jackass, Jackass' next to him.

I lowered my eyes and did my best to fight down a smile. 'Yes, sir.'

'Dismissed.'

Ambrose turned on his heel and stormed off, but before he made it through the door, Elodin burst out singing:

> 'He's a well-bred ass, you can see it in his stride!
> And for a copper penny he will let you take a ride!'

The thought of writing a public apology was galling to me. But, as they say, the best revenge is living well. So I decided to ignore Ambrose and enjoy my new luxurious lifestyle at the Horse and Four.

But I only managed two days of revenge. On the third day the Horse and Four had a new owner. Short, jolly Caverin was replaced with a tall, thin man who informed me that my services were no longer required. I was told to vacate my rooms before nightfall.

It was irritating, but I knew of at least four or five inns of a similar quality on this side of the river that would jump at the chance to employ a musician with his talent pipes.

But the innkeeper at Hollybush refused to speak with me. The White Hart and Queen's Crown were content with their current musicians. At the Golden Pony I waited for over an hour before I realised I was being politely ignored. By the time I was turned away by the Royal Oak I was fuming.

It was Ambrose. I didn't know how he'd done it, but I knew it was him. Bribes perhaps, or a rumour that any inn employing a certain red-haired musician would be losing the business of a large number of wealthy noble customers.

So I began working my way through the rest of the inns this side of the river. I'd already been turned away by the upper-class ones, but there were many respectable places left. Over the next several hours, I tried the Shepherd's Rest, the Boar's Head, Dog in the Wall, Staves Inn, and The Tabard. Ambrose had been very thorough; none of them were interested.

It was early evening by the time I came to Anker's, and by that time the only thing keeping me going was pure black temper. I was determined to try every single inn on this side of the river before I resorted to paying for a bunk and a meal chit again.

When I came to the inn, Anker himself was up on a ladder nailing a long piece of cedar siding back into place. He looked down at me as I came to stand near the foot of the ladder.

'So you're the one,' he said.

'Beg your pardon?' I said, puzzled.

'Fellow stopped by and told me that hiring a young red-haired fellow would make for a great pile of unpleasantness.' He nodded at my lute. 'You must be him.'

'Well then,' I said, adjusting the shoulder strap of my lute case. 'I won't waste your time,'

'You aren't wasting it yet,' he said as he climbed down the ladder, wiping his hands on his shirt. 'The place could use some music.'

I gave him a searching look. 'Aren't you worried?'

He spat. 'Damn little gadflies think they can buy the sun out the sky, don't they?'

'This particular one could probably afford it,' I said grimly. 'And the moon too, if he wanted the matched set to use as bookends.'

He snorted derisively. 'He can't do a damn thing to me. I don't cater to his sort of folk, so he can't scare off my business. And I own this place my own self, so he can't buy it and fire me off like he did to poor old Caverin . . .'

'Someone bought the Horse and Four?'

Anker gave me a speculative look. 'Ye din't know?'

I shook my head slowly, taking a moment to digest this piece of information. Ambrose had bought the Horse and Four just to spite me out of a job. No, he was too clever for that. He had probably loaned the money to a friend and passed it off as a business venture.

How much had it cost? A thousand talents? Five thousand? I couldn't even guess how much an inn like the Horse and Four was worth. What was even more disturbing was how quickly he had managed it.

It put things in sharp perspective for me. I'd known Ambrose was rich, but honestly, *everyone* was rich compared to me. I'd never bothered thinking about *how* wealthy he was, or how he could use it against me. I was getting a lesson in the sort of influence a wealthy baron's firstborn son could bring to bear.

For the first time I was glad for the University's strict code of conduct. If Ambrose was willing to go to these lengths, I could only imagine what drastic measures he would take if he didn't need to maintain a semblance of civility.

I was jolted out of my reverie by a young woman leaning out the front door of the inn, 'Damn you, Anker!' she shouted. 'I'm not going to pull and carry while you stand out here scratching your ass! Get in here!'

Anker muttered something under his breath as he picked up the ladder and he stowed it around the corner in the alleyway. 'What'd you do to this fellow anyway? Tup his mum?'

'Wrote a song about him, actually.'

As Anker opened the door of the inn, a gentle welter of conversation poured out onto the street. 'I'd be curious to hear a song like that.' He grinned. 'Why don't you come give it a play?'

'If you're sure,' I said, not quite believing my luck. 'There's bound to be trouble.'

'Trouble,' he chuckled. 'What does a boy like you know about trouble? I was in trouble afore you were born. I been in trouble you don't even got words for.' He turned to face me, still standing in the doorway. 'It's been a while since we've had music in here regular. Can't say as I like to go without. A proper tavern has music.'

I smiled. 'I have to agree with you there.'

'Truth is, I'd have you in just to twist that rich tit's nose,' Anker said. 'But if you can play worth half a damn . . .' He pushed the door open farther, making it an invitation. I could smell sawdust and honest sweat and baking bread.

By the end of the night it was all arranged. In exchange for playing four nights a span, I earned a tiny room on the third floor and the assurance that if I was around at mealtimes I would be welcome to a bit of whatever was cooking in the pot. Admittedly, Anker was getting the services of a talented musician for a bargain price, but it was a deal I was happy to make. Anything was better than going back to Mews and the silent scorn of my bunkmates.

The ceiling of my tiny room slanted downward in two corners, making it seem even smaller than it really was. It would have been cluttered if there had been more than the few sticks of furniture: a small desk with a wooden chair and a single shelf above it. The bed was flat and narrow as any bunk in the Mews.

I set my slightly battered copy of *Rhetoric and Logic* on the shelf over the desk. My lute case leaned comfortably in the corner. Through the window I could see the lights of the University unblinking in the cool autumn air. I was home.

———————

Looking back, I count myself lucky that I ended up in Anker's. True, the crowds were not as wealthy as those at the Horse and Four, but they appreciated me in a way the nobles never had.

And while my suite of rooms at the Horse and Four had been luxurious, my tiny room at Anker's was *comfortable*. Think in terms of shoes. You don't want the biggest you can find. You want the pair that fits. In time, that tiny room at Anker's came to be more of a home to me than anywhere else in the world.

But at that particular moment, I was furious at what Ambrose had cost me. So when I sat down to write my public letter of apology, it dripped with venomous sincerity. It was a work of art. I beat my breast with remorse. I wailed and gnashed my teeth over the fact that I had maligned a fellow student. I also included a full copy of the lyrics, along with two new verses and full musical notation. I then apologised in excruciating detail about every vulgar, petty innuendo included in the song.

I then spent four precious jots of my own money on paper and ink and called in the favour Jaxim owed me for trading him my late admissions slot. He had a friend that worked in a print shop, and with his help we printed over a hundred copies of the letter.

Then, the night before fall term began, Wil, Sim, and I posted them on every flat surface we could find on both sides of the river. We used a lovely alchemical adhesive Simmon had cooked up for the occasion. The stuff went on like paint, then dried clear as glass and hard as steel. If anyone wanted to remove the posts, they'd need a hammer and chisel.

In hindsight, it was as foolish as taunting an angry bull. And, if I had to guess, I'd say this particular piece of insolence was the main reason Ambrose eventually tried to kill me.

CHAPTER SIXTY-TWO

Leaves

UNDER POINTED ADVICE FROM several sources, I limited myself to three fields of study in the upcoming term. I continued Advanced Sympathy with Elxa Dal, held a shift in the Medica, and continued my apprenticeship under Manet. My time was pleasantly full, but not overburdened as it had been last term.

I studied my artificing more doggedly than anything else. Since my search for a patron had come to a dead end, I knew my best chance for self-sufficiency lay in becoming an artificer. Currently I worked for Kilvin and was given relatively menial jobs at relatively low pay. Once I finished my apprenticeship, that would improve. Better still, I would be able to pursue my own projects then sell them on commission for a profit.

If. If I was able to keep ahead of my debt to Devi. If I could somehow continue to muster enough money for tuition. If I could finish my apprenticeship under Manet without getting myself killed or crippled by the dangerous work that was done in the Fishery every day . . .

Forty or fifty of us gathered in the workshop, waiting to see the new arrival. Some sat on the stone worktables to get a good view, while a dozen or so students gathered on the iron catwalks in the rafters among Kilvin's hanging lamps.

I saw Manet up there. He was hard to miss: three times older than any of the other students with his wild hair and grizzled beard. I headed up the stairs and made my way to his side. He smiled and clapped me on the shoulder.

'What are you doing here?' I asked. 'I thought this was just for the greenwood who haven't seen this stuff before.'

'I thought I'd play the dutiful mentor today,' he shrugged. 'Besides, this particular display is worth watching, if only for the expressions on everyone's faces.'

Sitting atop one of the shop's heavy worktables was a massive cylindrical container about four feet high and two feet across. The edges were sealed without any bulky welds, and the metal had a dull, burnished look that made me guess it was more than simple steel.

I let my gaze wander the room and was surprised to see Fela standing in the crowd, waiting for the demonstration to begin along with the rest of the students.

'I didn't know Fela worked here,' I said to Manet.

Manet nodded. 'Oh sure. What, two terms now?'

'I'm surprised I haven't noticed,' I mused as I watched her talking to one of the other women in the crowd.

'So am I,' Manet said with a low, knowing chuckle. 'But she's not here very often. She sculpts and works with cut tile and glass. She's here for the equipment, not the sygaldry.'

The belling tower struck the hour outside, and Kilvin looked around, marking the faces of everyone there. I didn't doubt for a moment that he took note of exactly who was missing. 'For several span we will have this in the shop,' he said simply, gesturing to the metal container that stood nearby. 'Nearly ten gallons of a volatile transporting agent: *Regim Ignaul Neratum.*'

'He's the only one that calls it that,' Manet said softly. 'It's bone-tar.'

'Bone-tar?'

He nodded. 'It's caustic. Spill it on your arm and it'll eat through to the bone in about ten seconds.'

While everyone watched, Kilvin donned a thick leather glove and decanted about an ounce of dark liquid from the metal canister into a glass vial. 'It is important to chill the vial prior to decanting, as the agent boils at room temperature.'

He quickly sealed off the vial and held it up for everyone to see. 'The pressure cap is also essential, as the liquid is extremely volatile. As a gas it exhibits surface tension and viscosity, like mercury. It is heavier than air and does not dissipate. It coheres to itself.'

With no further preamble Kilvin tossed the vial into a nearby firewell, and there was the sharp, clear sound of breaking glass. From this height, I could see the firewell must have been cleaned out specially for this occasion. It was empty, just a shallow, circular pit of bare stone.

'It's a shame he's not more of a showman,' Manet said softly to me. 'Elxa Dal could do this with a little more flair.'

The room was filled with a sharp crackling and hissing as the dark liquid warmed itself against the stone of the firewell and began to boil. From my high vantage, I could see a thick, oily smoke slowly filling the bottom of the well. It didn't behave like fog or smoke at all. Its edges didn't diffuse. It pooled, and hung together like a tiny, dark cloud.

Manet tapped me on the shoulder, and I looked at him just in time to avoid being blinded by the initial burst of flame as the cloud caught fire. There were dismayed noises from all around and I guessed most of the others had been caught unaware. Manet grinned at me and gave a knowing wink.

'Thanks,' I said and turned back to watch. Jagged flames danced across the surface of the fog, coloured a bright sodium-red. The additional heat made the dark fog boil faster, and it swelled until the flames were licking towards the top of the waist-high lip of the firewell. Even from where I stood on the catwalk I could feel a gentle heat on my face.

'What the hell do you call that?' I asked him quietly. 'Fire-fog?'

'We could,' he responded. 'Kilvin would probably call it an atmospherically activated incendiary action.'

The fire flickered and died all at once, leaving the room filled with the acrid smell of hot stone.

'In addition to being highly corrosive,' Kilvin said, 'in its gaseous state the reagent is flammable. Once it warms sufficienctly, it will burn on contact with air. The heat that this produces can cause a cascading exothermic reaction.'

'Cascading huge Goddamn fire,' Manet said.

'You're better than a chorus,' I said softly, trying to keep a straight face.

Kilvin gestured. 'This container is designed to keep the agent cold and under pressure. Be mindful while it remains in the workshop. Avoid excessive heat in its immediate vicinity.' With that, Kilvin turned and headed back into his office.

'That's it?' I asked.

Manet shrugged. 'What else needs to be said? Kilvin doesn't let anyone work here unless they're careful, and now everyone knows what to be careful of.'

'Why is it even here?' I asked. 'What's it good for?'

'Scares the hell out of the first-termers.' He grinned.

'Anything more practical than that?'

'Fear is plenty practical,' he said. 'But you can use it to make a different type of emitter for sympathy lamps. You get a bluish light instead of the ordinary red. A little easier on the eyes. Fetch outrageous prices.'

I looked down into the workshop, but couldn't see Fela anywhere in the milling bodies. I turned back to Manet. 'Want to keep playing dutiful mentor and show me how?'

He absently ran his hands through his wild hair and shrugged. 'Sure.'

I was playing at Anker's later that night when I caught the eye of a beautiful girl sitting at one of the crowded tables in back. She looked remarkably like Denna, but I knew that to be nothing more than my own fancy. I hoped to see her enough that I had been catching glimpses of her out of the corner of my eye for days.

My second glance told me the truth . . .

It *was* Denna, singing along with half the folk in Anker's to 'Drover's Daughters'. She saw I was looking in her direction and waved.

Her appearance caught me so much by surprise that I completely forgot what my fingers were doing and my song fell to pieces. Everyone laughed, and I took a grand bow to hide my embarrassment. They cheered and booed me in equal amounts for a minute or so, enjoying my failure more than they had the song itself. Such is human nature.

I waited for their attention to drift away from me, then made my way casually to where Denna was sitting.

She stood to greet me. 'I'd heard you were playing on this side of the river,' she said. 'But I can't imagine how you keep the job if you fall apart every time a girl gives you a wink.'

I felt myself flush a little. 'It doesn't happen that often.'

'The winking or the falling apart?'

Unable to think of a response, I felt myself flush redder, and she laughed. 'How long will you be playing tonight?' She asked.

'Not much longer,' I lied. I owed Anker at least another hour.

She brightened. 'Good. Come away with me afterward, I need someone to walk with.'

Hardly believing my good luck, I made a bow to her. 'At your service certainly. Let me go and finish up.' I made my way to the bar where Anker and two of his serving girls were busy pulling drinks.

Unable to catch his eye, I grabbed hold of his apron as he hurried past me. He jerked to a stop and barely avoided spilling a tray of drinks onto a table of customers. 'God's teeth boy. What's the matter w'ye?'

'Anker, I've got to go. I can't stay till closing tonight.'

His face soured. 'Crowds like this don't come for the askin'. They ain't goin' to stay without a little song or summat to entertain 'em.'

'I'll do one more song. A long one. But I've got to go after that.' I gave him a desperate look. 'I swear I'll make it up to you.'

He looked at me more closely. 'Are ye in trouble?' I shook my head. 'It's a girl then.' He turned his head at the sound of voices calling for more drinks, then waved me away, briskly. 'Fine, go. But mind you, make it a good, long song. And you'll owe me.'

I moved to the front of the room and clapped my hands for the room's attention. Once the room was moderately quiet I began to play. By the time I struck the third chord everyone knew what it was: 'Tinker Tanner'. The oldest song in the world. I took my hands from the lute and began to clap. Soon everyone was pounding out the rhythm in unison, feet against the floor, mugs on tabletops.

The sound was almost overwhelming, but it faded appropriately when I sang the first verse. Then I led the room in the chorus with everyone singing along, some with their own words, some in their own keys. I moved to a nearby table as I finished my second verse and led the room in the chorus again.

Then I gestured expectantly towards the table to sing a verse of their own. It took a couple of seconds for them to realise what I wanted, but the expectation of the whole room was enough to encourage one of the more tipsy students to shout out a verse of his own. It gained him thunderous applause and cheers. Then, as everyone sang the chorus again, I moved to another table and did the same thing.

Before too long folk were taking initiative to sing out their own verses when the chorus was over. I made my way to where Denna waited by the outer door, and together we slipped out into the early evening twilight.

'That was cleverly done,' she said as we began to stroll away from the tavern. 'How long to you think they'll keep it up?'

'That will all depend on how quickly Anker manages to pull down drinks for the lot of them.' I came to a stop at the edge of the alley that ran between the back of Anker's tavern and the bakery next door. 'If you will excuse me a moment, I have to put my lute away.'

'In an alley?' she asked.

'In my room.' Stepping lightly, I moved quickly up the side of the building. Right foot rain barrel, left foot window ledge, left hand iron drainpipe, and I swung myself onto the lip of the first story roof. I hopped across the alley to the roof of the bakery and smiled at her startled intake of breath. From there it was a short stroll upward and I hopped back across to the second story roof of Anker's. Tripping the latch to my window, I reached through and set my lute lightly on my bed before heading back down the way I had come.

'Does Anker charge a penny every time you use his stairs?' she asked as I neared the ground.

I stepped down from the rainbarrel and brushed my hands against my trousers. 'I come and go at odd hours,' I explained easily as I fell into step beside her. 'Am I correct in understanding that you are looking for a gentleman to walk with you tonight?'

A smile curved her lips as she looked sideways at me. 'Quite.'

'That is unfortunate,' I sighed. 'I am no gentleman.'

Her smile grew. 'I think that you are close enough.'

'I would like to be closer.'

'Then come walking with me.'

'It would please me greatly. However . . .' I slowed my walk a bit, my smile fading into a more serious expression. 'What about Sovoy?'

Her mouth made a line. 'He's staked a claim on me then?'

'Well, not as such. But there are certain protocols involved . . .'

'A gentleman's agreement?' she asked acidly.

'More like honour among thieves, if you will.'

She looked me in the eye. 'Kvothe,' she said seriously. 'Steal me.'

I bowed and made a sweeping gesture towards the world. 'At your command.' We continued our walk, the moon was shining, making the houses and shops around us seem washed and pale. 'How is Sovoy anyway? I haven't seen him for a while.'

She waved a hand to dismiss the thought of him. 'I haven't either. Not for lack of trying on his part.'

My spirits rose a bit. 'Really?'

She rolled her eyes. 'Roses! I swear you men have all your romance from the same worn book. Flowers are a good thing, a sweet thing to give a lady.

But it is always roses, always red, and always perfect hothouse blooms when they can come by them.' She turned to face me. 'When you see me do you think of roses?'

I knew enough to shake my head, smiling.

'What then? If not a rose what do you see?'

Trapped. I looked her up and down once, as if trying to decide. 'Well,' I said slowly. 'You'll have to forgive us men. You see, it's not an easy thing to pick a flower to fit a girl, if you'll excuse my expression. . . .'

She grimaced. '*Pick a flower.* Yes, I'll excuse it this time.'

'The trouble is, when you gift a girl with flowers your choice can be construed so many different ways. A man might give you a rose because he feels you are beautiful, or because he fancies their shade or shape or softness similar to your lips. Roses are expensive, and perhaps he wishes to show through a valuable gift that you are valuable to him.'

'You make a good case for roses,' she said. 'The fact remains I do not like them. Pick another flower to suit me.'

'But what suits? When a man gives you a rose what you see may not be what he intends. You may think he sees you as delicate or frail. Perhaps you dislike a suitor who considers you all sweet and nothing else. Perhaps the stem is thorned, and you assume he thinks you likely to hurt a hand too quick to touch. But if he trims the thorns you might think he has no liking for a thing that can defend itself with sharpness. There's so many ways a thing can be interpreted,' I said. 'What is a careful man to do?'

She cast a sidelong look to me. 'If the man is you, I'd guess he would spin clever words and hope the question was forgotten.' She tilted her head. 'It isn't. What flower would you pick for me?'

'Very well, let me think.' I turned to look at her, then away. 'Let's run down a list. Dandelion might be good; it is bright, and there is a brightness about you. But dandelion is common, and you are not a common creature. Roses we have dealt with and discarded. Nightshade, no. Nettle . . . perhaps.'

She made a face of mock outrage and showed me her tongue.

I tapped a finger to my lips as if reconsidering. 'You are correct, except for your tongue it doesn't suit you.'

She huffed and crossed her arms.

'Wild oat!' I exclaimed, startling a laugh from her. 'It's wildness suits you, but it is a small flower, and bashful. For that as well as other,' I cleared my throat, 'more obvious reasons, I think we'll pass the wild oat by.'

'Pity,' she said.

'Daisy is a good one,' I bulled ahead, not letting her distract me. 'Tall and slender, willing to grow by roadsides. A hearty flower, not too delicate. Daisy is self-reliant. I think it might suit you . . . But let us continue in our list. Iris? Too gaudy. Thistle, too distant. Violet, too brief. Trillium? Hmmm, there's a thing. A fair flower. Doesn't take to cultivation. The texture of the petals . . .' I made the boldest motion of my young life and brushed the side of her neck gently with a pair of fingers. '. . . smooth enough to match your skin, just barely. But it is too close to the ground.'

'This is quite a bouquet you've brought for me,' she said gently. Unconsciously, she raised a hand to the side of her neck where I had touched her, held it there a moment, then let it fall.

A good sign or a bad one? Was she wiping my touch away or pressing it close? Uncertainty filled me more strongly than before and I decided to press ahead with no more blatant risks. I stopped walking. 'Selas flower.'

She stopped and turned to look at me. 'All this and you pick a flower I don't know? What is a selas flower? Why?'

'It is a deep red flower that grows on a strong vine. Its leaves are dark and delicate. They grow best in shadowy places, but the flower itself finds stray sunbeams to bloom in.' I looked at her. 'That suits you. There is much of you that is both shadow and light. It grows in deep forests, and is rare because only skilled folk can tend one without harming it. It has a wondrous smell and is much sought and seldom found.' I paused and made a point of examining her. 'Yes, since I am forced to pick, I would choose selas.'

She looked at me. Looked away. 'You think too much of me.'

I smiled. 'Perhaps you think too little of yourself.'

She caught a piece of my smile and shone it back at me. 'You were closer early in your list. Daisies, simple and sweet. Daisies are the way to win my heart.'

'I will remember it.' We started walking again. 'What flower would you bring me?' I teased, thinking to catch her off guard.

'A willow blossom,' she said without a second's hesitation.

I thought for a long minute. 'Do willows have blossoms?'

She looked up and to the side, thinking. 'I don't think so.'

'A rare treat to be given one then.' I chuckled. 'Why a willow blossom?'

'You remind me of a willow.' She said easily. 'Strong, deep-rooted, and hidden. You move easily when the storm comes, but never farther than you wish.'

I lifted my hands as if fending off a blow. 'Cease these sweet words,' I protested. 'You seek to bend me to your will, but it will not work. Your flattery is naught to me but wind!'

She watched me for a moment, as if to make sure my tirade was complete. 'Beyond all other trees,' she said with a curl of a smile on her elegant mouth, 'the willow moves to the wind's desire.'

The stars told me five hours had passed. But it seemed hardly any time at all before we came to the Oaken Oar where she was staying in Imre. At the doorway there was a moment that lasted for an hour as I considered kissing her. I had been tempted by the thought a dozen times on the road as we talked: when we paused on Stonebridge to watch the river in the moonlight, underneath a linden tree in one of Imre's parks . . .

At those times I felt a tension building between us, something almost tangible. When she looked sideways at me with her secret smile, the tilt of her head, the way she almost faced me made me think she must be hoping for me to do . . . something. Put my arm around her? Kiss her? How did one know? How could I be certain?

I couldn't. So I resisted the pull of her. I did not want to presume too much, did not want to offend her or embarrass myself. What's more, Deoch's warning had made me uncertain. Perhaps what I felt was nothing more than Denna's natural charm, her charisma.

Like all boys of my age, I was an idiot when it came to women. The difference between me and the others is that I was painfully aware of my ignorance, while others like Simmon bumbled around, making asses of themselves with their clumsy courting. I could think of nothing worse than making some unwelcome advance toward Denna and having her laugh at the awkwardness of my attempt. I hate nothing more than doing things badly.

So I made my good-byes and watched her enter the side door of the Oaken Oar. I took a deep breath and could hardly keep from laughing or dancing about. I was so full of her, the smell of the wind through her hair, the sound of her voice, the way the moonlight cast shadows across her face.

Then, slowly, my feet settled to the ground. Before I had taken six steps I sagged like a sail when the wind fades. As I walked back through the town, past sleeping houses and dark inns, my mood swung from elation to doubt in the space of three brief breaths.

I had ruined everything. All the things I had said, things that seemed so clever at the time, were in fact the worst things a fool could say. Even now she was inside, breathing a sigh of relief to finally be rid of me.

But she had smiled. Had laughed.

She hadn't remembered our first meeting on the road from Tarbean. I couldn't have made that much of an impression on her.

Steal me, she had said.

I should have been bolder and kissed her at the end. I should have been more cautious. I had talked too much. I had said too little.

CHAPTER SIXTY-THREE

Walking and Talking

WILEM AND SIMMON WERE already well into their lunches when I arrived at our usual spot in the courtyard. 'Sorry,' I said as I set my lute on the cobblestones near the bench. 'Got caught up haggling.'

I had been on the other side of the river buying a dram of quicksilver and a pouch of sea salt. The last had cost me dearly, but for once I wasn't concerned about money. If fortune smiled on me, I would be moving up the ranks in the Fishery soon, and that meant my money troubles would soon be over.

While shopping in Imre, I had also, quite by coincidence, wandered past the inn where Denna was staying, but she hadn't been there, or at the Eolian, or in the park where we'd stopped to talk last night. All the same, I was in a fine mood.

I tipped my lute case onto its side and flipped it open so the sun could warm the new strings, helping them stretch. Then I settled onto the stone bench under the pennant pole next to my two friends.

'So where were you last night?' Simmon asked too casually.

It was only then I remembered that the three of us had planned to meet up with Fenton and play corners last night. Seeing Denna had completely driven the plan from my mind. 'Oh God, I'm sorry Sim. How long did you wait for me?'

He gave me a look.

'I'm sorry,' I repeated, hoping I looked as guilty as I felt. 'I forgot.'

Sim grinned, shrugging it off. 'It's not a big deal. When we figured out you weren't going to show, we went to the Library to drink and look at girls.'

'Was Fenton mad?'

'Furious,' Wilem said calmly, finally entering the conversation. 'Said he was going to box your ears next time he saw you.'

Sim's grin widened. 'He called you a fluff-headed E'lir with no respect for his betters.'

'Made claims about your parentage and sexual tendency towards animals,' Wilem said with a straight face.

' ". . . in the Tehlin's cassock!" ' Simmon sang with his mouth full. Then he laughed and started to choke. I pounded him on the back.

'Where were you?' Wilem asked while Sim tried to get his breath back. 'Anker said you left early.'

For some reason, I found myself reluctant to talk about Denna. 'I met someone.'

'Someone more important than us?' Wilem asked in a flat tone that could be taken for dry humour or criticism.

'A girl,' I admitted.

One of his eyebrows went up. 'The one you've been chasing around?'

'I haven't been *chasing* anyone,' I protested. 'She found me, at Anker's.'

'Good sign,' Wilem said.

Simmon nodded wisely then looked up with a playful glint in his eye. 'So did you make any music?' He nudged me with an elbow and wagged his eyebrows up and down. 'A little duet?'

He looked too ridiculous for me to be offended. 'No music. She just wanted someone to walk her home.'

'Walk her home?' He said suggestively, wagging his eyebrows again.

I found it less amusing this time. 'It was dark out,' I said seriously. 'I just escorted her back to Imre.'

'Oh,' Sim said, disappointed.

'You left Anker's early,' Wil said slowly. 'And we waited for an hour. Does it take you two hours to walk to Imre and back?'

'It was a long walk,' I admitted.

'How long is long?' Simmon asked.

'A few hours.' I looked away. 'Six.'

'Six hours?' Sim asked. 'Come on, I think I'm entitled to a few details after listening to you ramble on about her for the last two span.'

I began to bristle. 'I don't ramble. We just walked,' I said. 'Talked.'

Sim looked doubtful. 'Oh come *on*. For six hours?'

Wilem tapped Simmon's shoulder. 'He's telling the truth.'

Simmon glanced over at him. 'Why do you say that?'

'He sounds more sincere than that when he lies.'

'If the two of you will be quiet for a minute or so I'll tell you the whole of it. Fair?' They nodded. I looked down at my hands, trying to collect my thoughts, but they wouldn't fall into any sort of orderly pattern. 'We took the long way back to Imre, stopped on Stonebridge for a while. Went to a park outside town. Sat by the river. We talked about . . . nothing really. Places we've been. Songs . . .' I realised I was rambling and shut my mouth. I picked my next words carefully. 'I thought about doing more than walking and talking but—' I stopped. I had no idea what to say.

They were both silent for a moment. 'I'll be,' Wilem marvelled. 'The mighty Kvothe, brought low by a woman.'

'If I didn't know you, I'd think you were scared,' Simmon said not quite seriously.

'You're damn right I'm scared,' I said in a low voice, wiping my hands nervously against my trousers. 'You'd be too if you'd ever met her. It's all I can do to sit here instead of running off to Imre, hoping to see her through a store window, or pass her crossing the street.' I gave a shaky smile.

'Go then.' Simmon smiled and gave me a little push. 'Godspeed. If I knew a woman like that I wouldn't be here eating lunch with the likes of you two.' He brushed his hair away from his eyes and gave me another push with his free hand. 'Go on.'

I stayed where I was. 'It's not that easy.'

'Nothing's ever easy with you,' Wilem muttered.

'Of course it's that easy,' Simmon laughed. 'Go tell her some of what you just told us.'

'Right,' I said with dark sarcasm. 'As if it were simple as singing. Besides, I don't know if she would want to hear it. She's something special . . . What would she want with me?'

Simmon gave me a frank stare, 'She came looking for you. She obviously wants something.'

There was a moment of silence and I hurried to change the subject while I had the chance. 'Manet's given me permission to start my journeyman project.'

'Already?' Sim gave me an anxious look. 'Will Kilvin go along with it? He's not a big one for cutting corners.'

'I didn't cut any corners,' I said. 'I just pick things up quickly.'

Wilem gave an amused snort and Sim spoke up before the two of us started to bicker. 'What are you doing for your project? Sympathy lamp?'

'Everyone does a lamp,' Wilem said.

I nodded. 'I wanted to do something different, maybe a gearwin, but Manet told me to stick to the lamp.' The belling tower struck four. I got to my feet and gathered up my lute case, ready to head to class.

'You should tell her,' Simmon said. 'If you like a girl you have to let her know.'

'How's that working out for you so far?' I said, irritated that Sim of all people would presume to give me relationship advice. 'Statistically speaking, how often has that strategy paid off, in your vast experience?'

Wilem made a point of looking elsewhere while Sim and I glared at each other. I looked away first, feeling guilty.

'Besides, there's nothing to tell,' I muttered. 'I like spending time with her, and now I know where she's staying. That means I can find her when I go looking.'

CHAPTER SIXTY-FOUR

Nine in the Fire

THE NEXT DAY, as luck would have it, I made a trip to Imre. Then, since I just happened to be in the neighbourhood, I stopped by the Oaken Oar.

The owner didn't know the name 'Denna' or 'Dianne', but a young, lovely dark-haired girl named 'Dinnah' was renting a room there. She wasn't in right now, but if I cared to leave a note . . . I declined his offer, comforted by the fact that since I now knew where Denna was staying, finding her would be relatively easy.

However, I had no luck catching Denna at the Oaken Oar over the next two days. On the third day, the owner informed me that Denna had left in the middle of the night, taking all her things and leaving her bill unpaid. After stopping by a few taverns at random and not finding her, I walked back to the University, not knowing if I should be worried or irritated.

Three more days and five more fruitless trips to Imre. Neither Deoch nor Threpe had heard any news of her. Deoch told me that it was her nature to disappear like this, and that looking for her would serve about as much purpose as calling for a cat. I knew it to be good advice, and ignored it.

———————

I sat in Kilvin's office trying to look calm as the great, shaggy master turned my sympathy lamp over in his huge hands. It was my first solo project as an artificer. I'd cast the plates and ground the lenses. I'd doped the emitter without giving myself arsenic poisoning. Most importantly, mine was the Alar and the intricate sygaldry that turned the individual pieces into a functioning handheld sympathy lamp.

If Kilvin approved of the finished product, he would sell it and I would receive part of the money as a commission. More importantly, I would become an artificer in my own right, albeit a fledgling one. I would be trusted to pursue my own projects with a large degree of freedom. It was a big step forward in the ranks of the Fishery, a step towards gaining the rank of Re'lar, and more importantly, my financial freedom.

Finally he looked up. 'This is finely made, E'lir Kvothe,' he said. 'But the design is not typical.'

I nodded. 'I made a few changes, sir. If you turn it on you'll see—'

Kilvin made a low sound that could have been an amused chuckle or an irritated grunt. He set the lamp down on the table and walked around the room, snuffing all the lamps but one. 'Do you know how many sympathy lamps I have had explode in my hands over the years, E'lir Kvothe?'

I swallowed and shook my head. 'How many?'

'None,' he said gravely. 'Because I am always careful. I am always absolutely sure of what I hold in my hands. You must learn patience, E'lir Kvothe. A moment in the mind is worth nine in the fire.'

I dropped my eyes and tried to look appropriately chastised.

Kilvin reached out and extinguished the one remaining lamp, bringing the room to near total darkness. There was a pause, then a distinctive reddish light welled from the hand lamp to shine against a wall. The light was very dim, less than that of a single candle.

'The action on the switch is graded,' I said quickly. 'It's more of a rheostat than a switch, really.'

Kilvin nodded. 'Cleverly done. That is not something most bother with on a small lamp such as this.' The light grew brighter, then dimmer, then brighter again. 'The sygaldry itself seems quite good,' Kilvin said slowly as he set the lamp down on the table. 'But the focus of your lens is flawed. There is very little diffusion.'

It was true. Instead of lighting the whole room, as was typical, my lamp revealed a narrow slice of the room: the corner of the worktable and half of the large black slate that stood against the wall. The rest of the room remained dark.

'It's intentional.' I said. 'There are lanterns like that, bull's-eye lanterns.'

Kilvin was little more than a dark shape across the table. 'Such things are known to me, E'lir Kvothe,' his voice held a hint of reproach. 'They are much used for unsavoury business. Business arcanists should have no mingling with.'

'I thought sailors used them,' I said.

'Burglars use them,' Kilvin said seriously. 'And spies, and other folk who do not wish to reveal their business during the dark hours of night.'

My vague anxiety grew suddenly sharper. I had considered this meeting mostly a formality. I knew I was a skilled artificer, better than many who had worked much longer in Kilvin's shop. Now I was suddenly worried that I might have made a mistake and wasted nearly thirty hours of work on the lamp, not to mention over a whole talent of my own money that I'd invested in materials.

Kilvin made a noncommittal grunt and muttered under his breath. The half-dozen oil lamps around the room sputtered back into life, filling the room with natural light. I marvelled at the master's casual execution of a six-way binding. I couldn't even guess where he had drawn the energy from.

'It's just that everyone makes a sympathy lamp for their first project,' I said to fill the silence. 'Everyone always follows the same old schema. I wanted to do something different. I wanted to see if I could make something new.'

'I expect what you wanted was to demonstrate your extreme cleverness,' Kilvin said matter-of-factly. 'You wished to not only finish your apprenticeship in half the usual time, you wanted to bring me a lamp of your own improved design. Let us be frank, E'lir Kvothe. Your making this lamp is an attempt to show that you are better than the ordinary apprentice, is it not?' As he said this, Kilvin looked directly at me, and for a moment there was none of his characteristic distraction lurking behind his eyes.

I felt my mouth go dry. Underneath his shaggy beard and heavily accented Aturan, Kilvin had a mind like a diamond. What had made me think I could lie to him and get away with it?

'Of course I wanted to impress you, Master Kilvin,' I said, looking down. 'I would think that that goes without saying.'

'Do not grovel,' he said. 'False modesty does not impress me.'

I looked up and squared my shoulders. 'In that case, Master Kilvin, I *am* better. I learn faster. I work harder. My hands are more nimble. My mind is more curious. However, I also expect you know this for yourself without my telling you.'

Kilvin nodded. 'That is better. And you are right, I do know these things.' He thumbed the lamp on and off while pointing it at different things around the room. 'And in all fairness, I am duly impressed with your skill. The lamp is tidily made. The sygaldry is quite cunning. The engraving precise. It is clever work.'

I flushed with pleasure at the compliments.

'But there is more to artificing than simply skill,' Kilvin said as he lay the lamp down and spread his huge hands out flat on either side of it. 'I cannot sell this lamp. It would gravitate to the wrong people. If a burglar were caught with such a tool it would reflect badly on all arcanists. You have completed your apprenticeship, and distinguished yourself in terms of skill.' I relaxed a bit. 'But your greater judgment is still somewhat in question. The lamp itself we will melt down for metals, I suppose.'

'You're going to melt down my lamp?' I had worked for a full span on the lamp and invested almost all the money I had on the purchase of raw materials. I had been counting on making a tidy profit once Kilvin sold it, but now . . .

Kilvin's expression was firm. 'We are all responsible for maintaining the University's reputation, E'lir Kvothe. An item like this in the wrong hands would reflect badly on all of us.'

I was trying to think of some way to persuade him when he waved a hand at me, shooing me towards the door. 'Go tell Manet your good news.'

Disheartened, I made my way out into the workshop and was greeted by the sounds of a hundred hands busily chiselling wood, chipping stone, and hammering metal. The air was thick with the smell of etching acids, hot iron, and sweat. I spotted Manet off in the corner, loading tile into a kiln. I waited until he closed the door and backed away, mopping sweat off his forehead with the sleeve of his shirt.

'How did it go?' he asked. 'Did you pass or am I going to be stuck holding your hand for another term?'

'I passed,' I said dismissively. 'You were right about the modifications. He wasn't impressed.'

'Told you,' he said without any particular smugness. 'You have to remember that I've been here longer than any ten students. When I tell you the masters are conservatives at heart, I'm not just making noise. I know.' Manet ran a hand idly over his wild, grey beard as he eyed the heat waves rolling off the brick kiln. 'Any thoughts on what you're going to do with yourself now that you're a free agent?'

'I was thinking of doping a batch of the blue-lamp emitters,' I said.

'The money is good,' Manet said slowly. 'Risky though.'

'You know I'm careful,' I reassured him.

'Risky is risky,' Manet said. 'I trained a fellow maybe ten years back, what was his name . . . ?' He tapped his head for a moment, then shrugged. 'He made a little slip.' Manet snapped his fingers sharply. 'But that's all it takes. Got burned pretty badly and lost a couple fingers. Wasn't much of an artificer afterwards.'

I looked across the room at Cammar, with his missing eye and bald, scarred head. 'Point taken.' I flexed my hands anxiously as I looked over at the burnished metal canister. People had been nervous around it for a day or two after Kilvin's demonstration, but it had soon become just another piece of equipment. The truth was, there were ten thousand different ways to die in the Fishery if you were careless. Bone-tar just happened to be the newest, most exciting way to kill yourself.

I decided to change the subject. 'Can I ask you a question?'

'Fire away,' he said, glancing at the nearby kiln. 'Get it? Fire away?'

I rolled my eyes. 'Would you say you know the University as well as anyone?'

He nodded. 'As well as anyone alive. All the dirty little secrets.'

I lowered my voice a bit. 'So if you wanted to, could you get into the Archives without anyone knowing?'

Manet's eyes narrowed. 'I could,' he said, 'but I wouldn't.'

I started to say something but he cut me off with more than a hint of exasperation. 'Listen my boy, we've talked about this before. Just be patient. You need to give Lorren more time to cool off. It's only been a term or so . . .'

'It's been half a year!'

He shook his head. 'That only seems like a long time to you because you're young. Believe me, it's fresh in Lorren's mind. Just spend another term or so impressing Kilvin, then ask him to intercede on your behalf. Trust me. It'll work.'

I put on my best hangdog expression. 'You could just . . .'

He shook his head firmly. 'No. No. No. I won't show you. I won't tell you. I won't draw you a map.' He softened his expression and lay a hand on my shoulder, obviously trying to take some of the sting out of his bald refusal. 'Tehlu anyway, why all the hurry? You're young. You have all the time in the world.' He levelled a finger at me. 'But if you get expelled it's forever. And that's what'll happen if you're caught sneaking into the Archives.'

I let my shoulders slump, dejected. 'You're right, I suppose.'

'That's right, I'm right,' Manet said, turning back to look at the kiln. 'Now run along. You're giving me an ulcer.'

I walked away, thinking furiously about Manet's advice and what he had let slip in our conversation. In general I knew his advice was good. If I were well-behaved for a term or two, I would get access to the Archives. It was the safe, simple route to what I wanted.

Unfortunately, I couldn't afford patience. I was painfully aware of the fact that this term would be my last unless I could find a way to make a great deal of money rather quickly. No. Patience wasn't an option for me.

On my way out, I peered inside Kilvin's office and saw him sitting at his worktable, idly thumbing my lamp on and off. His expression was distracted again, and I didn't doubt that his vast machine of a brain was busy thinking about a half dozen things all at once.

I knocked on the door frame to get his attention. 'Master Kilvin?'

He didn't turn to look at me. 'Yes?'

'Could *I* buy the lamp?' I asked. 'I could use it to read at night. Right now I'm still spending money on candles.' I briefly considered wringing my hands before deciding against it. Too melodramatic.

Kilvin thought for a long moment. The lamp in his hand gave a soft, *t-tick* as he switched it on again. 'You cannot buy what your own hands build,' he said. 'The time and materials that made it were yours.' He held it out to me.

I stepped into the room to take it, but Kilvin drew his hand back and met my eye. 'I must make clear one thing,' he said seriously. 'You cannot sell or lend this. Not even to someone you trust. If this is lost, it would eventually end up in the wrong hands and be used for skulking about in the dark, doing dishonest things.'

'I give you my word, Master Kilvin. No one will be using it but me.'

As I left the shop I was careful to keep my expression neutral, but inside I was wearing a wide, satisfied smile. Manet had told me exactly what I needed to know. There was another way into the Archives. A hidden way. If it existed, I could find it.

CHAPTER SIXTY-FIVE

Spark

I LURED WIL AND Sim to the Eolian with the promise of free drinks, the one piece of generosity I could afford.

You see, while Ambrose's interference might keep me from gaining a wealthy noble as a patron, there were still plenty of regular music lovers who bought me more drinks than I could comfortably consume on my own.

There were two simple solutions to this. I could become a drunk, or use an arrangement that has been around for as long as there have been taverns and musicians. Attend to me as I draw back the curtain to reveal a long-kept minstrel's secret . . .

Let's say you are out at an inn. You listen to me play. You laugh, cry, and generally marvel at my craft. Afterwards, you want to show your appreciation, but you don't have the wherewithal to make a substantial gift of money like some wealthy merchant or noble. So you offer to buy me a drink.

I, however, have already had a drink. Or several drinks. Or perhaps I am trying to keep a clear head. Do I refuse your offer? Of course not. That would just waste a valuable opportunity and most likely leave you feeling snubbed.

Instead I graciously accept and ask bartender for a Greysdale Mead. Or a Sounten. Or a particular vintage of white wine.

The name of the drink isn't the important thing. The important thing is that the drink doesn't really exist. The bartender gives me water.

You pay for the drink, I thank you graciously, and everyone walks away happy. Later, the bartender, the tavern, and the musician share your money three ways.

Better yet, some sophisticated drinking establishments allow you to keep drinks as a sort of credit for future use. The Eolian was just such a place.

That is how, despite my poverty-stricken state, I managed to bring an entire dark bottle of scutten back to the table where Wil and Sim waited.

Wil eyed it appreciatively as I sat down. 'What's the special occasion?'

'Kilvin approved my sympathy lamp. You're looking at the Arcanum's newest journeyman artificer,' I said a little smugly. Most students spend at least three or four terms finishing their apprenticeships. I kept my mixed success with the lamp to myself.

'About time,' Wil said dryly. 'Took you what, almost three months? People were beginning to say that you had lost your touch.'

'I thought you'd be more pleased,' I said as I peeled the wax off the top of the bottle. 'My days of being a pinchpenny might be coming to an end.'

Sim made a dismissive noise. 'You stand your round well enough,' he said.

'I drink to your continued success as an artificer,' Wil said, sliding his cup towards me. 'Knowing it will lead to more drinks in the future.'

'Plus,' I said as I stripped the last of the wax away, 'there's always the chance that if I get you drunk enough you'll let me slip into the Archives someday when you're working the desk.' I kept my tone carefully jovial as I glanced up at him to gauge his reaction.

Wil took a slow drink, not meeting my eye. 'I can't.'

Disappointment nestled sourly in the pit of my stomach. I made a dismissive gesture, as if I couldn't believe he'd taken my joke seriously. 'Oh, I know—'

'I thought about it,' Wilem interrupted. 'Seeing as how you didn't deserve the punishment you got, and I know how much it's been bothering you.' Wil took a drink. 'Lorren occasionally suspends students. A handful of days for too loud talking in the Tombs. A few span if they are careless with a book. But banned is different. That hasn't happened in years. Everyone knows. If anyone saw you . . .' He shook his head. 'I'd lose my position as scriv. We could both get expelled.'

'Don't beat yourself up,' I said. 'Just the fact that you considered it means—'

'We're getting maudlin here,' Sim broke in, knocking his glass against the table. 'Open the bottle and we'll drink to Kilvin being so impressed that he talks to Lorren and gets you unbanned from the Archives.'

I smiled and began to work a screw into the cork. 'I have a better plan,' I said. 'I vote we drink to the perpetual confusation and botherment of a certain Ambrose Jakis.'

'I think we can all agree to that,' Wil said, raising his glass.

'Great God,' Simmon said in a hushed tone. 'Look what Deoch found.'

'What's that?' I asked, concentrating on getting the cork out all in one piece.

'He's managed to get the most beautiful woman in the place again.' Sim's grumble was uncharacteristically surly. 'It's enough to make you hate a man.'

'Sim, your taste in women is questionable at best.' The cork came free with a pleasing sound and I held it up triumphantly for them to see. Neither of them paid me any attention, their eyes pinned to the doorway.

I turned to look. Paused. 'That's Denna.'

Sim turned back to look at me. 'Denna?'

I frowned. 'Dianne. Denna. She's the one I told you about before. The one who sang with me. She goes by a lot of different names. I don't know why.'

Wilem gave me a flat look. '*That's* your girl?' he asked, his voice thick with disbelief.

'Deoch's girl,' Simmon amended gently.

It seemed to be the case. Handsome, muscular Deoch was talking to her in that easy way he had. Denna laughed and put an arm around him in a casual embrace. I felt a heavy weight settle in my chest as I watched them talk.

Then Deoch turned and pointed. She followed his gesture, met my eyes, and lit up as she smiled at me. I returned the smile by reflex alone. My heart began to beat again. I waved her over. After a quick word to Deoch she began to make her way through the crowd towards us.

I took a quick drink of scutten as Simmon turned to look at me with an almost reverent disbelief.

I had never seen Denna dressed in anything other than travelling clothes. But tonight she was wearing a dark green dress that left her arms and shoulders bare. She was stunning. She knew it. She smiled.

The three of us stood as she approached. 'I was hoping to find you here,' she said.

I gave a small bow. 'I was hoping to be found. These are two of my best friends. Simmon.' Sim smiled sunnily and brushed his hair away from his eyes. 'And Wilem.' Wil nodded. 'This is Dianne.'

She lounged into a chair. 'What brings such a group of handsome young men out on the town tonight?'

'We're plotting the downfall of our enemies,' Simmon said.

'And celebrating,' I hurried to add.

Wilem raised his glass in a salute. 'Confusion to the enemy.'

Simmon and I followed suit, but I stopped when I remembered Denna didn't have a glass. 'I'm sorry,' I said. 'Can I buy you a drink?'

'I was hoping you would buy me dinner,' she said. 'But I would feel guilty about stealing you away from your friends.'

My mind raced as I tried to think of a tactful way to extricate myself.

'You're making the assumption that we want him here,' Wilem said with a straight face. 'You'd do us a favour if you took him away.'

Denna leaned forward intently, a smile brushing the pink corners of her mouth. 'Really?'

Wilem nodded gravely. 'He drinks even more than he talks.'

She darted a teasing look at me. 'That much?'

'Besides,' Simmon chimed in innocently. 'He'd sulk for days if he missed a chance to be with you. He'll be completely worthless to us if you leave him here.'

My face grew hot and I had the sudden urge to throttle Sim. Denna laughed sweetly. 'I suppose I'd better take him then.' She stood with a motion like a willow wand bending to the wind and offered me her hand. I took it. 'I hope to see you again, Wilem, Simmon.'

They waved and we started to make our way to the door. 'I like them,' she said. 'Wilem is a stone in deep water. Simmon is like a boy splashing in a brook.'

Her description startled a laugh from me. 'I couldn't have said it better. You mentioned dinner?'

'I lied,' she said with an easy delight. 'But I would love the drink you offered me.'

'How about the Taps?'

She wrinkled her nose. 'Too many old men, not enough trees. It is a good night to be out of doors.'

I gestured towards the door. 'Lead the way.'

She did. I basked in her reflected light and the stares of envious men. As we left the Eolian, even Deoch looked a little jealous. But as I passed him I caught a glimmer of something other in his eye. Sadness? Pity?

I spared no time for it. I was with Denna.

We bought a loaf of dark bread and a bottle of Avennish strawberry wine. Then found a private place in one of the many public gardens scattered throughout Imre. The first of autumn's falling leaves danced along the streets beside us. Denna removed her shoes and danced lightly through the shadows, delighting in the feel of the grass beneath her feet.

We settled on a bench beneath a great spreading willow, then abandoned it and found more comfortable seats on the ground at the foot of the tree. The bread was thick and dark, and tearing chunks of it gave us distraction for our hands. The wine was sweet and light, and after Denna kissed the bottle it left her lips wet for an hour.

It had the desperate feel of the last warm night of summer. We spoke of everything and nothing, and all the while I could hardly breathe for the nearness of her, the way she moved, the sound of her voice as it touched the autumn air.

'Your eyes were far away just then,' she said. 'What were you thinking?'

I shrugged, buying a moment to think. I couldn't tell her the truth. I knew every man must compliment her, bury her in flattery more cloying than roses. I took a subtler path. 'One of the masters at the University once told me that there were seven words that would make a woman love you.' I made a deliberately casual shrug. 'I was just wondering what they were.'

'Is that why you talk so much? Hoping to come on them by accident?'

I opened my mouth to retort. Then, seeing her dancing eyes, I pressed my lips together and tried to fight down my embarrassed flush. She lay a hand on my arm. 'Don't go quiet on my account, Kvothe,' she said gently. 'I'd miss the sound of your voice.'

She took a drink of wine. 'Anyway, you shouldn't bother wondering. You spoke them to me when first we met. You said, *I was just wondering why you're here.*' She made a flippant gesture. 'From that moment I was yours.'

My mind flashed back to our first meeting in Roent's caravan. I was stunned. 'I didn't think you remembered.'

She paused in tearing a piece of dark bread away from the loaf and looked up at me quizzically. 'Remember what?'

'Remembered me. Remembered our meeting in Roent's caravan.'

'Come now,' she teased. 'How could I forget the red-haired boy who left me for the University?'

I was too stunned to point out that I hadn't left her. Not really. 'You never mentioned it.'

'Neither did you,' she countered. 'Perhaps I thought that you had forgotten me.'

'Forget you? How could I?'

She smiled at that, but looked down at her hands. 'You might be surprised what men forget,' she said, then lightened her tone. 'But then again, perhaps not. I don't doubt that you've forgotten things, being a man yourself.'

'I remember your name, Denna.' It sounded good to say it to her. 'Why did you take a new one? Or was Denna just the name that you were wearing on the road to Anilin?'

'Denna,' she said softly. 'I'd almost forgotten her. She was a silly girl.'

'She was like a flower unfolding.'

'I stopped being Denna years ago, it seems.' She rubbed her bare arms and looked around as if she was suddenly uneasy that someone might find us here.

'Should I call you Dianne, then? Would you like it better?'

The wind stirred the hanging branches of the willow as she cocked her head to look at me. Her hair mimicked the motion of the trees. 'You are kind. I think I like Denna best from you. It sounds different when you say it. Gentle.'

'Denna it is,' I said firmly. 'What happened in Anilin, anyway?'

A leaf floated down and landed in her hair. She brushed it away absentmindedly. 'Nothing pleasant,' she said, avoiding my eyes. 'But nothing unexpected either.'

I held out my hand and she passed me back the loaf of bread. 'Well I'm glad you made it back,' I said. 'My Aloine.'

She made a decidedly unladylike noise. 'Please, if either of us is Savien, it's me. I'm the one that came looking for you,' she pointed out. 'Twice.'

'I look,' I protested. 'I just don't seem to have a knack for finding you.' She rolled her eyes dramatically. 'If you could recommend an auspicious time and place to look for you, it would make a world of difference . . .' I trailed off gently, making it a question. 'Perhaps tomorrow?'

Denna gave me a sideways glance, smiling. 'You're always so cautious,' she said. 'I've never known a man to step so carefully.' She looked at my face as if it were a puzzle she could solve. 'I expect noon would be an auspicious time tomorrow. At the Eolian.'

I felt a warm glow at the thought of meeting her again. '*I was just wondering why you're here*,' I mused aloud, remembering the conversation that seemed so long ago. 'You called me a liar, afterwards.'

She leaned forward to touch my hand in a consoling way. She smelled of strawberry, and her lips were a dangerous red even in the moonlight. 'How well I knew you, even then.'

We talked through the long hours of night. I spoke subtle circles around the way I felt, not wanting to be overbold. I thought she might be doing the same, but I could never be sure. It was like we were doing one of those elaborate Modegan court dances, where the partners stand scant inches apart, but − if they are skilled − never touch.

Such was our conversation. But not only were we lacking touch to guide us, it was as if we were also strangely deaf. So we danced very carefully, unsure what music the other was listening to, unsure, perhaps, if the other was dancing at all.

———

Deoch was standing vigil at the door, same as always. He waved to see me. 'Master Kvothe. I'm afraid you've missed your friends.'

'I thought I might've. How long have they been gone?'

'Only an hour.' He stretched his arms above his head, grimacing. Then let them fall to his sides with a weary sigh.

'Did they seem put out that I abandoned them?'

He grinned. 'Not terribly. They happened on a couple lovelies of their own. Not as lovely as yours, of course.' He looked uncomfortable for a moment, then spoke slowly as if he were picking his words with great care. 'Look, s . . . Kvothe. I know it's not my place, and I hope you don't take it wrong.' He looked around and suddenly spat. 'Damn. I'm no good at this sort of thing.'

He looked back at me and gestured vaguely with his hands. 'You see, women are like fires, like flames. Some women are like candles, bright and friendly. Some are like single sparks, or embers, like fireflies for chasing on summer nights. Some are like campfires, all light and heat for a night and willing to be left after. Some women are like hearthfires, not much to look at but underneath they are all warm red coal that burns a long, long while.

'But Dianne . . . Dianne is like a waterfall of spark pouring off a sharp iron edge that God is holding to the grindstone. You can't help but look, can't help but want it. You might even put your hand to it for a second. But you can't hold it. She'll break your heart . . .'

The evening was too fresh in my memory for me to pay much heed to Deoch's warning. I smiled, 'Deoch, my heart is made of stronger stuff than glass. When she strikes she'll find it strong as iron-bound brass, or gold and adamant together mixed. Don't think I am unaware, some startled deer to stand transfixed by hunter's horns. It's she who should take care, for when she strikes, my heart will make a sound so beautiful and bright that it can't help but bring her back to me in winged flight.'

My words startled Deoch into bemused laugher. 'God you're brave,' he shook his head. 'And young. I wish I were as brave and young as you.' Still smiling, he turned to enter the Eolian. 'Good night then.'

'Good night.'

Deoch wished that he were more like me? It was as great a compliment as any I had ever been given.

But even better than that was the fact that my days of fruitlessly searching for Denna were at an end. Tomorrow at noon in the Eolian: 'lunch and talking and walking' as she had phrased it. The thought filled me with a giddy excitement.

How young I was. How foolish. How wise.

CHAPTER SIXTY-SIX

Volatile

I WOKE EARLY THE next morning, nervous at the thought of lunch with Denna. Knowing it would be useless to attempt to get back to sleep, I headed to the Fishery. Last night's extravagant spending had left me with exactly three pennies in my pocket, and I was eager to take advantage of my newly earned position.

Usually I worked nights in the Fishery. It was a different place in the mornings. There were only fifteen or twenty people there pursuing their individual projects. In the evenings there were usually twice that many. Kilvin was in his office, as always, but the atmosphere was more relaxed: busy, but not bustling.

I even saw Fela off in the corner of the shop, chipping carefully away at a piece of obsidian the size of a large loaf of bread. Small wonder I'd never seen her here before if she made a habit of being in the shop this early.

Despite Manet's warning, I decided to make a batch of blue emitters for my first project. Tricky work, as it required the use of bone-tar, but they would sell fairly quickly, and the whole process would only take me four or five hours of careful work. Not only could I be done in time to meet with Denna at the Eolian for lunch, but I might be able to get a small advance from Kilvin so I could have a bit of money in my purse when I went to meet her.

I gathered the necessary tools and set up in one of the fume hoods along the eastern wall. I chose a place near a drench, one of the five-hundred-gallon tanks of twice-tough glass that were spaced throughout the workshop. If you spilled something dangerous on yourself while working in the hoods, you could simply pull the drench's handle and rinse yourself clean in a stream of cool water.

Of course I would never need the drench so long as I was careful. But it was nice having it close, just in case.

After setting up the fume hood, I made my way to the table where the bone-tar was kept. Despite the fact that I knew it was no more dangerous than a stone saw or the sintering wheel, I found the burnished metal container unnerving.

And today something was different. I caught the attention of one of the more experienced artificers as he walked past. Jaxim had the haggard look common to most artificers in the middle of large projects, as if he were putting off sleep until it was entirely finished.

'Should there be this much frost?' I asked him, pointing out the tar canister. Its edges were covered in fine white tufts of frost, like tiny shrubs. The air around the metal actually shimmered with cold.

Jaxim peered at it, then shrugged. 'Better too cold than not cold enough,' he said with a humourless chuckle. 'Heh heh. Kaboom.'

I couldn't help but agree, and guessed that it might have something to do with the workshop being cooler this early in the morning. None of the kilns had been fired up yet, and most of the forge fires were still banked and sullen.

Moving carefully, I ran through the decanting procedure in my head, making sure I hadn't forgotten anything. It was so cold that my breath hung white in the air. The sweat on my hands froze my fingers to the canister's fastenings the same way a curious child's tongue sticks to a pump handle in the dead of winter.

I decanted about an ounce of the thick, oily liquid into the pressure vial and quickly applied the cap. Then I made my way back to the fume hood and started preparing my materials. After a few tense minutes, I began the long, meticulous process of preparing and doping a set of blue emitters.

My concentration was broken two hours later by a voice behind me. It wasn't particularly loud, but it held a serious tone you never ignore in the Fishery.

It said, 'Oh my God.'

Because of my current work, the first thing I looked at was the bone-tar canister. I felt a flash of cold sweat roll over me when I saw black liquid leaking from one corner and running down the worktable's leg to pool on the floor. The thick timber of the table's leg was almost entirely eaten away, and I heard a light popping and crackling as the liquid pooling on the floor began to boil. All I could think of was Kilvin's statement during the demonstration: *In addition to being highly corrosive, the gas burns when it comes in contact with air . . .*

Even as I turned to look, the leg gave way and the worktable began to tip. The burnished metal canister tumbled down. When it struck the stone floor, the metal was so cold it didn't simply crack or dent, it shattered like glass. Gallons of the dark fluid burst out in a great splay across the workshop floor. The room filled with sharp crackling and popping sounds as the bone-tar spread across the warm stone floor and started to boil.

Long ago, the clever person who designed the Fishery placed about two dozen drains in the workshop to help with cleaning and managing spills. What's more, the workshop's stone floor rose and fell in a gentle pattern of peaks and troughs to guide the spills toward those drains. That meant as soon as the container shattered, the wide spill of oily liquid began to run off in two different directions, heading for two different drains. At the same time it continued to boil, forming thick, low clouds, dark as tar, caustic, and ready to burst into flame.

Trapped between these two spreading arms of dark fog was Fela, who had been working by herself at an out-of-the-way table in the corner of the shop. She stood, her mouth half open in shock. She was dressed practically for work in the shop, light trousers and a gauzy linen shirt cuffed at the elbow. Her long, dark hair was pulled back into a tail, but still hung down to nearly the small of her back. She would burn like a torch.

The room began to fill with frantic noise as people realised what was happening. They shouted orders or simply yelled in panic. They dropped tools and knocked over half-finished projects as they scrambled around.

Fela hadn't screamed or called for help, which meant no one but me had noticed the danger she was in. If Kilvin's demonstration was any indication, I guessed the whole shop could be a sea of flame and caustic fog in less than a minute. There wasn't any time . . .

I glanced at the scattered projects on the nearby worktable, looking for anything that could be of some help. But there was nothing: a jumble of basalt blocks, spools of copper wire, a half-inscribed hemisphere of glass that was probably destined to become one of Kilvin's lamps . . .

And as easy as that, I knew what I had to do. I grabbed the glass hemisphere and dashed it against one of the basalt blocks. It shattered and I was left with a thin, curved shard of broken glass about the size of my palm. With my other hand I grabbed my cloak from the table and strode past the fume hood.

I pressed my thumb against the edge of the piece of glass and felt an unpleasant tugging sensation followed by a sharp pain. Knowing I'd drawn blood, I smeared my thumb across the glass and spoke a binding. As I came to stand in front of the drench I dropped the glass to the floor, concentrated, and stepped down hard, crushing it with my heel.

Cold unlike anything I'd ever felt stabbed into me. Not the simple cold you feel in your skin and limbs on a winter day. It hit my body like a clap of thunder. I felt it in my tongue and lungs and liver.

But I got what I wanted. The twice-tough glass of the drench spiderwebbed into a thousand fractures, and I closed my eyes just as it burst. Five hundred gallons of water struck me like a great fist, knocking me back a step and soaking me through to the skin. Then I was off, running between the tables.

Quick as I was, I wasn't quick enough. There was a blinding crimson flare from the corner of the workshop as the fog began to catch fire, sending up strangely angular tongues of violent red flame. The fire would heat the rest of the tar, causing it to boil more quickly. This would make more fog, more fire, and more heat.

As I ran, the fire spread. It followed the two trails the bone-tar made as it ran towards the drains. The flames shot up with startling ferocity, sending up two curtains of fire, effectively cutting off the far corner of the shop. The flames were already as tall as me, and growing.

Fela had worked her way out from behind the workbench and hurried along the wall towards one of the floor drains. Since the bone-tar was pouring down the grate, there was a gap close to the wall clear of flame or fog. Fela was just about to sprint past when dark fog began to boil up out of the grate. She gave a short, startled shriek as she backed away. The fog was burning even as it boiled up, engulfing everything in a roiling pool of flame.

I finally made my way past the last table. Without slowing I held my breath, closed my eyes, and jumped over the fog, not wanting to let the horrible corrosive stuff touch my legs. I felt a brief, intense flash of heat on my hands and face, but my wet clothing kept me from being burned or catching fire.

Since my eyes were closed, I landed awkwardly, banging my hip against the stone top of a worktable. I ignored it and ran to Fela.

She had been backing away from the fire towards the outer wall of the shop, but now she was staring at me, hands half-raised protectively. 'Put your arms down!' I shouted as I ran up to her, spreading my dripping-wet cloak with both hands. I don't know if she heard me over the roar of the flames, but regardless, Fela understood. She lowered her hands and stepped towards the cloak.

As I closed the final distance between us, I glanced behind and saw the fire was growing even faster than I'd expected. The fog clung to the floor, over a foot deep, black as pitch. The flames were so high I couldn't see to the other side, let alone guess how thick the wall of fire had become.

Just before Fela stepped into the cloak, I lifted it to completely engulf her head. 'I'm going to have to carry you out.' I shouted as I bundled the cloak around her. 'Your legs will burn if you try to wade through.' She said something in reply, but it was muffled by the layers of wet cloth and I couldn't make it out over the roar of the fire.

I picked her up, not in front of me, like Prince Gallant out of some storybook, but over one shoulder, the way you carry a sack of potatoes. Her hip pressed hard into my shoulder and I pelted towards the fire. The heat battered the front of my body, and I threw my free arm up to protect my face, praying the moisture on my trousers would save my legs from the worst of the corrosive nature of the fog.

I drew a deep breath just before I hit the fire, but the air was sharp and acrid. I coughed reflexively and sucked down another lungful of the burning air just as I entered the wall of flame. I felt the sharp chill of the fog around my lower legs and there was fire all around me as I ran, coughing and drawing in more bad air. I grew dizzy and tasted ammonia. Some distant, rational part of my mind thought: *of course, to make it volatile.*

Then nothing.

When I awoke, the first thing that sprang to my mind was not what you might expect. Then again, it may not be that much of a surprise if you have ever been young yourself.

'What time is it?' I asked frantically.

'First bell after noon,' a female voice said. 'Don't try to get up.'

I slumped back against the bed. I was supposed to have met with Denna at the Eolian an hour ago.

Miserable and with a sour knot in my stomach, I took in my surroundings. The distinctive antiseptic tang in the air let me know that I was somewhere in the Medica. The bed was a giveaway too: comfortable enough to sleep in, but not so comfortable that you'd want to lie around.

I turned my head and saw a familiar pair of striking green eyes framed by close-cropped blond hair. 'Oh,' I relaxed back onto the pillow. 'Hello, Mola.'

Mola stood next to one of the tall counters that lined the edges of the room. The classic dark colours of those who worked at the Medica made her pale complexion seem even more so. 'Hello Kvothe,' she said, continuing to write her treatment report.

'I heard you finally got promoted to El'the,' I said. 'Congratulations. Everyone knows you deserved it a long time ago.'

She looked up, her pale lips curving into a small smile. 'The heat doesn't seem to have damaged the gilding on your tongue.' She lay down her pen. 'How does the rest of you feel?'

'My legs feel fine, but numb, so I'm guessing I got burned but you've already done something about it.' I lifted up the bedsheet, looked under it, then tucked it carefully back into place. 'I also seem to be in an advanced state of undress.' I felt a momentary panic. 'Is Fela alright?'

Mola nodded seriously and moved closer to stand by the side of the bed. 'She has a bruise or two from when you dropped her, and is a little singed around the ankles. But she came out of it better than you did.'

'How is everyone else from the Fishery?'

'Surprisingly good, all things considered. A few burns from heat or acid. One case of metal poisoning, but it was minor. Smoke tends to be the real troublemaker with fires, but whatever was burning over there didn't seem to give off any smoke.'

'It did give off a sort of ammonia fume.' I took a few deep, experimental breaths. 'But my lungs don't seem to be burned,' I said, relieved. 'I only got about three breaths of it before I passed out.'

There was a knock on the door and Sim's head popped in. 'You're not naked are you?'

'Mostly,' I said. 'But the dangerous parts are covered up.'

Wilem followed in, looking distinctly uncomfortable. 'You're not nearly as pink as you were before,' he said. 'I'm guessing that's a good sign.'

'His legs are going to hurt for a while, but there's no permanent damage,' she said.

'I brought fresh clothes,' Sim said cheerily. 'The ones you were wearing were ruined.'

'I hope you chose something suitable from my vast wardrobe?' I said dryly to hide my embarrassment.

Sim shrugged off my comment. 'You showed up without shoes, but I couldn't find another pair in your room.'

'I don't have a second pair,' I said as I took the bundle of clothes from Sim. 'It's fine. I've been barefoot before.'

I walked away from my little adventure without any permanent damage. However, right now there wasn't a part of me that didn't hurt. I had flash burn across the backs of my hands and neck and mild acid burns across my lower legs from where I'd waded through the fire-fog.

Despite all this, I made my limping way the long three miles across the river to Imre, hoping against hope that I might still find Denna waiting.

Deoch eyed me speculatively as I crossed the courtyard toward the Eolian. He looked me up and down pointedly. 'Lord, boy. You look like you fell off a horse. Where are your shoes?'

'A good morning to you too,' I said sarcastically.

'A good afternoon,' he corrected, with a significant glance up at the sun. I began to brush past him, but he held up a hand to stop me. 'She's gone, I'm afraid.'

'Black . . . sodding damn.' I slumped, too weary to curse my luck properly.

Deoch gave me a sympathetic grimace. 'She asked about you,' he said consolingly. 'And waited for a good long while too, almost an hour. Longest I've ever seen that one sit still.'

'Did she leave with someone?'

Deoch looked down at his hands, where he was toying with a copper penny, rolling it back and forth over his knuckles. 'She's not really the sort of girl who spends a lot of time alone . . .' He gave me a sympathetic look. 'She turned a few away, but did eventually leave with a fellow. I don't think she was really *with* him, if you catch my meaning. She's been looking for a patron, and this fellow had that sort of look about him. White-haired, wealthy, you know the type.'

I sighed. 'If you happen to see her, could you tell her . . .' I paused, trying to think of how I could describe what had happened. 'Can you make "unavoidably detained" sound a little more poetic?'

'I reckon I can. I'll describe your hangdog look and shoeless state for her too. Lay you a good solid groundwork for some grovelling.'

I smiled despite myself. 'Thanks.'

'Can I buy you a drink?' he asked. 'It's a little early for me, but I can always make an exception for a friend.'

I shook my head. 'I should be getting back. I've got things to do.'

———

I limped back to Anker's and found the common room buzzing with excited folk talking about the fire in the Fishery. Not wanting to answer any questions, I slunk into an out-of-the-way table and got one of the serving girls to bring me a bowl of soup and some bread.

As I ate, my finely tuned eavesdropper's ears picked out pieces of the stories people were telling. It was only then, hearing it from other people, that I realised what I had done.

I was used to people talking about me. As I've said, I had been actively building a reputation for myself. But this was different; this was real. People were already embroidering the details and confusing parts, but the heart of the story was still there. I had saved Fela, rushed into the fire and carried her to safety. Just like Prince Gallant out of some storybook.

It was my first taste of being a hero. I found it quite to my liking.

CHAPTER SIXTY-SEVEN

A Matter of Hands

AFTER LUNCH AT ANKER'S, I decided to return to the Fishery and see how much damage had been done. The stories I'd overheard implied that the fire had been brought under control fairly quickly. If that was the case, I might even be able to finish work on my blue emitters. If not, I might at least be able to reclaim my missing cloak.

Surprisingly, the majority of the Fishery made it through the fire without much damage at all, but the northeast quarter of the shop was practically destroyed. There was nothing left but a jumble of broken stone and glass and ash. Bright blurs of copper and silver spread over broken tabletops and portions of the floor where various metals had been melted by the heat of the fire.

More unsettling than the wreckage was the fact that the workshop was deserted. I'd never seen the place empty before. I knocked on Kilvin's office door, then peered inside. Empty. That made a certain amount of sense. Without Kilvin, there was no one to organise the clean up.

Finishing the emitters took hours longer than I'd expected. My injuries distracted me, and my bandaged thumb made my hand slightly clumsy. As with most artificing, this job required two skilled hands. Even the minor encumbrance of a bandage was a serious inconvenience.

Still, I finished the project without incident and was just preparing to test the emitters when I heard Kilvin in the hallway, cursing in Siaru. I glanced over my shoulder just in time to see him stomp through the doorway towards his office, followed by one of Master Arwyl's gillers.

I closed the fume hood and walked toward Kilvin's office, mindful of where I set my bare feet. Through the window, I could see Kilvin waving his arms like a farmer shooing crows. His hands were swathed in white bandages nearly to the elbow. 'Enough,' he said. 'I will tend them myself.'

The man caught hold of one of Kilvin's arms and made adjustments to the bandages. Kilvin pulled his hands away and held them high in the air, out of reach. '*Lhinsatva*. Enough is enough.' The man said something too quiet for me to hear, but Kilvin continued to shake his head. 'No. And no more of your drugs. I have slept long enough.'

Kilvin motioned me inside. 'E'lir Kvothe. I need to speak to you.'

Not knowing what to expect, I stepped into his office. Kilvin gave me a dark look. 'Do you see what I find after the fire is quenched?' He asked, gesturing towards a mass of dark cloth on his private worktable. Kilvin lifted one corner of it carefully with a bandaged hand and I recognised it as the charred remains of my cloak. Kilvin shook it once, sharply, and my hand lamp tumbled free, rolling awkwardly across the table.

'We spoke about your thieves' lamp not more than two days ago. Yet today I find it lying about where anyone of questionable character might take it for their own.' He scowled at me. 'What do you have to say for yourself?'

I gaped. 'I'm sorry Master Kilvin. I was . . . They took me away . . .'

He glanced at my feet, still scowling. 'And why are you unshod? Even an E'lir should have better sense than to wander naked-footed in a place such as this. Your behaviour lately has been quite reckless. I am dismayed.'

As I fumbled about for an explanation, Kilvin's grim expression spread into a sudden smile. 'I am joking with you, of course,' he said gently. 'I owe you a great weight of thanks for pulling Re'lar Fela from the fire today.' He reached out to pat me on the shoulder, then thought better of it when he remembered the bandages on his hand.

I felt my body go limp with relief. I picked up the lamp and turned it over in my hand. It didn't seem to have been damaged by the fire or corroded by the bone-tar.

Kilvin brought out a small sack and lay it on the table as well. 'These things were also in your cloak,' he said. 'Many things. Your pockets were full as a tinker's pack.'

'You seem in a good mood, Master Kilvin,' I said cautiously, wondering what painkiller he'd been given at the Medica.

'I am,' he said cheerfully. 'Do you know the saying "*Chan Vaen edan Kote*"?'

I tried to puzzle it out. 'Seven years . . . I don't know *Kote*.'

' "Expect disaster every seven years",' he said. 'It is an old saying, and true enough. This has been two years overdue.' He gestured to the wreckage of his shop with a bandaged hand. 'And now that it has come, it proves a mild disaster. My lamps were undamaged. No one was killed. Of all the small injuries, mine were the worst, as it should be.'

I eyed his bandages, my stomach clenching at the thought of something happening to his skilled artificer's hands. 'How are you?' I asked carefully.

'Second-grade burns,' he said, then waved away my concerned exclamation before it hardly began. 'Just blisters. Painful, but no charring, no long-term loss of mobility.' He gave an exasperated sigh. 'Still, I will have a damned time getting any work done for the next three span.'

'If all you need is hands, I could lend them, Master Kilvin.'

He gave a respectful nod. 'That is a generous offer, E'lir. If it were merely a matter of hands I would accept. But much of my work involves sygaldry that would be . . .' he paused, choosing his next word carefully, '. . . *unwise* for an E'lir to have contact with.'

'Then you should promote me to Re'lar, Master Kilvin.' I said with a smile. 'So I might better serve you.'

He gave a deep chuckle. 'I may at that. If you continue your good works.'

I decided to change the subject, rather than push my luck. 'What went wrong with the canister?'

'Too cold,' Kilvin said. 'The metal was just a shell, protecting a glass container inside and keeping the temperature low. I suspect that the canister's sygaldry was damaged so it grew colder and colder. When the reagent froze . . .'

I nodded, finally understanding. 'It cracked the inner glass container. Like a bottle of beer when it freezes. Then ate through the metal of the canister.'

Kilvin nodded. 'Jaxim is currently under the weight of my displeasure,' he said darkly. 'He told me you brought it to his attention.'

'I was sure the whole building would burn to the ground,' I said. 'I can't imagine how you managed to get it under control so easily.'

'Easily?' he asked, sounding vaguely amused. 'Quickly, yes. But I did not know it was *easily.*'

'How did you manage it?'

He smiled at me. 'Good question. How do you think?'

'Well, I heard one student say that you strode out of your office and called the fire's name, just like Taborlin the Great. You said, "fire be still" and the fire obeyed.'

Kilvin gave a great laugh. 'I like that story,' he said, grinning widely behind his beard. 'But I have a question for you. How did you make it through the fire? The reagent produces a most intense flame. How is it you are not burned?'

'I used a drench to wet myself, Master Kilvin.'

Kilvin looked thoughtful. 'Jaxim saw you leaping through the fire just moments after the reagent spilled. The drench is quick, but not so quick as that.'

'I'm afraid I broke it, Master Kilvin. It seemed the only way.'

Kilvin squinted through the window of his office, frowned, then left and walked to the other end of the shop toward the shattered drench. Kneeling down, he picked up a jagged piece of glass between his bandaged fingers. 'How in all the four corners did you manage to break my drench, E'lir Kvothe?'

His tone was so puzzled that I actually laughed. 'Well, Master Kilvin, according to the students, I staved it in with a single blow from my mighty hand.'

Kilvin grinned again. 'I like that story too, but I do not believe it.'

'More reputable sources claim I used a piece of bar-iron from a nearby table.'

Kilvin shook his head. 'You are a fine boy, but this twice-tough glass was made by my own hands. Broad-shouldered Cammar could not break it with an anvil hammer.' He dropped the piece of glass and came back to his feet. 'Let the others tell whatever stories they wish, but between us let us share secrets.'

'It's no great mystery,' I admitted. 'I know the sygaldry for twice-tough glass. What I can make, I can break.'

'But where was your source?' Kilvin said. 'You could have nothing ready on such short notice . . .' I held up my bandaged thumb. 'Blood,' he said, sounding surprised. 'Using the heat of your blood could be called reckless, E'lir Kvothe. What of binder's chills? What if you had gone into hypothermic shock?'

'My options were rather limited, Master Kilvin,' I said.

Kilvin nodded thoughtfully. 'Quite impressive, to unbind what I have wrought with nothing more than blood.' He started to run a hand through his beard, then frowned in irritation when the bandages made this impossible.

'What of you, Master Kilvin? How did you manage to get the fire under control?'

'Not using the name of fire,' he conceded. 'If Elodin had been here, matters would have been much simpler. But as the name of fire is unknown to me, I was left to my own devices.'

I gave him a cautious look, not sure whether he was making another joke or not. Kilvin's deadpan humour was hard to detect at times. 'Elodin knows the name of fire?'

Kilvin nodded. 'There may be one or two others here at the University, but Elodin has the surest grip of it.'

'The name of fire,' I said slowly. 'And they could have called it and the fire would have done what they said, like Taborlin the Great?'

Kilvin nodded again.

'But those are just stories,' I protested.

He gave me an amused look. 'Where do you think stories come from, E'lir Kvothe? Every tale has deep roots somewhere in the world.'

'What sort of a name is it? How does it work?'

Kilvin hesitated for a moment, then shrugged his massive shoulders. 'It is troublesome to explain in this language. In any language. Ask Elodin – he makes a habit of studying such things.'

I knew firsthand how helpful Elodin would be. 'So how *did* you stop the fire?'

'There is little mystery in it,' he said. 'I was prepared for such an accident and had a small vial of the reagent in my office. I used it as a link and drew heat from the spill. The reagent grew too cold to boil and the remaining fog burned away. The lion's share of the reagent drained down the grates while Jaxim and the others scattered lime and sand to control what was left.'

'You can't be serious,' I said. 'It was a furnace in here. You couldn't have moved that many thaums of heat. Where would you have put it?'

'I had an empty heat-eater ready for just such an emergency. Fire is the simplest of troubles I have prepared for.'

I waved his explanation aside. 'Even so, there's no way. It must have been . . .' I tried to calculate how much heat he would have had to move, but stalled out, not knowing where to begin.

'I estimate eight hundred fifty million thaums,' Kilvin said. 'Though we must check the trap for a more accurate number.'

I was speechless. 'But . . . how?'

'Quickly,' he made a significant gesture with his bandaged hands, 'but not easily.'

CHAPTER SIXTY-EIGHT

The Ever-Changing Wind

I TRUDGED THROUGH THE next day barefoot, cloakless, and thinking grim thoughts about my life. The novelty of playing hero faded quickly in light of my situation. I had one ragged suit of clothes. My flash burns were minor but incessantly painful. I had no money to buy painkillers or new clothes. I chewed bitter willow bark and bitter was my mood.

My poverty hung around my neck like a heavy stone. Never before had I been more aware of the difference between myself and the other students. Everyone attending the University had a safety net to fall back on. Sim's parents were Aturan nobility. Wil came from a wealthy merchant family in the Shald. If things got rough for them, they could borrow against their families' credit or write a letter home.

I, on the other hand, couldn't afford shoes. I only owned one shirt. How could I hope to stay in the University for the years it would take me to become a full arcanist? How could I hope to advance in the ranks without access to the Archives?

By noon, I had worked myself into such a grim mood that I snapped at Sim during lunch and we bickered like an old married couple. Wilem offered no opinion, keeping his eyes carefully on his food. Finally, in a blatant attempt to dispel my foul mood they invited me to go see *Three Pennies for Wishing* across the river tomorrow evening. I agreed to go, as I'd heard the players were doing Feltemi's original and not one of the expurgated versions. It was well suited to my mood, full of dark humour, tragedy, and betrayal.

After lunch I found Kilvin had already sold half my emitters. Since they were going to be the last blue emitters made for some time, the price was high, and my share was slightly over a talent and a half. I expected Kilvin might have padded the price a little, which rankled my pride a bit, but I was in no position to look a gift horse in the mouth.

But even this did nothing to improve my mood. Now I could afford shoes and a secondhand cloak. If I worked like a dog for the remainder of the term I might be able to earn enough to eke out my interest to Devi and tuition as well. The thought brought me no joy. More than ever I was aware how tenuous my situation was. I was a hairsbreadth away from disaster.

My mood spiralled downward and I skipped Advanced Sympathy in favour of going over the river to Imre. The thought of seeing Denna was the only thing that had the potential to raise my spirits a little. I still needed to explain to her why I'd missed our lunch date.

On my way to the Eolian I bought a pair of low boots, good for walking and warm enough for the winter months ahead. It nearly emptied my purse again. I sullenly counted my money as I left the cobbler's shop: three jots and a drab. I'd had more money living on the streets of Tarbean . . .

'Your timing's good today,' Deoch said as I approached the Eolian. 'We've got someone waiting for you.'

I felt a foolish grin spread to my face and clapped him on the shoulder as I headed inside.

Instead of Denna I spotted Fela sitting at a table by herself. Stanchion stood nearby, chatting with her. When he saw me approaching, he waved me over and wandered back to his usual perch at the bar, clapping me affectionately on the shoulder as he walked by.

When she saw me, Fela came to her feet and rushed toward me. For a second I thought she was going to run into my arms as if we were reunited lovers in some overacted Aturan tragedy. But she pulled up short of that, her dark hair swinging. She was lovely as always, but with a heavy, purpling bruise darkening one of her high cheekbones.

'Oh no,' I said, my hand going to my face in sympathetic pain. 'Is that from when I dropped you? I'm so sorry.'

She gave me an incredulous look, then burst out laughing. 'You're apologising for pulling me out of a fiery hell?'

'Just the part where I passed out and dropped you. It was sheer stupidity. I forgot to hold my breath and sucked down some bad air. Were you hurt anywhere else?'

'Nowhere I can show you in public,' she said with a slight grimace, shifting her hips in a way I found most distracting.

'Nothing too bad, I hope.'

She put on an fierce expression. 'Yes, well. I expect you to do a better job next time. A girl gets her life saved, she expects gentler treatment all-round.'

'Fair enough,' I said, relaxing. 'We'll treat this as a practice run.'

There was a heartbeat of silence between us, and Fela's smile faded a bit. She reached out halfway to me with one hand, then hesitated and let it fall back to her side. 'Seriously, Kvothe. I . . . that was the worst moment of my whole life. There was fire everywhere . . .'

She looked down, blinking. 'I knew I was going to die. I really knew it. But I just stood there like . . . like some scared rabbit.' She looked up, blinking away tears and her smile burst out again, dazzling as ever. 'Then you were there, running through the fire. It was the most amazing thing I've ever seen. It was like . . . have you ever seen *Daeonica*?'

I nodded and smiled.

'It was like watching Tarsus bursting out of hell. You came through the fire and I knew everything was going to be alright.' She took a half step toward me and rested her hand on my arm. I could feel the warmth of it through my shirt. 'I was going to die there—' she broke off, embarrassed. 'I'm just repeating myself now.'

I shook my head. 'That's not true. I saw you. You were looking for a way out.'

'No. I was just standing there. Like one of those silly girls in those stories my mother used to read me. I always hated them. I used to ask, "Why doesn't she push the witch out of the window? Why doesn't she poison the ogre's food?" ' Fela was looking down at her feet now, her hair falling to hide her face. Her voice grew softer and softer until it was barely louder than a sigh. ' "Why does she just sit there waiting to be saved? Why doesn't she save herself?" '

I lay my hand on top of hers in what I hoped was a comforting way. When I did, I noticed something. Her hand wasn't the delicate, fragile thing I had expected. It was strong and calloused, a sculptor's hand that knew hard hours of work with hammer and chisel.

'This isn't a maiden's hand,' I said.

She looked up at me, her eyes luminous with the beginning of tears. She gave a startled laugh that was half sob. 'I . . . what?'

I flushed with embarrassment as I realised what I'd said, but pushed ahead. 'This isn't the hand of some swooning princess who sits tatting lace and waiting for some prince to save her. This is the hand of a woman who would climb a rope of her own hair to freedom, or kill a captor ogre in his sleep.' I looked into her eyes. 'And this is the hand of a woman who would have made it through the fire on her own if I hadn't been there. Singed perhaps, but safe.'

I brought her hand to my lips and kissed it. It seemed like the thing to do. 'All the same, I am glad I was there to help.' I smiled. 'So . . . like Tarsus?'

Her smile dazzled me again. 'Like Tarsus, Prince Gallant, and Oren Velciter all rolled into one,' she said laughing. She gripped my hand. 'Come see. I have something for you.'

Fela pulled me back to the table where she'd been sitting and handed me a bundle of cloth. 'I asked Wil and Sim what I could get you as a gift, and it seemed somehow appropriate . . .' She paused, suddenly shy.

It was a cloak. It was a deep forest green, rich cloth, fine cut. It hadn't been bought off the back of some fripperer's cart, either. This was the sort of clothing I could never hope to afford for myself.

'I had the tailor sew a bunch of little pockets into it,' she said nervously. 'Wil and Sim both mentioned how that was important.'

'It's lovely,' I said.

Her smile beamed out again. 'I had to guess at the measurements,' she admitted. 'Let's see if it fits.' She took the cloak out of my hands and stepped close to me, spreading it over my shoulders, her arms circling me in something very near to an embrace.

I stood there, to use Fela's words, like a scared rabbit. She was close enough that I could feel the warmth of her, and when she leaned to adjust the way the cloak lay across my shoulders, one of her breasts brushed my arm. I stood still as a statue. Over Fela's shoulder I saw Deoch grin from where he leaned in the doorway across the room.

Fela stepped back, eyed me critically, then stepped close again and made a small adjustment to the way the cloak fastened across my chest. 'It suits you,' she said. 'The colour brings out your eyes. Not that they need it. They're the greenest thing I've seen today. Like a piece of spring.'

As Fela stepped back to admire her handiwork, I saw a familiar shape leaving the Eolian through the front door. Denna. I only caught a brief glimpse of her profile, but I recognised her as surely as I know the backs of my own hands. What she had seen, and what conclusions she had drawn from it, I could only guess.

My first impulse was to bolt out the door after her. To explain why I had broken our date two days ago. To say I was sorry. To make it clear that the woman with her arms around me had just been giving me a gift, nothing more.

Fela smoothed the cloak over my shoulder and looked at me with eyes that only moments before had been luminous with the beginnings of tears.

'It fits perfectly,' I said, taking the cloth between my fingers and fanning it out to the side. 'It's much better than I deserve, and you shouldn't have, but I thank you.'

'I wanted to show you how much I appreciated what you did.' She reached out to touch my arm again. 'This is nothing, really. If there's anything I can ever do for you. Any favour. You should stop by . . .' She paused, looking at me quizzically. 'Are you alright?'

I glanced past her towards the doorway. Denna could be anywhere by now. I'd never be able to catch her.

'I'm fine,' I lied.

Fela bought me a drink and we chatted for a while about small things. I was surprised to learn that she'd been working with Elodin for the last several months. She did some sculpting for him, and in exchange he occasionally tried to teach her. She rolled her eyes. He woke her in the middle of the night and took her to an abandoned quarry north of town. He put wet clay in her shoes and made her spend the entire day walking around in them. He even . . . she flushed and shook her head, breaking off the story. Curious, but not wanting to make her uncomfortable, I didn't pursue it any further and we agreed between the two of us that he was more than half mad.

All the while, I sat facing the door, vainly hoping that Denna might return and I could explain the truth of matters to her.

Eventually Fela headed back to the University for Abstract Maths. I stayed at the Eolian, nursing a drink and trying to think how I could make things right between Denna and myself. I would have liked to have a good, maudlin drunk, but I couldn't afford it, so I made my slow, limping way back across the river as the sun was setting.

It wasn't until I was getting ready to make one of my regular trips to the roof of Mains that I realised the significance of something Kilvin had said to me. If the majority of the bone-tar had gone down the grates . . .

Auri. She lived in the tunnels underneath the University. I bolted to the Medica, moving as quickly as I could despite my weary, footsore state. Halfway there I had a stroke of luck and spotted Mola crossing the courtyard. I shouted and waved to get her attention.

Mola eyed me suspiciously as I approached. 'You're not going to serenade me, are you?'

I shifted my lute self-consciously and shook my head. 'I need a favour,' I said. 'I have a friend that might be hurt.'

She gave a weary sigh. 'You should . . .'

'I can't go to the Medica for help.' I let my anxiety creep into my voice. 'Please, Mola? I promise it won't take more than a half hour or so, but we have to go now. I'm worried I might be too late already.'

Something in my tone convinced her. 'What's the matter with your friend?'

'Maybe burns, maybe acid, maybe smoke. Like the people who were caught in the Fishery fire yesterday. Maybe worse.'

Mola started walking. 'I'll get my kit from my room.'

'I'll wait here if you don't mind,' I took a seat on a nearby bench. 'I'll just slow you down.'

I sat and tried to ignore my various burns and bruises, and when Mola returned I led her to the southwestern side of Mains where there were a trio of decorative chimneys. 'We can use these to get on the roof.'

She gave me a curious look but seemed content to hold onto her questions for now.

I made my slow way up the chimney, using the protruding pieces of field-stone as hand- and footholds. This was one of the easiest ways onto the roof of Mains. I'd chosen it partly because I wasn't sure of Mola's climbing ability, and partly because my own injuries had left me feeling less than athletic.

Mola joined me on the roof. She still wore her dark uniform from the Medica, but had added a grey cloak from her room. I took a roundabout path so we could stay on the safer sections of Mains. It was a cloudless night, and there was a sliver of moon to light our way.

'If I didn't know better,' Mola said as we made our way around a tall brick chimney. 'I'd think that you were luring me somewhere quiet for a sinister purpose.'

'What makes you think I'm not?' I asked lightly.

'You don't seem like the type,' she said. 'Besides, you can barely walk. If you tried anything, I'd just push you off the roof.'

'Don't spare my feelings,' I said with a chuckle. 'Even if I weren't half-crippled, you could still throw me off this roof.'

I stumbled a little on an unseen ridge and nearly fell because my battered body was slow to respond. I sat on a piece of roof slightly higher than the rest and waited for the momentary dizziness to pass.

'Are you alright?' Mola asked.

'Probably not.' I pushed myself to my feet. 'It's just over this next roof,' I said. 'It might be best if you stood back a ways and stayed quiet. Just in case.'

I made my way to the edge of the roof. I looked down at the hedges and the apple tree. The windows were dark.

'Auri?' I called softly. 'Are you there?' I waited, growing more nervous by the second. 'Auri, are you hurt?'

Nothing. I began to curse under my breath.

Mola crossed her arms. 'Right, I think I've been plenty patient here. Care to tell me what's going on?'

'Follow me and I'll explain.' I headed for the apple tree and began to climb carefully down. I walked around the hedge to the iron grate. The ammonia smell of bone-tar wafted up from the grate, faint but persistent. I tugged on the grate, and it lifted a few inches before catching on something. 'I made a friend a few months ago,' I said, nervously sliding my hand between the bars. 'She lives down here. I'm worried that she might be hurt. A lot of the reagent went down the drains from the Fishery.'

Mola was silent for a while. 'You're serious.' I felt around in the dark under the grate, trying to figure out how Auri kept it closed. 'What sort of person would live down there?'

'A frightened person,' I said. 'A person who's afraid of loud noises, and people, and the open sky. It took me nearly a month to coax her out of the tunnels, let alone get close enough to talk.'

Mola sighed. 'If you don't mind I'll have a seat.' She walked over to the bench. 'I've been on my feet all day.'

I continued to feel around under the grate, but try as I might, I couldn't find a clasp anywhere. Growing increasingly frustrated, I grabbed the grate and tugged on it hard, again and again. It made several echoing metallic thumps but didn't come free.

'Kvothe?' I looked up to the edge of the roof and saw Auri standing there, a silhouette against the night sky, her fine hair made a cloud around her head.

'Auri!' The tension poured out of me, leaving me feeling weak and rubbery. 'Where have you been?'

'There were clouds,' she said simply as she walked around the edge of the roof toward the apple tree. 'So I went looking for you on top of things. But the moon's coming out, so I came back.'

Auri scampered down the tree, then pulled up short when she saw Mola's cloaked form sitting on the bench.

'I brought a friend to visit, Auri,' I said in my gentlest tones. 'I hope you don't mind.'

There was a long pause. 'Is he nice?'

'It's a she. And yes, she's nice.'

Auri relaxed a bit and came a few steps closer to me. 'I brought you a feather with the spring wind in it, but since you were late . . .' she looked at me gravely, 'you get a coin instead.' She held it out at arm's length, pinched between her thumb and forefinger. 'It will keep you safe at night. As much as anything can, that is.' It was shaped like an Aturan penance piece, but it gleamed silver in the moonlight. I'd never seen a coin like it.

Kneeling, I opened my lute case and brought out a small bundle. 'I've got some tomatoes, beans, and something special.' I held out the small sack I'd spent most of my money on two days ago, before all my troubles had started. 'Sea salt.'

Auri took it, and peered inside the small leather sack. 'Why this is lovely, Kvothe. What lives in the salt?'

Trace minerals, I thought. *Chromium, bassal, malium, iodine . . . everything your body needs but probably can't get from apples and bread and whatever you manage to scrounge up when I can't find you.*

'The dreams of fish,' I said. 'And sailor's songs.'

Auri nodded, satisfied, and sat down, spreading out the small cloth and arranging her food with the same care as always. I watched her as she began to eat, dipping a green bean into the salt before taking a bite. She didn't seem hurt, but it was hard to tell by the pale moonlight. I needed to be sure. 'Are you okay, Auri?'

She cocked her head at me, curious.

'There was a big fire. A lot of it went down the grates. Did you see it?'

'Holy God, yes,' she said, her eyes wide. 'It was all over, and all the shrews and raccoons were running everyway, trying to get out.'

'Did any of it get on you?' I asked. 'Did you get burned?'

She shook her head, grinning a child's sly smile. 'Oh no. It couldn't catch me.'

'Were you close to the fire?' I asked. 'Did you breathe any of the smoke?'

'Why would I breathe smoke?' Auri looked at me as if I were simple. 'The whole Underthing smells like cat piss now.' She wrinkled her nose. 'Except by Downing and in the Belows.'

I relaxed a bit, but I saw Mola begin to fidget where she was sitting on the bench. 'Auri, can my friend come over?'

Auri froze with a bean halfway to her mouth, then relaxed and bobbed her head once, sending her fine hair swirling around her.

I beckoned to Mola who began to walk slowly toward us. I was a little uneasy at how their meeting would go. It had taken me over a month of gentle coaxing to draw Auri out from the tunnels underneath the University where she lived. I worried that a bad reaction from Mola might startle her back underground where I would have no chance of finding her.

I gestured to where Mola stood. 'This is my friend Mola.'

'Hello, Mola.' Auri looked up and smiled. 'You have sunny hair like me. Would you like an apple?'

Mola's expression was carefully blank. 'Thank you, Auri. I'd like that.'

Auri jumped up and ran back to where the apple tree overhung the edge of the roof. Then ran back toward us, her hair flying behind her like a flag. She handed Mola an apple. 'This one has a wish inside it,' she said matter-of-factly. 'Make sure you know what you want before you take a bite.' That said, she settled back down and ate another bean, chewing primly.

Mola looked over the apple for a long moment before taking a bite.

Auri finished her meal quickly after that, and tied up the bag of salt. 'Now play!' she said, excited. 'Play!'

Smiling, I brought out my lute and brushed my hands over the strings. Thankfully my injured thumb was on my chording hand, where it would be a relatively minor inconvenience.

I looked at Mola as I tuned the strings. 'You can go if you like,' I told her. 'I wouldn't want to accidentally serenade you.'

'Oh you musn't go.' Auri turned to Mola, her expression deathly serious. 'His voice is like a thunderstorm, and his hands know every secret hidden deep beneath the cool, dark earth.'

Mola's mouth quirked into a smile. 'I suppose I could stay for that.'

So I played for both of them, while overhead the stars continued in their measured turning.

———————

'Why haven't you told anyone?' Mola asked me as we made our way across the rooftops.

'It didn't seem like anyone's business,' I said. 'If she wanted people to know she was there, I imagine she'd tell them herself.'

'You know what I mean,' Mola said, irritated.

'I know what you mean,' I sighed. 'But what good would come of it? She's happy where she is.'

'Happy?' Mola sounded incredulous. 'She's ragged and half-starved. She needs help. Food and clothes.'

'I bring her food,' I said. 'And I'll bring her clothes too, as soon . . .' I hesitated, not wanting to admit my abject poverty, at least not in so many words. 'As soon as I can manage it.'

'Why wait? If you just told someone . . .'

'Right,' I said sarcastically. 'I'm sure Jamison would rush out here with a box of chocolates and a featherbed if he knew there was a starveling half-cracked student living under his University. They'd crock her and you know it.'

'Not necessarily . . .' She didn't even bother finishing, knowing what I'd said was true.

'Mola, if people come looking for her, she'll just rabbit down into the tunnels. They'll scare her away and I'll lose what chance I have to help her.'

Mola looked down at me, her arms folded across her chest. 'Fine. For now. But you'll have to bring me back here later. I'll bring her some of my clothes. They'll be too big for her, but they'll be better than what she has.'

I shook my head. 'It won't work. I brought her a secondhand dress a couple span ago. She says wearing someone else's clothes is filthy.'

Mola looked puzzled. 'She didn't look Cealdish. Not even a little.'

'Maybe she was just raised that way.'

'Do you feel any better?'

'Yes,' I lied.

'You're shaking.' She stretched out a hand. 'Here, lean on me.'

Pulling my new cloak close around me, I took her arm and made my slow way back to Anker's.

CHAPTER SIXTY-NINE

Wind or Women's Fancy

OVER THE NEXT TWO span my new cloak kept me warm on my occasional walks to Imre, where I was consistently unsuccessful in finding Denna. I always had some reason to cross the river: borrowing a book from Devi, meeting Threpe for lunch, playing at the Eolian. But Denna was the real reason.

Kilvin sold the rest of my emitters, and my mood improved as my burns healed. I had money to spare for luxuries such as soap and a second shirt to replace the one I'd lost. Today I had gone to Imre for some bassal filings I needed for my current project: a large sympathy lamp using two emitters I'd saved for myself. I hoped to turn a tidy profit.

It may seem odd that I was constantly buying materials for my artificing over the river, but the truth was merchants near the University frequently took advantage of the students' laziness and raised their prices. It was worth the walk for me if I could save a couple of pennies.

After I finished my errand I headed to the Eolian. Deoch was at his usual post, leaning against the doorway. 'I've been keeping an eye out for your girl,' he said.

Irritated at how transparent I must seem, I muttered, 'She's *not* my girl.'

Deoch rolled his eyes. 'Fine. *The* girl. Denna, Dianne, Dyanae . . . whatever she's calling herself these days. I haven't seen hide nor hair of her. I even asked around a little, nobody's seen her in a full span. That means she's probably left town. It's her way. She does it at the drop of a hat.'

I tried not to let my disappointment show. 'You didn't have to go to the trouble,' I said. 'But thanks all the same.'

'I wasn't asking entirely on your account,' Deoch admitted. 'I've a fondness for her myself.'

'Do you now?' I said as neutrally as I could manage.

'Don't give me that look. I'm not any sort of competition.' He gave a crooked smile. 'Not this time around at any rate. I might not be one of you University folk, but I can see the moon on a clear night. I'm smart enough not to stick my hand in the same fire twice.'

I struggled to get my expression back under control, more than slightly embarrassed. I don't usually let my emotions go parading around on my face. 'So you and Denna . . .'

'Stanchion still gives me a hard time about chasing after a girl half my age.' He shrugged his broad shoulders sheepishly. 'For all that, I am still fond of her. These days she reminds me of my littlest sister more than anything.'

'How long have you known her?' I asked, curious.

'I wouldn't say I really *know* her, lad. But I met her what, about two years back? Not that long, maybe a year and little change . . .' Deoch ran both of his hands through his blond hair and arched his back in a great stretch, the muscles in his arms straining against his shirt. Then he relaxed with an explosive sigh and looked out at the nearly empty courtyard. 'The door won't be busy for hours yet. Come give an old man an excuse to sit and have a drink?' He jerked his head in the direction of the bar.

I looked at Deoch: tall, muscular, and tan. 'Old man? You've still got all your hair and your teeth, don't you? What are you, thirty?'

'Nothing makes a man feel older than a young woman.' He laid a hand on my shoulder. 'Come on, share a drink with me.' We made our way over to the long mahogany bar and he muttered as he looked over the bottles. 'Beer dulls a memory, brand sets it burning, but wine is the best for a sore heart's yearning.' He paused and turned to looked at me, his brow furrowed. 'I can't remember the rest of that. Can you?'

'Never heard it before,' I said. 'But Teccam claims that out of all the spirits, only wine is suited to reminiscence. He said a good wine allows clarity and focus, while still allowing a bit of comforting coloration of the memory.'

'Fair enough,' he said, picking through the racks before drawing out a bottle and holding it up to a lamp, peering through it. 'Let's view her in a rosy light, shall we?' He grabbed two glasses and led us off to a secluded booth in the corner of the room.

'So you've known Denna for a while,' I prompted as he poured each of us a glass of pale red wine.

He slouched back against the wall. 'Off and on. More off, honestly.'

'What was she like back then?'

Deoch spent several long moments pondering his answer, giving the question more serious consideration than I'd expected. He sipped his wine. 'The same,' he said at last. 'I suppose she was younger, but I can't say she seems any older now. She always struck me as being older than her years.' He frowned. 'Not *old* really, more . . .'

'Mature?' I suggested.

He shook his head. 'No. I don't know a good word for it. It's like if you look at a great oak tree. You don't appreciate it because it's older than the other trees, or because it's taller. It just has something that other younger trees don't. Complexity, solidity, significance.' Deoch scowled, irritated. 'Damn if that isn't the worst comparison I've ever made.'

A smile broke onto my face. 'It's nice to see I'm not the only one who has trouble pinning her down with words.'

'She's not much for being pinned down,' Deoch agreed and drank off the rest of his wine. He picked up the bottle and tapped the mouth of it lightly against my glass. I emptied it, and he poured again for both of us.

Deoch continued, 'She was just as restless then, and wild. Just as pretty, prone to startle the eye and stutter the heart.' He shrugged again. 'As I said, largely the same. Lovely voice, light of foot, quick of tongue, men's adoration and women's scorn in roughly equal amounts.'

'Scorn?' I asked.

Deoch looked at me as if he didn't understand what I was asking. 'Women hate Denna,' he said plainly, as if repeating something we both already knew.

'Hate her?' The thought baffled me. 'Why?'

Deoch looked at me incredulously, then burst out laughing. 'Good lord, you really don't know anything about women, do you?' I would ordinarily have bristled at his comment, but Deoch was nothing but good natured. 'Think of it. She's pretty and charming. Men crowd round her like stags in rut.' He made a flippant gesture. 'Women are bound to resent it.'

I remembered what Sim had said about Deoch not a span ago. *He's managed to get the most beautiful woman in the place again. It's enough to make you hate a man.* 'I've always felt she was rather lonely,' I volunteered. 'Maybe that's why.'

Deoch nodded solemnly. 'There's truth to that. I never see her in the company of other womenfolk, and she has about as much luck with men as . . .' He paused, groping for a comparison. 'As . . . damn.' He gave a frustrated sigh.

'Well, you know what they say: Finding the right analogy is as hard as . . .' I put on a thoughtful expression. 'As hard as . . .' I made an inarticulate grasping gesture.

Deoch laughed and poured more wine for both of us. I began to relax. There is a sort of camaraderie that rarely exists except between men who have fought the same enemies and known the same women. 'Did she tend to disappear back then, too?' I asked.

He nodded. 'No warning, just suddenly gone. Sometimes for a span. Sometimes for months.'

' "No fickleness in flight like that of wind or women's fancy",' I quoted. I meant it to be musing, but it came out bitter. 'Do you have any guess as to why?'

'I've given some thought to that,' Deoch said philosophically. 'In part I think it is her nature. It could be she simply has wandering blood.'

My irritation cooled a bit at his words. Back in my troupe, my father occasionally made us pull up stakes and leave a town despite the fact that we were welcome and the crowds were generous. Later, he would often explain his reasoning to me: a glare from the constable, too many fond sighs from the young wives in town . . .

But sometimes he had no reason. *We Ruh are meant to travel, son. When my blood tells me to wander, I know enough to trust it.*

'Her circumstances are probably responsible for most of it,' Deoch continued.

'Circumstances?' I asked, curious. She never talked of her past when we were together, and I was always careful not to press her. I knew what it was like, not wanting to talk too much about your past.

'Well, she doesn't have any family or means of support. No long-standing friends able to help her out of a tight spot if the need arises.'

'I haven't got any of those things either,' I groused, the wine making me a little surly.

'There's more than a little difference there,' Deoch said with a hint of re-proach. 'A man has a great many opportunities to make his way in the world. You've found yourself a place at the University, and if you hadn't you would still have options.' He looked at me with a knowing eye. 'What options are available to a young, pretty girl with no family? No dowry? No home?'

He began to hold up fingers. 'There's begging and whoring. Or being some lord's mistress, which is a different slice of the same loaf. And we know our Denna doesn't have it in her to be a kept woman or someone's dox.'

'There's other work to be had,' I said holding up fingers of my own. 'Seamstress, weaver, serving girl . . .'

Deoch snorted and gave me a disgusted look. 'Come now lad, you're smarter than that. You know what those places are like. And you know that a pretty girl with no family ends up being taken advantage of just as often as a whore, and paid less for her trouble.'

I flushed a bit at his rebuke, more than I would have normally, as I was feeling the wine. It was making my lips and the tips of my fingers a little numb.

Deoch filled our glasses again. 'She's not to be looked down on for moving where the wind blows her. She has to take her opportunities where she finds them. If she gets the chance to travel with some folk who like her singing, or with a merchant who hopes her pretty face will help him sell his wares, who's to blame her for pulling up stakes and leaving town?

'And if she trades on her charm a bit, I'll not look down on her because of it. Young gents court her, buy her presents, dresses, jewellery.' He shrugged his broad shoulders. 'If she sells those things for money to live, there's nothing wrong in that. They are gifts freely given, and hers to do with as she pleases.'

Deoch fixed me with a stare. 'But what is she to do when some gent gets too familiar? Or gets angry at being denied what he considers bought and paid for? What recourse does she have? No family, no friends, no standing. No choice. None but to give herself over to him, all unwilling . . .' Deoch's face was grim. 'Or to leave. Leave quickly and find better weather. Is it any surprise then that she is harder to lay hands on than a windblown leaf?'

He shook his head, looking down at the table. 'No, I do not envy her her life. Nor do I judge her.' His tirade seemed to have left him spent and slightly embarrassed. He didn't look up at me as he spoke. 'For all that, I would help her, if she would let me.' He glanced up at me and gave a chagrined smile. 'But she's not the sort to be beholden to anyone. Not one whit. Not a hairsbreadth.' He sighed and dribbled the last drops of the bottle evenly into our glasses.

'You've shown her to me in a new light,' I said honestly. 'I'm ashamed I didn't see it for myself.'

'Well, I've had a head start on you,' he said easily. 'I've known her longer.'

'Nevertheless, I thank you,' I said holding up my glass.

He held up his own. 'To Dyanae,' he said. 'Most lovely.'

'To Denna, full of delight.'

'Young and unbending.'

'Bright and fair.'

'Ever sought, ever alone.'

'So wise and so foolish,' I said. 'So merry and so sad.'

'Gods of my fathers,' Deoch said reverently. 'Keep her always so: unchanging, past my understanding, and safe from harm.'

We both drank and set down our glasses.

'Let me buy the next bottle,' I said. It would tap out my slowly hoarded line of credit with the bar, but I found myself increasingly fond of Deoch and the thought of not standing my round with him was too galling to consider.

'Stream, stone, and sky,' he swore, rubbing at his face. 'I dare not. Another bottle and we'd be slitting our wrists into the river before the sun goes down.'

I made a gesture to a serving girl. 'Nonsense,' I said. 'We'll just change to something less maudlin than wine.'

I didn't notice I was being followed when I returned to the University. Perhaps my head was so full of Denna that there was little room left for anything else. Perhaps I had been living civilised for so long that the hard-earned reflexes I'd picked up in Tarbean were starting to fade.

The blackberry brand probably had something to do with it as well. Deoch and I had talked for a long while, and between us drank half a bottle of the stuff. I had brought the remainder of the bottle back with me, as I knew Simmon had a taste for it.

Small matter why I didn't notice them, I suppose. The result was the same. I was strolling down a poorly lit part of Newhall Lane when something blunt struck me on the back of the head and I was bundled off into a nearby alley, half-senseless.

I was only stunned for a moment, but by the time I had re-gathered my wits, I had a heavy hand clamped over my mouth.

'Alright, cully,' the huge man behind me spoke into my ear. 'I've got a knife on you. You struggle, I stick you. That's all there is to it.' I felt a gentle prod against my ribs under my left arm. 'Check the finder,' he said to his companion.

A tall shape was all I could see in the dim light of the alley. He bowed his head, looking at his hand. 'I can't tell.'

'Light a match, then. We have to be sure.'

My anxiety began to blossom into full-blown panic. This wasn't some simple back-alley coshing. They hadn't even checked my pockets for money. This was something else.

'We know it's him,' the tall one said impatiently. 'Let's just do this and have it over with. I'm cold.'

'Like hell. Check it now, while he's close. We've lost him twice already. I'm not having another cock-up like in Anilin.'

'I hate this thing,' the tall man said as he went through his pockets, presumably looking for a match.

'You're an idiot,' the one behind me said. 'It's cleaner this way. Simpler. No confusing descriptions. No names. No worrying about disguises. Follow the needle, find our man, and have done with it.'

The matter-of-fact tone of their voices terrified me. These men were professionals. I realised with sudden certainty that Ambrose had finally taken steps to ensure I would never bother him again.

My mind raced for a moment, and I did the only thing I could think of: I dropped the half-full bottle of brand. It shattered on the cobblestones and the night air was suddenly filled with the smell of blackberries.

'That's great,' the tall man hissed. 'How about you let him ring a bell while you're at it?'

The man behind me tightened his grip on my neck and shook me hard, just once. The same way you would do to a naughty puppy. 'None of that,' he said, irritated.

I went limp, hoping to lull him, then concentrated and muttered a binding against the man's thick hand.

'Tough tits,' the man replied. 'If you stepped in glass it's your own damn *faaaaaah!*' He let out a startled shout as the pool of brand around our feet caught fire.

I took advantage of his momentary distraction and twisted away from him. But I wasn't quite quick enough. His knife tore a bright line of pain across my ribs as I pulled away and began pelting down the alley.

But my flight was short-lived. The alley dead-ended against a sheer brick wall. There were no doors, no windows, nothing to hide behind or use to get a leg up on the wall. I was trapped.

I turned to see the two men blocking the mouth of the alley. The large one was stamping his leg furiously, trying to extinguish it.

My left leg was burning as well, but I didn't spare a thought for it. A little burn would be the least of my problems if I didn't do something quick. I looked around again, but the alley was distressingly clean. Not even any decent garbage to use as a makeshift weapon. I frantically ran through the contents of my cloak's pockets, desperately trying to form some sort of plan. Some pieces of copper wire were useless. Salt, could I throw it in their eyes? No. Dried apple, pen and ink, a marble, string, wax . . .

The large man finally beat out the flames and the two of them began to make their slow way down the alley. The light from the circle of burning brand flickered across the blades of their knives.

Still going over my countless pockets, I found a lump that I didn't recognise. Then I remembered – it was the a sack of bassal shavings I had bought to use for my sympathy lamp.

Bassal is a light, silvery metal, useful in certain alloys that I would be using to construct my lamp. Manet, ever the careful teacher, had taken care to describe the dangers of every material we used. If it gets hot enough, bassal burns with an intense, white-hot flame.

I hurriedly untied the pouch. The trouble was, I didn't know if I could make this work. Things like candle wicking or alcohol are easy to light. They just need a focused flash of heat to get them going. Bassal was different. It needed a great deal of heat to ignite, which is why I wasn't worried about carrying it around in my pocket.

The men came a few slow steps closer and I flung the handful of bassal shavings in a wide arc. I tried to get it close to their faces, but didn't hold much hope. The shavings had no real heft, it was like throwing a handful of loose snow.

Lowering one hand to the flame licking at my leg, I focused my Alar. The wide pool of burning brand winked out behind the two men, leaving the alley in pitch darkness. But there still wasn't enough heat. Reckless with desperation, I touched my bloody side, concentrated, and felt a terrible cold tear through me as I pulled more heat from my blood.

There was an explosion of white light, blinding in the dark of the alley. I'd closed my eyes, but even through my lids the burning bassal was piercingly bright. One of the men screamed, high and terrified. When I opened my eyes I could see nothing but blue ghosts dancing over my vision.

The scream faded to a low moaning, and I heard a thump as if one of the men had stumbled and fallen. The tall man began to babble, his voice little more than a terrified sobbing. 'Oh God. Tam, my eyes. I'm blind.'

As I listened, my vision cleared enough for me to see the vague outlines of the alley. I could see the dark shapes of both men. One was kneeling with his hands in front of his face, the other was sprawled motionless on the ground farther down the alley. It looked like he had run headlong into a low rafter beam at the mouth of the alley and knocked himself unconscious. Scattered around the cobblestones, the remnants of bassal were sputtering out like tiny blue-white stars.

The kneeling man was only flash-blind, but it would last for several minutes: long enough for me to get well away from here. I moved slowly around him, being careful to step quietly. My heart leapt into to my throat as he spoke up again.

'Tam?' The man's voice was high and frightened. 'I swear Tam, I'm blind. The kid called down lightning on me.' I saw him go down on to all fours and begin to feel around with his hands. 'You were right, we shouldn'ta come here. No good comes of meddling with these sort of folk.'

Lightning. Of course. He didn't know a thing about real magic. It gave me a thought.

I took a deep breath, settling my nerves. 'Who sent you?' I demanded in my best Taborlin the Great voice. It wasn't as good as my father's, but it was good.

The big man gave a wretched moan and stopped feeling around with his hands. 'Oh sir. Don't do anything that—'

'I am not asking again.' I cut him off angrily. 'Tell me who sent you. And if you lie to me, I'll know.'

'I don't know a name,' he said quickly. 'We just get half the coin and a hair. We don't know names. We don't actually meet. I swear . . .'

A hair. The thing they had called a 'finder' was probably some sort of dowsing compass. Though I couldn't make anything that advanced, I knew the principles involved. With a piece of my hair, it would point towards me no matter where I ran.

'If I ever see either of you again, I will call down worse than fire and lightning,' I said menacingly as I edged toward the mouth of the alley. If I could get hold of their finder I wouldn't have to worry about them tracking me down again. It had been dark and the hood of my cloak had been up. They might not even know what I looked like.

'Thank you, sir,' he babbled. 'I swear you won't see hide or hair of us after this. Thank you . . .'

I looked down at the fallen man. I could see one of his pale hands against the cobblestones, but it was empty. I looked around, wondering if he had dropped it. It was more likely that he'd tucked it away. I moved closer still, holding my breath. I reached into his cloak, feeling for pockets, but his cloak was pinned under his body. I took gentle hold of his shoulder and eased him slowly . . .

Just then, he let out a low moan and rolled the rest of the way onto his back under his own power. His arm flopped loosely onto the cobbles, bumping my leg.

I would like to say I simply took a step away, knowing that the tall man would be groggy and still half-blind. I'd like to tell you I remained calm and did my best to intimidate them further, or at the very least that I said something dramatic or witty before I left.

But that would not be the truth. The truth was, I ran like a frightened deer. I made it nearly a quarter mile before the darkness and my dazzled vision betrayed me and I ran headlong into a horse tether, crumpling to the ground in a painful heap. Bruised, bleeding, and half-blind, I lay there. Only then did I realise I wasn't being chased at all.

I dragged myself to my feet, cursing myself for a fool. If I'd kept my wits about me, I could have taken their dowsing compass away, ensuring my safety. As it was, I'd have to take other precautions.

I made my way back to Anker's, but when I arrived all the inn's windows were dark and the door was locked. So, half drunk and wounded I made my way up to my window, tripped the latch and tugged . . . but it wouldn't open.

It had been at least a span of days since I'd come back to the inn so late that I'd been forced to use my window route. Had the hinges rusted?

Bracing myself against the wall, I drew out my hand lamp and thumbed it on to its dimmest setting. Only then did I see something lodged firmly into the crack of the windowframe. Had Anker's wedged my window shut?

But when I touched it, I realised it wasn't wood. It was a piece of paper, much folded over. I tugged it free and the window came open easily. I clambered inside.

My shirt was ruined, but when I stripped it off I was relieved by what I saw. The cut wasn't particularly deep – painful and messy, but less serious than when I'd been whipped. Fela's cloak was torn too, which was irritating. But, everything said, it would be easier to patch that than my kidney. I made a mental note to thank Fela for choosing a nice, thick fabric.

Stitching it up could wait. For all I knew the two men had recovered from the little scare I'd given them and were already dowsing for me again.

I left through the window, leaving my cloak behind so as not to get any blood on it. I hoped the lateness of the hour and my natural stealth would keep me from being seen. I couldn't begin to guess what rumours would start if someone saw me running across the rooftops late at night, bloody and naked to the waist.

I gathered up a handful of leaves as I made my way to the roof of a livery overlooking the pennant courtyard near the Archives.

In the dim moonlight I could see the dark, shapeless shadows of leaves swirling over the grey of the cobblestones below. I ran my hand roughly through my hair, ending up with a few loose strands. Then I dug at a seam of tar on the roof with my fingernails and used some to stick the hair to a leaf. I repeated this a dozen times, dropping the leaves off the roof, watching as the wind took them away in a mad dance back and forth across the courtyard.

I smiled at the thought of anyone trying to dowse for me now, trying to make sense of the dozens of contradictory signals as the leaves swirled and spun in a dozen different directions.

I'd come to this particular courtyard because the wind moved oddly here. I'd only noticed it after the autumn leaves began to fall. They moved in a complex, chaotic dance across the cobblestones. First one way, then another, never falling into a predictable pattern.

Once you noticed the wind's odd swirlings, it was hard to ignore. In fact, viewed from the roof like this, it was almost hypnotic. The same way flowing water or a campfire's flames can catch your eye and hold it.

Watching it tonight, weary and wounded, it was rather relaxing. The more I watched it, the less chaotic it seemed. In fact, I began to sense a greater underlying pattern to the way the wind moved through the courtyard. It only looked chaotic because it was vastly, marvellously complex. What's more, it seemed to be always changing. It was a pattern made of changing patterns. It was—

'You're up studying awfully late,' said a quiet voice from behind me.

Startled out of my reverie, my body tensed, ready to bolt. How had someone managed to get up here without my noticing?

It was Elodin. Master Elodin. He was dressed in a patched set of trousers and a loose shirt. He waved idly in my direction and crouched down to sit cross-legged on the edge of the roof as casually as if we were meeting for a drink in a pub.

He looked down into the courtyard. 'It's particularly good tonight, isn't it?'

I folded my arms, ineffectually trying to cover my bare, bloody chest. Only then did I notice the blood on my hands was dry. How long had I been sitting here, motionless, watching the wind?

'Master Elodin,' I said, then stopped. I had no idea what I could possibly say in a situation like this.

'Please, we're all friends here. Feel free to call me by my first name: Master.' He gave a lazy grin and looked back down towards the courtyard.

Hadn't he noticed the state I was in? Was he being polite? Maybe . . . I shook my head. There was no use guessing with him. I knew better than anyone that Elodin was cracked as the potter's cobbles.

'Long ago,' Elodin said conversationally, not taking his eyes from the courtyard below. 'When folk spoke differently, this used to be called the Quoyan Hayel. Later they called it the Questioning Hall, and students made a game of writing questions on slips of paper and letting them blow about. Rumour had it you could divine your answer by which way the paper left the square.' He pointed to the roads that left gaps between the grey buildings. 'Yes. No. Maybe. Elsewhere. Soon.'

He shrugged. 'It was all a mistake though. Bad translation. They thought Quoyan was an early root of *quetentan*: question. But it isn't. Quoyan means "wind". This is rightly named "the House of the Wind".'

I waited a moment to see if he intended to say any more. When nothing was forthcoming I got slowly to my feet. 'That's interesting, Master . . .' I hesitated, not sure how serious he had been before. 'But I should be going.'

Elodin nodded absently and gave a wave that was half farewell, half dismissal. His eyes never left the courtyard below, following the ever-changing wind.

———

Back in my room at Anker's, I sat on my bed for a long minute in the dark, trying to decide what to do. My thoughts were muddy. I was weary, wounded, and still a little drunk. The adrenaline that had kept me going earlier was slowly turning sour and my side burned and stung.

I took a deep breath and tried to focus my thoughts. I'd been moving on instinct so far, but now I needed to think things through carefully.

Could I go to the masters for help? For a moment hope rose in my chest, then fell. No. I had no proof that Ambrose was responsible. What's more, if I told them the whole story, I would have to admit that I had used sympathy to blind and burn my attackers. Self-defense or no, what I'd done was unquestionably malfeasance. Students had been expelled for less than that just to preserve the University's reputation.

No. I couldn't risk being expelled over this. And if I went to the Medica, there would be too many questions. And word of my injury would get around if I went in to get stitched. That meant Ambrose would know how close he had come to succeeding. It would be better to give the impression that I had walked away unscathed.

I had no idea how long Ambrose's hired killers had been following me. One of them had said, 'We already lost him twice.' That means they could know I had a room here at Anker's. I might not be safe here.

I locked the window and drew the curtain before turning on my hand lamp. The light revealed the forgotten piece of paper that had been wedged into my window. I unfolded it and read:

Kvothe,

Getting up here is every bit as much fun as you made it look. However, springing your window took some time. Finding you not at home, I hope you do not mind me borrowing paper and ink enough to leave this note. As you are not playing downstairs, or peacefully abed, a cynical person might wonder what you are doing at this late hour, and if you are up to no good. Alas, I shall have to walk back home tonight without the comfort of your escort or the pleasure of your company.

I missed you this Felling past at the Eolian, but though denied your company, I had the good fortune to meet someone quite interesting. He is a quite singular fellow, and I am eager to tell you what little I can of him. When next we meet.

I currently have rooms at the Swan and Swale (Swail?) in Imre. Please call on me, before the 23rd of this month, and we will have our lunch, belated. After that I will be about on my business.

Your friend and apprentice housebreaker,

Denna,

pstscrpt – Please rest assured that I did not notice the disgraceful condition of your bed linens, and did not judge your character thereby.

Today was the 28th. The letter didn't have a date, but it had probably been there for at least a span and a half. She must have left it only a few days after the fire in the Fishery.

I briefly tried to decide how I felt about it. Flattered that she had tried to find me? Furious that the note had gone unfound until now? As to the matter of the 'fellow' that she had met . . .

It was far too much for me to deal with at the moment, weary, wounded, and still somewhat the worse for drink. Instead I quickly cleaned the shallow cut as best I could using my washbasin. I would have put some stitches in it myself, but I couldn't get a good angle. It started bleeding again, and I cut off the cleaner pieces of my ruined shirt to fashion a makeshift bandage.

Blood. The men who tried to kill me still had the dowsing compass, and I'd undoubtedly left some of my blood on his knife. Blood would be vastly more effective in a dowsing compass than a simple hair; that meant that even if they didn't already know where I lived, they might be able to find me despite the precautions I'd taken.

I moved around my room quickly, stuffing everything of value into my travelsack, as I didn't know when it would be safe to return. Under a stack of papers I found a small folding knife I'd forgotten about, after I'd won it off Sim playing corners. It would be worth next to nothing in a fight, but that was better than nothing at all.

Then I grabbed my lute and cloak and snuck downstairs into the kitchen, where I was lucky enough to find an empty Velegen wine pot with a wide mouth. It was a minor piece of luck, but I was glad for whatever I could get at this point.

I headed east and crossed the river, but didn't go all the way into Imre proper. Instead I headed south a bit to where a few docks, a seedy inn, and a handful of houses perched on the bank of the wide Omethi River. It was a small port that serviced Imre, too small to have a name of its own.

I stuffed my bloody shirt into the wine pot and made it watertight with a piece of sympathy wax. Then I dropped it in the Omethi River and watched it bob slowly downstream. If they were dowsing for my blood, it would seem like I was heading south, running. Hopefully they'd follow it.

CHAPTER SEVENTY

Signs

I CAME SUDDENLY AWAKE early the next morning. I didn't know exactly where I was, only that I wasn't where I should be, and that something was wrong. I was hiding. Someone was after me.

I was curled up in the corner of a small room. I lay on a blanket and I was wrapped in my cloak. This was an inn . . . it slowly came back to me. I had rented a room at an inn near Imre's docks.

I came to my feet, stretching carefully so as not to aggravate my wound. I'd pushed the dresser against the room's only door and tied the window shut with a length of rope despite the fact that it was too small for a grown man to fit through.

Seeing my precautions in the cool blue light of early morning, I was a little embarrassed. I couldn't remember whether I'd slept on the floor out of fear of assassins or bedbugs. Either way, it was clear that I hadn't been thinking too clearly towards the end of the night.

I gathered up my travelsack and lute and headed downstairs. I had some planning to do, but before that, I needed breakfast and a bath.

Despite my busy night, I'd barely slept past sunrise, so I had easy access to the bathhouse. After cleaning myself up and rewrapping the bandage around my side, I felt mostly human. A plate of eggs, a couple of sausages, and some fried potatoes later, I felt I could begin to think rationally about my situation. It's amazing how much easier it is to think productively when your belly is full.

I sat in the far corner of the little dockside inn and sipped a mug of fresh-pressed apple cider. I was no longer worried that hired killers were going to leap out and assault me. Still, I was sitting with my back to the wall with a good view of the door.

Yesterday had left me shaken mostly because it had caught me so unprepared. In Tarbean I'd lived each day expecting people would try to kill me. The civilised atmosphere of the University had lulled me into a false sense of security. I never would have been caught off my guard a year ago. I certainly wouldn't have been surprised by the attack itself.

My hard-won instincts from Tarbean were urging me to run. Leave this place. Leave Ambrose and his vendetta far behind. But that feral part of me cared only for safety. It had no plan.

I couldn't leave. I had too much invested here. My studies. My vain hopes for gaining a patron and my stronger hopes of entry to the Archives. My precious few friends. Denna . . .

Sailors and dockworkers began to filter into the inn to get the morning meal, and the room slowly filled with the gentle buzz of conversation. I heard a bell ringing dimly in the distance and it occurred to me that my shift in the Medica would be starting in an hour. Arwyl would notice if I was absent, and he was not forgiving of such things. I fought down the urge to run back to the University. It was well known that absent students were punished with higher tuitions the following term.

To give myself something to do while I was thinking through my situation, I brought out my cloak along with needle and thread. The knife from last night had made a straight cut about two handspan across. I began to sew it closed, using tiny stitches so the seam wouldn't be obvious.

While my hands worked, my thoughts wandered. Could I confront Ambrose? Threaten him? Not likely. He knew I couldn't successfully bring charges against him. But maybe I could persuade a few of the masters of what had really happened. Kilvin would be outraged at the thought of hired killers using a dowsing compass, and perhaps Arwyl . . .

'. . . all blue fire. Every one of them dead, thrown around like rag dolls and the house falling to pieces around them. I was glad to see the end of the place. I can tell you that.'

I jabbed my finger with the needle as my eavesdropper's ears picked the conversation out of the common room's general din. A few tables over, two men were drinking beer. One was tall and balding, the other was fat with a red beard.

'Yer such an old woman,' the fat one laughed. 'You'll listen to any piece of gossip.'

The tall man shook his head somberly. 'I was in the tavern when they came in with the news. They were gatherin' folk with wagons so they could go get the bodies. The whole wedding party dead as leather. Over thirty folks gutted like pigs and the place burned down in a blue flame. And that weren't the least oddness from what . . .' He dropped his voice and I lost what he was saying among the general noise of the room.

I swallowed against the sudden dryness in my throat. I slowly tied off the last stitch on my cloak and set it down. I noticed my bleeding finger and absently put it in my mouth. I took a deep breath. I took a drink.

Then I walked over to the table where the two men sat talking. 'Did you gentlemen come downriver by any chance?'

They looked up, obviously irritated by the interruption. *Gentlemen had been a mistake, I should have said fellows, fellas.* The bald one nodded.

'Did you come by way of Marrow?' I asked, picking a northern town at random.

'No,' the fat one said. 'We're down from Trebon.'

'Oh good.' I said, my mind racing for a plausible lie. 'I have family up in those parts I was thinking of visiting.' My mind went blank as I tried to think of a way to ask him for the details of the story I'd overheard.

My palms were sweaty. 'Are they getting ready for the harvest festival up that way, or have I already missed it?' I finished lamely.

'Still in the works,' the bald one said and pointedly turned his shoulder to me.

'I'd heard there was some problem with a wedding up in those parts . . .'

The bald one turned back to look at me. 'Well I don't know how you'd have heard that. As the news was fresh last night and we just docked down here ten minutes ago.' He gave me a hard look. 'I don't know what you're sellin', boy. But I ain't buyin'. Piss off or I'll thump you.'

I went back to my seat, knowing I'd made an irrecoverable mess of things. I sat, keeping my hands flat on the table to keep them from shaking. A group of people brutally killed. Blue fire. Oddness . . .

Chandrian.

Less than a day ago the Chandrian were in Trebon.

———————

I finished my drink more out of reflex than anything else, then stood and made my way to the bar.

I was quickly coming to grips with the reality of the situation. After all these years I finally had the opportunity to learn something about the Chandrian. And not just a mention of them pressed flat between the pages of a book in the Archives. I had the chance to see their work firsthand. This was an opportunity that might never come again.

But I needed to get to Trebon soon, while things were still fresh in people's memories. Before curious or superstitious townsfolk destroyed what evidence remained. I didn't know what I hoped to find, but anything I learned about the Chandrian would be more than I knew now. And if I were to have a chance at anything useful, I had to be there as soon as possible. Today.

The morning crowd was keeping the innkeeper busy, so I had to lay an iron drab on the bar before she paid me any attention at all. After paying for a private room last night and breakfast and bath this morning, the drab represented a good portion of my worldly wealth, so I kept my finger on it.

'What'll you have?' she asked, as she came up to me.

'How far is it to Trebon?' I asked.

'Upriver? A couple days.'

'I didn't ask how long it was. I need to know how *far* . . .' I said, stressing the last word.

'No need to get snippy,' she said, wiping her hands on her grubby apron. 'By river it's forty miles or so. Could take more than two days depending on if you're on a barge or a billow-boat, and what the weather's like.'

'How far by road?' I asked.

'Blacken me if I know,' she muttered, then called down the bar. 'Rudd, how far to Trebon by road?'

'Three or four days,' said a weathered man without looking up from his mug.

'I asked how *far,*' she snapped at him. 'Is it longer than the riverway?'

'Damn sight longer. About twenty-five leagues by road. A hard road too, uphill.'

God's body, who measured things in leagues these days? Depending on where that fellow grew up, a league could be anywhere between two to three and a half miles. My father always claimed that a league wasn't really a unit of measurement at all, just a way for farmers to attach numbers to their rough guesses.

Still, it let me know Trebon was somewhere between fifty and eighty miles to the north. It was probably best to assume the worst, at least seventy miles.

The woman behind the bar turned back to me. 'There you have it. Now can I get you something?'

'I need a waterskin, if you have one, or a bottle of water if you don't. And some food that will keep on the road. Hard sausage, cheese, flatbread . . .'

'Apples?' she asked. 'Got some lovely Red Jennies this morning. Good for the road.'

I nodded. 'And whatever else you have that's cheap and will travel.'

'A drab doesn't go far . . .' she said with a glance down at the bar. I shook out my purse and was surprised to see four drabs and a copper ha'penny I hadn't accounted for. I was practically rich.

She gathered up my money and headed back to the kitchen. I fought off the momentary pang at being utterly destitute again and ran a quick mental inventory of what I had in my travelsack.

She came back with two loaves of flatbread, a thick, hard sausage that smelled of garlic, a small cheese sealed in wax, a bottle of water, half a dozen gorgeous bright red apples, and a small sack of carrots and potatoes. I thanked her kindly and stuffed the lot into my sack.

Seventy miles. I could make it today if I had a good horse. But good horses cost money . . .

I breathed in the smell of rancid fat as I knocked on Devi's door. I stood there for a minute, fighting the urge to fidget impatiently. I had no idea if Devi would be awake at such an early hour, but it was a risk I had to take.

Devi opened the door and smiled when she saw me. 'Well here's a pleasant surprise.' She opened the door wider. 'Come in. Sit down.'

I gave her my best smile. 'Devi, I just—'

She frowned. 'Come in,' she said more firmly. 'I don't discuss business on the landing.'

I came in and she closed the door behind me. 'Take a seat. Unless you'd rather have a bit of a lie down.' She nodded playfully toward the huge curtained bed in the corner of the room. 'You won't believe the story I heard this morning,' she said, laughter hiding in her voice.

Despite the urgency I felt, I forced myself to relax. Devi was not one to be rushed, if I tried, it would only irritate her. 'What did you hear?'

She sat on her side of the desk and folded her hands. 'Apparently last night a pair of ruffians tried to lift a purse off a young student. Much to their dismay, it turns out he's the next Taborlin in training. He called down fire and lightning. Blinded one and gave the other such a mighty blow to the head that he still hasn't woken up.'

I sat quietly for a moment as I absorbed the information. An hour ago this would have been the best news I could have heard. Now it was hardly more than a distraction. Still, despite the urgency of my other errand, I couldn't ignore the chance to gather some information about the crisis closer to home. 'They weren't just trying to rob me,' I said.

Devi laughed. 'I knew it was you! They didn't know anything about him except for that he had red hair. But that was enough for me.'

'Did I really blind the one?' I asked. 'And the other still unconscious?'

'I honestly don't know,' Devi admitted. 'News travels quickly among us unsavoury types, but it's mostly gossip.'

My mind was spinning quickly along a new plan now. 'Would you care to spread a little gossip of your own?' I asked.

'That depends,' she gave a wicked smile. 'Is it terribly exciting?'

'Drop my name,' I said. 'Let them know exactly who it was. Let them know I'm mad as hell, and I'll kill the next ones that come after me. I'll kill them and whoever hired them, the middlemen, their families, their dogs, the whole lot.'

Devi's delighted expression faded to something closer to distaste. 'That's a little grim, don't you think? I appreciate that you're attached to your purse,' she gave me a playful look, 'and I have a vested interest there myself. But there's no—'

'They weren't thieves,' I said. 'They were hired to kill me.' Devi gave me a skeptical look. I tugged up the corner of my shirt to show my bandage. 'I'm serious. I can show you where one of them cut me before I got away.'

Frowning, she stood up and came around to the other side of the desk. 'Alright, show me.'

I hesitated, then decided that I was better off humouring her, as I still had favours to ask. I took off my shirt and lay it on the desk.

'That bandage is filthy,' she said, as if it was a personal offense. 'Get rid of it.' She walked to a cabinet at the back of the room and came back with a black physicker's kit and a washbasin. She washed her hands, then looked at my side. 'You haven't even had it stitched?' She said incredulously.

'I've been rather busy,' I said. 'With the running like hell and hiding all night.'

She ignored me and set about cleaning my side with a cool efficiency that let me know she'd studied in the Medica. 'It's messy, but not deep,' she said. 'It's not even all the way through the skin in some places.' She stood up and pulled a few things out of her bag. 'You'll still need stitches.'

'I would have done it myself,' I said. 'But . . .'

'. . . but you're an idiot who didn't even make sure this was cleaned properly,' she finished. 'If this gets infected, it would serve you right.'

She finished cleaning my side and rinsed her hands in the bowl. 'I want you to know I'm doing this because I have a soft spot for pretty boys, the mentally infirm, and people who owe me money. I consider this protecting my investment.'

'Yes ma'am.' I sucked in air when she applied the antiseptic.

'I thought you weren't supposed to bleed,' she said matter-of-factly. 'There's another legend proven false.'

'Speaking of.' Moving as little as possible, I reached out and pulled a book out of my travelsack, then laid it on her desk. 'I brought back your copy of *Mating Habits of the Common Draccus*. You were right, the engravings added a lot to it.'

'I knew you'd like it.' There was a moment of silence as she began stitching me back together. When she spoke again, most of the playfulness was gone from her voice. 'Were these fellows *really* hired to kill you, Kvothe?'

I nodded. 'They had a dowsing compass and some of my hair. That's how they knew I was a redhead.'

'Lord and lady, wouldn't that just send Kilvin into a froth?' She shook her head. 'Are you sure they weren't just hired to scare you? Rough you up a little to teach you to mind your betters?' She paused in her stitching and looked up at me. 'You weren't stupid enough to borrow money off Heffron and his boys, were you?'

I shook my head. 'You're the only hawk for me, Devi.' I smiled. 'In fact that's why I stopped by today—'

'And here I thought you merely enjoyed my company,' she said, turning back to her needlework. I thought I detected a tinge of irritation in her voice. 'Let me finish this first.'

I thought about what she'd said for a long moment. The tall man had said, 'let's do him' but that could mean any number of things. 'It's possible they weren't trying to kill me,' I admitted slowly. 'He had a knife though. You don't need a knife to give someone a beating.'

Devi snorted. 'And I don't need blood to get people to settle their debts. But it certainly helps.'

I thought about it as she tied off the final stitch and began to wrap me in a fresh bandage. Maybe it was meant to be a simple beating. An anonymous message from Ambrose telling me to mind my betters. Maybe it was a simple attempt to scare me off. I sighed, trying not to move too much as I did so. 'I'd like to believe that's the case, but I really don't think so. I think they were really after blood. That's what my gut tells me.'

Her expression grew serious. 'In that case I will spread the word a little,' she said. 'I don't know about the part about killing their dogs, but I'll drop a few things into the rumour mill so people will think twice about taking that sort of job.' She chuckled low in her throat. 'Actually, they're already thinking twice after last night. This will make them think three times.'

'I appreciate it.'

'Small trouble to me,' she said dismissively as she stood up and brushed off her knees. 'A small favour to help a friend.' She washed her hands in the basin, then dried them carelessly on her shirt. 'Let's hear it,' she said as she sat behind the desk, her expression suddenly businesslike.

'I need money for a fast horse,' I said.

'Leaving town?' She arched a pale eyebrow. 'You never struck me as the running away sort.'

'I'm not running,' I said. 'But I need to cover some ground. Seventy miles before it gets much after noon.'

Devi widened her eyes a bit. 'A horse that could make that trip is going to cost,' she said. 'Why not just buy a post note and switch out fresh horses all the way? Faster and cheaper.'

'There's no post stations where I'm going,' I said. 'Upriver then into the hills. Little town called Trebon.'

'Alright,' she said. 'How much are you looking for?'

'I'll need money to buy a fast horse with no dickering. Plus lodging, food, maybe bribes . . . Twenty talents.'

She burst out laughing, then regained her composure and covered her mouth. 'No. I'm sorry but no. I do have a soft spot for charming young men like yourself, but it's not on my head.'

'I have my lute,' I said, sliding the case forward with my foot. 'For collateral. Plus anything else in here.' I put my travelsack on the desk.

She drew a breath, as if to refuse me out of hand, then shrugged and looked into the bag, poking around. She pulled out my copy of *Rhetoric and Logic,* and a moment later my handheld sympathy lamp. 'Hello,' she said curiously, thumbing on the switch and pointing the light towards the wall. 'This is interesting.'

I grimaced. 'Anything except that,' I said. 'I promised Kilvin I wouldn't ever let that out of my hands. I gave my word.'

She gave me a frank look. 'Have you ever heard the expression beggars can't be choosers?'

'I gave my word,' I repeated. I unpinned my silver talent pipes from my cloak and slid them across her desk so they lay near *Rhetoric and Logic*. 'Those aren't easy to come by, you know.'

Devi looked at the lute, the book, and the pipes, and drew a long, slow breath. 'Kvothe, I can tell that this is important to you, but the numbers just don't add. You're not good for that much money. You're barely good for the four talents you owe me.'

That stung, mostly because I knew it to be the truth.

Devi thought about it for another second, then shook her head firmly. 'No, just the interest . . . In two months you'd owe me over thirty-five talents.'

'Or something equally valuable in trade,' I said.

She gave me a gentle smile. 'And what do you have worth thirty-five talents?'

'Access to the Archives.'

Devi sat. Her slightly patronising smile frozen on her face. 'You're lying.'

I shook my head. 'I know there's another way in. I haven't found it yet, but I will.'

'That's a lot of *if*.' Devi's tone was skeptical. But her eyes were full of something more than simple desire. It was closer to hunger, or lust. I could tell she wanted into the Archives just as badly as I did. Perhaps even moreso.

'That's what I'm offering,' I said. 'If I can pay you back, I will. If not, when I find a way into the Archives I'll share it with you.'

Devi looked up at the ceiling, as if calculating odds in her head. 'With these things as collateral, and the possibility of access to the Archives, I can loan you a dozen talents.'

I stood up and swung my travelsack over my shoulder. 'I'm afraid we're not bargaining here,' I said. 'I'm just informing you as to the conditions of the loan.' I gave her an apologetic smile. 'It's twenty talents or nothing. I'm sorry I didn't make that clear from the beginning.'

CHAPTER SEVENTY-ONE

Strange Attraction

THREE MINUTES LATER I strode towards the doors of the nearest livery. A well-dressed Cealdish man smiled at my approach and stepped forward to greet me. 'Ah, young sir,' he said holding out his hand. 'My name is Kaerva. Might I ask—'

'I need a horse,' I said, shaking his hand quickly. 'Healthy, well-rested, and well-fed. One that can take six hours of hard riding today.'

'Certainly, certainly,' Kaerva said, rubbing his hands together and nodding. 'All things are possible with the will of God. I'd be pleased to—'

'Listen,' I interrupted again. 'I'm in a hurry, so we're going to skip the preliminaries. I won't pretend to be uninterested. You won't waste my time with a parade of hacks and nags. If I have not bought a horse in ten minutes, I will leave and buy one elsewhere.' I met his eye. '*Lhinsatva?*'

The Cealdish man was aghast. 'Sir, the purchase of a horse should never be so rushed. You would not pick a wife in ten minutes, and on the road, a horse is more important than a wife.' He gave a bashful smile. 'Even God himself didn't—'

I cut him off yet again. 'God's not buying a horse today, I am.'

The thin Cealdish man paused to collect his thoughts. 'Right,' he said softly, more to himself than to me. '*Lhin,* come around and see what we have.'

He led me around the outside of the stables to a small corral. He gestured near the edge of the fence. 'That dapple mare is as steady a horse as any you could hope for. She'll take you . . .'

I ignored him and looked over the half-dozen hacks that stood idly inside the fence. Though I had neither means nor reason to keep a horse, I knew good from bad, and nothing I saw here came close to suiting my needs.

You see, troupers live and die by the horses that pull their wagons, and my parents had not neglected my education in this area. I could size up a horse by the time I was eight, and a good thing too. Townsfolk regularly tried to pass off half-dead or gingered up nags to us, knowing that by the time we discovered our mistakes we'd be miles and days away. There was a world of trouble waiting for a man who sold his neighbour some sickly hobble, but what was the harm of swindling one of the filthy, thieving Ruh?

I turned to face the cavler, frowning. 'You have just wasted two precious minutes of my time, so I'm guessing you still don't understand my position here. Let me be as plain as possible. I want a fast horse ready for hard riding today. For this I will pay quickly, in hard coin, and without complaint.' I held up my newly heavy purse in one hand and shook it, knowing he could tell the ring of true Cealdish silver inside.

'If you sell me a horse that throws a shoe, or starts to limp, or spooks at shadows, I will miss a valuable opportunity. A quite unrecoverable opportunity. If that happens, I will not come back and demand a refund. I will not petition the constable. I will walk back to Imre this very night and set fire to your house. Then, when you run out the front door in your nightshirt and stockle-cap, I will kill you, cook you, and eat you. Right there on your lawn while all your neighbours watch.'

I gave him a deadly serious look. 'This is the business arrangement I am proposing, Kaerva. If you are not comfortable with it, tell me and I will go elsewhere. Otherwise, leave off this parade of drays and show me a real horse.'

The short Ceald looked at me, more stunned than horrified. I could see him trying to come to grips with the situation. He must think I was either a raving lunatic, or the son of some important noble. Or both.

'Very well,' he said, letting all the ingratiating charm fall from his voice. 'When you say hard riding, how hard do you mean?'

'Very hard,' I said. 'I need to go seventy miles today. Dirt roads.'

'Will you need saddle and tack too?'

I nodded. 'Nothing fancy. Nothing new.'

He drew a deep breath. 'Fine, and how much do you have to spend?'

I shook my head and gave a tight smile. 'Show me the horse and name your price. A Vaulder would do nicely. If he's a little wild, I won't mind if it means he's got energy to spare. Even a good Vaulder mix could serve me, or a Khershaen forth horse.'

Kaerva nodded and led me back towards the wide doors of the stable. 'I do have a Khershaen. A full-blood actually.' He made a gesture to one of the stablehands. 'Bring out our black gentleman, double-quick.' The boy sprinted off.

The cavler turned back to me. 'Gorgeous animal. I ran him through the traces before I bought him, just to be sure. Galloped him a full mile and he hardly even worked up a sweat, smooth a gait as ever I've felt, and I'd not lie to your lordship on that account.'

I nodded, a full-blooded Khershaen was exactly suited to my purpose. They had a legendary endurance, but there would be no avoiding the price, either. A well-trained forth horse was worth a dozen talents. 'How much are you asking for him?'

'I'll want two solid marks,' he said without any hint of apology or wheedling in his voice.

Merciful Tehlu, twenty talents. He'd have to have silver shoes to be worth that much. 'I'm in no mood for a lengthy dicker, Kaerva,' I said shortly.

'You've made me well aware of that, milord,' he said. 'I'm telling you my honest price. Here. You'll see why.'

The boy hurried out leading a sleek monster of a horse. At least eighteen hands tall, proud head, and black from his nose to the tip of his tail. 'He loves to run,' Kaerva said with genuine affection in his voice. He ran a hand along the smooth black neck. 'And look at that colour. Not so much as a pale whisker, that's why he's worth twenty if he's worth a single shim.'

'I don't care about the colour,' I said absentmindedly while I looked him over for signs of injury or old age. There was nothing. He was glossy, young, strong. 'I just need to move quickly.'

'I understand,' he said apologetically. 'But I can't just ignore the colouring. If I wait a span or two, some young lord will pay just for the snappy look of him.'

I knew it was true. 'Does he have a name?' I asked moving slowly towards the black horse, letting him smell my hands and get used to me. Bargaining can be hurried, but befriending a horse cannot. Only a fool rushes first impressions with a spirited young Khershaen.

'Not one that's stuck on him,' he said.

'What's your name, boy?' I asked gently, just so he could get used to the sound of my voice. He snuffed delicately at my hand, keeping close watch with one large, intelligent eye. He didn't back away, but he certainly wasn't at his ease either. I kept talking as I came closer, hoping he would relax at the sound of my voice. 'You deserve a good name. I hate to see some lordling with delusions of wit saddle you with some terrible name like Midnight or Sooty or Scut.'

I came closer and lay one hand along his neck. His skin twitched, but he didn't pull away. I needed to be sure of his temperament as much as his stamina. I couldn't take the risk of jumping on the back of a skittish horse. 'Someone half clever might dub you Pitch or Scuttle, ill-favoured names. Or Slate, a sedentary name. Heaven forbid you end up Blackie, that's an ill-fitting name for a prince like you.'

My father always talked to new horses in this way, in a steady calming litany. As I stroked his neck, I kept speaking without giving any mind to what I said. Words don't matter to the horse, the tone of your voice is the important thing. 'You've come a long way. You should have a proud name, so folk won't think of you as common. Was your previous owner Cealdish?' I asked. '*Ve vanaloi. Tu teriam keta. Palan te?*'

I could sense him relax a bit at the sound of the familiar language. I walked onto his other side, still looking him over carefully and letting him get used to my presence. '*Tu Ketha?*' I asked him. *Are you coal?* '*Tu mahne?*' *Are you a shadow?*

I wanted to say twilight, but I couldn't bring the Siaru word to mind. Rather than pause, I just bulled ahead, faking it as best I could as I eyed his hooves to see if they were chipped or cracked. '*Tu Keth-Selhan?*' *Are you first night?*

The big black lowered his head and nuzzled me. 'You like that one, do you?' I said with a bit of a laugh, knowing that what really happened was that he had caught scent of the package of dried apple I had tucked in one of the pockets of my cloak. The important thing was that he had a feel for me now. If he was comfortable enough to nuzzle at me for food, we could get along well enough for a hard day's ride.

'Keth-Selhan seems to suit him for a name,' I said, turning back to Kaerva. 'Anything else I need to know?'

Kaerva seemed disconcerted. 'He shies a bit on his right side.'

'A bit?'

'Just a bit. It stands to reason that he's probably a bit prone to spooking on that side too, but I haven't seen him do it.'

'How's he trained? Close rein or trouper style?'

'Close.'

'Fine. You've got one minute left to make this deal. He's a good animal, but I'm not paying twenty talents for him.' I spoke with certainty in my voice, but no hope in my heart. He was a gorgeous animal, and his colouring made him worth at least twenty talents. Still, I'd go through the motions and hope to squeeze the man down to nineteen. That at least would leave me money for food and lodging when I got to Trebon.

'Very well,' Kaerva said. 'Sixteen.'

Only my years of stage training kept me from gaping openly at his sudden drop. 'Fifteen,' I said, feigning irritation. 'And that will include the saddle, tack, and a bag of oats.' I began pulling money out of my purse as if the deal was already finished.

Unbelievably, Kaerva nodded and called for one of the boys to bring a saddle and tack.

I counted the money into Kaerva's hand as his assistant saddled the big black. The Ceald seemed uncomfortable meeting my eye.

If I didn't know horses as well as I do, I would have thought I was being swindled. Maybe the horse was stolen, or the man was desperate for money.

Whatever the reason, I didn't care. I was due a bit of good luck. Best of all, this meant that I might be able to resell the horse at a bit of a profit after I reached Trebon. Honestly, I would need to sell him as soon as I could manage, even if I lost money on the deal. Stabling, food, and grooming for a horse like this would cost me a penny a day. I couldn't afford to keep him.

I strapped my travelsack into a saddlebag, checked the cinch and stirrups, then swung myself up onto Keth-Selhan's back. He danced slightly to the right, eager to be off. That made two of us. I twitched the reins and we were on our way.

———

Most problems with horses have nothing to do with the horses themselves. They stem from the ignorance of the rider. Folk shoe their horses badly, saddle them improperly, feed them poorly, then complain that they were sold a half-lame, swayback, ill-tempered hack.

I knew horses. My parents had taught me to ride and care for them. While most of my experience had been with sturdier breeds, bred to pull rather than to race, I knew how to cover ground quickly when I needed to.

When they're in a hurry, most folk push their mount too hard too soon. They head out at a dead gallop, then find themselves with a horse lame or half dead inside an hour. Pure idiocy. Only a twelve-colour bastard treats a horse that way.

But to be entirely truthful, I would have ridden Keth-Selhan to death if it would have brought me to Trebon in a timely fashion. There are some times when I am willing to be a bastard. I would have killed a dozen horses if it would have helped me get more information about the Chandrian and why they had killed my parents.

But ultimately, there was no sense in thinking that way. A dead horse wouldn't get me to Trebon. A live one would.

So I started Keth-Selhan at a nice walk to warm him up. He was eager to go faster, probably sensing my own impatience, and that would have been fine if I'd only needed to go a mile or three. But I needed him for at least fifty, maybe seventy, and that meant patience. I had to rein him back down to a walk twice before he resigned himself to it.

After a mile, I trotted him for a bit. His gait was smooth, even for a Kershaen, but a trot is jarring no matter what, and it pulled at the new stitches in my side. I urged him up to a canter after another mile or so. Only after we were three or four miles out of Imre and we came to a good, straight stretch of flat road did I nudge him up to a gallop.

Finally given the chance to run, he surged ahead. The sun had just finished burning away the morning dew, and farmers harvesting wheat and barley in the fields looked up as we thundered past. Keth-Selhan was fast; so fast that the wind tore at my cloak, stretching it behind me like a flag. Despite the fact that I knew I must cut quite the dramatic figure, I quickly grew tired of the drag on my neck, unfastened the cloak, then stuffed it into a saddlebag.

When we passed through a stand of trees, I brought Selhan back down to a trot. That way he got a little rest, and we didn't run the risk of rounding a corner and barrelling into a fallen tree or slow-moving cart. When we came out into pastureland and could see our way clear, I gave him his head again and we practically flew.

After an hour and a half of this, Selhan was sweating and breathing hard, but he was doing better than I was. My legs were a rubbery mess. I was fit enough, and young, but I hadn't been in the saddle for years. Riding uses different muscles than walking, and riding at a gallop is just as hard as running unless you want to make your horse work twice as hard for every mile.

Suffice to say I welcomed the next stretch of trees. I hopped out of the saddle and walked to give both of us a well-deserved break. I cut one of my apples down the middle and gave him the larger half. I figured we'd come about thirty miles, and the sun wasn't even fully at zenith.

'That's the easy bit,' I told him, stroking his neck fondly. 'Lord, but you are lovely. You're not half blown yet, are you?'

We walked for about ten minutes, then we had the good luck to come across a little creek with a wooden bridge running across it. I let him drink for a long minute, then pulled him away before he took too much.

Then I mounted up and gaited him back up to a gallop by slow stages. My legs burned and ached as I leaned over his neck. The drumming of his hooves was like a counterpoint to the slow song of the wind, endlessly burning past my ears.

The first snag came about an hour later when we had to cross a wide stream. It wasn't treacherous by any means, but I had to unsaddle him and carry everything across rather than risk it getting wet. I couldn't ride him for hours wearing a wet harness.

On the other side of the river I dried him off with my blanket and re-saddled him. It took half an hour, which meant he had gone from being rested to being cold, so I had to warm him up gently, slow walk to trot to canter. That stream cost me an hour all told. I worried if there was another one the chill would get into Selhan's muscles. If that happened, Tehlu himself wouldn't be able to bring him up to a gallop again.

An hour later I passed through a small town, hardly more than a church and a tavern that happened to be next to each other. I stopped long enough to let Selhan drink a bit from a trough. I stretched my numb legs and looked up anxiously at the sun.

After that, the fields and farms grew fewer and farther between. The trees grew thicker and denser. The road narrowed and was not in good repair, rocky in places, washed out in others. It made for slower and slower going. But, truth be told, neither myself or Keth-Selhan had much more galloping left in us.

Eventually we came to another stream crossing the road. Not much more than a foot deep at the most. The water had a sharp, foul smell that let me know there was a tannery upstream, or a refinery. There wasn't any bridge, and Keth-Selhan made his way slowly across, placing his hooves gingerly on the rocky bottom. I wondered idly if it felt good, like when you dandle your feet in the water after a long day's walking.

The stream didn't slow us down much, but over the next half hour we had to cross it three separate times as it wound back and forth across the road. It was an inconvenience more than anything, never much deeper than a foot and half. Each time we crossed it the acrid smell of the water was worse. Solvents and acids. If not a refinery, then at least a mine. I kept my hands on the reins, ready to pull Selhan's head up if he tried to drink, but he was smarter than that.

A long canter later I came up over a hill and looked down onto a crossroads at the bottom of a small grassy valley. Right under the signpost was a tinker with a pair of donkeys, one of them loaded so high with bags and bundles that it looked ready to tip over, the other conspicuously unburdened. It stood by the side of the dirt road grazing with a small mountain of gear piled beside it.

The tinker sat on a small stool at the side of the road, looking dispirited. His expression brightened when he saw me riding down the hill.

I read the signpost as I came closer. North was Trebon. South was Temfalls. I reined in as I approached. Keth-Selhan and I could both use the rest, and I was not in enough of a hurry to be rude to a tinker. Not by half. If nothing else the fellow could tell me how far I had left to go before I came to Trebon.

'Hello there!' he said, looking up at me, shading his eyes with one hand. 'You've got the look of a lad that's wanting something.' He was older, balding, with a round, friendly face.

I laughed. 'I'm wanting a lot of things, tinker, but I don't think you've got any of them in your packs.'

He gave me an ingratiating smile. 'Well now, don't go assuming . . .' He stopped and looked down for a moment, thoughtfully. When he met my eyes again his expression was still kind, but more serious than before. 'Listen, I'll be honest with you, son. My little donkey has got herself a stone bruise in her forehoof and can't carry her load. I'm stuck here until I come by some manner of help.'

'Normally nothing would make me happier than to help you, tinker,' I said. 'But I need to get to Trebon as quickly as I can.'

'That won't take much doing.' He nodded over the hill to the north. 'You're only about a half mile out. If the wind was blowing southerly you could smell the smoke.'

I looked in the direction he gestured and saw chimney smoke rising from behind the hill. A great wave of relief washed over me. I'd made it, and it was barely an hour after noon.

The tinker continued. 'I need to get to the Evesdown docks.' He nodded to the east. 'I've made arrangements to ship downriver and I'd dearly love to catch my boat.' He eyed my horse significantly. 'But I'll need a new pack animal to carry my gear . . .'

It seems my luck had finally turned. Selhan was a fine horse, but now that I was in Trebon, he would be little more than a constant drain on my limited resources.

Still, it's never wise to look eager to sell. 'This is an awful lot of horse to be used for packing,' I said, patting Keth-Selhan's neck. 'He's a full-blooded Khershaen, and I can tell you I've never seen a better horse in all my days.'

The tinker looked him over skeptically. 'He's knackered is what he is,' he said. 'He hasn't got another mile left in him.'

I swung off the saddle, staggering a bit when my rubbery legs almost buckled underneath me. 'You should give him some credit, tinker. He's come all the way from Imre today.'

The tinker chuckled. 'You're not a bad liar, boy, but you need to know when to stop. If the bait's too big, the fish won't bite.'

I didn't need to pretend to be horrified. 'I'm sorry I didn't properly introduce myself.' I held out my hand. 'My name is Kvothe, I am a trouper and one of the Edema Ruh. Never on my most desperate day would I lie to a tinker.'

The tinker shook my hand. 'Well,' he said, slightly taken aback, 'my sincere apologies to you and your family. It's rare to see one of your folk alone on the road.' He looked the horse over critically. 'All the way from Imre, you say?' I nodded. 'That's what, almost sixty miles? Hell of a ride . . .' He looked at me with a knowing smile. 'How are your legs?'

I grinned back at him. 'Let's just say I'll be glad to be on my own feet again. He's good for another ten miles I'd guess. But I can't say the same for myself.'

The tinker looked over the horse again and gave a gusty sigh. 'Well, as I said, you've got me over a bit of a barrel. How much do you want for him?'

'Well,' I said. 'Keth-Selhan here's a full-blood Khershaen, and his colour is lovely, you have to admit. Not a patch on him but isn't black. Not a white whisker—'

The tinker burst out laughing. 'I take it back,' he said. 'You're a terrible liar.'

'I don't see what's so funny,' I said a little stiffly.

The tinker gave me an odd look. 'Not a white whisker, no.' He nodded past me toward Selhan's hindquarters. 'But if he's all black then I'm Oren Velciter.'

I turned to look and saw that Keth-Selhan's left hind foot had a distinct white sock that went halfway up to his hock. Stupefied, I walked back and bent down to look. It wasn't a clean white, more of a washed-out grey. I could smell the faint odour of the stream we had splashed through on the last leg of our journey: solvents.

'That shim bastard,' I said incredulously. 'He sold me a dyed horse.'

'Didn't the name tip you off?' the tinker chuckled. '*Keth-Selhan*? Lord boy, someone's been thumbing their nose at you.'

'His name means twilight,' I said.

The tinker shook his head, 'Your Siaru is rusty. *Ket-Selem* would be "first-night". *Selhan* means "sock". His name is one sock.'

I thought back to the horse-trader's reaction when I'd picked the name. No wonder the fellow had seemed so disconcerted. No wonder he had dropped the price so quickly and easily. He thought I knew his little secret.

The tinker laughed at my expression and clapped me on the back. 'Don't sweat it, lad. It happens to the best of us from time to time,' he turned away and began to rummage through his bundles. 'I think I have something you'll like. Let me offer you a trade.' He turned around and held out something black and gnarled like a piece of driftwood.

I took it from him and looked it over. It was heavy and cold to the touch. 'A lump of slag iron?' I asked. 'Are you out of magic beans?'

The tinker held out a pin in his other hand. He held it about a handspan away then let go. Instead of falling, the pin snapped to the side and clung to the smooth blob of black iron.

I drew in an appreciative breath. 'A loden-stone? I've never seen one of these.'

'Technically, it's a Trebon-stone,' he said matter-of-factly. 'As it's never been near Loden, but you're near enough. There's all manner of people who would be interested in that beauty down Imre-way . . .'

I nodded absently as I turned it over in my hands. I'd always wanted to see a drawstone, ever since I was a child. I pulled the pin away, feeling the strange attraction it had to smooth black metal. I marvelled. A piece of star-iron in my hand. 'How much do you figure it's worth?' I asked.

The tinker sucked his teeth a little. 'Well I'm figuring right here and now it's worth just about one full-blooded Kershaen pack mule . . .'

I turned it over in my hand, pulled the pin away and let it snap back again. 'Trouble is tinker, I put myself into debt with a dangerous woman in order to buy this horse. If I don't sell it well, I'm going to be in a desperate way.'

He nodded. 'Piece of sky-iron of that size, if you take less than eighteen talents you're cutting a hole in your own purse. Jewellers will buy it, or rich folk who want it for the novelty.' He tapped the side of his nose. 'But if you head to the University you'll do better. Artificers have a great love for loden-stone. Alchemists too. If you find one in the right mood you'll get more.'

It was a good deal. Manet had taught me loden-stone was quite valuable and difficult to come by. Not only for its galvanic properties, but because pieces of sky-iron like this often had rare metals mingled with the iron. I held out my hand. 'I'm willing to make it a deal.'

We shook hands solemnly, then just as the tinker began to reach for the reins, I asked, 'And what will you give me for his tack and saddle?'

I was a little worried that the tinker might take offense at my wheedling, but instead he smiled a sly smile. 'That's a clever lad,' he chuckled. 'I like a fellow who's not afraid to push for a little extra. What would you like then? I've got a lovely woolen blanket here. Or some nice rope?' He pulled a coil of it out of the donkey's packs. 'Always good to have a piece of rope with you. Oh, how about this?' He turned around with a bottle in his hands and winked at me. 'I've got some lovely Avennish fruit wine. I'll give you all three for your horse's gear.'

'I could use a spare blanket,' I admitted. Then a thought occurred to me. 'Do you have any clothes near my size? I seem to be going through a lot of shirts lately.'

The old man paused, holding the rope and bottle of wine, then shrugged and began to dig around in his packs.

'Have you heard anything about a wedding around these parts?' I asked. Tinkers always have their ears to the ground.

'The Mauthen wedding?' He tied off one pack and began to dig through another. 'I hate to tell you but you missed it. Happened yesterday.'

My stomach clenched at his casual tone. If there had been a massacre the tinker would certainly have heard. I suddenly had the horrible thought that I'd put myself in debt and run halfway to the mountains on a goose chase. 'Were you there? Did anything odd happen?'

'Here we are!' The tinker turned around holding up a shirt of plain grey homespun. 'Nothing fancy, I'm afraid, but it's new. Well, newish.' He held it up to my chest to judge the fit.

'The wedding?' I prompted.

'What? Oh no. I wasn't there. Bit of an event though, from what I understand. Mauthen's only daughter and they were sending her off proper. Been planning it for months.'

'So you didn't hear of anything odd happening?' I asked, a sinking feeling in my gut.

He shrugged helplessly. 'Like I said, I wasn't there. I've been up around the ironworks the last couple days,' he nodded to the west. 'Trading with panners and folk up in the high rock.' He tapped the side of his head as if he'd just remembered something. 'That reminds me, I found a brassie up in the hills.' He rummaged in his packs again and brought out a flat, thick bottle. 'If you don't care for wine, maybe something a little stronger . . . ?'

I started to shake my head, then realised that some homemade brand would be useful cleaning my side tonight. 'I might be . . .' I said. 'Depending on the offer on the table.'

'Honest young gent like yourself,' he said grandly. 'I'll give you blanket, both bottles, and the coil of rope.'

'You're generous, tinker. But I'd rather have the shirt than the rope and the fruit wine. They'd just be dead weight in my bag and I've got a lot of walking ahead of me.'

His expression soured a little, but he shrugged. 'Your call, of course. Blanket, shirt, brand, and three jots.'

We shook hands, and I took time to help him load Keth-Selhan because I had the vague feeling that I'd insulted him by turning down his previous offer. Ten minutes later he was heading east, and I made my way north over the green hills into Trebon.

I was glad to walk the last half-mile under my own power as it helped me work the stiffness from my legs and back. As I crested the hill, I saw Trebon sprawling out below, tucked into a low bowl made by the hills. It wasn't a large town by any means, perhaps a hundred buildings sprawling around a dozen winding, packed-dirt streets.

In the early days with the troupe, I'd learned how to size up a town. It's a lot like reading your audience when you're playing in a tavern. The stakes are higher of course, play the wrong song in a tavern and people might hiss you, but misjudge an entire town and things can get uglier than that.

So I sized up Trebon. It was off the beaten path, halfway between a mining town and a farming town. They weren't likely to be instantly suspicious of strangers, but it was small enough that everyone knew by looking at you that you weren't one of the locals.

I was surprised to see people setting up straw-stuffed shamble-men outside their homes. That meant that despite the proximity to Imre and the University, Trebon was truly a backwater community. Every town has a harvest festival of some sort, but these days most folk settle for having a bonfire and getting drunk. The fact that they were following old folk traditions meant people in Trebon were more superstitious than I would usually expect.

Despite that, I liked seeing the shamble-men. I have a fondness for the traditional harvest festivals, superstitions and all. They're a type of theater, really.

The Tehlin church was the nicest building in town, three stories tall and made of quarried stone. Nothing odd about that, but bolted above the front doors, high above the ground, was one of the biggest iron wheels I'd ever seen. It was real iron too, not just painted wood. It was ten feet tall and must have weighed a solid ton. Ordinarily such a display would have made me nervous, but since Trebon was a mining town I guessed it showed civic pride more than fanatic piety.

Most of the other buildings in town were low to the ground, built of rough timber with cedar-shingle roofs. The inn was respectable though, two stories tall, with plaster walls and red clay tiles on the roof. There was bound to be someone in there who would know more about the wedding.

There was a bare handful of people inside, not surprising as harvest was in full swing and there were still five or six hours of good daylight left. I put on my best anxious expression as I made my way over to the bar where the innkeeper stood.

'Excuse me,' I said. 'I hate to trouble you, but I'm looking for someone.'

The innkeeper was a dark-haired man with a perpetual scowl. 'Who's that then?'

'My cousin was here for a wedding,' I said, 'and I heard there was some trouble.'

At the word *wedding* the innkeeper's scowl turned stony. I could feel the two men farther down the bar not looking at me, pointedly not looking anywhere in my direction. It was true then. Something terrible had happened.

I saw the innkeeper reach out and press his fingers onto the bar. It took me a second to realise he was touching the iron head of a nail driven into the wood. 'Bad business,' he said shortly. 'Nothing I care to say about it.'

'Please,' I said, letting worry bleed into my tone. 'I was visiting family in Temfalls when the rumour came down that something had happened. They're all busy pulling in the last of the wheat, so I promised I'd come up and see what the trouble was.'

The innkeeper looked me up and down. A gawker he could turn away, but he couldn't deny me the right to know what had happened to a family member. 'There's the one upstairs who was there,' he said shortly. 'Not from around here. Might be your cousin.'

A witness! I opened my mouth to ask another question, but he shook his head. 'I don't know a thing about it,' he said firmly. 'Don't care to, either.' He turned and made himself suddenly busy with the taps of his beer barrels. 'Up at the far end of the hall, on the left.'

I headed across the room and up the stairs. I could feel everyone not looking at me now. Their silence and the innkeeper's tone made it clear that whoever was upstairs was not *one of the many* who had been there, it was *the one*. One survivor.

I went to the end of the hallway and knocked on the door. First softly, then again, louder. I opened the door slowly, so as not to startle whoever might be inside.

It was a narrow room with a narrow bed. A woman lay on it, fully clothed, one arm wrapped in a bandage. Her head was turned towards the window, so I could only see her profile.

Still I recognised her. Denna.

I must have made some noise, because she turned to look at me. Her eyes went wide and for once she was the one who was at a loss for words.

'I heard you were in some trouble,' I said nonchalantly. 'So I thought I'd come and help.'

Her eyes went wide for a moment, then narrowed. 'You're lying,' she said with a wry twist to her lips.

'I am,' I admitted. 'But it's a pretty lie.' I took a step into the room and closed the door softly. 'I would have come, if I'd known.'

'Anyone can make the trip after they get the news,' she said dismissively. 'It takes a special sort of man to show up when he doesn't know there's trouble.' She sat up and turned to face me, swinging her legs over the side of the bed.

Now that I looked more closely, I noticed that she had a bruise high on one temple in addition to the bandage on her arm. I took another step toward her, 'Are you alright?' I asked.

'No,' she said bluntly. 'But I could be a damn sight worse off.' She came to her feet slowly, as if she was unsure how steady she would be. She took a cautious step or two and seemed more or less satisfied. 'Right. I can walk. Let's get out of here.'

CHAPTER SEVENTY-TWO

Borrorill

DENNA TURNED LEFT INSTEAD of right as she came out of her room. At first I thought she was disoriented, but when she came to a back stairway I saw she was actually trying to leave without heading through the taproom. She found the alley door, but it was locked fast.

So we headed out the front. As soon as we entered the taproom I was pointedly aware of everyone's attention on us. Denna made a beeline for the front door, moving but with the slow determination of a storm cloud.

We were almost out when the man behind the bar called out. 'Hoy! Hey now!'

Denna's eyes flickered to the side. Her mouth made a thin line and she continued her walk to the door as if she hadn't heard.

'I'll deal with him,' I said softly. 'Wait for me. I'll be out in just a second.'

I walked over to where the barman stood scowling. 'That your cousin then?' he asked. 'Has the constable said she can go?'

'I thought you didn't want to know anything about it,' I said.

'I surely don't. But she's had use of the room, and meals, and I had the doctor out to patch her up.'

I gave him a hard look. 'If there's a doctor in this town worth more than ha'penny, then I'm the King of Vint.'

'I'm out half a talent in all,' he insisted. 'Bandages ain't free, and I had a woman by to sit with her, waiting for her to wake up.'

I doubted very much that he was out half that, but I certainly didn't want trouble with the constable. In truth, I didn't want any sort of delay. Given Denna's tendencies, I was worried that if I lost sight of her for more than a minute she would disappear like morning fog.

I took five jots from my purse and scattered them onto the bar. 'Knackers profit from a plague,' I said scathingly, and left.

I felt a ridiculous amount of relief when I saw Denna waiting outside, leaning against the horse post. Her eyes were closed and she had her face tilted toward the sun. She sighed contentedly and turned towards the sound of my approaching footsteps.

'Was it that bad?' I asked.

'They were kind enough at first,' Denna admitted, gesturing with her bandaged arm. 'But this old woman kept checking in on me.' She frowned and brushed her long black hair back, giving me a clear view of the purpling bruise that spread from her temple all the way back to her hairline. 'You know the type, some tight-laced spinster with a mouth like a cat's ass.'

I burst out laughing, and Denna's sudden smile was like the sun peering from behind a cloud. Then her face grew dark again as she continued. 'She kept giving me this look. Like I should've had the decency to die with all the other folk. Like all this was my fault.'

Denna shook her head. 'But she was better than the old men. The constable put his hand on my leg!' She shuddered. 'Even the mayor came, clucking over me like he cared, but he was only there to badger me with questions. "What were you doing there? What happened? What did you see . . . ?" '

The scorn in Denna's voice made me bite back my own questions so quickly that I almost caught my tongue between my teeth. It's my nature to ask questions, not to mention that the whole purpose of this mad dash into the foothills was to investigate what had happened.

Still, the tone of Denna's voice made it clear she was in no mood to give answers right now. I shrugged my travelsack higher up onto my shoulder and something occurred to me. 'Wait. Your things. You left them all back in your room.'

Denna hesitated for a heartbeat. 'I don't think anything of mine was there,' she said as if the thought hadn't even occurred to her before.

'Are you sure you don't want to go back and check?'

She shook her head firmly. 'I leave where I'm not welcome,' she said matter-of-factly. 'Everything else I can make up along the way.'

Denna started to walk down the street and I fell in beside her. She turned onto a narrow side street heading west. We passed an old woman hanging a shamble-man made of oat sheaves. It wore a crude straw hat and a pair of sackcloth pants. 'Where are we headed?' I asked.

'I need to see if my things are out at the Mauthen farm,' she said. 'After that I'm open to suggestions. Where were you planning to go before you found me?'

'Honestly, I was heading out to the Mauthen farm myself.'

Denna gave me a sideways look. 'Fair enough. It's only about a mile out to the farm. We can be there and still have plenty of light.'

The land around Trebon was rough, mostly thick forest broken by stretches of rocky ground. Then the road would round a corner and there would be a small, perfect field of golden wheat tucked among the trees, or nestled into a valley surrounded by dark stone bluffs. Farmers and hands dotted the fields, covered in chaff and moving with the slow weariness that comes from knowing half the day's harvest was still to come.

We'd only been walking a minute when I heard a familiar thump of hooves behind us. I turned to see a small open-topped cart bumping slowly up the road. Denna and I stepped off into the scrub, as the road was barely wide enough for the cart. A bone weary farmer eyed us suspiciously from where he sat, hunched over the reins.

'We're heading to the Mauthen farm,' Denna called out as he came closer. 'Would you mind if we caught a ride?'

The man eyed us grimly, then nodded towards the back of the cart. 'I'm heading past old Borrorill. Ye'll have to make your own way from there.'

Denna and I clambered on and sat facing backwards on the clapboard with our feet dangling over the edge. It wasn't much faster than walking, but we were both glad to be off our feet.

We rode in silence. Denna obviously wasn't interested in discussing things in front of the farmer, and I was glad to have a moment to think things over. I had planned on telling whatever lies were necessary to get the information I wanted from the witness. Denna complicated things. I didn't want to lie to her, but at the same time I couldn't risk telling her too much. The last thing I wanted to do was convince her I was crazy with wild stories of the Chandrian . . .

So we rode in silence. It was nice just being near her. You wouldn't think a girl in bandages with a blackened eye could be beautiful, but Denna was. Lovely as the moon: not flawless, perhaps, but perfect.

The farmer spoke up, breaking my reverie. 'Here's Borrorill.'

I looked around for the rill, but couldn't see it. Which was a shame, as I wouldn't mind a cool drink or a bit of a wash. Hours of hard riding had left me sweaty and smelling of horse.

We thanked the farmer and hopped off the back of the cart. Denna led the way along the dirt track that wound back and forth up the side of the hill, between the trees and the occasional outcrop of worn, dark stone. Denna seemed steadier than when we'd left the tavern, but kept her eyes on the ground, choosing her steps with deliberate care as if she didn't quite trust her balance.

A sudden thought came to me. 'I got your note,' I said, pulling the folded piece of paper out of a pocket in my cloak. 'When did you leave it for me?'

'Nearly two span ago.'

I grimaced, 'I only got it last night.'

She nodded to herself. 'I worried about that when you never showed up. I thought it might have fallen out, or got wet so you couldn't read it.'

'I just haven't used the window lately,' I said.

Denna shrugged nonchalantly. 'Silly of me to assume you would, really.'

I tried to think of something to add, something that would explain what she might have seen when Fela had given me my cloak in the Eolian. I couldn't think of anything. 'I'm sorry I missed our lunch.'

Denna looked up, amused. 'Deoch said you were caught in a fire or something. Told me you looked positively wretched.'

'I felt wretched,' I said. 'More from missing you than from the fire . . .'

She rolled her eyes. 'I'm sure you were *terribly* distraught. You did me a favour in a way. While I was sitting there . . . alone . . . pining away . . .'

'I said I was sorry.'

'. . . an older gentleman introduced himself to me. We talked, got to know each other . . .' She shrugged and looked sideways at me, almost bashfully. 'I've been meeting with him ever since. If things continue smoothly, I think he'll be my patron before the year is out.'

'Really?' I said, relief splashing over me like cold water. 'That's wonderful, and long overdue. Who is he?'

She shook her head, her dark hair falling down around her face. 'I can't say. He's obsessed with his privacy. He wouldn't tell me his real name for more than a span. Even now I don't know if the name he's given me is real.'

'If you're not sure who he really is,' I said slowly. 'How do you know he's a gentleman?'

It was a foolish question. We both knew the answer, but she said it anyway. 'Money. Clothes. Bearing.' She shrugged. 'Even if he's only a wealthy merchant, he'll still make a good patron.'

'But not a great one. Merchant families don't have the same stability . . .'

'. . . and their names don't carry the same weight,' she finished with another, knowing shrug. 'Half a loaf is better than none, and I'm tired of having no loaf at all.' She sighed. 'I've been working hard to reel him in. But he's so dodgy . . . We never meet in the same place twice, and never in public. Sometimes he'll set up a meeting and never even show up for it. Not that that's anything new in my life . . .'

Denna staggered as a rock shifted under her foot. I grabbed for her, and she caught hold of my arm and shoulder before she fell. For a moment we were pressed against each other, and I was very aware of her body against mine as she took a moment to balance herself.

I steadied her, and we moved apart. But after she regained her footing, she kept her hand resting lightly on my arm. I moved slowly, as if a wild bird had landed there and I was desperately trying to avoid startling it into flight.

I considered putting my arm around her, partly for support and partly for other more obvious reasons. I quickly discarded the idea. I still remembered the look on her face when she mentioned the constable touching her leg. What would I do if she had a similar response to me?

Men flocked around Denna, and I knew from our conversations how tiresome she found them. I couldn't bear the thought of making the same mistakes they made, simply because I didn't know any better. It was better not to risk offending her, better to be safe. As I've said before, there is a great difference between being fearless and being brave.

We followed the path as it doubled back on itself, continuing up the hill. All was silent except for the wind moving in the tall grass.

'So he's secretive?' I prompted gently, worried that the silence would soon become uncomfortable.

'*Secretive* doesn't cover it by half,' Denna said, rolling her eyes. 'Once a woman offered me money for information about him. I played dumb, and later when I told him about it he said it had been a test to see how much I could be trusted. Another time some men threatened me. I'm guessing that was another test.'

The fellow sounded rather sinister to me, like a fugitive from the law or someone hiding from his family. I was about to say so when I saw Denna looking at me anxiously. She was worried, worried that I would think less of her for pandering to the whimsy of some paranoid lordling.

I thought about my talk with Deoch, about the fact that, hard as my lot was, hers was undoubtedly harder. What would I put up with if I could win a powerful noble's patronage? What would I go though to find someone who would give me money for lute strings, see that I was dressed and fed, and protect me from vicious little bastards like Ambrose?

I bit back my previous comments and gave her a knowing grin. 'He'd better be rich enough to be worth your trouble,' I said. 'Bags of money. Pots of it.'

Her mouth quirked up at the corner, and I felt her body relax, glad that I wasn't judging her. 'Well that would be telling, now, wouldn't it?' Her eyes danced, saying: *yes*.

'He's the reason I'm here,' she continued. 'He told me to show up at this wedding. It's a lot more rural than I expected, but . . .' She shrugged again, a silent comment about the inexplicable desires of the nobility. 'I expected my patron-to-be to be there—' She stopped, laughing. 'Did that even make any sense?'

'Just make up a name for him,' I suggested.

'You pick one,' she said. 'Don't they teach you about names at the University?'

'Annabelle,' I suggested.

'I will not,' she said, laughing, 'refer to my potential patron as Annabelle.'

'The Duke of Richmoney.'

'Now you're just being flippant. Try again.'

'Just tell me when I hit one you like . . . Federick the Flippant. Frank. Feran. Forue. Fordale . . .'

She shook her head at me as we climbed the crest of the hill. As we finally reached the top, the wind gusted past us. Denna gripped my arm for balance and I held up a hand to shield my eyes from dust and leaves. I coughed in surprise as the wind forced a leaf straight into my mouth, causing me to choke and splutter.

Denna thought this was particularly funny. 'Fine,' I said, as I fished the leaf out of my mouth. It was yellow, shaped like a spearhead. 'The wind has decided for us. Master Ash.'

'Are you sure it isn't Master Elm?' she asked, eyeing the leaf. 'It's a common mistake.'

'Tastes like an ash,' I said. 'Besides, elm is feminine.'

She nodded seriously, though her eyes were dancing. 'Ash it is then.'

As we made it out of the trees and over the top of the hill the wind gusted again, pelting us with more debris before it died down. Denna took a step away from me, muttering and rubbing at her eyes. The part of my arm where her hand had rested suddenly felt very cold.

'Black hands,' she said, scrubbing at her face. 'I've got chaff in my eyes.'

'Not chaff,' I said, looking across the top of the hill. Not fifty feet away was a cluster of charred buildings that must have once been the Mauthen farm. 'Ash.'

I led Denna to a little stand of trees that blocked the wind and the sight of the farm. I gave her my water bottle and we sat on a fallen tree, resting as she rinsed her eyes clean.

'You know,' I said hesitantly, 'you don't need to go over there. I could look for your things if you tell me where you left them.'

Her eyes narrowed a little. 'I can't tell if you're being considerate or condescending . . .'

'I don't know what you saw last night. So I don't know how delicate I should be.'

'I don't need much delicacy, as a rule,' she said shortly. 'I'm no blushing daisy.'

'Daisies don't blush.'

Denna looked at me, blinking her red eyes.

'You're probably thinking of "shrinking violet" or "blushing virgin". Either way, daisies are white. They can't blush . . .'

'That,' she said flatly, 'was condescending.'

'Well, I thought I'd let you know what it looked like,' I said. 'For comparison. So there's less confusion when I'm trying to be considerate.'

We stared at each other for a bit, eventually she looked away, rubbing at her eyes. 'Fair enough,' she admitted. She tilted her head back and splashed more water onto her face, blinking furiously.

'I really didn't see much,' she said as she daubed her face on her shirtsleeve. 'I played before the wedding, then again while they were getting ready for supper. I kept expecting my . . .' she gave a faint smile, '. . . Master Ash to make an appearance, but I knew I couldn't dare ask about him. For all I knew, the whole thing was another test of his.'

She trailed off, frowning. 'He has a way of signalling me. A way of letting me know when he's around. I excused myself and found him over by the barn. We headed into the woods for a bit and he asked me questions. Who was there, how many people, what they looked like.' She looked thoughtful.

'Now that I'm thinking of it, I think that was the real test. He wanted to see how observant I was.'

'He almost sounds like a spy,' I mused.

Denna shrugged. 'We wandered for about half an hour, talking. Then he heard something and told me to wait for him. He headed off towards the farmhouse and was gone for a long while.'

'How long?'

'Ten minutes?' she shrugged. 'You know how it is when you're waiting for someone. It was dark and I was cold and hungry.' She wrapped her arms around her stomach and leaned forward a little. 'Gods, I'm hungry now, too. I wish I would've . . .'

I pulled an apple out of my travelsack and handed it to her. They were gorgeous, red as blood, sweet, and crisp. The sort of apples you dream about all year but can only get for a few weeks during the fall.

Denna gave me a curious look. 'I used to travel a lot,' I explained as I took one for myself. 'And I used to be hungry a lot. So I usually carry something to eat. I'll fix you a real dinner when we set camp for the night.'

'And he cooks, too . . .' She bit into the apple and took a drink of water to wash it down. 'Anyway, I thought I heard shouting, so I headed back in the direction of the farm. When I came out from behind a bluff, I could definitely hear screaming and shouting. Then I got closer and smelled smoke. And I saw the light of the fire through the trees—'

'What colour was it?' I asked, my mouth half full of apple.

Denna looked at me sharply, her expression suddenly suspicious. 'Why do you ask that?'

'I'm sorry, I interrupted,' I said swallowing my mouthful of apple. 'Finish your story first and I'll tell you afterwards.'

'I've been talking an awful lot,' she said. 'And you haven't made any mention at all of why you're up in this little corner of the world.'

'The masters down at the University heard some odd rumours and sent me here to find out if they were true,' I said. There was no awkwardness or hesitation in the lie. I didn't even plan it, really, it just came out. Forced to make a snap decision, I couldn't safely tell her the truth about my search for the Chandrian. I couldn't bear the thought of Denna thinking I was brain-addled.

'The University does that sort of thing?' Denna asked. 'I thought you lot just sat around reading books.'

'Some folks read,' I admitted. 'But when we hear strange rumours, some-one needs to go out and find out what's really happened. When people get superstitious, they start to look toward the University and think, *Who around here is meddling with dark powers better left alone? Who should we toss into a great, blazing bonfire?*'

'So you do this sort of thing a lot?' She made a gesture with her half-eaten apple. 'Investigate things?'

I shook my head. 'I just got on a master's bad side. He made sure I drew the short straw for this little trip.'

Not a bad lie, considering it was off the cuff. It would even hold up if she did any asking around, as parts of it were true. When necessity demands it, I'm an excellent liar. Not the noblest of skills, but useful. It ties closely to acting and storytelling, and I learned all three from my father, who was a master craftsman.

'You are so full of horseshit,' she said matter-of-factly.

I froze with my teeth halfway into my apple. I pulled back, leaving white impressions in the red skin. 'I beg your pardon?'

She shrugged. 'If you don't want to tell me, that's fine. But don't fabricate some story out of a misguided desire to pacify or impress me.'

I drew a deep breath, hesitated, and let it out slowly. 'I don't want to lie to you about why I'm here,' I said. 'But I worry what you might think if I tell you the truth.'

Denna's eyes were dark, thoughtful, and gave nothing away. 'Fair enough,' she said at last with an almost imperceptible nod. 'I believe that.'

She took a bite of her apple and gave me a long look as she chewed, never looking away from my eyes. Her lips were wet and redder than the apple. 'I heard some rumours.' I said at last. 'And I want to know what happened here. That's all really. I just . . .'

'Listen Kvothe, I'm sorry.' Denna sighed and ran a hand through her hair. 'I shouldn't have pushed you. It's none of my business, really. I know what it's like to have secrets.'

I almost told her everything then. The whole story about my parents, the Chandrian, the man with black eyes and a nightmare smile. But I worried it might seem like the desperate elaboration of a child caught in a lie. So instead I took the coward's way out and stayed silent.

'You'll never find your true love that way,' Denna said.

I snapped out of my reverie, confused. 'I'm sorry, what?'

'You eat the core of your apple,' she said, amused. 'You eat it all around, then from the bottom to the top. I've never seen anyone do that before.'

'Old habit,' I said dismissively, not wanting to tell her the truth. That there had been a time in my life when the core was all of the apple I was likely to find, and I'd been glad of it. 'What did you mean before?'

'Didn't you ever play that game?' she held up her own apple core and grabbed the stem with two fingers. 'You think of a letter and twist. If the stem stays on you think of another letter and twist again. When the stem breaks off . . .' hers did, '. . . you know the first letter of the name of the person you're going to fall in love with.'

I looked down at the tiny piece of apple I had left. Not enough to grip and twist. I bit off the last of the apple and tossed the stem. 'Looks like I'm destined to be loveless.'

'There you go with seven words again,' she said with a smile. 'You do realise you always do that?'

It took me a minute to realise what she was referring to, but before I could respond Denna had moved on. 'I heard the seeds are supposed to be bad for you,' she said. 'They have arsenic in them.'

'That's just a wives' tale,' I said. It was one of the ten thousand questions I'd asked Ben when he'd travelled with the troupe. 'It's not arsenic. It's cyanide, and there's not enough to hurt you unless you eat bucketsful.'

'Oh.' Denna gave the remains of her apple a speculative look, then began to eat it from the bottom up.

'You were telling me about what happened to Master Ash before I rudely interrupted,' I prompted gently as I could.

Denna shrugged. 'There isn't much left to tell. I saw the fire, came closer, heard more shouting and commotion . . .'

'And the fire?'

She hesitated. 'Blue.'

I felt a sort of dark anticipation rise up in me. Excitement at finally being close to answers about the Chandrian, fear at the thought of being close to them. 'What did the ones look like who attacked you? How did you get away?'

She gave a bitter laugh. 'Nobody attacked me. I saw shapes outlined against the fire and ran like billy-hell.' She lifted her bandaged arm and touched the side of her head. 'I must have gone headfirst into a tree and knocked myself out. I woke up in town this morning.

'That's the other reason I needed to come back,' she said. 'I don't know if Master Ash might still be out here. I didn't hear anyone in town talking about finding an extra body, but I couldn't ask without making everyone suspicious . . .'

'And he wouldn't like that,' I said.

Denna nodded. 'I don't doubt he'll turn this into another test to see how well I can keep my mouth shut.' She gave me a significant look. 'Speaking of which . . .'

'I'll make a point of being terribly surprised if we find anyone,' I said. 'Don't worry.'

She smiled nervously. 'Thanks. I just hope he's alive. I've invested two whole span trying to win him over.' She took a final drink out of my water bottle and handed it back to me. 'Let's go have a look around, shall we?'

Denna came unsteadily to her feet, and I tucked my water bottle back into my travelsack, watching her out of the corner of my eye. I had worked in the Medica for the better part of a year. Denna had been struck on her left temple hard enough to blacken her eye and bruise her well past her ear into her hairline. Her right arm was bandaged, and from the way she carried herself, I guessed she had some serious bruises along her left side, if not a few broken ribs.

If she had run into a tree, it must have been an oddly shaped tree.

But still, I didn't make a point of it. Didn't press her.

How could I? I too knew what it was like to have secrets.

———————

The farm was nowhere near as gruesome as it could have been. The barn was nothing but a jumble of ash and planking. To one side a water trough stood next to a charred windmill. The wind tried to spin the wheel, but it only had three fins left, and it simply swayed back and forth, back and forth.

There were no bodies. Only the deep ruts wagon wheels had cut into the turf when they had come to haul them away.

'How many people were at the wedding?' I asked.

'Twenty-six, counting the bride and groom.' Denna kicked idly at a charred timber half buried in ashes near the remains of the barn. 'Good thing it usually rains in the evenings here, or this whole side of the mountain would be on fire by now . . .'

'Any simmering feuds lurking around here?' I asked. 'Rival families? Another suitor looking for revenge?'

'Of course,' Denna said easily. 'Little town like this, that's what keeps things on an even keel. These folk will carry a grudge for fifty years about what their Tom said about our Kari.' She shook her head. 'But nothing of the killing sort. These were normal folks.'

Normal but wealthy, I thought to myself as I walked toward the farmhouse. This was the sort of house only a wealthy family could afford to build. The foundation and the lower walls were solid grey stone. The upper story was plaster and timber with stone reinforcing the corners.

Still, the walls sagged inward on the verge of collapse. The windows and door gaped with dark soot licking out around the edges. I peered through the doorway and saw the grey stone of the walls charred black. There was broken crockery scattered among the remains of furniture and charred floorboards.

'If your things were in there,' I said to Denna. 'I think they're as good as gone. I could go in for a look . . .'

'Don't be stupid,' she said. 'This whole thing is about to come down.' She knocked a knuckle against the doorframe. It echoed hollowly.

Curious at the odd sound of it, I went over to look. I picked at the doorpost with a fingernail and a long splinter the size of my palm peeled away with little resistance. 'This is more like driftwood than timber,' I said. 'After spending all this money, why skimp on the doorframe?'

Denna shrugged. 'Maybe the heat of the fire did it?'

I nodded absently and continued to wander around, looking things over. I bent to pick up a piece of charred shingle and muttered a binding under my breath. A brief chill spread up my arms and flame flickered to life along the rough edge of the wood.

'That's something you don't see every day,' Denna said. Her voice was calm, but it was a forced calm, as if she was trying hard to sound nonchalant.

It took me a moment to figure out what she was talking about. Simple sympathy like this was so commonplace in the University that I hadn't even thought about how it would look to someone else.

'Just a little meddling with dark forces better left alone,' I said lightly, holding up the burning shingle. 'The fire was blue last night?'

She nodded. 'Like a coal-gas flame. Like the lamps they have in Anilen.'

The shingle was burning an ordinary, cheerful orange. No trace of blue about it, but it could have been blue last night. I dropped the shingle and crushed it out with my boot.

I circled the house again. Something was bothering me, but I couldn't put my finger on it. I wanted to go inside for a look around. 'The fire really wasn't that bad,' I called out to Denna. 'What did you end up leaving inside?'

'Not that bad?' she said incredulously, as she came around the corner. 'The place is a husk.'

I pointed. 'The roof isn't burned through except right by the chimney. That means the fire probably didn't damage the second story very much. What of yours was in there?'

'I had some clothes and a lyre Master Ash bought for me.'

'You play lyre?' I was surprised. 'How many strings?'

'Seven. I'm just learning.' She gave a brief, humorless laugh. 'I *was* learning. I'm good enough for a country wedding and that's about it.'

'Don't waste yourself on the lyre,' I said. 'It's an archaic instrument with no room for subtlety. Not to disparage your choice of instrument,' I said quickly. 'It's just that your voice deserves better accompaniment than a lyre can give you. If you're looking for a straight-string instrument you can carry with you, go for a half-harp.'

'You're sweet,' she said. 'But I didn't pick it. Mr. Ash did. I'll push him for a harp next time.' She looked around aimlessly and sighed. 'If he's still alive.'

I peered in one of the gaping windows to look around, only to have a chunk of the windowsill snap off in my hands when I leaned on it. 'This one's rotten through too.' I said, crumbling it in my hands.

'Exactly,' Denna took hold of my arm and pulled me away from the window. 'The place is just waiting to fall in on you. It's not worth going in. Like you said, it's just a lyre.'

I let myself be led away. 'Your patron's body might be up there.'

Denna shook her head. 'He's not the sort to run into a burning building and get himself trapped.' She gave me a hard look. 'What do you think you're going to find in there, anyway?'

'I don't know,' I admitted. 'But if I don't go inside, I don't know where else to look for clues about what really happened here.'

'What rumours did you hear, anyway?' Denna asked.

'Not much,' I admitted, thinking back to what the bargeman had said. 'A bunch of people were killed at a wedding. Everyone dead, torn apart like rag dolls. Blue fire.'

'They weren't really torn apart,' Denna said. 'From what I heard in town, it was a lot of knife and sword work.'

I hadn't seen anyone wearing so much as a belt knife since I'd been in town. The closest thing had been farmers with sickles and scythes in the fields. I looked back at the sagging farmhouse, sure that I was missing something . . .

'So what do you think happened here?' she asked.

'I don't know,' I said. 'I was half expecting to find nothing. You know how rumours get blown out of proportion.' I looked around. 'I would have written the blue fire off to rumour if you hadn't been here to confirm it.'

'Other people saw it last night,' she said. 'Things were still smouldering when they came for the bodies and found me.'

I looked around, irritated. I still felt like I was missing something, but I couldn't think of what in the world it could be. 'What do they think in town?' I asked.

'Folk weren't really talkative around me,' she said bitterly. 'But I caught a bit of the conversation between the constable and the mayor. Folk are whispering about demons. The blue fire made sure of that. Some folk were talking about shamble-men. I expect the harvest festival will be more traditional than usual this year. Lots of fires and cider and straw men . . .'

I looked around again. The collapsed wreckage of the barn, a windmill with three fins, and a burned-out husk of a house. Frustrated I ran my hands through my hair, still sure I was missing something. I'd expected to find . . . something. Anything.

As I stood there, it occurred to me how foolish the hope was. What had I hoped to find? A footprint? A scrap of cloth from someone's cloak? Some crumpled note with a vital piece of information conveniently written out for me to find? That sort of thing only happened in stories.

I pulled out my water bottle and drank off the last of it. 'Well, I'm done here,' I said as I walked over to the water trough. 'What are you planning to do next?'

'I need to look around a bit,' she said. 'There's a chance my gentleman friend is out there, hurt.'

I looked out over the rolling hills, gold with autumn leaves and wheat fields, green with pasture and stands of pine and fir. Scattered throughout were the dark scars of bluffs and stone outcroppings. 'There's a lot of ground to cover . . .' I said.

She nodded, her expression resigned. 'I've got to at least make an effort.'

'Would you like some help?' I asked. 'I know a little woodcraft . . .'

'I certainly wouldn't mind the company,' she said. 'Especially considering the fact that there may be a troupe of marauding demons in these parts. Besides, you already offered to make me dinner tonight.'

'That I did.' I made my way past the charred windmill to the iron hand pump. I grabbed the handle, leaned my weight against it, and staggered as it snapped off at the base.

I stared at the broken pump handle. It was rusted through to the center, crumbling away in gritty sheets of red rust.

In a sudden flash I remembered coming back to find my troupe killed that evening so many years ago. I remembered reaching out a hand to steady myself and finding the strong iron bands on a wagon's wheel rusted away. I remembered the thick, solid wood falling to pieces when I touched it.

'Kvothe?' Denna's face was close to mine, her expression concerned. 'Are you alright? Tehlu blacken, sit down before you fall down. Are you hurt?'

I moved to sit on the edge of the water trough, but the thick planking crumbled under my weight like a rotten stump. I let gravity pull me the rest of the way down and sat on the grass.

I held the rusted-through pump handle up for Denna to see. She frowned at it. 'That pump was new. The father was bragging about how much it had cost to get a well set up here at the top of the hill. He kept saying that no daughter of his would have to carry buckets uphill three times a day.'

'What do you think happened here?' I asked. 'Truthfully.'

She looked around, the bruise on her temple a sharp contrast against her pale skin. 'I think when I'm done looking for my patron to be, I'm going to wash my hands of this place and never look back.'

'That's not an answer,' I said. 'What do you think happened?'

She looked at me for a long moment before responding. 'Something bad. I've never seen a demon, and I don't ever expect to. But I've never seen the King of Vint either . . .'

'Do you know that children's song?' Denna looked at me blankly, so I sang:

> 'When the hearthfire turns to blue,
> What to do? What to do?
> Run outside. Run and hide.
>
> When your bright sword turns to rust?
> Who to trust? Who to trust?
> Stand alone. Standing stone.'

Denna grew paler as she realised what I was implying. She nodded and chanted the chorus softly to herself:

> *'See a woman pale as snow?*
> *Silent come and silent go.*
> *What's their plan? What's their plan?*
> *Chandrian. Chandrian.'*

———————

Denna and I sat in the patchwork shade of the autumn trees, out of sight of the ruined farm. *Chandrian. The Chandrian were really here.* I was still trying to collect my thoughts when she spoke.

'Is this what you were expecting to find?' she asked.

'It's what I was looking for,' I said. *The Chandrian were here less than a day ago.* 'But I didn't expect this. I mean, when you're a child and you go digging for buried treasure, you don't expect to find any. You go looking for dennerlings and faeries in the forest, but you don't find them.' *They'd killed my troupe, and they'd killed this wedding party.* 'Hell, I go looking for you in Imre all the time, but I don't actually expect to find you . . .' I trailed off, realising that I was blathering.

Some of the tension bled out of Denna as she laughed. There was no mocking in it, only amusement. 'So am I lost treasure or a faeling?'

'You're both. Hidden, valuable, much sought and seldom found.' I looked up at her, my mind hardly attending to what was coming out of my mouth. 'There's much of the fae in you as well.' *They are real. The Chandrian were real.* 'You're never where I look for you, then you appear all unexpected. Like a rainbow.'

Over the last year I'd held a silent fear in my secret heart. I worried at times that the memory of my troupe's death and the Chandrian had just been a strange sort of grief-dream my mind had created to help me deal with the loss of my entire world. But now I had something resembling proof. They were real. My memory was real. I wasn't crazy.

'When I was I child I chased a rainbow for an hour one evening. Got lost in the woods. My parents were frantic. I thought I could catch up to it. I could see where it should touch the ground. That's what you're . . .'

Denna touched my arm. I felt the sudden warmth of her hand through my shirt. I drew a deep breath and smelled the smell of her hair, warm with the sun, the smell of green grass and her clean sweat and her breath and apples. The wind sighed through the trees and lifted her hair so that it tickled my face.

Only when sudden silence filled the clearing did I realise that I'd been keeping up a steady stream of mindless chatter for several minutes. I flushed with embarrassment and looked around, suddenly remembering where I was.

'You were a little wild around the eyes there,' she said gently. 'I don't think I've ever seen you out of sorts before.'

I took another slow breath. 'I'm out of sorts all the time,' I said. 'I just don't show it.'

'My point exactly.' She took a step back, her hand slowly sliding down the length of my arm until it fell away. 'So what now?'

'I . . . I have no idea.' I looked around aimlessly.

'That doesn't sound like you either,' she said.

'I'd like a drink of water,' I said, then gave a sheepish grin at how childish it sounded.

She grinned back at me. 'That's a good place to start,' she teased. 'After that?'

'I'd like to know why the Chandrian attacked here.'

'*What's their plan,* eh?' She looked serious. 'There isn't much middle ground with you, is there? All you want is a drink of water and the answer to a question that folk have been guessing at since . . . well, since forever.'

'What do you think happened here?' I asked. 'Who do you think killed these folks?'

She crossed her arms in front of her chest. 'I don't know,' she said. 'It could have been all manner of . . .' She stopped, chewing on her lower lip. 'No. That's a lie,' she said at last. 'It sounds strange to say, but I think it was them. It sounds like something out of a story, so I don't want to believe it. But I do.' She looked at me nervously.

'That makes me feel better.' I stood up. 'I thought I might be a little crazy.'

'You still might be,' she said. 'I'm not a good touchstone to use for judging your sanity.'

'Do you feel crazy?'

She shook her head, a half smile curling the corner of her mouth. 'No. How about you?'

'Not particularly.'

'That's either good or bad, depending,' she said. 'How do you propose we go about solving the mystery of the ages?'

'I need to think on it for a while,' I said. 'In the meantime, let's find your mysterious Master Ash. I'd love to ask him a few questions about what he saw back at the Mauthen farm.'

Denna nodded. 'I was thinking I would head back to where he left me, behind that bluff, then look between there and the farm.' She shrugged. 'It's not much of a plan . . .'

'It gives us a place to start,' I said. 'If he came back and found you were gone, he might have left a trail that we could pick up.'

Denna led the way through the woods. It was warmer here. The trees kept the wind at bay but the sun could still peer through as many of the trees were nearly bare. Only the tall oaks were still holding all their leaves, like self-conscious old men.

As we walked, I tried to think of what reason the Chandrian could have had for killing these people. Was there any similarity between this wedding party and my troupe?

Someone's parents have been singing the entirely wrong sort of songs . . .

'What did you sing last night?' I asked. 'For the wedding.'

'The usual,' Denna said, kicking through a pile of leaves. 'Bright stuff. "Pennywhistle." "Come Wash in the River." "Copper Bottom Pot." ' She chuckled. ' "Aunt Emme's Tub" . . .'

'You didn't,' I said, aghast. 'At a *wedding*?'

'A drunk grandfather asked for it,' she shrugged as she made her way though a thick tangle of yellowing banerbyre. 'There were a few raised eyebrows, but not many. They're earthy folk around here.'

We walked a little longer in silence. The wind gusted in the high branches above us, but where we trudged along it was just a whisper. 'I don't think I've ever heard "Come Wash" before . . .'

'I'd have thought . . .' Denna looked over her shoulder at me. 'Are you trying to trick me into singing for you?'

'Of course.'

She turned and smiled warmly at me, her hair falling into her face. 'Maybe later. I'll sing for my supper.' She led us around a tall outcrop of dark stone. It was chillier here, out of the sun. 'I think he left me here,' she said, looking around uncertainly. 'Everything looks different during the day.'

'Do you want to search the route back toward the farm, or circle out from here?'

'Circles,' she said. 'But you'll have to show me what I'm supposed to be looking for. I'm a city girl.'

I briefly showed her what little I knew of woodcraft. I showed her the sort of ground where a boot will leave a scuff or a print. I pointed out how the pile of leaves she had walked through were obviously disturbed, and how the branches of the banerbyre were broken and torn where she'd struggled through.

We stayed close together, as two pairs of eyes are better than one, and neither of us was eager to set off alone. We worked back and forth, making larger and larger arcs away from the bluff.

After five minutes I began to sense the futility of it. There was just too much forest. I could tell that Denna quickly came to the same conclusion. The storybook clues we hoped to find once again failed to show themselves. There were no torn scraps of cloth clinging to branches, no deep bootprints or abandoned campsites. We did find mushrooms, acorns, mosquitoes, and raccoon scat cleverly concealed by pine needles.

'Do you hear water?' Denna asked.

I nodded. 'I could really do with a drink,' I said. 'And a bit of a wash.'

We wandered wordlessly away from our search, neither one of us wanting to admit that we were eager to give it up, both of us feeling in our bones how pointless it was. We followed the sound of running water down the hill until we pushed through a thick stand of pine trees and came upon a lovely, deep stream about twenty feet across.

There was no scent of foundry runoff in this water, so we drank and I topped off my water bottle.

I knew the shape of stories. When a young couple comes to a river there is a definite shape to what will happen next. Denna would bathe on the other side of the nearby fir tree, out of sight on a sandy bit of shore. I would move off a discrete distance, out of sight, but within easy talking distance. Then . . . *something* would happen. She would slip and turn her ankle, or cut her foot on a sharp stone, and I'd be forced to rush over. And then . . .

But this was not a story of two young lovers meeting by the river. So I splashed some water on my face and changed into my clean shirt behind a tree. Denna dipped her head in the water to cool off. Her glistening hair was dark as ink until she wrung it out with her hands.

Then we sat on a stone, dandling our feet in the water and enjoying each other's company as we rested. We shared an apple, passing it back and forth between bites, which is close to kissing, if you've never kissed before.

And, after some gentle goading, Denna sang for me. One verse of 'Come Wash', a verse I had never heard before, which I suspect she made up on the spot. I will not repeat it here, as she sang it to me, not to you. And since this is not the story of two young lovers meeting by the river, it has no particular place here, and I will keep it to myself.

CHAPTER SEVENTY-THREE

Pegs

NOT LONG AFTER THE apple was gone, Denna and I pulled our feet out of the water and gathered ourselves to leave. I considered leaving off my boots, as feet that can run bare over Tarbean's rooftops are in no danger of being hurt by the roughest forest floor. But I didn't want to appear uncivilised, so I pulled on my socks despite the fact that they were damp and clammy with sweat.

I was lacing up my boot when I heard a faint noise off in the forest, out of sight behind a stand of thick pine trees.

Quietly, I reached out to Denna, touched her shoulder lightly to get her attention, and held my finger to my lips.

What? She mouthed silently.

I moved closer, stepping carefully to make as little sound as possible. 'I think I hear something,' I said, my head close to hers. 'I'm going to go have a look.'

'Like hell you are,' she whispered, her face pale in the shadow of the pines. 'That's exactly what Ash said before he left last night. I'll be damned if you're going to disappear on me too.'

Before I could reply, I heard more movement through the trees. Brush rustling, the sharp snap of a dry pine branch. As the noises got louder, I could pick out the sound of something big breathing heavily. Then a low, animal grunt.

Not human. Not the Chandrian. My relief was short-lived as I heard another grunt and some snuffling. A wild boar, probably heading for the river.

'Get behind me,' I said to Denna. Most people don't realise how dangerous wild boars are, especially in the fall, when the males are fighting for dominance. Sympathy wouldn't be any good. I had no source, no link. I didn't have so much as a stout stick. Would it be distracted by the few apples I had left?

The boar shouldered aside the low hanging boughs of the nearby pine, snuffling and huffing. It probably weighed twice as much as me. It gave a great guttural grunt as it looked up and saw us. It lifted its head, nose wriggling, trying to catch our scent.

'Don't run or it'll chase you,' I said softly, stepping slowly in front of Denna. At a loss for anything better, I brought out my folding knife and worked it open with my thumb. 'Just back up and get into the river. They aren't good swimmers.'

'I don't think she's dangerous,' Denna said in a normal tone behind me. 'She looks more curious than angry.' She paused. 'Not that I don't appreciate your noble urges and all.'

At second glance I saw Denna was right. It was a sow, not a boar, and under a patina of mud it was the pink of a domestic pig, not the brown bristle of a wild one. Bored, it lowered its head and began to root around among the shrubbery below the pines.

Only then did I realise I was poised in a sort of half-crouch, one hand out like a wrestler. In the other hand I held my pitiful folding knife, so small it needed several runs at halving a good-sized apple. Worst of all I was only wearing one boot. I looked ridiculous: crazy as Elodin on his worst day.

My face flushed hot and I knew I must be red as a beet. 'Merciful Tehlu, I feel like an idiot.'

'It's rather flattering, actually,' Denna said. 'With the exception of some rather irritating posturing in bars, I don't know if I've ever had anyone actually leap to my defense before.'

'Yes of course.' I kept my eyes down as I tugged on my other sock and boot, too embarrassed to look her in the eye. 'It's every girl's dream to be rescued from someone's pet pig.'

'I'm serious.' I looked up and saw some gentle amusement in her face, but no mocking. 'You looked . . . fierce. Like a wolf with all its hackles up,' she stopped, looking up at my head. 'Or a fox, I suppose. You're too red for a wolf.'

I relaxed a bit. A bristling fox is better than a deranged, half-shod idiot.

'You're holding your knife wrong though,' she said matter-of-factly, nodding toward my hand. 'If you actually stabbed anyone, your grip would slip and you'd cut your own thumb.' Reaching out, she took hold of my fingers and moved them slightly. 'If you hold it like this, your thumb is safe. The down side is that you lose a lot of the mobility in your wrist.'

'Been in a lot of knife fights, have you?' I asked, bemused.

'Not as many as you might think,' she said with a sly smile. 'It's another page out of that worn book you men are so fond of using to court us.' She rolled her eyes, exasperated. 'I can't count the men who have tried to seduce me away from my virtue by teaching me how to defend it.'

'I've never seen you wearing a knife,' I pointed out. 'Why is that?'

'Why would I wear a knife?' Denna asked. 'I am a delicate blossom and all that. A woman who goes around wearing a knife is obviously looking for trouble.' She reached deep into her pocket and brought out a long, slender piece of metal, glittering all along one edge. 'However a woman who *carries* a knife is *ready* for trouble. Generally speaking, it's easier to appear harmless. It's less trouble all around.'

Only the fact that she was so matter-of-fact kept me from being startled. Her knife wasn't much larger than mine, but hers wasn't a folding knife. It was a straight piece of metal, with thin leather wrapping the grip. It clearly wasn't designed for eating or performing odd jobs around the campfire. It looked more like one of the razor-sharp surgical knives from the Medica. 'How do you keep that in your pocket without cutting yourself to shreds?' I asked.

Denna turned sideways so show me. 'My pocket is slit all along the inside. It straps to my leg. That's why it's so flat. So you can't see I'm wearing it.' She gripped the leather handle and held her knife in front of her for me to see. 'Like this. You want to keep your thumb along the flat.'

'Are you trying to seduce me away from my virtue by teaching me how to defend it?' I asked.

'Like you have any virtue,' she laughed. 'I'm trying to keep you from cutting up your pretty hands the next time you have to save a girl from a pig.' She cocked her head to the side. 'Speaking of. Did you know that when you're angry your eyes—'

'*Loo pegs!*' A voice came through the trees accompanied by the dull clank of a bell. '*Peg peg peg . . .*'

The great sow perked up and trotted back through the brush towards the sound of the voice. Denna took a moment to replace her knife while I picked up my travelsack. Following the pig through the trees, we spotted a man downstream with a half dozen large sows milling around him. There was an old bristling boar too, and a score of assorted piglets scampering underfoot.

The swineherd eyed us suspiciously. 'Hulloo!' he shouted. 'Dain't be afeerd. Tae wain't baet.'

He was lean and leathery from the sun, with a scraggling beard. His long stick had a crude bronze bell hanging from it, and he wore a tattered bag over one shoulder. He smelled better than you'd probably expect, as ranging pigs keep themselves cleaner than those kept penned. Even if he had smelled like a penned pig, I couldn't really hold it against him, as I had no doubt smelled worse at various points in my life.

'Oi taut Oi heard sommat daen tae water aways,' he said, his accent so thick and oily you could almost taste it. My mother referred to it as a deep valley accent since you only found them in towns that didn't have much contact with the outside world. Even in small rural towns like Trebon, folk didn't have much of an accent these days. Living in Tarbean and Imre for so long, I hadn't heard a dialect this thick in years. The fellow must have grown up in a truly remote location, probably tucked far back into the mountains.

He came up to where we stood, his weathered face grim as he squinted at us. 'Wat are the tae o' yeh daen oot here?' he said suspiciously. 'Oi taut Oi heard sengen.'

'At twere meh coosin,' I said, making a nod toward Denna. 'Shae dae have a loovlie voice far scirlin, dain't shae?' I held out my hand. 'Oi'm greet glad tae meet ye, sar. Y'clep me Kowthe.'

He looked taken aback when he heard me speak, and a good portion of the grim suspicion faded from his expression. 'Pleased Oi'm certain, Marster Kowthe,' he said, shaking my hand. 'Et's a rare troit tae meet a fella who speks propper. Grummers round these ports sound loik tae've got a mouth fulla wool.'

I laughed. 'Moi faether used tae sae: "Wool en tae mouth and wool en tae head".'

He grinned and shook my hand. 'Moi name es Skoivan Schiemmelpfenneg.'

'Yeh've got name enough far a keng,' I said. 'Would yeh be turible offenced if'n Oi pared et down tae Schiem?'

'All moi friends dae,' he grinned at me, clapping me on the back. 'Schiem'll do foin fur loovlie young folk loik yusselfs.' He looked back and forth between Denna and myself.

Denna, much to her credit, hadn't so much as batted an eye at my sudden change in dialect. 'Fargive meh,' I said making a gesture in her direction. 'Schiem, thas es moi most favorite coosin.'

'Dinnaeh,' Denna said.

I dropped my voice to a stage whisper. 'A swee lass, but shae es turible shy. Yeh woon't be heeren mekel out o' her, Oi'm afeerd . . .'

Denna picked up her part without the least hesitation, looking down at her feet and twining her fingers together nervously. She glanced up long enough to smile at the swineherd, then dropped her eyes again, making such a picture of awkward bashfulness that I was almost fooled myself.

Schiem touched his forehead politely and nodded, 'Pleased tae meet yeh, Dinnaeh. Oi hain't naever heard a voice sae loovlie in awl moi loif,' he said, pushing his shapeless hat back onto his head a bit. When Denna still wouldn't meet his eye, he turned back to me.

'Foin looken herd.' I nodded in the direction of the scattered pigs that were meandering through the trees.

He shook his head, chuckling. 'Nae a *herd*. Shep an' cows mak a herd. Pegs make a *sounder*.'

'Es at soo?' I said. 'Es there a chance, friend Schiem, that Oi moit buy a foin wee peg from yeh? Moi coosin and Oi messed our danner today . . .'

'Might do,' he said cautiously, his eyes flickering to my purse.

'If yeh dress et for us, Oi'll gie ye four jots,' I said, knowing it to be a generous price. 'But that's only if yeh'll do us the faivor o setten doon and sharin' a bite wit us.'

It was a casual testing of the waters. People in solitary jobs like shepherds or swineherds tend to either enjoy their own company, or be starved for conversation. I hoped Schiem was the latter. I needed information about the wedding and none of the people in town seemed likely to talk.

I gave him a sly grin and dipped my hand into my travelsack, bringing out the bottle of brand I'd bought from the tinker. 'Oi've even got a dram o' somethin' tae season et. Ef yeh're not opposed tae taking a drop wit a couple o' strangers sae early in tae day . . .'

Denna caught her cue and glanced up in time to catch Schiem's eye, smile shyly, then look down again.

'Weel moi moither raised me propper,' the swineherd said piously, laying a hand flat on his chest. 'Oi dan't drenk but when Oi'm tharsty or when the wind's blowin'.' He tipped his shapeless hat dramatically off his head and made a half-bow to us. 'Yeh seem tae be good folk. Oi'd love tae share a bit of danner wit ye.'

———

Schiem collared a young pig and carried it off a ways, where he killed and dressed it using a long knife from his bag. I cleared away leaves and stacked some rocks to make a quick firepit.

After a minute, Denna came over with an armload of dry wood. 'I assume we're pumping this fellow for every scrap of information we can get?' she said quietly over my shoulder.

I nodded. 'Sorry about the shy cousin bit, but . . .'

'No, it was good thinking. I don't speak fluent bumpkin and he'll be more likely to open up to someone who does.' Her eyes flickered behind me. 'He's almost done.' She wandered away towards the river.

I covertly used some sympathy to start the fire while Denna cobbled together a couple of cooking skewers out of forked willow branches. Scheim returned with the piglet neatly quartered.

I passed around the bottle of brand while the pig cooked over the fire, smoking and dripping fat onto the coals. I made a show of drinking, just raising the bottle and wetting my mouth. Denna tipped it when it passed her by as well, and there was some rosy colour in her cheeks afterward. Schiem was as good as his word, and since the wind was blowing, it wasn't too long before his nose was comfortably red.

Schiem and I chatted about nothing in particular until the pig was crispy and crackling on the outside. The more I listened, the more Schiem's accent faded into the back of my awareness and I didn't need to concentrate so much on maintaining my own. By the time the pig was done, I was hardly aware of it at all.

'You're roight handy wit a knife,' I complimented Schiem. 'But Oi'm surprised you'd gut the little fella roit here with tae pegs close by . . .'

He shook his head. 'Pegs is vicious bastards.' He pointed to one of the sows trotting over to the patch of ground where he'd dressed the pig. 'See? Shae's after this little one's lights. Pegs is clever, but tae hain't a touch sentimental.'

Declaring the pig nearly done, Schiem brought out a round farmer's loaf and shared it three ways. 'Mutton,' he grumbled to himself. 'Who wants mutton when yeh can hae a nice piece o' bacon?' He got to his feet and began to carve the pig with his long knife. 'Wot would you loik, little lady?' Schiem said to Denna.

'Oi'm nae partial, mesself,' she said. 'Oi'll take wheteer yeh have handy there.'

I was glad Schiem wasn't looking at me when she spoke. Her accent wasn't perfect, a little too long on the *ohs* and too tight in the back of the throat, but it was really quite good.

'Nae need tae be shy aboot it,' Schiem said. 'There'll be plenty and tae spare.'

'Oi've always had a likin' for tae hinder parts, mesself,' Denna said, then flushed in embarrassment and looked down. Her *ohs* were better this time.

Schiem showed his true gentlemanly nature by refraining from any crude comments as he lay a thick slice of steaming meat atop her piece of bread. 'Moind yer fingers. Give't a minute tae cool.'

Everyone set to, Schiem served up seconds, then thirds. Before too long we were licking the grease from our fingers and filling in the corners. I decided to get to business. If Scheim wasn't ready for some gossip now, he never would be.

'Oi'm surprised tae see yeh out and aboot wit all tae bad business lately.'

'Wot business is that?' he asked.

He didn't know about the wedding massacre yet. Perfect. While he couldn't give me particulars about the attack itself, it meant he would be more willing to talk about the events leading up to the wedding. Even if everyone in town wasn't scared to death, I doubted I'd be able to find anyone willing to speak with frank honesty about the dead.

'Oi heard they had some trouble up on Mauthen farm,' I said, keeping my information as vague and inoffensive as possible.

He snorted. 'Can't say as Oi find that startlen in the leest.'

'How's that?'

Schiem spat to the side. 'Mauthens are a right lot o' bastards, an' no better than they should be.' He shook his head again. 'I keep off Borrorill cause Oi've got one lick o' good sense me mum beat into me. Mauthen dain't even have that.'

It wasn't until I heard Schiem say the name of the place in his thick accent that I heard it properly. It wasn't borro-rill. It had nothing to do with a rill. It was barrow-hill.

'Oi don't even graze my pegs there, but that daft bastard builds a house . . .' He shook his head, disgusted.

'Didn't folk troi an' stop 'em?' Denna prompted.

The swineherd made a rude noise. 'Mauthen ain't much for listenen. Nothin' plugs a man's ears like money.'

'Still, et's just a house,' I said dismissively. 'Nae much harm in that.'

'Man wants his daughter tae have a fine house wit a view, that's all tae the good,' Schiem conceded. 'But when ye're diggen the foundation an' yeh find bones an' such, an' yeh don't stop . . . that's a whole new type of stupid.'

'He didn't!' Denna said, aghast.

Schiem nodded, leaning forward. 'An that weren't the worst o' it. He keeps diggen, an' he hits stones. Then does he stop?' He sniffed. 'He starts pullen 'em up, looken for more so he can use them for the house!'

'Why wouldn't he want tae use the stones he found?' I asked.

Schiem looked at me like I was daft. 'Would'e build a house wit barrow stones? Would yeh dig something out o' a barrow an' give it to your daughter as a wedding present?'

'He found something? What was it?' I passed him the bottle.

'Well that's the greet damn secret, hain't it?' Schiem said bitterly, taking another drink. 'From wot I hear, he was out there, diggen the house foundation, an' pullen up stones. Then he finds a little stone room all sealed up toight. But he makes everybody keep mum about what he finds there on account he wants et tae be this greet surprise at the wedding.'

'Some sort o' treasure?' I asked.

'Nae money.' He shook his head. 'Mauthen's never been quiet aboot that. Et were probably some sort o' . . .' his mouth opened and closed a bit, searching for a word, '. . . what de ye call something old that rich folk put on a shelf tae impress all their grummer friends?'

I gave a helpless shrug.

'An heirloom?' Denna said.

Schiem laid his finger alongside his nose and then pointed to her, smiling. 'That's et. Some flash thing tae impress folk. He's a showy bastard, Mauthen is.'

'So nobody knew what et was?' I asked.

Schiem nodded. 'There was only the handful that knew. Mauthen and his brother, two o' the sons, an' mebbe his woife. The lot o' them been lording the big secret over folk for half a year, smug as pontiffs.'

This cast everything in a new light. I needed to get back up to the farm and look at things again.

' 'Ave yeh seen anyone around these parts today?' Denna asked. 'We're looken for moi uncle.'

Schiem shook his head. 'Can't say as Oi've had the pleasure.'

'Oi'm really worried about him,' she pressed.

'Oi won't lie tae yeh, dearie,' he said. 'Yeh've got reason tae be worried ef he's alone in these woods.'

'Are there bad folk around?' I asked.

'Nae like yeh're thinkin',' he said. 'I don't get down here but once a year in the fall. Forage for the hogs makes it worth moi while, but only just. There's strange things in these woods. Especial off tae the north.' He looked at Denna, then down at his feet, obviously unsure as to whether or not he should continue.

This is exactly the sort of thing I wanted to know about, so I waved his comment away, hoping to provoke him. 'Dan't go telling us faerie stories, Schiem.'

Schiem frowned. 'Two nights ago, when I got up tae—' he hesitated, glancing at Denna, '—attend tae moi personals, I saw lights off tae the north. A big wash o' blue flame. Big as a bonfire, but all o' a sudden.' He snapped his fingers. 'Then nothing. Happened three times. Sent a chill roight down the middle of my back.'

'*Two* nights ago?' I asked. The wedding had only been last night.

'Oi said two nights, din't Oi?' Schiem said. 'Oi've been making my way south ever since. Oi want nae part of whatever it es making blue fire in the night up there.'

'Schiem, really. Blue fire?'

'Oi'm not some lying Ruh, spinning stories to scare yeh out o' pennies, boy,' he said, plainly irritated. 'I spent moi loife in these hills. Everyone knows that there's somethen out in the north bluffs. There's a reason folk stay away from there.'

'Aren't there any farms out there?' I asked.

'There's no place tae farm on the bluffs, unless yoor growen rocks,' he said hotly. 'Yeh think Oi dan't know a candle or a campfire when I see one? Et was blue, Oi tell ye. Greet billows o' et,' he made an expansive gesture with his arms. 'Loik when yeh pour liquor on a fire.'

I let it go, and turned the conversation elsewhere. Before too long Sheim gave a deep sigh and got to his feet. 'The pegs'll have picked this place clean by now,' he said, picking up his walking stick and shaking it so the crude bell clanked loudly. Pigs came trotting up obediently from all directions. 'Loo pegs!' He shouted. 'Pegs pegs pegs! C'man ye counts!'

I wrapped up the remains of the cooked pig in a piece of sackcloth, and Denna made a few trips with the water bottle and doused the fire. By the time we were finished, Schiem had his sounder in order. It was larger than I'd thought. More than two dozen full-grown sows, plus the young pigs and the boar with the grey, bristling back. He gave a brief wave, and without any further word headed off, the bell on his walking stick clanking as he walked and his pigs trailing in a loose mob behind him.

'Well that wasn't terribly subtle,' Denna said.

'I had to push him a bit,' I said. 'Superstitious folk don't like to talk about things they're afraid of. He was about to clam up, and I needed to know what he'd seen in the forest.'

'I could have got it out of him,' she said. 'More flies with honey and all that.'

'You probably could have,' I admitted as I shouldered my travelsack and began to walk. 'I thought you said you didn't speak bumpkin.'

'I've got a mimic's ear,' she said with an indifferent shrug. 'I pick up things like that pretty quickly.'

'Surprised the hell out of moi . . .' I spat. 'Damn. I'm going to be a whole span of days getting rid of that accent. Like a piece of gristle in my teeth.'

Denna was eyeing the surrounding landscape despondently. 'I guess we should get back to beating the bushes, then. Find my patron and find you some answers.'

'No point, really,' I said.

'I know, but I can't give up without at least trying.'

'That's not what I mean. Look . . .' I pointed to where the pigs had rooted around in the dirt and leaves, going after some choice morsel. 'He's been letting his pigs graze all over. Even if there is a trail, we'd never find it.'

She drew a long breath and let it out in a tired sigh. 'Is there anything left in that bottle?' she asked wearily. 'My head still aches.'

'I'm an idiot,' I said, looking around. 'I wish you'd mentioned it was bothering you sooner.' I walked over to a young birch tree, cut off several long strips of bark, and brought them back to her. 'The inside of the bark is a good painkiller.'

'You're a handy fellow to have around.' She peeled some off with a fingernail and put it in her mouth. She wrinkled her nose. 'Bitter.'

'That's how you know it's real medicine,' I said. 'If it tasted good it would be candy.'

'Isn't that the way of the world?' she said. 'We want the sweet things, but we need the unpleasant ones.' She smiled when she said it, but only with her mouth. 'Speaking of,' she said, 'how am I going to find my patron? I'm open to suggestions.'

'I have an idea,' I said, shouldering my travelsack. 'But first we have to head back up to the farm. There's something I need to take a second look at.'

We made our way back to the top of Barrow Hill, and I saw how it had come by its name. Odd, irregular lumps rose and fell despite the fact that there weren't any other rocks nearby. Now that I was looking for them, they were impossible to miss.

'What is it you needed to look at?' Denna said. 'Realise that if you attempt to go inside the house I might be forced to physically restrain you.'

'Look at the house,' I said. 'Now look at the bluff that's sticking out of the trees behind it.' I pointed. 'The rock around here is dark . . .'

'. . . and the stones of the house are grey,' she finished.

I nodded.

She continued to look at me expectantly. 'And that means what, exactly? Like he said, they found barrow stones.'

'There aren't any barrows around here,' I said. 'People build barrows in Vintas, where it's traditional, or in low, marshy places where you can't dig a grave. We're probably five hundred miles away from a real barrow.'

I walked closer to the farmhouse. 'Besides, you don't use stones to build barrows. Even if you did, you wouldn't use quarried, finished stone like this. This was brought from a long ways off.' I ran a hand over the smooth grey stones of the wall. 'Because someone wanted to build something that would last. Something solid.' I turned back to face Denna. 'I think there's an old hill fort buried here.'

Denna thought about it for a moment. 'Why would they call it barrow hill if there weren't real barrows?'

'Probably because folk around here haven't ever seen a real barrow, just heard about them in stories. When they find a hill with big mounds on it . . .' I pointed out the oddly shaped hillocks. 'Barrow Hill.'

'But this is nowhere.' She looked around aimlessly. 'This is the outside edge of nowhere . . .'

'Now it is,' I agreed. 'But back when this was built?' I gestured to a break in the trees to the north of the burned farmhouse. 'Come over here for a second. I want to look at something else.'

Walking past the trees on the northern ridge of the hill gave a gorgeous view of the surrounding countryside. The red and yellow of autumn leaves were breathtaking. I could see a few houses and barns scattered about, surrounded by golden fields, or pale green pieces of pasture with dots of white sheep. I could see the stream where Denna and I had dandled our feet.

Looking north, I could see the bluffs Schiem had mentioned. The land looked rougher there.

I nodded mostly to myself. 'You can see thirty miles in every direction here. The only hill with a better view is that one.' I pointed to a tall hill obscuring my view of the northern bluffs. 'And that one practically comes to a point. It's too narrow on top for any decent sized fortification.'

She looked around thoughtfully, then nodded. 'Fair enough, you've sold me. There was a hill fort here. What now?'

'Well, I'd like to make it to the top of that hill before we set camp tonight.' I pointed at the tall narrow hill that was currently hiding part of the bluffs from our sight. 'It's only a mile or two, and if there's anything strange going on in the north bluffs, we'll have a clear view of it from there.' I thought for a moment. 'Plus, if Ash is anywhere within twenty miles he could see our fire and come to us. If he's trying to keep a low profile and doesn't want to go into town, he might still approach a campfire.'

Denna nodded. 'That certainly beats the hell out of stumbling around in the brush.'

'I have my moments,' I said, making a grand gesture down the hill. 'Please, ladies first.'

CHAPTER SEVENTY-FOUR

Waystone

DESPITE OUR GENERAL WEARINESS, Denna and I made good time and came to the top of the northern hill just as the sun was setting behind the mountains. Though trees ringed the hill on all sides, its peak was bald as a priest's head. The unrestricted view in all directions was breathtaking. My only regret is that the clouds had blown in while we walked, leaving the sky flat and grey as slate.

To the south I could see a handful of small farms. A few streams and narrow roads cut meandering paths through the trees. The western mountains were like a distant wall. To the south and east I could see smoke rising into the sky and the low, brown buildings of Trebon.

Turning north I saw that what the swineherd had said was true. There were no signs of human habitation in that direction. No roads or farms or chimney smoke, just increasingly rough ground, exposed rock, and trees clinging to the bluffs.

The only thing on the top of the hill was a handful of greystones. Three of the massive stones were stacked together to form a huge arch, like a massive doorway. The other two lay on their sides, as if lounging in the thick grass. I found their presence comforting, like the unexpected company of old friends.

Denna sat on one of the fallen greystones as I stood looking out over the countryside. I felt a slight prickle of rain against my face and muttered a curse, flipping the hood of my cloak up.

'It won't last long,' Denna said. 'It's done this the last couple nights. Clouds up, soaks for about half an hour, then blows over.'

'Good,' I said. 'I hate sleeping in the rain.'

I set my travelsack on the leeward side of one of the greystones and the two of us began to set up camp. We each went about our business as if we'd done this a hundred times before. Denna cleared a space for a fire and gathered stones. I brought back an armload of wood and got the fire going quickly. On my next trip I gathered some sage and dug up a few wild onions I'd noticed on the way up the hill.

The rain came down hard, then tapered off as I started to make supper. I used my small cookpot to make a stew with the leftover pork from lunch, some carrots and potatoes, and the onions I'd found. I seasoned it with salt, pepper, and sage, then warmed a loaf of flatbread near the fire and broke open the wax on the cheese. Last of all, I tucked two apples in among the hot rocks of the fire. They'd be baked in time for dessert.

By the time dinner was ready, Denna had amassed a small mountain of firewood. I spread out my blanket for her to sit on, and she made appreciative noises over the food as we set about eating.

'A girl could get used to this sort of treatment,' Denna said after we'd finished. She leaned contentedly back against one of the greystones. 'If you had your lute here, you could sing me to sleep and everything would be perfect.'

'I met a tinker on the road this morning, and he tried to sell me a bottle of fruit wine,' I said. 'I wish I'd taken him up on his offer.'

'I love fruit wine,' she said. 'Was it strawberry?'

'I think it was,' I admitted.

'Well that's what you get for not listening to a tinker on the road,' she chided, her eyes drowsy. 'Clever boy like you has heard enough stories to know better . . .' She sat up suddenly, pointing over my shoulder. 'Look!'

I turned. 'What am I looking for?' I asked. The sky was still thick with clouds, so the surrounding countryside was just a sea of black.

'Just keep looking. Maybe it will . . . There!'

I saw it. A flicker of blue light off in the distance. I got to my feet and put the fire behind me so it wouldn't dull my vision. Denna came to stand beside me and we waited breathlessly for a moment. Another swell of blue light, stronger.

'What do you think that is?' I asked.

'I'm pretty sure all the iron mines are off to the west,' Denna mused. 'It can't be that.'

There was another flare. It did seem to be coming from the bluffs, which meant that if it was a flame, it was a big one. At least several times larger than our own fire.

'You said your patron had a way of signalling you,' I said slowly. 'I don't mean to pry, but it's not . . .'

'No. It's nothing to do with blue fire,' she said with a low chuckle at my discomfiture. 'That would be altogether too sinister, even for him.'

We watched for a while longer, but it didn't happen again. I took a branch about as big around as my thumb, broke it in half, then used a rock to pound both halves into the earth like tent stakes. Denna raised a questioning eyebrow.

'It points towards where we saw the light,' I said. 'I can't see any land-marks in this dark, but in the morning this will show us what direction it was in.'

We reclaimed our previous seats and I threw more wood on the fire, send-ing sparks twinkling up into the air. 'One of us should probably stay up with the fire,' I said. 'In case anyone shows up.'

'I don't tend to sleep through the night anyway,' Denna said. 'So that shouldn't be a problem.'

'You have trouble sleeping?'

'I have dreams,' she said in a tone of voice that made it clear that was all she had to say on the subject.

I picked at some brownbur that clung to the edge of my cloak, pulling it out and tossing it into the fire. 'I think I've got an idea about what happened at the Mauthen farm.'

She perked up. 'Do tell.'

'The question is: Why would the Chandrian attack at that specific place and time?'

'The wedding, obviously.'

'But why this particular wedding? Why this night?'

'Why don't you just tell me?' Denna said, rubbing her forehead. 'Don't try to tease me into some sort of sudden burst of understanding like you're my schoolmaster.'

I felt myself flush hot with embarrassment again. 'I'm sorry.'

'Don't be. Normally I'd love nothing more than some witty back and forth with you, but I've had a long day and my head aches. Just skip to the end . . .'

'It's whatever Mauthen found while he was digging up the old hill fort, looking for stones,' I said. 'He dug something out of the ruins and gossiped about it for months. The Chandrian heard and showed up to steal it.' I finished with a bit of a flourish.

Denna frowned. 'Doesn't hold together. If all they wanted was the item, they could have waited until after the wedding and just killed the newly-weds. Much easier.'

That took some of the wind out of my sails. 'You're right.'

'It would make more sense if what they really wanted was to get rid of all knowledge of the thing. Like Old King Celon when he thought his regent was going to expose him for treason. Killed the fellow's whole family and burned down their estate to make sure no word got out or evidence was left for anyone to find.'

Denna gestured off to the south. 'Since everyone who knew the secret would be at the wedding, the Chandrian can come in, kill everyone who knows anything, and either destroy or steal whatever it is.' She made a motion with the flat of her hand. 'Clean sweep.'

I sat stunned. Not so much by what Denna had said, which was, of course, better than my own guess. I was remembering what had happened to my own troupe. *Someone's parents have been singing entirely the wrong sort of songs.* But they hadn't just killed my parents. They killed everyone who had been close enough to hear even a part of the song.

Denna rolled herself into my blanket and curled up with her back to the fire. 'I will allow you to ponder my vast cleverness while I sleep. Wake me when you need anything else figured out.'

I stayed awake mostly through an effort of will. I'd had a long, grueling day, riding sixty miles and walking a half dozen more. But Denna was hurt and needed her sleep more. Besides, I wanted to keep an eye out for any more signs of the blue light to the north.

There weren't any. I fed the fire and wondered vaguely if Wil and Sim were worried about my sudden disappearance back at the University. What of Arwyl and Elxa Dal and Kilvin? Would they wonder what happened to me? I should have left a note . . .

I had no way to track the time, as the clouds still hid the stars. But I had fed the fire at least six or seven times when I saw Denna stiffen and come suddenly awake. She didn't bolt upright, but her breathing stopped and I saw her dark eyes dart about wildly, as if she didn't know where she was.

'Sorry,' I said, mostly to give her something familiar to focus on. 'Did I wake you?'

She relaxed and sat up. 'No, I . . . no. Not at all. I'm done sleeping for a bit. You want a turn?' She rubbed at her eyes and peered at me over the fire. 'Silly question. You look like hell.' She began to unwrap the blanket from around herself. 'Here . . .'

I waved it off. 'Keep it. My cloak is good enough for me.' I put my hood up and lay down on the grass.

'What a gentleman,' she teased gently, wrapping it across her shoulders.

I pillowed my head with my arm, and while I was trying to think of a clever response, I fell asleep.

———————

I woke from a dim dream of moving through a crowded street to the sight of Denna's face above me, rosy and sharply shadowed by the firelight. All in all, a very pleasant way to wake up.

I was about to say something to that effect when she put her finger over my lips, distracting me in about eighteen different ways.

'Quiet,' she said softly. 'Listen.'

I sat up.

'Do you hear it?' she asked after a moment.

I cocked my head. 'Just the wind . . .'

She shook her head and cut me off with a gesture. 'There!'

I did hear it. At first I thought it was some disturbed rocks sliding down the hill, but no, this didn't fade into the distance like that would. It sounded more like something being dragged up the side of the hill.

I got to my feet and looked around. While I'd slept the clouds had blown away, and now the moon lit the surrounding countryside in pale silver light. Our wide firepit was brim full of shimmering coals.

Just then, not far down the hillside, I heard . . . to say I heard a branch breaking would mislead you. When a person moving through the woods breaks a branch, it makes a short, sharp *snap*. This is because any branch a man breaks accidentally is small and breaks quickly.

What I heard was no twig snapping. It was a long cracking sound. The sound a leg-thick branch makes when it's torn from a tree: *kreek-kerrrka-krraakkk*.

Then, as I turned to look at Denna, I heard the other noise. How can I describe it?

When I was young my mother took me to see a menagerie in Senarin. It was the only time I had ever seen a lion, and the only time I had heard one roar. The other children in the crowd were frightened, but I laughed, delighted. The sound was so deep and low that I could feel it rumble in my chest. I loved the feeling and remember it to this day.

The sound I heard on the hill near Trebon was not a lion's roar, but I felt it in my chest the same way. It was a grunt, deeper than a lion's roar. Closer to the sound of thunder in the distance.

Another branch broke, almost on the crest of the hill. I looked in that direction and saw a huge shape dimly lined by the firelight. I felt the ground shudder slightly under my feet. Denna turned to look at me, her eyes wide with panic.

I grabbed hold of her arm and ran toward the opposite side of the hill. Denna kept up with me at first, then planted her feet when she saw where I was headed. 'Don't be stupid,' she hissed. 'We'll break our necks if we run down that in the dark.' She cast around wildly, then looked up at the nearby greystones. 'Get me up there and I'll haul you up after.'

I laced my fingers together to make a step. She put her foot into it, and I heaved so hard I almost threw her into the air where she could catch the edge of the stone. I waited a brief moment until she swung her leg up, then I slung my travelsack over my shoulder, and scrambled up the side of the massive stone.

Rather I should say I scrambled *at* the side of the massive stone. It was worn smooth by ages of weather and didn't have any handholds to speak of. I slid to the ground, my hands scrabbling ineffectually.

I bolted to the other side of the arch, hopped up onto one of the lower stones, and made another leap.

I hit the rock hard, all along the front of my body, knocking the wind out of me and banging my knee. My hands gripped at the top of the arch, but I couldn't find any purchase—

Denna caught me. If this were some heroic ballad, I would tell you how she clasped my hand firmly and pulled me to safety. But the truth is she got hold of my shirt with one hand while the other made a tight fist in my hair. She hauled hard and kept me from falling long enough for me to catch a grip and scramble to the top of the stone with her.

As we lay there, panting, we peered over the edge of the stone. Down on the hilltop, the dim shape was beginning to move into the circle of our firelight. Half hidden in the shadows, it looked larger than any animal I had ever seen, big as a loaded wagon. It was black, with a massive body like a bull's. It came closer, moving in an odd shuffle, not like a bull or a horse. The wind fanned the fire, causing it to flare up, and I saw it carried its thick body close to the ground, legs out to the side, like a lizard.

When it came farther into the light the comparison was impossible to avoid. It was a huge lizard. Not long like a snake, it was squat like a cinder brick, its thick neck blending into a head shaped like a massive flat wedge.

It covered half the distance from the crest of the hill to our fire in a single, spastic burst of speed. It grunted again, deep like rumbling thunder, and I felt it in my chest. As it came closer it moved past the other greystone that lay in the grass, and I realised my eyes weren't playing tricks on me. It was bigger than the greystone. Six feet high at the shoulder, fifteen feet long. Big as a horsecart. Massive as a dozen bulls tied together.

It moved its thick head back and forth working its wide mouth open and closed, tasting the air.

Then there was a burst of blue flame. The sudden light of it was blinding, and I heard Denna cry out beside me. I ducked my head and felt a wash of heat roll over us.

Rubbing at my eyes, I looked down again and saw the thing move closer to the fire. It was black, scaled, massive. It grunted again like thunder, then bobbed its head and breathed another great gout of billowing blue fire.

It was a dragon.

CHAPTER SEVENTY-FIVE

Interlude – Obedience

IN THE WAYSTONE INN, Kvothe paused expectantly. The moment stretched out until Chronicler looked up from his page.

'I'm giving you the opportunity to say something,' Kvothe said. 'Something along the lines of, "That can't be!" or "There's no such thing as dragons . . ." '

Chronicler wiped the nib of his pen clean, 'It's not really my place to comment on the story,' he said placidly. 'If you say you saw a dragon . . .' He shrugged.

Kvothe gave him a profoundly disappointed look. 'This from the author of *The Mating Habits of the Common Draccus?* This from Devan Lochees, the great debunker?'

'This from Devan Lochees who agreed not to interrupt or change a single word of the story he is recording.' Chronicler lay his pen down and massaged his hand. 'Because those were the only conditions under which he could get access to a story he very much desired.'

Kvothe gave him a level look. 'Have you ever heard the expression white mutiny?'

'I have,' Chronicler said with a thin smile.

'I could say it, Reshi,' Bast said brightly. 'I haven't agreed to anything.'

Kvothe looked back and forth between them, then sighed. 'There are few things as nauseating as pure obedience,' he said. 'Both of you would do well to remember that.' He gestured for Chronicler to pick his pen up again. 'Very well . . . It was a dragon.'

CHAPTER SEVENTY-SIX

The Mating Habits of the Common Draccus

'IT'S A DRAGON,' Denna whispered. 'Tehlu hold and overroll us. It's a dragon.'

'It's not a dragon,' I said. 'There's no such thing as dragons.'

'Look at it!' she hissed at me. 'It's right there! Look at the huge Goddamn dragon!'

'It's a draccus,' I said.

'It's Goddamn huge,' Denna said with a tinge of hysteria in her voice. 'It's a Goddamn huge dragon and it's going to come over here and eat us.'

'It doesn't eat meat,' I said. 'It's an herbivore. It's like a big cow.'

Denna looked at me and started to laugh. Not hysterical laughter, but the helpless laugher of someone who's just heard something so funny they can't help but bubble over with it. She put her hands over her mouth and shook with it, the only sound was a low huffing that escaped through her fingers.

There was another flash of blue fire from below. Denna froze midlaugh, then took her hands away from her mouth. She looked at me, her eyes wide, and spoke softly with a slight quaver in her voice, 'Mooooo.'

We had both gone from terrified to safe so quickly that we were close to laughing from sheer relief anyway. So when she convulsed with laughter again, muffling it with her hands, I started to laugh too, my belly shaking as I tried not to make any noise. We lay there like two giggling children while below us the great beast grunted and snuffed around our fire, occasionally sending up gouts of flame.

After a long several minutes, we regained control of ourselves. Denna wiped tears away from her eyes and drew a deep, shaky breath. She slid closer to me until the left side of her body was pressed close up against my right.

'Listen,' she said softly as we both looked over the edge of the stone. 'That thing does not graze,' she said. 'It's huge. It could never get enough food. And look at its mouth. Look at those teeth.'

'Exactly. They're flat, not pointed. It eats trees. Whole trees. Look at how big it is. Where could it possibly find enough meat? It would have to eat ten deer every day. There's no way it could survive!'

She turned her head to look at me. 'How the hell do you know this?'

'I read about it at the University,' I said. 'A book called *The Mating Habits of the Common Draccus*. It uses the fire in a mating display. It's like a bird's plumage.'

'You mean that that thing down there,' she groped for words, her mouth working silently for a moment, 'is going to try and tup our campfire?' She looked for a moment as if she was going to burst into laughter again, but she drew a deep, shuddering breath instead, regaining her composure. 'Now that's something I have to see . . .'

We both felt a shudder in the stone underneath us, coming up from the ground below. At the same time, things grew noticeably darker.

Looking down, we saw the draccus rolling in the fire like a hog in a wallow. The ground shook as it wriggled around, crushing the fire underneath itself.

'That thing must weigh . . .' Denna stalled out, shaking her head.

'Maybe five tons,' I guessed. 'Five at least.'

'It could come get us. It could push over these stones.'

'I don't know about that,' I said, slapping the stone under my hand, trying to sound more certain than I really was. 'These have been here for a long time. We're safe.'

While rolling in our overlarge campfire, the draccus had scattered burning branches around the top of the hill. It now wandered to where a half-charred log lay smoldering in the grass. The draccus snuffed, then rolled, crushing the log into the earth. Then it came back to its feet, snuffed the log again, and ate it. It didn't chew. It bolted the log whole, like a frog getting a cricket down into its gullet.

It did this several times, moving in a circle around the now largely extinguished fire. It snuffed, rolled on the burning pieces, then ate them after they were extinguished.

'That makes sense, I suppose,' Denna said, watching it. 'It starts fires and lives in the woods. If it didn't have something in its head that made it want to put out fires, it wouldn't survive very long.'

'That's probably why it came here,' I said. 'It saw our fire.'

After several minutes of snuffing and rolling, the draccus came back to the flat bed of coals that was all that remained of our fire. It circled it a few times, then walked over it and lay down. I cringed, but it just shifted back and forth like a hen settling into a nest. The hilltop below was now entirely dark except for the pale moonlight.

'How can I never have heard of these things?' Denna asked.

'They're very rare,' I said. 'People tend to kill them because they don't understand they're relatively harmless. And they don't reproduce very quickly. That one down there is probably two hundred years old, about as big as they get.' I marvelled at it. 'I bet there aren't more than a couple hundred draccus that size in the whole world.'

We watched for another couple minutes, but there was no movement from below. Denna gave a jaw-popping yawn. 'Gods, I'm exhausted. There's nothing like the certain knowledge of your own death to tucker you out.' She rolled over onto her back, then onto her side, then back facing towards me, trying to get comfortable. 'Lord it's cold up here.' She shivered visibly. 'I can see why it's cuddled up on our fire.'

'We could go down and get the blanket,' I suggested.

She snorted. 'Not likely.' She shivered visibly, wrapping her arms around her chest.

'Here,' I stood up and took off my cloak. 'Wrap up in this. It's not much, but it's better than the bare stone.' I held it out to her. 'I'll watch you while you sleep and make sure you don't fall off.'

She stared at me for a long moment, and I half expected her to beg off. But after a moment she took it and wrapped it around herself. 'You, Master Kvothe, certainly know how to show a girl a good time.'

'Wait until tomorrow,' I said. 'I'm just getting started.'

I sat there quietly, trying not to shiver, and eventually Denna's breathing leveled off. I watched her sleep with the calm contentment of a boy who has no idea of how foolish he is, or what unexpected tragedies the following day will bring.

CHAPTER SEVENTY-SEVEN

Bluffs

I WOKE WITHOUT REMEMBERING when I had fallen asleep. Denna was shaking me gently. 'Don't move too quickly,' she said. 'It's a long way down.'

I slowly uncurled, nearly every muscle in my body complaining at how it had been treated yesterday. My thighs and calves were tight, hard knots of pain.

Only then did I realise I was wearing my cloak again. 'Did I wake you up?' I asked Denna. 'I don't remember . . .'

'In a way you did,' she said. 'You nodded off and tipped right onto me. You didn't even flicker a lid when I cussed you out . . .' Denna trailed off as she watched me slowly come to my feet. 'Good lord, you look like someone's arthritic grandfather.'

'You know how it is,' I said. 'You're always stiffest when you wake up.'

She smirked. 'We womenfolk don't have that problem, as a rule.' Her expression grew serious as she watched me. 'You're serious, aren't you?'

'I rode about sixty miles yesterday, before I met up with you,' I said. 'I'm not really used to that. And when I jumped last night I hit the rock pretty hard.'

'Are you hurt?'

'Absolutely,' I said. 'Especially in my everywhere.'

'Oh,' she gasped, her hands going to her mouth. 'Your beautiful hands!'

I looked down and saw what she meant. I must have hurt them rather badly in my wild attempt to climb the greystone last night. My musician's calluses had saved my fingertips for the most part, but my knuckles were scraped badly and crusted with blood. Other parts of me hurt so much that I hadn't even noticed.

My stomach clenched at the sight of them, but when I opened and closed my hands I could tell they were just painfully skinned, not seriously injured. As a musician, I always worried that something might happen to my hands, and my work as an artificer had doubled that anxiety. 'It looks worse than it is,' I said. 'How long has the draccus been gone?' I asked.

'At least a couple of hours. It wandered away a little after the sun came up.'

I looked down from my high vantage on the greystone arch. Last evening the hilltop had been a uniform expanse of green grass. This morning it looked like a battlefield. The grass was crushed in places, burned to stubble in others. There were deep furrows dug in the earth where the lizard had rolled or dragged its heavy body across the turf.

Getting down from the greystone was harder than getting up had been. The top of the arch was about twelve feet off the ground, higher than was convenient for jumping. Normally I wouldn't have worried about it, but in my stiff, bruised condition I worried I'd land awkwardly and turn my ankle.

Eventually we managed it by using the strap of my travelsack as a makeshift rope. While Denna braced herself and held one end, I lowered my-self down. The sack ripped wide open, of course, scattering my belongings, but I made it to the ground with nothing more serious than a grass stain.

Then Denna hung from the lip of the rock and I grabbed her legs, letting her slide down slowly. Despite the fact that I was bruised all down my front side, the experience did a lot to improve my mood.

I gathered up my things and sat down with needle and thread to sew my travelsack back together. After a moment Denna returned from her brief trip into the trees, pausing briefly to pick up the blanket we'd left below. It had several large claw rents from when the draccus had walked over it.

'Have you ever seen one of these before?' I asked, holding out my hand.

She raised an eyebrow at me. 'How many times have I heard that one?' Grinning, I handed her the lump of black iron I'd got from the tinker. She looked it over curiously. 'Is this a loden-stone?'

'I'm surprised you recognise it.'

'I knew a fellow who used one as a paperweight.' She sighed disparagingly. 'He made a special point of how, despite the fact that it was so valuable and exceedingly rare, he used it as a paperweight.' She sniffed. 'He was a prat. Do you have any iron?'

'Fish around in there.' I pointed to my jumbled possessions. 'There's bound to be something.'

Denna sat on one of the low greystones and played with the loden-stone and a piece of broken iron buckle. I slowly sewed up my travelsack, then reattached the strap, stitching it several times so it wouldn't come loose.

Denna was thoroughly engrossed by the loden-stone. 'How does it work?' she asked, pulling the buckle away and letting it snap back. 'Where does the pulling come from?'

'It's a type of galvanic force,' I said, then hesitated. 'Which is a fancy way of saying that I've got no idea at all.'

'I wonder if it only likes iron because it's made of iron,' she mused, touching her silver ring to it with no effect. 'If someone found a loden-stone made of brass would it like other brass?'

'Maybe it would like copper and zinc,' I said. 'That's what brass is made of.' I turned the bag rightside out and began packing up my things. Denna handed me back the loden-stone and wandered off toward the destroyed remains of the fire pit.

'It ate all the wood before it left,' she said.

I went over to look too. The area around the firepit was a churned-up mess. It looked like an entire legion of cavalry had ridden across it. I prodded a great piece of overturned sod turf with the toe of my boot, then bent to pick something up. 'Look at this.'

Denna came closer and I held something up for her to see. It was one of the draccus' scales, smooth and black, roughly as big as my palm, and shaped like a teardrop. It was a quarter inch thick in the middle, tapering to the edges.

I held it out to Denna. 'For you, m'lady. A memento.'

She hefted it in her hand. 'It's heavy,' she said. 'I'll go find one for you . . .' She skipped back to prod through the remains of the firepit. 'I think it ate some of the rocks along with the wood. I know I gathered more than this to line the fire last night.'

'Lizards eat rocks all the time,' I said. 'It's how they digest their food. The rocks grind up the food in their guts.' Denna eyed me skeptically. 'It's true. Chickens do it, too.'

She shook her head, looked away as she prodded in the churned-up earth. 'You know, at first I was kind of hoping you would turn this encounter into a song. But the more you talk about this thing, I'm not so sure. Cows and chickens. Where's your flair for the dramatic?'

'It does well enough without exaggeration,' I said. 'That scale is mostly iron, unless I miss my guess. How can I make that more dramatic than it already is?'

She held up the scale, looking at it closely. 'You're kidding.'

I grinned at her. 'The rocks around here are full of iron,' I said. 'The draccus eats the rocks and slowly they get ground down in its gizzard. The metal slowly filters into the bones and scales.' I took the scale and walked over to one of the greystones. 'Year after year it sheds its skin, then eats it, keeping the iron in its system. After two hundred years . . .' I tapped the scale against the stone. It made a sharp ringing sound somewhere between a bell and a piece of glazed ceramic.

I handed it back to her. 'Back before modern mining people probably hunted them for their iron. Even nowadays I'm guessing an alchemist would pay a pretty penny for the scales or bones. Organic iron is a real rarity. They could probably do all sorts of things with it.'

Denna looked down at the scale in her hand. 'You win. You can write the song.' Her eyes lit with an idea. 'Let me see the loden-stone.'

I dug it out of my bag and handed it to her. She brought the scale close to it and they snapped sharply together, making the same odd, ceramic ring again. She grinned and walked back over to the firepit and started pushing the loden-stone through the debris, hunting for more scales.

I looked out toward the northern bluffs. 'I hate to be the bearer of bad news,' I said, pointing off to a faint smudge of smoke rising from the trees. 'But something's smoldering down there. The marker stakes I planted are gone, but I think that's the direction we saw the blue fire last night.'

Denna moved the loden-stone back and forth over the ruins of the fire pit. 'The draccus couldn't have been responsible for what happened at the Mauthen farm.' She gestured at the churned up earth and sod. 'There wasn't any of this sort of wreckage there.'

'I'm not thinking about the farm,' I said. 'I'm thinking someone's patron might have been roughing it last night with a cheery little campfire . . .'

Denna's face fell. 'And the draccus saw it.'

'I wouldn't worry,' I said quickly. 'If he's as clever as you say, he's probably safe as houses.'

'Show me a house that's safe from that thing,' she said grimly, handing me back my loden-stone. 'Let's go have a look.'

It was only a few miles to where the faint line of smoke rose from the forest, but we made bad time. We were sore and tired, and neither of us was hopeful about what we would find when we reached our destination.

While we walked we shared my last apple and half of my remaining loaf of flatbread. I cut strips of birch bark and Denna and I both picked at them and chewed. After an hour or so, the muscles in my legs relaxed to the point where walking was no longer painful.

As we got closer our progress slowed. Rolling hills were replaced with sharp bluffs and scree-covered slopes. We had to climb or go the long way around, sometimes doubling back before we found a way through.

And there were distractions. We stumbled onto a patch of ripe ashberry that slowed us down for almost a full hour. Not long after that we found a stream and stopped to drink and rest and wash. Again my hope for a storybook dalliance was thwarted by the fact that the stream was only about six inches deep. Not ideal for proper bathing.

It was early afternoon before we finally came to the source of the smoke, and what we found was not at all what we expected.

It was a secluded valley tucked into the bluffs. I say valley, but in truth it was more like a gigantic step among the foothills. On one side was a high cliff wall of dark rock, and on the other was a sheer drop-off. Denna and I came at it from two different, unapproachable angles before we finally found a way in. Luckily the day was windless, and the smoke rose straight as an arrow into the clear blue sky. If not for that to guide us, we probably never would have found the place.

Once it had probably been a pleasant little piece of forest, but now it looked like it had been struck by a tornado. Trees were broken, uprooted, charred, and smashed. Huge furrows of exposed earth and rock were dug everywhere, as if some giant farmer had gone raving mad while plowing his field.

Two days ago I wouldn't have been able to guess what would cause such destruction. But after what I had seen last night . . .

'I thought you said they were harmless?' Denna said, turning to me. 'It went on a rampage here.'

Denna and I began to pick our way through the wreckage. The white smoke rose from the deep hole left by a large maple tree that had been tipped over. The fire was nothing more than a few coals smouldering in the bottom of the hole where the roots had been.

I idly kicked a few more clods of dirt into the hole with the toe of my boot. 'Well, the good news is that your patron isn't here. The bad news is . . .' I broke off, drawing a deeper breath. 'Do you smell that?'

Denna took a deep breath and nodded, wrinkling her nose.

I climbed up onto the side of the fallen maple and looked around. The wind shifted and the smell grew stronger, something dead and rotten.

'I thought you said they don't eat meat,' Denna said, looking around nervously.

I hopped down from the tree and made my way back to the cliff wall. There was a small log cabin there, smashed to flinders. The rotting smell was stronger.

'Okay,' Denna said, looking over the wreckage. 'This does not look harmless at all.'

'We don't know if the draccus was responsible for this,' I said. 'If the Chandrian attacked here, the draccus could have been lured by the fire and caused the destruction while putting it out.'

'You think the Chandrian did this?' she asked. 'That doesn't fit with anything I've ever heard of them. They're supposed to strike like lightning then disappear. They don't visit, set some fires, then come back later to run a few errands.'

'I don't know what to think. But two destroyed houses . . .' I began to sift through the wreckage. 'It seems reasonable that they're related.'

Denna drew in a sharp breath. I followed her line of sight and saw the arm protruding from under several heavy logs.

I moved closer. Flies buzzed up and I covered my mouth a bit in a futile attempt to stave off the smell. 'He's been dead for about two span.' I bent and picked up a tangle of shattered wood and metal. 'Look at this.'

'Bring it here and I'll look at it.'

I brought it back to where she stood. The thing was broken almost beyond recognition. 'Crossbow.'

'Didn't do him much good,' she said.

'The question is why did he have it in the first place?' I looked at the thick piece of blue steel that made the crossbar. 'This wasn't some hunting bow. This is what you use to kill a man in armour from across a field. They're illegal.'

Denna snorted. 'Those sorts of laws don't get enforced out here. You know that.'

I shrugged. 'The fact remains that this was an expensive piece of machinery. Why would someone living in a tiny cabin with a dirt floor own a crossbow worth ten talents?'

'Maybe he knew about the draccus,' Denna said looking around nervously. 'I wouldn't mind a crossbow right about now.'

I shook my head. 'Draccus are shy. They stay away from people.'

Denna gave me a frank look, gesturing sarcastically at the wreckage of the cabin.

'Think about every wild creature in the forest,' I said. 'All wild creatures avoid contact with people. Like you said, you've never even heard of the draccus. There's a reason for that.'

'Maybe it's rabid?'

That brought me up short. 'That's a terrifying thought.' I looked around at the ruined landscape. 'How on earth would you put something like that down? Can a lizard even catch the froth?'

Denna shifted uncomfortably from one foot to the other, looking around nervously. 'Is there anything else you'd like to look at here? Because I'm done with this place. I don't want to be here when that thing gets back.'

'Part of me feels like we should give this fellow a decent burial . . .'

Denna shook her head. 'I'm *not* staying here that long. We can tell someone in town and they can take care of it. It could come back any minute.'

'But why?' I asked. 'Why does it keep coming back here?' I pointed. 'That tree's been dead for a span of days, but that one just got torn up a couple days ago . . .'

'Why do you care?' Denna asked.

'The Chandrian,' I said firmly. 'I want to know why they were here. Do they control the draccus?'

'I don't think they were here,' Denna said. 'At the Mauthen farm, maybe. But this is just the work of a rabid cow-lizard.' She gave me a long look, searching my face. 'I don't know what you came here looking for. But I don't think you're going to find it.'

I shook my head, looking around. 'I feel like this has to be connected to the farm.'

'I think you *want* it to be connected,' she said gently. 'But this fellow's been dead a long while. You said so yourself. And remember the doorframe and the water trough at the farm?' She bent down and rapped a knuckle against one of the logs from the ruined cabin. It made a solid sound. 'And look at the crossbow – the metal isn't rusted away. They weren't here.'

I felt my heart sink in my chest. I knew she was right. Deep down I knew I'd been grasping at straws. Still, it felt wrong giving up without trying everything possible.

Denna took hold of my hand. 'Come on. Let's go.' She smiled and tugged on me. Her hand was cool and smooth in my own. 'There's more interesting things to do than hunt . . .'

There was a loud splintering noise off in the trees: *kkkrek-ke-krrk*. Denna dropped my hand and turned to face the way we'd come. 'No . . .' she said. 'No, no, no . . .'

The sudden threat of the draccus brought me back into focus. 'We're fine,' I said looking around. 'It can't climb. It's too heavy.'

'Climb what? A tree? It's been knocking those down for fun!'

'The bluffs.' I pointed to the cliff wall that bordered this little section of forest. 'Come on . . .'

We scrambled to the base of the cliff, stumbling through furrows and jumping over fallen trees. Behind us I heard the rumbling, thunderlike grunt. I darted a glance over my shoulder, but the draccus was still somewhere among the trees.

We got to the base of the cliff and I started searching for a section both of us could climb. After a long frantic minute we emerged from a thick patch of sumac to find a swath of wildly churned-up dirt. The draccus had been digging there.

'Look!' Denna pointed to a break in the cliff, a deep crack about two feet across. It was wide enough for a person to squeeze through, but too narrow for the huge lizard. There were sharp claw marks on the cliff wall and broken rocks scattered around the churned-up earth.

Denna and I squeezed into the narrow gap. It was dark, the only light coming from the narrow strip of blue sky high overhead. As I crept along I was forced to turn sideways in places to make it through. When I brought my hands away from the walls my palms were covered in black soot. Unable to dig its way in, apparently the draccus had breathed fire down into the narrow passage.

After only a dozen feet, the crevasse widened slightly. 'There's a ladder,' Denna said. 'I'm going up. If that thing breathes fire at us it will be like rainwater down a gully.'

She climbed and I followed her. The ladder was crude but sturdy, and after twenty feet it opened out onto a piece of level ground. Dark stone surrounded us on three sides, but there was a clear view of the ruined cabin and the destroyed trees below. A wooden box was set against the cliff wall.

'Can you see it?' Denna asked, peering down. 'Tell me I didn't just skin my knees running from nothing.'

I heard a dull *whump* and I felt a wave of hot air rise up against my back.

The draccus grunted again, and another wash of fire ran through the narrow gap below. Then there came a sudden, furious sound like nails on a slate as the draccus clawed madly against the base of the cliff.

Denna gave me a frank look. 'Harmless.'

'It's not after us,' I said. 'You saw. It was digging at that wall long before we ever got here.'

Denna sat down. 'What is this place?'

'Some sort of lookout,' I said. 'You can see the whole valley from here.'

'Obviously it's a lookout,' she sighed. 'I'm talking about the whole place.'

I opened the wooden box that was up against the cliff wall. Inside was a rough wool blanket, a full waterskin, some dried meat, and a dozen wickedly sharp crossbow bolts.

'I don't know either,' I admitted. 'Maybe the fellow was a fugitive.'

The noise stopped below. Denna and I peered out over the ruined valley. Eventually the draccus moved away from the cliff. It walked slowly, its huge body digging an irregular rut into the ground.

'It's not moving as quickly as it did last night,' I said. 'Maybe it *is* sick.'

'Maybe it's tired from a hard day's trying to track us down and kill us.' She looked up at me. 'Sit down. You're making me nervous. We're not going anywhere for a while.'

I sat down and we watched the draccus make its plodding way to the middle of the valley. It went up to a tree about thirty feet tall and pushed it over without any noticeable effort.

Then it began to eat it, leaves first. Next it crunched up branches thick as my wrist as easily as a sheep would tear up a mouthful of grass. When the trunk was finally stripped bare, I assumed it would have to stop. But it simply clamped its huge, flat mouth down on one end of the trunk and twisted its massive neck. The trunk splintered and broke, leaving the draccus with a large but manageable mouthful that it bolted down more or less whole.

Denna and I took the opportunity to eat some lunch of our own. Just some flatbread, sausage, and the rest of my carrots. I was hesitant to trust the food in the box, as there was the distinct possibility that the fellow living here had been some manner of crazy.

'It still amazes me that no one around here has ever seen it,' Denna said.

'People have probably caught glimpses,' I said. 'The swineherd said everyone knows there's something dangerous in these woods. They probably just assumed it was a demon or some nonsense like that.'

Denna glanced back at me, an amused curl to her mouth. 'Says the fellow who came to town looking for the Chandrian.'

'That's different,' I protested hotly. 'I don't go around spouting faerie stories and touching iron. I'm here so I can learn the truth. So I can have information that comes from somewhere more reliable than thirdhand stories.'

'I didn't mean to touch a nerve,' Denna said, taken aback. She looked back down below. 'It really is an incredible animal.'

'When I read about it I didn't really believe about the fire,' I admitted. 'It seemed a little far-fetched to me.'

'More far-fetched than a lizard big as a horse cart?'

'That's just a matter of size. But fire isn't a natural thing. If nothing else, where does it keep the fire? It's obviously not burning inside.'

'Didn't they explain it in that book you read?' Denna asked.

'The author had some guesses, but that's all. He couldn't catch one to dissect it.'

'Understandable,' Denna said as she watched the draccus casually nudge over another tree and begin eating that one as well. 'What sort of a net or a cage would hold it?'

'He had some interesting theories though,' I said. 'You know how cow manure gives off a gas that burns?'

Denna turned to look at me and laughed. 'No. Really?'

I nodded, grinning. 'Farm kids will strike sparks onto a fresh cow pat and watch it burn. That's why farmers have to be careful about storing manure. The gas can build up and explode.'

'I'm a city girl,' she said chuckling. 'We didn't play those sorts of games.'

'You missed some big fun,' I said. 'The author suggested that the draccus just stores that gas in a bladder of some kind. The real question is how it lights the gas. The author has a clever idea about arsenic. Which makes sense, chemically. Arsenic and coal gas will explode if you put them together. That's how you get marsh lights in swamps. But I think that's a little unreasonable. If it had that much arsenic in its body, it would poison itself.'

'Mmmm-hmm,' Denna said, still watching the draccus below.

'But if you think about it, all it needs is a tiny spark to ignite the gas,' I said. 'And there are plenty of animals that can create enough galvanic force for a spark. Clip eels, for example, can generate enough to kill a man, and they're only a couple of feet long.' I gestured toward the draccus. 'Something that big could certainly generate enough for a spark.'

I was hoping that Denna would be impressed by my ingenuity, but she seemed distracted by the scene below.

'You're not really listening to me, are you?'

'Not so much,' she said, turning to me and giving a smile. 'I mean, it makes perfect sense to me. It eats wood. Wood burns. Why wouldn't it breathe fire?'

While I tried to think of a response to that, she pointed down into the valley. 'Look at the trees down there. Do they look odd to you?'

'Aside from being destroyed and mostly eaten?' I asked. 'Not particularly.'

'Look how they're arranged. It's hard to see because the place is a shambles, but it looks like they were growing in rows. Like someone planted them.'

Now that she pointed it out, it did look like a large section of the trees had been in rows before the draccus came. A dozen rows with a score of trees each. Most of them were now only stumps or empty holes.

'Why would someone plant trees in the middle of a forest?' She mused. 'It's not an orchard . . . Did you see any fruit?'

I shook my head.

'And those trees are the only ones the draccus has been eating,' she said. 'There's the big clear spot in the middle. The others he knocks down, but those he knocks down and eats.' She squinted. 'What kind of tree is it eating right now?'

'I can't tell from here,' I said. 'Maple? Does it have a sweet tooth?'

We looked for a while longer, then Denna got to her feet. 'Well, the important thing is that it's not going to run over and breathe fire down our backs. Let's go see what's at the other end of that narrow path. I'm guessing it's a way out of here.'

We headed down the ladder and made our slow, winding way along the bottom of the tiny crevasse. It twisted and turned for another twenty feet before opening up into a tiny box canyon with steep walls rising away on every side.

There was no way out, but it was obviously being put to some use. The place had been cleared of plants, leaving a packed dirt floor. Two long fire pits had been dug, and resting over the pits on brick platforms were large metal pans. They almost resembled the rendering vats that knackers use for tallow. But these were wide, flat, and shallow, like baking pans for enormous pies.

'It does have a sweet tooth!' Denna laughed. 'This fellow was making maple candy here. Or syrup.'

I moved closer to look. There were buckets laying around, of the sort that could carry maple sap so it could be boiled down. I opened the door of a tiny ramshackle shed and saw more buckets, long wooden paddles for stirring the sap, scrapers for getting it out of the pans . . .

But it didn't feel right. There were plenty of maple trees in the forest. It didn't make sense to cultivate them. And why pick such an out-of-the-way place?

Maybe the fellow was simply crazy. Idly, I picked up one of the scrapers and looked at it. The edge was smeared dark, like it had been scraping tar . . .

'Eech!' Denna said behind me. 'Bitter. I think they burned it.'

I turned around and saw Denna standing by one of the firepits. She had pried a large disk of sticky material out of the bottom of one of the pans and taken a bite out of it. It was black, not the deep amber color of maple candy.

I suddenly realised what was really going on here. '*Don't!*'

She looked at me, puzzled. 'It's not *that* bad.' She said, her words muffled through her sticky mouthful. 'It's strange, but not really unpleasant.'

I stepped over to her knocked it out of her hand. Her eyes flashed angrily at me. '*Spit it out!*' I snapped. '*Now! It's poison!*'

Her expression went from angry to terrified in a flash. She opened her mouth and let the wad of dark stuff fall to the ground. Then she spat, her saliva thick and black. I pressed my water bottle into her hands. 'Rinse your mouth out,' I said. 'Rinse and spit it out.'

She took the bottle, and then I remembered it was empty. We'd finished it during lunch.

I took off running, scrambling through the narrow passage. I darted up the ladder, grabbed the waterskin, then down and back to the small canyon.

Denna was sitting on the canyon floor, looking very pale and wide-eyed. I thrust the waterskin into her hands and she gulped so quickly that she choked, then gagged a bit as she spat it out.

I reached into the fire pit, pushing my hand deep into the ashes until I found the unburned coals underneath. I brought up a handful of unburned charcoal. I shook my hand, scattering most of the ashes away, then thrust the handful of black coals at her. 'Eat this,' I said.

She looked at me blankly.

'Do it!' I shook the handful of coals at her. 'If you don't chew this up and swallow it, I'll knock you out and force it down your throat!' I put some in my own mouth. 'Look, it's fine. Just do it.' My tone softened, became more pleading than commanding. 'Denna, trust me.'

She took some coals and put them in her mouth. Face pale and eyes beginning to brim with tears, she gritted up a mouthful and took a drink of water to wash it down, grimacing.

'They're harvesting Goddamn ophalum here,' I said. 'I'm an idiot for not seeing it sooner.'

Denna started to say something, but I cut her off. 'Don't talk. Keep eating. As much as you can stomach.'

She nodded solemnly, her eyes wide. She chewed, choked a little, and swallowed the charcoal with another mouthful of water. She ate a dozen mouthfuls in quick succession, then rinsed her mouth out again.

'What's ophalum?' she asked softly.

'A drug. Those are denner trees. You just had a whole mouthful of denner resin.' I sat down next to her. My hands were shaking. I lay them flat against my legs to hide it.

She was quiet at that. Everyone knew about denner resin. In Tarbean the knackers had to come for the stiff bodies of sweet-eaters that overdosed in the Dockside alleys and doorways.

'How much did you swallow?' I asked.

'I was just chewing it, like toffee.' Her face went pale again. 'There's still some stuck in my teeth.'

I touched the waterskin. 'Keep rinsing.' She swished the water from cheek to cheek before spitting and repeating the process. I tried to guess at how much of the drug she had in her system, but there were too many variables, I didn't know how much she had swallowed, how refined this resin was, if the farmers had taken any steps to filter or purify it.

Her mouth worked as her tongue felt around her teeth. 'Okay, I'm clean.'

I forced a laugh. 'You're anything but clean,' I said. 'Your mouth is all black. You look like a kid that's been playing in the coal bin.'

'You aren't much better,' she said. 'You look like a chimney sweep.' She reached out to touch my bare shoulder. I must have torn my shirt against the rocks in my rush to get the waterskin. She gave a wan smile that didn't touch her frightened eyes at all. 'Why do I have a belly full of coals?'

'Charcoal is like a chemical sponge,' I said. 'It soaks up drugs and poisons.'

She brightened a little. 'All of them?'

I considered lying, then thought better of it. 'Most. You got it into you pretty quickly. It will soak up a lot of what you swallowed.'

'How much?'

'About six parts in ten,' I said. 'Hopefully a little more. How do you feel?'

'Scared,' she said. 'Shaky. But other than that, no different.' She shifted nervously where she sat and put her hand on the sticky disk of resin I'd knocked away from her earlier. She flicked it away and wiped her hand nervously on her trousers. 'How long will it be before we know?'

'I don't know how much they refined it,' I said. 'If it's still raw, it will take longer to work its way into your system. Which is good, as the effects will be spread out over a longer period of time.'

I felt for her pulse in her neck. It was racing, which didn't tell me anything. Mine was racing too. 'Look up here.' I gestured with my raised hand and watched her eyes. Her pupils were sluggish responding to the light. I lay my hand on her head and under the pretext of lifting her eyelid a little, I pressed my finger against the bruise on her temple, hard. She didn't flinch or show the least hint that it pained her.

'I thought I was imagining it before,' Denna said, looking up at me. 'But your eyes really do change colour. Normally they're bright green with a ring of gold around the inside . . .'

'I got them from my mother,' I said.

'But I've been watching. When you broke the pump handle yesterday they went dull green, muddy. And when the swineherd made that comment about the Ruh they went dark for just a moment. I thought it was just the light, but now I can see it's not.'

'I'm surprised you noticed,' I said. 'The only other person to ever point it out was an old teacher of mine. And he was an arcanist, which means it's pretty much his job to notice things.'

'Well it's my job to notice things about you.' She cocked her head a bit. 'People probably are distracted by your hair. It's so bright. It's pretty . . . pretty distracting. And your face is really expressive. You're always in control of it, even the way your eyes behave. But not the colour.' She gave a faint smile. 'They're pale now. Like green frost. You must be terribly afraid.'

'I'm guessing it's old-fashioned lust,' I said in my roughest tones. 'It's not often a beautiful girl lets me get this close to her.'

'You always tell me the most beautiful lies,' she said, looking away from me and down to her hands. 'Am I going to die?'

'No,' I said firmly. 'Absolutely not.'

'Could . . .' she looked up at me and smiled again, her eyes wet but not overflowing. 'Could you just say it out loud for me?'

'You aren't going to die,' I said, getting to my feet. 'Come on, let's see if our lizard friend is gone yet.'

I wanted to keep her moving around and distracted, so we each had another little drink and headed back to the lookout. The draccus lay sleeping in the sun.

I took the opportunity to stuff the blanket and the dried meat into my travelsack. 'I felt guilty about stealing from the dead before,' I said. 'But now . . .'

'At least now we know why he was hiding in the middle of nowhere with a crossbow and a lookout and all that,' Denna said. 'A minor mystery solved.'

I started to fasten up my travelsack then, as an afterthought, packed the crossbow bolts as well.

'What are those for?' she asked.

'They're worth something,' I said. 'I'm in debt to a dangerous person. I could use every penny . . .' I trailed off, my mind working.

Denna looked at me, and I could see her mind jumping to the same conclusion. 'Do you know how much that much resin would be worth?' she asked.

'Not really,' I said thinking about the thirty pans, each with a wafer of black, sticky resin congealed in the bottom, big as a dinner plate. 'I'm guessing a lot. An awful lot.'

Denna shifted back and forth on her feet. 'Kvothe, I don't know how I feel about this. I've seen girls get hooked on this stuff. I need money.' She gave a bitter laugh. 'I don't even have a second set of clothes right now.' She looked worried. 'But I don't know if I need it this badly.'

'I'm thinking of apothecaries,' I said quickly. 'They'd refine it into medicine. It's a powerful painkiller. The price won't be nearly as good as if we went to the other sort of people, but still, half a loaf . . .'

Denna smiled broadly. 'I'd love half a loaf. Especially since my cryptic prick of a patron seems to have disappeared.'

We headed back down into the canyon. This time as I emerged from the narrow passageway, I saw the evaporating pans in a different light. Now each of them was the equivalent of a heavy coin in my pocket. Next term's tuition, new clothes, freedom from my debt with Devi . . .

I saw Denna looking at the trays with the same fascination, though hers was somewhat more glassy-eyed than mine. 'I could live comfortably for a year off this,' she said. 'And not be beholden to anyone.'

I went to the tool shed and grabbed a scraper for each of us. At the end of a few minutes work we had combined all of the black, sticky pieces into a single wad the size of a sweetmelon.

She shivered a bit, then looked at me, smiling. Her cheeks were flushed. 'I suddenly feel really good.' She crossed her arms across her chest, rubbing her hands up and down. 'Really, really good. I don't think it's just the thought of all that money.'

'It's the resin,' I said. 'It's a good sign that it's taken this long to hit you. I'd have been worried if it had happened sooner.' I gave her a serious look. 'Now listen. You need to let me know if you feel any heaviness in your chest, or have any trouble breathing. So long as neither of those things happens, you should be fine.'

Denna nodded, then drew a deep breath and let it out again. 'Sweet angel Ordal above, I feel great.' She gave me an anxious expression, but the wide grin kept spilling out. 'Am I going to get addicted from this?'

I shook my head and she sighed with relief. 'You know the damnedest thing? I'm scared about getting addicted, but I don't care that I'm scared. I've never felt like this before. No wonder our big scaly friend keeps coming back for more . . .'

'Merciful Tehlu,' I said. 'I didn't even think of that. That's why it was trying to claw its way in here. It can smell the resin. It's been eating the trees for two span, three or four a day.'

'The biggest sweet-eater of them all, coming back to get his fix.' Denna laughed, then her expression went horrified. 'How many trees were left?'

'Two or three,' I said, thinking of the rows of empty holes and broken stumps. 'But it may have eaten another since we've been back here.'

'Have you ever seen a sweet-eater when they've got the hunger on them?' Denna said, her face stricken. 'They go crazy.'

'I know,' I said, thinking of the girl I'd seen in Tarbean dancing naked in the snow.

'What do you think it's going to do when the trees run out?'

I thought for a long moment. 'It's going to go looking for more. And it's going to be desperate. And it knows the last place where it found the trees had a little house that smelled like people . . . We're going to have to kill it.'

'Kill it?' She laughed, then pressed her hands against her mouth again. 'With nothing but my good singing voice and your manly bravado?' She started to giggle uncontrollably, despite the fact that she was holding both her hands in front of her mouth. 'God, I'm sorry Kvothe. How long am I going to be like this?'

'I don't know. The effects of ophalum are euphoria . . .'

'Check.' She winked at me, grinning.

'Followed by mania, some delirium if your dose was high enough, then exhaustion.'

'Maybe I'll sleep through the night for once,' she said. 'You can't seriously expect to kill this thing. What are you going to use? A pointy stick?'

'I can't just let it run wild. Trebon's only about five miles from here. And there's smaller farms closer than that. Think of the damage it would do.'

'But how?' she repeated. 'How do you kill a thing like that?'

I turned to the tiny shed. 'If we're lucky this fellow had the good sense to buy a spare crossbow . . .' I began to dig around, throwing stuff out the door. Stirring paddles, buckets, scrapers, spade, more buckets, a barrel . . .

The barrel was about the size of a small keg of ale. I carried it outside the shed and pried off the lid. In the bottom was an oilcloth sack containing a large gummy mass of black denner resin, at least four times as much as Denna and I had already scraped together.

I pulled out the sack and rested it on the ground, holding it open for Denna to look. She peered in, gasped, then jumped up and down a little bit. 'Now I can buy a pony!' she said, laughing.

'I don't know about a pony,' I said, doing some calculations in my head. 'But I think before we split up the money, we should buy you a good half-harp out of this,' I said. 'Not some sad lyre.'

'Yes!' Denna said, then she threw her arms around me in a wild, delighted hug. 'And we'll get you . . .' She looked at me curiously, her sooty face inches away from my own. 'What do you want?'

Before I could say anything, do anything, the draccus roared.

CHAPTER SEVENTY-EIGHT

Poison

THE ROAR OF THE draccus was like a trumpet, if you can imagine a trumpet big as a house, and made of stone, and thunder, and molten lead. I didn't feel it in my chest. I felt it in my feet as the earth shook with it.

The roar made us jump nearly out of our skins. The top of Denna's head banged into my nose, and I staggered, blinded with pain. Denna didn't notice, as she was busy tripping and falling over into a loose, laughing tangle of arms and legs.

As I helped Denna to her feet I heard a distant crashing, and we made our way carefully back up to the lookout.

The draccus was . . . cavorting, bounding around like a drunken dog, knocking over trees like a boy would topple cornstalks in a field.

I watched breathlessly as it came to an ancient oak tree, a hundred years old and massive as a greystone. The draccus reared up and brought its front legs down on one of the lower branches, as if it wanted to climb. The branch, big as a tree itself, practically exploded.

The draccus reared again, coming down hard on the tree. I watched, certain that it was about to impale itself on the broken limb, but the jagged spear of hard wood barely dimpled its chest before splintering. The draccus crashed into the trunk, and though it didn't snap, it fractured with a sound like a crack of lightning.

The draccus threw itself around, hopped and fell, rolling over jagged spurs of rock. It belched a huge gout of flame and charged the fractured oak tree again, striking with its great blunt wedge of a head. This time, it knocked the tree over, causing an explosion of earth and rock as the tree's roots tore out of the ground.

All I could think of was the futility of trying to hurt this creature. It was bringing more force to bear against itself than I could ever hope to muster.

'There's no way we can kill that,' I said. 'It would be like trying to attack a thunderstorm. How could we possibly hurt it?'

'We lure her over the side of a cliff,' Denna said matter-of-factly.

'She?' I asked. 'Why do you think it's a *she*?'

'Why do you think it's a *he*?' she replied, then shook her head as if to clear it. 'Never mind, it doesn't matter. We know it's drawn to fires. We just build one and hang it from a branch.' She pointed to a few trees overhanging the cliff below. 'Then, when it rushes over to put it out . . .' She made a pantomime with both hands of something falling.

'Do you think even that would hurt it?' I asked dubiously.

'Well,' Denna said, 'when you flick an ant off a table it doesn't get hurt even though for an ant that has to be like dropping off a cliff. But if one of us jumped off a roof, we'd get hurt because we're heavier. It makes sense that bigger things fall even harder.' She gave a pointed look down at the draccus. 'You don't get much bigger than that.'

She was right, of course. She was talking about the square-cube ratio, though she didn't know what to call it.

'It should at least injure it,' Denna continued. 'Then, I don't know, we could roll rocks down onto it or something.' She looked at me. 'What? Is there something wrong with my idea?'

'It's not very heroic,' I said dismissively. 'I was expecting something with a little more flair.'

'Well I left my armour and warhorse at home,' she said. 'You're just upset because your big University brain couldn't think of a way, and my plan is brilliant.' She pointed behind us, to the box canyon. 'We'll build the fire in one of those metal pans. They're wide and shallow and they'll take the heat. Was there any rope in that shed?'

'I . . .' I felt the familiar sinking feeling in my gut. 'No. I don't think so.'

Denna patted me on the arm. 'Don't look like that. When it leaves we'll check the wreckage of the house. I'll bet there's some rope in there.' She looked at the draccus. 'Honestly, I know how she feels. I feel a little like running around and jumping on things too.'

'That's the mania I was talking about,' I said.

After a quarter-hour the draccus left the valley. Only then did Denna and I emerge from our hiding place, me carrying my travelsack, she with the heavy oilskin bag that held all the resin we'd found, nearly a full bushel of it.

'Give me your loden-stone,' she said, setting down the sack. I handed it over. 'You find some rope. I'm going to go get you a present.' She skipped away lightly, her dark hair flying behind her.

I made a quick search of the house, holding my breath as much as possible. I found a hatchet, broken crockery, a barrel of wormy flour, a mildewy straw tick, a ball of twine, but no rope.

Denna gave a delighted shout from the trees, ran up to me, and pressed a black scale into my hand. It was warm with the sun, slightly larger than hers but more oval than tear-shaped.

'Thank you kindly, m'lady.'

She bobbed a charming curtsey, grinning. 'Rope?'

I held up a ball of rough twine. 'This is as close as I could find. Sorry.'

Denna frowned, then shrugged it off. 'Oh well. Your turn for a plan. You have any strange and wonderful magics from the University? Any dark powers better left alone?'

I turned the scale over in my hands and thought about it. I had wax, and this scale would make as good a link as any hair. I could make a simulacrum of the draccus, but then what? A hotfoot wasn't going to bother a creature that was perfectly comfortable lying on a bed of coals.

But there are more sinister things you can do with a mommet. Things no good arcanist was ever supposed to consider. Things with pins and knives that would leave a man bleeding even though he was miles away. True malfeasance.

I looked at the scale in my hand, considering it. The thing was mostly iron and thicker than my palm in the middle. Even with a mommet and a hot fire for energy, I didn't know if I could make it through the scales to hurt the thing.

Worst of all, if I tried I wouldn't know if it had worked. I couldn't bear the thought of sitting idly by some fire, sticking pins into a wax doll while miles away a drug-crazed draccus rolled in the flaming wreckage of some innocent family's farm.

'No,' I said. 'No magic I can think of.'

'We can go tell the constable that he needs to deputise about a dozen men with bows to come kill a drug-crazed big-as-a-house dragon-chicken.'

It came to me in a flash. 'Poison,' I said. 'We'll have to poison it.'

'You've got two quarts of arsenic on you?' she asked skeptically. 'Would that even be enough for something big as that?'

'Not arsenic.' I nudged the oilskin sack with my foot.

She looked down. 'Oh,' she said, crestfallen. 'What about my pony?'

'You'll probably have to skip your pony,' I said. 'But we'll still have enough to buy you a half-harp. In fact, I bet we'll be able to make even more money from the draccus' body. The scales will be worth a lot. And the naturalists at the University will love to be able—'

'You don't need to sell me,' she said. 'I know it's the right thing to do.' She looked up at me and grinned. 'Besides, we get to be heroes and kill the dragon. Its treasure is just a perk.'

I laughed. 'Right then,' I said. 'I think we should head back to the grey-stone hill and build a fire there to lure it in.'

Denna looked puzzled. 'Why? We know it's going to come back here. Why don't we just camp here and wait?'

I shook my head. 'Look at how many denner trees are left.'

She looked around. 'It ate all of them?'

I nodded. 'If we kill it this evening, we can be back in Trebon by tonight,' I said. 'I'm tired of sleeping outdoors. I want to get a bath, a hot meal, and a real bed.'

'You're lying again,' she said cheerfully. 'Your delivery's getting better, but to me you're clear as a shallow stream.' She prodded my chest with a finger. 'Tell me the truth.'

'I want to get you back to Trebon,' I said. 'Just in case you ate more resin than is good for you. I wouldn't trust any doctor living there, but they probably have some medicines I could use. Just in case.'

'My hero.' Denna smiled. 'You're sweet, but I feel fine.'

I reached out and flicked her ear with the tip of my finger, hard.

Her hand went to the side of her head, her expression outraged. 'Ow . . . oh.' She looked confused.

'Doesn't hurt at all, does it?'

'No,' she said.

'Here is the truth,' I said seriously. 'I think you're going to be fine, but I don't know for certain. I don't know how much of that stuff you have left working its way into your system. In an hour I'll have a better idea, but if something goes wrong I'd rather be an hour closer to Trebon. It means I won't have to carry you as far.' I looked her square in the eye. 'I don't gamble with the lives of people I care for.'

She listened to me, her expression somber. Then the grin blossomed back onto her face. 'I like your manly bravado,' she said. 'Do it some more.'

CHAPTER SEVENTY-NINE

Sweet Talk

IT TOOK US ABOUT two hours to get back to the greystone hill. It would have been faster, but Denna's mania was growing stronger, and all her extra energy was more of a hindrance than a help. She was highly distractible and prone to larking off in her own direction if she saw something interesting.

We crossed the same small stream that we had before, and, despite the fact that it wasn't much more than ankle deep, Denna insisted on bathing. I washed up a little, then moved a discreet distance away and listened to her sing several rather racy songs. She also made several none-too-subtle invitations that I could join her in the water.

Needless to say, I kept my distance. There are names for people who take advantage of women who are not in full control of themselves, and none of those names will ever rightfully be applied to me.

————

Once we reached the peak of the greystone hill, I put Denna's surplus of energy to use and sent her to gather firewood while I made an even larger fire pit than our previous one. The bigger the fire, the quicker it would draw the draccus close.

I sat down next to the oilskin bag and opened it. The resin gave off an earthy smell, like sweet, smoky mulch.

Denna returned to the top of the hill and dropped an armload of wood. 'How much of that are you going to use?' she asked.

'I still have to figure that out,' I said. 'It's going to require some guesswork.'

'Just give him all of it,' Denna said. 'Better safe than sorry.'

I shook my head. 'There's no reason to go that far. It would just be wasteful. Besides, the resin makes a powerful painkiller when properly refined. People could use the medicine . . .'

'. . . and you could use the money,' Denna said.

'I could,' I admitted. 'But honestly, I was thinking more about your harp. You lost your lyre in that fire. I know what it's like to be without an instrument.'

'Did you ever hear the story about the boy with the golden arrows?' Denna asked. 'That always bothered me when I was young. You must want to kill someone really badly to shoot a gold arrow at him. Why not just keep the gold and go home?'

'It certainly shines a new light on that story,' I said, looking down at the sack. I guessed this much denner resin would be worth at least fifty talents to an apothecary. Maybe as much as a hundred, depending on how refined it was.

Denna shrugged and headed back into the trees for more firewood and I began the elaborate guesswork of how much denner it would take to poison a five ton lizard.

It was a nightmare of educated guessery, complicated by the fact that I had no way to make accurate measurements. I started with a bead the size of the last digit of my little finger, my guess as to how much resin Denna had actually swallowed. However, Denna had been liberally dosed with charcoal, which effectively reduced that by a half. I was left with a ball of black resin slightly larger than a pea.

But that was just the amount required to make a human girl euphoric and energetic. I wanted to kill the draccus. For that I tripled the dose, then tripled it again to be sure. The end result was a ball the size of a large, ripe grape.

I guessed the draccus weighed five tons, eight hundred stone. I guessed Denna at eight or nine stone, eight to be on the safe side. That meant I needed a hundred times that grape-size dose to kill the draccus. I made ten grape-size pellets, then mashed them together. It was the size of an apricot. I made nine more apricot-size balls and set them in the wooden bucket we had brought from the denner plantation.

Denna dropped another load of wood and peered down into the bucket. 'That's it?' she asked. 'It doesn't look like very much.'

She was right. It didn't look like much at all compared to the draccus' huge bulk. I explained how I'd come up with my estimate. She nodded.

'That seems about right, I guess. But don't forget that it's been eating trees for the better part of a month. It probably has a tolerance.'

I nodded and added five more apricot-size balls to the bucket.

'And it might be tougher than you think. The resin might work different on lizards.'

I nodded again and added another five balls to the bucket. Then, after a moment's consideration, I added one more. 'That brings us up to twenty-one,' I explained. 'A good number. Three sevens.'

'Nothing wrong with having luck on your side,' Denna agreed.

'We want it to die quickly, too,' I said. 'It will be more humane for the draccus and safer for us.'

Denna looked at me. 'So we double it?' I nodded and she headed back into the trees while I made another twenty-one balls and dropped them into the bucket. She came back with more wood just as I was rolling up the last ball.

I packed the resin down into the bottom of the bucket. 'That should be more than enough,' I said. 'That much ophalum would kill the entire population of Trebon twice over.'

Denna and I looked at the bucket. It contained about a third of all the resin we'd found. What was left in the oilskin sack would be enough to buy Denna a half-harp, pay off my debt to Devi, and still have enough left over so that we could live comfortably for months. I thought of buying new clothes, a full set of new strings for my lute, a bottle of Avennish fruit wine . . .

I thought of the draccus brushing aside trees as if they were sheaves of wheat, shattering them casually with its weight.

'We should double it again,' Denna said, echoing my own thoughts, 'just to be sure.'

I doubled it yet again, rolling out another forty-two balls of the resin while Denna fetched armload after armload of wood.

I got the fire blazing just as the rain started to come down. We built it larger than our last one with the hope that a brighter fire would attract the draccus more quickly. I wanted to get Denna back to the relative safety of Trebon as soon as possible.

Lastly I cobbled together a rough ladder using the hatchet and twine I'd found. It was ugly but serviceable, and I leaned it up against the side of the greystone arch. This time, Denna and I would have an easy route to safety.

———————

Our dinner was nowhere near as grand as last night's. We made do with the last of my now-stale flatbread, dried meat, and the last potatoes baked on the edge of the fire.

While we ate, I told Denna the full story of the fire in the Fishery. Partly because I was young, and male, and desperately wanted to impress her, but I also wanted to make it clear that I had missed our lunch due to circumstances completely outside my control. She was the perfect audience, attentive and gasping at all the right moments.

I was no longer worried about her overdosing. After gathering a small mountain of firewood, her mania was fading, leaving her in a content, almost dreamy lethargy. Still, I knew the aftereffects of the drug would leave her exhausted and weak. I wanted her safely in bed in Trebon for her recovery.

After we finished eating I made my way over to where she sat with her back against one of the greystones. I cuffed up my shirtsleeves. 'Alright, I need to check you over,' I said pompously.

She smiled lazily at me, her eyes half-closed. 'You really do know how to sweet talk a girl, don't you?'

I felt for her pulse in the hollow of her slender throat. It was slow, but steady. She shied away a little from my touch. 'You tickle.'

'How do you feel?' I asked.

'Tired,' she said, her voice slightly slurred. 'Good and tired and a little cold . . .'

While this wasn't unexpected, it was still a little surprising considering the fact that we were only feet away from a blazing bonfire. I fetched the extra blanket from my bag and brought it back to her. She snuggled into it.

I leaned close so that I could look into her eyes. Her pupils were still wide and sluggish, but no more than before.

She reached up and lay her hand on my cheek. 'You have the sweetest face,' she said, looking at me dreamily. 'It's like the perfect kitchen.'

I fought not to smile. This was the delirium. She'd fade in and out of it before the profound exhaustion dragged her down into unconsciousness. If you see someone spouting nonsense to themselves in an alleyway in Tarbean, odds are they're not actually crazy, just a sweet-eater deranged by too much denner. 'A kitchen?'

'Yes,' she said. 'Everything matches and the sugar bowl is right where it should be.'

'How does it feel when you breathe?' I asked.

'Normal,' she said easily. 'Tight but normal.'

My heart beat a little faster at that. 'What do you mean by that?'

'I have trouble breathing,' she said. 'My chest gets tight sometimes and it's like breathing through pudding.' She laughed. 'Did I say pudding? I meant molasses. Like a sweet molasses pudding.'

I fought off the urge to point out angrily that I'd asked her to tell me if she felt anything wrong with her breathing. 'Is it hard to breathe now?'

She shrugged indifferently.

'I need to listen to your breathing,' I said. 'But I don't have any tools here, so if you could unbutton your shirt a little, I'll need to press my ear against your chest.'

Denna rolled her eyes and unbuttoned more of her shirt than was altogether necessary. 'Now that one is entirely new,' she said archly, sounding for a moment like her normal self. 'I've never had anyone try that before.'

I turned and pressed my ear up against her breastbone.

'What does my heart sound like?' she asked.

'It's slow but strong,' I said. 'It's a good heart.'

'Is it saying anything?'

'Nothing I can hear,' I said.

'Listen harder.'

'Take a few deep breaths and don't talk,' I said. 'I need to listen to your breathing.'

I listened. The air rushed in and I felt one of her breasts pressing against my arm. She exhaled and I felt her breath, warm against the back of my neck. Gooseflesh broke out over my whole body.

I could picture Arwyl's disapproving stare. I closed my eyes and tried to concentrate on what I was doing. In and out, it was like listening to the wind through the trees. In and out, I could hear a faint crackling, like paper crumpling, like a faint sigh. But there was no wetness, no bubbling.

'Your hair smells really nice,' she said.

I sat up. 'You're fine,' I said. 'Make sure to let me know if it gets any worse or feels different.'

She nodded amiably, smiling dreamily.

Irritated that the draccus seemed to be taking its sweet time making an appearance, I heaped more wood on the fire. I looked out at the northern bluffs, but there was nothing to see in the dim light but the outlines of trees and rocks.

Denna laughed suddenly. 'Did I call your face a sugar bowl or something?' she asked, peering at me. 'Am I even making any sense right now?'

'It's just a little delirium,' I reassured her. 'You'll fade in and out of it before you go to sleep.'

'I hope it's as much fun for you as it is for me,' she said pulling the blanket closer around herself. 'It's like a cottony dream, but not as warm.'

I climbed the ladder to the top of the greystone where we had stashed our possessions. I took a handful of the denner resin out of the oilskin sack, carried it down, and threw it on the edge of the fire. It burned sullenly, giving off an acrid smoke that the wind brushed away to the north and west, toward the unseen bluffs. Hopefully the draccus would smell it and come running.

'I had pneumonia when I was just a tiny baby,' Denna said with no particular inflection. 'That's why my lungs aren't good. It's horrible not being able to breathe sometimes.'

Denna's eyes were half closed as she continued, almost as if she were talking to herself. 'I stopped breathing for two minutes and died. Sometimes I wonder if this all isn't some sort of mistake, if I should be dead. But if it isn't a mistake I have to be here for a reason. But if there is a reason, I don't know what that reason is.'

There was the distinct possibility that she didn't even realise that she was talking, and an even greater possibility that most of the important parts of her brain were already asleep and she wouldn't remember any of what was happening now in the morning. Since I didn't know how to respond, I simply nodded.

'That's the first thing you said to me. *I was just wondering why you're here.* My seven words. I've been wondering the same thing for so long.'

The sun, already hidden by the clouds, finally set behind the western mountains. As the landscape faded into darkness, the top of this small hill felt like an island in a great ocean of night.

Denna was beginning to nod where she sat, her head slowly sinking to her chest, then bobbing back up. I walked over and held out my hand. 'Come on, the draccus will be here soon. We should get up onto the stones.'

She nodded and came to her feet, blankets still wrapped around her. I followed her to the ladder and she made her slow, stumbling way up to the top of the greystone.

It was chilly up on the stone, away from the fire. The wind brushed past, making the slight chill worse. I spread one blanket across the stone and she sat down, huddled in the other blanket. The cold seemed to rouse her a little and she looked around peevishly, shivering. 'Damn chicken. Come eat your dinner. I'm cold.'

'I was hoping to have you tucked into a warm bed in Trebon by now,' I admitted. 'So much for my brilliant plan.'

'You always know where you're doing,' she said muzzily. 'You're important with your green eyes looking at me like I mean something. It's okay that you have better things to do. It's enough that I get you sometimes. Once in a while. I know I'm lucky for that, to get you just a little.'

I nodded agreeably, as I watched the hillside for signs of the draccus. We sat for a while longer, staring off into the dark. Denna nodded a little, then pulled herself upright again and fought off another violent shiver. 'I know you don't think of me . . .' She trailed off.

It's best to humour people in delirium, lest they turn violent. 'I think about you all the time, Denna,' I said.

'Don't patronise me,' she said crossly, then her tone softened again. 'You don't think of me like that. That's fine. But if you're cold too, you could come over here and put your arms around me. Just a little.'

My heart in my mouth, I moved closer and sat behind her, wrapping my arms around her. 'That's nice,' she said, relaxing. 'I feel like I've always been cold.'

We sat looking to the north. She leaned against me, delightful in my arms. I drew shallow breaths, not wanting to disturb her.

Denna stirred slightly, murmuring. 'You're so gentle. You never push . . .' She trailed off agian, resting more heavily against my chest. Then she roused herself. 'You could, you know, push more. Just a little.'

I sat there in the dark, holding her sleeping body in my arms. She was soft and warm, indescribably precious. I had never held a woman before. After a few moments my back began to ache with the pressure of supporting her weight and my own. My leg started to go numb. Her hair tickled my nose. Still, I didn't move for fear of ruining this, the most wonderful moment of my life.

Denna shifted in her sleep, then started to slide sideways and jerked awake. 'Lie down,' she said, her voice clear again. She fumbled with the blanket, pulling it away so it was no longer between us. 'Come on. You've got to be cold too. You're not a priest, so you're not going to get in trouble for it. We'll be fine. Just a little fine in the cold.'

I put my arms around her and she draped the blanket over both of us.

We lay on our sides, like spoons nesting in a drawer. My arm ended up under her head, like a pillow. She curled snugly along the inside of my body, so easy and natural, as if she had been designed to fit there.

As I lay there, I realised I had been wrong before, *this* was the most wonderful moment of my life.

Denna stirred in her sleep. 'I know you didn't mean it,' she said clearly.

'Mean what?' I asked softly. Her voice was different, no longer dreamy and tired. I wondered if she was talking in her sleep.

'Before. You said you'd knock me down and make me eat coals. You'd never hit me.' She turned her head a little. 'You wouldn't, would you? Not even if it was for my own good?'

I felt a chill go through me. 'What do you mean?'

There was a long pause, and I was beginning to think she'd fallen asleep when she spoke up again. 'I didn't tell you everything. I know Ash didn't die at the farm. When I was heading toward the fire he found me. He came back and said that everyone was dead. He said that people would be suspicious if I was the only one who survived . . .'

I felt a hard, dark anger rise up in me. I knew what came next, but I let her talk. I didn't want to hear it, but I knew she needed to tell someone.

'He didn't just do it out of the blue,' she said. 'He made sure it was what I really wanted. I knew it wouldn't look convincing if I did it to myself. He made sure I really wanted him to. He made me ask him to hit me. Just to be sure.

'And he was right.' She didn't move at all as she spoke. 'Even this way they thought I had something to do with it. If he hadn't done it, I might be in jail right now. They would've hanged me.'

My stomach churned acid. 'Denna,' I said. 'A man who could do that to you – he's not worth your time. Not one moment of it. It's not a matter of him being only half a loaf. He's rotten through. You deserve better.'

'Who knows what I deserve?' she said. 'He's not my best loaf. He's it. Him or hungry.'

'You have other options,' I said, then stalled, thinking of my conversation with Deoch. 'You've . . . you've got . . .'

'I've got you,' she said dreamily. I could hear the warm, sleepy smile in her voice, like a child tucked into bed. 'Will you be my dark-eyed Prince Gallant and protect me from pigs? Sing to me? Whisk me away to tall trees . . .' she trailed off to nothing.

'I will,' I said, but I could tell by the heavy weight of her against my arm that she had finally fallen asleep.

CHAPTER EIGHTY

Touching Iron

I LAY AWAKE, feeling Denna's gentle breath against my arm. I couldn't have slept even if I'd wanted to. The closeness of her filled me with a crackling energy, a low warmth, a gentle thrumming hum. I lay awake savouring it, every moment precious as a jewel.

Then I heard the distant crack of a breaking branch. Then another. Earlier I wanted nothing more than the draccus to hurry to our fire. Now, I would have traded my right hand to have it go on its merry way for another five minutes.

Still, it came. I began gently untangling myself from Denna. She barely stirred in her sleep. 'Denna?' I shook her gently, then harder. Nothing. I wasn't surprised. There are few things deeper than a sweet-eater's sleep.

I covered her in the blanket, then set my travelsack on one side, the oil-skin bag on the other, like bookends. If she rolled in her sleep, she would butt into those before getting close to the edge of the greystone.

I moved to the other side of the stone and looked out to the north. The clouds were still thick overhead, so I couldn't see anything outside the circle of firelight.

Feeling carefully with my fingers, I located the piece of twine I had laid across the top of the greystone. The other end was tied to the rope handle of the wooden bucket below, midway between the fire and the greystones. My main fear was that the draccus might accidentally crush the bucket before it smelled it. I planned to haul the bucket to safety if that happened, then cast it out again. Denna had laughed at my plan, referring to it as chicken-fishing.

The draccus came to the top of the hill, moving noisily through the brush. It stopped just inside the circle of firelight. Its dark eyes shone red, and there was red on its scales. It made a deep huffing sound and began to circle the fire, slowly rocking its head back and forth. It blew a wide plume of fire in what I was coming to recognise as either some sort of greeting or a challenge.

It darted towards our fire. Despite the fact that I'd watched it at some length, I was still surprised by how quickly the huge animal could move. It pulled up short of the fire, huffed again, then advanced on the bucket.

Despite the fact that the bucket was sturdy wood and built to hold at least two gallons, it looked tiny as a teacup next to the draccus' massive head. It sniffed again, then butted the bucket with its nose, tipping it over.

The bucket rolled in a half-circle, but I'd packed the sticky resin in tightly. The draccus took another step, huffed again, and took the whole thing into its mouth.

I was so relieved that I almost forgot to let go of the twine. It was jerked out of my hands as the draccus chewed the bucket a little, crushing it in its massive jaws. Then it worked its head up and down, forcing the sticky mass down its gullet.

I breathed a huge sigh of relief and sat down to watch as the draccus circled the fire. It gushed out a billow of blue flame, then another, then turned and rolled in the fire, wriggling and crushing it into the dirt.

Once the fire was flattened, the draccus began to follow the same pattern as before. It sought out the scattered pieces of the fire, rolled in them until they were extinguished, then ate the wood. I could almost imagine each new stick and stump it swallowed forcing the denner resin deeper into its gizzard, mixing it around, breaking it up, forcing it to dissolve.

A quarter-hour passed as I watched it complete its circuit of the fire. I'd hoped it would have showed the effects of the resin by now. By my best guess, it had eaten six times a lethal dose. It should rush quickly past the initial stages of euphoria and mania. Then would follow delirium, paralysis, coma, and death. By all my calculations it should be over within an hour, hopefully sooner.

I felt a pang of regret as I watched it go about the business of crushing out the scattered fires. It was a magnificent animal. I hated to kill it even more than I hated to waste upwards of sixty talents worth of ophalum. But there was no denying what would happen if events were left to run their course. I didn't want the deaths of innocents on my conscience.

Soon it stopped eating. It merely rolled on the scattered branches, extinguishing them. It was moving more vigorously now, a sign that the denner was beginning to take effect. It started to grunt, low and deep. *Grunt. Grunt.* A wash of blue fire. Roll. *Grunt.* Roll.

Finally there was nothing left but the bed of glimmering coals. As before, the draccus positioned itself on top of them and laid down, extinguishing all the light on the top of the hill.

It lay there quietly for a moment. Then grunted again. *Grunt. Grunt.* Wash of fire. It wriggled its belly farther into the coals, almost like it was fidgeting. If this was the onset of mania, it was coming too slowly for my liking. I'd hoped that it would be well on its way to delirium by now. Had I underestimated the dosage?

As my eyes slowly adjusted to the dark, I realised there was another source of light. At first I thought the clouds had blown over, and the moon was peering in from the horizon. But when I turned away from the draccus to look behind me, I saw the truth.

Off to the southwest, barely two miles away, Trebon was full of firelight. Not just dim candlelight from windows, there were tall flames leaping everywhere. For a moment I thought the city was ablaze.

Then I realised what was happening: the harvest festival. There was a tall bonfire in the middle of town, and smaller ones outside the houses where people would be giving cider to the weary workers. They would drink and throw their shamble-men into the fires. Dummies made of wheat sheaves, of barley shocks, of straw, of chaff. Dummies built to flare up bright and sudden, a ritual to celebrate the end of the year, something that was supposed to keep demons away.

Behind me I heard the draccus grunt. I looked down at it. Just as I had been, it was facing away from Trebon, towards the dark cliffs to the north.

I am not a religious person, but I will admit that I prayed then. I prayed earnestly to Tehlu and all his angels, asking for the draccus to die, just slide quietly asleep and pass on without turning around to see the city's fires.

I waited for several long minutes. At first I thought the draccus was asleep, but as my eyes sharpened I could see its head weaving steadily back and forth, back and forth. As my eyes grew more accustomed to the dark, the fires of Trebon seemed to grow brighter. It had been half an hour since it had eaten the resin. Why wasn't it dead yet?

I wanted to throw down the rest of the resin, but I didn't dare. If the draccus turned toward me, it would be facing south, toward the town. Even if I threw the sack of resin directly in front of it, it might turn around to resettle itself on the fire. Perhaps if—

The draccus roared then, deep and powerful as before. I had no doubt they heard it in Trebon. I wouldn't have been surprised to learn that they had heard it in Imre. I glanced at Denna. She shifted in her sleep but didn't wake.

The draccus bounded off the bed of coals, looking for all the world like a frisking puppy. The coals still glimmered in places, giving me enough light to see the great beast roll around, flip. Bite at the air. Turn . . .

'No,' I said. 'No, no, no.'

It looked out toward Trebon. I could see the leaping flames of the town's fires reflected in its huge eyes. It breathed another gout of blue fire in a high arc. The same gesture it had made before: a greeting or a challenge.

Then it was running, tearing down the hillside with demented abandon. I heard it crashing and snapping through the trees. Another roar.

I thumbed on my sympathy lamp and went to Denna, shaking her roughly. 'Denna. Denna! You have to get up!'

She barely stirred.

I lifted her eyelid and checked her pupils. They showed none of their earlier sluggishness and shrank quickly in response to the light. That meant the denner resin had finally worked its way out of her system. This was simple exhaustion, nothing else. Just to be sure I lifted both lids and brought the light back around again.

Yes. Her pupils were fine. She was fine. As if to confirm my opinion, Denna scowled fiercely and squirmed away from the light, muttering something indistinct and decidedly unladylike. I couldn't make out all of it, but the words 'whoremonger' and 'soddoff' were used more than once.

I scooped her up, blankets and all, and carefully made my way down to the ground. I bundled her up again between the arch of the greystones. She seemed to rouse herself slightly as I jostled her around. 'Denna?'

'Moteth?' she muttered around a mouthful of sleep, her eyes barely moving under her lids.

'Denna! The draccus is going down to Trebon! I have to . . .'

I stopped. Partly because it was obvious she had dropped back into unconsciousness, but also because I wasn't entirely sure what it was I had to do.

I had to do something. Normally the draccus would avoid a town, but drug-crazed and manic, I had no idea what its reaction to the harvest fires would be. If it rampaged through the town it would be my fault. I had to do something.

I dashed to the top of the greystone, grabbed both bags, and came back down. I upended the travelsack, emptying everything onto the ground. I grabbed the crossbow bolts, wrapped them in my torn shirt, and stuffed them into my travelsack. I threw in the hard iron scale too, then stuffed the bottle of brand into the oilskin sack for padding and put that in my travelsack as well.

My mouth was dry, so I took a quick swallow of water from the water-skin, recapped it, and left it for Denna. She would be terribly thirsty when she woke up.

I slung the travelsack over my shoulder and cinched it tight across my back. Then I thumbed on my sympathy lamp, picked up the hatchet, and began to run.

I had a dragon to kill.

————————

I ran madly through the woods, the light from my sympathy lamp bobbing wildly, revealing obstacles ahead of me bare moments before I was on top of them. Small wonder that I fell, tumbling down the hill, ass over teakettle. When I got up I easily found my lamp, but I abandoned the hatchet, know-ing deep in my heart that it wouldn't be of any use against the draccus.

I fell twice more before I made it to the road, then I tucked my head like a sprinter and ran towards the distant light of the city. I knew the draccus could move faster than me, but I hoped it would be slowed by the trees, or disori-ented. If I made it to the town first I could warn them, get them ready . . .

But as the road emerged from the trees, I could see the fires were brighter, wilder. Houses were burning. I could hear the draccus' near-constant bellowing punctuated by shouting and high-pitched screams.

I slowed to a trot as I came into town, catching my breath. Then I scam-pered up the side of a house to one of the few two-story rooftops so I could see what was really happening.

In the town square the bonfire had been scattered everywhere. Several nearby houses and shops were staved in like rotten barrels, most of them burning fitfully. Fire flickered on the wooden shingles of a handful of roofs. If not for the evening's earlier rain, the town would already be ablaze instead of just a few scattered buildings. Still, it was just a matter of time.

I couldn't see the draccus, but I could hear the great crunching it made as it rolled in the wreckage of a burning house. I saw a gush of blue flame rise high above the rooftops and heard it roar again. The sound made me sweat. Who knew what was going through its drug-addled mind right now?

There were people everywhere. Some were simply standing, confused, others panicked and ran to the church, hoping to find shelter in the tall stone building or the huge iron wheel that hung there, promising them safety from demons. But the church doors were locked, and they were forced to find shelter elsewhere. Some people watched, horrified and weeping, from their windows, but a surprising number kept their heads and were forming a bucket line from the town's cistern atop the city hall to a nearby burning building.

And just like that I knew what I had to do. It was like I had suddenly stepped onto a stage. Fear and hesitation left me. All that remained was for me to play my part.

I jumped to a nearby roof, then made my way across several others until I came to a house near the town square where a scattered piece of bonfire had set the roof burning. I pried up a thick shingle burning along one edge and took off running for the roof of the town hall.

I was only two roofs away when I slipped. Too late I realised I'd jumped to the inn's roof – no wood shingles here, but clay tiles slippery with rain. I held tight to the burning shingle as I fell, unwilling to let it go to brace my fall. I slid nearly to the edge of the roof before I came to a stop, heart pounding.

Breathless, I kicked off my boots as I lay there. Then with the familiar feel of rooftop under my calloused feet I ran, jumped, ran, slid, and jumped again. Finally I swung myself one-handed by an eave-pipe onto the flat stone roof of the town hall.

Still clutching the burning shingle, I made my way up the ladder to the top of the cistern, whispering a breathless thanks to whoever had left it open to the sky.

As I'd sprinted across the rooftops, the flame on the shingle had gone out, leaving a thin line of red ember along the edge. I puffed it carefully back to life and soon it was blazing merrily again. I broke it down the middle and dropped half to the flat roof below.

Turning to survey the town, I made note of the biggest fires. There were six especially bad ones, blazing up into the dark sky. Elxa Dal had always said that all fires are one fire, and all fires are the sympathist's to command. Very well then, all fires were one fire. *This* fire. *This* piece of burning shingle. I murmured a binding and focused my Alar. I used my thumbnail to scratch a hasty ule rune onto the wood, then doch, then pesin. In the brief moment it took to do that the entire shingle was smoldering and smoking, hot in my hand.

I hooked my foot around the ladder rung and leaned deep into the cistern, quenching the shingle in the water. For a brief moment I felt the cool water surround my hand, then it quickly warmed. Even though the shingle was under water, I could see the faint line of red ember still smoldering along its edge.

I pulled out my pocketknife with my other hand and drove it through the shingle into the wooden wall of the cistern, pinning my makeshift piece of sygaldry under the water. I have no doubt it was the quickest, most slapdash heat-eater ever created.

Pulling myself back onto the ladder, I looked around to a town blessedly dark. The flames had dimmed, and in most places had subsided to sullen coals. I hadn't doused the fires, merely slowed them down enough to give the townsfolk and their buckets a fighting chance.

But my job was only half done. I dropped to the roof and picked up the other half of the still-burning shingle I'd dropped. Then I slid down a drainpipe and legged it away through the dark streets, across the town square to the front of the Tehlin church.

I stopped under the huge oak that stood before the front door, still holding its full array of autumn leaves. Kneeling, I opened my travelsack and brought out the oilskin bag with all the remaining resin. I poured the bottle of brand onto it and set it afire with the burning shingle. It flared up quickly, billowing acrid, sweet-smelling smoke.

Then I put the blunt end of the shingle between my teeth, jumped to catch a low branch, and began to climb the tree. It was easier than making my way up the side of a building, and took me high enough to where I could jump to the wide stone window ledge on the church's second floor. I broke off a twig from the oak tree and stuffed it into my pocket.

I edged along the window ledge to where the huge iron wheel hung, bolted to the stone of the wall. Climbing that was quicker than a ladder, though the iron spokes were startlingly cold against my still-wet hands.

I made my way to the top of the wheel, and from there pulled myself onto the flat peak of the highest roof in town. The fires were still dark for the most part, and most of the shouting had died down to sobs and a low murmur of urgent, hurried talk. I took the piece of shingle out of my mouth and blew on it until it was flaming again. Then I concentrated, muttered another binding, and held the oak twig above the flame. I looked out over the town and saw the glimmering coals dim even further.

A moment passed.

The oak tree below burst into sudden, brilliant flame. It flared brighter than a thousand torches as all its leaves caught fire at the same time.

In the sudden light I saw the draccus raise its head two streets away. It bellowed and blew a cloud of blue flame even as it started to run toward the fire. It turned a corner too quickly and caromed wildly into the wall of a shop, smashing through with little resistance.

It slowed as it approached the tree, blowing flame again and again. The leaves flared and faded quickly, leaving nothing but a thousand embers, making the tree look like an immense extinguished candelabrum.

In the dim red light, the draccus was hardly more than a shadow. But I could still see the beast's attention wander, now that the bright flames were gone. The massive wedge of a head swayed back and forth, back and forth. I cursed under my breath. It wasn't close enough . . .

Then the draccus huffed loud enough for me to hear from where I stood a hundred feet above. The head snapped around as it smelled the sweet smoke of the burning resin. It snuffed, grunted, and took another step towards the smoking bag of resin. It didn't show nearly the restraint it had earlier, and practically pounced on it, snapping up the smoldering sack in its great wide mouth.

I took a deep breath and shook my head, trying to clear away some of the sluggishness I felt. I had performed two rather substantial pieces of sympathy in quick succession and was feeling rather thickheaded because of it.

But as they say, third time pays for all. I broke my mind into two pieces, then, with some difficulty, into a third. Nothing less than a triple binding would do for this.

As the draccus worked its jaw, trying to swallow the sticky mass of resin, I fumbled in my travelsack for the heavy black scale, then brought the loden-stone out from my cloak. I spoke my bindings clearly and focused my Alar. I brought the scale and stone up in front of me until I could feel them tugging at each other.

I concentrated, focused.

I let go of the loden-stone. It shot toward the iron scale. Below my feet was an explosion of stone as the great iron wheel tore free from the church wall.

A ton of wrought iron fell. If anyone had been watching, they would have noticed that the wheel fell faster than gravity could account for. They would have noticed that it fell at an angle, almost as if it were drawn to the draccus. Almost as if Tehlu himself steered it toward the beast with a vengeful hand.

But there was no one there to see the truth of things. And there was no God guiding it. Only me.

CHAPTER EIGHTY-ONE

Pride

LOOKING DOWN I SAW the draccus pinned beneath the great wrought-iron wheel. It lay motionless and dark in front of the church, and despite the necessity of it all, I felt a pang of regret for killing the poor beast.

I had one long moment of exhausted pure relief. The autumn air was fresh and sweet despite the woodsmoke, and the stone roof of the church was cool under my feet. Feeling rather smug, I tucked the scale and loden-stone back into my travelsack. I drew a deep breath and looked out over the town I had saved.

Then I heard a grating noise and felt the roof shift beneath me. The front of the building sagged, crumbled, and I staggered as the world fell out from underneath me. I looked for a safe roof to leap to, but there were none close enough. I scrambled backward as the roof disintegrated into a mass of falling rubble.

Desperate, I leapt for the charred branches of the oak tree. I grabbed one, but it snapped under my weight. I tumbled through the branches, struck my head, and fell into darkness.

CHAPTER EIGHTY-TWO

Ash and Elm...

I WOKE IN A BED. In a room. In an inn. More than that was not immediately clear to me. It felt exactly like someone had hit me in the head with a church.

I had been cleaned and bandaged. Very thoroughly bandaged. Someone had seen fit to treat all my recent injuries no manner how minor. I had white linen around my head, my chest, my knee, and one of my feet. Someone had even cleaned and wrapped the mild abrasions on my hands and the knife wound from three days ago when Ambrose's thugs had tried to kill me.

The lump on my head seemed to be the worst of the lot. It throbbed and left me dizzy when I lifted my head. Moving was a lesson in punitive anatomy. I swung my feet off the edge of the bed and grimaced: *deep tissue trauma to the medial-poloni in the right leg.* I sat up: *oblique strain to the cartilage between the lower ribs.* I got to my feet: *minor spraining of the sub ... trans ... damn, what was that called?* I pictured Arwyl's face, frowning behind his round spectacles.

My clothes had been washed and mended. I put them on, moving slowly to savour all the exciting messages my body was sending me. I was glad there wasn't a mirror in the room, knowing I must look completely battered. The bandage around my head was rather irritating, but I decided to leave it on. From the way things felt, it might be the only thing keeping my head from falling into several different pieces.

I went to the window. It was overcast, and in the grey light the town looked awful, soot and ash everywhere. The shop across the street had been smashed like a dollhouse under a soldier's boot. People moved about slowly, sifting through the wreckage. The clouds were thick enough that I couldn't tell what time it was.

I heard a faint rush of air as the door opened, and I turned to see a young woman standing in the doorway. Young, pretty, unassuming, the sort of girl that always worked at little inns like this: a Nellie. Nell. The sort of girl who spent her life in a perpetual flinch because the innkeeper had a temper and a sharp tongue and wasn't afraid to show her the back of his hand. She gaped at me, obviously surprised that I was out of bed.

'Was anyone killed?' I asked.

She shook her head. 'The Liram boy got his arm broke pretty bad. And some folk got burned and such . . .' I felt my whole body relax. 'You shouldn't be up, sir. Doctor said you weren't likely to wake up at all. You should rest.'

'Is . . . has my cousin come back to town?' I asked. 'The girl who was out at the Mauthen farm. Is she here too?'

The young woman shook her head. 'It's just you, sir.'

'What time is it?'

'Supper's not quite ready, sir. But I can bring you something if you like.'

My travelsack had been left by the side of the bed. I lifted it up onto my shoulder, it felt odd with nothing inside except the scale and loden-stone. I looked around for my boots until I remembered I'd kicked them off to get better traction running around the rooftops last night.

I left the room with the girl trailing behind me and headed down to the common room. It was the same fellow behind the bar as before, still wearing his scowl.

I walked up to him. 'My cousin,' I said. 'Is she in town?'

The barman turned the scowl towards the doorway behind me as the young girl emerged. 'Nell, what in God's hell are you doing letting him up? I swear you haven't got the sense God gave a dog.'

So her name really was Nell. I would have found that amusing under different circumstances.

He turned to me and gave a smile that was really just a different sort of scowl. 'Lord boy, does your face hurt? It's killing me.' He chortled at his own joke.

I glared at him. 'I asked about my cousin.'

He shook his head. 'She hasn't come back. Good riddance to bad luck, I say.'

'Bring me bread, fruit, and whatever meat you have ready in the back,' I said. 'And a bottle of Avennish fruit wine. Strawberry if you have it.'

He leaned up against the bar and raised an eyebrow at me. His scowl reshaped itself into a small, patronising smile. 'No sense rushing about, son. The constable will be wanting to talk to you now that you're up.'

I clenched my teeth against my first choice of words and took a deep breath. 'Listen, I've had an exceptionally irritating couple of days, my head hurts in ways you don't have the full wit to understand, and I have a friend who might be in trouble.' I stared at him, icy in my calm. 'I have no desire to have things turn unpleasant. So I am asking you, kindly, to get me what I asked for.' I brought out my purse. 'Please.'

He looked at me, anger slowly bubbling up onto his face. 'You mouthy little swaggercock. If you don't show me a little respect, I'll sit you down and tie you to a chair until the constable comes.'

I tossed an iron drab onto the bar, keeping another clenched tight in my fist.

He scowled at it. 'What's that?'

I concentrated and felt a chill begin to bleed up my arm. 'That is your tip,' I said as a thin curl of smoke began to curl up from the drab. 'For your quick and courteous service.'

The varnish around the drab began to bubble and char in a black ring around the piece of iron. The man stared at it, mute and horrified.

'Now fetch me what I asked for,' I said, looking him in the eye. 'And a skin of water too. Or I will burn this place down around your ears and dance among the ashes and your charred, sticky bones.'

I came to the top of the greystone hill with my travelsack full. I was barefoot, out of breath, and my head was throbbing. Denna was nowhere to be seen.

Making a quick search of the area, I found all my scattered possessions where I'd left them. Both blankets. The waterskin was mostly empty but other than that, everything was here. Denna might have just stepped away for a call of nature.

I waited. I waited for longer than was entirely sensible. Then I called for her, softly at first, then louder, though my head throbbed when I shouted. Finally I just sat. All I could think about was Denna waking alone, aching, thirsty, and disoriented. What must she have thought?

I ate a little then, trying to think of what I could do next. I considered opening the bottle of wine, but knew it was a bad idea, as I undoubtedly had a mild concussion. I fought off the irrational worry that Denna might have wandered into the woods in a delirium, and that I should go look for her. I considered lighting a fire, so she would see it and come back . . .

But no. I knew she was simply gone. She woke, saw that I wasn't there, and left. She had said it herself when we left the inn in Trebon. *I leave where I'm not wanted. The rest I can make up as I go.* Did she think I had abandoned her?

Regardless, I knew in my bones that she was long gone from here. I packed up my travelsack. Then, just in case I was wrong, I wrote a note explaining what had happened and that I would wait for her in Trebon for a day. I used a piece of coal to write her name on one of the greystones, then drew an arrow down to where I left all the food I had brought, a bottle of water, and one of the blankets.

Then I left. My mood was not a pleasant one. My thoughts were not gentle or kind.

———————

When I came back to Trebon, dusk was closing over the city. I made my way onto the rooftops with a little more care than usual. I wouldn't be able to trust my balance until my head had a few days to mend itself.

Still it was no great feat to make it to the roof of the inn where I collected my boots. From this vantage, in the dim light, the town looked grim. The front half of the church had completely collapsed and nearly a third of the town had been scarred by fire. Some buildings were merely singed, but others were little more than ash and cinders. Despite my best efforts, the fire must have raged out of control after I was knocked unconscious.

I looked to the north and saw the peak of the greystone hill. I hoped to see the flicker of a fire, but there was nothing, of course.

I made my way over to the flat roof of the town hall and climbed the ladder to the cistern. It was almost empty. A few feet of water rippled near the bottom, far below where my knife pinned a charred shingle to the wall. That explained the state the town was in. When the water level had dropped below my makeshift sygaldry, the fire had flared up again. Still, it had slowed things down. If not for that, there might not be any town left at all.

Back at the inn a great many somber, sooty people were gathering to drink and gossip. My scowling friend was nowhere to be seen, but a cluster of folk were gathered around the bar, excitedly discussing something they saw there.

The mayor and constable were there too. As soon as they spotted me, they rushed me into a private room to talk.

I was tight-lipped and grim, and, after the events of the last several days, not terribly intimidated by the authority of two paunchy old men. They could tell, and that made them nervous. I had a headache and didn't feel like explaining myself, and was quite comfortable tolerating an uncomfortable silence. Because of this, they talked quite a bit, and in asking their own questions, they told me most of what I wanted to know.

The town's injuries were blessedly minor. Because it had been the harvest festival, no one had been caught sleeping. There were a lot of bruises, singed hair, and folk that had breathed more smoke than was good for them, but aside from a few bad burns and the fellow whose arm had been crushed by a falling timber, I looked to have had the worst of it.

They knew beyond all certainty that the draccus was a demon. A huge black demon breathing fire and poison. If there had been any slim sliver of doubt as to that fact, it had been laid to rest when the beast had been struck down by Tehlu's own iron.

It was also agreed upon that the demon beast had been responsible for the destruction of the Mauthen farm. A reasonable conclusion despite the fact that it was dead wrong. Trying to convince them of anything else would be a pointless waste of my time.

I had been found unconscious atop the iron wheel that had killed the demon. The local sawbone doctor had patched me up as best he could, and, unfamiliar with the remarkable thickness of my skull, expressed serious doubts as to whether or not I would ever wake.

At first the general opinion was that I was merely an unlucky bystander, or that I had somehow pried the wheel off the church. However, my miraculous recovery combined with the fact that I had charred a hole into the bar downstairs encouraged people to finally take notice of what a young boy and an old widow had been saying all day: that when the old oak had gone up like a torch, they had seen someone standing on the roof of the church. He was lit by the fire below. His arms were raised in front of him, almost as if he were praying . . .

Eventually the mayor and constable ran out of things to say to fill the silence, and merely sat there looking anxiously back and forth from me to each other.

It occurred to me they didn't see a penniless, ragged boy sitting across from them. They saw a mysterious battered figure who had killed a demon. I saw no reason to dissuade them. In fact it was high time I caught a piece of luck in this business. If they considered me some sort of hero or holy man, it gave me useful leverage.

'What did you do with the demon's body?' I asked and watched them relax. Until this point I had barely spoken a dozen words, responding to most of their tentative questions with grim silence.

'No worry about that, sir,' the constable said. 'We knew what to do with it.'

My stomach knotted, and I knew before they told me: they'd burned and buried it. The creature was a scientific marvel, and they had burned and buried it like trash. I knew naturalist scrivs in the Archives who would have cut off their hands to study such a rare creature. I had even hoped, deep in my heart, that bringing such an opportunity to their attention might win me my way back into the Archives.

And the scales and bones. Hundreds of pounds of denatured iron that alchemists would have fought over . . .

The mayor nodded eagerly and singsonged, 'Dig a pit that's ten by two. Ash and elm and rowan too.' He cleared his throat. 'Though it had to be a bigger hole than that, of course. Everyone took a turn to get it done as quickly as possible.' He held up his hand, proudly displaying a set of fresh blisters.

I closed my eyes and fought down the urge to throw things around the room and curse them in eight languages. That explained why the town was still in such a sorry state. Everyone had been busy burning and burying a creature worth a king's ransom.

Still, there was nothing to be done about it. I doubted my new reputation would be enough to protect me if they caught me trying to dig it up. 'The girl that survived the Mauthen wedding,' I said. 'Has anyone seen her today?'

The mayor looked at the constable questioningly. 'Not that I've heard. Do you think she was connected to the beast in some way?'

'What?' the question was so absurd I didn't understand it at first. 'No! Don't be ridiculous.' I scowled at them. The last thing I needed was to somehow implicate Denna in all this. 'She was helping me in my work.' I said, careful to keep things ambiguous.

The mayor glared at the constable, then looked back to me. 'Is your . . . work finished here?' He asked carefully, as if afraid of giving offense. 'I certainly don't mean to pry into your affairs . . . but . . .' He licked his lips nervously. 'Why did this happen? Are we safe?'

'You're as safe as I can make you,' I said ambiguously. It sounded like a heroic thing to say. If all I was going to gain from this was a bit of reputation, I might as well make sure it was the right sort.

Then I had an idea. 'To be certain of your safety, I need one thing.' I leaned forward in my chair, lacing my fingers together. 'I need to know what Mauthen dug up on Barrow Hill.'

I saw them look at each other, thinking: *How does he know about that?*

I leaned back in the chair, fighting the urge to smile like a tomcat in a dovecote. 'If I know what Mauthen found up there, I can take steps to make sure that this sort of thing doesn't happen again. I know it was a secret, but someone in town is bound to know more. Spread the word, and have anyone who knows anything come talk to me.'

I came to my feet smoothly. It took a conscious effort not to wince at the various twinges and aches. 'But have them come quickly. I leave tomorrow evening. I have pressing business to the south.'

Then I swept out the door, my cloak trailing rather dramatically behind me. I am a trouper to my bones, and when the scene is set, I know how to make an exit.

I spent the next day eating good food and dozing in my soft bed. I took a bath, tended to my various wounds, and generally took a well-deserved rest. A few people stopped by to tell me what I already knew. Mauthen had dug up barrow stones and found something buried there. What was it? Just something. No one knew more than that.

I was sitting beside my bed toying with the idea of writing a song about the draccus when I heard a timid tapping at my door, so faint I almost missed it. 'Come in.'

The door opened a crack, then wider. A young girl of thirteen or so looked around nervously and scurried inside, closing the door softly behind her. She had curling, mousy brown hair and a pale face with two spots of colour high on each cheek. Her eyes were hollow and dark, as if she had been crying, or missing sleep, or both.

'You wanted to know what Mauthen dug up?' She looked at me, then away.

'What's your name?' I asked gently.

'Verainia Greyflock,' she said dutifully. Then dropped a hurried curtsey, looking at the floor.

'That's a lovely name,' I said. 'A verian is a tiny red flower.' I smiled, trying to set her at her ease. 'Have you ever seen one?' She shook her head, eyes still on the floor. 'I'm guessing no one calls you Verainia though. Are you a Nina?'

She looked up at that. A faint smile showed itself on her stricken face. 'That's what my gran calls me.'

'Come sit, Nina.' I nodded to the bed, as it was the only other place to sit in the room.

She sat, her hands twisting nervously in her lap. 'I seen it. The thing they got out of the barrow.' She looked up at me, then down at her hands again. 'Jimmy, Mauthen's youngest boy, he showed me.'

My heart beat faster. 'What was it?'

'It was a big fancy pot,' she said softly. 'About this high.' She held her hand about three feet off the ground. It was shaking. 'It had all sorts of writings and pictures on it. Really fancy. I haven't ever seen colors like that. And some of the paints were shiny like silver and gold.'

'Pictures of what?' I asked, fighting to keep my voice calm.

'People,' she said. 'Mostly people. There was a woman holding a broken sword, and a man next to a dead tree, and another man with a dog biting his leg . . .' she trailed off.

'Was there one with white hair and black eyes?'

She looked at me wide-eyed, nodded. 'Gave me the all-overs.' She shivered.

The Chandrian. It was a vase showing the Chandrian and their signs.

'Can you remember anything else about the pictures?' I asked. 'Take your time, think hard.'

She thought about it. 'There was one with no face, just a hood with nothing inside. There was a mirror by his feet and there was a bunch of moons over him. You know, full moon, half moon, sliver moon.' She looked down, thinking. 'And there was a woman . . .' She blushed. 'With some of her clothes off.'

'Can you remember anything else?' I asked. She shook her head. 'What about the writing?'

Nina shook her head. 'This was all foreign writing. It didn't say anything.'

'Do you think you could draw any of the writing you saw on it?'

She shook her head again. 'I only saw it for half a moment,' she said. 'Me and Jimmy knew we'd catch a beating if his da caught us.' Her eyes welled up with sudden tears. 'Are demons going to be coming for me too, cause I seen it?'

I shook my head reassuringly, but she burst into tears anyway. 'I been so scared since what happened out at Mauthen's,' she sobbed. 'I keep having dreams. I know they're going to come get me.'

I moved to sit next to her on the bed and put my arm around her, making comforting noises. Her sobbing slowly wound down. 'Nothing is going to come and get you.'

She looked up at me. She was no longer crying, but I could see the truth of things in her eyes. Underneath it all she was still terrified. No amount of gentle words would be enough to reassure her.

I stood and went over to my cloak. 'Let me give you something,' I said, reaching into one of the pockets. I brought a piece of the sympathy lamp I was working on in the Fishery, it was a disk of bright metal covered with intricate sygaldry on one side.

I brought it back to her. 'I got this charm when I was in Veloran. Far away, across the Stormwal mountains. It is a most excellent charm against demons.' I took her hand and pressed it into her palm.

Nina looked down at it, then up at me. 'Don't you need it?'

I shook my head. 'I have other ways of keeping safe.'

She clutched it, tears spilling down her cheeks again. 'Oh thank you. I'll keep it with me all the time.' Her hands were white-knuckled around it.

She would lose it. Not soon, but in a year, or two, or ten. It was human nature, and when that happened, she would be even worse off than before. 'There's no need for that,' I said quickly. 'Here's how it works.' I took her hand that clutched the piece of metal and wrapped it in my own. 'Close your eyes.'

Nina closed her eyes, and I slowly recited the first ten lines of *Ve Valora Sartane*. Not very appropriate really, but it was all I could think of at the time. Tema is an impressive sounding language, especially if you have a good dramatic baritone, which I did.

I finished and she opened her eyes. They were full of wonder, not tears.

'Now it's tuned to you,' I said. 'No matter what, no matter where it is, it will protect you and keep you safe. You could even break it and melt it down and the charm would still hold.'

She threw her arms around me and kissed my cheek. Then stood suddenly, blushing. No longer pale and stricken, her eyes were bright. I hadn't noticed before, but she was beautiful.

She left soon after that and I sat for a while on my bed, thinking.

Over the last month I had pulled a woman from a blazing inferno. I had called fire and lighting down on assassins and escaped to safety. I had even killed something that could have been either a dragon or a demon, depending on your point of view.

But there in that room was the first time I actually felt like any sort of hero. If you are looking for a reason for the man I would eventually become, if you are looking for a beginning, look there.

CHAPTER EIGHTY-THREE

Return

THAT EVENING I GATHERED up my things and made my way down to the common room. The townsfolk eyed me and murmured excitedly among themselves. I overheard a few comments as I walked to the bar, and realised that yesterday most of them had seen me wrapped in bandages, presumably with terrible wounds underneath. Today the bandages were gone, and all they saw were some minor bruises. Another miracle. I fought to keep from smiling.

The sullen innkeeper told me that he couldn't possibly dream of charging me, seeing as how the entire town was in my debt and all that. I insisted. No, no. Absolutely not. He wouldn't hear of it. If only there was something else he could do to show his gratitude.

I put on a thoughtful expression. Now that he mentioned it, I said, if he happened to have another bottle of that lovely strawberry wine . . .

I made my way to Evesdown docks and got a seat on a barge heading downriver. Then, while I was waiting, I asked if any of the dockworkers had seen a young woman come through here in the last couple days. Dark haired, pretty . . .

They had. She had been by yesterday afternoon and shipped downriver. I felt a certain amount of relief, knowing that she was safe and relatively sound. But other than that, I didn't know what to think. Why hadn't she come to Trebon? Did she think I had abandoned her? Did she remember anything we had talked about that night as we lay on the greystone together?

We docked in Imre a few hours after dawn, and I went straightaway to Devi's. After some spirited bargaining, I gave her the loden-stone and a single talent in order to wipe out my extremely short term loan of twenty talents. I still owed my original debt, but after all I'd been through, a four-talent debt no longer seemed terribly ominous, despite the fact that my purse was largely empty again.

It took a while to put my life back together. I'd only been gone four days, but I needed to make apologies and give explanations to all manner of people. I'd missed an appointment with Count Threpe, and two meetings with Manet, and a lunch with Fela. Anker's had gone without a musician for two nights. Even Auri reproached me gently for not coming to visit her.

I'd missed classes with Kilvin, Elxa Dal, and Arwyl. They all accepted my appologies with gracious disapproval. I knew that when next term's tuitions were set, I would end up paying for my sudden, largely unexplained absence.

Most important were Wil and Sim. They had heard rumours of a student attacked in an alley. Given Ambrose's smugger-than-usual expression of late, they expected I had been run out of town, or, at worst, that I was weighted down with rocks at the bottom of the Omethi.

They were the only ones that got a real explanation of what had happened. Though I didn't tell them the entire truth about why I was interested in the Chandrian, I did tell them the whole story, and showed them the scale. They were appropriately amazed, though they did tell me in plain terms that next time I would leave a note for them or there would be hell to pay.

And I looked for Denna, hoping to make my most important explanation of all. But, as always, looking did no good.

CHAPTER EIGHTY-FOUR

A Sudden Storm

IN THE END I found Denna as I always do, through pure accident.

I was walking hurriedly along, my mind full of other things, when I turned a corner and had to pull up short to keep from running headlong into her.

We both stood there for a half-second, startled and speechless. Despite the fact that I'd been searching out her face in every shadow and carriage window for days, the sight of her stunned me. I'd remembered the shape of her eyes, but not the weight of them. Their darkness, but not their depth. Her closeness pressed the breath out of my chest, as if I'd suddenly been thrust deep underwater.

I'd spent long hours thinking about how this meeting might go. I had played the scene a thousand times in my mind. I feared she would be distant, aloof. That she would spurn me for leaving her alone in the woods. That she would be silent and sullenly hurt. I worried that she might cry, or curse me, or simply turn and leave.

Denna gave me a delighted smile. 'Kvothe!' She caught up my hand and pressed it between her own. 'I've missed you. Where have you been?'

I felt myself go weak with relief. 'Oh, you know. Here and there.' I made a nonchalant gesture. 'Around.'

'You left me dry in the dock the other day,' she said with a mock-serious glare. 'I waited, but the tide never came.'

I was about to explain things to her when Denna gestured to a man standing beside her. 'Forgive my rudeness. Kvothe, this is Lentaren.' I hadn't even noticed him. 'Lentaren, Kvothe.'

Lentaren was tall and lean. Well muscled, well dressed, and well-bred. He had a jawline a mason would have been proud of and straight, white teeth. He looked like Prince Gallant out of a storybook. He reeked of money.

He smiled at me, his manner easy, friendly. 'Nice to meet you, Kvothe,' he said with a graceful half-bow.

I returned the bow on pure reflex, smiling my most charming smile. 'At your service, Lentaren.'

I turned back to Denna. 'We should have lunch one of these days,' I said blithely, arching one eyebrow ever so slightly, asking, *is this Master Ash?* 'I have some interesting stories for you.'

'Absolutely,' she shook her head slightly, telling me, *No.* 'You left before you could finish your last one. I was terribly disappointed that I missed the end. Distraught, in fact.'

'Oh it's just the same thing you've heard before a hundred times before,' I said. 'Prince Gallant kills the dragon but loses the treasure and the girl.'

'Ah, a tragedy,' Denna looked down. 'Not the ending I'd hoped for, but no more than I expected, I suppose.'

'It would be something of a tragedy if it stopped there,' I admitted. 'But it depends on how you look at it, really. I prefer to think of it as a story that's waiting for an appropriately uplifting sequel.'

A carriage trundled by on the road and Lentaren stepped out of the way, incidentally brushing up against Denna as he moved. She took hold of his arm absentmindedly. 'I don't generally go in for serial stories,' she said, her expression momentarily serious and unreadable. Then she shrugged and gave me a hint of a wry smile. 'But I've certainly changed my mind about these things before. Maybe you'll convince me otherwise.'

I gestured to the lute case I carried slung over my shoulder. 'I still play at Anker's most nights if you'd like to stop in . . .'

'I will.' Denna sighed and looked up at Lentaren. 'We're already late, aren't we?'

He squinted up at the sun and nodded. 'We are. But we can still catch them if we hurry.'

She turned back to me. 'I'm sorry, we have a riding appointment.'

'I would never dream of keeping you,' I said, graciously stepping to one side, out of their way.

Lentaren and I nodded politely to each other. 'I'll come find you before too long,' she said, turning to face me as they walked past.

'Go on.' I nodded in the direction they'd been heading. 'Don't let me keep you.'

They turned to go. I watched them walk through the cobbled streets of Imre. Together.

———————

Wil and Sim were waiting for me by the time I arrived. They had already claimed a bench with a good view of the fountain in front of the Eolian. Water flared up around statuary nymphs being chased by a satyr.

I laid my lute case down beside the bench and absentmindedly flipped open the lid, thinking my lute might enjoy the feel of a little sun on its strings. If you aren't a musician, I don't expect you to understand.

Wil handed me an apple as I took a seat next to them. The wind brushed though the square and I watched the spray from the fountain move like gauzy curtains in the wind. A few red maple leaves danced circles on the cobblestones. I watched them as they skipped and twirled, tracing strange, complicated patterns in the empty air.

'I'm guessing you finally found Denna?' Wilem asked after a while.

I nodded without looking away from the leaves. I didn't really feel like explaining.

'I can tell because you're quiet,' he said.

'Didn't go well?' Sim asked gently.

'Didn't turn out the way I'd hoped,' I said.

They nodded sagely and there was another moment of silence.

'I was thinking about what you told us,' Wil said. 'What your Denna said. There is a hole in her story.'

Sim and I looked at him, curious.

'She said she was looking for her patron,' Wilem pointed out. 'She was travelling with you to look for him. But later she said she knew he was safe because he—' Wil hesitated significantly, '—met with her as she was heading back to the burning farm. It does not fit. Why would she hunt for him if she knew he was safe?'

I hadn't considered that. Before I could think of a response, Simmon shook his head. 'She was just making an excuse to spend time with him,' he said as if it were plain as day.

Wilem frowned a little.

Sim looked back and forth between us, plainly surprised he had to explain himself. 'It's obvious she has a thing for you,' he said, and began counting on his fingers. 'She finds you at Anker's. She comes to get you that night at Eolian when we're drinking. She makes up an excuse to wander around the middle of nowhere with you for a couple of days . . .'

'Sim,' I said, exasperated. 'If she was interested I'd be able to find her more than once in a month of searching.'

'That's a logical fallacy,' Sim pointed out eagerly. 'False cause. All that proves is that you're lousy at finding her, or that she's hard to find. Not that she's not interested.'

'In fact,' Wilem pointed out, taking up Simmon's side, 'since she finds you more often, it seems likely that she must spend a fair amount of time looking for you. You are not easy to track down. That indicates interest.'

I thought about the note she had left me, and for a moment I entertained the thought that Sim might be right. I felt a faint hope flicker in my chest, remembering that night we lay atop the greystone.

Then I remembered that Denna had been delirious out of her mind that night. And I remembered Denna on Lentaren's arm. I thought of tall, handsome, wealthy Lentaren and all the other countless men who had something worthwhile to offer her. Something more than a good singing voice and manly bravado.

'You know I'm right!' Simmon pushed his hair out of his eyes, laughing boyishly. 'You can't argue your way out of this one! She's obviously stupid for you. And you're just plain stupid, so it's a great match.'

I sighed. 'Sim, I'm happy to have her as a friend. She's a delightful person and I'm glad to spend time with her. That's all there is.' I forced the proper amount of jovial unconcern into my voice so Sim would take me at my word and drop the subject for the time being.

Sim looked at me for a moment, then shrugged it off. 'If that's the case,' he said, gesturing with his piece of chicken, 'Fela talks about you all the time. Thinks you're a hell of a guy. Plus the whole saving her life thing. I'm pretty sure you have a chance there.'

I shrugged, watching the patterns the wind made in the fountain's spray.

'You know what we should . . .' Sim stopped midthought, staring past me, his expression going suddenly blank.

I turned to see what he was looking at and saw my lute case, empty. My lute was gone. I looked around wildly, ready to spring to my feet and dash off searching for it. But there was no need – a few feet away stood Ambrose and a few of his friends. He held my lute loosely in one hand.

'Oh, merciful Tehlu,' Simmon muttered behind me. Then at a normal volume he said, 'Give it back, Ambrose.'

'Quiet, E'lir,' Ambrose snapped. 'This is none of your concern.'

I got to my feet, keeping my eyes on him, on my lute. I had come to think of Ambrose as taller than me, but when I stood I saw that we were eye level with each other. Ambrose seemed a bit surprised as well.

'Give it to me,' I said, and stretched out my hand. I was surprised to see that it wasn't shaking. I was shaking inside: half fear, half fury.

Two parts of me tried to speak at the same time. The first part cried, *Please don't do anything to it. Not again. Don't break it. Please give it back. Don't hold it by the neck like that.* The other half of me was chanting, *I hate you, I hate you, I hate you,* like spitting out mouthfuls of blood.

I took a step forward. 'Give it to me.' My voice sounded odd to my own ears, emotionless and flat. Flat as my outstretched palm. I had stopped shaking inside.

He paused for a moment, caught unaware by something in my tone. I could sense his unease – I wasn't acting the way he had expected. Behind me, I could hear Wilem and Simmon hold their breath. Behind Ambrose, his friends paused, suddenly unsure.

Ambrose smiled and cocked an eyebrow. 'But I've written a song for you, and it needs to be accompanied.' He gripped the lute roughly and dragged his fingers across the strings with no thought for rhythm or tune. People stopped to watch as he sang:

> *'There once was a ravel named Kvothe*
> *Whose tongue was quick at quipping.*
> *The masters thought him clever*
> *And rewarded him with whipping.'*

Quite a few passersby had stopped to watch by this point, smiling and laughing at Ambrose's little show. Encouraged, Ambrose made a sweeping bow.

'Everyone sing!' he shouted, raising his hands like an orchestra conductor, gesturing with my lute like a baton.

I took another step forward. 'Give it back, or I will kill you.' At that moment, I meant it in perfect earnest.

Everything grew quiet again. Seeing he wasn't going to get the rise he had expected from me, Ambrose affected nonchalance. 'Some people have no sense of humour,' he said with a sigh. 'Catch.'

He tossed it to me, but lutes are not meant to be tossed. It twisted awkwardly in the air, and when I grabbed, there was nothing in my hands. Whether he was clumsy or cruel makes not the slightest difference to me. My lute hit the cobblestones bowl first and made a splintering noise.

The sound reminded me of the terrible noise my father's lute had made, crushed beneath my body in a soot-streaked alley in Tarbean. I bent to pick it up and it made a noise like a wounded animal. Ambrose half-turned to look back at me and I saw flickers of amusement play across his face.

I opened my mouth to howl, to cry, to curse him. But something *other* tore from my throat, a word I did not know and could not remember.

Then all I could hear was the sound of the wind. It roared into the courtyard like a sudden storm. A nearby carriage slid sideways across the cobblestones, its horses rearing up in panic. Sheet music was torn from someone's hands to streak around us like strange lightning. I was pushed forward a step. Everyone was pushed by the wind. Everyone but Ambrose, who pinwheeled to the ground as if struck by the hand of God.

Then everything was still again. Papers fell, twisting like autumn leaves. People looked around, dazed, their hair tousled and clothes in disarray. Several people staggered as they braced against a storm that was no longer there.

My throat hurt. My lute was broken.

Ambrose staggered to his feet. He held his arm awkwardly at his side and blood was running down from his scalp. The look of wild, confused fear he gave me was a brief, sweet pleasure. I considered shouting at him again, wondering what would happen. Would the wind come again? Would the ground swallow him up?

I heard a horse whinnying in panic. People began to pour from the Eolian and the other buildings around the courtyard. Musicians looked around wildly, and everyone was talking at once.

'. . . was that?'

'. . . notes are all over. Help me before they get . . .'

'. . . did it. Him over there, with the red . . .'

'. . . demon. A demon of wind and . . .'

I looked around in mute confusion until Wilem and Simmon hurried me away.

'We didn't know where to take him,' Simmon said to Kilvin.

'Say it all to me again,' Kilvin said calmly. 'But this time only one talks.' He pointed at Wilem. 'Try to put the words all in a tidy row.'

We were in Kilvin's office. The door was closed and the curtains drawn. Wilem began to explain what had happened. As he gained speed he switched to Siaru. Kilvin kept nodding along, his face thoughtful. Simmon listened intently, occasionally interjecting a word or two.

I sat on a stool nearby. My mind was a whirl of confusion and half-formed questions. My throat was sore. My body was weary and full of sour adrenaline. In the middle of it all, deep in the center of my chest, a piece of me burned in anger like a forge coal fanned red and hot. All around me there was a great numbness, as if I were sealed in wax ten inches thick. There was no Kvothe, only the confusion, the anger, and the numbness wrapping him. I was like a sparrow in a storm, unable to find a safe branch to cling to. Unable to control the tumbling motion of my flight.

Wilem was reaching the end of his explanation when Elodin entered the room without knocking or announcing himself. Wilem fell silent. I spared the Master Namer half a glance then looked back toward the shattered lute in my hands. As I turned it over in my hands, one of its sharp edges cut my finger. I blankly watched the blood well up and fall to the floor.

Elodin came to stand directly in front of me, not bothering to speak to anyone else. 'Kvothe?'

'He's not right, Master,' Simmon said, his voice shrill with worry. 'He's gone all dumb. He won't say a thing.' While I heard the words, knew they had meaning, even knew the meanings that belonged to them, I couldn't pull any sense from them.

'I think he struck his head,' Wilem said. 'He looks at you, but nothing is there. His eyes are like a dog's eyes.'

'Kvothe?' Elodin repeated. When I didn't respond or look up from my lute he reached forward and gently tipped my chin up until I met his eye. 'Kvothe.'

I blinked.

He looked at me. His dark eyes steadied me somewhat. Slowed the storm inside me. '*Aerlevsedi*,' he said. 'Say it.'

'What?' Simmon said somewhere in the distant background. 'Wind?'

'*Aerlevsedi*,' Elodin repeated patiently, his dark eyes intent upon my face.

'*Aerlevsedi*,' I said numbly.

Elodin closed his eyes briefly, peacefully. As if he were trying to catch a faint strain of music wafting gently on a breeze. Unable to see his eyes, I began to drift. I looked back down toward the broken lute in my hands, but before my gaze wandered too far he caught my chin again, tilting my face up.

His eyes caught mine. The numbness faded, but the storm still turned inside my head. Then Elodin's eyes changed. He stopped looking toward me and looked *into* me. That is the only way I can describe it. He looked deep into me, not into my eyes, but through my eyes. His gaze went into me and settled solidly in my chest, as if he had both his hands inside me, feeling the shape of my lungs, the movement of my heart, the heat of my anger, the pattern of the storm that thundered inside me.

He leaned forward and his lips brushed my ear. I felt his breath. He spoke . . . and the storm stilled. I found a place to land.

There is a game all children try at some time or another. You fling out your arms and spin round and round, watching as the world blurs. First you are disoriented, but if you continue to spin long enough the world resolves itself, and you are no longer dizzy as you spin with the world blurring around you.

Then you stop and the world lurches into regular shape. The dizziness strikes you like a thunderclap, everything lurches, moves. The world tilts around you.

That is what happened when Elodin stilled the storm in my head. Suddenly, violently dizzy I cried out and raised my hands to keep myself from falling sideways, falling upward, falling inward. I felt arms catch me as my feet tangled in the stool and I began to topple to the floor.

It was terrifying, but it faded. By the time I recovered, Elodin was gone.

CHAPTER EIGHTY-FIVE

Hands Against Me

SIMMON AND WILEM TOOK me to my room at Anker's where I fell into bed and spent eighteen hours behind the doors of sleep. When I woke the next day I felt surprisingly good, considering I had slept in my clothes and my bladder felt stretched to the size of a sweetmelon.

Fortune smiled on me, giving me enough time for a meal and a bath before one of Jamison's errand boys tracked me down. I was needed in the Masters' Hall. I was due to be on the horns in half an hour.

Ambrose and I stood before the masters' table. He had accused me of malfeasance. In retaliation I had accused him of theft, destruction of property, and Conduct Unbecoming a Member of the Arcanum. After my previous experience on the horns I had familiarised myself with the *Rerum Codex*, the University's official rules. I had read them twice to be certain of how things were done around here. I knew them like the backs of my hands.

Unfortunately, this meant I knew exactly how much trouble I was in. The charge of malfeasance was a serious one. If they found me guilty of intentionally harming Ambrose, I would be whipped and expelled from the University.

There was little doubt that I had hurt Ambrose. He was bruised and limping. A garish red abrasion colored his forehead. He wore a sling as well, but I was fairly certain that was merely a piece of drama he had added on his own.

The trouble was, I didn't have the slightest idea what had really happened. I hadn't had the opportunity to speak with anyone. Not even to thank Elodin for helping me yesterday in Kilvin's shop.

The masters allowed each of us to speak our piece. Ambrose was on his best behaviour, which meant he was very polite when he spoke at all. After a while, I began to suspect that his sluggishness might be from a too-liberal dose of painkiller. By the glaze in his eyes, my guess was laudanum.

'Let's deal with the grievances in order of their severity,' the Chancellor said after we had related our sides of the story.

Master Hemme made a gesture, and the Chancellor nodded for him to speak. 'We should pare the charges down before we vote,' Hemme said. 'E'lir Kvothe's complaints are redundant. You cannot charge a student with both theft *and* destruction of the same property, it is either one or the other.'

'Why do you say that, Master?' I asked politely.

'Theft implies the possession of another's property,' Hemme said in reasonable tones. 'How can you possess something that you have destroyed? One charge or the other should be set aside.'

The Chancellor looked at me. 'E'lir Kvothe, do you wish to set aside one of your complaints?'

'No sir.'

'Then I call for a vote to set aside the charge of theft,' Hemme said.

The Chancellor glared at Hemme, chastising him silently for speaking out of turn, then turned back to me. 'Stubbornness in the face of reason is hardly laudable E'lir, and Master Hemme makes a convincing argument.'

'Master Hemme makes a flawed argument,' I said evenly. 'Theft implies *acquisition* of another's property. It is ridiculous to imply you cannot destroy what you have stolen.'

I saw a few of the masters nod at this, but Hemme persisted. 'Master Lorren, what is the punishment for theft?'

'The student may be given no more than two single lashes across the back,' Lorren recited. 'And must return the property or the price of the property plus a fine of one silver talent.'

'And the punishment for destruction of property?'

'The student must pay for the replacement or repair of the property.'

'You see?' Hemme said. 'There is the possibility that he would have to pay twice for the same lute. There is no justice in that. It would be punishing him twice for the same thing.'

'No Master Hemme,' I interjected. 'It would be punishing him for theft and for destruction of property.' The Chancellor gave me the same look Hemme had earned before for speaking out of turn, but I bulled ahead. 'If I had lent him my lute and he had broken it, that would be one matter. If he had stolen it and left it intact, that would be another. It is not one or the other. It is both.'

The Chancellor rapped his knuckles on the table to quiet us. 'I take it then, that you will not set aside one of the charges?'

'I will not.'

Hemme raised a hand and was recognised. 'I call for a vote to strike the charge of theft.'

'All in favour?' the Chancellor said wearily. Hemme raised his hand, as did Brandeur, Mandrag, and Lorren. 'Five and a half to four: grievance stands.'

The Chancellor pressed on before anyone could slow things down. 'Who finds Re'lar Ambrose guilty of destruction of property?' Everyone raised their hands but Hemme and Brandeur. The Chancellor looked at me. 'How much did you pay for your lute?'

'Nine talents and six.' I lied, knowing it to be a reasonable price.

Ambrose roused himself at this. 'Come now. You've never held ten talents in your life.'

Annoyed, the Chancellor rapped his knuckles at the interruption. But Brandeur raised a hand to speak. 'Re'lar Ambrose does raise an interesting point. How does a student who came to us destitute come by such money?'

A few of the masters looked at me speculatively. I looked down as if embarrassed. 'I won it playing corners, sirs.'

There was an amused mutter. Elodin laughed out loud. The Chancellor rapped the table. 'Re'lar Ambrose to be fined nine talents and six. Does any master oppose this action?'

Hemme raised his hand and was voted down.

'On the grievance of theft. Number of lashes sought?'

'None,' I said, raising a few eyebrows.

'Who finds Re'lar Ambrose guilty of theft?' the Chancellor called out. Hemme, Brandeur, and Lorren kept their hands down. 'Re'lar Ambrose to be fined ten talents and six. Does any master oppose this action?'

Hemme kept his hand down this time, looking sullen.

The Chancellor took a deep breath and let it out in a rush. 'Master Archivist, what is the punishment for Conduct Unbecoming a Member of the Arcanum?'

'Student may be fined, lashed, suspended from the Arcanum, or expelled from the University depending on the severity of grievance,' Lorren said calmly.

'Punishment sought?'

'Suspension from the Arcanum,' I said as if it were the most sensible thing in the world.

Ambrose's composure broke. 'What?' he said incredulously, turning to face me.

Hemme chimed in. 'Herma, this is growing ridiculous.'

The Chancellor looked at me with a tinge of reproach. 'I'm afraid I must agree with Master Hemme, E'lir Kvothe. I hardly think that this is grounds for suspension.'

'I disagree,' I said, attempting to bring all my powers of persuasion to bear. 'Think on what you've heard. For no other reason than his personal distaste for me, Ambrose chose to publicly mock me, then steal and destroy the only thing I owned of any value.

'Is this the sort of behaviour that a member of the Arcanum should exhibit? Is this the attitude you wish to cultivate in the rest of the Re'lar? Are petty meanness and spite characteristics you approve of in students who seek to become arcanists? It has been two hundred years since we have seen an arcanist burned. If you succeed in giving guilders to petty children such as this,' I gestured to Ambrose. 'That long-standing peace and safety will be over in a scant handful of years.'

It swayed them. I could see it on their faces. Ambrose moved nervously beside me, his eyes darting from face to face.

After a moment of silence the Chancellor called for the vote. 'Those in favor of suspension for Re'lar Ambrose?'

Arwyl's hand went up, followed by Lorren's, Elodin's, Elxa Dal's . . . There was a tense moment. I looked from Kilvin to the Chancellor, hoping to see one of their hands join the others.

The moment passed. 'Grievance failed.' Ambrose let out a breath. I was only slightly disappointed. In fact, I was rather surprised I had managed to carry it as far as I had.

'Now,' the Chancellor said as if preparing himself for a great effort. 'The grievance of malfeasance against E'lir Kvothe.'

'From four to fifteen single lashes and mandatory expulsion from the University,' Lorren recited.

'Lashes sought?'

Ambrose turned to look at me. I could see the wheels in his mind turning, trying to calculate how heavy a price he could make me pay and still have the masters vote in his favour. 'Six.'

I felt a leaden fear settle into the pit of my stomach. I didn't care one whit about the lashes. I would take two dozen if it would keep me from being expelled. If I were thrown from the University my life was over. 'Chancellor?' I said.

He gave me a tired, kindly look. His eyes said he understood, but that he had no choice but to see things through to their natural end. The gentle pity in his look frightened me. He knew what was going to happen. 'Yes, E'lir Kvothe?'

'Might I say a few things?'

'You have already given your defense,' he said firmly.

'But I don't even know what I did!' I burst out, panic overwhelming my composure.

'Six lashes and expulsion,' the Chancellor carried on in an official voice, ignoring my outburst. 'All those in favour?'

Hemme raised his hand. Brandeur and Arwyl followed. My heart sank as I saw the Chancellor raise his hand, and Lorren, and Kilvin, and Elxa Dal. Last of all was Elodin who smiled lazily and waggled the fingers of his upraised hand, as if waving. All nine hands against me. I was to be expelled from the University. My life was over.

CHAPTER EIGHTY-SIX

The Fire Itself

'SIX LASHES AND EXPULSION,' the Chancellor said heavily.

Expulsion, I thought numbly, as if I had never heard the word before. *To expel, to cast violently away.* I could feel Ambrose's satisfaction radiating outward. For a second I was afraid that I was going to be violently ill right there in front of everyone.

'Does any master oppose this action?' the Chancellor asked ritualistically as I looked down at my feet.

'I do,' the stirring voice could only be Elodin's.

'All in favour of suspending expulsion?' I looked up again in time to see Elodin's hand. Elxa Dal's. Kilvin, Lorren, the Chancellor. All hands save Hemme's. I almost laughed out of shock and sheer disbelief. Elodin gave me his boyish smile again.

'Expulsion repealed,' the Chancellor said firmly and I felt Ambrose's satisfaction flicker and wane beside me. 'Are there any further issues?' I caught an odd note in the Chancellor's voice. He was expecting something.

It was Elodin who spoke. 'I move that Kvothe be raised to the rank of Re'lar.'

'All in favour?' All hands save Hemme's were raised in a single motion. 'Kvothe is raised to Re'lar with Elodin as sponsor on the fifth of Fallow. Meeting adjourned.' He pushed himself up from the table and made his way to the door.

'What?!' Ambrose yelled, looking around as if he couldn't decide who he was asking. Finally he scampered off after Hemme, who was making a quick exit behind the Chancellor and the majority of the other masters. I noticed he wasn't limping nearly as much as he had before the trial began.

Bewildered, I stood stupidly until Elodin came over and shook my unresponsive hand. 'Confused?' he asked. 'Come walk with me. I'll explain.'

———

The bright afternoon sunlight was a shock after the shadowy cool of Hollows. Elodin awkwardly pulled his master's robes up over his head. Underneath he was wearing a simple white shirt and a pair of rather disreputable looking pants held up by a piece of frayed rope. I saw for the first time that he was barefoot. The tops of his feet showed the same healthy tan as his arms and face.

'Do you know what *Re'lar* means?' he asked me conversationally.

'It translates as "speaker",' I said.

'Do you know what it *means*?' he stressed the word.

'Not really,' I admitted.

Elodin drew a deep breath. 'Once upon a time, there was a University. It was built in the dead ruins of an older University. It wasn't very big, perhaps fifty people in all. But it was the best University for miles and miles, so people came and learned and left. There was a small group of people who gathered there. People whose knowledge went beyond mathematics and grammar and rhetoric.

'They started a smaller group inside the University. They called it the Arcanum and it was a very small, very secret thing. They had a ranking system among themselves, and your rise through those ranks was due to prowess and nothing else. One entered this group by proving they could see things for what they really were. They became E'lir, which means see-er. How do you think they became Re'lar?' He looked at me expectantly.

'By speaking.'

He laughed. 'Right!' He stopped and turned to face me. 'But speaking what?' His eyes were bright and sharp.

'Words?'

'Names,' he said excitedly. 'Names are the shape of the world, and a man who can speak them is on the road to power. Back in the beginning, the Arcanum was a small collection of men who understood things. Men who knew powerful names. They taught a few students, slowly, carefully encouraging them toward power and wisdom. And magic. Real magic.' He looked around at the buildings and milling students. 'In those days the Arcanum was a strong brandy. Now it is well-watered wine.'

I waited until I was sure he was finished. 'Master Elodin, what happened yesterday?' I held my breath and hoped beyond hope for an intelligible answer.

He gave me a quizzical look. 'You called the name of the wind,' he said as if the answer were obvious.

'But what does that mean? And what do you mean by *name*? Is it just a name like "Kvothe" or "Elodin"? Or is it more like "Taborlin knew the names of many things." '

'Like both,' he said, waving to a pretty girl leaning out of a second-story window.

'But how can a name do something like that? "Kvothe" and "Elodin" are just sounds we make, they don't have any power by themselves.'

Elodin raised his eyebrows at this. 'Really? Watch.' He looked down the street. 'Nathan!' he shouted. A boy turned to look in our direction. I recognised him as one of Jamison's errand boys. 'Nathan, come here!'

The boy trotted over and looked up at Elodin. 'Yes sir?'

Elodin handed the boy his master's robe. 'Nathan, would you take this to my rooms for me?'

'Certainly sir,' the boy took the robe and hurried away.

Elodin looked at me. 'Do you see? The names we call each other are not *Names*. But they have some power nonetheless.'

'That's not magic,' I protested. 'He had to listen to you. You're a master.'

'And you're a Re'lar,' he said implacably. 'You called the wind and the wind listened.'

I struggled with the concept. 'You're saying the wind is alive?'

He made a vague gesture. 'In a way. Most things are alive in one way or another.'

I decided to take a different tack. 'How did I call the wind if I didn't know how?'

Elodin clapped his hands together, sharply. '*That* is an excellent question! The answer is that each of us has two minds: a waking mind and a sleeping mind. Our waking mind is what thinks and talks and reasons. But the sleeping mind is more powerful. It sees deeply to the heart of things. It is the part of us that dreams. It remembers everything. It gives us intuition. Your waking mind does not understand the nature of names. Your sleeping mind does. It already knows many things that your waking mind does not.'

Elodin looked at me. 'Remember how you felt after you called the name of the wind?'

I nodded, not enjoying the memory.

'When Ambrose broke your lute, it roused your sleeping mind. Like a great hibernating bear jabbed with a burning stick, it reared up and roared the name of the wind.' He swung his arms around wildly, attracting odd looks from passing students. 'Afterwards your waking mind did not know what to do. It was left with an angry bear.'

'What did you do? I can't remember what you whispered to me.'

'It was a name. It was a name that settled the angry bear, eased it back to sleep. But it is not sleeping so soundly now. We need to rouse it slowly and bring it under your control.'

'Is that why you moved to suspend my expulsion?'

He made a dismissive gesture. 'You were in no real danger of being expelled. You are not the first student to call the name of the wind in anger, though you are the first in several years. Some strong emotion usually wakes the sleeping mind for the first time.' He smiled. 'The name of the wind came to me when I was arguing with Elxa Dal. When I shouted it his braziers exploded in a cloud of burning ash and cinder,' he chuckled.

'What did he do to make you so angry?'

'He refused to teach me the advanced bindings. I was only fourteen and an E'lir. He told me I would have to wait until I was a Re'lar.'

'There are advanced bindings?'

He grinned at me. 'Secrets, Re'lar Kvothe. That is what being an arcanist is all about. Now that you are a Re'lar you are entitled to certain things that were withheld before. The advanced sympathetic bindings, the nature of names. Some smattering of dubious runes, if Kilvin thinks you're ready.'

Hope rose in my chest. 'Does this mean I'm allowed access to the Archives now?'

'Ah,' Elodin said. 'No. Not in the least. You see, the Archives are Lorren's domain, his kingdom. Those secrets are not mine to give away.'

At his mention of secrets my mind settled on one that had been bothering me for months. The secret at the heart of the Archives. 'What about the stone door in the Archives?' I asked. 'The four-plate door. Now that I'm a Re'lar can you tell me what's behind it?'

Elodin laughed. 'Oh no. No, no. You don't aim for small secrets do you?' He clapped me on the back as if I'd just made an especially good joke. '*Valaritas*. God. I can still remember what it was like, standing down there looking at the door, wondering.'

He laughed again. 'Merciful Tehlu, it almost killed me.' He shook his head. 'No. You don't get to go behind the four-plate door. But,' he gave me a conspiratorial look. 'Since you are a Re'lar . . .' He looked from side to side as if afraid that someone might overhear us. I leaned closer. 'Since you are a Re'lar, I will admit that it exists.' He gave me a solemn wink.

Disappointed as I was, I couldn't help but smile. We walked for a while in silence past Mains, past Anker's. 'Master Elodin?'

'Yes?' His eyes followed a squirrel across the road and up a tree.

'I still don't understand about names.'

'I will teach you to understand,' he said easily. 'The nature of names cannot be described, only experienced and understood.'

'Why can't it be described?' I asked. 'If you understand a thing, you can describe it.'

'Can you describe all the things you understand?' he looked sideways at me.

'Of course.'

Elodin pointed down the street. 'What colour is that boy's shirt?'

'Blue.'

'What do you mean by blue? Describe it.'

I struggled for a moment, failed. 'So *blue* is a name?'

'It is a word. Words are pale shadows of forgotten names. As names have power, words have power. Words can light fires in the minds of men. Words can wring tears from the hardest hearts. There are seven words that will make a person love you. There are ten words that will break a strong man's will. But a word is nothing but a painting of a fire. A name is the fire itself.'

My head was swimming by this point. 'I still don't understand.'

He laid a hand on my shoulder. 'Using words to talk of words is like using a pencil to draw a picture of itself, on itself. Impossible. Confusing. Frustrating.' He lifted his hands high above his head as if stretching for the sky. 'But there are other ways to understanding!' he shouted, laughing like a child. He threw both arms to the cloudless arch of sky above us, still laughing. 'Look!' he shouted tilting his head back. 'Blue! Blue! Blue!'

CHAPTER EIGHTY-SEVEN

A Heavy Question

'HE'S QUITE, quite mad,' I said to Simmon and Wilem later that afternoon at Anker's.

'He's a master,' Sim responded tactfully. 'And your sponsor. And from what you've told us he's the reason you weren't expelled.'

'I'm not saying that he isn't intelligent, and I've seen him do things that I can't begin to explain. But the fact remains that he is completely off his nut. He talks in circles about names and words and power. It sounds good while he's saying it. But it doesn't really mean anything.'

'Quit complaining,' Simmon said. 'You beat both of us to Re'lar, even if your sponsor is cracked. And you got paid two span of silver for breaking Ambrose's arm. You got away free as a bird. I wish I had half your luck.'

'Not quite free as a bird,' I said. 'I'm still going to be whipped.'

'What?' Sim said. 'I thought you said that they suspended it?'

'They suspended my expulsion,' I said. 'Not the whipping.'

Simmon gaped. 'My God, why not?'

'Malfeasance,' Wilem said in a low voice. 'They can't let a student get off bird-free after they've voted him guilty of malfeasance.'

'That's what Elodin said.' I took a drink. Took another.

'I don't care,' Simmon said hotly. 'It's barbaric.' He hammered out his last word on the table with his fist, upsetting his glass and spilling a dark pool of scutten across the table. 'Shit.' He scrambled to his feet and tried to keep it from spilling on the floor with his hands.

I laughed helplessly until there was water in my eyes and my stomach ached. I felt a weight lift off my chest as I finally regained my breath. 'I love you, Sim,' I said earnestly. 'Sometimes I think you're the only honest person I know.'

He looked me over. 'You're drunk.'

'No, it's the truth. You're a good person. Better than I'll ever be.' He gave me a look that said he couldn't tell if he was being made fun of or not. A serving girl came over with wet rags, wiped the table clean, and made a few barbed comments. Sim had the decency to look embarrassed enough for all of us.

——————

By the time I made it back to the University, it was fully dark. I stopped briefly at Anker's to pick up a few things, then made my way onto the roof of Mains.

I was surprised to find Auri waiting for me on the roof despite the clear sky. She sat on a short brick chimney, swinging her bare feet idly. Her hair made a gauzy cloud around her tiny form.

She hopped down when I came closer and gave a little half step sideways that was almost like a curtsey. 'Good evening, Kvothe.'

'Good evening, Auri,' I said. 'How are you?'

'I am lovely,' she said firmly, 'and it is a lovely night.' She held both her hands behind her back and shifted from foot to foot.

'What have you brought me tonight?' I asked.

She gave her sunny smile. 'What have you brought *me*?'

I pulled a narrow bottle from underneath my cloak. 'I brought you some honey wine.'

She took hold of it with both hands. 'Why, this is a princely gift.' She peered down at it wonderingly. 'Think of all the tipsy bees.' She pulled the cork and sniffed it. 'What's in it?'

'Sunlight,' I said. 'And a smile, and a question.'

She held the mouth of the bottle up to her ear and grinned at me.

'The question's at the bottom,' I said.

'A heavy question,' she said, then held her hand out to me. 'I brought you a ring.'

It was made of warm, smooth wood. 'What does it do?' I asked.

'It keeps secrets,' she said.

I held it to my ear.

Auri shook her head seriously, her hair swirling around her. 'It doesn't tell them, it keeps them.' She stepped close to me and took the ring, sliding it onto my finger. 'It's quite enough to have a secret,' she chided me gently. 'Anything more would be greedy.'

'It fits,' I said, somewhat surprised.

'They're your secrets,' she said, as if explaining something to a child. 'Who else would it fit?'

Auri brushed her hair away behind her and made her curious half step to the side again. Almost like a curtsey, almost like a tiny dance. 'I was wondering if you would join me for dinner tonight, Kvothe,' she said, her face serious. 'I have brought apples and eggs. I can also offer a lovely honey wine.'

'I'd love to share dinner with you, Auri,' I said formally. 'I have brought bread and cheese.'

Auri scampered down into the courtyard and in a few minutes returned with a delicate porcelain teacup for me. She poured the honey wine for both of us, drinking hers in a series of dainty sips from a silver beggar's cup hardly bigger than a thimble.

I sat down on the roof and we shared our meal. I had a large loaf of brown barley bread and a wedge of hard white Dalonir cheese. Auri had ripe apples and a half dozen brown-spotted eggs that she had somehow managed to hard-boil. We ate them with salt I brought out from a pocket in my cloak.

We shared most of the meal in silence, simply enjoying each other's company. Auri sat cross-legged with her back straight and her hair fanning out to all sides. As always, her careful delicacy somehow made this makeshift meal on a rooftop seem like a formal dinner in some nobleman's hall.

'The wind has been bringing leaves into the Underthing lately,' Auri said conversationally toward the end of the meal. 'Through the grates and tunnels. They settle in the Downings, so things are all a-rustle there.'

'Is that so?'

She nodded. 'And a mother owl has moved in. Made her nest right in the middle of the Grey Twelve, bold as brass.'

'She's something of a rarity then?'

She nodded. 'Absolutely. Owls are wise. They are careful and patient. Wisdom precludes boldness.' She sipped from her cup, holding the handle daintily between her thumb and forefinger. 'That is why owls make poor heroes.'

Wisdom precludes boldness. After my recent adventures in Trebon I couldn't help but agree. 'But this one is adventurous? An explorer?'

'Oh yes,' Auri said, her eyes wide. 'She is fearless. She has a face like a wicked moon.'

She refilled her tiny silver cup with honey wine and emptied the last of it into my teacup. After tipping the bottle all the way upside-down, she pursed her lips and blew across the top of it in two sharp bursts so that it made a hooting noise. 'Where's my question?' she demanded.

I hesitated, unsure as to how she would respond to my request. 'I was wondering, Auri. Would you mind showing me the Underthing?'

Auri looked away, suddenly shy. 'Kvothe, I thought you were a gentleman,' she said, tugging self-consciously at her ragged shirt. 'Imagine, asking to see a girl's underthing.' She looked down, her hair hiding her face.

I held my breath for a moment, choosing my next words carefully lest I startle her back underground. While I was thinking, Auri peeked at me through the curtain of her hair.

'Auri,' I asked slowly, 'are you joking with me?'

She looked up and grinned. 'Yes I am,' she said proudly. 'Isn't it wonderful?'

Auri took me through the heavy metal grate in the abandoned courtyard, down into the Underthing. I brought out my hand lamp to light the way. Auri had a light of her own, something she held in her cupped hands that gave off a soft, blue-green glow. I was curious about what she held but didn't want to press her for too many secrets at once.

At first the Underthing was exactly what I had expected. Tunnels and pipes. Pipes for sewage, water, steam, and coal gas. Great black pig-iron pipes a man could crawl through, small, bright brass pipes no bigger around than your thumb. There was a vast network of stone tunnels, branching and connecting at odd angles. If there were any rhyme or reason to the place, it was lost on me.

Auri gave me a whirlwind tour, proud as a new mother, excited as a little girl. Her enthusiasm was infectious and I soon lost myself in the excitement of the moment, ignoring my original reasons for wanting to explore the tunnels. There is nothing quite so delightfully mysterious as a secret in your own backyard.

We made our way down three spiral staircases made of black wrought iron to reach the Grey Twelve. It was like standing in the bottom of a canyon. Looking up I could see faint moonlight filtering in through drain grates far overhead. The mother owl was gone, but Auri showed me the nest.

The deeper we went, the stranger things became. The round tunnels for drainage and pipes disappeared and were replaced with squared-off hallways and stairways strewn with rubble. Rotting wooden doors hung off rusted hinges, and there were half-collapsed rooms filled with mouldering tables and chairs. One room had a pair of bricked-up windows despite the fact that we were, at my best guess, at least fifty feet below ground.

Deeper still, we came to Throughbottom, a room like a cathedral, so big that neither Auri's blue light nor my red one reached the highest peaks of the ceiling. All around us were huge, ancient machines. Some lay in pieces: broken gears taller than a man, leather straps gone brittle with age, great wooden beams that were now explosions of white fungus, huge as hedgerows.

Other machines were intact but worn by centuries of neglect. I approached an iron block as big as a farmer's cottage and broke off a single flake of rust large as a dinner plate. Underneath was nothing but more rust. Nearby there were three great pillars covered in green verdigris so thick it looked like moss. Many of the huge machines were beyond identifying, looking more melted than rusted. But I saw something that might have been a waterwheel, three stories tall, lying in a dry canal that ran like a chasm through the middle of the room.

I had only the vaguest of ideas as to what any of the machines might have done. I had no guess at all as to why they had lain here for uncounted centuries, deep underground. There didn't seem—

CHAPTER EIGHTY-EIGHT

Interlude — Looking

THE SOUND OF HEAVY boots on the wooden landing startled the men sitting in the Waystone Inn. Kvothe bolted to his feet midsentence and was halfway to the bar before the front door opened and the first of the Felling night crowd made their way inside.

'You've got hungry men here, Kote!' Cob called out as he opened the door. Shep, Jake, and Graham followed him inside.

'We might have a little something in the back,' Kote said. 'I could run and fetch it straightaway, unless you'd like drinks first.' There was a chorus of friendly assent as the men settled onto their stools at the bar. The exchange had a well-worn feel, comfortable as old shoes.

Chronicler stared at the red-haired man behind the bar. There was nothing left of Kvothe in him. It was just an innkeeper: friendly, servile, and so unassuming as to almost be invisible.

Jake took a long drink before noticing Chronicler sitting at the far end of the room. 'Well look at you, Kote! A new customer. Hell, we're lucky to have got any seats at all.'

Shep chuckled. Cob swiveled his stool around and peered at where Chronicler sat next to Bast, pen still poised over his paper. 'Is he a scribe or sommat?'

'He is,' Kote said quickly. 'Came into town late last night.'

Cob squinted toward them. 'What's he writing?'

Kote lowered his voice a bit, drawing the attention of the customers away from the guest and back to his side of the bar. 'Remember that trip Bast made to Baedn?' They nodded attentively. 'Well, turns out he had a scare with the pox, and he's been feeling his years a bit since then. He thought he'd best get his will writ down while he had the chance.'

'Sense enough in that, these days,' Shep said darkly. He drank off the last of his beer and knocked the empty mug down. 'I'll do another of those.'

'Whatsoever monies I have saved at the time of my death shall go to the Widow Sage,' Bast said loudly across the room. 'To help in raising and dowering her three daughters, as they are soon to be of marriaging age.' He gave Chronicler a troubled look. 'Is "marriaging" a word?'

'Little Katie certainly has grown up a bit this last year, hasn't she?' Graham mused. The others nodded in agreement.

'To my employer, I leave my best pair of boots,' Bast continued magnanimously. 'And whatsoever of my trousers he finds fit him.'

'Boy does have a fine pair of boots,' Cob said to Kote. 'Always thought so.'

'I leave it to Pater Leoden to distribute the remainder of my worldly goods among the parish, as, being an immoral soul, I will have no further need of them.'

'You mean, *immortal,* don't you?' Chronicler asked uncertainly.

Bast shrugged. 'That's all I can think of for now.' Chronicler nodded and quickly shuffled the paper, pens, and ink into his flat leather satchel.

'Come on over then,' Cob called to him. 'Don't be a stranger.' Chronicler froze, then made his way slowly toward the bar. 'What's your name, boy?'

'Devan,' he said, then looked stricken and cleared his throat. 'Excuse me, Carverson. Devan Carverson.'

Cob made introductions all around, then turned back to the newcomer. 'Which way you from, Devan?' Cob asked.

'Off past Abbott's Ford.'

'Any news from that way?'

Chronicler shifted uncomfortably in his seat while Kote eyed him darkly from the other side of the bar. 'Well . . . the roads are rather bad . . .'

This sparked a chorus of familiar complaints, and Chronicler relaxed. While they were still grousing, the door opened and the smith's prentice came in, boyish and broad-shouldered with the smell of coalsmoke in his hair. A long rod of iron rested on his shoulder as he held the door open for Carter.

'You look a fool, boy,' Carter groused as he made his way slowly through the door, walking with the stiff care of the recently injured. 'You keep hauling that around, and folk'll start talking about you like they do Crazy

Martin. You'll be that crazy boy from Rannish. You want to listen to that for the next fifty years?'

The smith's prentice shifted his grip on the iron bar self-consciously. 'Let 'em talk,' he mumbled with a hint of defiance. 'Since I went out and took care of Nelly I've been having dreams about that spider thing.' He shook his head. 'Hell, I'd think you'd be carrying one in each hand. That thing could've killed you.'

Carter ignored him, his expression stiff as he walked gingerly toward the bar.

'Good to see you up and about, Carter,' Shep called out, raising his mug. 'I thought we might not see you out of bed for another day or two.'

'Take more than a few stitches to keep me down,' Carter said.

Bast made a show of offering up his stool to the injured man, then quietly took a seat as far from the smith's prentice as possible. There was a warm murmur of welcome from everyone.

The innkeeper ducked into the back room and emerged a few minutes later carrying a tray loaded with hot bread and steaming bowls of stew.

Everyone was listening to Chronicler. '. . . if I remember right, Kvothe was off in Severen when it happened. He was walking home—'

'It weren't Severen,' Old Cob said. 'It was off by the University.'

'Could have been,' Chronicler conceded. 'Anyway, he was walking home late at night and some bandits jumped him in an alleyway.'

'It was broad daylight,' Cob said testily. 'In the middle of town. All manner of folk were around to see it.'

Chronicler shook his head stubbornly. 'I remember an alley. Anyway, the bandits surprised Kvothe. They wanted his horse,' he paused and rubbed his forehead with the tips of his fingers. 'Wait, that's not right. He wouldn't have his horse in an alley. Maybe he was on the road to Severen.'

'I told you, it weren't Severen!' Cob demanded, slapping his hand down on the bar, plainly irritated. 'Tehlu anyway, just stop. You've got it all mixed up.'

Chronicler flushed in embarrassment. 'I only heard it once, years ago.'

Shooting Chronicler a dark look, Kote clattered the tray down loudly onto the bar and the story was momentarily forgotten. Old Cob ate so quickly he almost choked himself, and washed it down with a long swallow of beer.

'Seeing as how you're still working on your dinner there,' he said none too casually to Chronicler as he wiped his mouth on his sleeve. 'Would you mind terrible if I picked up the story? Just so's the boy can hear it?'

'If you're sure you know it . . .' Chronicler said hesitantly.

'Of course I know it,' Cob said as he spun his stool around to face more of his audience. 'Alright. Way back when Kvothe was just a pup, he went to the University. But he didn't live in the University proper, you see, on account of the fact that he was just ordinary folk. He couldn't afford all the fancy living that went on there.'

'How come?' the smith's prentice asked. 'You said before that Kvothe was so smart they paid him to stay even though he was just ten years old. They gave him a purse full of gold, and a diamond big as his thumb knuckle, and a brand new horse with a new saddle and tack and new shoes and a full bag of oats and everything.'

Cob gave a conciliatory nod. 'True, that's true. But this was a year or two after Kvothe had got all that. And you see, he'd gave a lot of that gold to some poor folk whose houses had all burned down.'

'Burned down during their wedding,' Graham interjected.

Cob nodded. 'And Kvothe had to eat, and rent a room, and buy more oats for his horse. So his gold was all used up by then. So he—'

'What about the diamond?' the boy insisted.

Old Cob gave the barest of frowns. 'If you've got to know, he gave that diamond to a special friend of his. A special lady friend. But that's a whole different story than the one I'm telling now.' He glared at the boy, who dropped his eyes contritely and spooned up a mouthful of stew.

Cob continued, 'Since Kvothe couldn't afford all that rich living in the University, he stayed in the town nextby instead, place called *Amary*.' He shot Chronicler a pointed look. 'Kvothe had a room in a inn where he got to stay there for free because the widow who owned the place took a shine to him, and he did chores to help earn his keep.'

'He played music there too,' Jake added. 'He was all sorts of clever with his lute.'

'Get your dinner into your gob and let me finish my say, Jacob,' Old Cob snapped. 'Everyone knows Kvothe was clever with a lute. That's why the widow had taken such a shine to him in the first place, and playing music every night was *part* of his chores.'

Cob took a quick drink and continued. 'So one day Kvothe was out running errands the widow, when a fellow pulls out a knife and tells Kvothe if he doesn't hand over the widow's money, he'll spill Kvothe's guts all over the street.' Cob pointed an imaginary knife at the boy and gave him a menacing look. 'Now you've got to remember, this is back when Kvothe was just a pup. He ain't got no sword, and even if he did, he ain't learned to fight proper from the Adem yet.'

'So what did Kvothe do?' the smith's prentice asked.

'Well,' Cob leaned back. 'It was the middle of the day, and they were smack in the middle of Amary's town square. Kvothe was about to call for the constable, but he always had his eyes wide open, you see. And so he noticed that this fellow had white, white teeth . . .'

The boy's eyes grew wide. 'He was a sweet-eater?'

Cob nodded. 'And even worse, the fellow was starting to sweat like a hard-run horse, his eyes were wild, and his hands . . .' Cob widened his own eyes and held out his hands, making them tremble. 'So Kvothe knew the fellow had the hunger something fierce, and that meant he'd stab his own mum for a bent penny.' Cob took another long drink, drawing out the tension.

'Whatever did he do?' Bast burst out anxiously from the far end of the bar, wringing his hands dramatically. The innkeeper glared at his student.

Cob continued, 'Well, first he hesitates, and the man comes closer with the knife and Kvothe can see the fellow ain't going to ask again. So Kvothe uses a dark magic that he found locked away in a secret book in the University. He speaks three terrible, secret words and calls up a demon—'

'A demon?' the prentice's voice was almost a yelp. 'Was it like the one . . .'

Cob shook his head, slowly. 'Oh no, this one weren't spiderly at all. It was worse. This one was made all of shadows, and when it landed on the fellow it bit him on the chest, right over his heart, and it drank all the blood out of him like you'd suck the juice out of a plum.'

'Blackened hands, Cob,' Carter said, his voice thick with reproach. 'You're going to give the boy nightmares. He'll be carrying around that damn iron stick for a year with all your nonsense stuffed in his head.'

'That's not how I heard it,' Graham said slowly. 'I heard there was a woman trapped in a burning house, and Kvothe called up a demon to protect him from the fire. Then he ran inside and pulled the lady out of the fire and she wasn't burned at all.'

'Listen to yourselves,' Jake said, disgusted. 'You're like kids at Midwinter. "Demons stole my doll". "Demons spilled the milk". Kvothe didn't meddle with demons. He was at the University learning all manner of names, right?

The fellow came at him with a knife and he called out fire and lightning, just like Taborlin the Great.'

'It was a demon, Jake,' Cob said angrily. 'Otherwise the story don't make a lick of sense. It was a demon he called up, and it drank up the fellow's blood, and everyone who saw was powerful shook up by it. Someone told a priest, then the priests went to the constable, and the constable went and pulled him out of the widow's inn that night. Then they slapped him into jail for consorting with dark forces and such.'

'Folk probably just saw the fire and thought it was a demon,' Jake persisted. 'You know how folk are.'

'No I don't, Jacob,' Cob snapped, crossing his arms in front of his chest and leaning back against the bar. 'Why don't you tell me how folk are? Why don't you just go ahead and tell this whole damn story while . . .'

Cob stopped at the sound of heavy boots clumping on the wooden landing outside. After a pause, someone fumbled with the latch.

Everyone turned around to look at the door, curious, as all the regular customers were already there. 'Two new faces in one day,' Graham said gently, knowing he was touching on a delicate subject. 'Looks like your dry spell might be over, Kote.'

'Roads must be getting better,' Shep said into his drink, a hint of relief in his voice. 'About time we got a touch of luck.'

The latch clicked and the door swung slowly open, moving in a slow arc until it struck the wall. A man stood outside in the dark, as if deciding whether or not to come in.

'Welcome to the Waystone,' the innkeeper called out from behind the bar. 'What can we do for you?'

The man stepped into the light and the farmers' excitement was smothered by the sight of the piecemeal leather armour and heavy sword that marked a mercenary. A lone mercenary was never reassuring, even in the best of times. Everyone knew that the difference between an unemployed mercenary and a highwayman was mostly one of timing.

What's more, it was obvious this mercenary had fallen on hard times. Brownburr clung thick to the bottoms of his trousers and the rough leather of his boot's laces. His shirt was fine linen dyed a deep, royal blue, but mud-spattered and bramble-torn. His hair was a greasy snarl. His eyes were dark and sunken, as if he hadn't slept in days. He moved a few steps farther into the inn, leaving the door open behind him.

'Looks like you've been on the road a while,' Kvothe said cheerily.

'Would you like a drink or some dinner?' When the mercenary made no reply, he added, 'None of us would blame you if you wanted to catch a bit of sleep first, either. It looks like you've had a rough couple days.' Kvothe glanced at Bast, who slid off his stool and went to close the inn's front door.

After slowly looking over everyone sitting at the bar, the mercenary moved to the empty space between Chronicler and Old Cob. Kvothe gave his best innkeeper's smile as the mercenary leaned heavily against the bar and mumbled something.

Across the room, Bast froze with his hand on the door handle.

'Beg your pardon?' Kvothe asked, leaning forward.

The mercenary looked up, his eyes meeting Kvothe's then sweeping back and forth behind the bar. His eyes moved sluggishly, as if he had been addled by a blow to the head. '*Aethin tseh cthystoi scthaiven vei.*'

Kvothe leaned forward, 'I'm sorry, what was that again?' When nothing was forthcoming from the mercenary, he looked around at the other men at the bar. 'Did anyone catch that?'

Chronicler was looking the mercenary over, eyeing the man's armour, the empty quiver of arrows, his fine blue linen shirt. The scribe's stare was intense, but the mercenary didn't seem to notice.

'It's Siaru,' Cob said knowingly. 'Funny. He don't look like a shim.'

Shep laughed, shaking his head. 'Naw. He's drunk. My uncle used to talk like that.' He nudged Graham with an elbow. 'You remember my Uncle Tam? God, I've never known a man who drank like that.'

Bast made a frantic, covert gesture from where he stood near the door, but Kvothe was busy trying to catch the mercenary's eye. 'Speak Aturan?' Kvothe asked slowly. 'What do you want?'

The mercenary's eyes rested momentarily on the innkeeper. '*Avoi—*' he began, then closed his eyes and tilted his head, as if listening. He opened his eyes again. '*I . . . want . . .*' he began, his voice slow and thick. '*I . . . look . . .*' He trailed off, his gaze wandering aimlessly around the room, his eyes unfocused.

'I know him,' Chronicler said.

Everyone turned to look at the scribe. 'What?' Shep asked.

Chronicler's expression was angry. 'This fellow and four of his friends robbed me about five days ago. I didn't recognise him at first. He was clean-shaven then, but it's him.'

Behind the man's back, Bast made a more urgent gesture, trying to catch his master's attention, but Kvothe was intent on the befuddled man. 'Are you sure?'

Chronicler gave a hard, humourless laugh. 'He's wearing my shirt. Ruined it too. Cost me a whole talent. I never even got a chance to wear it.'

'Was he like this before?'

Chronicler shook his head. 'Not at all. He was almost genteel as high-waymen go. I had him pegged as a low-ranking officer before he deserted.'

Bast gave up signaling. 'Reshi!' He called out, a hint of desperation in his voice.

'Just a moment, Bast,' Kvothe said as he tried to catch the stupefied mercenary's attention. He waved a hand in front of the man's face, snapped his fingers. 'Hello?'

The man's eyes followed Kvothe's moving hand, but seemed oblivious to everything being said around him. '*I . . . am . . . look . . .*' he said slowly. '*I look . . .*'

'What?' Cob demanded testily. 'What are you looking for?'

'*Looking . . .*' the mercenary echoed vaguely.

'I imagine he's looking to give me my horse back,' Chronicler said calmly as he took a half step closer to the man and grabbed the hilt of his sword. With a sudden motion he yanked it free, or rather, he tried to. Instead of sliding easily free it of its scabbard, it came halfway out and stuck.

'No!' Bast cried from across the room.

The mercenary stared vaguely at Chronicler, but made no attempt to stop him. Standing awkwardly, still gripping the hilt of the man's sword, the scribe tugged harder and the sword pulled slowly free. The broad blade was mottled with dried blood and rust.

Taking a step back, Chronicler regained his composure and levelled the sword at the mercenary. 'And my horse is just for starters. Afterwards I think he's looking to give me my money back and have a nice chat with the constable.'

The mercenary looked at the point of the sword where it swayed unsteadily in front of his chest. His eyes followed the gently swaying motion for a long moment.

'Just leave him be!' Bast's voice was shrill. 'Please!'

Cob nodded. 'Boy's right, Devan. Fella's not right in his head. Don't go pointing that at him. He looks likely to pass out on top of it.'

The mercenary absentmindedly lifted a hand. '*I am looking . . .*' he said, brushing the sword aside as if it were a branch blocking his path. Chronicler sucked in a breath and jerked the sword away as the man's hand ran along the edge of the blade, drawing blood.

'See?' Old Cob said. 'What I tell you? Sod's a danger to hisself.'

The mercenary's head tilted to the side. He held up his hand, examining it. A slow trickle of dark blood made its way down his thumb, where it gathered and swelled for a moment before dripping onto the floor. The mercenary drew a deep breath through his nose, and his glassy sunken eyes came into sudden, sharp focus.

He smiled wide at Chronicler, all the vagueness gone from his expression. '*Te varaiyn aroi Seathaloi vei mela,*' he said in a deep voice.

'I . . . I don't follow you,' Chronicler said, disconcerted.

The man's smile fell away. His eyes hardened, grew angry. '*Te-tauren sciyr-loet? Amauen.*'

'I can't tell what you're saying,' Chronicler said. 'But I don't care for your tone.' He brought the sword back up between them, pointing at the man's chest.

The mercenary looked down at the heavy, notched blade, his forehead furrowing in confusion. Then sudden understanding spread across his face and the wide smile returned. He threw back his head and laughed.

It was no human sound. It was wild and exulting, like a hawk's shrill cry.

The mercenary brought up his injured hand and grabbed the tip of the sword, moving with such sudden speed that the metal rang dully with the contact. Still smiling, he tightened his grip, bowing the blade. Blood ran from his hand, down the sword's edge to patter onto the floor.

Everyone in the room watched in stunned disbelief. The only sound was the faint grating of the mercenary's finger bones grinding against the bare edges of the blade.

Looking Chronicler full in the face, the mercenary twisted his hand sharply and the sword broke with a sound like a shattered bell. As Chronicler stared dumbly at the ruined weapon the mercenary took a step forward and laid his empty hand lightly on the scribe's shoulder.

Chronicler gave a choked scream and jerked away as if he had been jabbed with a hot poker. He swung the broken sword wildly, knocking the hand away and notching it deep into the meat of the mercenary's arm. The man's face showed no pain or fear, or any sign of awareness that he'd been wounded at all.

Still holding the broken tip of the sword in his bloody hand, the mercenary took another step toward Chronicler.

Then Bast was there, barreling into the mercenary with one shoulder, striking him with such force that the man's body shattered one of the heavy barstools before slamming into the mahogany bar. Quick as a blink, Bast grabbed the mercenary's head with both hands and slammed it into the edge of the bar. Lips pulled back in a grimace, Bast drove the man's head viciously into the mahogany: once, twice . . .

Then, as if Bast's action had startled everyone awake, chaos erupted in the room. Old Cob pushed himself away from the bar, tipping his stool over as he backed away. Graham began shouting something about the constable. Jake tried to bolt for the door and tripped over Cob's fallen stool, sprawling to the floor in a tangle. The smith's prentice grabbed for his iron rod and ended up knocking it to the floor where it rolled in a wide arc and came to rest under a table.

Bast gave a startled yelp and was thrown violently across the room to land on one of the heavy timber tables. It broke under his weight and he lay sprawled in the wreckage, limp as a rag doll. The mercenary came to his feet, blood flowing freely down the left-hand side of his face. He seemed utterly unconcerned as he turned back to Chronicler, still holding the tip of the broken sword in his bleeding hand.

Behind him, Shep picked up a knife from where it lay next to the half-eaten wheel of cheese. It was just a kitchen knife, its blade about a handspan long. Face grim, the farmer stepped close behind the mercenary and stabbed down hard, driving the whole of the short blade deep into the mercenary's body where the shoulder meets the neck.

Instead of collapsing, the mercenary spun around and lashed Shep across the face with the jagged edge of the sword. Blood sprayed and Shep lifted his hands to his face. Then, moving so quickly it was little more than a twitch, the mercenary brought the piece of metal back around, burying it in the farmer's chest. Shep staggered backward against the bar, then collapsed to the floor with the broken end of the sword still jutting between his ribs.

The mercenary reached up and curiously touched the handle of the knife lodged in his own neck. His expression more puzzled than angry, he tugged at it. When it didn't budge, he gave another wild, birdlike laugh.

As the farmer lay gasping and bleeding on the floor, the mercenary's attention seemed to wander, as if he had forgotten what he was doing. His eyes slowly wandered around the room, moving lazily past the broken tables, the black stone fireplace, the huge oak barrels. Finally the mercenary's gaze came to rest on the red-haired man behind the bar. Kvothe did not blanch or back away when the man's attention settled onto him. Their eyes met.

The mercenary's eyes sharpened again, focusing on Kvothe. The wide, humourless smile reappeared, made macabre by the blood running down his face. '*Tè aithiyn Seathaloi?*' he demanded. '*Tè Rhintae?*'

With an almost casual motion, Kvothe grabbed a dark bottle from the counter and flung it across the bar. It struck the mercenary in the mouth and shattered. The air filled with the sharp tang of elderberry, dousing the man's still-grinning head and shoulders.

Reaching out one hand, Kvothe dipped a finger into the liquor that spattered the bar. He muttered something under his breath, his forehead furrowed in concentration. He stared intently at the bloody man standing on the other side of the bar.

Nothing happened.

The mercenary reached across the bar, catching hold of Kvothe's sleeve. The innkeeper simply stood, and in that moment his expression held no fear, no anger or surprise. He only seemed weary, numb, and dismayed.

Before the mercenary could get a grip on Kvothe's arm, he staggered as Bast tackled him from behind. Bast managed to get one arm around the mercenary's neck while the other raked at the man's face. The mercenary let go of Kvothe and laid both hands on the arm that circled his neck, trying to twist away. When the mercenary's hands touched him, Bast's face became a tight mask of pain. Teeth bared, he clawed wildly at the mercenary's eyes with his free hand.

At the far end of the bar, the smith's prentice finally retrieved his iron rod from under the table and stretched to his full height. He charged over the fallen stools and strewn bodies on the floor. Bellowing, he lifted the iron rod high over one shoulder.

Still clinging to the mercenary, Bast's eyes grew wide with sudden panic as he saw the smith's prentice approaching. He released his grip and backed away, his feet tangling in the wreckage of the broken barstool. Falling backward, he scuttled madly away from the both of them.

Turning, the mercenary saw the tall boy charging. He smiled and stretched out a bloody hand. The motion was graceful, almost lazy.

The smith's prentice swatted the arm away. When the iron bar struck him, the mercenary's smile fell away. He clutched at his arm, hissing and spitting like an angry cat.

The boy swung the iron rod again, striking the mercenary squarely in the ribs. The force of it knocked him away from the bar, and he fell to his hands and knees, screaming like a slaughtered lamb.

The smith's prentice grabbed the bar with both hands and brought it down across the mercenary's back like a man splitting wood. There was the gristly sound of bones cracking. The iron bar rang softly, like a distant, fog-muffled bell.

Back broken, the bloody man still tried to crawl toward the inn's door. His face was blank now, his mouth open in a low howl as constant and unthinking as the sound of wind through winter trees. The prentice struck again and again, swinging the heavy iron rod lightly as a willow switch. He scored a deep groove in the wooden floor, then broke a leg, an arm, more ribs. Still the mercenary continued to claw his way toward the door, shrieking and moaning, sounding more animal than human.

Finally the boy landed a blow to the head and the mercenary went limp. There was a moment of perfect quiet, then the mercenary made a deep, wet, coughing sound and vomited up a foul fluid, thick as pitch and black as ink.

It was some time before the boy stopped battering at the motionless corpse, and even when he did stop, he held the bar poised over one shoulder, panting raggedly and looking around wildly. As he slowly caught his breath, the sound of low prayers could be heard from the other side of the room where Old Cob crouched against the black stone of the fireplace.

After a few minutes even the praying stopped, and silence returned to the Waystone Inn.

For the next several hours the Waystone was the center of the town's attention. The common room was crowded, full of whispers, murmured questions, and broken sobbing. Folk with less curiosity or more propriety stayed outside, peering through the wide windows and gossiping over what they'd heard.

There were no stories yet, just a roiling mass of rumour. The dead man was a bandit come to rob the inn. He'd come looking for revenge against Chronicler, who'd deflowered his sister off in Abbott's Ford. He was a woodsman gone rabid. He was an old acquaintance of the innkeeper, come to collect a debt. He was an ex-soldier, gone tabard-mad while fighting the rebels off in Resavek.

Jake and Carter made a point of the mercenary's smile, and while denner addiction was a city problem, folk had still heard of sweet-eaters here. Three-finger Tom knew about these things, as he'd soldiered under the old king nearly thirty years ago. He explained that with four grains of denner resin, a man could have his foot amputated without a twinge of pain. With eight grains he'd saw through the bone himself. With twelve grains he'd go for a jog afterward, laughing and singing 'Tinker Tanner'.

Shep's body was covered with a blanket and prayed over by the priest. Later, the constable looked at it as well, but the man was clearly out of his depth, and was looking because he felt he should rather than because he knew what to look for.

The crowd began to thin after an hour or so. Shep's brothers showed up with a cart to collect the body. Their grim, red-eyed stares drove away most of the remaining spectators who were idling about.

Still, there was much to be done. The constable tried to piece together what had happened from witnesses and the more opinionated onlookers. After hours of speculation, the story finally began to coalesce. Eventually it was agreed that the man was a deserter and denner addict come to their little town just in time to go crazy.

It was clear to everyone that the smith's prentice had done the right thing, a brave thing in fact. Still, the iron law demanded a trial, so there'd be one next month, when the quarter court came through these parts on its rounds.

The constable went home to his wife and children. The priest took the mercenary's remains off to the church. Bast cleared the wrecked furniture away, stacking it near the kitchen door to be used as firewood. The innkeeper mopped the inn's hardwood floor seven times, until the water in the bucket no longer tinged red when he rinsed it out. Eventually even the most dedicated gawkers drifted away, leaving the usual Felling night crowd, minus one.

Jake, Cob, and the rest made halting conversation, speaking of everything other than what had happened, clinging to the comfort of each other's company.

One by one, exhaustion drove them out of the Waystone. Eventually only the smith's prentice remained, looking down into the cup in his hands. The iron rod lay near his elbow on the top of the mahogany bar.

Nearly half an hour passed without anyone speaking. Chronicler sat at a nearby table, making a pretense of finishing a bowl of stew. Kvothe and Bast puttered about, trying to look busy. A vague tension built in the room as they snuck glances at each other, waiting for the boy to leave.

The innkeeper strolled over to the boy, wiping his hands on a clean linen cloth. 'Well boy, I guess—'

'Aaron,' the smith's prentice interjected, not looking up from his drink. 'My name's Aaron.'

Kvothe nodded seriously. 'Aaron, then. I suppose you deserve that.'

'I don't think it was denner,' Aaron said abruptly.

Kvothe paused. 'Beg pardon?'

'I don't think that fellow was a sweet-eater.'

'You with Cob then?' Kvothe asked. 'Think he was rabid?'

'I think he had a demon in him,' the boy said with careful deliberation, as if he'd been thinking about the words for a long time. 'I didn't say anything before 'cause I didn't want folk to think I'd gone all cracked in the head like Crazy Martin.' He looked up from his drink. 'But I still think he had a demon in him.'

Kvothe put on a gentle smile and gestured to Bast and Chronicler. 'Aren't you worried we'll think the same?'

Aaron shook his head seriously. 'You aren't from around here. You've been places. You know what sort of things are out in the world.' He gave Kvothe a flat look. 'I figure you know it was a demon too.'

Bast grew still where he stood sweeping near the hearth. Kvothe tilted his head curiously without looking away. 'Why would you say that?'

The smith's prentice gestured behind the bar. 'I know you got a big oak drunk-thumper under the bar there. And, well . . .' His eyes flickered upward to the sword hanging menacingly behind the bar. 'There's only one reason I can think you'd grab a bottle instead of that. You weren't trying to knock that fellow's teeth in. You were gonta light him on fire. 'Cept you didn't have any matches, and there weren't any candles closeby.

'My ma used to read to me from the *Book of the Path*,' he continued. 'There's plenty of demons in there. Some hide in men's bodies, like we'd hide under a sheepskin. I think he was just some regular fella who'd got a demon inside him. That's why nothing hurt him. It'd be like someone poking holes in your shirt. That's why he din't make no sense, either. He was talking demon talk.'

Aaron's eyes slid back to the cup he held in his hands, nodding to himself. 'The more I think, the better it makes sense. Iron and fire. That's for demons.'

'Sweet-eaters are stronger than you'd think,' Bast said from across the room. 'Once I saw—'

'You're right,' Kvothe said. 'It was a demon.'

Aaron looked up to meet Kvothe's eye, then nodded and looked down into his mug again. 'And you didn't say anything because you're new in town, and business is shy enough.'

Kvothe nodded.

'And it won't do me any good to tell folk, will it?'

Kvothe drew a deep breath, then let it out slow. 'Probably not.'

Aaron drank off the last swallow of his beer and pushed the empty mug away from himself on the bar. 'Alright. I just needed to hear it. Needed to know I hadn't gone all crazy.' He came to his feet and picked up the heavy iron rod with one hand resting it on his shoulder as he turned toward the door. No one spoke as he made his way across the room and let himself out, closing the door behind him. His heavy boots sounded hollowly on the wooden landing outside, then there was nothing.

'There's more to that one than I would've guessed,' Kvothe said at last.

'It's because he's big,' Bast said matter-of-factly as he gave up the pretense of sweeping. 'You people are easily confused by the look of things. I've had my eye on him for a while now. He's cleverer than folk give him credit for. Always looking at things and asking questions.' He carried the broom back toward the bar. 'He makes me nervous.'

Kvothe looked amused. 'Nervous? You?'

'The boy reeks of iron. Spends all day handling it, baking it, breathing its smoke. Then comes in here with clever eyes.' Bast gave a profoundly disapproving look. 'It's not natural.'

'Natural?' Chronicler finally spoke up. There was a tinge of hysteria in his voice. 'What do you know about natural? I just saw a demon kill a man, was that natural?' Chronicler turned to face Kvothe. 'What the hell was that thing doing here anyway?' Chronicler asked.

' *"Looking"*, apparently,' Kvothe said. 'That's about all I got. How about you, Bast? Could you understand it?'

Bast shook his head. 'I recognised the sound more than anything, Reshi. Its phrasing was very old, archaic. I couldn't make heads or tails of it.'

'Fine. It was looking,' Chronicler said abruptly. 'Looking for what?'

'Me, probably,' Kvothe said grimly.

'Reshi,' Bast admonished him, 'you're just being maudlin. This isn't your fault.'

Kvothe gave his student a long, weary look. 'You know better than that, Bast. All of this is my fault. The scrael, the war. All my fault.'

Bast looked like he wanted to protest, but couldn't find the words. After a long moment, he looked away, beaten.

Kvothe leaned his elbows onto the bar, sighing. 'What do you think it was, anyway?'

Bast shook his head. 'It seemed like one of the *Mahael-uret*, Reshi. A skin dancer.' He frowned as he said it, sounding anything but certain.

Kvothe raised an eyebrow. 'It isn't one of your kind?'

Bast's normally affable expression sharpened into a glare. 'It was *not* "my kind",' he said indignantly. 'The Mael doesn't even share a border with us. It's as far away as anywhere can be in the Fae.'

Kvothe nodded a hint of an apology. 'I just assumed you knew what it was. You didn't hesitate to attack it.'

'All snakes bite, Reshi. I don't need their names to know they're dangerous. I recognised it as being from the Mael. That was enough.'

'So, probably a skin dancer?' Kvothe mused. 'Didn't you tell me they'd been gone for ages and ages?'

Bast nodded. 'And it seemed sort of . . . dumb, and it didn't try to escape into a new body.' Bast shrugged. 'Plus, we're all still alive. That seems to indicate that it was something else.'

Chronicler watched the conversation incredulously. 'You mean neither of you know what it was?' He looked at Kvothe. 'You told the boy it was a demon!'

'For the boy it's a demon,' Kvothe said, 'because that's the easiest thing for him to understand, and it's close enough to the truth.' He began to slowly polish the bar. 'For everyone else in town it's a sweet-eater because that will let them get some sleep tonight.'

'Well it's a demon for me too then,' Chronicler said sharply. 'Because my shoulder feels like ice where it touched me.'

Bast hurried over. 'I forgot it got a hand on you. Let me see.'

Kvothe closed the window's shutters while Chronicler removed his shirt; there were bandages stripping the backs of his arms from where he had been wounded by the scrael three nights ago.

Bast looked closely at his shoulder. 'Can you move it?'

Chronicler nodded, rolling it around. 'It hurt like twelve bastards when he touched me, like something was tearing up inside.' He shook his head in irritation at his own description. 'Now it just feels strange. Numb. Like it's asleep.'

Bast prodded his shoulder with a finger, looking it over dubiously.

Chronicler looked back at Kvothe. 'The boy was right about the fire, wasn't he? Until he mentioned it, I didn't under*aaaaggghhhh!*' the scribe shouted, jerking away from Bast. 'What in God's name was that?' he demanded.

'Your brachial nerve plexus, I'm guessing,' Kvothe said dryly.

'I needed to see how deep the damage went,' Bast said, unruffled. 'Reshi? Would you get me some goose grease, garlic, mustard. . . . Do we have any of those green things that smell like onions but aren't?'

Kvothe nodded. 'Keveral? I think there's a few left.'

'Bring them, and a bandage too. I should get a salve on this.'

Kvothe nodded and stepped through the doorway behind the bar. As soon as he was out of sight, Bast leaned close to Chronicler's ear. 'Don't ask him about it,' he hissed urgently. 'Don't mention it at all.'

Chronicler looked puzzled. 'What are you talking about?'

'About the bottle. About the sympathy he tried to do.'

'So he *was* trying to light that thing on fire? Why didn't it work? What's—'

Bast tightened his grip, his thumb digging into the hollow beneath Chronicler's collarbone. The scribe gave another startled yelp. 'Don't talk about that,' Bast hissed in his ear. 'Don't ask questions.' Holding both the scribe's shoulders, Bast shook him once, like an angry parent with a stubborn child.

'Good lord, Bast. I can hear him howling all the way in the back,' Kvothe called from the kitchen. Bast stood upright and pulled Chronicler straight in his chair as the innkeeper emerged from the doorway. 'Tehlu anyway, he's white as a sheet. Is he going to be okay?'

'It's about as serious as a frostburn,' Bast said disparagingly. 'It's not my fault if he screams like a little girl.'

'Well, be careful with him,' Kvothe said, setting a pot of grease and a handful of garlic cloves on the table. 'He'll need that arm for at least another couple days.'

Kvothe peeled and crushed the garlic. Bast mixed the salve and smeared the foul-smelling concoction onto the scribe's shoulder before wrapping a bandage around it. Chronicler sat very still.

'Do you feel up for a little more writing tonight?' Kvothe asked after the scribe was wearing his shirt again. 'We're still days away from any true ending, but I can tie up a few loose ends before we call it a night.'

'I'm good for hours yet.' Chronicler hurried to unpack his satchel without so much as a glance in Bast's direction.

'Me too.' Bast turned to face Kvothe, his face bright and eager. 'I want to know what you found under the University.'

Kvothe gave a shadow of a smile. 'I supposed you would, Bast.' He came to the table and took a seat. 'Underneath the University, I found what I had wanted most, yet it was not what I expected.' He motioned for Chronicler to pick up his pen. 'As is often the case when you gain your heart's desire.'

CHAPTER EIGHTY-NINE

A Pleasant Afternoon

THE NEXT DAY I was whipped in the wide cobblestone courtyard that used to be called the Quoyan Hayel. The House of the Wind. I found it oddly appropriate.

As predicted, there was an impressive crowd for the event. Hundreds of students filled the courtyard to overflowing. They peered out of windows and doorways. A few even found their way onto the rooftops for a better view. I don't blame them, really. Free entertainment is hard to pass by.

I was lashed six times, singly, across the back. Not wanting to disappoint, I gave them something to talk about. A repeat performance. I did not cry out, or bleed, or faint. I left the courtyard walking on my own two feet with my head held high.

After Mola laid fifty-seven tidy stitches across my back, I found consolation in a journey to Imre where I spent Ambrose's money on an extraordinarily fine lute, two nice sets of used clothing for me, a small bottle of my own blood, and a warm new dress for Auri.

It was, all in all, a very pleasant afternoon.

CHAPTER NINETY

Half-Built Houses

EVERY NIGHT I WENT exploring underground with Auri. I saw many interesting things, some of which may bear mentioning later, but for now suffice to say that she showed me all the vast and varied corners of the Underthing. She took me to Downings, Vaults, the Woods, Delving, Cricklet, Tenners, Candlebear . . .

The names she gave them, nonsensical at first, fit like a glove when I finally saw what they described. The Woods didn't resemble a forest in any way. It was just a series of crumbling halls and rooms where ceilings were propped up with thick wooden support beams. Cricklet had a tiny trickle of fresh water running down one wall. The moisture attracted crickets, who filled the long low room with their tiny songs. Vaults was a narrow hallway with three deep cracks running across the floor. I only understood the name after watching Auri jump all three in quick secession to make it to the other end.

It was several days before Auri took me to Belows, a maze of intersecting tunnels. Despite the fact that we were at least a hundred feet below ground, they were filled with a steady, rushing wind that smelled of dust and leather.

The wind was the clue I needed. It let me know I was close to finding what I'd come here looking for. Still, it bothered me that I didn't understand the name of this place, I knew I must be missing something.

'Why do you call this Belows?' I asked Auri.

'That's its name,' she said easily. The wind made her fine hair stream out behind her like a gauzy pennant. 'You call things by their names. That's what names are for.'

I smiled despite myself. 'Why does it have that name? Isn't everything here "below"?'

She turned to look at me, head cocked to one side. Her hair blew around her face and she brushed it back with her hands. 'It's not *belows,*' she said. 'It's *belows.*'

I couldn't hear the distinction. 'Blows?' I asked puffing out my cheeks as if blowing out air.

Auri laughed, delighted. 'That's a piece.' She grinned. 'Try for more.'

I tried to think of what else made sense. 'Bellows?' I made a gesture with both arms as if working a forge bellows.

Auri thought about that for a moment, looking up and tilting her head back and forth. 'That's not as good. This is a quiet place.' She reached out a small hand and took hold of the edge of my cloak, pulling it out to the side so the slow wind caught it, filling it like a sail.

Auri looked up at me, grinning as if she'd just done a magic trick.

Billows. Of course. I grinned back, laughing.

That minor mystery put to rest, Auri and I began a meticulous investigation of Billows. After several hours I began to get a feel for the place, an understanding of which way I needed to go. It was just a matter of finding the tunnel that led there.

It was maddening. The tunnels twisted, leading in wide, unhelpful detours. Those rare times when I found a tunnel that stayed true to its course, the way was blocked. Several passages turned straight up or straight down, leaving me with no way to follow them. One passage had thick iron bars driven deep into the surrounding stone, blocking the way. Another grew steadily narrower until it was barely a handspan across. A third ended with a cave-in of tangled wood and soil.

After days of searching, we finally found an ancient mouldering door. The damp wood crumbled to pieces when I tried to open it.

Auri wrinkled her nose and shook her head. 'I'll skin my knees.'

Shining my sympathy lamp past the ruined door, I saw what she meant. The room beyond slanted down until the ceiling was only three feet high.

'Will you wait for me?' I asked her as I took off my cloak and cuffed up my shirtsleeves. 'I don't know if I can find my way up to the top without you.'

Auri nodded, looking worried. 'Ins are easier than outs, you know. There's tight places. You can get stuck.'

I was trying not to think of that. 'I'm just going for a look. I'll be back in half an hour.'

She cocked her head. 'What if you're not?'

I smiled. 'You'll have to come and rescue me.'

She nodded, her face as solemn as an earnest child.

I put my sympathy lamp in my mouth, shining the red light out against the pitch blackness in front of me. Then I got down on all fours and headed forward, my knees rubbing against the rough stone of the floor.

After several turnings, the ceiling went lower still, too low for crawling. After a long moment of consideration, I dropped to my belly and pressed on, pushing my lamp ahead of me. Each twist of my body pulled at the rows of stitches all across my back.

If you have never been deep underground, I doubt you can understand what it is like. The darkness is absolute, almost tangible. It lurks outside the light, waiting to rush in like a sudden flood. The air is still and stale. There's no noise except what you make yourself. Your breathing becomes loud in your own ears. Your heart thumps. And all the while there is the overwhelming knowledge that thousands of tons of earth and stone are pressing down above you.

Still I continued to worm my way ahead, moving by inches. My hands were grimy, and sweat dripped into my eyes. The crawlway grew smaller yet, and I foolishly let one of my arms get pinned to my side. Cold sweat burst out across my whole body as I panicked. I struggled, trying to get it stretched out in front of me . . .

After several terrifying minutes I managed to get my arm free. Then, after lying there for a moment, trembling in the dark, I pressed ahead.

And found what I'd been looking for . . .

———————

After emerging from the Underthing, I made my careful way through a window and a locked door into the women's wing of the Mews. I knocked softly on Fela's door, not wanting to wake anyone accidentally. Men were not allowed unescorted in the women's wing of the Mews, especially not during the late hours of night.

I knocked three times before I heard a gentle stirring in her room. After a moment, Fela opened the door, her long hair in wild disarray. Her eyes were still half-closed as she peered into the hallway with a puzzled expression. She blinked when she saw me standing there, as if she hadn't really expected anyone.

She was unmistakably naked, with a bedsheet half-wrapped around herself. I will admit that the sight of gorgeous, full-breasted Fela half-naked in front of me was one of the most startlingly erotic moments in my young life.

'Kvothe?' she said, maintaining a remarkable degree of composure. She tried to cover herself more fully and met with mixed success, pulling the sheet up to her neck in exchange for exposing a scandalous amount of long, shapely leg. 'What time is it? How did you get in here?'

'You said that if I ever needed anything, I could call on you for a favour,' I said urgently. 'Did you mean it?'

'Well, yes. Of course,' she said. 'God, you're a mess. What happened to you?'

I looked down at myself, only then realising the state I was in. I was grimy, the front of my body streaked with dirt from sliding across the floor. I'd torn open my trousers across one knee, and it looked like I was bleeding underneath. I'd been so excited that I hadn't even noticed or thought to change into my new clothes before I came.

Fela took a half step back and swung the door wider, making room for me to enter. As it opened, the door made a tiny wind that pressed the sheet against her body, outlining her nudity in perfect profile for a moment. 'Do you need to come in?'

'I can't stay,' I said without thinking, struggling against the urge to gawk openly. 'I need you to meet a friend of mine in the Archives tomorrow evening. Fifth bell, by the four-plate door. Can you do that?'

'I have class,' she said. 'But if it's important, I can skip it.'

'Thank you,' I said quietly as I backed away.

It says a great deal about what I had found in the tunnels underneath the University that I was halfway back to my room at Anker's before I realised I had turned down an invitation from a near-naked Fela to join her in her room.

———

The next day Fela skipped her lecture on Advanced Geometries and made her way to the Archives. She climbed down several flights of stairs and through a maze of corridors and shelves to find the only section of stone wall in the entire building that wasn't lined with books. The four-plate door stood there, silent and immobile as a mountain: *Valaritas*.

Fela looked around nervously, shifting her weight from foot to foot.

After a long moment, a hooded figure stepped out of the dark and into the ruddy light of her hand lamp.

She smiled anxiously. 'Hello,' she said softly. 'A friend asked me to . . .' she paused and ducked her head a little, trying to glimpse the face under the shadow of the hood.

You probably wouldn't be surprised at who she saw.

'Kvothe?' she said incredulously, looking around in sudden panic. 'My God, what are you doing in here?'

'Trespassing,' I said flippantly.

She grabbed hold of me and pulled me through a maze of shelves until we came to one of the reading holes scattered throughout the Archives. She pushed me in and closed the door firmly behind us and leaned against it. 'How did you get in here? Lorren will burst a vessel! Do you want to get us both expelled?'

'They wouldn't expel you,' I said easily. 'You're guilty of Willful Collusion at the very most. They can't expel you for that. You'd probably get off with a fine, since they don't whip women.' I shifted my shoulders a little, feeling the dull tug of the stitches across my back. 'Which seems a little unfair if you ask me.'

'How did you get in here?' she repeated. 'Did you sneak past the desk?'

'You're better off not knowing,' I hedged.

It had been Billows, of course. Once I smelled old leather and dust on the wind there I knew I was close. Hidden away in the maze of tunnels was a door that lead directly into the lowest level of the stacks. It was there so the scrivs would have easy access to the ventilation system. The door had been locked, of course, but locked doors have never proved much of a hindrance to me. More's the pity.

I didn't tell Fela any of that, however. I knew my secret route would only work as long as it remained secret. Telling a scriv, even a scriv who owed me a favour, simply wasn't a good idea.

'Listen,' I said quickly. 'It's safe as houses. I've been here for hours and no one's come even close to me. Everyone carries their own light so it's easy to avoid them.'

'You just surprised me,' Fela said, as she brushed her dark hair back over her shoulders. 'You're right though, it's probably safer out there.' She opened the door and peered outside, making sure the coast was clear. 'Scrivs spot-check the reading holes periodically to make sure no one's sleeping in here, or having sex.'

'What?'

'There's a lot you don't know about the Archives.' She smiled as she opened the door the rest of the way.

'That's why I need your help,' I said as we headed out into the stacks. 'I can't make heads or tails of this place.'

'What are you looking for?' Fela asked.

'About a thousand things,' I said honestly. 'But we can start with the history of the Amyr. Or any nonfictional reports of the Chandrian. Anything about either one really. I haven't been able to find a thing.'

I didn't bother trying to keep the frustration from my voice. To finally get inside the Archives after all this time and not be able to find any of the answers I was looking for was maddening. 'I thought things would be better organised,' I groused.

Fela chuckled deep in her throat. 'And how would you do that, exactly? Organise everything, I mean.'

'I've been thinking about it for the last couple hours, actually,' I said. 'It'd be best to do it by subject. You know: histories, memoirs, grammars . . .'

Fela stopped walking and gave a deep sigh. 'I guess we should get this over with.' She pulled a slim book off a shelf at random. 'What's the subject of this book?'

I opened it and glanced over the pages. It was written in an old scribe's hand, spidery and hard to follow. 'It looks like a memoir.'

'What type of memoir? Where do you put it in relationship to the other memoirs?'

Still flipping pages, I spotted a carefully drawn map. 'Actually, it looks more like a travelogue.'

'Fine,' she said. 'Where do you put it in the memoir-travelogue-section?'

'I'd organise them geographically,' I said, enjoying the game. I flipped more pages. 'Atur, Modeg, and . . . Vint?' I frowned and looked at the spine of the book. 'How old is this? The Aturan Empire absorbed Vint over three hundred years ago.'

'Over four hundred years,' she corrected. 'So where do you put a travelogue that refers to a place that doesn't exist any more?'

'It would be more of a history, really,' I said more slowly.

'What if it isn't accurate?' Fela pressed. 'Based on hearsay rather than personal experience? What if it's purely fictional? Novel travelogues were quite a fashion in Modeg a couple hundred years ago.'

I closed the book and slowly slid it back onto the shelf. 'I'm beginning to see the problem,' I said thoughtfully.

'No, you don't,' Fela said frankly. 'You're just glimpsing the edges of the problem.' She gestured to the stacks around us. 'Let's say you became Master Archivist tomorrow. How long would it take you to organise all this?'

I looked around at the countless shelves retreating off into the darkness. 'It would be a lifetime's work.'

'Evidence suggests it takes more than just one lifetime,' Fela said dryly. 'There are over three quarters of a million volumes here, and that's not even taking into consideration the clays or scrolls or fragments from Caluptena.'

She made a dismissive gesture. 'So you spend years developing the perfect organisational system, which even has a convenient place for your historical-fictional-travelogue-memoir. You and the scrivs spend decades slowly identifying, sorting and reordering tens of thousands of books.' She looked me in the eye. 'And then you die. What happens then?'

I began to see where she was going. 'Well, in a perfect world, the next Master Archivist would pick up where I left off,' I said.

'Hurrah for the perfect world,' Fela said sarcastically, then turned and began leading me through the shelves again.

'I'm guessing the new Master Archivist usually has his own ideas about how to organise things?'

'Not *usually*,' Fela admitted. 'Sometimes there are a several in a row who work toward the same system. But sooner or later you get someone who's sure they have a better way of doing things and everything starts from scratch again.'

'How many different systems have there been?' I spotted a faint red light bobbing in the distant shelves and pointed towards it.

Fela changed directions to take us away from the light and whoever was carrying it. 'It depends on how you count them,' she said softly. 'At least nine in the last three hundred years. The worst was about fifty years ago when there were four new Master Archivists within five years of each other. The result was three different factions among the scrivs, each using a different cataloging system, each firmly believing theirs was the best.'

'Sounds like a civil war,' I said.

'A holy war,' Fela said. 'A very quiet, circumspect crusade where each side was sure they were protecting the immortal soul of the Archives. They would steal books that had already been cataloged in each other's systems. They would hide books from each other, or confuse their order on the shelves.'

'How long did this go on?'

'Almost fifteen years,' Fela said. 'It might still be going on today if Master

Tolem's scrivs hadn't finally managed to steal the Larkin ledger books and burn them. The Larkins couldn't keep going after that.'

'And the moral of the story is that people get passionate around books?' I teased gently. 'Hence the need to spot-check the reading holes?'

Fela stuck out her tongue at me. 'The moral of the story is that things are a mess in here. We effectively "lost" almost two hundred thousand books when Tolem burned the Larkin ledgers. They were the only records on where those books were located. Then, five years later, Tolem dies. Guess what happens then?'

'A new Master Archivist looking to start over with a clean slate?'

'It's like an endless chain of half-built houses,' she said, exasperated. 'It's easy to find books in the old system, so that's how they build the new system. Whoever's working on the new house keeps stealing lumber from what's been built before. The old systems are still there in scattered bits and pieces. We're still finding pockets of books scrivs hid from each other years ago.'

'I sense this is a sore spot with you,' I said with a smile.

We reached a flight of stairs and Fela turned to look at me. 'It's a sore spot with every scriv who lasts more than two days working in the Archives,' she said. 'People down in the Tomes complain when it takes us an hour to bring them what they want. They don't realise it's not as easy as going to the "Amyr History" shelf and pulling down a book.'

She turned and began to climb the stairs. I followed her silently, appreciating the new perspective.

CHAPTER NINETY-ONE

Worthy of Pursuit

AUTUMN TERM SETTLED INTO a comfortable pattern after that. Fela slowly introduced me to the inner workings of the Archives and I spent what time I could spare skulking about, trying to dig up answers to my thousand questions.

Elodin did something that could, conceivably, be referred to as teaching, but for the most part he seemed more interested in confusing me than shedding any real light on the subject of naming. My progress was so nonexistent that I wondered at times if there was any progress to be made at all.

What time I didn't spend studying or in the Archives I spent on the road to Imre, braving the coming winter wind, if not looking for its name. The Eolian was always my best bet for finding Denna, and as the weather worsened I found her there more and more. By the time the first snow fell, I usually managed to catch her one trip of three.

Unfortunately, I rarely managed to have her wholly to myself, as she usually had someone with her. As Deoch had mentioned, she was not the sort who spent a lot of time alone.

Still I kept coming. Why? Because whenever she saw me some light would go on inside her, making her glow for a moment. She would jump to her feet, run to me, and catch hold of my arm. Then, smiling, bring me back to her table and introduce me to her newest man.

I came to know most of them. None were good enough for her, so I held them in contempt and hated them. They in turn hated and feared me.

But we were pleasant to each other. Always pleasant. It was a game of sorts. He would invite me to sit, and I would buy him a drink. The three of us would talk, and his eyes would slowly grow dark as he watched her smile towards me. His mouth would narrow as he listened to the laughter that leapt from her as I joked, spun stories, sang . . .

They would always react the same way, trying to prove ownership of her in small ways. Holding her hand, a kiss, a too-casual touch along her shoulder.

They clung to her with desperate determination. Some of them merely resented my presence, saw me as a rival. But others had a frightened knowledge buried deep behind their eyes from the beginning. They knew she was leaving, and they didn't know why. So they clutched at her like shipwrecked sailors, clinging to the rocks despite the fact that they are being battered to death against them. I almost felt sorry for them. Almost.

So they hated me, and it shone in their eyes when Denna wasn't looking. I would offer to buy another round of drinks, but he would insist, and I would graciously accept, and thank him, and smile.

I have known her longer, my smile said. *True, you have been inside the circle of her arms, tasted her mouth, felt the warmth of her, and that is something I have never had. But there is a part of her that is only for me. You cannot touch it, no matter how hard you might try. And after she has left you I will still be here, making her laugh. My light shining in her. I will still be here long after she has forgotten your name.*

There were more than a few. She went through them like a pen through wet paper. She left them, disappointed. Or, frustrated, they abandoned her, leaving her heartsore, moved to sadness but never as far as tears.

There were tears once or twice. But they were not for the men she had lost or the men she had left. They were quiet tears for herself, because there was something inside her that was badly hurt. I couldn't tell what it was and didn't dare to ask. Instead I simply said what I could to take the pain away and helped her shut her eyes against the world.

———————

Occasionally I would talk about Denna with Wilem and Simmon. Being true friends they gave me sensible advice and compassionate sympathy in roughly equal amounts.

The compassion I appreciated, but the advice was worse than useless. They urged me toward the truth, told me to open my heart to her. To pursue her. Write her poetry. Send her roses.

Roses. They didn't know her. Despite the fact that I hated them, Denna's men taught me a lesson that I might never have learned otherwise.

'What you don't understand,' I explained to Simmon one afternoon as we sat under the pennant pole, 'is that men fall for Denna all the time. Do you know what that's like for her? How tiresome it is? I am one of her few friends. I won't risk that. I won't throw myself at her. She doesn't want it. I will not be one of the hundred cow-eyed suitors who go mooning after her like love-struck sheep.'

'I just don't understand what you see in her,' Sim said carefully. 'I know she's charming. Fascinating and all of that. But she seems rather,' he hesitated, 'cruel.'

I nodded. 'She is.'

Simmon watched me expectantly, finally said. 'What? No defense for her?'

'No. Cruel is a good word for her. But I think you are saying cruel and thinking something else. Denna is not wicked, or mean, or spiteful. She is cruel.'

Sim was quiet for a long while before responding. 'I think she might be some of those other things, and cruel as well.'

Good, honest, gentle Sim. He could never bring himself to say bad things about another person, just imply them. Even that was hard for him.

He looked up at me. 'I talked with Sovoy. He's still not over her. He really loved her, you know. Treated her like a princess. He would have done anything for her. But she left him anyway, no explanation.'

'Denna is a wild thing,' I explained. 'Like a hind or a summer storm. If a storm blows down your house, or breaks a tree, you don't say the storm was mean. It was cruel. It acted according to its nature and something unfortunately was hurt. The same is true of Denna.'

'What's a hind?'

'A deer.'

'I thought that was a hart?'

'A hind is a female deer. A wild deer. Do you know how much good it does you to chase a wild thing? None. It works against you. It startles the hind away. All you can do is stay gently where you are, and hope in time that the hind will come to you.'

Sim nodded, but I could tell he didn't really understand.

'Did you know they used to call this place the Questioning Hall?' I said, pointedly changing the subject. 'Students would write questions on slips of paper and let the wind blow them around. You would get different answers depending on the way the paper left the square.' I gestured to the gaps between the grey buildings Elodin had shown to me. 'Yes. No. Maybe. Elsewhere. Soon.'

The belling tower struck and Simmon sighed, sensing it was pointless to pursue the conversation further. 'Are we playing corners tonight?'

I nodded. After he was gone I reached into my cloak and pulled out the note Denna had left in my window. I read it again, slowly. Then carefully tore away the bottom of the page where she had signed it.

I folded the narrow strip of paper with Denna's name, twisted it, and let the courtyard's ever-present wind tug it out of my hand to spin among the few remaining autumn leaves.

It danced along the cobblestones. It circled and spun, making patterns too wild and varied for me to understand. But though I waited until the sky grew dark, the wind never took it away. When I left, my question was still wandering in the House of the Wind, giving no answers, hinting at many. *Yes. No. Maybe. Elsewhere. Soon.*

———————————

Lastly, there was my ongoing feud with Ambrose. I walked on pins and needles every day, waiting for him to take his revenge. But the months passed and nothing happened. Eventually, I came to the conclusion that he had finally learned his lesson and was keeping a safe distance from me.

I was wrong, of course. Perfectly and completely wrong. Ambrose had merely learned to bide his time. He did manage to get his revenge, and when it came, I was caught flatfooted and forced to leave the University.

But that, as they say, is a story for another day.

CHAPTER NINETY-TWO

The Music that Plays

'THAT SHOULD DO FOR now, I imagine,' Kvothe said, gesturing for Chronicler to lay down his pen. 'We have all the groundwork now. A foundation of story to build upon.'

Kvothe came to his feet and rolled his shoulders, stretching his back. 'Tomorrow we'll have some of my favorite stories. My journey to Alveron's court. Learning to fight from the Adem. Felurian . . .' He picked up a clean linen cloth and turned to Chronicler. 'Is there anything you need before you turn in for the night?'

Chronicler shook his head, knowing a polite dismissal when he heard one. 'Thank you, no. I'll be fine.' He gathered everything into his flat leather satchel and made his way upstairs to his rooms.

'You too, Bast,' Kvothe said. 'I'll take care of the cleaning up.' He made a shooing motion to forestall his student's protest. 'Go on. I need time to think about tomorrow's story. These things don't plan themselves you know.'

Shrugging, Bast headed up the stairs as well, his footsteps sounding hard on the wooden stairs.

Kvothe went about his nightly ritual. He shovelled ashes out of the huge stone fireplace and brought in wood for tomorrow's fire. He went outside to extinguish the lamps beside the Waystone's sign, only to find that he'd forgotten to light them earlier that evening. He locked the inn, and after a moment's consideration, left the key in the door so Chronicler could let himself out if he woke early in the morning.

Then he swept the floor, washed the tables, and rubbed down the bar, moving with a methodical efficiency. Last came the polishing of the bottles.

As he went through the motions his eyes were far away, remembering. He did not hum or whistle. He did not sing.

———————

In his room, Chronicler moved about restlessly, tired but too full of anxious energy to let sleep take him. He removed the finished pages from his satchel and stowed them safely in the heavy wooden chest of drawers. Then he cleaned all his pen's nibs and set them out to dry. He carefully removed the bandage on his shoulder, threw the foul-smelling thing in the chamber pot, and replaced the lid before washing his shoulder clean in the hand basin.

Yawning, he went to the window and looked out at the little town, but there was nothing to see. No lights, no movement. He opened the window a crack, letting in the fresh autumn air. Drawing the curtains, Chronicler undressed for bed, lying his clothes over the back of a chair. Last of all he removed the simple iron wheel from around his neck and laid it on the nightstand.

Turning down his bed, Chronicler was surprised to see the sheets had been changed sometime during the day. The linen was crisp and smelled pleasantly of lavender.

After a moment's hesitation, Chronicler moved to the door of his room and locked it. He laid the key on the nightstand, then frowned and picked up the stylised iron wheel and put it back around his neck before snuffing the lamp and crawling into bed.

For the better part of an hour, Chronicler lay sleepless in his sweet-smelling bed, rolling restlessly from side to side. Finally he sighed and threw off the covers. He relit the lamp with a sulfur match and climbed back out of bed. Then he walked over to the heavy chest of drawers beside the window and pushed at it. It wouldn't budge at first, but when he put his back into it, he managed to slide it slowly across the smooth wooden floor.

After a minute the weighty piece of furniture was pressed against the door of his room. Then he climbed back into bed, rolled down the lamp, and quickly fell into a deep and peaceful sleep.

———————

It was pitch black in the room when Chronicler woke with something soft pressing against his face. He thrashed wildly, more a reflex than an attempt to get away. His startled shout was muffled by the hand clamped firmly over his mouth.

After his initial panic, Chronicler went quiet and limp. Breathing hard through his nose, he lay there, eyes wide in the darkness.

'It's just me,' Bast whispered without removing his hand.

Chronicler said something muffled.

'We need to talk.' Kneeling beside the bed, Bast looked down at the dark shape Chronicler made, twisted in his blankets. 'I'm going to light the lamp and you're not going to make any loud noises. Alright?'

Chronicler nodded against Bast's hand. A moment later a match flared, filling the room with jagged red light and the acrid smell of sulfur. Then gentler lamp-light welled up. Bast licked his fingers and pinched the match between them.

Trembling slightly, Chronicler sat up in the bed and put his back against the wall. Bare-chested, he gathered the blankets self-consciously around his waist and glanced toward the door. The heavy dresser was still in place.

Bast followed his gaze. 'That shows a certain lack of trust,' he said dryly. 'You better not have scratched up his floors. He gets mad as hell about that sort of thing.'

'How did you get in here?' Chronicler demanded.

Bast flailed his hands franticly at Chronicler's head. 'Quiet!' he hissed. 'We have to be quiet. He has ears like a hawk.'

'How . . .' Chronicler began more softly, then stopped. 'Hawks don't have ears.'

Bast gave him a puzzled look. 'What?'

'You said he has ears like a hawk. That doesn't make any sense.'

Bast frowned and made a dismissive gesture. 'You know what I mean. He can't know that I'm here.' Bast sat on the edge of the bed and smoothed down his trousers self-consciously.

Chronicler gripped the blankets bunched around his waist. 'Why *are* you here?'

'Like I said, we need to talk.' Bast looked at Chronicler seriously. 'We need to talk about why you're here.'

'This is what I do,' Chronicler said, irritated. 'I collect stories. And when I get the chance I investigate odd rumours and see if there's any truth behind them.'

'Out of curiosity, which rumour was it?' Bast asked.

'Apparently you got soppy drunk and let something slip to a wagoneer,' Chronicler said. 'Rather careless, all things considered.'

Bast gave Chronicler a profoundly pitying look. 'Look at me,' Bast said, as if talking to a child. 'Think. Could some wagon herder get me drunk? Me?'

Chronicler opened his mouth. Closed it. 'Then . . .'

'He was my message in a bottle. One of many. You just happened to be the first person to find one and come looking.'

Chronicler took a long moment to digest this piece of information. 'I thought you two were hiding?'

'Oh we're hiding alright,' Bast said bitterly. 'We're tucked away so safe and sound that he's practically fading into the woodwork.'

'I can understand you feeling a little stifled around here,' Chronicler said. 'But honestly, I don't see what your master's bad mood has do to with the price of butter.'

Bast's eyes flashed angrily. 'It has everything to do with the price of butter!' he said through his teeth. 'And it's a damn sight more than a bad mood, you ignorant, wretched *anhaut-fehn*. This place is killing him.'

Chronicler went pale at Bast's outburst. 'I . . . I'm not . . .'

Bast closed his eyes and drew a deep breath, obviously trying to calm himself. 'You just don't understand what's going on,' he said, speaking to himself as much as Chronicler. 'That's why I came, to explain. I've been waiting for months for someone to come. Anyone. Even old enemies come to settle scores would be better than him wasting away like this. But you're better than I'd hoped for. You're perfect.'

'Perfect for what?' Chronicler asked. 'I don't even know what the problem is.'

'It's like . . . have you ever heard the story of Martin Maskmaker?' Chronicler shook his head and Bast gave a frustrated sigh. 'How about plays? Have you seen *The Ghost and the Goosegirl* or *The Ha'penny King*?'

Chronicler frowned. 'Is that the one where the king sells his crown to an orphan boy?'

Bast nodded. 'And the boy becomes a better king than the original. The goosegirl dresses like a countess and everyone is stunned by her grace and charm.' He hesitated, struggling to find the words he wanted. 'You see, there's a fundamental connection between *seeming* and *being*. Every Fae child knows this, but you mortals never seem to see. We understand how dangerous a mask can be. We all become what we pretend to be.'

Chronicler relaxed a bit, sensing familiar ground. 'That's basic psychology. You dress a beggar in fine clothes, people treat him like a noble, and he lives up to their expectations.'

'That's only the smallest piece of it,' Bast said. 'The truth is deeper than that. It's . . .' Bast floundered for a moment. 'It's like everyone tells a story about themselves inside their own head. Always. All the time. That story makes you what you are. We build ourselves out of that story.'

Frowning, Chronicler opened his mouth, but Bast held up a hand to stop him. 'No, listen. I've got it now. You meet a girl: shy, unassuming. If you tell her she's beautiful, she'll think you're sweet, but she won't believe you. She knows that beauty lies in your beholding.' Bast gave a grudging shrug. 'And sometimes that's enough.'

His eyes brightened. 'But there's a better way. You *show* her she is beautiful. You make mirrors of your eyes, prayers of your hands against her body. It is hard, very hard, but when she truly believes you . . .' Bast gestured excitedly. 'Suddenly the story she tells herself in her own head changes. She transforms. She isn't *seen as beautiful*. She is *beautiful, seen*.'

'What the hell is that supposed to mean?' Chronicler snapped. 'You're just spouting nonsense now.'

'I'm spouting too much sense for you to understand,' Bast said testily. 'But you're close enough to see my point. Think of what he said today. People saw him as a hero, and he played the part. He wore it like a mask but eventually he believed it. It became the truth. But now . . .' he trailed off.

'Now people see him as an innkeeper,' Chronicler said.

'No,' Bast said softly. 'People saw him as an innkeeper a year ago. He took off the mask when they walked out the door. Now he sees *himself* as an innkeeper, and a failed innkeeper at that. You saw what he was like when Cob and the rest came in tonight. You saw that thin shadow of a man behind the bar tonight. It used to be an act . . .'

Bast looked up, excited. 'But you're perfect. You can help him remember what it was like. I haven't seen him so lively in months. I know you can do it.'

Chronicler frowned a bit. 'I'm not sure . . .'

'I know it will work,' Bast said eagerly. 'I tried something similar a couple of months ago. I got him to start a memoir.'

Chronicler perked up. 'He wrote a memoir?'

'*Started* a memoir,' Bast said. 'He was so excited, talked about it for days. Wondering where he should begin his story. After his first night's writing he was like his old self again. He looked three feet taller with lightning on his shoulders.' Bast sighed. 'But something happened. The next day he read what he'd written and went into one of his dark moods. Claimed the whole thing was the worst idea he'd ever had.'

'What about the pages he wrote?'

Bast made a crumpling motion with his hands and tossed imaginary papers away.

'What did they say?' Chronicler asked.

Bast shook his head. 'He didn't throw them away. He just . . . threw them. They've been lying on his desk for months.'

Chronicler's curiosity was almost palpable. 'Can't you just . . .' he waggled his fingers. 'You know, tidy them up?'

'*Anpauen.* No.' Bast looked horrified. 'He was furious after he read them.' Bast shivered a little. 'You don't know what he's like when he's really angry. I know better than to cross him on something like that.'

'I suppose you know best,' Chronicler said dubiously.

Bast gave an emphatic nod. 'Exactly. That's why I came to talk to you. Because I know best. You need to keep him from focusing on the dark things. If not . . .' Bast shrugged and repeated the motion of crumpling and throwing away a piece of paper.

'But I'm collecting the story of his life. The *real* story.' Chronicler made a helpless gesture. 'Without the dark parts it's just some silly f—' Chronicler froze halfway through the word, eyes darting nervously to the side.

Bast grinned like a child catching a priest midcurse. 'Go on,' he urged, his eyes were delighted, and hard, and terrible. 'Say it.'

'Like some silly faerie story,' Chronicler finished, his voice thin and pale as paper.

Bast smiled a wide smile. 'You know nothing of the Fae, if you think our stories lack their darker sides. But all that aside, this *is* a faerie story, because you are gathering it for me.'

Chronicler swallowed hard and seemed to regain some of his composure. 'What I mean is that what he's telling is a true story, and true stories have unpleasant parts. His more than most, I expect. They're messy, and tangled, and . . .'

'I know you can't get him to leave them out,' Bast said. 'But you can hurry him along. You can help him dwell on the good things: his adventures, the women, the fighting, his travels, his music . . .' Bast stopped abruptly. 'Well . . . not the music. Don't ask about that, or why he doesn't do magic anymore.'

Chronicler frowned. 'Why not? His music seems . . .'

Bast's expression was grim. 'Just don't,' he said firmly. 'They're not productive subjects. I stopped you earlier,' he tapped Chronicler's shoulder meaningfully, 'because you were going to ask him what went wrong with his sympathy. You didn't know any better. Now you do. Focus on the heroics, his cleverness.' He waved his hands. 'That sort of thing.'

'It's really not my place to be steering him one way or another,' Chronicler said stiffly. 'I'm a recorder. I'm just here for the story. The story's the important thing, after all.'

'Piss on your story,' Bast said sharply. 'You'll do what I say, or I'll break you like a kindling stick.'

Chronicler froze. 'So you're saying I work for you?'

'I'm saying you belong to me.' Bast's face was deadly serious. 'Down to the marrow of your bones. I drew you here to serve my purpose. You have eaten at my table, and I have saved your life.' He pointed at Chronicler's naked chest. 'Three ways I own you. That makes you wholly mine. An instrument of my desire. You will do as I say.'

Chronicler's chin lifted a bit, his expression hardening. 'I will do as I see fit,' he said, slowly raising a hand to the piece of metal that lay against his naked chest.

Bast's eyes flickered down, then up again. 'You think I'm playing at some game?' His expression was incredulous. 'You think iron will keep you safe?' Bast leaned forward, slapped Chronicler's hand away, and grabbed the circle of dark metal before the scribe could move. Immediately Bast's arm stiffened and his eyes clenched shut in a grimace of pain. When he reopened them they were solid blue, the colour of deep water or the darkening sky.

Bast leaned forward, bringing his face close to Chronicler's. The scribe panicked and tried to scrabble sideways out of the bed, but Bast took hold of his shoulder and held him fast. 'Hear my words, manling,' he hissed. 'Do not mistake me for my mask. You see light dappling on the water and forget the deep, cold dark beneath.' The tendons in Bast's hand creaked as he tightened his grip on the circle of iron. 'Listen. You cannot hurt me. You cannot run or hide. In this I will not be defied.'

As he spoke, Bast's eyes grew paler, until they were the pure blue of a clear noontime sky. 'I swear by all the salt in me: if you run counter to my desire, the remainder of your brief mortal span will be an orchestra of misery. I swear by stone and oak and elm: I'll make a game of you. I'll follow you unseen and smother any spark of joy you find. You'll never know a woman's touch, a breath of rest, a moment's peace of mind.'

Bast's eyes were now the pale blue-white of lightning, his voice tight and fierce. 'And I swear by the night sky and the ever-moving moon: if you lead my master to despair, I will slit you open and splash around like a child in a muddy puddle. I'll string a fiddle with your guts and make you play it while I dance.'

Bast leaned closer until their faces were mere inches apart, his eyes gone white as opal, white as a full-bellied moon. 'You are an educated man. You know there are no such things as demons.' Bast smiled a terrible smile. 'There is only my kind.' Bast leaned closer still, Chronicler smelled flowers on his breath. 'You are not wise enough to fear me as I should be feared. You do not know the first note of the music that moves me.'

Bast pushed himself away from Chronicler and took several steps back from the bed. Standing at the edge of the candle's flickering light, he opened his hand and the circle of iron fell to the wooden floor, ringing dully. After a moment, Bast drew a slow, deep breath. He ran his hands through his hair.

Chronicler remained where he was, pale and sweating.

Bast bent to pick up the iron ring by its broken cord, knotting it together again with quick fingers. 'Listen, there's no reason we can't be friends,' he said matter-of-factly as he turned and held the necklace out to Chronicler. His eyes were a human blue again, his smile warm and charming. 'There's no reason we can't all get what we want. You get your story. He gets to tell it. You get to know the truth. He gets to remember who he really is. Everyone wins, and we all go our separate ways, pleased as peaches.'

Chronicler reached out to take hold of the cord, his hand trembling slightly. 'What do you get?' he asked, his voice a dry whisper. 'What do you want out of this?'

The question seemed to catch Bast unprepared. He stood still and awkward for a moment, all his fluid grace gone. For a moment it looked as if he might burst into tears. 'What do I want? I just want my Reshi back.' His voice was quiet and lost. 'I want him back the way he was.'

There was a moment of awkward silence. Bast scrubbed at his face with both hands and swallowed hard. 'I've been gone too long,' he said abruptly, walking to the window and opening it. He paused with one leg over the sill and looked back at Chronicler. 'Can I bring you anything before you go to sleep? A nightcap? More blankets?'

Chronicler shook his head numbly and Bast waved as he stepped the rest of the way out the window, closing it gently behind him.

A Silence of Three Parts

IT WAS NIGHT AGAIN. The Waystone Inn lay in silence, and it was a silence of three parts.

The first part was a hollow, echoing quiet, made by things that were lacking. If there had been horses stabled in the barn they would have stamped and champed and broken it to pieces. If there had been a crowd of guests, even a handful of guests bedded down for the night, their restless breathing and mingled snores would have gently thawed the silence like a warm spring wind. If there had been music . . . but no, of course there was no music. In fact there were none of these things, and so the silence remained.

Inside the Waystone a man huddled in his deep, sweet-smelling bed. Motionless, waiting for sleep, he lay wide-eyed in the dark. In doing this he added a small, frightened silence to the larger, hollow one. They made an alloy of sorts, a harmony.

The third silence was not an easy thing to notice. If you listened for an hour, you might begin to feel it in the thick stone walls of the empty taproom and in the flat, grey metal of the sword that hung behind the bar. It was in the dim candlelight that filled an upstairs room with dancing shadows. It was in the mad pattern of a crumpled memoir that lay fallen and unforgotten atop the desk. And it was in the hands of the man who sat there, pointedly ignoring the pages he had written and discarded long ago.

The man had true-red hair, red as flame. His eyes were dark and distant, and he moved with the weary calm that comes from knowing many things.

The Waystone was his, just as the third silence was his. This was appropriate, as it was the greatest silence of the three, wrapping the others inside itself. It was deep and wide as autumn's ending. It was heavy as a great river-smooth stone. It was the patient, cut-flower sound of a man who is waiting to die.